CHASE RYDER

COMPLETE SERIES (EXPANDED EDITION)

JO HO

*This book is dedicated to my other half, Matt, who is quite possibly, the sweetest guy there ever was. He has shown me what unconditional love is and brings joy and silliness to every day. I don't even mind that
my cats love him more than me now.
(I do, really).*

I also want to thank Dawn for sticking with me since we were seven years old, showing she had great taste, even then! She has been the biggest cheerleader in my life and I wouldn't have written this book, or made this giant leap without her support.

THE CHASE RYDER SERIES BOOK 1

WANTED

JO HO

AWARD-WINNING SCREENWRITER

WANTED

BOOK 1

1
———

PROLOGUE

NEW YORK CITY, NY
He had been running now for days.

The hot asphalt stung his cracked soles and the burning sun pounded onto his thinning frame, but he knew he couldn't stop. He had to get away.

A battered blue truck thundered past, and he flinched. No matter how often it happened, he still wasn't prepared for the rush of sound that roared into his ears. Where he was from, there were no cars. No vehicles of any kind.

He lifted his nose to the wind and welcomed the heady sensation of another new smell to add to his collection. Juicy, with a hint of smoke. He licked his lips, mouth watering in anticipation. Crossing onto the sidewalk, he moved towards the aroma, to where an overweight man in a greasy apron cooked on a stand. Meat patties sizzled on the grill.

He hadn't eaten since the escape, and now his stomach protested painfully. He padded up to the man and gave him a hopeful look, but clapping eyes on him, the vendor grabbed a broom and started shaking it in warning.

"Get lost, you filthy beast!"

Red from the heat of the flames, perspiration slid down his wobbly chin and landed with a plop an inch away from the meat. When his target failed to move, he glared down at the optimistic hopeful and—

WHAAM! Steel-capped boots lashed out onto his rump.

The sharp stabbing pain shocked the brown and white dog who had never felt anything like it in his life.

He blinked back tears and howled.

2
———

THE CEO

The CEO wasn't pleased.

Though considered an attractive man by many, The CEO had an eerie way of smiling that never reached his blue-gray eyes. Of slim build, he took great pains with his appearance, which showed in the Saville Row tailored suits he'd had shipped in from London. Custom made, a single suit could feed a starving African nation for a week — not that he ever would, abhorring charity as he did.

Deceptively soft-spoken, The CEO's calm exterior masked a ruthless streak that terrified men twice his size. Any who failed to do his bidding had a way of vanishing, never to be seen again.

The CEO stood by his desk in the glass office overlooking The Facility. Pouring himself a glass of Cognac, he sipped at the drink, letting the warmth of the liquid slide down his throat.

For all intents and purposes, The Facility was a high-tech laboratory where secretive experiments were being conducted on a daily basis. White-coated scientists rushed around below conducting wide-ranging research, but few knew the real reason for The Facility's existence. Only The CEO's most trusted advisors had the key to that secret, which essentially included only two people: the muscle, and Dr. Elora Robins, the brain.

After years of research, they had finally created the perfect specimen, only for him to escape. The CEO frowned, remembering the ineptitude of the staff member who was ultimately responsible. His name was Julio, and he was one of the night janitors.

Julio had worked at The Facility for close to twenty years when its number one focus was genetic engineering and DNA splicing. An illegal immigrant, The CEO had hired him specifically (as he had done with all low-level staff) as he knew Julio couldn't afford NOT to keep quiet about what went on in the lab. As an added bonus, Julio also worked for below minimum wage. The CEO had never understood anyone who paid higher rates to such low dwellers unless they liked flushing company profits down the drain.

On the night of the escape, Julio had been suffering from a bout of food poisoning. It seemed he'd left out some food at home that had been visited by houseflies. On his fourth trip to the toilets, when nausea and diarrhea had almost forced its way out, Julio had left a security gate unlocked.

This was all the opportunity that the resourceful dog had needed. Sticking to the air shafts and lesser used walkways, the dog had snuck out of The Facility before the alarm was even raised.

Needless to say, when it was discovered that Julio was to blame, The CEO had had him disposed of. His family is still searching for him to this day.

The CEO fingered his sleeve now as he waited for the call to be patched through. *The Mercenary wouldn't let him down. He knew what was at risk.* They had lost the dog for a few days, but a new sighting had pinpointed him in New York City. Feeling the beginnings of a headache, The CEO took another sip of his drink, a three-hundred-year-old brand of Cognac that cost the same as a small car.

Finally, Suzanne, his assistant, spoke through the intercom.

"Sir, he's on one."

The CEO activated the speakerphone and spoke one quiet word.

"*Well?*"

The Mercenary's voice was strained.

"Alpha escaped."

The glass slid out of his hand, smashing onto the granite floor. Shards of glass flew in every direction. Almost immediately, the office door flung open and Suzanne bustled inside. In her forties, she was his right hand and prepared for every eventuality. Including this, it seemed. Suzanne had entered carrying paper towels, which she now used to mop up the spilled liquid. He watched her in silence before issuing The Mercenary's next command in a voice loaded with threat.

"Find him, or don't bother coming back."

$$\frac{3}{}$$

CHASE

G*REENWICH, FAIRFIELD COUNTY*
Everyone loved sunsets. Everyone, that is, but me, Chase Ryder, to whom sunsets signaled that yet another hard night was approaching.

In the leafy upmarket park surrounding a man-made lake, wealthy couples strolled hand-in-hand admiring the mottled orange sky. I stirred, waking from my nap beneath a towering oak. Oaks were best as they provided plenty of foliage to protect against sudden showers and prying eyes. There was also the added bonus of load-bearing lower branches that someone nimble could scramble onto should trouble come calling... and you should know, trouble had me on speed-dial.

I stared at my reflection in the water. The face that stared back at me was fourteen but looked younger. A button nose and blue eyes gave the illusion of innocence. My mouth was plump; a little bigger than I'd like, but at least I'd never need collagen. The shoulder length hair would be a glossy chestnut if it weren't hanging in one big, greasy streak. Despite my current condition, I knew I was above average, but I'm not exactly what you'd call vain, usually choosing to hide my face rather than show it.

My stomach emitted a low rumble. I slipped a hand into a pocket and retrieved the last of my money, a hundred bucks or so. All that's left of my stash. It might seem like a good amount, but I'd already been on the road for eight months. In that time, I learned to only spend when I absolutely had to. *If only I was rich, I wouldn't be in this mess.*

I looked around at my surroundings. Yummy mommies with Pilate's-honed bodies bouncing designer-clad babies on tanned knees. The only hunger they knew was self-inflicted. I compared my figure to that of a passing cyclist, frowning when I realized that the only difference between us was our ages.

Originally from "The Paper City" Holyoke in Hampden County — one of the poorest cities in Massachusetts — I'd come here thinking I would receive more charity in affluent Greenwich, which had seen Mel Gibson and Meryl Streep among its wealthy residents, but these people, so caught up in their self-made dramas, barely noticed me. I'd totaled less here than if I'd stayed home.

I frowned as a shadow fell over the water, obscuring my face. *Strange.* The shadow didn't encompass the whole park, just me. Too late, the danger signs came into my head as a hand clamped down on my shoulder. The nails were ripped and blackened with dirt. I noticed the smell next, pungent, like raw sewage mixed with a brewery.

"Spare some change?"

I spun around to find myself gripped, vice-like, in the arms of a guy who was maybe seventeen. His glazed eyes focused on the money in my hands. I looked at his arms — yup, mottled with needle tracks. I scanned the area quickly, searching for help, but help wasn't coming. *Note to self: if trees are leafy enough to shield you from prying eyes, they'll also shield the nasty druggie who has you in his grasp.*

I froze in terror.

The druggie eyeballed the money in my hand and snatched it from me. He hesitated then, doubt clouding his eyes, but when he realized we were isolated from the rest of the park, they narrowed shrewdly.

"That it, or you holding out on me?"

Without waiting for an answer, his hands started patting me down. Here's something you should know about me: no one, but no one touches me without my consent. Instantly, a surge of white-hot fury broke through the fear. I screamed into his face.

"Don't you touch me!" and struggled like a wildcat. He was startled but much stronger than he seemed and moved like I was nothing but a mild annoyance. As he reached into my pockets, I saw my opportunity and plunged two fingers into his windpipe, slamming the palm of my other hand under his nose, snapping the weak cartilage there. Eyes wide with shock, he released me instantly.

Groaning in pain, he sank to the ground, hands around his now bloody nose. Fallen, he looked much younger. Not much bigger than me and nothing like the terrifying beast I'd thought he was. I swooped in and snatched my money back.

Shooting a quick prayer to the YouTube gods of Krav Maga, I grabbed my backpack and got the hell out of Dodge.

4

SULLY

ELLINGTON, CONNECTICUT
    I tossed aside the thin sheet that covered my body and glanced at the bedside clock's digital display: 1:47. Those seemingly innocuous numbers filled me with a sudden, though expected, weariness. I stared up at the ceiling and sighed.

Every night, the same goddamn thing.

As I rolled over to stare out of the window, a stray beam of moonlight caught the wedding band on my finger. The ring glinted, a tiny spark in the inky blackness, but I ignored it, the same way I ignored the framed picture that was currently lying face down on the vanity table. I didn't need to see it to know what it contained; the image was seared into my brain.

Taking care not to disturb the empty side of the bed, I picked up my watch, absently running my fingers over the engraved inscription on the back. "To Sully, with love and thanks from the Bauer family". The watch was a gift from a grateful family whose beloved cat I had saved. Although my actual name is Jake Sullivan, no one but my father calls me that, and anything that helped distance myself from that tool was a good thing in my mind. I slipped on the watch, grabbed a pair of tracksuit bottoms from the floor, and tugged them on.

Moments later, I jogged out into the dark. With my mussed brown hair, week's facial growth, and sweat encrusted gym clothes, I knew I wasn't quite the poster boy this prestigious neighborhood insisted upon, but to hell with it. There were extenuating circumstances.

The barren streets were silent, but in their own way, welcoming. Out here, in the dark, I could let the full range of my emotions run riot.

And tonight it was anger.

They say grief comes in seven stages, but for me, they alternated each night. Days were tough, especially the sunny ones that taunted me with how life could have been. On those occasions, I stayed away from parks and beaches, anywhere that might prove too nostalgic. The memories would flash up, stabbing like a knife in the chest even now, almost a full year later.

Things were changing, though. I was beginning to find the odd moment to be grateful for: the scent of freshly cut flowers, a traffic-free Route 83 during an emergency callout. Little by little, I was learning to cope... but as soon as my head hit the pillow, the demons would come.

Placing one foot in front of the other, I stared up at the stars and wondered how much longer it would be before I would get used to sleeping alone.

5

―――――

CHASE

The sun had barely risen, but I was already on the hunt for breakfast. Like they say, it's the most important meal of the day.

It had taken me all night to shake off the druggie incident. I knew I was lucky this time, but I couldn't afford another slip-up. In the future, I would stay away from trees, bushy or otherwise.

From experience, I knew Monday mornings were the most fruitful, with restaurants tossing whatever hadn't sold from the week before. It was with this promise of delectable treasure that I jogged into the back end of a strip of restaurants and climbed into the dumpster behind The Blessed Palace, a popular Asian establishment. The place was kinda tacky looking, covered with gold and red dragons that looked more like a distorted fish than those epic mythological characters, but they do a weekend buffet that never failed to impress, judging by the length of the waiting line that curved around the block on a regular basis.

Sadly for me, Lady Luck hadn't just left the building, she'd taken a slow boat to China, as a deep dumpster dive only delivered some decomposed fish heads *(seriously gross)*, half a fortune cookie *(semi-gross, and empty, so no good fortune for me — figures)* and something I'd prefer not to examine in closer detail. All you need to know is it looked like Swamp Thing's illegitimate lovechild with a roach.

Enough said.

I sighed with irritation. *Damn greedy staff must have taken the leftovers home with them.* That's the problem with Asians. Never waste a thing.

Shoving the cookie into my mouth, I picked my way over the remaining mess of empty cartons and boxes. As I grabbed hold of the skip to haul myself out, I heard a sound and froze. Someone had just yelped. Loudly. In a that-really-hurt kind of way.

I raised my head and peeked over the edge of the dumpster. A mangy dog, some kind of collie mix, was backing away from a man. There was a bone in his mouth, but the guy had one hand on it. He wore the uniform of The Blessed Palace and struck repeatedly at the dog with a wet dishtowel.

THWACK! The towel made a whipping sound as it connected with the collie's flank. The dog whimpered but didn't let go. He didn't attack either, just kept backing away. It's like the thing didn't know he had two rows of sharp teeth.

My eyes narrowed into slits. From the collie's thin frame, I could tell he was starving, maybe even more so than me. It could have been my own lack of food or the injustice of it all, but I felt a sudden rage building.

Stealthily, I crawled out of the dumpster and dropped silently, landing behind the guy in my Kmart sneakers. He twirled the towel, readying another strike. Neither of them had noticed me yet, so I took full advantage of the situation. I reached for the nearest trashcan, snatched the lid off, and HURLED it at the guy's head. The dull sound it made on contact made us all wince. He dropped like a hot spring roll. I looked at the dog. "RUN MUTT!"

And took off. I only glanced back when I reached the end of the block, so it was a shock to see the dog panting right behind me.

"Shoo! Scram!" I waved my hands at him, but he just cocked his head at me. Seeing that we were alone, I slowed my running to a jog. Clearly Angry Chinese Man wasn't after us. Which, come to think of it, was weird.

I suddenly stopped. What if I'd hit him too hard? Heads are pretty soft and not the best defense against steel. What if I'd... *killed* him? My life didn't flash in front of my eyes so much as my mugshot.

Muttface suddenly dropped his bone. That alone was shocking enough, but then he clamped his jaws around my wrist and started tugging.

"Hey, dufus! I just saved you! What kind of gratitude is that?"

And then I heard it. Furious shouts. Furious *foreign* shouts. I glanced back and saw Angry Chinese Man was not dead after all, but alive and kicking — and he had brought friends. *With cleavers.* The dog and I stared at each other, the same expression mirrored in our eyes... holy crap.

Muttface tore off, stopping a few yards ahead of me. He looked at me and barked once before tearing off again. Didn't need a membership to Mensa to figure out what he meant. Having no Plan B, I sprinted after him.

The dog ran fast, but never in a straight line. It was like he had experience evading capture. Already light-headed, I was becoming dizzy with all the twists and turns we were taking. *I* had no idea where we were any more, so Angry Chinese Man and chums had no chance. I followed Muttface down a side street.

And suddenly I collapsed.

One minute I was running, the next I tasted tarmac. I felt a wet, sandpapery tongue on my face.

And then there was darkness.

6

SULLY

S taring moodily into a mug of black coffee, I stifled a yawn. I sat at a kitchen table, eyes staring blankly at a newspaper open in front of me. My next client was due any second, but I found it difficult to care. While the late-night workout sessions meant my body was in its prime, my mind felt groggy, and I wished I could sleep the day away. But duty called.

"Your eleven thirty canceled," came a shout from the next room.

Or maybe not. It was Florence, my elderly, no-nonsense receptionist-come-assistant. This was a small practice that didn't require much staff, so multi-tasking Florence was a Godsend, though her domineering attitude wore me thin on occasion. Her long floral dress made slapping sounds against her legs now as she marched into the kitchen. An image of Florence doing a Hitler salute flashed into my mind before I shook it guiltily away. When I caught the determined look on her face, however, I steeled myself, ready for trouble.

"Since there's nothing in the diary until three, now would be a good time for you to do some spring cleaning. Clear out anything you don't need," she suggested. She gestured upstairs at my house above the practice. Her eyes bored into me, but I refused to take the bait, lowering my gaze to the paper.

"Another time. I'm busy."

She glared at me, but not without some sympathy. It was quite the feat and a Florence special. With a sigh of impatience, she snatched the paper away, grabbed my chin, and raised it to meet her gaze. But when she spoke again, it was unnervingly soft.

"It's unhealthy, dear."

I swallowed. I knew she was right, but just the thought of clearing *her* things away caused my chest to constrict. Experience meant I knew Florence wouldn't be dropping this anytime soon, however. With no energy for a fight, I nodded meekly.

"I'll make a start," I conceded and made my way slowly up the stairs.

At the top of the stairs, I shut the door that separated work from home and walked into the living area. The room was decorated eclectically, the result of many happy weekends perusing the local flea market, but right now, it seemed as if a tornado had left its devastation in its wake, with empty microwave trays and beer cans littering the floor. I stepped over them and turned the television on, finding comfort in the inane infomercial chatter. Tossing a crusty pizza box from the sofa, I lay down and shut my eyes. I'd get to it, but first I needed a snooze...

7
____

CHASE

I don't know how long I was out for, but it was the smell that woke me. My mouth was as dry as parchment, and my eyes felt like they were stapled shut, but I forced them open. I had to see what was causing the delicious aroma wafting towards me.

There was a something on the ground. It took a second for my vision to clear, but when it did, I thought I must still be in La La Land. There, in front of me, lay a carton of STEAMING DUMPLINGS! I blinked. The dog sat next to them patiently, as if waiting for me to react. When I gaped stupidly, he nudged the carton towards me and *grinned*. I spotted the Blessed Palace logo on the side of the box and pulled what can only be described as a comical double take.

No way...

I forced myself into a sitting position, dusted the street scum from my face, and reached for the food. My fingers closed around the edge of the box.

It felt real enough?

Muttface woofed and pawed the ground as if to say get a move on. I needed no further urging and shoved a dumpling into my mouth. Holy taste bud explosions! Turns out, those lines were onto something! I inhaled the box of deliciousness, even giving a few pieces to my new best furry friend, surprised to see how delicately he ate them. Clearly, I could learn a thing or two. Together, we *woofed* them down. In no time at all, the carton was empty. I tipped it upside down, just in case there was another sucker hiding in there, but nada. C'est finito. I looked at the dog.

"That was the best meal I've had in… just the longest time. If only we had some fritters too, huh? I could die and go to foodie heaven." Muttface cocked his head like he was actually considering my words, then suddenly took off without a backward glance. I felt a pang of crushing disappointment. "Thought we had something going here," I called after him — but I was talking to thin air. Littlest Hobo was long gone. Feeling kinda bereft, I thought about how I was humanizing the dog. Me. Miss. Anti-Dolittle. Eight months on the streets could sure change a person.

As a kid, the only pet I'd ever had was a baby duck, and that lasted for all of a week. One day, as a treat, I decided to let him swim in the gutter (The Paper City = Poor = No Paddling Pool for Ducky), only he got swept away by the current and into a drain. I'd lain on the sidewalk, ear pressed to the drain, listening to his cries until they were all but swallowed by the gushing water. I cried for months after. OK, I was five, but still.

Back to my present situation. Muttface is just a dumb animal. So, somehow, he brought me food from the same restaurant we ran away from. Ironic, but hardly rocket science. Maybe he'd already stashed them some place when Angry Chinese Man caught him. And while I was having my tarmac nap, he'd fetched provisions. It made sense. Kind of.

I could stay here waiting for Big Trouble in Little China to happen, or I could move on and find a bed for the night. It was a no-brainer. I staggered to my feet, swaying a bit, my blood sugar still low despite the recent meal. I'm one of those annoying girls who can eat whatever she wants without putting on a pound, but that also meant my high metabolism required more sustenance than the average girl of my size, which, being homeless, sucks big time.

I made my way back onto the main street and spotted a bus shelter on the other side of the road. It wasn't great, but it might do. I just needed to check if it was watertight — nothing worse than waking up to a mouthful of rain.

Expensive cars roared past, not in the least concerned by my bedraggled state. Car-jacking was low in this part of town, but these guys weren't going to risk a higher insurance premium just to test out that statistic, especially for pungent moi. I wasn't counting, but it had been at least five days since my body had seen any water, and that was even before the dumpster dive. I waited for a break in the traffic.

"Woof."

The sound came from behind. I took an involuntary gasp and spun around — but a bit *too* fast. Balance and co-ordination fled me as my foot slipped from the curb. I caught a brief glimpse of my furry best friend before I felt myself tumbling backward into the sea of cars.

Time slowed to a crawl.

When you're about to die, adrenaline pounds through your body and details fly out at you in what can only be described as supersonic vision. Like Muttface's eyes, which I only just noticed were an emerald green with gold flecks. And the see-through plastic tub he gripped in his mouth containing banana fritters, covered in sesame seeds that formed the initials BP.

While I was in slo-mo, the dog, conversely, seemed to be moving at super speed. In one quick motion, he dropped the fritters and lunged for my chest, snagging a mouthful of T-shirt. I hung there, suspended over the road, just inches away from my demise, anchored only by this animal's teeth and a prayer that the cheap polyester fabric wouldn't give out. A car horn blared to tell us to quit messing around. As if.

And then the dog pulled me to safety.

I sank to my knees, shaken, gasping for the breath I hadn't known I was holding. I couldn't believe it. I wasn't dead. I was alive. The dog had saved me.

Muttface tapped his paw on the tub of fritters, which had landed unscathed on the sidewalk, and chuffed softly like he was inordinately pleased with himself.

My jaw hit the floor.

8

───

CHASE

I admit I was freaked.

Too much was happening, and I wasn't prepared for any of it. A million questions swam through my already taxed brain. I found myself eyeballing the dog constantly. There was no other logical explanation than the conclusion I'd come up with for his talents, and trust me, I'd exhausted all the possibilities in the hour since my near miss with the reaper.

Muttface was an alien disguised as man's best friend.

Which was kind of brilliant, if you think about it. What better way to spy on a different species than to camouflage yourself as the number one pet in America? Just look at him: head swiveled around, sniffing his butt like a real dog. He couldn't be more disarming. Or gross.

We'd discarded the bus shelter idea due to both our discomforts of it being so overlooked *(well, I'm assuming Muttface had objections; he was definitely restless)* and we were now camped out in a shopping mall's mother and baby room, which to me felt like The Hilton.

I was trying to ignore Muttface — who had suddenly taken a great interest in sniffing each of the toilet stalls — and turned my attention to the room instead.

There were marble walls, a glass-domed ceiling, and hanging baskets overflowing with dried flowers. Opposite the stalls stood a floor-to-ceiling mirror etched in gold, while the far wall was covered with posters of upcoming movies in steel frames. An entire area of the room was kitted out with sofas and bean bags. *I mean seriously, why would anyone put sofas in a restroom?*

I was hoping the security guards would forget to check this place so we could stay the night. I'd gotten lucky previously once or twice, though they were never as nice as this. I was pretty sure I could fit on one of those gigantic baby-changers if I rolled my legs up. Could probably fit on there *with* the dog. I figured that along with mansions and cars, rich people must have bigger babies.

Feeling uncustomarily light-hearted, I plucked a flower from a basket and tucked it behind my ear. Turning to the mirror, I meant to mock my own reflection. Instead, I was shocked at how I'd taken dirt to a whole new level. Quickly, with Muttface guarding the door, I gave myself a flannel wash (one of the things I always carried in my trusty backpack) and dried off using an air blade dryer thingy. There was even a classy hand cream dispenser—

—Which promptly disappeared into my bag. It's not like I condone stealing, but this place wasn't going to miss it. Besides, it smelled like *coconuts.* Then I turned to my furry friend, who was busying himself with his own version of a bath. I'd put things off for as long as I could, but I knew it was time to get some answers, whether I was ready for them or not. I perched on the edge of a baby changer and cleared my throat.

"Hey, dog. Could you stop that? We need to talk."

Muttface immediately ceased licking and fixed his intelligent eyes on me. Then he waited, head tilted. It was disconcerting, to tell the truth.

"I'm going to ask some questions. I'm assuming you can't actually speak?"

He barked. I heard the chastisement in his tone.

"Correction, you can speak. I just don't understand what you're saying."

He barked again and wagged his tail.

"We're going to need to establish some rules for this to work. How about I take one bark as yes and two for no?"

"Woof." His butt shook with excitement. I grinned in spite of myself, pretty sure we were making history here. Shame about the restroom though, nice as it was. Maybe, in years to come, they'll rewrite this whole event and make the setting more palatable. I heard they change things all the time.

He pranced on his feet before settling back down.

"Let's begin. Are you... an alien?" I waited expectantly, but he said nothing. I suddenly realized the possible flaw of my questioning. "You know what that is, right? Creature from outer space? Not of this Earth? Little green man? Or furry in your case?"

One bark.

"So, you're not an alien, but you know what one is." I felt the need to clarify, for my own sanity if not his.

Another bark. Hmmm.

"But clearly you're super intelligent."

The resounding "WOOF!" was obviously something he was very proud of. And who could blame him?

"Were you born that way?" The question was greeted by two barks. Our first no. I tried to decipher what else it could be. My eyes landed on one of the movie posters. Some sci-fi thing to do with DNA splicing. I felt the hairs raise on the back of my neck.

"Did someone make you like this?"

"Woof."

This time, his bark was somber, like he was remembering something deeply sad. The ramifications of this hit me pretty hard. If he was made, it was for a reason, and I don't think it was to perform at Rocco's Traveling Circus. I reached out and stroked his head. He leaned into me, pink tongue hanging out in a goofy expression. Honestly, you'd think he'd never been petted before.

"Did you run away from the people who made you?"

Another bark. This one more determined. He stared at me and tensed his body as if how I responded would determine his next move. I thought about what he'd just revealed and realized we had more in common than I'd initially thought. I dropped down from my perch and cupped his face in my hands.

"Just because someone made you, doesn't mean they deserve you. If that was the case, I'd be back in Massachusetts. If you're worried I'll send you back, don't. I wouldn't do that to you."

He regarded me solemnly. Then his tail twitched suddenly, swinging from side to side in the biggest wag I'd seen to date. When I smiled, the dog leaped up, and I got my first whiff of doggy breath as he licked my nose to my forehead. Not an inch of my face escaped unscathed. It wasn't the most pleasant experience of my life.

"Stop that! Rule number 1, no licking!" I wiped my face on my sleeve, trying to rid it of any excess saliva. "So," I asked nonchalantly, "are you planning on sticking around, or is this a flying visit?"

"WOOF!"

I managed not to smile, but honestly? I felt a huge sense of relief at his answer. It kind of surprised even me.

"Then we need to call you something other than Muttface. I should warn you, Lassie and Hooch have been used to death." Several other possibilities ran through my head; Beethoven, Bruiser, and Bingo, but none of those felt right. And then I was hit with a spark of genius. And the cherry on top? It was still a B name!

"How about... Bandit? That means outlaw, in case you don't know, except you probably do, seeing as you seem to know a lot for your type..." I was babbling, suddenly nervous, surprised by how much it mattered to me what he thought of my choice.

Next thing I knew I was on the ground, the wind knocked out of me as a giant tongue slobbered over my face again.

We probably needed to run through our rules of engagement a few more times.

9

SULLY

The hands on the antique brass clock revealed it was a little after six in the evening. A freestanding monolith that took up the whole of one wall, it was the one luxury I kept in the practice. A little ostentatious for the simple surroundings of the workplace, but I didn't care. Besides, there was no room for it upstairs. It was a family heirloom passed down from my father and had sentimental value. That we both treasured it was the only thing we had ever agreed upon.

I sighed at the time. I had thought I'd be done with work by now. The Red Sox were playing tonight, and I had planned on watching the game, but instead, here I was, rifling through the cabinets, compiling a medicine list. Really, this fell under Florence's job description, but after our earlier altercation, I had avoided her for the rest of the day. Childish, I knew, but I was the boss. I was almost done when the doorbell rang. Irritated by the interruption, I growled down the hall.

"Unless someone's dying, we're closed. Come back tomorrow."

"Sul, it's me," a familiar voice said. "Open up."

I frowned but put down the list and unlocked the front door. Mark Armstrong stood outside. All chiseled jaw line and broad shoulders, he was a regular hit with the ladies, though, unlike me, Mark was a player who cherished his freedom. We had been firm friends since college. Mark worked as a consultant down on Wall Street. I never really understood what his job was, only that it involved ridiculous amounts of money and offshore accounts. Mark had the kind of lifestyle most people envied. And the icing on the cake? He only worked three days a week. Today must have been a work day, as Mark was still dressed in an Armani suit in lieu of his usual shirts and slacks, and instead of a briefcase, he carried a perspex tray of lasagna.

"Figured you could do with some home cooking."

I pulled a face. "Like I haven't been through enough already."

Mark sidestepped smoothly past me, not waiting for an invitation. "Relax," he said. "I didn't say it was *my* cooking."

I closed the door as Mark made his way up the stairs. "Then I hope you gave her a good time at least. First, there's mothering, then comes the smothering. That's your saying, right?"

Mark ignored me. He stood in the living area, taking in the empty junk food wrappers and general mess. I felt some embarrassment, but I knew Mark wouldn't make this into a thing. "I keep asking to borrow your cleaner..." I cleared a space on a chair for Mark, but he shook his head.

"I'll heat this up, get some beers going. You, my friend, are heading for the shower." He moved into the open-plan kitchen. Once a safe distance away, he tossed a look back at me. "You're pretty ripe."

I sniffed under my arms and had to agree that I wasn't at my best. Mark set the dial on the oven and placed the dish inside.

"Instead of food, I'll bring you a case of Axe next time."

I grabbed a tennis ball from a shelf and aimed it at Mark's head. Anticipating a comeback, Mark side-stepped. The ball went wide, sailed over his shoulder, bounced off of the kitchen tiles and rolled into the sink.

"If you could only score like that the rest of the time," Mark quipped.

I mumbled something unintelligible as I stepped into the bathroom, slamming the door behind me.

10
____

SULLY

W hen I stepped out of the bathroom fresh from my shower, dressed in a pair of jeans and a cotton shirt, I had to admit I felt almost human again. The rich aroma of the reheating lasagna caused my stomach to flip-flop. *Real food,* I thought. *Not something out of a box.* I padded barefoot into the kitchen but was surprised to find it empty. Two beers and place settings were neatly laid out on the table, but Mark was nowhere in sight. Hearing a sound across the hall, I followed it to my bedroom... where I froze in the doorway.

Having erected several removal boxes, Mark was rifling through the closets at a rack of women's clothing. He had an armload when the floorboards beneath my feet creaked, revealing my presence. Mark spun around guiltily.

"What the hell are you doing?" My eyes glittered angrily.

Mark dropped the clothes onto the bed. "You can't avoid this forever." He stepped towards me, palms held outwards, placating. "We hoped you'd arrive here yourself, but it's been ten months. You needed a push."

"We?" My breath caught as it came to me. "Florence."

"She's worried about you. We both are."

"So you thought you'd *ambush* me?"

Mark took a step back, sensing my building rage.

"Sully, come on. I only want to help. Let me help you."

A range of conflicting emotions flickered across my face. Anger, fear, and then pain. Mark made an attempt to continue when his leg knocked against the pile of clothes, sending them tumbling to the ground.

I reacted like a man possessed. Darting forward, I scrambled around, snatching the clothes from the floor as if they were made of a precious material that would disintegrate if left there a second too long.

"Sully." Mark's voice was pained, struggling to watch his friend's desperate behavior. He cleared his throat. "They won't bring her back. Nothing will."

But I was beyond hearing, now methodically sorting the clothes into a neat pile. My touch was gentle, reverent.

Mark steeled himself. Clenching his fists, he braced himself.

"Emma's gone," he said flatly. "You need to accept it."

I suddenly rounded on him.

"You think I don't know that? There isn't one second of any day where I haven't thought about her cold body lying in a box instead of with me. I can't sleep, I can barely function, but her things keep me sane. Having them here keeps her close to me." My voice cracked, raw with pain.

But Mark refused to bend.

"You're holding on when you need to let go." He slipped a business card from his wallet, offering it to me. "Look, just... call them. They're expecting you."

I didn't move. Sighing, Mark set the card onto the table. Unbidden, my eyes roamed over the typed lettering. *Dr. Philip Grass, Psychologist. Specialist in grieving.*

"Get out," I said softly.

Mark hesitated. Then placed a hand on my shoulder.

It was the wrong thing to do.

ROARING, I flew at him, shoving him back through the hallway to the top of the stairs.

"Jesus, stop!" Mark cast a startled look over his shoulder at the fast approaching steps, but my rage knew no bounds. Mark reached for the banisters, fingers closing around the sturdy wood. He held on, anchoring himself even as I continued to push.

"I want you gone! Leave us alone!"

Unable to withstand my fury and at a disadvantage beneath me, Mark stumbled down the steps, all the while pleading with me.

"Can you hear yourself? There is no more 'us'."

With a determination built of desperation, I forced him through the hallway and out of the practice. No sooner had Mark's foot landed outside than I slammed the door on him.

Mark walked slowly back to his car. I waited until he unlocked the car, then I slid open the upstairs window. The lasagna flew at Mark with unnerving aim, landing inches from him. Hitting pavement, the dish smashed into a thousand pieces. Meat sauce and glass splashed onto his pants.

"Nothing wrong with my aim now," I said.

Gritting his teeth, Mark climbed into his car and drove away.

11

CHASE

I woke to find dog hair in my mouth and the smelly beast stretched out by my side. At some point during the night, he must have crawled onto the baby changer with me. He must've been cold and needed the added warmth. *Note to self: Give him a blanket, or at least a towel, next time.*

I yawned and stretched. Light streamed in through high set windows, showering the bathroom in iridescent sunlight. I blinked, somewhat taken aback. The place was practically sparkly. I was entertaining the possibility of this being our nightly stay when Bandit suddenly sat up and cocked his ear.

"What is it?" I asked.

Bandit looked towards the door, gave a low warning growl, and bolted into a toilet cubicle. I scrambled after him and had just enough time to climb onto the toilet before a cleaner entered, pushing a cart. Tacky salsa blared out from her cheap headphones. I peeked through the crack in the door to see a Hispanic woman wielding a mop, dancing to her phone. Good. At least she wouldn't hear us over that racket. I waited until the cleaner entered the first cubicle and signaled Bandit to follow. Quickly, we snuck out, darted around the cart, and escaped into the mall outside.

A scattering of early morning staff was trickling in. I knew we had to get out before we were spotted - a girl and her dog would stick out like a sore thumb. Seeing a sign for the exit, we started for it, when a gorgeous smell assaulted our nostrils. Practically drooling, Bandit sighed and gave me a pleading look.

I craned my head for the source of the heavenly scent and found it just a few feet away; a pastry stand, being looked after by one lone worker with his back to us. I was figuring out how we could sneak some goods when Bandit darted ahead. I watched in amazement as Bandit slunk closer, always keeping out of sight. Within seconds he had reached the stand. He snatched three pretzels into his mouth and made it back to me before anyone had seen a thing. I beamed at him.

"You sneaky little thief!"

I swear he grinned at me.

Shoving the stolen goods into my bag, we bolted for freedom and didn't stop until we were at least two blocks away. I found a nice spot by a green and handed a whole pretzel to Bandit. His eyes went so wide with happiness I thought they would explode out of his head.

Stupid dog.

CHASE

fter breakfast, we headed downtown. My newfound companion's special abilities had got me thinking. Like me, Bandit knew a thing or two about survival. Also, like me, he had sticky fingers — or paws — and could lift things better than anyone. Clearly, we could survive just taking what we needed when we needed it, but I realized we should aim higher. Here was a goldmine waiting to happen!

Having been broke my entire life, I had always craved money. And right then, I considered the various ways we could utilize Bandit's skills. Obviously, there was street performing, but that was just one step away from begging, which I draw the line at (there was that small matter of pride). I could enter him into a dog competition, but that would bring too much attention to us. I doubt my mom would care enough to find me, but Bandit's real owner, that was another story. I knew I still needed the full lowdown from the dog, but somehow I kept putting it off. Some sixth sense told me he or she was way bad news.

I looked at him now, padding next to me. His tongue lolled out in a sign of contentment, and he seemed for all the world just a normal dumb dog, but I could see he held his posture differently to other mutts. No matter what he was doing — goofing around, resting, or eating — Bandit was constantly aware of danger.

In my experience, there were only two types of people in the world: one's who had suffered by the hands of others, and one's who hadn't. Bandit fell into my camp.

We arrived outside a grand stone building with an ornate welcome sign that read: "Welcome to Ashdale Library."

Perfect.

I reached up and unwrapped my scarf, then tied it around Bandit's neck. He cocked his head at me in question, but I didn't elaborate. As I headed inside, I called back to him.

"Come on, Boy, time for some schooling."

At the word "school", Bandit pricked up his ears and bounded after me.

13

CHASE

I let out an impressed whistle.

The old stone facade disguised a thoroughly modern interior. A glass ceiling hung over the central chamber. Shelves filled with books formed a maze across the floor. I could make out some familiar-sounding titles — The Hunger Games, Harry Potter, Twilight — but I had no interest in those.[1] My gaze swept the room until I found what I was looking for... a bank of computers. Happily, there were only a few other web geeks around. I started towards them when a voice stopped me dead.

"Young lady, there are no dogs allowed in here."

This had come from a prickly looking librarian. I casually studied the name on the badge pinned to her chest. Miss. Thorne. *How apt.* I stared over Miss. Thorne's shoulder and allowed my gaze to drift to one side.

"Even guide dogs? I'm partially blind." The lie came with no effort at all.

Miss. Thorne blinked at me behind wide-rimmed glasses, her expression horrified. What a terrible faux pas she had just committed! Her face flushed an ugly red. She took a step back and stammered.

"I'm sorry... I didn't know."

I smiled sadly at thin air.

"No worries. I get it all the time. Glaucoma," I explained helpfully. Miss. Thorne took another step away from me as if to keep my eye disease at bay.

"Can I assist you with anything? Our braille texts are on the next floor up?"

So someone who couldn't see would have to stumble up a flight of stairs all on their lonesome? Whoever designed the layout of this place should be given an award. I shook my head.

"That's very kind of you, but my dog is trained to look after me."

Miss. Thorne cleared her throat.

"Excellent. Well, I'll be here if you need me. You just have to call."

I waited patiently for her to go, and after a few moments, she finally got the hint. Spinning on her heel so fast it was a miracle she didn't snap her ankle, Miss. Thorne walked stiffly to the check-out desk.

Stooping down, I clutched hold of the scarf around Bandit's neck and spoke into his ear. "Lead the way, Fella." Bandit snapped to attention and — quite literally — pranced to the computers, enjoying the charade. I rolled my eyes at his antics. Someone had to teach this dog, less is more. Happily, the computers were out of Miss. Thorne's line of vision, so we wouldn't be getting any questioning looks sent our way.

The computer was already on, so I pulled up Google and searched for some money-making schemes. Windows popped up with helpful banners like: "Earn $1000 a day working from home!"; "Get paid for surveys!"; and my own personal favorite, "How to gamble your way to a fortune!" While I was pretty sure I couldn't get into a casino for that last one, the gambling thing struck a chord in my brain. Poker!

I looked at Bandit by my side, his back ramrod straight. He was taking this acting thing very seriously. If I could teach him to understand poker, he could be my spy on the inside. I could have him perched somewhere incon-spicuous and he could spy on the game for me. I'd just have to teach him a few basic signals... Excitement flooded my body. This could work!

I cleared the unhelpful pop-up windows and opened YouTube. I honestly don't know what I would have done without this site. I've learned self-defense, the best techniques of dumpster diving, and even how to collage. Yes, I'm an artist. Surprised?

Although I'd drawn the short straw in most everything else, one thing I had going for me was my photographic memory. Didn't matter what I saw, heard, or read. Once it went into my brain, it would stay ingrained in there forever. Hence the glaucoma reference.

I loaded various how-to videos and hit play.

"Boy, pay attention. You're getting a quiz later."

A whine of excitement escaped his lips.

Seriously.

What a freak.

14

CHASE

We had been walking now for hours.

The day had long since disappeared, having been swallowed by the night, taking along with it the green lawns, flower displays, and coffee shops of Nicetown, Connecticut. Here, the streets were littered with trash. Run down properties were boarded up and covered with graffiti. Others fared little better, as decaying stoops and overgrown, over-junked, front yards battled for attention. Scantily clad women crawled the curb, attempting to flag down passing cars.

Yes, folks, we'd arrived in Ghettoville.

My foot lashed out at an empty Coke can. It flipped over three times before landing into a blocked gutter with a splash. Bandit had to stifle his urge to chase after it. I gave him an apologetic look.

"Sorry. Wasn't thinking."

He shot me a look — he couldn't understand the sudden need to pursue the can. The need left him uneasy.

"You're a dog. Dog's chase. Deal with it."

He woofed, and I could tell my answer displeased him. Earlier, when we'd left the library, his tail was alert and wagging; now it barely even twitched. We'd only been together a short while, but already I was starting to read his body language, and man, was he dog tired.

After Bandit had digested what seemed like every poker video under the sun, we left the library for a jaunt in Walmart[2], where we obtained our own pack of cards. Then, in a nearby park (gotta love Greenwich for the amount of square parkage), I proceeded to teach Bandit sign language,

Chase Ryder style: a cocked right ear meant I should raise, both ears facing behind means I fold, and a cocked left ear, call. I knew this amounted to cheating, but you try eating days-old meat crawling with maggots then get back to me.

A couple of shady looking guys walked past. I gave them a wide berth, but they paid me zero attention. They headed towards a dive of a place where a flashing neon sign above the entrance read "McCall's". The guys strolled inside. I was about to move on when I spotted the poker chip one of the guys was tossing in his hand.

This was it, I thought to myself. *This was the place.* No fancy doorman, no dress code. No one would notice a girl and her dog... I hoped.

I waited for a few beats, and when the coast was clear, I slipped in with Bandit.

Like I figured it would be, the place was dimly lit. Tables littered the room in a haphazard fashion, where a dozen or so customers sat drinking amber colored beer. Despite the rock music emanating from a jukebox that had seen better days, the dance floor was empty. A baseball game blared from an ancient television set overlooking the bar — which was lucky really, as the sole barman had his full attention on it. There was a distinct air of despair in this place, and I didn't need Bandit's nose to smell it. I felt a pang of sympathy for the drunk drowning his sorrows in the corner. He looked like how I usually felt. Beaten.

I moved quickly to a cigarette dispenser, pretending to study the brands inside. Bandit stuck close by my side, but we didn't need to be so cautious. The patrons were so deep in their alcohol-induced stupor that there wasn't even one curious glance our way.

From the central bar, two corridors lead off: one to the restrooms and the other some sort of private room. I watched as the shady guys marched up to a closed door and knocked three times. The door was opened by a man whose giant head seemed to float on a cloud of heavy cigarette smoke. When the smoke cleared, I saw the poker game that was in progress beyond. I stared down at Bandit and grinned.

"This is it. You ready?"

He pawed the ground, and his butt shook with excitement.

Despite the lack of attention thrown our way, we kept to the shadows as we crossed the bar and made our way to the closed door. I gave Bandit one last look, then before I could chicken out, I knocked three times. As before, the door opened, but this time, a guy with a patch over one eye shot us a startled look.

"This ain't no nursery. Get outta here, kid."

He turned his back on me, figuring I would heed his words, however, I shoved my foot in the door and forced my way inside. Eight grown men zeroed in on me, including the guys we had followed.

"I'm here to play." I'm sure I would have sounded more convincing if my voice hadn't wavered at the end of that sentence.

Patch grinned at me, revealing a gaping set of black teeth. I cringed and mentally affirmed I would take better care of my own molars in the future.

"This is a private game, young lady."

I gave him the best glower I could manage.

"I have money," I said. Then I pushed past and marched up to the surprised table. I gestured, and Bandit immediately took his position behind the other players. But he couldn't keep still. I think he was nervous, picking up on my vibes.

A big guy with the dealer's pin smirked at me.

"You're pretty gutsy for a kid."

"And you're pretty chirpy for a guy who's going to lose it all," I shot back. Dealer continued to smirk at me, though there was now a hardness in his eyes. Guess he didn't like being shown up.

"Alright kid. Show us what you've got or get out."

I tensed. This was it. Bandit must have sensed my sudden indecision as he stole back to my side. I reached into my backpack, withdrew my carefully saved stash, and slammed it onto the table with as much force as I could muster.

"Here." I kept my eyes level with his. *Show no fear,* I chanted to myself.

Dealer broke his gaze to take in the money I had slammed down... and burst out laughing. One by one, the men around the table joined him in laughter until the whole room was in an uproar. Except for me. I kept my face a mask of defiance, refusing to show my confusion.

"A hundred and twelve dollars?" he choked out in between laughs. "A hundred and twelve?"

Patch left his position by the door. His grin wider — and even grosser — than before.

"What's so funny?" I demanded.

Dealer leaned back against his seat and pointed to the current betting pot on the table.

"See that? That's just the starting bets for this hand. We open with fifty which means, you wouldn't even last one round." He smiled a slimey smile before continuing.

"While I do find your naivety charming, I think it's time for you and the fleabag to leave."

Patch grabbed my shoulder and started steering me to the door, but I twisted away from him, dived towards the table and grabbed my money. The other men made as if to stop me, but Dealer held them off.

"No. Let her take her hard earned cash. We are men of honor."

At that, the room erupted again. Bandit, not understanding what was happening, whined unhappily.

I shoved the money into my pockets, then tore out of there with Bandit close at my heels. To my fury, I felt tears pricking at the corners of my eyes. Determined that none of them would see me crying, I found a door marked FIRE EXIT and pushed it open. We stumbled out into a back alley.

"I can't believe those jerks!"

Bandit circled me and shoved his nose into my hand. I petted him without thinking and automatically started to feel a bit better. I remembered reading an article on how pets were great stress relievers in a copy of Reader's Digest before. I took several deep breaths and calmed down. *Oh well. Not all of my plans were winners, but at least we didn't lose our money. Could've been worse.*

Bandit bared his teeth at me and growled.

I snatched my hand back, confused by the complete change in him. And then I smelled it. Hard liquor breath.

Breathing down my neck.

I spun around to find the drunk from earlier standing behind me — only now he didn't seem so pitiful. He staggered towards me, reeking of desperation and whiskey. Bandit growled warningly again, baring his sharp white teeth.

"I don't want to hurt you, just give me the money," he pleaded.

Here's the thing you should know about me. I'd managed to make four hundred bills last eight months. You do the math. With a hundred and twelve still left, that meant I'd used roughly a dollar a day to live on, which I think you'll agree is pretty hardcore. I could go four days on what you spend on a coffee. I take nothing more seriously in life than cash. So was I going to hand it over to this drunk? You bet I wasn't.

Seeing the determination on my face, he looked almost apologetic.

"You don't understand. I need that money. It's a matter of life and death."

I almost snorted in his face.

"Welcome to my world, scumbag."

OK. Here's another thing you should know. My mouth shoots off before I even know what I'm doing. It's one of my worst traits and something I really should work on.

All niceness faded from his face, and he lunged for me. Bandit started barking like a crazed thing. I tried to run, but he snagged hold of my backpack and wouldn't let go. Then I tried to elbow him, but my bag got in the way. He must've slipped as I felt his crushing weight land on top of me. We tumbled onto a crate of empty bottles.

I managed to twist around until I was facing him. I kicked out, getting him on his side. It must have hurt as he suddenly shrieked and backhanded me across my face. My head snapped back as stars clouded my vision. There was a metallic taste in my mouth — blood — and I realized I must have bitten my cheek. His hands went for my pockets, where he must have seen me stash the money when a ball of fur suddenly flew towards him.

A scream of agony pierced the night. I watched with fascinated horror as Bandit clamped his fangs around the drunk's right hand — the hand that had hit me and was about to strike again. The drunk was frantically trying to shake him off, but Bandit wasn't letting go for no one. I felt a moment of deep pride. *Go, Boy!*

I was pushing myself up when I saw the drunk reach for a bottle that had had its base smashed off. Jagged edges glinted, caught by an overhead streetlight. It took a split second to realize what his intentions were, but by then I was already too late. I flung myself forward at the same time the bottle flashed through the air and stabbed into Bandit's stomach. He yelped and dropped like a stone.

The drunk stood over him with the bottle raised high, preparing to stab again. Blood pounded in my ears as I realized Bandit wouldn't last another round. I screamed.

"Here! Take it! Leave him alone!" I threw the money at him. A cloud of paper bills rained onto the ground. He scrambled on all fours for the money. When he had taken every last bill, he disappeared down the alley without a second glance.

I bolted to Bandit's side.

15

CHASE

There was so much blood.

My hand pressed tightly against the deep wound, but it barely stemmed the flow. Bandit whined, his whole body trembling in pain. He panted loudly, the white of his eyes showing. Did that mean something? Was he dying? My encyclopedic brain ran through everything I'd ever learned on first aid, but it was no use - the data filed up in there applied only to people.

"Hold on, Boy. You'll be OK," I choked out.

Bandit looked at me like he knew I was lying. Cold panic ripped through me. *No God, please, please let him be OK.* My heart was thumping so loudly I thought it would explode from my chest. There was a high-pitched ringing in my ears that dulled the world around me. Abruptly the ringing died down and I could hear with crystal clarity: nearby cars screeching to a halt as the drunk skidded into traffic, followed by car horns blaring, and screeching tires. In a white rage, I hoped for the resounding thump that would signal a collision, but it never came. Why do the bad guys always get away?

Unwrapping the scarf from his neck, I turned it into a tight bandage and tied it over the wound, but I'd barely finished the knots before his blood seeped through, blossoming over the thin material and staining it red. I had to get help. He wouldn't last much longer like this.

I wrapped my arms around his body and tried to lift, but he was so heavy, my legs started to buckle from the effort. A whimper escaped his lips as I tried unsuccessfully to lay him down again gently. I spun around, taking in the junk in the alley: there were multiple trash cans, some boxes, and something half hidden behind a doorway. I jogged forward a few steps and had to stop myself from bursting into tears of relief. It was a little worn, but there was no denying the Whole Foods shopping cart!

Quickly, I grabbed a box, flattened it, and shoved it inside the cart. Shrugging out of my denim jacket, I lay it on top. It wasn't much, but it was the best I could do to soften what was going to be a very bumpy ride. With a strength I didn't know I possessed, I maneuvered Bandit onto the makeshift gurney. He flopped loosely in my arms and barely made a sound. This I knew was a very bad sign. I slid a hand under his nose and felt a weak blast of hot air against my fingers. Still breathing.

"Hang on, I'm getting you help."

Seizing the handles of the cart, I thundered out of the alley.

16
———

CHASE

Shop fronts blurred past, but none were what we needed. I didn't stop for anyone. There was no time. Pedestrians dived out of my way, shouting insults. Did they think this was some kind of sick game? I shot another glance at Bandit and paled at the blood that was turning my jacket red. He wasn't even that big. *How could he have so much blood?* The thought briefly crossed my mind that Bandit wasn't fully grown. He was probably quite young. I shook my head and focused.

Where were we going?

Suddenly, I knew what to do. My eyes swept up and down the streets until I pinpointed a telephone booth across the road. I swung the cart so hard the wheels shrieked in protest. Then, not waiting for a gap in the traffic, I ran into the road.

Brakes screamed. Horns blared. An irate driver leaned out of the window and yelled some pretty foul things at me. I ignored them all and pushed the cart over the street. Bandit's tongue was hanging completely out of his mouth now. It was pale. Almost white. Definitely not a good sign.

Making it to the booth, relief flooded through me when I saw the phone directory hanging by a cord. I flung it open and prayed I'd find what I needed.

17

SULLY

I stared into the carton of another unappetizing takeout. Oily noodles with burned pieces of rubber that masqueraded as chicken. That home-cooked lasagna sounded mighty good right about now. Shame it was nothing but a stain on the sidewalk.

I let out a long sigh. I shouldn't have flipped like that. In the last ten months, I had systematically severed ties to all our friends — anything that reminded me of my previous life with Emma. A few had stubbornly hung on in there, but I had managed to push away every one of them until Mark was the only friend I had left. Except maybe now that bridge was burned too.

I reached for a Coors and gulped the sweetness down. Tomorrow I'd call and eat humble pie. But not tonight. Tonight was terrible-Chinese-and-get-drunk-in-front-of-the-box night. All day, Florence had spoken to me in a clipped tone of voice laced with disappointment. I had tried explaining my side, but Florence wasn't interested in anything I had to say. She was so steaming mad that — despite being her boss — I had given her a wide berth. What that woman couldn't do for Catholic guilt.

I got up from the dining table and moved to the window. Emma had always loved this view. I stared past the perfectly manicured neighborhood lawns and into the distance, where just below the horizon, the New York skyline blazed with lights. This view was the reason we had bought this place. "A little piece of heaven," she had called it.

I thought Emma had lost her mind when she first set eyes on the rundown property and declared that this would be our forever home. Its previous elderly owner had long given up on the upkeep, and time had taken its toll on the bricks and mortar. The neighborhood disliked the eyesore, but put up with it due to their love and respect for the old coot.

Like many other times in her life, Emma had seen the potential of the place and had haggled like a pro until the real estate agents — disarmed by her tenacity and charm — finally caved. I thought of the happy months we'd spent renovating the property to change it from the dump it used to be.

I closed my eyes so I could see her again. Hair piled messily on top of her head, she wore those painted-splattered dungarees she liked for decorating. She waved a loaded paint brush around - narrowly missing my face — and painted different color patches on the wall, which in fairness all looked yellow to me. Then she stood back to study them. I loved the way her nose wrinkled whenever she was thinking. When she had finally decided on a tone, I had grabbed her hand and twirled her around as we'd danced to the radio in celebration. Our marriage had been filled with silly, wonderful moments like these.

My eyes flashed open, filled with tears. *Oh Em. It should've been me.*

The familiar, crushing ache began to build inside. I grabbed my head and squeezed. My head pounded with the pain I was physically causing, but I kept up the pressure until I couldn't take it anymore. My hands dropped to my sides, relieved that the raw pain in my heart had momentarily been interrupted.

But the pounding continued.

I frowned as I slowly came to the realization that the pounding wasn't in my head anymore.

It was real.

18

CHASE

I could see the lights on the floor upstairs. So why wasn't he coming?

The sign on the window confirmed that this was the place I was looking for. Although the clinic was closed now, I knew someone lived above. I had seen his silhouette by the window.

I stabbed at the bell with a bloody finger while pounding on the door with my other hand.

"Please," I cried desperately. "We need help!"

Finally, a hazy figure appeared through the glazed glass and began moving forwards. Lights flooded on, blinding me. Then I heard the furious voice of whom I assumed was the vet.

"Why the hell are you pounding on my door? Do you know what time..."

His sentence trailed off. I could feel, rather than see, him looking over my shoulder.

"What the—?"

"You've got to help him. He's been stabbed."

19

SULLY

I barely registered the sight before me.

The kid — she must've been all of fifteen — was covered in blood and hysterical. A quick scan of her body revealed she wasn't harmed. However, I couldn't say the same for the dog lying in the shopping cart.

He was a tri-colored liver Border Collie. Pedigree, and very rare judging by his green eyes. He was also dying of a gaping wound in his stomach. Normally I wouldn't take house calls this time of night, but this was clearly an emergency, and if I didn't do anything, the dog was going to die.

The girl was babbling at me, but I'd already tuned her out, my professional head taking over. I grabbed the cart and wheeled it inside.

"Close the door and come with me," I commanded.

Surprisingly, the girl shut her mouth and complied.

I steered the dog into the operating theater and hoisted him onto the table. I felt for his pulse; it was weak, but it was there. A quick examination of the wound revealed a laceration deep enough that it exposed both muscle and tissue. He'd lost a lot of blood. I pursed my lips. Infection, along with possible organ failure, was a very real concern right now.

"I'll need to operate to have any chance of saving him."

"Do it," she said. "Whatever you need to do, just don't let him die!"

"Go wait in the lounge."

This time, however, she wouldn't comply, shaking her head violently. "I'm not leaving him! This only happened because of me. I was attacked. He saved me." The Girl's voice cracked as she struggled to hold back the tears. I had seen upset kids before, especially when I'd had to put down their beloved pets, but this was something else. This level of desperation reminded me of myself at the hospital, at Emma's bedside, holding onto her pale and non-responsive hand... Shaking my head to clear the unwelcome memory, I took in her battered clothing and general griminess. She was a street kid, I would bet my life on it. This dog was probably her only friend in the world.

I softened my voice.

"I'll do the best I can, but you can't be in here. He has an open wound. You could risk infecting him."

My words sliced into her panic. She looked up at me then and must have been reassured by what she saw there. She swallowed, then nodded, moving across the room. When she reached the door, she shot me a pleading look.

"You have to save him, OK? He's special."

I nodded and got to work. Reaching across the bench, I snapped on a pair of gloves then set up a donor blood bag, measuring out the correct dose of anesthetic for a dog this size.

When I looked up again, she had gone.

20

CHASE

I left the operating theater, but there was no way I could just sit there, twiddling my thumbs. Bandit's life was hanging by a thread, and I couldn't believe there was nothing I could do! Flashes of our recent travels came into my head like a movie of our best moments that was being projected directly into my mind. I could feel myself on the verge of a panic attack and had to clamp down on it. *Breathe!*

I ran my tongue over parched lips to discover how dry they were. Like someone whose brain's been lobotomized, I didn't even know how I had gotten there. All I can remember is seeing the details for this place in the directory then running the eight blocks here. For the first time, I noticed my surroundings.

I was standing in a waiting area. There was no hiding the fact I was in a veterinary clinic, but someone had given it a good try. The room was painted a cheery yellow, and a giant bulletin board wrapped around the four walls with hundreds of photographs pinned onto it. I moved in for a closer look.

They were all snapshots of healthy animals and their happy owners. Scribbled on some were messages addressed to "Sully" thanking him for his great work with Fido, Gizmo, and Dodo. I scanned the many messages and felt a tiny spark of relief at the sheer number of success stories contained on the board. I decided right then that when this was all over, there'd be one more photograph stuck on this board.

I glanced at the name again — Sully — and guessed that that must be the guy with his hands inside Bandit now. The thought of that brought a vivid image to mind that struck me with renewed terror as a wave of nausea overcame me.

I bolted into the next room, hoping it was a restroom, but found myself inside a kitchen. I ran to the sink and got there just in time for the acrid bile to fly out of my mouth. I retched until my stomach cramped and there was nothing left inside.

Afterward, I wiped my mouth on my sleeve and drank a glass of water, giving myself a few moments to recover. My forehead was clammy, and I suddenly noticed my hands were shaking. Maybe my sugar level was low. Come to think of it, I hadn't eaten since the pretzel that morning. Driven by the natural instinct to survive, I pulled open the kitchen cupboards and investigated their contents.

The first had neatly lined rows of mugs advertising different pet food brands. I marveled that someone — clearly with nothing better to do — had taken the time to face them outward and turn their handles to the right. Somehow I didn't think it was that Sully guy.

The next cupboard contained a mixture of hot drinks and powdered milk. I actually contemplated taking the milk since it was still a source of protein, but then I arrived at the final cupboard and hit the jackpot! Inside, there was a smattering of energy bars, a box of cereal, and a couple of packs of cookies. I swiped the bars and cookies and snagged a handful of cereal, which I crammed into my starving mouth. I must've swallowed half the box before I reluctantly set it aside. I'd stripped the entire cupboard in under a minute, which must've been a record.

A part of me felt bad about what I was doing. Sully was in the next room attempting to save Bandit's life, and here I was thieving, but something told me if he knew the truth, he wouldn't really have minded. Judging by what I'd found here, he could more than afford to eat. Besides, if Bandit survived, he'd need all the food I could salvage.

I fingered an energy bar, sorely tempted. Saliva flooded my mouth, and I could almost taste the sweetness, but I stopped short of tearing open the wrapper. Although my stomach churned with hunger, I decided I would save it for Bandit. It was the least I could do.

I opened the fridge. Instead of the food I expected to find, there were boxes and boxes of medical vials and syringes. As they were of no value to me, I closed the fridge and resumed my exploration of the house. Two doors lead out of the kitchen: one opened into a no-frills bathroom, the other onto the base of some carpeted stairs. I wondered if I should keep going - the stairs didn't have the same feel as the rest of the clinic. Framed certificates and memorabilia lined the walls, which weren't yellow anymore, but a pale green. I hesitated, but then I convinced myself that if I kept myself occupied,

I wouldn't think about the scene next door — and the potentially devastating result.

Cocking my head, I listened for any sounds of life from upstairs, but there was nothing. I'm usually pretty stealthy, and this carpet would muffle any excess sound, even if I weren't unusually light on my feet. I headed up, telling myself I only meant to have a peek.

When I reached the top, I found myself in a living room. Huge windows looked out onto the upmarket neighborhood. I guess this was a nice place. Kinda hard to see it though, covered in trash like it was. Takeout cartons and burger wrappers littered the place. I picked up the nearest carton. Whatever it was had long died and was now a congealed green soup. Nice. I set the box down.

The room was painted in yet another cheerful color, this time a spring orange. Drooping plants with brown encrusted leaves overflowed from every window. Whoever had the green thumb hadn't cared for them in quite some time. I moved past a sofa covered with workout clothes and investigated the many framed photographs on a bookshelf. Sully had his arms around a pretty woman in every one. There they were running down a beach; sharing a dog at a Red Sox game; sipping coconut shell cocktails in an exotic far eastern place (Thailand?). I stopped on the last photograph on their wedding day. Could two people look more in love?

Would I ever experience love like that?

I carried on through the living room into a hallway, past the bathroom, and found myself in Sully's bedroom. Like the rest of the house, it was messy. *Why do people have nice homes if all they're going to do is trash them?*

Yes, I felt weird in a grown man's room. I knew I had to keep myself occupied though, so my mind wouldn't play the "what if" game. You know like, "What if Bandit doesn't make it?"

See, not good, is it?

The walk-in closet stood out, as it was the only tidy thing in here. Inside, dresses and shirts hung neatly on hangers, all arranged in the same direction, and in ascending length order. So cropped tops started on the far left, mid length shirts took up the middle section, and by the time you got to the right, the hems of full length dresses draped on the floor.

I noted Sully's wife was petite; only a size bigger than me. I hoped she wasn't one of those who starved herself to look good and thought back to the happy face in the pictures I had seen. No, she seemed much more sensible than that.

My fingers reached out, itching to feel the fabric of a beautiful white dress, but before they could make contact, I whipped them back in horror. Dried blood covered my hands.

Bandit's blood.

I spun around and staggered into the bathroom to see my gruesome reflection staring back at me. There was blood all over my top, on my face, and in my hair. How had I not noticed this before?

I blasted the tap and frantically started scrubbing.

21

SULLY

I had been working on the collie now for close to two hours.

My mind was a blur. I wasn't even sure how I'd managed it on my own. I'd set up a blood transfusion — taking blood from a healthy dog who was in for a broken paw. Putting an animal under can be tricky on even a healthy animal, but on one as injured as this, well, there's a lot of luck and prayer involved. Sometimes the animals reacted to the anesthetic and never woke up again.

I hoped that wasn't the case here.

The nasty gashes in his stomach were caused by a sharp, serrated instrument. Amazingly, no internal organs were punctured. I concluded that whatever had sliced into him hadn't penetrated his intestines. I cleaned the wound the best I could, sewed it up, and covered it with a bandage. I'd have to check on the wound regularly. The worst thing that could happen now was for it to get infected. Having done everything I could to save him, all we could do now was wait. Hopefully, he'd come around in a few hours.

After I disinfected the instruments and pulled off the rubber gloves, I took my first unhurried look at him. He really was a gorgeous thing. Glossy white coat with brown patches. Unusually, his face was white, barring the top right section, dissected in a perfect diagonal under his nose. His eyes were closed now, but I knew they were a brilliant jade green. He was worth a lot to someone. Somehow I didn't think he belonged to the girl.

Although the dog was currently malnourished, there were signs it wasn't always this way. His blood pressure was low, but that was par for the course with blood loss to this degree. The cracks on his feet were new, which was unusual in and of itself. I'd pegged him for about two years old and never had I seen soles so smooth. Almost as if he'd never stepped foot outside before.

His teeth were so pristine you'd think his owner had used whitener on them. No buildup, only slight doggy breath. I looked inside his left ear. As expected, it was spotless — also unusual for a dog that's been on the streets. Tugging gently on the dog's right ear, I looked inside to see a row of numbers and letters tattooed into his ear. It was some kind of identifying code. I jotted it onto a notepad I kept handy and made a mental note to look into this when I knew more about the dog's condition.

My neck muscles complained wearily. I reached up to massage them, surprised to find it was almost eleven at night. Suddenly my thoughts drifted to the girl, and my stomach twisted into knots. I'd let a complete stranger — and a homeless one at that — loose in my home.

Stupid, Sully. Stupid.

I ran from the operating room.

22

SULLY

I ran into the waiting room, but the girl wasn't there (not that I had really expected her to be, but sometimes, it's nice to be proven wrong). She wasn't in the hallway or kitchen, and my office was empty, which just left *upstairs*. I swallowed as a bitterness began a party in my mouth. Taking two steps at a time, I raced upstairs...

And gave a huge sigh of relief. Everything was as I had left it. ~~We~~ I hadn't been burgled. The room was still a bomb site, except now, buried under my workout clothes on the sofa, the girl slept. I froze and gave what Em had fondly dubbed my bug out face.

She dressed tough, but it couldn't hide the fact she was a naturally cute kid, albeit one who'd had it rough. The bottoms of her jeans were worn, and the soles of her baseball boots, coming apart. A dirty backpack lay on the floor next to her. Even in sleep, its strap was looped tightly around her wrist.

It was that single detail that undid me. Explained a lot about her life. I wondered what horror made her run away from wherever she was from.

I didn't want to wake her, but I couldn't just hop into bed either, so I did the next best thing. I opened the fridge and took out a loaf of bread, some butter, and a block of cheese.

Moments later, two packed grilled cheese sandwiches were toasting in a skillet. Before Em had passed, I was the cook in the house, but it had been a while since I'd wanted to do anything this domestic. If my instincts were right, I figured the girl would be hungry.

Besides, I had questions, and answers were always more forthcoming when softened with a bribe.

23

———

CHASE

I was dreaming.

Bandit and I were stuck in this weird Matrix style world, only instead of computer binary codes, we were surrounded by drunks hurling playing cards at us, and in the background, there was this sizzling sound, like someone was cooking a BBQ, except the meat smelled liked burned cheese.

My nose wrinkled involuntarily. It was like a magic compass and always did that when food was on the horizon. Dimly, I was aware of more noises: the scraping of plates and pots banging. My eyes flashed open, and I leaped up with a snarl, ready to fight.

Sully was standing at the sink, a tea towel over one shoulder, his mouth wide open, startled by my aggressive stance. I blinked at him, completely disoriented.

"Hi there," he said.

I didn't reply, glancing wearily around the room instead. *Well, this was pretty stupid of me. Alone. In a stranger's home.*

"You hungry? I made grilled cheese." He gestured at the dining table where the sandwiches waited with two glasses of milk.

My stomach made an involuntary sound. Something between a growl and all out shouting. I wanted nothing more than to sink my teeth into that sticky cheesiness, but there was something I had to know first.

"Bandit, my dog..." Fear constricted my throat so tightly, the words got stuck, and I couldn't finish the full sentence.

Sully's expression was grave but hopeful.

"I did what I could. He just has to rest now. If he comes out of the anesthetic, there's a good chance he'll make it."

"*If* he comes out?" I questioned.

Sully held my gaze as he spoke. "It can be hit and miss for a healthy dog and Bandit, you said?"

I nodded.

"He was cut pretty bad," he continued. "All we can do is give him time."

I flung my bag onto my shoulder and started for the stairs.

"So we should be by his side, right? What if he wakes up and no one's there? What if he's in pain?" Clearly, I had forgotten my own rules of that game. I made it to the top step when Sully stopped me.

"That much trauma, combined with the anesthetic, he'll be out for at least four hours. Plenty of time for us to eat and get to know each other."

I must've shot him a hard look, as he suddenly backed off, mortified.

"I meant that in a far less creepy way than it sounded," he said.

I hesitated, but honestly? I was growing so faint from hunger that the only thing stopping me from falling down the stairs was my hand clutching hold of the banister. Gruffly, I nodded and went across to the table. He sat opposite me.

"I'm Sully."

"Chase," I mumbled as I grabbed the sandwich nearest to me and bit into it. The taste was so overwhelmingly good, so fresh, that if I had any tears left in me, I would've cried.

Sully tried not to watch me as he started on his own. We ate quietly for a few seconds. Just two strangers enjoying a meal. He was good, I'd give him that. Not one question so far, but I knew they were coming. I braced myself. He polished off his sandwich in five or six bites while I was determined to savor mine. Who knew when I'd be eating like this again? He gulped down his milk and wiped a hand across his mouth.

"What happened?" he asked simply.

Usually, whenever a grown-up asks me anything, my first instinct is to lie. I'm not even sure why. Call it my healthy distrust of them. But this guy seemed different. After all, he could've called the cops on me the minute I turned up at his door, but instead, he'd helped Bandit and cooked me a meal. Figured I owed him the truth, if nothing else.

"A drunk attacked me, took all my money. Bandit tried to protect me, but the drunk stabbed him with a bottle." My voice was flat. I could've been reciting the weather report for all the emotion I showed.

Sully looked shocked. There was a well of sadness reflected in his eyes, but all he uttered was "Tough break."

I appreciated he didn't try to make this into a thing. I finished my sandwich, drank the milk, and pushed back my chair. The food was a nice gesture, but it didn't make us bff's. I was determined to put a little distance between us. As I stood up, there was a strange expression on Sully's face. Took me a while before I realized he was staring at my bloodstained shirt. I plucked at it self-consciously.

"There's a washer downstairs. I can take care of that?" he volunteered.

I looked down, embarrassed by his kindness.

"I don't have anything else to wear while it's in the wash."

He studied me for what seemed an indeterminable amount of time before speaking again. "Wait here." He disappeared from the room, returning moments later with a pair of jeans, a tank top, and an olive green sweater. I'd seen those clothes earlier, in the closet, but didn't want him to know I'd been snooping. He handed me the clothes.

"Probably a bit big, but... you can keep these." The words seemed to stick in his throat.

I couldn't hide my surprise.

"Won't your wife be mad?"

Pain flashed in his eyes. I knew instantly I'd said something wrong. He clenched his fists and closed his eyes. I guess he was counting in his head or something. When he spoke it again, it was barely a whisper.

"She doesn't need them anymore."

Things suddenly fell into place. The terrible mess in the nicely decorated house. The decaying plants. Sully's wife wasn't around anymore. I didn't know whether she had left or died, but I knew not to ask. The guy looked like he was hanging by a thread.

His shoulders slumped as he piled dirty plates into the sink.

"I'll wait with Bandit. You can use the bathroom if you want. Up to you."

With that, he turned and went downstairs.

I stood there, the clothes clutched in my arms. A huge part of me was thrilled at the thought of a hot shower, but this guy was still a stranger. I looked at the pretty clothes he'd given me. They smelled of lavender. There was no way I could change into them as I was. The blood in my hair had dried, giving me unwanted red low lights with a disgusting, crunchy texture. He'd said Bandit wouldn't wake for a while. What was the harm?

Still, I hadn't survived so long on the streets without learning a thing or two. I dragged a chair into the bathroom with me, locked the door, and wedged the chair up against it. If he tried to break in while I was in the shower... well, he wouldn't be able to.

I turned the water on full blast, peeled the blood-soaked clothes off my body, and stepped into the shower.

24

SULLY

I couldn't believe how I'd reacted to her simple question. I'd played it off, but the truth was, I'd needed to be alone for a while. Pretending everything was fine was exhausting, and that was on top of the long day I'd already had. I knew I would have to pull an all-nighter to watch over the dog. Usually, I'd farm that out to staff, but since I was the only one around tonight... at least I wouldn't have my nightly sleep struggle.

I checked in on Bandit. He was still out, but his color had improved somewhat. I placed my fingers on the inner side of Bandit's thigh and felt for a pulse on the femoral artery. The beat was slow and steady. Another positive sign.

The old boiler kicked into gear, the ancient pipes rattling within the confines of the walls. Chase was taking me up on the shower. Good. She'd smelled pretty foul, but I hadn't wanted to put her on edge any more than she already was.

With nothing else to do, I suddenly remembered the serial number tattooed into Bandit's ear and fetched the laptop from my office. Firing up the MacBook, I typed the numbers into a veterinary database of found animals. I hit return and waited, not really expecting to get a result.

I was wrong.

Within seconds, a warning flashed across the screen:

If you see this dog, call us immediately on the following number.
He has escaped from a medical facility and carries a contagious virus.

The virus is NOT transmittable to humans. Repeat. It is NOT transmittable to
humans. However, you should not approach him.
Please call and we will handle the extraction.
On his safe return, you will be handsomely rewarded.

The warning was followed by a picture of Bandit at full health. I was right; he was a stunning dog, and now I knew why.

He was a lab dog. A virus carrying medical experiment.

Despite the wrench in my gut and how I knew this would kill the young girl upstairs, I did what any professional in my line of work would do.

I picked up the phone and dialed.

25

———

SULLY

After a few rings, the call was answered by a curt female voice.

"HPA, how can I be of assistance?"

"Hi," I began. "I'm calling about a warning you filed with the National Pets Registrar about a missing Tri-colored border collie."

There was a sudden silence on the line. When she spoke again, it was with barely controlled enthusiasm.

"I'm a vet with a clinic in Connecticut. A girl just arrived with an injured dog, pretty sure it's the one you're looking for."

"Could you give me your name, sir?" she asked.

"Jake Sullivan. I run Ellington Pet Care in Sudbury Park Estate."

"Thank you, sir. Now, I have a few questions for our extraction team. Have you come in close contact with the dog?"

"Yes. He was injured. I performed a basic op and sewed up the wound. He'd lost quite a bit of blood, but I performed a single transfusion."

"I see." She didn't sound pleased by my having saved his life. I got the distinct feeling the dog was nothing but an experiment to her. It made my betrayal to Chase all the harder. "And either before or during the operation, did you communicate with the dog at all?"

I paused, perplexed. *What kind of question was that?* She must have felt my hesitation as she quickly tried to cover it up.

"What I mean to say is, was the dog awake when he was brought to you?"

"Barely," I replied.

"So you didn't speak to him, he didn't respond?"

OK. This was getting weird. I frowned at her line of questioning.

"I'm sorry, what kind of medical facility is this?" I asked.

"Please hold, sir."

Cheesy elevator music piped down the line. I was stunned. I'd asked a simple question, and she'd put me on hold? Something felt wrong about this whole scenario. I held the phone in my hand, wondering how long it would be before she got back to me when the music abruptly cut out. I sat there, shocked, hearing nothing but the dead dial tone. *She'd cut me off?!* Turning around on my stool, my eyes followed the cord to the phone — and stopped dead.

Bandit sat next to the phone, awake, his paw nestled firmly in the cradle. It was he who had cut me off.

26

SULLY

T he dog and I traded looks. Then slowly — slowly — Bandit lifted his paw off the cradle, planted his foot on the ground, and shot me what I could only describe as a hurt look.

Though I was puzzling over what had happened, my work instincts took over. My eyes ran over him, performing a quick check. All things considered, he was in great form. More than great if you considered he shouldn't be able to stand right now. This was one driven dog.

Bandit started sniffing the air anxiously. I wondered what he was doing before it came to me.

"She's upstairs," I informed him. "Chase. She's having a shower."

As if he understood exactly what I was saying, he stared straight up at the ceiling and cocked his head, listening for any movement above him. He must've heard something that confirmed my words because the anxiousness disappeared, replaced by a weariness he directed at me.

I wasn't sure why I was talking to him like a human, but I couldn't deny there was keen intelligence that shone from his eyes. We kept a watchful eye on each other until the door cracked open behind him, followed by the appearance of Chase. The change in Bandit was immediate. His tail wagged back and forth so vigorously that it almost threw his whole balance — he was still shaking off the effects of the anesthetic.

"Bandit!" Chase went to hug the dog, but I grabbed her arm and physically stopped her.

"Wait. There's something you need to know about him," I began. Chase turned to Bandit then, a reproachful look on her face.

"What did I say about keeping it secret? What did you do?" she demanded.

To my surprise, Bandit acted like a child being reprimanded. He lowered onto all fours (showing submission) and whined pitifully. Though he couldn't speak, his actions were clear. *It wasn't me. I didn't do anything.*

"Yeah, right," Chase chided. "Couldn't wait to show off, I'll bet."

Bandit barked twice.

"At least you're alive, though. That's what counts."

One bark. Followed by a long, relieved sigh.

I saw animals respond to their owners all the time. Florence had three cats who talked to her nonstop, even mimicked the sounds and tones of her voice. It's the highest form of compliment a pet can ever give their owner.

I love you so much I'm going to learn to speak the way you do.

But what was happening here wasn't the same. I looked questionably at Chase. She sighed too as if the game was up.

"One bark is yes, two means no."

"What?" I managed to mumble.

She turned to the dog. "Boy, are you hungry?"

One bark.

"What about a drink, you thirsty?"

One bark.

"Did you like the man who hurt you earlier?"

Two angry sounding barks.

"Am I glad you're alive?"

One joyful bark.

I watched the whole exchange with my mouth open, but Chase didn't catch my reaction. She busied herself at the sink and gave Bandit a bowl of water, which he slurped up gratefully. To me, she asked, "Can he eat something?"

I nodded mutely and grabbed a tin of doggie chow from a shelf. Inside, my mind was racing. There was no way in hell they'd rehearsed that little charade, no way, but then... how was that possible? Was this some kind of hustle these two did? Was the dog just a distraction, and I was about to get robbed? I shook my head. No, there were plenty of richer houses in this neighborhood, and Bandit's wound could not be faked, and neither could Chase's very real concern.

My thoughts a tangled mess, and unable to make sense of it all, I focused on the one thing I could do — pouring the dog food onto a plate — but as I went towards him, Bandit bared his teeth at me. Startled by his reaction, Chase frowned.

"Sully's our friend, Boy."

Two barks.

"He is, he saved you."

Two barks and a worried whine. Chase looked up at me in apology.

"I'm sorry, I don't know why he has a problem with you."

"I do," I said quietly. Suddenly the phone call with "HPA" resounded in my head. One sentence in particular which hadn't made much sense at first, but now cast a whole new light on things: *did you communicate with the dog at all?* Could it be? Could this dog have the same intelligence level as a human?

"I... I think I might've made a mistake."

One loud bark.

Chase didn't understand a thing I was saying, but she was a smart girl and fear was fast sinking in. I could tell by her sudden sped up breathing.

"Oh no. Who did you tell?" she asked.

I shook my head, still unwilling to accept what my mind was starting to rationalize.

"There was a warning. They said he escaped from a medical facility. That he carried a virus."

Bandit shot two barks at me and pawed the ground, agitated. Chase was staring at me in utter horror.

"No, they were doing horrible things to him. He escaped yes, but he doesn't have a virus. They're lying!"

"But... how do you know that's true?"

Chase all but wrung her hands at me. "Just look at him! What more proof do you need?!"

The dog was pacing agitatedly, Chase matching him stride for stride. A gnawing ache appeared in my stomach.

Doubt.

"It's too late," I said. "I've already called them."

Chase flung her bag over her shoulder, cold determination on her face. "Then we have to go."

Bandit stood up immediately, ready to leave with her when suddenly, two vehicles screeched into the drive. I ran to the nearest window and looked through a crack in the blind.

Two unmarked gray vans sat outside. The doors slid open, revealing six or so swarthy men in black combat gear. They spilled out of the vans welding tranquilizer guns and took formation on the front porch. My trained eyes recognized the darts on the guns — Ketamine — but at that dosage, it'd be enough to knock out a horse. Grimly, I remembered Keta-mine could also be used on humans.

The doorbell rang.

We all froze.

A clipped baritone called in through the letter-box.

"Good evening, Mr. Sullivan. We're from HPA, and we're here for the extraction. Could you let us in?"

27

CHASE

"What're we going to do?" I whispered. *"We can't let them take him."*
Bandit chuffed softly in agreement. I flung an arm around his neck, hugging him close. Sully watched us guiltily from his position by the window.

"I'm sorry. I don't see any way out of this."

Indignant fury made me brave. "You were the one who caused this! You can't *not* help us now!"

"Legally, he's their property, and you have no idea what virus it is he's carrying. He could be dangerous," Sully said.

I threw my hands up in the air, exasperated. "They're lying to get him back, can't you see that? It's not like they can say he's super intelligent!"

Sully peeked out of the window again. Then back at us. He obviously still didn't believe the four-legged truth that was staring him in the face. "Do you know what they'll do to him if they get him back?" I pleaded. "They'll lock him in a cage, and he'll never be free again!"

My words must have struck a chord, as involuntarily, Bandit started shaking with fear. It was awful to see, but so was the resigned expression on Sully's face.

"I've done what I can..." He trailed off, unable to find the words to finish the sentence, but I already knew where he was going with this. Glaring at him, I unzipped my bag.

"Give me the meds I'll need for him. At least do that for us." I gestured at him impatiently as anger and fear flooded my body. Coming to a decision, Sully sprang into action and started tossing things inside.

"You'll need to change his bandage twice a day. Clean the wound with disinfectant and cover it up again." He shoved a bottle of pills into the bag. "He also needs one of these, three times a day, preferably with food." Sully zipped up my bag and steered me to the kitchen. "Take the back door and head right. There's a path behind the back yard that's pretty overlooked by the trees. They won't see you there."

He stopped suddenly. "Look, whatever this is about, I really am sorry."

Bandit must have decided he was being sincere as his tongue snaked out and licked Sully's hand. And in that tiny gesture, all was forgiven. Sully's eyes turned bright with something that looked suspiciously like tears, but before I could get a proper look, he took off.

"Where are you going?" I called after him.

"To buy you time," he replied.

28

SULLY

I had no idea what I was doing. I knew I should hand Bandit over to the men at the door, but I couldn't shake the doubt that had crept into my mind. Things just weren't adding up.

As I moved slowly down the hall, I ran over the things that were bothering me: like the conversation with HPA and the bizarre line of questioning that had come from the receptionist. And now the men standing on my front porch. How on Earth had they gotten here so quickly when not even an hour had passed since my call?

I stared at the silhouettes of the men outside. Virus or not, did they really need so many of them? Wasn't that overkill? They looked more like a SWAT team than the animal wranglers a lab might have. I took a deep breath and moved the last few steps towards them when THE DOOR EXPLODED INWARD.

Splintered wood flew past my face, narrowly missing my cheek. Reacting on pure instinct, I ran back into the clinic, into the waiting area. Dazed, my ears ringing, I briefly wondered how tranquilizer guns could've done that to the door. Staring down the hall, I got my first close-up look at the men and saw that a few carried not tranquilizer guns, but *shotguns*. Well, that would explain how my door was now hanging off its hinges. Realizing with a growing horror that these men weren't what they seemed, I knew I was in grave danger.

I bolted into my office, to the work desk where two phones (a landline and my cell), my wallet, and a dock for my laptop lay. I snatched up the phone intending to call the police, but instead of a dial tone, there was a scratchy whine. I dropped it back onto its cradle and snatched up the cell, flipping it open only to find that same scratchy noise.

They were blocking my phone lines!

Sounds of crashing came from the room next door. The men were storming my home now, overturning furniture and destroying everything in their path. They would be here in seconds.

Not knowing what else to do, I snatched up my wallet and started heading for the back door, through the recovery room, when one of the men pounced on me. Though I was taller, my adversary had at least thirty pounds on me. I swiveled on my feet until I faced him. The guy snarled into my face.

"Stop fighting, Doc. It'll go better for you."

I hated people telling me what to do at the best of times, but this jerk was in *my* house. Glowering at him, I stomped on his toes, then swept my foot up behind his knee, knocking him off balance. He went down like a fallen tree. I hopped over him, but the guy's hand snaked out and caught me around the ankle. I grabbed the water bowl Bandit had been using and swung it at the guy's head. *One, two, three times!* Steel smashed into his skull until the guy was out for the count.

"He's in here!" I heard someone shout.

I bolted through the recovery room towards the exit when Chase's panicked voice cried out suddenly. "Help, help!!" A cacophony of dog and cat cries blanketed the night, distressed from the attack.

They were in the kennels.

I crept towards them silently, hoping the animal calls would mask any sound I made. Plastering myself to the corner, I saw Chase gripped by two men. One had a deep scar on the left side of his face. The other had the build and stature of ex-military. He had a commanding and menacing presence and only spoke when necessary. This must be the scumbag in charge.

Scarface shook Chase roughly.

"Where's the dog, kid?"

"You're too late," Chase cried. "He's long gone."

I had to hand it to her. Nothing fazed this girl. Scarface didn't seem as impressed though as his hand lashed across her face, leaving an angry red imprint of his palm. Chase's head snapped back violently. Just seeing it made my teeth jar; I don't know what it must have felt like for Chase.

"That all you got?" she taunted, eyes flashing.

A vein in Scarface's forehead throbbed. His hand clenched into a fist as he went to punch her again. But suddenly a sea of cats and dogs spilled out of the kennels, swarming around their feet! Scarface tried to find Bandit but couldn't keep up with them.

"Boss?" he asked.

"Go," the military man instructed. "I'll deal with the girl." His hand slid into his Kevlar vest to retrieve a wicked looking syringe.

I didn't know what was in the needle this time, but I knew it couldn't be good. While the last thing I wanted was to become embroiled in whatever the heck was going on here, I couldn't in all good conscience let them hurt the girl; Emma would turn in her grave. If I was going to do anything, I had to act now.

Using the animals as cover, I stole behind Military Man and struck at his syringe-wielding hand. Not expecting the move, the needle dropped to the ground, where, stampeded by a heavy-footed Bull Mastiff, it shattered into a million pieces. Military Man roared furiously, turning his attention to me, flinging Chase to one side.

"Run!' I screamed.

Chase bolted down the hall as Military Man barreled into me, crushing the breath from my windpipe. Grabbing me in a headlock, he squeezed. I felt a wall of muscle constricting my airway, pushing down on my chest. This must be what a car feels like in a steel compactor, came my distant thought. I clawed feebly at Military Man, but he held on with vice-like arms.

As the world began to swim, and I started seeing stars, there came a chorus of ferocious barking. I felt the pressure easing slightly and twisted my face in the direction of the sound. Some escaped dogs had formed a circle and were snarling at us.

Wait, not at us. At Military Man.

Globules of thick saliva dripped out of the Bull Mastiff's mouth. Low, threatening growls reverberated in the back of his throat. Unsurprisingly, Military Man took a step back.

It was a mistake. The dogs advanced as one.

In one smooth move, Military Man released me and sprinted for the operating theater. The dogs raced past me, bounding after him.

I was in shock and stood there, gaping stupidly after them. After a few moments, I looked towards the exit to see Chase and Bandit running away. I stared back at the clinic, at the home I had made with Emma and which was now being destroyed. My heart seized in my chest. I knew it was just panic, but it felt as serious as a heart attack. Every instinct in my body screamed at me to rush upstairs and save Emma's precious things. Her smiling face on our wedding day — my favorite picture of her, and the one that I had had to place face down as the sight of it tore me apart — flashed up in my head. All I had to do was run up those stairs, and into the bedroom, and the picture would be there...

Then another image flashed up. Chase's anxious, tear-streaked face when she had first appeared on my doorstep, with Bandit, bleeding out in the shopping cart.

As I fought with myself over what to do, a gunshot blasted into my reverie, causing me to crash back down to Earth.

Tearing my gaze away from my home, I ran after them.

29

CHASE

We ran for what seemed like miles until blisters formed on my feet and my lungs were on fire.

Within a few short minutes, Sully had caught up to us and was now leading us down meandering footpaths, behind opulent backyards with swimming pools and double garages. He had obviously come this way many times before. He never hesitated, taking each turn and corner confidently, stopping just in time as we reached a road with traffic. We zig-zagged across the neighborhood until he finally took us uphill to a secluded clearing where we could see all the way down to NYC. It was here where we saw the mushroom cloud of smoke billowing into the sky. Sully squinted at the direction of the smoke, taking it all in. Pain flashed over his face.

"They're burning down my home," he'd said quietly.

And I realized he was right. We hadn't run nearly as far as I'd thought. From here, we had a perfect view of the blazing fire that consumed his clinic. Lights from neighboring houses flooded on as concerned residents gathered around. In the far off distance, the screaming sirens of an approaching fire truck blared, but I knew it was already too late. It wouldn't reach the clinic in time to save it.

It was a shock when I'd first realized he was running after us. Back in the clinic, Sully had been so reluctant to help that I had been ready to burn the place down myself, but when they started blasting holes in his home, I understood how much danger we were in. Despite how I had some major trust issues when it came to adults, I kept my misgivings to myself. Besides, they had almost killed him. It wasn't safe for him back home anymore, even if the home were still standing.

I sank to my knees, from emotion or exhaustion, I wasn't sure. Maybe both. Bandit pressed up against me as if offering his strength. Sully tore his eyes from the fire and looked down at him.

"What was that down there?"

"The thing with the dogs? Pretty sure he got them to attack the bad guys. He probably just asked," I said.

"Woof," came Bandit's reply.

I stroked him, gratefully. "Thank you, Boy. You saved us."

Bandit flopped onto his side and raised his legs in the air. I reached down and scratched the uninjured part of his stomach. Sully didn't say anything, just continued staring at the blaze in the distance, anger and pain rolling off of him in waves. It was uncomfortable to watch.

I opened my backpack, rifling through it until I came up with a pack of cookies that I fed to Bandit, conscious he still hadn't eaten yet and needed to keep up his strength. He gobbled them down so fast I thought he would take my fingers with them. I was relieved by Bandit's appetite, though. Wanting food = good. It meant he was on the road to recovery. Sully finally looked back at us and frowned at my choice of food.

"What, it's not like I have a wide menu available," I said, opening my bag to show him my stash.

Suddenly, he reacted, recognizing the contents inside. "You stole from me? While I was saving your dog? That's what you were doing in my clinic?"

My cheeks started flushing, but I felt justified in my actions. "Bandit needs to eat, and you looked like you could afford it."

Sully looked outraged by my response, but I wasn't backing down. What else was I supposed to do? Suddenly, Sully laughed, incredulous. "You come knocking on my door, covered in blood, Bandit in your arms. I help you save him and in return, you steal from me. And now my home is gone. Everything. There's nothing left of her."

And wow, if that didn't feel like he had sucker-punched me in the stomach. It was like I could feel everything he was feeling, and I did not like it one bit. In a bid to change the subject, I forced myself up, despite my calves screaming in protest. Since my lungs didn't feel like they would burst anymore, I knew I had to make a move. If those guys were searching for us, I had to put as much distance between us as possible.

"Bandit and I need to keep moving. We're too close still. I can't risk them finding us," I said. "Boy, are you OK to move again?" I asked Bandit.

His tail wagged, and he stood up, if a little wearily. My guilt escalated another notch. "We'll rest once we're a safe distance away." He licked my hand to tell me he was OK. He understood. I turned to face Sully, biting my lip as I struggled to find the words.

"I'm sorry," was all I finally managed.

Sully didn't respond. Didn't move a muscle, in fact. Just stood there, frozen, unblinking. The thought came then that maybe he wasn't so much shell-shocked anymore, but in *physical* shock.

My mind ran through what it knew about the condition. Keep the patient warm. Well, it was pretty hot out here tonight so, check. My eyes took in the condition of his face. Was the skin clammy or just sweating from the run here? I didn't know. I was about to reach out to take his pulse when he suddenly turned and focused his dark eyes on me.

"I'm coming with you."

I was so shocked by his words, I didn't know what to say. I pulled back and shared a look with Bandit. "Er, heck no," came my instant response. "I know you helped us, but I don't know you, and I trust no one. Nada."

Sully ignored me, warming to his decision.

"Those men are after me now too! You think they'll let me go if they catch me? There's nothing left here for me now, and Bandit needs my help. His wound will need to be regularly dressed. If it gets infected, which is likely out here, you won't have a clue how to fix it."

What he was saying wasn't unreasonable, but every nerve in my body was crying out NO! People had a way of screwing me over, and I really wasn't comfortable with the idea of us rolling on together. A girl and her dog didn't draw much attention, but add a man to the equation and it was all up for grabs.

"Look," he continued. "I've lost too much not to see this through. I want to know who those men are, and what they want with Bandit. I want to see the face of the person who took away the last link I have with Emma."

I didn't reply, brain in panic mode. He must have realized I wasn't caving any day soon, however, as he came at me with my biggest weakness.

"What about money? Do you have any? Because I do."

So then we were three.

30

THE MERCENARY

After the mutts had gone for him, The Mercenary had retreated into the operating theater. They'd trapped him into a corner, but The Mercenary had completed two tours in Iraq and wasn't about to be taken down by these fur on legs.

He'd tipped over the operating table and, using it for cover, he'd taken shots at the dogs with the tranq gun. Of course, he would've preferred a real gun, but the boss had commanded no casualties. Not out of the kindness of his heart, but to keep the clean-up down. Boss ran a near invisible operation, and that's how he liked to keep it.

The first row of dogs dropped fast, and once the others saw their fate, they scampered off in terror. Stupid animals. The Mercenary rounded up his men and sent half into the night to search for the dog while he and the rest ransacked the place. Among the things he found that could be of use was Sullivan's cell. While they searched, Sullivan's full background had been downloaded to his PDA. There was only one piece of information The Mercenary found of interest — Sullivan was a recent widower.

With this knowledge in mind, The Mercenary searched the apartment above with fresh eyes. This was a man clinging onto his dead wife; her things were everywhere. Since The Mercenary was a man who didn't like to lose — and yes, he had lost tonight — The Mercenary decided to have some fun and torched the clinic. Boss hadn't said anything about building casualties so, The Mercenary figured it was fair game. Besides, this Sullivan jerk deserved nothing less for giving him so much trouble.

Once the clinic had been set alight, he and his men had piled back into the vans and were off before a crowd had even gathered. Shadows in the night, that's what they were. The Mercenary took one last look at the blaze. It was quite the beaut, now spreading to the surrounding houses.

Good, The Mercenary thought, smiling. *If Sullivan ever returned, he'd have angry neighbors to contend with.*

Blackman, his guy with the scar on the right side of his face, suddenly handed him a phone, expression grim. "It's the boss," he said.

The smile was wiped instantly from The Mercenary's mouth.

31

CHASE

After we'd walked another two hours, we made our way to Scantic River State Park. Sully mentioned quietly that he used to come here with his wife. He figured we'd be safe here for the night, though when we passed a sign that revealed we were in one hundred and sixty-seven acres of open ground for deer and turkey hunting, I sincerely hoped no one would mistake us for dinner, not after all we'd already gone through tonight.

Sully checked Bandit's wound, said it was coping well under the conditions, fed him a pill, then redressed the dressing. He said he'd keep watch for the first few hours and if no one came, then he'd allow himself to rest. Since he was forcing himself on us, I'd asked what our plan was for tomorrow, but all he managed was to mumble he'd figure something out by the time the sun rose. I would've preferred to know what our next steps were right then and there — what if I didn't like what he was planning? Sully, however, wasn't forthcoming with any more information and seemed to shut right down. After instructing Bandit not to leave my side (you never know, some trigger-happy fool might think he was a deer), I found myself musing over the day's insane events.

It was strange. Most of the adults I'd met in my life weren't the responsible type. Heck, they were downright degenerates (especially my folks), and not surprisingly, I'd developed a healthy mistrust of them all. With Sully, I wasn't sure. Yeah, he really cared about his wife, but that didn't make him a good person. Judging by the constant flip-flopping in my stomach, my gut didn't know what to make of him as yet, so I'd be wary, just in case. People have a habit of turning on you when you least expected it. This I knew from experience.

Bandit curled up by my side and was asleep almost instantly. Poor guy, from being stabbed to escaping capture within minutes of his life-saving operation. I realized we had a lot in common. We were both survivors. It'd take a lot more than a few armed men to break us.

I stared across at Sully's profile. Outwardly he seemed calm, but his hands were clenched into fists, and his jaw set into a tense line. He was still staring into space when my eyes finally closed and I fell asleep.

32

SULLY

orning light streamed in through tall oak trees, bathing us in a
warm glow. Chase and Bandit were curled together, much as
they had been the whole night.

I had barely slept. All night, my mind had raced with vivid flashbacks of
the day before. From the moment of Chase's bloody arrival to my near
brush with death. Military Man's sneering face regularly interrupted my
flow of thoughts, causing me to wonder what kind of corporation he worked
for that would condone such violence.

Obviously, one that didn't care one iota for the rules.

I'd told Chase I'd come up with a plan for them, and I had one, of sorts.
Just not a very good one. I knew I was being irrational. This was crazy! A
huge part of my brain was screaming at me: *go back! This won't end well!* But
every time I considered leaving, a picture of Emma going up in flames
entered my mind, and it made me madder than a wet hen. I wanted, no,
needed to find the people who had done this to me. If I were honest, I also
felt a flicker of excitement.

All year I had been a shadow of myself. Just motivating myself to do
normal things, like cleaning up the house and taking a shower, had seemed
monumentally hard. I felt nothing, only numb. Had been that way for so
long now, I wondered if I'd ever feel anything again. Yet tonight, despite all
logic, I was feeling a rush of emotions so intense, they threatened to overwhelm me. And that was before I considered the possibility of Bandit's
super intellect. For sure, I was going to test that. As soon as I figured
out how.

I looked at the sleeping girl and dog. I knew without a doubt that they needed me. As resourceful as she was, they wouldn't last long out here without help. Not that I felt beholden to them. It would take a while before I would get over how Chase had stolen from me. The defiance in her eyes when I'd caught her out!

I pulled out my wallet and counted out my money. Not much. Enough for food and some place to stay tomorrow, but they'd need more. I had a credit card, but I wasn't keen on the idea of surfacing for now. Better to stay out of sight until the heat had died down. Or at least until those soldier thugs weren't around.

Bandit stirred, waking. He got up, performed an all body shake, then padded over to greet me. I couldn't help smiling. As a boy, I had been one of those kids who couldn't get enough of animals. Soon as I could walk, I would chase after anything furry and on four legs. Sadly, neither parent was particularly into animals, so my early interactions only consisted of friends' pets. After I had met Emma (we were college sweethearts), we'd discussed getting a dog, but the timing was never right. And when the clinic opened, well, I had had plenty of animals to look after. We had decided to give the clinic time to establish itself, and maybe in a year or so, we would adopt a pet.

Well, Em, how d'you like me now? Instant father of two.

Chase woke, instantly alert. She gave me a wary look. "Morning," she said, as she dove into her bag before surfacing with several energy bars that she handed out to us. At least the girl had some manners.

"We're going to have to get him more appropriate food. That much sugar isn't good for him."

Stomach cramping from hunger, I nibbled on my own bar, though the sickly sweetness made me wince. I wasn't a breakfast guy normally, but I needed the energy. What I wouldn't have done for a cup of java.

"So what's the plan," Chase asked.

I forced the rest of the granola bar down my throat.

"We need to find a way to communicate with Bandit that's a little more than yes and no. Those men will probably be coming after us, and the more we know about them, the better off we'll be."

"But what can we use?" Chase wondered aloud.

"Something cheap. We don't have much." I replied.

At that, Chase grinned.

"Well, I'm kinda an expert on that." She stood up. "Come on."

33

THE MERCENARY

The Mercenary raged inside the empty van.

After they'd set fire to the clinic, The Mercenary's men had combed the streets until dawn, but the trio had disappeared. Vanished into thin air.

The Mercenary thumped the steering wheel with his fist. Pain shot through his hand, but he welcomed it with a twisted delight. *He had had them in his grasp! If only those damned dogs hadn't attacked!*

He knew for sure what had happened: Alpha had set those mutts on them. The worrying thought wormed through his brain, boring into the back of his eyes, making his head throb. In all the tests run at The Facility, nothing like this had ever happened. Could Alpha control other dogs, or had he simply asked? The Mercenary reported his findings to Dr. Robbins, but her reaction had disgusted him. She had been excited! She considered the dog an ever-evolving marvel, but The Mercenary knew the truth. Alpha was a freak who needed to be put down. And he was the man to do it.

The Mercenary flipped open his cell and dialed a number he kept for special occasions. The call was answered after a few rings by a curt male voice.

"Chicago PD?"

"Well, if it isn't Danny boy! How's pop?" he asked with something as close to enthusiasm as he could muster.

"Uncle? Hey, how are you, old man?"

"Less of the old, thank you," he retorted.

"We're all doing great. Dad caught a twenty-pound rock bass over the weekend. Hasn't shut up about it since."

The Mercenary smiled thinly, tapping his foot, impatient to get to the crux of the call. "But did he skin and cook it, or toss it back into the river?"

"What do you think?"

"Always the weakest link, my kid brother."

"So what can I do for you? Is this a social call?" Daniel asked.

Finally! "Afraid not, son. I need a favor. I'm on a case about a missing girl. Young Caucasian, around fourteen? First name's Chase, but that's all I got."

"No worries. I'll run it through the database, see what we can dig up."

The Mercenary smiled dangerously.

"Thanks, son. And when you've done that, I'm going to need another favor from you..."

34

CHASE

On a scale of one to crazy, this was definitely in the insane range. I felt like every person in the place was watching us.

We were in another generic mall. It was a Saturday, so the place was heaving with kids and families out to damage their wallets. Just like us. Me, my dad, and our guide dog. Only Sully's wallet was looking pretty empty, so our mission today? Get to a cashpoint and withdraw the hell outta it.

While Sully and I were on edge, constantly looking over our shoulders for any soldier types who might be after us, Bandit was having a dog of a time. This was only his second time in a place like this (the first being practically empty), but here, Bandit couldn't get enough of the noise, the bright lights, and smells. He was sniffing everything he could get his nose on. Including people. It was hugely embarrassing.

For his part, Sully tried to act like this was no big deal, but there was something in the way his shoulders slumped, how he dragged his feet. I would never admit it, but I was feeling kinda bad for him. I'm not really the touchy-feely type though, so I focused on the mall directory and located what we needed on the map with a finger.

"It's just down there," I pointed.

Sully looked at where my finger was.

"*That's* your big idea?" He didn't bother to hide his skepticism.

"Look, this is my area of expertize. I guess you wouldn't know that living where you lived, but this is what I know." I headed off before he could ask any more inane questions and looked down at Bandit. "What do you say,

Boy, want to go shopping?" I asked. He grinned at me and picked up the
pace. Sully saw his reaction and patted his pockets worriedly.

"Let's keep it light, OK?"

Moments later we stepped into my favorite place in the whole world,
The Dollar Store. Seriously, if you've never been in one, you don't know
what you're missing. They have everything in this place. *E-very-thing.*

On my left was the cleaning section containing all kinds of amazing
products that you've never heard of. From an eraser sponge to white vinegar
spray — the most organic and best cleaner out there apparently, but whiffy
I'd bet. Ahead of me stood the gardening section where tools were going for
a dollar! And plastic nets for growing vegetables, and ooh, a red gnome! On
the far side was the food aisle, where my feet naturally wanted to head, but
that wasn't what we came here for. I silently commanded them to obey, and
we — my feet and I — were about to move to the back of the store when
Bandit took off down an aisle. Sully stopped me from following.

"I think I know where he's going. I'll go after him, you get the stuff."

Sensing there wasn't anything to fear in this place, I nodded and ambled
to the back, following the signs until I found what I was looking for —
books. But not thick, heavy tomes — who reads those, right? I grabbed
bright and colorful children's books, ones suitable for a child just learning
how to read. I wasn't sure what Bandit's reading age would be, so I grabbed
one of each up until age six. After that, the books had fewer pictures and
weighed a ton more.

I made my way to the cashier, but the quickest route there was to detour
past the food. I took that as a sign from the Universe. Juices flooded my
mouth as soon as I saw the breathtaking range on offer. It's just insane what
you could get in here, especially when you compared it to other places. I
once snuck into a Wholefoods just to see what the fuss was all about. The
prices made my eyes water, no joke.

Almost of their own accord, my fingers plucked several heart attack-
inducing cakes from the shelves, curling around the satisfying weight of
them. *We had to eat,* I justified to myself and chocolate is good for energy.
It's what rock climbers and survivalists carry for emergencies.

Within seconds, my arms were piled so high, I could barely see over
them. You're probably wondering why I didn't just use one of those baskets?
Well, I normally don't get to shop for more than a handful of things at a
time, so it never crossed my mind. Rounding a corner, I almost crashed into
the others. Bandit had the goofiest grin I'd ever seen on him, and in his
mouth, he carried a bone so big, it looked like it could've been the leg of a
horse or something. Sully's arms were loaded up too, with dog kibble, some
other random stuff, and a backpack of his own. Despite everything he was
going through, Sully's face was a picture of amazement.

"They have bags in here, for a few dollars! I've bought coffee that costs more than this!"

I couldn't help my grin. "Told ya."

Sully's eyes were wide, unable to comprehend it all.

"How do they make money at these prices?"

"I don't think they're doing badly," I replied, gesturing at the heaving store full of customers. We dumped everything in front of a cashier and she tallied up the items. Her hands moved so fast they were almost a blur.

"That's twenty-five dollars," she said. We looked at the four bags full of stuff we'd just packed. Sully couldn't keep the smile off his face as he handed the bills to her.

"First time in a dollar store. Won't be my last."

The cashier gave him a baleful look and kept silent. Clearly, she wasn't as excited by this place as we were. Fool. She forked over his change.

"Thanks for coming to your one stop family shop," she intoned emotionlessly, already reaching for the next customer's purchases.

Sully shoved everything into his new backpack, and we left the store.

35

CHASE

We'd gone a little way when Sully pointed across the mall at a Bank of America. I knew it was too risky for us to go inside, what with all the cameras banks usually had. We wanted to draw as little attention to ourselves as possible, so Bandit and I were back in "disguise."

Still, a blind kid with a dog gets noticed.

He handed me his backpack, and I decided to wait by the indoor water fountain while Sully made the withdrawal. Well, technically, Bandit decided this for us when he forgot our little charade for a moment and bounded towards the gushing display.

Luckily, a kindly woman helped "guide" me to him. I had to explain he was still young and in the process of being trained. Afterward, Bandit hung his head like I'd berated him when I really hadn't.

Who knew the dog would be so sensitive?

We sat by the fountain and watched as Sully slipped his card into an ATM. He keyed in his password, but something flashed across the screen that I couldn't make out. I could see the concerned expression on Sully's face though, all the way from over here. I stood up as a metallic taste flooded my mouth; I had bitten the inside of my cheek. Happens a lot when I get nervous.

Like now.

Sully tried his password again. This time the whole screen flashed red. Then a high-pitched alarm sounded from within the bank.

So much for not drawing attention.

Everyone in the mall was now looking in his direction. Sully backed away from the ATM, looking stunned. He turned, found my face in the crowd, and mouthed one word at me.

"*RUN.*"

36

SULLY

It all happened so fast, I hadn't had time to process it. I typed in the correct password, but the following message had flashed up on the screen:

Return the dog to us now and you and the girl will be spared.
We only want the dog.
Press #1 for our team to begin extraction.

The message stayed on the screen just long enough for me to take it all in, before it vanished, swallowing my card in the process. I could barely fathom it. They'd gotten into my account! The speed these people worked at, and how wide their net had been cast, was absolutely terrifying.

I had just begun to register the fact that we wouldn't get far without any cash when the alarm had sounded. It seemed every face in the mall turned to me. Even though I had done nothing wrong, I froze, and it was this moment of hesitation that undid me. A flurry of activity came from within the bank. Security guards raced towards me, guns raised.

I turned and searched frantically for Chase. Picking out her face from the crowd, I mouthed *RUN*, then bolted in the *opposite* direction, clear, even in the heat of the moment, that our best chance of not being caught would be if we split up.

I charged past startled shoppers and hurdled over a bench, but it had been some time since I'd participated in any school sports days. Technique all wrong, I came down heavy on one foot. A sharp pain shot through my ankle. I winced and pushed on, but at a slower pace, favoring my left leg. Seeing a guard approaching my flank, I swerved into a packed food hall.

"Hey, you! Stop right there!" The guard shouted.

I ignored him, weaving quickly through the shocked diners. Every step causing increasing pain, when I finally saw a way out, sequestered between the Chinese and Italian booths. I was three feet from the exit when a tattooed-covered cook swung a steel pan at me.

Pain EXPLODED in my stomach.

I crashed to the floor, hands over my stomach, gasping for breath.

37

SULLY

The pain ricocheted inside my stomach, tearing through my guts. I could do nothing but try to breathe through it all. The cook stood over me, holding the pan, grinning smugly.

"He's over here!" Applause broke out among the diners, enjoying the impromptu show. Boots thundered to my side, and I felt myself hoisted unceremoniously onto my feet. My arms were jerked behind me, and hand-cuffs slapped onto my wrists. The cool metal bit into me, threatening to cut off my circulation.

"Loosen up on the shackles," I growled, but my captor, an overweight rent-a-guard, only pulled tighter on my binds, enjoying the grimace this caused. Still winded from the chase, his cheeks were flushed an ugly red. Perspiration dripped from his forehead and ran in rivulets down his face. I noted the name sewn onto his uniform: "Sholtz, Henry".

Sholtz breathed into my face.

"Looky here, first catch of the day." It wasn't a pleasant experience since his breath reeked of smoke and coffee. Throw in a doughnut and we'd have ourselves every cop cliche under the sun, I thought. I leaned away from the other man.

"Someone could do with a mint."

Sholtz's cheeks turned even redder, if that was possible. All niceness disappeared from his eyes. "This way, scumbag."

He shoved me through the food hall, past the cheering diners, and into an elevator. With every step, my eyes roamed the area, searching for a blind girl and her dog, feeling relieved when I couldn't see them. Hopefully, they were long gone by now.

Sholtz punched B on the control panel and the elevator doors pinged closed. I watched the floor numbers descending. *Basement. Why does it have to be the basement?*

"Exactly what am I being detained for?" I asked.

My guard shot me a disgusted look.

"Like you don't know."

"Tell you what, let's assume I'm innocent until proven otherwise and oblivious to the crime. What exactly are the charges? Failure to retrieve money from my account?"

Sholtz shot me another look filled with loathing and spat out the words.

"Kidnapping of a minor."

38

THE MERCENARY

L ike a spider who has spun his web and was now waiting patiently for his prey to land, The Mercenary sat in his van, drumming his fingers on the wheel.

A few hours ago, his ever reliable nephew, Daniel, had come good, sending through an email with information on the mystery girl. While it wasn't exactly a dossier, there was enough for The Mercenary to formulate a plan.

Her name was Chase Ryder. Fourteen years old, born in Holyoke, Hampden County to one Tracy Blueman. No father listed, Blueman was typical trailer trash, living off the state. Her employment history was as sporadic as her personal relationships; the woman couldn't hold down a job or a man it seemed, not until a few years ago when one Frank Tubble was added to the home rental agreement. There were two reports of domestic disturbances which hadn't led anywhere, but other than that, there was no more listed information until ten months ago, when Chase was reported as missing, a suspected runaway.

Local uniforms had interviewed the couple. Despite noting that they weren't particularly savory characters (the home was a wreck and there was evidence of alcohol abuse), they were not suspected of misconduct, and any questioning at Chase's school only revealed that the girl was a loner and seemed unhappy. Despite being described as bright from her teachers, Chase's grades were failing, and she seemed headed in a downward spiral.

The Mercenary didn't need to be a shrink to see the pattern. Desperate mom brings home a new stepdad who turns out to be less knight-in-shining-armor, and more abusive drunk. It was a story as old as time, though The Mercenary felt no sympathy; everyone had their cross to bear.

Blueman hadn't checked in on the progress to find her child in months now, something that pleased The Mercenary. *Good.* The last thing he needed was a busybody parent, nosing in on his plan. An absentee, uncaring parent was *exactly* what he wanted.

Having created a missing child report, The Mercenary had sent it to Daniel to distribute among the police stations across several states.

He had taken liberties with the report, describing Sullivan as a suspected kidnapper, painting him in a very bad light indeed since nothing was more abhorred than a predator of children.

When Sullivan and the kid eventually surfaced, it wouldn't be long before The Mercenary was informed...

39

CHASE

We watched the whole takedown in shock.

One minute Sully was at the ATM, the next he was being pursued by mall cops.

I signaled Bandit, and he came to my side immediately. Since everyone's attention was on the pursuit at hand, it wasn't hard for us to follow behind discreetly.

Sully sure could run fast! He put so much distance between himself and the out-of-shape cops that I thought he'd get well clear of them, but then he leaped over a bench and stumbled on the landing. I saw his ankle buckle — just a bit — but it was enough that he was in trouble. Still, he would've gotten away if it weren't for Slugger.

It was like I could feel the blow in my own stomach. I flinched as Sully went down. Hopefully, the guy hadn't cracked any ribs, or we'd be in serious trouble.

A hysterical laugh escaped my lips. *Like we weren't already.* Bandit tossed me a confused look. I didn't have time to reassure him of my sanity. I stood there, rooted to the spot, torn by my natural instinct to flee and my guilty conscience, which was shouting at me, telling me we couldn't leave Sully like this. Bandit must have realized what I was struggling with, as he barked twice, loudly, and stamped his paw in Sully's direction. I hesitated, then nodded. He was right, we couldn't leave him. We hurried after them.

A fat cop shackled Sully and marched him inside an elevator. I watched the numbers until they stopped at B, then we darted out of sight and into a stairwell. Taking the steps two at a time, we shot down them until we

arrived outside a door marked "Basement". I grabbed the handle and twisted. As quietly as I could manage, I tugged the door opened, and we stole
inside.

We found ourselves in a gray, windowless, stone security block. Cut off
from the sunshine, the temperature down here plummeted, and I found
myself shivering. I studied the reception desk up ahead. It was manned by a
lone female cop. Behind her, there were a bunch of adjoining glass offices
where I could see Sully being escorted into a holding cell.

I scanned the floor and located two cameras. One pointed at reception,
the other overlooked the corridor that Sully had disappeared down. *So our
problem was threefold. We needed to bust Sully out of there while avoiding both
cops and cameras.* I was thinking the odds were majorly against us when I
remembered I had a furry secret weapon on four legs.

As I stared at the cameras, a plan came together in my mind.

"Bandit..." I whispered. He pressed up against me and whined, waiting
for my next command.

"How's your night vision?" I asked.

40

SULLY

I stared around my small cell.

With nothing to do and no possible means of escaping, I contemplated how my life had changed over the course of only a few days. From hero to zero.

At least that's what the cops around here thought of me. HPA, the organization behind this whole shebang — if that was even their real name — were prolific with their lies. As I was marched into my cell, the passing cops glared at me like the leper they thought I was. One guy almost spat in my face. I wasn't entirely sure whether he had missed on purpose or not.

As soon as I was shunted into the cell, Sholtz had reluctantly released my hands from the cuffs. Out of protocol, I knew, as opposed to the kindness of his heart. I was no longer considered a threat now that I was locked up in a 12x12 cell. A tiny barred window stood nine feet from the floor. Even if I could've gotten up there and somehow managed to tear the bars away, no amount of watching my diet and exercising would have made me fit through that small square. Other than the window, my prison contained a steel urinal that stank to high heaven and a flat bench that was wide enough to sleep on but not enough to be comfortable. If I managed to get out of this alive, I knew I would never complain about Motel 6 ever again.

I rubbed at the purple welts on my wrists, surprised they were all the injury I had sustained. Well, that, and the giant bruise that now covered my midsection. I poked gingerly at my side and inhaled a sharp intake of breath at the pain that caused, but happily, no ribs were cracked. I would take every small win right now.

Sholtz had warned me that the FBI had been notified of my capture, and several agents were now on route to extract me. I couldn't help the involuntary shudder the word "extract" had caused. Not knowing the real reason behind my reaction, Sholtz had grinned like the Cheshire Cat. Here was a man who enjoyed the suffering of others. The term "innocent until proven guilty" didn't seem to cross his mind. Then again, I didn't think Sholtz had much of a mind inside that gaping large head of his. I started pacing the small cell as panic set in.

HPA's men thought nothing of breaking into a person's home and attacking them. Hell, they'd burned my clinic down. Once they had me in their hands, what would they do to "extract" the information they wanted? I stopped pacing suddenly and hoped to God Chase had managed to escape. If they ever got a hold of that girl...

I shook myself, surprised by the level of my feelings. Since the day I had buried my wife, I had carefully cultivated a sense of detachment. Self-preservation really, so this new concern for the two's welfare came as quite the shock. As did the realization that, for the first time in eight months, the thought of Emma didn't bring a searing pain in my chest.

I was still marveling at this not-so-small miracle when the lights blew out, plunging the floor into darkness.

41

SULLY

I could hear shouts of alarm rising around me, though I knew it would only be moments before a backup generator kicked in. Even small-town mall cops have a contingency plan. I sat onto the cold bench, waiting for the commotion to die down, when I heard the sound of heavy breathing.

Wait, not breathing. Panting.

My nose caught an undeniable scent. *Dog breath.* In disbelief, I called out quietly.

"Bandit?"

My reply was a soft, "*Woof.*"

Something metallic clattered onto the floor. I dropped on all fours, moving towards the general direction of the sound, until my fingers brushed against a set of keys. Relief swam through me in waves. Feeling my way around, I found the lock and inserted a key. It wasn't the right one. Fingering a larger key, I tried that next.

"Come on, we don't have much time," came Chase's bodiless voice.

She had appeared like a ghost. I hadn't even heard her arrive. Someone not too far away shouted.

"We found the breaker!"

As power surged back into the building, I inserted the right key and twisted.

By the time the lights flickered back on, the cell was empty.

42

CHASE

Bandit couldn't contain his excitement as Sully snuck out of the cell and did several circuits around him, but if I was expecting gratitude, I had another thing coming.

"Of all the stupid... I told you to run," Sully hissed at me through the dark.

"Seriously?" I managed back. "I think the words you're looking for are, thank you!"

"This isn't a game, Chase! They could catch you both... I can't believe you came back..."

I was too concerned with our predicament to do this particular dance right now. "There's no time to argue, let's just get out of here," I instructed. My eyes had grown accustomed to the darkness, but even then, I could barely make out three steps ahead of me. I grabbed onto Bandit's makeshift collar with one hand and Sully with the other. "Hurry, Boy, get us out of here."

Bandit barked softly, then shot into action, weaving quickly and surely through the corridors. We'd been going maybe five seconds when the strip lights above us started to flicker.

"Duck!" Sully cried out.

We dropped into a crouch, flattening ourselves against the wall, Bandit pressed up against me. Light flooded the room. In preparation for this, I had shielded my eyes. Consequently, my recovery time was fast. I blinked the haze away and took in our surroundings.

We were in one of the glass offices. Luckily, this one was empty. Unluckily, we were surrounded by four glass walls. If anyone came down either of the flanking corridors, we'd be seen. Sully pointed ahead of us.

"That's the reception desk. If we can make it there, the exit's just beyond."

I nodded. So now we had a plan.

"Bandit. You first. Head for the door."

Knowing stealth was of the utmost importance, he didn't bark, but pawed the ground at me. At my nod, he took off, a streak of brown across the floor. He was going so fast, he almost overshot the door. I saw him dig in his back heels and skid to a stop. He leaped up, grasped the fire exit door handle in his mouth, and tugged down. The door opened silently. He waited, propping the door ajar, head tilted towards us.

Sully gestured, and now it was my turn to make a run for it. I kept low, which wasn't hard for me since I'm pretty short, anyway. My sneakers squeaked on the linoleum floor, but I figured they wouldn't hear that over the noise the cops were generating: self congratulations and war stories if you can believe that. I made it to Bandit and slid past him into the stairwell.

Sully came after us. He was halfway across the floor when his injured ankle gave out. He dropped, and a cry escaped his lips, drawing the attention of the reception cop.

"What the... you! Stop right there!" she yelled.

Sully scrambled up and half ran, half hopped over to us. I lunged forward to help him, but he shook me off, pointing at the wall behind me.

"The fire axe!" he shouted.

I bolted to the cabinet housing the axe in question and smashed my elbow inside. Safety glass shattered into shards, raining harmlessly over my feet. I wrenched the axe from its moorings and rushed back to Sully. He grabbed it from my hands and wedged it between the handle of the door we'd just come through and the top step.

The cop came flying into the door just then, but the axe held. She threw herself at the door but wasn't able to get it open more than a foot. She pressed her face into the gap.

"You're in enough trouble as it is! We can do a deal if you stop running and turn yourselves in."

I stared her directly in the face. "Whatever they've told you about him, it's all lies. Sully hasn't done anything." Before she could respond, I slid under Sully's arm to ease some weight off of his injured ankle, and together, we hobbled up the stairs as more cops threw themselves at the door.

Moments later we burst onto the mall's main parade and headed quickly but discreetly to an exit. A few shoppers cast raised eyebrows our way, but no one intervened.

When we got outside, a bus was just pulling up. We didn't even see the destination sign, we just climbed on and hunkered down by the back. Only when the bus pulled away did we allow ourselves to breathe again. I couldn't believe we'd just engineered our first jail break.

Sadly, it wouldn't be our last.

43

THE MERCENARY

The Mercenary popped an aspirin and chased it down with a can of Red Bull that he downed in one gulp. He flexed his fingers until the can flattened into a metal disc, compressed in his gorilla-like hand.

He'd picked up news of Sullivan's capture on his police scanner and was heading to the mall when the blackout had happened. The Mercenary had been at this line of work almost his entire life and knew better than to believe in coincidences.

It was that damn dog again. He was sure of it.

He swung the unlicensed sedan into the parking lot and opened the glove compartment. Inside was a multitude of fake ID's. The Mercenary fished around until he found the one he was looking for. He stared down at his own face, only the one in the photo was neater and dressed, as he was now, in an all-black suit. The Mercenary checked his reflection in the rearview mirror. He wasn't a vain man, but took pride in pulling off a passable disguise. The face he saw smiling back at him was strong, with eyes that challenged anyone foolish enough to disagree with him. He nodded to himself, pleased. *A believable official.*

Sliding a government-issued firearm into his shoulder holster, The Mercenary emerged from the car and made his way inside.

A few minutes later he was standing by the reception desk. A frazzled young cop stared back at him. Seems she hadn't had a good day and was now taking it out on him. Or so she thought. The Mercenary wasn't anyone's punching bag. Unsmiling, The Mercenary flipped her his FBI badge, gestured at the cameras, and demanded to see the CCTV footage of their prisoner's escape.

She took offence at his tone but called her superior, a man named Sholtz. Sholtz was typical of these generic mall staff. Overweight and full of self-importance. The Mercenary would have fun taking him down a peg or two.

Sholtz reluctantly lead The Mercenary into the CCTV booth. A bank of monitors were already cued up with the requested footage. The Mercenary leaned forward and twisted the navigational cog. On the screens, the images sprang to life. The Mercenary recognized the corridor he had walked down only moments before, but as the camera panned left and settled on the reception desk, the screens fell black.

"We found a bunch of wires pulled from the breaker box. The kid, no doubt, but it doesn't make sense. If he kidnapped her, why would she sneak back to help him?"

The Mercenary stared down his nose at him. This fool hadn't noticed the girl or the dog, despite The Mercenary's fake police report. As far as he was concerned, Sholtz wasn't good enough to lick his shoes. "You haven't heard of Stockholm Syndrome, when a victim begins feeling trust and affection towards their captor? That's unfortunately what must be happening here." The Mercenary hoped that would be enough to shut him up, but Sholtz however, had no idea the repulsion he caused in The Mercenary and continued talking in his irritating voice.

"Not sure what you're hoping for unless you can see in the dark."

Without a word, The Mercenary retrieved a pair of glasses from his pocket. They had a retro wayfarer style, though the lenses were tinted red. If truth be told, they were far too hipster-looking for his taste, but since they weren't a vanity item, The Mercenary slipped them onto his face and triggered a barely perceivable switch on the right arm. Electricity hummed through the frame as the glasses powered up. He stared through the red lenses until the augmented imaging kicked in. Suddenly, he could clearly see the reception desk on the monitors. The glasses were a high-tech IED — Image Enhancement Device — designed and created by one of the Boss's many genius lackeys, and The Mercenary's favorite weapon of choice.

"Are those what I think they are?" the hapless cop asked.

"Yes," came The Mercenary's curt reply.

"Always wondered what they would be like to use."

In response, The Mercenary deliberately turned his back on him. "You may leave."

Sholtz bristled, finally comprehending the brush off. From the corner of his eye, The Mercenary could see Sholtz hesitating, wondering if he should retort back. He must have thought better of it, as he spun on his heel and left. The Mercenary turned his attention to the screen and proceeded to watch Sullivan breakout.

44

CHASE

We'd been riding silently on the bus for hours. Sully stared moodily out of the window, hands gripped into fists that only seemed to squeeze tighter the farther we got from his home.

He didn't say anything, but I knew his mind was on his wife and the life he'd left behind. While I still wasn't super keen on the idea of his tagging along, part of me was learning to deal with it. Like, what was I going to do? Send him away? The man could barely function. Besides, we had bigger problems to deal with, like how he didn't have a clue where we were heading. My mind wasn't much help either, drawing blanks as it was.

I shifted my position. Not for the first time, I wondered why the seats were designed to be so uncomfortable. It's like they didn't want you to ride the bus for a long journey. I looked down at Bandit, lying on the floor between my feet. He seemed more subdued than usual. I think something was bothering him, but he wasn't able to voice what.

Which reminded me.

I took out the easiest book we'd bought from the Dollar Store and laid it by his feet. The bus was pretty empty, and most passengers preferred to sit up front. I think actually because of Bandit. Seems the public don't like to be near a dog in a contained space. Made me wonder what kinds of dogs they were accustomed to. Bandit instantly perked up and pricked his ears forward. I bent down and whispered at him.

"We'll do a quiz later, OK?"

His tongue snaked out and licked my nose, making me regret being so nice to him.

The bus chugged through several New England neighborhoods. We passed a cheerful sign that said SCRANTON, Pennsylvania. WELCOME HOME! It looked like a nice enough place. The sidewalks were free from litter, shopfronts were clean with fresh coats of paint. Any people I could see were busy moving to and from work or meeting up with friends. I only counted one homeless person, which is generally how I measure a town's success rate. I felt the bus slow down and craned my head around. We were turning into a bus terminal, where a small strip of sad looking businesses did trade.

"End of the line, folks," the bus driver called out.

Somewhere along our ride we'd lost most of the passengers, so there was only an elderly couple who made their way to the exit with us. I moved aside to let them pass first. The old woman smiled at me, then looked at Sully.

"What a polite daughter you have."

Sully's eyebrows shot up so high I worried they would shoot right off his face. He went to correct her, but I elbowed him silent.

"Thank you ma'am. I try." *Why draw more attention to ourselves, right?* Our motley "family" descended the bus and headed into the adjoining diner which was clean, if uninspiring. Tablecloths covered plastic furniture that was yellow with age. We found a table whose leg somebody had shoved a piece of cardboard coaster under to keep it steady. We sat down. I instantly grabbed a menu and pored over the offerings. That was the thing about being broke and homeless; food is a BIG deal. The biggest.

Sully signaled a nearby waitress. She was a big-chested woman, with even bigger red hair, all done up in a towering beehive. I couldn't stop staring. Must've been a whole can of hairspray up in there.

"I'm Rose, what can I do for ya?" she said, chewing a piece of gum noisily with her mouth open.

"Can I just get a bowl of water for the dog while we look at the menu?" Sully barely looked at her, but he seemed to have an immediate effect on Red. She stopped chewing her gum and batted fake eyelashes at him.

"Well, of course, Sugar. I'll be right back for your order." She headed for the kitchen, swinging her hips as she went. I was pretty sure it was all for Sully's benefit; shame he wasn't looking. He opened his wallet and took out the remaining cash. It was a pitiful supply. We'd have enough for a light meal here, but there wouldn't be much left after eating. He rubbed at his eyes, the weight of the world sitting on his shoulders.

"What day is it?" I asked.

Sully frowned. "Why?"

"Cos if it's Tuesday, kids eat free as long as they're accompanied by one paying adult," I said, pointing at an offer stuck to the window.

"It's Wednesday," he replied.

"Figures," I grumbled. I slid lower into my seat as Red came back with a bowl of water for Bandit, and also something else: a big plate. On it was a juicy red bone with lots of meat still clinging to it. Smelling it, Bandit shot up and begged, one paw raised. A whine escaped from the back of his throat as a long glob of drool dripped from his mouth. Red laughed.

"Here you go, pooch. Swiped this from our chef. He'd just throw it away."

Sully finally looked at her and gave her a genuine smile of thanks. "Thank you."

She winked at him. "Pleasure. Now, what about you? Know what you'd like yet?'

She pouted those red lips suggestively. I would've slid further down my seat if I could have. This was painful to watch. Sully, on the other hand, seemed oblivious to her mad flirting.

"You know when you've run into one bad thing after another?"

Red nodded, though she obviously didn't know where he was heading with this. Come to think of it, neither did I.

"I only get my kid one week out of the month. Planned on taking her for a nice meal, maybe a movie after, but damn machine ate my card and the bank can't get it back to me until tomorrow. I've only a twenty to last us until then."

"How unlucky," she said, totally buying his story.

I was amazed. Sully had some skills! Red glanced at the near empty diner, where only a few old age pensioners sat, sipping soup, including the ones who had gotten off the bus with us. Then she must have made up her mind as she looked at us conspiratorially.

"You know, Cook made up a batch of chilli earlier, but he'd left it on the stove too long. The bottom almost burned right through the pan. We can't sell it, but I could probably give that to you for free? It's going to be hela smokey, I ain't going to lie, but the offer's there if you want it?"

Sully reached across and squeezed her hand, causing her cheeks to flush bright pink. "You are an angel."

Reluctantly, she removed her hand and went to get us our freebie food. I looked at Sully, unable to hide my utter amazement. He stared back at me, a knowing glint in his eye.

"Still think I'm useless?" he asked. I snapped my mouth shut. *What, he was a mind reader too now?*

Red came back with two giant bowls of chilli. She'd also added some warm bread rolls, fresh out of the oven. I don't feel much affection for people in general, but I could've kissed her. She set the bowls in front of us. The smell of them caused my toes to curl. There were actual pieces of meat in there! Without waiting to see if I should, I shoved a heaped spoonful into my mouth. It was so good, I almost fainted. Red seemed pleased by my enthusiasm.

"Nice to see a girl who likes to eat," she said.

"Food is highly underrated," I replied. "This is so good, I could eat an entire pot of it."

Red laughed. "Well there's plenty more, so just let me know if you want seconds."

I didn't even mind when she reached out and ruffled my hair. I make exceptions for anyone who feeds me.

Sully had better manners than me, so he actually waited for Red to leave before eating. We dunked the rolls into the chilli, mopping up the sauce. Under the table, Bandit, too, was in ecstasy. He was licking and chewing that bone like it was the best thing he'd ever tasted.

When I finished my bowl, I leaned back and sighed happily. My belly, not accustomed to so much food, was distended and straining against the belt. Sully was still eating, so I took a second to examine the diner.

Red was serving the old couple from the bus. Sully's flirtation must have cheered her right up, as she was now friendly to all her customers. She chatted and flitted around the place, keeping everyone happy. I looked away from her, to a bookcase loaded with leaflets.

"I'll be back," I said to Sully. Bandit looked up at me in question but never stopped chewing his bone. I felt his eyes follow me, however, as I made my way to the bookcase.

As I'd thought, there were timetables of all the buses from the terminal. I scanned the destinations. Some names I recognized: Baltimore, Pittsburgh, Syracuse. None of them seemed interesting until my eyes landed on the one destination and I felt excitement brewing in me. Grabbing the timetable, I headed back to our booth, where I found two new bowls of chilli and rolls had been set onto the table. God bless that woman!

"What've you got there?" Sully looked at the leaflet clutched in my hand. I slid it across the table to him.

"Where we're going next."

Sully read the words on the paper. "Atlantic City?" he enquired.

"The whole reason I let you join us is because you had money, except now you don't. Can you think of a better place to make money?" I replied.

"Gambling's an art form, and one I'm not particularly good at."

"Well it's lucky we've a secret weapon here." I glanced down at Bandit, and Sully suddenly got my drift.

"Seriously?"

"Seriously."

And that was it. End of discussion.

45

CHASE

I cleaned up in the bathroom, while Sully settled the bill. Well, there wasn't really a bill. We'd only drank tap water so Red hadn't charged us, but Sully gave her a tip anyway. I told him he shouldn't have as we needed every cent, but Sully said it wasn't right not to. Whatever. This is why I'd last longer on the streets than he would alone. He was clueless what it really took to survive.

Red seemed sad to see us go. I got the feeling she was a lonely girl. There wasn't a wedding ring on her finger, and judging by the clientele, it didn't seem like there were many eligible bachelors in this town. At least, none who were traveling by bus, anyway. I suppose anyone who was remotely successful would've been driving their own car, not using uncomfortable and tardy public transport like us losers.

Bandit — still chewing his bone — followed me outside. I found bus stop D and waited there for the bus to arrive. It wouldn't get here for another hour though, so I thought it was a good time to start Bandit's education. I fished out the book I'd decided on earlier. BRADLEY THE BUMBLE BEE, it announced in bright red letters. There was a drawing of a giant bee flitting from different things on the cover. Already, I had a pretty good inkling of how this story would go.

I found a seat on a wooden bench, and Bandit hopped up next to me. I looked across at the diner to see Sully had finally extracted himself from Red. I was amused to see him carrying a tub of what could only be more of the chilli. He sat down next to Bandit and quietly watched as I began to teach the dog how to read.

The first page had a picture of the Bee standing on a red apple. I spelled out each of the letters of "apple" to Bandit. He seemed to understand, but I wouldn't really be able to test him until we were alone.

Suddenly I noticed we had an audience. A man waiting by the next bus stop tossed us an interested look. A battered suitcase covered with travel stickers sat by his feet. He wore a shirt tucked into suit pants and had the air of a traveling salesman. I forced a heavy Russian accent into my voice and pointed at the picture book.

"Aaaa," I asked Sully hopefully, while flicking my eyes in the direction of our spectator.

"Good, now try the next letter. Paaaaa," he encouraged. He sure caught on fast. Dutifully, I copied his voice, exaggerating my pronunciation. Our act worked, as the salesman lost interest pretty soon after I reached "e", which I was thankful for. My mouth felt like it'd had a workout, and though we hadn't long finished eating, I found myself wanting a drink. I suddenly developed a newfound respect for actors. It wasn't as easy as it seemed.

I felt a wet nose on the side of my neck. It was Bandit's way of letting me know he was done with this word. It was pretty amazing how much he conveyed without a sound, but then, I guess that's what happens when you have a genius IQ dog. I turned the page. Bradley the Bumble Bee was now balancing precariously on a colorful beach ball. Three guesses on the word.

"Ball," I said quietly. "B...a...l...l." My finger moved along each letter as I pronounced them. Bandit's eyes followed closely. A bubble of excitement rose within me. This was really happening! Bandit was learning how to read! I could feel Sully all tensed up beside me. He was still struggling to believe that Bandit was special, even though to me it was pretty damn obvious. Something else was becoming apparent too, however; we were being hunted, and to stay one step ahead of them, we needed answers soon. And we would get them once we weren't quite so out in the open.

We sped through the book. We couldn't know for sure Bandit's reading age, but he was picking this up scarily fast. By the time we reached "S", our bus pulled up. The doors pinged open and our driver, a jolly man with a face lined with wrinkles from many summers spent behind the wheel, beamed at us.

"Howdy. Hop on up, folks. We'll be on our way in fifteen minutes" he said, gesturing into the vehicle. As Bandit climbed on, still carrying his bone, the driver reached down and gave him a giant scratch behind the ears. Bandit almost toppled over from happiness.

"Beautiful Collie, you got there. I've a German Shepherd myself. Best thing I ever did, getting a dog. Loyal to the bone and always happy to see you."

Bandit surprised us all next. He jumped up, placed a paw on either side of the driver's shoulders and vigorously sniffed at his neck. It wasn't a display of affection, as I first thought, but something else entirely. Sully was mortified and pulled Bandit down.

"No, Boy. We don't do that."

Bandit strained against Sully, scrabbling to get to the driver. For his part, the driver didn't seem concerned. He was quite liking all the attention, but Sully and I were worried. *What was he doing?*

Sully tugged — hard. I flinched, thinking of the pain this must be causing. Finally, Bandit whimpered and allowed Sully to drag him to the seats. Once more we sat at the back where we could have some privacy.

Sully bent his head close to Bandit's, his expression troubled.

"Why did you do that to the driver?"

Bandit dropped his bone, looked up at him, and licked his hand to reassure him that he was well. Still, there was something really bothering him. He circled the floor, agitated. An idea came to me. I fished out his learning book and asked if Bandit could show us anything in them that might help explain his concern. Bandit woofed. Using his paw, he began turning the pages of the book. When he got to "D" he stopped and placed his paw very deliberately on the center of the page.

We examined the picture. Bradley had been blown by a gust of strong wind and had hurt his wing. Luckily, a passing Doctor spotted him and helped bandage it up. In no time at all, Bradley was off flying again to "E".

I traded looks with Sully. He glanced over at the driver who was now chatting to another passenger as she ascended the steps.

"Is it the bee?" I asked.

Bandit chuffed twice, softly.

"If it's not him, then, the doctor? Is that it?"

Bandit chuffed once, but his whole body trembled. Whatever Doctor he had known had left him with some very bad memories. I rubbed his chin to reassure him.

"He's a driver, not a doctor, so why would you..." Sully trailed off suddenly. I looked at them both, no idea what was going on with them.

Bandit whined and shifted his paw slightly, so that the tip of one claw was now resting on top of Bradley's injured wing, like he was pointing to it.

Sully gave a sharp intake of breath and stared back at the driver.

"No way."

I couldn't take any more. "What? Are you going to tell me what's going on?"

Concern marred Sully's look of wonder. He continued staring at our driver as he explained. "We don't know how they do it, but some dogs can tell when a person is very sick. It's something to do with their extraordinary sense of smell. They're particularly good at spotting cancer."

I swallowed hard. Whatever I had expected, that wasn't it at all. "The driver has cancer? He's sick?"

"I think so."

And just to confirm what we'd already said, Bandit barked once. We turned back to our cheerful driver, welcoming more travelers onto the bus.

"Someone needs to tell him," came Sully's gentle reply.

46

SULLY

W e drove leisurely along route 476. Our driver didn't seem in any real hurry to reach our destination, and the passengers, too, seemed to be enjoying the ride. I, however, was dreading the moment we would arrive at Atlantic City. After so many years working as a vet, I was used to giving bad news to a pet's owner, but telling a person he was sick with a potentially life-threatening disease? This was something new entirely.

Maybe the dog was wrong? The hopeful thought flitted through my mind but disappeared just as quickly. I'd read countless studies on canine cancer detection. The dogs are able to do this by detecting the very low concentrations of the alkanes and aromatic compounds generated by tumors. It was a remarkable but well-documented fact. Torn up inside, I squeezed my eyes closed and lay back against the headrest.

Now that Bandit's message had been conveyed, the restlessness had disappeared, but he kept his eyes focused on the driver at all times. I could feel the concern radiating from him. For the first time, the truth was sinking in... Chase had been right all along. Somehow, Bandit had an intelligence level far exceeding any dog of his species, and that virus warning was just a story manufactured to cover up HPA's true intentions. I looked down at Bandit, cradling his bone between two paws but seemingly without an appetite any longer, and marveled at his ability to empathize. Intelligent or not, this was an ability some humans had not managed to master, so it was astonishing coming from a dog.

Just another thing to add to Bandit's list of talents.

We crossed into the heart of Philadelphia, the birthplace of the United States Marine Corps. I knew this little fact as I had considered running away to join it at twenty, when the difficulties at home had seemed unbearable. Staring at Chase, I felt ashamed now, realizing how good I had had it compared to her. Even during turbulent times, I had never known hunger, had never worried where I would be sleeping that night, or indeed, if I would ever wake again.

Oblivious to my musings, Chase sighed longingly at the many cheesesteak houses that passed by, drooling at the giant pictures of glistening, melted, yellow bites of heaven. Despite my dark thoughts, I couldn't stop my admiration; the kid could really eat.

The bus rolled past the eateries, down streets decorated with cheerful outdoor sculptures and murals, where small children played as their parents watched, chatting with friends and neighbors. In a moment of whimsy, I thought I might have liked to live here in another life. It was a sunny day, with the city blossoming under blue skies. We rode past several business blocks of polished black glass until a large green space came into view. Bandit tore his eyes from the driver to gape outside. We had reached Fairmont Park, a sign outside the park entrance announced. Seeing it, Chase's eyes lit up.

"That's the world's largest landscaped urban park."

"You learn that at school?" I asked.

"No. I read it somewhere once."

"Just once?" I raised my eyebrows, impressed. "And you've remembered it?"

Chase's thin shoulders lifted into a shrug. "I've got a photographic memory. Once something goes in, I can always find it again."

"That must come in useful," I said.

"Yeah. I usually ace my exams." She said it nonchalantly, like it was no big deal. While we were speaking, Bandit had pushed his nose as far out of the window as he could, gulping in big mouthfuls of air. It occurred to me that Bandit had probably never seen much of a natural environment before. I stroked Bandit's head.

"When all this is over, how about we take you to the countryside? There'll be rivers to swim in, mountains to climb, and animals to chase. First, we'll make some money, then we'll go on a trip."

Bandit grinned, pawing the ground. Liking the plan.

47

CHASE

The bus finally reached its last stop.

As the doors popped open, I could smell the salt in the air and see shimmering waves stretching out to the horizon. Gulls screeched overhead, soaring into the cloudless sky. Though we were officially here on business, I couldn't help but feel excited — this was only the second time I'd been to the sea!

When I was young, and before Tubs had entered our lives, my mom had taken me on a day trip to Provincetown in Cape Cod. I don't remember too much of that day. Just the red balloon a sidewalk performer had given me and the freedom I'd felt running barefoot along the beach. It was one of the few happy moments I had ever had with her. Not long after, Tubs had come along, and life had taken a downhill spiral to Crappytown.

This place reminded me of Provincetown, though it was way louder, like someone had ratcheted up the tacky counter to ten. Along the long boardwalk, brightly striped canopies shielded terraces packed with restaurant diners. Tourists took snapshot after snapshot, posing with cheesy smiles and peace signs.

Beside me, filled with excitement and desperate to leave, Bandit was darting up and down the length of the bus, bone still in his mouth, but first there was that conversation that needed to be had.

Sully waited until everyone else was off of the bus before approaching the driver.

The man smiled at us cheerfully, causing my stomach to twist in knots.

It didn't feel right for us to be standing there while they spoke about something so personal, so I led Bandit off the bus and we waited outside.

I couldn't hear the words Sully spoke, but I had a clear line of sight to the driver's face. He went through a whole gamut of emotions. Sunny, then questioning, which changed to concern, and finally fear. His dark eyes roamed the sidewalk for Bandit. When he found him, there was a gratefulness I didn't expect to see. News delivered, Sully reached across and shook his hand. The driver, though shell-shocked, remained calm and resolute as he took it. Sully climbed down the stairs and joined us outside.

"Did he believe you?" I asked him.

"Yeah."

"Did he know already?"

"No, but he suspected something was wrong. Been feeling a lump in that same region for a while. Didn't get it checked out in case it was nothing. Said he couldn't afford to waste the examination fee since his company doesn't provide insurance."

He fell silent, his thoughts with the jovial driver whose day he had just crushed. "I told him the best cure is to take preventative measures."

We both fell silent; anything we might have said felt redundant.

Suddenly, Bandit walked back onto the bus, and very deliberately, laid his bone down by the driver's feet. Licking the man's hand, he nudged him with his nose — guess that was his way of saying "take care of yourself" — then returned to us. The driver stared at Bandit, open-mouthed. I was feeling pretty awed myself.

Sully looked down at Bandit. "You may have just saved a man's life there."

For once Bandit looked solemn.

48

CHASE

We headed down the boardwalk, following the blinking lights of Caesar's Palace along the horizon. We'd been going a while when Sully stopped us outside a dive of a motel. I took in his choice of establishment, frowning. Of all the places on this street to choose... There was a much nicer bed-and-breakfast across the way, but Sully shook his head and pointed.

Of all the places here, this was the only one without CCTV cameras.

Rifling through his backpack, he fished out some items bought from the dollar store and handed a pair of scissors and hair dye to me. "Not sure how attached you are to being a blonde, but I think it's best if we alter our appearance."

I glanced at the box of dye and shrugged. "Brunette would make a nice change."

We headed to the reception desk, which was manned by a twenty-something guy with punk hair. Heavy metal blasted from his iPhone, which he didn't bother pausing to serve us. Just pointed at a sign, "$50 per night", got Sully to fill in a check-in form (he lied on just about everything), then handed us a key.

Sully took the key, and we moved past the reception desk and down the dark corridor. The decor was Icksville. Without thinking, I reached out and touched the raised wallpaper. It was a wine red color with an old-fashioned design, like something you'd see in an old Western movie. Made of some kind of brushed material, it felt greasy to touch, and I immediately regretted my decision to examine it without a pair of hazmat gloves. Yellow with age, wrought iron lamps flickered at us as dust collected on the rims. The floral carpet, which couldn't have seen a clean this side of the century, stuck to my sneakers as I walked over it. I waited until we were out of earshot before asking Sully the obvious question.

"How are we affording the room?"

Sully gave me a look that I think was meant to be confident, but he wasn't fooling anyone. "With our winnings."

I shot him a look. "You know that's the kind of thing a gamblerholic says, right?"

He shrugged. "I have every faith in Bandit."

Hearing his name, Bandit chuffed at us, though he still seemed a little down. I think he was feeling guilty about the driver. I made up my mind to cheer him up once we had some privacy.

Several identical doors passed by with faded brass numbers. When Sully reached twenty-eight, he stopped in front of it. "This is it."

He unlocked the door, and we stepped inside. Thankfully, the walls here were a lighter shade than the murder red in the hall. This was a pale green: I think the designers amongst you would consider it "mint". The carpet was the same as outside, but didn't look as sick-inducing with these walls. Two narrow single beds were separated by a dark wooden side table. On it lay a phone and a bible. Seeing the book, Bandit gave it an exploratory sniff.

"Don't think you're up to that yet," I said.

He shot me a questioning look but took my word for it as he padded off to investigate the adjoining bathroom. Sully had taken a seat on a battered armchair by the window. We had a nice view of a back alley, but at least there were no bars across the window. You get that a lot more in urban places like New York or Chicago. Guess Atlantic City didn't see too much excitement. I was relieved by this since my claustrophobic self didn't like to feel locked in. A flash of memory darted across my mind.

I was younger and locked in a small closet, punishment for one of the many crimes Tubs regularly decided I was guilty of. The darkness was suffocating. I lay down on my stomach and pressed my face to the thin crack at the base of the door, desperate for a hit of air. I could hear the radio blasting in the next room, while Tubs and Ma argued. From experience, I knew they would be some time. Fighting to remain calm, I chanted the alphabet backwards in my head until eventually, I fell into an exhausted sleep.

I shook myself from the unwanted trip down memory lane. See how much fun life was before now? Made running away from mercenaries with shotguns a picnic. Almost.

I turned my attention to a small TV that was fixed to a bracket on the wall. It looked as ancient as the carpet. If I turned it on, would the whole thing explode? Feeling brave, I plucked the remote from one of the beds and hit "on".

The monitor flickered to life. Despite appearances, it was working fine. A woman with glowing skin was extolling the virtues of a 12 step detox system which looked exactly like green puke in a bottle. You too could have a complexion like hers if you drank a puke drink three times a day! Seriously, is this what people get up to when they have money?

I pushed the channel button, flicking through until Jeopardy came on. This wasn't my type of show, but at least it wasn't inane infomercial chatter either. I left the TV on and moved into the bathroom to inspect Sully's recent purchases. The hair dye looked strong; I hoped it wouldn't sting. I'd read somewhere that some people had these crazy allergic reactions to the dye where their scalps literally burned off. I seriously hoped that wouldn't be the case with me. I was kinda attached to my hair. Grease and all.

Bandit, who had found nothing of interest in here, wandered back into the main area. Seeing the television, he jumped onto a bed, before he settled down with his head on his paws, and proceeded to watch the quiz show.

I almost slapped my head when I realized.

Quiz show.

"Boy, you are gonna *love* this."

49

SULLY

The sound of television babble drowned out the ache that was intermittently attacking my heart. Seeing Chase's joy on the boardwalk, I had had to turn my face away so she wouldn't see my pain. Emma had loved the wildness of the ocean. Our first trip away had been to a seaside similar to this. The colorful balloons and sweet smell of the cotton candy brought on another onslaught of bittersweet memories.

Emma would never experience this again.

A woman laughed close by, her voice clear and jubilant. Full of life, and so like Emma's.

I felt a tightness in my chest when I realized that as time passed, I would forget what her laughter sounded like, how she smelled like freshly washed cotton. I squeezed my eyes together and pictured her now, laughing with her arms outstretched, twirling in circles in our bedroom. I made a mental note: twirling. I must never forget how she was.

But then the bedroom burst into flames.

I flinched, rapidly crashing back to the present. Emma's things, the items I had been saving, evidence of our life together — it was all gone in a puff of smoke. I swallowed and turned my attention to the dog, who hadn't taken his eyes from the television set since he had first discovered it. As the presenter asked a question, Bandit fidgeted, making a low whining sound. He knew the answer. As the contestant answered correctly, Bandit chuffed, pleased with himself, tongue lolling out goofily.

Despite my mood, I smiled.

50

CHASE

I t took close to two hours, but when I emerged from the bathroom, I looked like a whole new person.

Gone was my shoulder length chestnut hair. In its place was a choppy, shorter cut that barely covered my ears. And I had black hair now. Surprisingly, this color and style made my eyes seem even bluer. As part of my new disguise, I had ringed them with heavy black kohl, but kept my cheeks and lips neutral (the goal was to look different and not like a clown). Although the dark dye was a little harsh on my skin and made me look paler than I actually am, I was still a total babe! And bonus, I looked several years older.

Jeopardy had long finished and Bandit was now watching an early episode of The Simpsons. When I appeared, he leaped off the bed and pranced around me, whining. I looked at Sully, who hadn't moved from his seat. He shook his head, no; he didn't know what was eating at Bandit either.

Bandit spun around and pawed at the alphabet book, opening it. His paw spun through the pages like lightning, so we could barely keep up with him.

"He's memorized them," Sully's said, awed.

"What?"

"He's memorized them. See how he's barely glancing at the pages?"

I gave this some consideration. "Are you telling me, on top of being Einstein, he has super powers?"

Bandit stopped pawing the book, looked up at us, and gave two strong barks.

"Guess he's just your run-of-the-mill genius dog then," Sully deadpanned. I think Bandit appreciated the joke as his tongue lolled out of the side of his mouth again.

He found the page he was looking for and pawed it deliberately. We were at P. Bradley the Bumble Bee was hovering over a Princess who sang to him, causing the bee to swoon deliriously mid-flight. My brows furrowed into a frown.

"You want me to *sing*?" I couldn't hide the incredulous tone in my voice.

Sully laughed. "I think he's paying you a compliment, Chase."

I looked back at the picture before I finally got it. "I look like a princess? But I'm in jeans."

Sully and the dog both rolled their eyes like a comical duo. If I'd had a camera to record the moment, I guarantee it would've got a billion hits on YouTube.

"He thinks you look pretty," Sully spelled out. Bandit barked once, confirming the translation. With horror, I felt the beginnings of a blush on my cheeks.

"Whatever," was my gracious reply, but neither of them seemed bothered by it. Sully looked away, allowing me some time to recover, but the dog just grinned at me. Needing to change the subject, I fixed critical eyes on Sully. "Well, that's one down. One to go."

His confused brown eyes met mine.

"Time for your quick change."

Sully glanced nervously at the scissors in my hand. "You do know how to use those, right?"

I nodded. "Course. Don't be such a baby."

51

SULLY

The wind whistled through my newly shorn hair. It was a pleasant, if unfamiliar, feeling.

Chase, it turned out, wasn't bad with the scissors.

She'd mumbled something about cutting her mom's hair before she realized what she was saying and clammed up. One day, I was going to have to talk to her about where she came from. Holding onto bad things wasn't good for the soul. This was something I knew very well.

We'd left the motel and headed down the sunny promenade with only one goal in mind — to make money. The kids were reveling in the sights and sounds of the vacation town, forgetting for a moment the predicament we were in. They marveled at the colorful, toy-like buildings, played hide and seek inside a life-size model of a Monopoly board, and splurged on a bag of cotton candy. I, however, had tuned everything out.

An idea was milling around inside my head, an end goal of sorts, but for me, it would be a last resort. I knew we couldn't keep running forever. We needed a safe location, somewhere remote, where we could blend into the countryside and wait until the heat died down. I knew the perfect place, but I needed time to get used to the idea. There was a reason the past stayed buried, but if we chose to go down that road, old wounds would be opened up.

The kids were now gaping at the flashy lights and tacky decor of the Taj Mahal Casino. Gold-etched domes battled against gaudy red lettering. I didn't need to look into my pockets to know how much money we had left. It was such a pittance, it wouldn't see us through another day. When we had first decided to come here, Chase had explained how Bandit had learned to play poker — and how they could use his special abilities to bend the rules. She was a resourceful and creative kid, and the idea certainly had merit, but since arriving here and doing a little reconnaissance, I knew it would never work. We wouldn't be able to cheat the system — not with all the guards and cameras in place, something we hadn't bargained on prior to hatching our plan. So now, it was onto Plan B... Despite how any attention drawn to us would be a bad thing; I knew we had to risk it. We would do this just once to see where it would get us.

Across the way was a convenience store, where a teenage boy exited, carrying a super-sized Big Gulp. Seeing him, I turned to the kids.

"Wait here."

I jogged over into the store, casually sauntered over to the soda fountain, and grabbed several paper cups. As I made my way to the exit, the store clerk yelled across to me.

"You can't take those unless you're buying a drink."

I waved and smiled. "My kid just bought one, but if I let him have the whole thing, we'll be stopping for restroom breaks every half hour. Better I share it with him."

The clerk stared at me, not buying the story. I pointed out the window, at the back of super-sized Big Gulp boy, who was now helpfully sitting outside on a bench, sipping his drink. Without waiting for another response, I left the store quickly and returned to Chase and Bandit, both watching me the whole time, full of questions.

My eyes searched the street until they landed on a corner that seemed perfect. No cameras, just a blocked off alley behind us. If we got into trouble, there would be plenty of time to see and get a head start. I gestured to the kids. "I have an idea how we can make some quick money, but it's risky."

Chase frowned at me, immediately concerned, while Bandit just looked at me, head tilted at an angle.

"Got the idea from you actually, Chase."

Her frown intensified. "OK, now I'm really worried," she said.

52

CHASE

Sully laid out his plan for us, but I was freaking out. We'd spent all this time keeping out of sight, and now he wanted us to solicit attention? How did that make sense?

"I'm not exactly comfortable with the idea myself, but we need cash and we need it now. What's the harm in trying?" He looked at me, not unreasonably, I hated to admit.

"Fine." It was anything but, however, he had a point. We sat on the ground, Bandit before us, as Sully handed me over two plastic cups that he'd lifted from the convenience store. He left one upturned on the ground before us, then took the remaining two cups for himself. I watched as he turned them upside down, then began hitting them on the ground in a catchy rhythm. His head nodded to the beat as he encouraged me to do the same. Seemed simple enough to do.

I fumbled a bit initially, but soon got the hang of it. When I had it down, Sully changed his own cupping to a beat that complemented my own. By this point, we had already caught the attention of a few passers-by. Sully cleared his throat, then started singing a well-known country song in a deep baritone. To my surprise, he was good — *really good*. The whole thing sounded great.

Then, our icing on the cake, our secret weapon, Bandit, began to sing.

He had impeccable timing and only howled when Sully nodded. The gathering audience who at first simply enjoyed the performance was now charmed by Bandit's antics. One by one, they dropped first coins, then bills into our cup.

Thrilled by our success, Bandit decided to crank it up a notch by adding dance moves to his repertoire, lifting opposite paws and prancing around. By now, folk were clapping and singing along. At the end of the performance, they gave us a huge round of applause. I was amazed! Some people moved on, but quite a few stayed for another track until the crowd grew even bigger.

Based on my reaction in the hotel room, you've probably gathered by now that singing isn't really a thing I do well, so hearing how naturally it came to Sully, I was a little jealous. I'd *love* to have a skill or talent that didn't involve just trying to stay alive.

Following Sully's lead, we blew through some twenty or so numbers. By the late afternoon, his voice was getting a little hoarse. Bandit too needed a break. He'd long stopped dancing, choosing just to howl along.

"I think that's a wrap," Sully said.

We crowded around the cup, which had been emptied a few times already and counted out the day's earnings. I couldn't believe my eyes.

"Two hundred bucks? All we did was sing?!"

Sully smiled, though he didn't seem quite as excited as I was.

"We're going to need more than that to get to where we need to go." He pocketed the cash, then threw the cups into a trash cash. My mouth fell open.

"What're you doing? We need those for tomorrow! Why would you throw them away?" I went to retrieve them, but Sully stopped me.

"We can't do it again. This was already a risky move. We need to move on. I have an idea where we can go, but two hundred bucks won't cover us getting there".

I frowned at him, while Bandit, picking up the concern between us, sneaked licks at our hands. "Well, how else are we going to make money, and more?"

He didn't respond right away, but there was clearly something on his mind. Something he wasn't particularly comfortable with, judging by the look that appeared on his face.

"You guys must be hungry."

Bandit barked "yes", wagging his tail with excitement. Sully probably thought he was pretty sneaky, using my biggest weakness against me as I did notice the rapid distraction technique he had just employed, however, the instant grumbling in my stomach wiped any objection clear out of my mind. Food first, questions later.

He led us to a cheap diner called NATE's. The flashing neon red sign was crusted over with dirt, and the N bulb had long blown, so the sign now read "ATE's", which kind of amused me. We sat at a vacant table to find that the menu was printed onto paper that covered the entire table. A sheet of scratched plastic sat on top, protecting it from spills. I couldn't read half of the descriptions due to the scratches, but that, it turns out, wouldn't be a problem.

"They have pictures of everything. Helpful."

"Yeah, I like how they've made a burrito look different by changing the sides that come with it." Sully joked, but it was half-hearted. Bandit laid his chin on Sully's hand, sighing loudly. Even the pooch was concerned. Absently, Sully reached over to scratch him behind the ears.

"You guys order. I've got something to attend to. I shouldn't be long."

He pushed back his chair and stood up to leave. I felt a moment of blind panic as the thought flashed across my mind that he wouldn't be coming back. I shot up from my seat as well, but too fast. My knee hit the table, knocking it. It screeched loudly across the floor a few inches, drawing a few perplexed glances our way. Sully must've sensed my fears then, as the distracted look that had been on his face went away.

"I'm just off to see about some money. I'll be back before you're done eating."

He patted Bandit once more, then took off across the street. I watched until he disappeared around the corner. My stomach gnawed at me, which wasn't unusual in and of itself, but I had a feeling this time that it wasn't from hunger. Bandit whined, liking Sully's absence about as much as me, which come to think of it, was weird. I hadn't wanted him to come along in the first place, so why was I acting all emo right now?

"He promised he'd be back, so let's just enjoy a meal. What do you fancy?"

Bandit looked down at the menu, nose so close to the plastic that his breath started fogging it up. Suddenly he stopped, lifted up his paw and very deliberately rested it on a picture. I slid his paw aside to see what it was.

"A burger. Good choice, buddy."

I signaled the waitress and focused on stroking Bandit, now sitting under the table. Sully said he'd be back. All I had to do was eat.

Simple, right?

53

SULLY

I knew Chase could take care of Bandit for an hour or two, but even then, it felt odd to be without them. I wasn't particularly sure I liked the feeling.

Motoring through the promenade at a rapid pace, my eyes scanned the lurid area for a certain establishment, as I tried not to think about what I was going to do. Instead, I mulled over how much my life had changed in the last forty-eight hours.

Aside from Florence and our animal patients, I had pretty much kept to myself this past year. Initially, when Emma had died, the sudden silence I had found myself in was crushing. Being at home was no longer relaxing. In fact, it induced outright panic. Thinking I didn't want to be alone, I had surrounded myself with family and friends. But pretty soon, the chatter, the constant battle to pretend I wasn't falling apart, exhausted me.

Without even realizing it, I began pushing people away. Just small things at first: not answering the phone; pretending I was asleep or wasn't home when well-wishers turned up at my door; to bailing out on last minute social functions until the invitations eventually stopped coming. Even Emma's family, reeling from their own loss and unable to deal with my standoffish behavior, began to avoid me.

Soon, I had no choice but to be alone since I had burned all bridges and no one wanted to be around me.

Except now I had two to protect.

I reached the end of another block when I saw the flashing sign across the road:

Pawn Shop. Instant Cash.

54

SULLY

Inside, the shop was dark and cramped.

The air tasted stale despite a row of opened windows. I assumed this was due to the sheer volume of items on display. Aisles of clothes, shoes and household objects dominated the front section. The back was filled with electronics, gaming consoles, and old television sets. Whoever was in charge of housekeeping could've done a better job as far as I was concerned — a fine layer of dust covered many of the items.

I worked through the maze until I reached the counter. A large, tattooed biker-type stood behind the counter. Around his thick neck rested a heavy gold chain with the name "Ed" on it.

"What have you got for me?" Ed mumbled. His tone wasn't rude, merely straight down to business. This wasn't a man who had time to fool around.

"You buy jewelry?" I asked.

Ed nodded. "Selling or pawning?"

"Selling," came my response. The word stuck in my throat.

"Let's see it." He stretched out a hand towards me, palm facing the ceiling. Waiting. I hesitated. As my mind raced, my eyes focused on the many lines and callouses on Ed's hand. This was it. No going backward.

I slipped the wedding ring off my finger.

The overhanging light bulb picked up the engraved writing on the inner band of the ring. I squinted to read the familiar words scorched into my heart: "Always and Forever." Her delicate voice sounded in my head, but it seemed far, far away, across an ocean of time. I waited until the last echo of her voice faded, then slid the ring across the counter.

Ed had been watching through my internal dialogue. He knew what I was going through. Though his expression never changed, Ed softened his voice when he spoke. "Nice piece. Shame the engraving knocks the price down."

I nodded, having guessed as much. "Just give me a ballpark."

The other man frowned, assessing the damage. "I know what it's worth, but no way can I match that. Best I can do today is three."

I couldn't hide my shock. "Three grand? That's a third what the ring's worth!" My fists tightened into balls as tension flooded through me.

Though Ed felt sympathy for me, he wasn't about to show it. Business was business after all, and there was a reason why Ed's had lasted long past the faddy shops he saw open, then close.

"It's my last and final offer. Take it or leave it."

55

CHASE

Bandit and I had long demolished our burgers and fries, but that weird ache in my stomach was still there.

Bandit lay beneath the table with his head on my feet. Throughout my meal, I had been sneaking him food. When she had taken my order, the waitress warned that dogs weren't supposed to be in the diner, but I started freaking out, rocking back and forth with my arms wrapped around myself, chanting "dog stays with me, dog stays with me."

I was pretending I had a form of Aspergers and only my dog's company would calm me. I know some of you might find that distasteful, but separation wasn't an option, and you know, I had already committed to eating... After that, she gave me a wide berth except to give Bandit a bowl of water after the urging from her boss, the greasy-looking cook, who kept peering at us from inside the kitchen.

An old clock ticked slowly above the entrance. I kept looking at it, counting the minutes, until I nearly drove myself crazy. I sipped water from a chipped glass, trying to make it last as long as possible.

I wasn't sure what Sully's new money-making scheme was, but in the event, it didn't work, I made sure that I had only ordered one meal, and it was one of the cheapest available. I had already drunk three glasses and was busting for the restroom when I finally saw him walking towards the diner.

At my questioning gaze, he shot me a barely perceivable nod. If he was successful, why, then, did he look so damn miserable?

He had barely entered the diner when Bandit's tail started thumping.

Pretty sure he couldn't have seen Sully from his position on the floor, so I'm guessing he must've caught Sully's scent. I remembered reading something about that this one time.

Did you know that to dogs, we're super stinky?

Not just our armpits, but our breath and genitals reek. Even our skin is covered in sweat and sebaceous glands (whatever those are) that churn out fluid and oils emitting our own particular scent.

As if that weren't icky enough, when we touch things, we leave a bit of ourselves on them, with our own bacteria steadily munching and excreting away. Next time your dog sniffs you, remember that.

Sully sat down next to me. "You done here?" he asked.

I nodded. "Don't worry, we didn't get much. Just enough to keep us here." Seeing his arrival, the waitress hurried over. I fell quickly silent.

"Are you her dad?" Off Sully's nod, she rushed to continue. "I'm sorry, but we might have had an incident here while you were gone. I didn't know about her... condition. I'm so sorry."

"Condition?"

Sully arched a brow, shooting looks at Bandit and I. I kept my gaze focused on the tabletop, saying nothing. Our waitress fussed over the table, picking up my plate, and cutlery as she shrugged apologetically.

"I tried to get her to remove the dog, which seemed to kick off some anxiety. My boss...," she gestured at the cook who made no pretense of watching us from inside his kitchen. "Said, as an apology, her meal is on us. He doesn't want no trouble."

Sully took the small win and nodded his thanks, though he was clearly burning with questions. Not unlike me, to be honest. He stood back up, offering me his hand. I was surprised until I realized he had no idea what my "condition" was and was hedging his bets.

Remembering that some people suffering from Aspergers hated to be touched, I recoiled and started making my way to the exit. Bandit followed immediately, not understanding what was happening, but game all the same. A few seconds later, Sully joined us outside.

"What was that all about?" he asked.

"I pretended I had Aspergers because she wanted Bandit to leave the diner."

He blinked at me. "Creative. Let me guess, you read about it once?"

"Yup."

I fidgeted on my feet. I had been patient all this time, but I couldn't wait any longer. "So, did your plan work? Did you get money?"

"I did."

I squealed and grabbed Bandit in a little dance. He chuffed happily at us. "How did you do it?"

A cloud of pain flashed over his eyes. As if he could feel it, Bandit stopped dancing immediately. "I don't want to talk about it."

So, of course, I wanted to plague him with a billion questions since his reply didn't tell me anything! But seeing his face, seeing how drained he looked, I shoved my curiosity down. I was pretty proud of myself, actually; I'm not known for my empathy. As we walked from the diner, a growl escaped from my stomach. Sully looked down, surprised.

"Are you kidding me? You just ate!"

"Not much, though. And I shared it with Bandit." I looked down. "I didn't know when you'd get back, and since I knew we didn't have much cash, I didn't want to risk ordering too much... in case we couldn't pay."

Sully looked at us both, eyes shining brightly. If I were a gambling girl (which from my disastrous previous attempt, we know I'm clearly not), I'd say those were tears in his eyes. His voice turned gruff as he cleared his throat.

"Well, we've got a decent amount now. How about we do something special?"

My eyes turned wide. "Like a main *and* dessert?"

I don't know what I'd said, but he for sure looked emotional suddenly. So I have a big appetite. He already knew this about me. He didn't answer, just inclined his head to follow, as he cleared his throat from the frog that had suddenly appeared in it.

56

CHASE

When Sully told me his idea of special, I couldn't believe it! This is what dreams are made of! Having seen numerous glorious ads for Caesar's restaurant, we headed straight there. We were sold before we'd even tasted a thing.

Their famous Bacchanal Buffet (*seriously, who comes up with these names?*) is apparently the best in the city, winning awards and everything. We walked into a massive hall of food. My eyes nearly popped out of my head when I saw the spread before me.

There were some nine restaurants in the one hall, each specializing in a different food, with a team of chefs preparing food right in front of us! My mouth salivated at the rows upon rows of dishes set out onto the tables: prime ribs, roasted South Carolina shrimp and grits, oak-grilled lamb chops, handmade dim sum and baked-to-order souffles (OK, I'm reading off labels now, and don't know what half of these things are. Still, they sound nice!).

One section contained only meat: both full sized and mini burgers, steak skewers (STEAK at a buffet!), sausages dripping with fat, stuffed and sliced roast chicken done in a million different ways, plus wings, ribs, and legs of every possible variety you could think of. Next was the seafood table where crustaceans were arranged artfully on mountains of ice and lemon slices. My taste buds are pretty simple though, and this was a little too fancy for me, if not outright gross. Don't you think king crabs look like giant alien spiders? Inside my mouth is the last place I'd want them to go.

Beside the seafood was a carb table filled with trays of mac and cheese, mashed potatoes, pasta, and freshly baked bread. There was even a section just for fries! Curly fries, thick cut fries, Southern fries, Steakhouse fries, wavy fries, and what I'd decided would be my favorite: tornado fries (basically a spiral cut fry on a stick). The thing was *huge!*

But then I realized, although I love my carbs, I couldn't possibly fill up on what was essentially the cheapest item there. I would eat what I usually couldn't afford on the street... and that meant *meat.*

And so it was that I loaded my plate with meat of every kind, taking care to source some for Bandit, who was doing a great job at being Sully's guide dog. His nose was going a hundred miles a minute, and he was practically swooning, but he was so good. His tongue didn't sneak a lick, not once.

Seems the other diners were also impressed with his restraint. I soon saw that they were "accidentally" dropping food on the ground, which Bandit dutifully hoovered up. He was having the best time, but then again, so was I, and I hadn't tasted a thing yet!

When there was a mountain of food on my plate, I gestured to Bandit, who guided Sully to an empty table. I dived into my meal, eating with my hands since I hadn't thought to bring cutlery. I must have looked like an animal, but I just didn't care. Sully used a fork to eat, but even he seemed to be enjoying himself, though he showed a ton more restraint than me.

I shared everything on my plate with Bandit and found that when he liked a food in particular, he would place his paw on my foot, applying gentle pressure. It was amazing, really, how we were learning our own sign language. Just think what we could do if we had the proper tools.

In no time, we devoured the first plate, and I went back for more, this time around allowing myself some of that amazingly gloopy looking mac and cheese. I even remembered a fork. And napkins, but mostly because my hands were sticky, and the servers were shuddering at the sight of them. I picked all of Bandit's favorites and sat back down to share, being careful to be stealthy all the while. There were so many diners, it was easy to get away with, really. Occasionally, someone caught on, but the fact that Bandit was a guide dog meant no one said a thing.

When we'd polished off four plates of food, I gave a loud belch and admitted defeat. No more food. I was fit to burst.

But then I saw the desserts.

Three cheesecakes, two pies, and one chocolate mint sundae later, I was done. Even Bandit — who could seriously compete in a food competition — had given up and was now lying contently on the ground. Sully had long stopped before either of us and had spent the rest of his time trying not to ogle at the amount of food I was shoveling down. *He was blind after all, remember?*

Sully's hands were wrapped around a mug of coffee that he sipped slowly from. He seemed to be savoring the flavor. He must be one of those caffeine addicts as the very act of drinking it soothed him. He put the mug down and focused at a distant point over my shoulder.

"Well, that is money well spent, even if I do say so myself."

I was just about to ask if this amazing meal had bankrupted us when Bandit suddenly tensed up. As I froze, worried at what he might have seen, he began frothing at the mouth. His eyes rolled into the back of his head as he fell onto his side, his body shaking with convulsions.

"What's happening?!" I screamed at Sully.

Forgetting all pretense of being blind, Sully leaped out of his chair. Pulling Bandit away from the wall, Sully shrugged out of his jacket and wrapped Bandit securely inside. He then slipped his hand under Bandit's face so that he wasn't slamming it against the hard ground, but other than that, he did nothing else.

"Why are you just sitting there? Do something!" I screamed at him again. By now, the other diners had stopped eating, some had gathered around to watch. Murmurs rose like a mumbled chorus. Most were concerned for Bandit, though a few wore confused expressions when they saw Sully didn't have a problem seeing with his eyes. I saw one kid filming everything on his phone but shoved the thought to one side.

"There's nothing else to do until the convulsion stops. The most important thing is to make sure he doesn't damage himself during the seizure." Seeing the panic in my eyes, he softened his voice. "It looks much worse than it is."

"Why is this happening to him? Is he... sick?" I meant to demand this of him, but I barely managed to whisper the words. Sully kept his face impassive, but I felt the concern rising from him in waves.

"I don't know. We need to see what's going on inside his head to find the cause of the seizure. It could be something as common as epilepsy..."

"Or it might have to do with the experiments they performed on him," I finished grimly.

He gave a curt nod. That was his guess.

I ran my fingers along Bandit's nose, hoping he wasn't in any pain. I hated that he was unconscious and unresponsive and possibly in pain, and willed him to look at me with his intelligent eyes again.

I heard a noise across the room and glanced over to find hotel staff coming our way. By the set of their shoulders, I knew we were about to be hit with more bad news. And I was right. Having discovered Sully wasn't blind, the staff reprimanded us for bringing Bandit inside. I ignored them and focused on my furry friend, who had finally stopped convulsing and was blinking sluggishly. After a few quivering breaths, he found me with his eyes. I ached at the fear and confusion I saw there.

"It's OK, Boy. You were sick, but you're good now." For what seemed the longest moment of my life, Bandit stared at me without any hint of the intelligence I had grown to know and love in him. The awful truth hit me like a ton of bricks.

He didn't recognize me.

Had the seizure done something to his brain? As I was running these terrifying scenarios in my head, Bandit forced himself to his feet and pressed against me. Feeling my anxiety, he had very deliberately trod on my foot. The relief flooding through me was palpable.

I tugged on Sully's sleeve — he was arguing with the security guards, refusing to move Bandit until he recovered — and let him know Bandit was good to go. Relief flashed over his face, echoing my own.

Though Bandit could walk, Sully decided to carry him. He didn't want Bandit to be any more taxed than he already was.

With the security guards at our backs, we hurried back to the motel.

57

CHASE

Sully was burning a path into the carpet. Since we'd arrived back, he hadn't stopped pacing the small room. I was getting whiplash just watching him.

"If I had my clinic, I could run the scans, find out what's wrong with Bandit."

"Can't we just take him to another vet?" I asked.

"And risk another attack by those thugs? No. We can't trust anyone."

I wrung my hands. Bandit had calmed since the convulsion and seemed back to himself, but there was a darkness in his eyes. A new awareness. He wanted to know what was wrong with him. "We can't keep running. We need a base, somewhere safe where they won't find us. Don't you have someplace we can go?"

Sully finally stopped pacing and tossed a look in my direction. Sighing, he hung his head low. "Yeah, but it's a last resort."

I snorted. "Think that train left a long while ago..." Sully didn't reply. I let out an exasperated breath. "What else is more important than saving Bandit? Whatever your problem is, get over it! We need a safe place, and we need it now!"

Sully shot me a look. I worried maybe I'd gone too far. My mouth shooting off again before my brain could catch up.

But then he began to pack our things. I jumped up to help. Since we didn't have much, we were pretty much done after a few minutes. He checked Bandit's wound and redressed it. It'd need to be bandaged for a few more days, but he seemed pleased by the progress.

I was relieved.

We needed all the wins we could get.

58

SULLY

An hour after we'd left the motel, we arrived at the Amtrak station. Tension caused my head to throb. On a scale of bad to worse, this idea was off the chart and yet, there really was no other choice. Not if we were to have a chance of saving the dog.

Chase stared at me, burning with questions, but knew enough not to ask. I appreciated her understanding. I'd get to the explanations in due course. I marched wearily to the ticket office where an agent waited with barely concealed boredom.

"How can I help, sir?"

"Two tickets to Montpelier."

The agent hit a few buttons on a screen and a price flashed up. "That'll be $156.75."

I was counting out the bills when the agent glanced behind me, noticing Chase retying Bandit's "collar".

"Is she under thirteen?"

I froze mid count and gave the guy an incredulous stare. "She's not my girlfriend if that's what you're asking."

The agent's mouth snapped shut, his cheeks flaming red.

"No, sir. I just meant... if she is, she can go for a child ticket.

I felt shame spreading through me. Poor guy was trying to help and here I was, ready to rip out his throat. "Right. Sorry. It's been that kind of day."

The agent nodded understandingly but didn't make any more eye contact. Once the tickets were printed, he quickly slid them under the counter.

"When's the next train?" I asked.

The agent glanced down at a timetable. "Four-thirty."

I looked at the clock behind me. "That's not for two hours."

The agent nodded. "We have a small waiting area, or if you prefer, there's a strip of shops one block away."

I took the tickets and change, nodded my thanks, and we went to kill time.

59

SULLY

We'd been wandering around aimlessly for what seemed like ten hours when Chase suddenly stopped dead in front of the Walmart window. Eyes wide, she took in the poster which advertised the week's best deals. She turned to Bandit and me, barely able to hide her excitement.

"I need some cash. I've got a great idea for something!"

I opened my wallet. "How much?"

Chase looked at the advertisement. "Four hundred and fifty."

I snapped the wallet shut. "Are you kidding me? What could we possibly need that would cost that much?"

"Please, Sully. I, of all people, know the value of money. You've got to trust me. It's a surprise."

She looked so honest, so excited, that I found myself forking over the bills despite my good sense. *What was the girl up to?*

"One sec..."

She disappeared inside, leaving me staring in bemusement at the dog. "Now I know what those dads with teenage daughters feel like. A chump."

Bandit woofed, though I knew he hadn't really understood my comment. He circled the sidewalk as if trying to find some clarity. We waited for close to fifteen minutes, but still, there was no sign of Chase. Just as I was beginning to feel a hint of concern, Chase reappeared with a shopping bag full of things. At my questioning face, Chase shook her head.

"Nope, not yet. Patience" was all she'd say.

I shrugged, fine. Far be it for me to pry. We did a slow lap around the shops, then headed back to the station, where our train was just pulling in.

Bandit's tail wagged from side to side. He'd read about a train in his book, but this was his first real life encounter. What with the engine sounds and seeing passengers climbing on and off the train, it was about all the excitement he could take. He pranced eagerly, anxiously waiting for our turn. Chase had to lay a restraining hand on his neck, in case the moment was too much for him. I had decided it would be pointless to warn them that too much excitement or stress could potentially cause another fit. There was nothing we could do if it happened. Better the two got to enjoy themselves while they could.

When it was finally time for them to board, Bandit shot off. Despite my reservations on our destination, I couldn't help but smile at Bandit's child-like enthusiasm. I traded a grin with Chase as we followed him onto the train.

60

THE MERCENARY

The Mercenary tugged at the designer suit he was wearing — a far cry from his usual combat gear. The soft fabric made him uncomfortable, offering no protection whatsoever.

Clutching a leather suitcase, he blended into the sea of suits that spilled onto the sidewalks of Wall Street, eagle eyes focused on the revolving door of one particular building. Patiently, he waited for the face he'd spent the last eight hours studying.

He ran through the details he'd memorized in his mind.

Suspect was born and raised in The Bronx to alcoholic parents who relied on the state. In spite of his troubling family life, suspect excelled at school and had an affinity with numbers. It was this skill that landed him a scholarship to college. After which, suspect joined one of Wall Street's top financial firms, where he spent his twenties billing the most hours of his peers.

He made his first million by twenty-five and now worked three days a week for an extortionate consultant fee. He played as hard as he worked and changed dates more frequently than his underwear. He was also Sullivan's longest-known friend and confidante.

The Mercenary's spine tingled, a sure sign that his prey was in sight. Spotting Mark's face in the crowd, The Mercenary smiled and skillfully navigated his way towards him. When he was inches from Mark, The Mercenary reached out a hand and clamped it onto the other man's shoulder.

"Well, I'll be a son of a gun, Mark? Mark Armstrong?"

Mark spun around, a questioning expression on his face.

"Yeah, who's asking?"

"Joel. Joel Miller. We have a mutual friend."

Mark smiled, his initial wariness vanishing. "Which friend is that?"

"Sully." Mark's smile wavered, the only outward sign of a problem. The Mercenary filed this away, knowing it would come in use later.

"How do you know him?"

"He helped out a dog, I know."

"That's Sully," Mark said, shaking his head. The Mercenary could see he wasn't going to get much out of him this way. He swapped tactics.

"Terrible news about Emma. She was so young, so full of life."

Pain flared in Mark's eyes. "Sully hasn't been the same since. It's like he's been gutted."

The Mercenary features softened sympathetically.

"Can't be easy on you either. Wouldn't know how to cope if our positions were reversed."

"Don't know how well I'm doing on that front either." Mark looked down, filled with worry. The Mercenary gave a moment's pause.

"Hey, I'm just on lunch break. You want to go grab a sandwich together?" Seeing the hesitation, The Mercenary's eye's twinkled kindly. "Man's gotta eat, and it's a lot more fun with company."

After a moment's pause, Mark nodded. The Mercenary hid his triumphant smile by gesturing across the way.

"I know this great little place..."

61

THE CEO

The CEO placed his hand on the reader. A quick scan and an automated voice welcomed him inside the secretive area known as the Genesis lab. A foot wide steel door swung inward, and he was immediately met with a sea of white.

Ceilings, counters, and lab coats; everything was blindingly white and sterile. The atmosphere was kept at an even temperature, and only select personnel were ever allowed inside. The CEO himself was not a frequent visitor, not wanting a constant reminder of The Facility's reason for being. His eyes searched the room until they found what they were looking for.

She was an attractive woman. Of average height and build with alabaster skin that barely saw the sun and dark, wavy, almost black hair that she kept tied back in a neat ponytail. Her brown eyes shone with intelligence from the rimless glasses she wore. Right now, they flicked over to him and tried to quell the anxiety that his appearance always brought.

Dr. Elora Robins. Who would know such a brain existed beneath that lovely facade?

She set down the clipboard in her hands and hurried across to him.

"Good afternoon, sir. I wasn't expecting you today."

The CEO merely smiled but did not offer an explanation. As lovely as she was, he enjoyed watching her squirm. Enjoyed wielding the power his wealth brought.

"Any news on Alpha?" She tried, but couldn't hide the concern that clouded her eyes. She loved Alpha. Had cared for him since he was a pup, hand rearing him from the minute he was "born" until the escape. She was the only mother he had ever known, and his disappearance hurt her almost as much as it had cost him.

"My man is on the hunt. Seems Alpha has made some friends, and they've all gone on the run."

62

ELORA

P ride surged inside of Elora before she quickly bolted it back down. Alpha wasn't alone! And if he'd revealed his intellect, he might be safe after all.

Since his escape, Elora had fretted like any mother whose child had run away. She worried how vulnerable the dog was. Worried he would get run over by a car, or worse, captured by unruly characters who might use him as a fighting dog (she had recently watched a documentary about just this horrifying subject). But now that he wasn't alone, Elora knew he was protected. She hoped he knew what to do, hoped she'd taught him enough.

The CEO's steely blue eyes focused on her face, trying to read her feelings. Elora kept her expression impassive. "At least he has more chance of survival now."

"Not if he's been talking to them." He waited several beats before speaking again. "Any news your end?"

Elora shook her head. "There was some movement with F-12, but no birth as yet." At her words, The CEO felt an unfamiliar emotion take hold. Something he had not felt since he was a penniless child living in the slums of Brooklyn.

Fear.

His hands shook. He tried to hide the action by clenching them into fists. "What's your ETA?"

"Three, maybe four days? It's hard to tell. This isn't an exact science."

A wave of exhaustion suddenly hit him. He took a step back to steady himself and hoped Elora hadn't seen. She hadn't, busy checking the figures on one of her endless charts. "If we don't find Alpha in time, this will all be for nothing."

"He never fails you." She was referring to The Mercenary. Her tone was placating, though not warm. The two had never gotten along.

"He knows what will happen if he did." The threat hovered in the air between them. Elora turned away to hide her distasteful expression.

"He won't fail. He'll find Alpha and bring him back."

He wanted to reach out to her. Wanted nothing more at that moment than to touch her hair and feel the silky skin of her face. Instead, he spun on his feet and stalked stiffly from the lab.

Elora let out a relieved breath. She knew he had feelings for her, but they weren't reciprocated. Elora could never love a man so coldly driven, even if she knew he had very good reasons for being the way he was.

She moved past the nameless scientists to the glass screen that separated her lab from their experiments, wincing inwardly at that word. Experiments. She looked into a room where thousands of test-tubes abounded. Inside each were embryos, all at different stages. Some were nothing more than a few combined cells, but others - such as F-15 - she could already make out their features. The long line of the jaw, the black snout, the curve of a tiny tail.

The light was low and a throbbing, vibrational sound played out via inset speakers - all to emulate the inside of a womb. Elora had hired a world-famous composer, who had worked many months to get the ambiance right. It all had to be perfect.

Elora pressed her hand to the glass and lovingly waited for her children to be born.

63

CHASE

The train rocketed us along at a hundred miles an hour. Having never been on one before, it wasn't just Muttface who was having a blast; I was enjoying every minute of the ride too.

Fields of green blurred into one. I reached up and pulled open the window, letting the air lash against my face. It brought tears to my eyes, but I didn't mind. Somehow, it made me feel more alive. I turned to Bandit, perched on the seat next to me, and grinned.

"You're supposed to be hanging *your* head out of the window."

In reply, Bandit cocked his head in question, then moved to join me. As soon as the wind was on his face, Bandit's eyes went wide with delight and his tongue fell out. I grinned and gestured to Sully to join us, but he only rolled his eyes at our antics. Killjoy.

Our tickets had already been checked, so I knew we wouldn't be disturbed for a while now, if not for the rest of our journey (we'd been on the train for an hour, so there was still another ten and a half to go). Deciding now was the time, I reached for the Walmart bag.

"Guys, I've got a present for Bandit."

At his name, Bandit tore himself from the window and bounded over to me, his face filled with expectation.

"What've you got? More books?" Sully asked.

At the word "books" Bandit jumped up at me and licked my face. His tail wagged so vigorously, I worried it would whip my face into shreds. I laughed and pushed him down. "No. Better."

Unable to wait for an unveiling, Bandit all but climbed into the bag. He emerged seconds later with a box clutched gingerly between his teeth. Sully gasped when he recognized the logo.

"An iPad? How rich do you think we are?"

I ignored his comment, refusing to let him spoil the moment. "Not the newest version, but I figured that wouldn't matter." I was practically buzzing with anticipation. Bandit didn't have a clue what was going on, but he seemed extraordinarily happy just to have been bought a present. I took the box from Bandit and slid the gleaming device out of the box.

"Figured Bandit would use up any and all books we could buy him in seconds, but with an iPad, we'll never run out. Plus there are the games and quizzes we can download." Bandit barked, and I pretty much got the gist of his excitement. *Books and quizzes, oh boy, oh boy!*

I turned on the iPad and tapped some pre-loaded icons. "But best of all, there's this little program..." and placed the device on the ground by Bandit's feet. Sully crowded around us for a better look.

An app had been opened, called Speak, Spell and Read. I tapped a tab, and a chart of common words appeared next to a diagram illustrating the word. I pressed one word, and the iPad said "hello" in a friendly male voice. I hit some more, and we heard "how are you today?" Bandit was so excited he couldn't keep still. His whole body shook, and he had pretty much slobbered all over me by this point.

"When you want to read, you hit the 'books' tab here and choose an age group for the correct reading level. Going by what you've read already, I'd say you're what, five or six years?"

Sully nodded in fascinated agreement.

"So we tap five, and look, hundreds and hundreds of books appear for you to read. Then later, when you're a little more advanced, there's stuff like Peter Pan, Charlotte's Web, Paddington Bear. Any word you don't understand, you just have to input it like so and..." Chase touched the word "robot".

The male voice explained, "Artificial life. A machine capable of carrying out a series of complicated commands automatically. In science fiction, it is a machine resembling a human being who is able to replicate certain human movements and functions automatically."

"Wow." Sully was blown away by the thing. "This is exactly what he needs to communicate with us."

"I know, right?" I practically beamed. "We can even pick the voice that suits him best." I pulled up a menu and started going through the options. The first was too clipped. The second, too mature. Another too corny. We went through what must have been twenty before the perfect voice materialized. It had a joyful tone, full of life, and sounded young and excitable.

Exactly how we thought of Bandit. He seemed to think it was right too as he laid his paw on my hand to stop me from moving to the next sample.

"But wait." Sully suddenly had a thought. "How will he be able to touch those buttons? Have you seen the size of his paws?" Bandit moved his paw away as if embarrassed by the enormity of it.

"Aha!" I dived into the bag once more, reappearing with a box of plastic styluses. "Like the ones they use with the Nintendo game thingies," I explained. But these things were tiny, something I had also given some thought to. I took out some cheap pens and some tape and taped the stylus onto the pen. I then offered the stylus pen to Bandit, who gripped it between his teeth.

Bandit lowered his head and tapped some buttons. "Hello. My name is..." There was a pause as Bandit tried to find his name, but it wasn't on the most common words list. I reached down and toggled a few menus.

"You press this button — learn — then type in the word. B-A-N-D-I-T. Hit save and look, there it is!" At this, Sully looked almost as excited as Bandit.

Bandit snuck another great big lick at my face, dropping his stylus in the excitement of the moment. He picked it back up daintily and tried again. "Hello. My name is Bandit and I love you."

Let's not lie; I practically melted at this, but he wasn't done. He looked pointedly at me, then down at the screen. Then back up to me. I understood immediately what he wanted, even though neither he nor the iPad had voiced his thoughts.

Bandit pressed learn. Then when the blank window appeared for my input, I spelled out my name. Bandit hit save, then his borrowed voice told me, "Chase. You are my best friend."

"And you mine, Muttface."

I threw my arms around him and buried my face in his fur.

64

SULLY

It was ironic.

Here we were on the run, heading to the one place I had tried to escape from so many years ago, and yet I hadn't felt this good since, well, since the day I'd married Emma.

The "kids" (as I was coming round to calling them) were lying on the floor having real conversations. In no time at all, Bandit's vocabulary had shot up. I estimated he was now reading and conversing at the level of a ten-year-old. It was all too easy to forget he was a dog.

"Hold up, I need a minute."

They looked up at me with such complete trust, I felt a pang in my chest. I lowered down to Bandit's side and peeled back the bandage. The skin was beginning to knit together around the stitches. I was relieved to find there wasn't a rotten smell — which would have indicated an infection. The wound was healing as well as it could under the circumstances. I would've preferred for Bandit to be resting in my clinic, not straining himself, but that wasn't an option anymore. I changed the bandage quickly, meaning to let the kids continue, but I noticed Bandit's eyes drooping. I sat back onto my seat and motioned to Chase.

"I think someone has had enough excitement and needs sixty winks."

Chase immediately rose. "You sleep," she told the dog. "We'll talk later."

"But I am not tired..." Bandit managed to get out before his chin sank onto the iPad and he closed his eyes.

65

CHASE

Grinning, I removed the stylus, tucked it into the iPad's case, and took a seat opposite Sully. Moments passed in companionable silence before I caught Sully staring at me. When I didn't say anything, Sully bit the bullet and asked, "Do you have any siblings?"

I knew we would eventually get around to this, but even this simple question caused tension to flood my body. I stared out at the trees blurring past, hoping he wouldn't pick up on it. "No. I'm an only child."

"No other family?"

"None that I know. We weren't exactly what you'd call close."

Sensing Sully wanted to ask more but was too polite to push, I let out a deep breath, my face finally expressing the sadness I'd been holding onto all this time.

"When I was little, I used to love Christmas. Not for the food, or the decorations, or even the toys — I never really had many toys — but for the movies. I loved watching happy families gathering together, being together. Even liked it when they argued 'cause that made them seem real, you know?" I took a breath before continuing.

"They were always such a unit. A real family. So different from my mom and me. I mean, we were OK. We never had enough money, and I was always hungry, but we were doing OK. Until she met Tubs."

Saying his name brought tension to my shoulders. Sully moved as if he wanted to reach out to me, but he didn't want to break the spell. He stayed in his seat, saying nothing, but encouraging me to continue with his eyes.

"He was a trucker. She met him at the diner she was working at part-time. Said he swept her off her feet, but all he did was pay her a little compliment. Mom was so starved of attention, she lapped it up like a dog." Bandit's ears pricked up at the word "dog", but his eyes stayed shut.

"Within a month he'd moved into our home. Mom doted on him, hand and foot. She loved that she now had a man paying the bills. I tried to have some kind of relationship with him, but Tubs was never interested in me. Far as I knew, he hated kids, and I was just one big annoyance. But then annoyance turned into out-and-out hate, especially when he was drunk — which he was becoming more and more frequent. Seemed I couldn't do anything right, and everything I did wrong would send him into a rage. Got so that I cut my hair just so he couldn't drag me by it anymore."

Sully's breath hissed out, and I saw him bite his lip. I turned back to the window and shrugged. "Anyway, things stayed like that a while, until one day, I realized Tubs was paying a bit *too* much attention to me. He was always watching, always leering. I tried telling mom, but she wasn't interested in hearing anything bad about him. I knew I wasn't safe there anymore, so I stole their savings — which wasn't much — and got outta there. Made do until I met Bandit. That's my story, really. Not very exciting."

By now Bandit was softly snoring and had missed my tale. I was glad. I didn't want him to lose the sweet naivety he had.

When Sully finally spoke, it was terse. "Some people just don't deserve to have kids."

"No, they don't," I agreed. I looked at him questioningly. "What about you and Emma? Did you guys ever want kids?"

Sully seemed to flinch at the question. "Yeah," he managed to get out. "We did."

"I'm sorry," I blurted out suddenly. "If I hadn't come to you, they wouldn't have destroyed your home. This is all my fault."

Sully shook his head. "You wanted to save Bandit. You weren't the thugs who burned my place down. You didn't start this. They did."

"But they wouldn't have done that if I hadn't chosen you."

"But you did choose me, and... I'm grateful for that."

My eyes were misting over with tears, but I felt hopeful now too. "You are?"

Sully smiled. "I've been living a lie, Chase. The last year, I've barely managed to survive, but now, I'm beginning to feel alive again. So no, I don't blame you for what happened."

"So you're not mad at me?" I had to get clarification, not being good at reading people at times.

Surprise broke over his face. "If I was, don't you think I'd have said something by now?"

"Tubs didn't," I said. "He'd stew over things until they boiled over."

Sully's features hardened. "Yeah, well, don't ever mistake me for that coward."

He fell silent for a moment, thinking. "The only thing I'm angry about is that I don't have anything left of Emma's. I was hoarding her things, holding on to them as if that kept her alive, and now there's nothing but my memories of us. Everything's gone."

I bit the side of my lip as I studied him, torn. Then, silently, I opened my backpack and reached inside. "You should have this." I handed a framed photograph to Sully. He stared down at the picture, overwhelmed to see Emma's smiling face looking back up at him. In the picture, he had his arm around her and they were strolling down a beach. A captured moment of normality, but one that now meant the world to him.

Tears erupted, tears he didn't even bother to hide. He ran a finger over Emma's face. "Why did you take it?"

I could feel myself squirming, uncomfortable. "I don't know. You both looked so happy."

Sully looked like he didn't know what he could say, so he kept it simple. "Thank you, Chase. Thank you."

66

THE MERCENARY

The Mercenary wasn't pleased.

After spending two hours listening to Armstrong drown his sorrows — the man really liked the sound of his own voice — one thing was clear: he had no idea where Sullivan had gone, and Sullivan himself was a ghost. No contacts listed under family outside of his wife, no mention of where he grew up. Digging through the national birth registry revealed some three hundred listings for a Jake Sullivan. The Mercenary was hitting a wall, and he didn't like it one bit.

After he paid for lunch, an act that felt alien to The Mercenary who wasn't known for his generosity but would be something his "character" would do, The Mercenary retreated back into his van, where his men were scanning airwaves and the internet for signs of any activity that would match their perpetrators.

As per standard operating procedure, The Mercenary had put eyes and ears on Armstrong and the annoying old woman who had worked at the clinic. The busybody spent her entire time on the phone, calling everyone she knew, telling them of her concern over Sullivan. So far, they had tallied up twenty hours of recordings. Thank God The Mercenary wouldn't need to listen to them himself. There wasn't enough money in the world to make him endure that torture.

All he could do now was wait.

And that was the worst part of his job.

67

CHASE

I'd never told anyone my sorry story before. It wasn't something I liked to think about. I'm not one of those "woe is me" people, you know? I just deal with it and move on with my life. Besides, if I spent my time mulling over the past, I'd be a seriously depressed person... or a drunk. And neither of those were possibilities for me. You see, I had long decided that I'd prove mom and Tubs wrong. I *was* someone special. I *was* worthwhile. And if they didn't want me, someone out there would.

Bandit snuck his head onto my lap, finally waking from his nap. A tuft of brown fur stood up messily on the top of his head, giving him a very human and comical look. Trust him to have bed head. I reached over and smoothed it down. His nose searched my pockets and fished out the stylus of his own accord. I watched him crawl eagerly to the charging iPad and turn it on. Don't think I'd ever not get a thrill watching him use it. Judging by the sappy expression woon Sully's face, he was thinking the same thing. He always looked at the dog like it was Christmas morning. Like the kids on those heart-warming holiday movies.

Bandit tapped a few words. "Hello again friends! I am hungry." I rubbed my stomach, feeling sympathy pangs.

"Do we have anything left?"

Sully rummaged around inside his bag but came up empty-handed. He shook his head. "We've got juice, water, and a few nuts, but that's it. There's a dining car on the train, though. We could give that a try."

I stood up and held out my hand for some cash. Sully opened up his wallet and forked over some more bills. I totally dug that. Getting money had never been this easy before.

Bandit nudged against my leg, wanting to come with me, but I figured we should keep a low profile. "No, Boy. Stay here. Keep out of sight." He whined, unhappy to leave me alone, but said "OK." I smiled. I would never get enough of this talking thing.

68

CHASE

I stepped out of our cabin and closed the door behind me. Though I wasn't anticipating any problems, it didn't hurt to be safe. Gorgeous scenery flew past the window, so beautiful that even *I* had to stop and admire.

Horses grazed on grassy fields beneath towering maple trees that arched over pockets of water. Every so often a quaint church or cluster of buildings interrupted the picturesque view, a reminder that even out here, in the most remote countryside, people could thrive. I wondered if we would find a place like this at the end of our travels. I wouldn't mind spending the rest of my life lounging under a tree, playing fetch with Bandit.

Briefly, I wondered if Sully would be there.

I wrapped my arms around myself and realized that for the first time since Tubs had appeared in my life; I felt hopeful. A smile snuck over my face.

Humming to myself, I made my way to the dining car, which, it turns out, sounds a lot more exciting than it actually is.

Plastic tables and molded seats lined one side of the carriage, where an elderly couple sat, nursing cups of coffee and slabs of a pasty-looking cake. The other half of the carriage contained a kiosk housing vending machines, a grill, and a display of ready-made deli-like dishes. The elderly couple looked up on my approach. Seeing my smile, they smiled back, which was a whole new thing for me too. Usually, they just grimaced, wrinkling their nose in disgust when they caught a whiff of me.

I arrived at the display cabinet and surveyed the contents inside. There were tubs of potato salad, slaw, and salad, and platters lined with slices of chicken and ham, with a mound of pickles decorating the center.

The bored service girl looked up from the National Enquirer she was reading. "Let me know when you've decided," she said, noisily popping a piece of gum. She didn't wait for a response and went right back to reading.

"I've decided."

She put the magazine down and came over. "That was quick."

"I don't mess around when it comes to food."

"Apparently not. So what're you having?"

I pointed at the tray of meat slices. "I'll take those, some turkey and lettuce sandwiches. Those brownies and juice boxes. Four. Might as well throw in a bag of Cheetos too. The extra large."

She looked at me, a pair of metal tongs in her gloved hand. "How many slices of the chicken and ham?"

"All of them."

She blinked, pausing a beat. "Like, *all* all?"

I nodded. "Just put them in saran wrap. That'll be great." She didn't respond but looked at me like she thought this was all some kind of sorority stunt. I figured some clarification was in order. "They're for my dog. We forgot to bring food for him."

At that, she unfroze. "I thought you were joking, but that makes sense now. I've got some nuggets in the fridge too. You think he'd want them?"

"Heck, I'd take 'em just for me, but yeah, nuggets would be great too. He's got a big appetite."

She grabbed the platter, tipped it on one end, and slid the meat into a plastic baggie. "They all do. We have a tiny terrier at home; she's smaller than a cat, but she can eat like a horse. Don't know where they put it all."

So we were sharing now. This was nice. I tried not to fidget, anxious to get back to Sully and Bandit. "So how much does that come to?"

She packed the rest of the items I'd ordered into a paper bag and rang up the total on a cash register. "Fourteen eighty-nine."

I counted out three fives and handed them over. "Keep the change." Although it gave me a bit of a thrill to say that, part of me already questioned my generosity. It wasn't that long ago when my only source of food was from a dumpster.

She nodded thanks, then immediately went back to her tabloid rag. I'm guessing she gets tipped a lot and eleven cents wasn't much of a big deal. Arms loaded up with supplies, I made my way back.

I caught a few curious stares. One lady commented, "you must have big appetites in your family." I faked a laugh and nodded but didn't stop or elaborate. She turned back to deal with her two kids, fighting over a PS Vita.

I was pretty thrilled by her response.

No suspicious stares, no worry that a cop was going to come along with questions. I was finally passing as a normal kid. I practically skipped back to our car, letting myself in with a clever use of my elbows since my hands were full.

"Well, I hope you're really hungry, 'cause I pretty much got us one of everything." My hip bumped the door closed, and I turned to face the seats, expecting everything to be the same as I'd left it.

Only it wasn't.

Sully was crouched on the floor, Bandit's head in his lap. His hands held Bandit securely as the last of the shaking eased from his body. White froth spilled out of his mouth, covering his jaw line. I looked at Bandit's eyes, but they were unfocused, glazed. The food tumbled out of my hands, crashing to the floor.

Sully tried to reassure me with a weak smile. "He had another seizure, but it's mostly done with now."

I fell onto my knees, wanting to comfort my furry friend, but worried that I would hurt him somehow, I only allowed myself to take hold of a paw, fearful that he would break if I applied even the faintest pressure.

"But this is so soon after the last one."

Sully nodded but kept silent, his brow knotted with tension. I could almost see the cogs in his mind turning over as he tried to make sense of it all. I knew if I asked, he wouldn't keep the truth from me.

"Why is this happening to him? Is he sick?"

"I don't know, but I'm sure as hell going to find out."

69

CHASE

It was a full ten minutes later when Bandit finally came to. In the back of my mind, I noted his recovery time was much longer than the first convulsion. I mentioned this to Sully, but he just nodded and pursed his lips. Judging by his expression, this wasn't a good thing. Though my stomach and heart were twisted up inside, I put on a bright smile.

"Hey, so I got tons of food. Anything you want to try first?"

Bandit blinked up at me as the fogged cleared. Sluggishly, he typed into the iPad. "It happened again?"

My first instinct was to lie. I wanted so badly to protect him, but Sully got there before me.

"Yeah. Sorry, Fella."

Bandit thought for a while. "Will it happen more?"

Sully steeled himself. "More and more frequently, I'm afraid. Once we arrive at our destination, you should get those scans we need. Until then, there's nothing else I can tell you for sure."

Bandit's little body shook. Sully and I tensed, each preparing for the worst when Bandit spoke again. "I am scared."

I wrapped my arms around him and squeezed tight, ignoring my instinct to treat him like a glass doll. "Me too."

It was a while before any of us could eat.

70

THE CEO

L ush lawns crunched underfoot as The CEO strolled through the grounds, carrying a bouquet of timeless white flowers. The cloudless sky was a vivid shade of blue, and the shining sun kept away the chill of the fall morning. He took in the familiar swaying oaks and immaculately tended rose beds. To the unobservant eye, this seemed like nothing more than a delightful park, one of those privately maintained ones that seemed to pop up in elite neighborhoods.

But he knew better.

He'd come here weekly for years now, always on Monday mornings, right after breakfast. He couldn't remember how this routine had started, but it was instinctual now. Like checking his stocks over his morning bowl of oatmeal, or the whiskey nightcap that he drank from a diamond shot glass, presented to him from Arab royalty after he had sold him the world's largest hotel chain. Yes, The CEO was a creature of habit, and he was fine with that.

An elderly man stared blankly as his caretaker engaged him in mindless chatter. They were feeding a flock of Eastern Bluebirds, a colorful bird with bright blue plumage and a red chest. The CEO only knew what they were as he had captured twenty or so of the birds once, keeping them in a cage at home to admire, but he had soon tired of their constant chirping...

He turned away, blocking out the sight of the man and his caretaker. He never looked here, never really wanted to know. The truth was already too much to bear without this constant reminder. He quickened his step, anxious to reach his destination, the wing named "Nightingale" after the historical figure. The sign loomed up ahead now. Discreet, like the rest of the place. Along with their reputation, it was the reason he had chosen this establishment. He approached the red-bricked building, noticing the ivy that covered the roof.

Reaching the door, he pushed it open and stepped inside, momentarily disoriented from the dark corridor ahead. Numbered rooms lead off from both sides of the corridor. The CEO didn't need to look to know what they said; he knew them all by heart. He counted in his head now as he moved past the rooms: *three... nine... thirteen...* At fourteen he stopped. The door was wide open.

He stepped inside. Light flooded the quaintly decorated room. Patterned curtains hung on the windows and inviting sofa's and armchairs were arranged into a seating area facing a large flat screen television. A bookshelf packed with framed photographs and mementos covered an entire wall, all featuring a woman lovingly embracing her child, a young boy, while a king-sized bed swamped in matching cushions stood opposite. Yet, despite all this effort, there was no denying that this was a hospital room.

And sitting up in the bed was an elderly woman.

Her gray hair was curled neatly, makeup dabbed carefully onto her face. Dressed in a pastel matching twinset — one of many The CEO had provided for her — she was hunched over the latest Nora Roberts' book when he stepped in. At his appearance, she stopped reading and looked up.

"Hello, mother. How are you today?" The CEO asked.

His mother, Irene, stared at him, confusion and fear in her eyes.

"Who are you, and what are you doing in my room?"

71

THE CEO

The CEO moved over to his mother, taking a seat next to her.

"It's me, Ma. Your son," he said, but she just frowned at him.

"Don't be ridiculous. My boy's only ten, and he's at school!"

He leaned closer, wanting to take her hands, but resisted the urge, knowing it might frighten her as it had so many times before. "I'm all grown now. And successful. I'm the wealthiest man in America. It's what you always wanted for me." He hated the way his voice sounded. Whiney and pleading. Weak. But then, outside of his empire, she was the only thing — and certainly the only person — he had ever cared about.

She looked at him, those violet eyes that used to shine so bright now dull from years of mindlessness. Sighing, he stopped trying to talk to her in the present. "Tell me about your boy."

It was like a light came on inside her. Her face turned animated, and she sat up a little taller. "He's so clever. Why, just the other day, his teacher told me he was functioning five times higher than his classmates. Five times! I'm just fit to burst. All these years juggling multiple jobs, it's been worth it to see how my boy is progressing."

Bitterness swept through him like a wave. This woman was his life: she was alive, and yet she might as well as be dead for all the good it did him. She would never know him as he was now.

Footsteps sounded in the corridor outside as a cheerful Nurse appeared, carrying a tray with several covered plates of delicious-smelling food. Seeing him, she shot him a big smile. "Back again. How're you today?"

The CEO managed a smile back at Ellie. At only thirty-something, she was already beginning to turn gray, but the endless care and devotion with which she took care of her patient was one of the reasons he kept her on staff. Ellie was a private nurse who he'd hired solely to look after his mother. "I'm well. How has she been?"

Ellie set the tray on a wheeled table, maneuvering it so that it sat in front of Irene. "Good. We played checkers yesterday, and she enjoyed her aqua workout. Didn't you, dear?" She said this to Irene, who nodded, even though she clearly couldn't remember. Ellie leaned forward to help her to sit higher. Fluffing up a pillow, she slipped it behind the older woman to support her back. Lifting the lids off the plates, Ellie described what the menu had to offer today: "French onion soup to start, followed by honey and mustard chicken with seasonal vegetables, and an apple pie for dessert."

Irene focused on the food, delighted. "Onion soup, my favorite! How did you know?" Ellie sneaked a wink at him, clearly her co-conspirator. Prior to enrolling his mother here, The CEO had given detailed instructions on what to feed her. Having made a list of some fifty of her favorite foods, her personal cook — another employee on The CEO's payroll — prepared these meals on rotation. The soup sat in a handcrafted bowl while the chicken was artfully arranged on top of the roasted vegetables. The pie too was elevated, sitting on a crumbed cookie bed with what looked like ice-cream foam on top. It was high-end, restaurant-quality, and a far cry from the meals typically served in such an establishment. Seeing how delectable the meals looked, he made a mental note to pay the cook more.

Irene reached for a spoon and scooped up a spoonful of soup, but as she raised it to her mouth, her eyes glazed over, and she blinked, startled. Lowering her hand, she looked across at him, suddenly angry. "Who are you and what are you doing in my room?!"

Unperturbed, Ellie took the spoon from her. "Here, let me help you with that." With patience and care, Ellie began feeding Irene, wiping her mouth with a napkin when the odd bit of liquid dribbled down her chin. The CEO turned away, pain stabbing at his heart.

It was unbearable to see his mother, the strong woman who had raised him, an invalid like this.

Ellie must have seen his reaction as she smiled at him reassuringly. "If it's any consolation, she doesn't remember any of this."

He knew her words were meant to comfort, but they had the opposite of the intended effect. He stood up, unable to bear anymore, and moved to the sink where he filled a vase full of water before setting the flowers he had brought with him inside. He placed the vase on the window beside Irene, letting it catch the sunlight. She looked up over her soup to admire them with delight.

"Oriental lilies, my favorites! How did you know?"
The CEO dropped a kiss on her forehead and left without another word.

72

SULLY

T he sky shone midnight blue when the train finally pulled into our destination.

On the train ride here, Chase had done a little research on my hometown, which she'd been keen to relay. Montpelier was the capital state of Vermont, best known for being the least populated state capital in the United States. Named after its cousin in France, for every one hundred women, there were only eighty-two men, which kind of sucked for those eighteen other women, Chase had thought. Unless they were gay. Which, come to think of it, how did they know the men surveyed were into women? What started off as a simple fact-finding mission soon turned into an epic debate which I was extremely reluctant to enter into. These were dangerous territories, and I wasn't primed for them yet.

Montpelier Station was an old-worldly place. Rickety benches lined the short platform. A vending machine, the only concession to the twentieth century, stood full and unused. Baskets hung from the rafters, exploding with bright flowers. I fixated on one, a bright red clover, the state flower. Seeing the familiar blossom, memories came flooding back to me.

As a six-year-old, I had loved surprising my mom with gifts. She delighted in simple pleasures, and I was only too happy to oblige. As far as I was concerned, mom was the center of my world and the greatest thing in the universe.

This particular afternoon, mom was baking my favorite dessert, a key lime pie. With the scent of the sweet pie teasing my taste buds, I had decided to gather the biggest bunch of wildflowers I could find. Plan created, I fidgeted on my feet, anticipating her delight.

I took my mission very seriously as I scoured the length and breadth of the land that I called home. I picked Wild Columbine, Milkweed, and Mountain Mint, saying each of the names out loud as I gathered them, proud that I remembered them all. Mom liked to try new things, and currently, she was working on some natural home remedies. It was she who had taught me about the plants.

When I thought I was done, I scrutinized my selection with a critical eye. It wasn't quite right; something was clearly missing. I walked around until I found what it was I wanted. Red Clover — but they were inside a dense cluster of bushes. Setting my bounty down, I squeezed myself through the bushes until I arrived at the bed of clovers. Grinning, I plopped myself onto a raised area on the ground and proceeded to pluck the best flowers.

It was while I was reaching for the biggest clover I felt something crawl across my thigh. Looking down, I saw a large black ant. I flicked it away with a finger and continued, but moments another ant found its way on me. Then another. And another. Within seconds, I looked down to see hundreds of them on me. I was sitting on an ant's nest!

Their legs tickled on my bare skin as the ants got under my clothing. As I swatted them away, they started to bite. And suddenly it wasn't ticklish any longer. Fire burst over my skin as the ant's jaws found soft flesh. Screaming with pain, I raced out of the clearing and ran for home.

That was how Mom found me. Screaming and sobbing as the ants tore into my young body. Later, after Mom had soothed my pain with hydrocortisone cream (she had tried one of her remedies first, but it had done nothing), Dad had laughed about my antics, though Mom was touched by my actions. When I had fully recovered, I went back to collecting flowers for Mom, though I was careful not to sit on an ant's nest again.

To this day, I didn't like those bright Red Clovers and gave them a wide berth.

I helped Bandit and Chase off the train and looked around. Aside from our traveling companions, only two other passengers descended onto the platform. Senses honed from the attack at the clinic, I shot the two passengers a cautious look. They were a middle-aged couple wheeling two large suitcases. As I watched, an elderly couple greeted them excitedly. "You finally made it home! How was London? You must tell us all about your trip!"

The coast was clear. We'd made it here without any issues. I allowed myself a brief moment of respite.

"Where to now?" Chase asked. Since Bandit's second seizure, she had kept one hand on the dog, as if she could keep the attacks at bay by doing so. I wished it were that simple.

"We've still some ways to go."

Rubbing shoulders stiff from the eleven-hour ride, Chase didn't seem thrilled by my reply.

"So, now what?"

"You had your fun. Now it's my turn to shop."

73

SULLY

The car dealership was two miles south of the station. I had driven past it on many occasions as a child, and I had admired the shining new paint jobs on the lot. Since we'd lived well off the beaten track, it was impossible to know what color our 4x4 had originally been, hidden, as it usually was, beneath a thick layer of dried mud. With their busy careers, my parents never cared much for simple chores like housekeeping. They had a cleaner for that, though the car never came under her remit.

I remembered the dealership's flashing neon sign, which used to blare out of the darkness. OPEN TWENTY-FOUR HOURS! It had announced cheerfully. I had often wondered what kind of people would need to buy a car in the middle of the night, never expecting for a moment that it would be me.

The roads here were quiet, with only the odd car passing by. Still, I made them walk single file down the edge of the road. As we were relatively near the train station, street lamps lit our path, but they would soon disappear, plunging us into darkness. I hoped we would reach the dealership before the lights ran out.

Crickets chirped into the night. An occasional bat swooped overhead, but otherwise, all was silent bar our own footsteps. Chase seemed unnerved by the stillness. She kept her shoulders hunched, expecting trouble with every sound.

"It's actually much safer out in the sticks than it is in town. Nowhere near as much crime," I offered.

"But everyone carries guns out here."

I couldn't deny that she was right. I shot a quick glance at Bandit, who seemed to have fully recovered from the early seizure. Sensing my concern, Bandit looked up at me and sneaked a quick lick of my fingers.

The silhouette of a building appeared on the horizon. I squinted and made out the open expanse of the car lot. Grinning, I upped my pace, only to fall to a crushing stop moments later at our destination.

The neon sign was still there, but now it hung at an angle, its moorings having rusted and fallen off from time. And it was dark, unlit. I took in the empty car lot. The only vehicle that remained was a rust bucket not fit for use, even if it could be started. I swore under my breath, massaging the back of my neck.

"Doesn't look like anyone's been here for a long time," Chase noted.

"I should've checked instead of assuming." I would've kicked myself if it were physically possible.

"Can we take a taxi?"

"Maybe if we had a number, but I doubt anyone's still working this hour."

Chase looked at Bandit. "Can I borrow your iPad?"

He woofed then stood still, head raised so she could pull it out of its case. Chase called up a website and Googled "taxis". Several hits turned up. She went to each one, looking at their hours of business, but sighed. "You're right. All closed. Plus they're in the next town over."

With nothing else for it, I led them back onto the road, where we continued walking. I tried to make light of our situation.

"It's nice to stretch our legs after being cooped up on the train so long."

"Yeah. Exercise. Woo." Chase's feigned enthusiasm raised a few brows.

"Well, we know one thing for sure. You can't lie worth a damn."

We walked for several hours until our legs felt fit to drop. I was about to announce that we camp down for the night when a vehicle approached from behind. Ignoring my earlier road safety lecture, I leaped into the road and started waving my arms. The vehicle kept approaching without altering its speed. Worried the driver might not see me, Chase flashed the iPad screen in their direction. That did the trick. The vehicle — a truck — slowed and an unruly head stuck out of the window.

"You folks broke down?"

She was around thirty, with the bluest eyes I had ever seen and a friendly smile the size of Texas. Freckles lined her nose, and the sun had lightened her already blonde hair. I didn't read any malicious intent in her eyes, but more than that, Bandit had already made his way below the window and was trying to lick her fingers.

"Wow, you are a gorgeous thing aren't you?"

Bandit woofed, which caused Chase and I to share a smile. The driver was too busy playing with him to notice.

"We're stranded, more like. Got off the train and was hoping to buy a car." I trailed off and gestured at the disused car lot.

"Old man Stanton closed that down when he retired some eight years ago now." She frowned, studying my face. "You from around here?"

I stiffened, weary about giving my information away to a complete stranger. Guess the years of living in a city had taught me some things after all. I smiled and said, "No, but I visited as a kid. We have family nearby."

She kept smiling, though a knowing look appeared in her eyes. Wherever we were from, we weren't up for swapping life stories. "My name's Sam, Sam Dubeau. I'm heading up to Middlesex. Can I offer you folks a ride?"

I hesitated, but Bandit answered for them with another loud woof. Before the humans could respond, he went around to the passenger side and scratched at the door until Sam opened it. Bandit leaped inside and settled next to Sam, who grinned and stroked the wacky dog. "Your pet seems to like me."

Chase clearly didn't like to see the other woman's hands on Bandit or him sitting in the car alone with her. She ran around the vehicle and leaped in after Bandit, leaving me standing alone on the road.

"Can I pick up a car there?" I asked.

"There isn't a dealership for another twenty miles, but I know someone who's selling a truck if that'll do you? I could drop you there."

I hesitated, unsure.

"It's on my way."

I finally smiled. "That'll be great. We'd appreciate it." I climbed in after Chase, and as she offered a hand to Sam.

"My name's Bella, and this is my dad, Charlie. The furball here is Ed." I shot her a look but otherwise kept up the pretense.

"It's nice to meet y'all. Where have you come from?"

Sam spoke to them both but aimed the question at Chase. Chase glanced at me and hesitated for a split second before answering.

"Washington, DC."

"You folks aren't in politics, are you? Cause I gotta say, I'm not terribly fond of politicians."

I offered my first genuine smile. "No. Not a suit among us."

"Well, that's a relief. So, you're here visiting family?"

"Sort of." I wanted to keep this as brief as possible. I also wanted to dissuade this whole line of questioning. Options flew through my mind until the perfect solution came to me.

"My father passed away. I'm here to settle up the estate and deal with the funeral."

Sam's eyes widened in sympathy. The joviality left her face and took on a respectful expression. "Sure am sad to hear that. My thoughts are with you and yours."

I glanced down as if to hide a tear. Surprising me, Chase leaned across and took my hand.

"It's alright, Dad. Pops wouldn't want you upset."

So I was wrong about her ability to act. She seemed to have the perfect mixture of empathy and sadness. Even Bandit joined in, blasting a sigh out of his nose and lowering his head onto our clasped hands.

If it wasn't in bad taste, I would have laughed.

74

SULLY

We drove in relative silence for the next hour — relative in that there was no talking. Sam, however, sang along to each song that played on the country radio. She was a hearty singer and kept a good melody with an impressive memory for song lyrics. I had to stop myself from joining in a few times because I felt this was an intimate thing to do. More importantly, Emma was the only woman I had previously sung for.

We drove past a small town with barely four shops on Main Street. All were closed up for the night. Out here in the sticks, it was a complete contrast to the bright lights and sounds of New York. There were no overnight food joints here, no late opening bars where one could drink themselves into a stupor only to stumble home at first light.

At last, we pulled up to a long and winding drive. The name on the mailbox read "Warrington." Sam switched off the ignition and climbed out.

"You guys wait here. I'll fetch Warrey."

Moments later, she returned with a man built like a brick house. With a checked shirt and ripped jeans, he wouldn't have looked amiss on the cover of GQ — if GQ were doing a blue collar special. I didn't know why, but Warrington's good looks made me anxious.

The other man's hands were covered in oil. He wiped them onto his clothes but managed to smear a line of black over his face. I elbowed Chase even as I began to feel her smirk. Warrey eyed the group suspiciously.

"Sam tells me you're on the lookout for transport?"

I nodded, then reached out to take Warrington's hand. We shook, but Warrington held on a moment longer than necessary, sizing me up. I extracted my hand and had to force myself not to wipe away the grime that now covered it.

"Well, let's not waste time." He gestured for us to follow him to where a truck waited. The paint job was peeling, and a few dents covered the body, but the defects seemed superficial.

"Had it six years, but since business is booming, I treated myself to a present."

I looked over Warrington's shoulder to see a brand new Chevrolet. At least it wasn't the convertible I was expecting.

"That's a nice looking ride. How much you want for this?"

"Two grand," came Warrington's instant response. Sam's reaction reflected what I was feeling. She simply dug her elbow into his ribs. Hard. Warrington flinched and stepped out of arm's reach. "What's your problem?"

"Two grand and he can have my truck!" Sam exclaimed. "Are you crazy? This isn't how you do business. These are good, honest folk."

I cringed inwardly at her blind faith in us and halted her defense with a hand on her shoulder. "My offer's 800, take it or leave it."

Warrington narrowed his eyes at them. "As I understand it, you don't have any other options. 1500."

Not to be outdone, I stared him down. "How bout I just pay Sam to drive us." I turned to Sam. "What do you say? I'll give you 200 just to get us there."

Before Sam could reply, Warrington stepped in and stopped her. "Fine! 1000 and you get off my land."

I grinned at Warrey, who didn't bother to hide the glower he was sending my way. "Nice doing business with you." Forking over the cash, I climbed into the truck to examine my new ride. Inside, the vehicle fared better. The upholstery was fine and everything seemed to be in working order. This wasn't a bad deal, not a bad deal at all. When Bandit and Chase settled beside me, Sam leaned in through the window.

"Guess I'll be seeing you then?" She gazed at me a split second too long to deny the interest simmering in her eyes. I could feel a jolt run through me. No one had looked at me like that since Emma, but I quickly pushed the feeling down. Now was not the time even if I could see her again. It was too soon.

"I doubt it, but it was great to meet you. Thanks for your help with the truck." To her credit, she didn't seem fazed by the rejection, though I couldn't understand the sudden disappointment I felt. Sam gave Bandit one last pet, shot Chase a smile, and nodded at me.

"You folks take care now." She turned and walked back to her own vehi-cle. I watched until Chase issued an impatient sigh.

"Are we going or are you just going to stare at her butt until it's gone?"

Cheeks flushing bright red, I started the engine and peeled out of there.

75

THE MERCENARY

L ooking down at his tablet, The Mercenary watched the video clip for the hundredth time.

Shaky footage started playing (the filmer wasn't much of a cameraman), as a busy food hall came into view. Mountains of delicious looking platters were attacked by greedy tourists, heaping food onto their already overflowing plates as the filmer, "xxGetGud420xx" judging by his handle, droned on in the background, explaining what he had already eaten and what he would be tackling next. The Mercenary found it a disturbing sign of the times that someone so clearly lacking in brain cells, with zero charisma, could have a YouTube following of thousands.

Frankly, he would pay just to shut the kid up so he wouldn't have to hear that monotonous voice again.

The kid was deliberating over the hot wings and whether he should go for BBQ instead, while The Mercenary was wondering if the Boss would object to an unauthorized hit when cries of alarm rose up from the crowd. The camera swung 180 degrees, the footage blurring until it auto-focused on the scene ahead.

There, on the ground, convulsing violently... Alpha.

The Mercenary watched as Sullivan administered aid while that skinny street kid screamed at him. She had dyed her hair and cut it, but he saw straight through the disguise. The Mercenary froze the footage on the girl's face: her mouth was open in a perpetual scream, eyes wide with fear. This wasn't the emotion of a kid who was just worried about a normal dog. No, this was the terror of someone who had already bonded with Alpha and knew how special he was.

It was enough to make The Mercenary scream, himself.

Thanks to Getgud, The Mercenary was able to determine where the action was taking place. Caesar's Palace. And not even the flagship casino, but its lesser-known, smaller cousin in Atlantic City. A part of him was impressed with their ingenuity - The Mercenary had cut them off from Sullivan's funds after all - though his team had already confirmed the trio hadn't had much luck scoring cash, as a hack into the hotel's security feed showed, they hadn't tried their luck on the tables or slots. Probably worried that a kid and her dog would be too conspicuous. Sensible really, but unluckily for them, The Mercenary's high-tech network of eagle-eyed IT geeks had spotted Getgud's video within minutes of it being uploaded.

One short flight later, and The Mercenary was stabbing his fork unenthusiastically into his own plate of food at the buffet. Wearing a new disguise as a Mexican tourist, The Mercenary had questioned the hotel staff and customers discreetly, as protocol required, but he already knew Sullivan & co would be long gone.

The last twenty-four hours had been spent fruitlessly searching bus garages and train stations for any sign of them. He had exhausted every possible lead bar one, which is how The Mercenary found himself now standing inside 30th Street Station in Philadelphia. It was a long shot, and a ways away from Atlantic City (for that, he was grateful). He glared at the bronze statue of an angel in front of him. The embossed plaque beneath it read: *Angel of the Resurrection by Walker Hancock*. Created to commemorate the 1,307 Pennsylvania Railroad employees who died in World War II, it was apparently the artist's favorite piece of work. The Mercenary thought it overwrought and distasteful.

He stormed through the Art déco styled hall, ignoring screaming children with their harassed parents. Their screams seemed to echo in the grand hall, something which displeased The Mercenary no end. Why did architects never consider these things before they designed their buildings?

Reaching the bank of ticket booths, The Mercenary made his way to each one, catching his reflection on a wall of glass. This afternoon he was dressed in a police uniform. It offered some benefits; the crowds parted like a wave, the public obeyed and never questioned his authority. In short, it made work like this far easier.

He took out a wanted poster his people had created using Sullivan's driving license, a recent photo Dr. Robins had supplied of Alpha, and a mockup of what the girl now looked like. With this, The Mercenary began questioning each ticket operator. It wasn't until he reached the sixth one that he caught a lead. The guy, a spotty, nerdy type who barely left his basement room by the looks of things, remembered Sullivan. Something about him being edgy and jumping to conclusions over a standard fare inquiry. He also remembered the girl. Said she was cute but seemed way too young for him.

The Mercenary wanted to know what train they had gotten onto, but the useless operator couldn't remember and made excuses about the amount of traffic that came his way. He did remember that they had some time to kill and had taken off to mosey around the nearby shops.

The Mercenary took a seat on a bench and made a phone call.

"Control, HS 031290 requesting assistance".

Within moments, the log of the operator's ticket sales over the last two days was downloaded onto his phone...

76

THE MERCENARY

Black as night and just as stealthy, the pilot steered the black-ops helicopter, not onto a helipad as one might expect, but into a retail car park.

A stunned late-night shopper loaded with bags froze mid-step, staring as the alien aircraft landed beside her car. Surprised, she lost her grip on the shopping. The bags dropped by her feet, spilling their contents. Oranges rolled across the tarmac in all directions. She watched in fascinated horror as one bright orange bumped into the military boots that had descended from the helicopter.

Boots which now flattened the fruit, leaving a sticky mess of pulp and juice on the ground.

The shopper's mouth snapped closed in shock, but she said nothing. Lowering her gaze to avoid eye contact, she scrambled around for her groceries but made sure she kept the black-clad man in her line of sight.

Single-minded, The Mercenary marched towards the supermarket entrance, caring nothing for the stunned glances cast his way. This particular part of his mission wasn't of a classified nature. The Mercenary glanced at a Swiss Army watch on his wrist. Time was of the essence, and too much of it had already been wasted.

A family of five exited the store just as The Mercenary arrived at the doors. Their chatter faded instantly. Except for the youngest, a three-year-old with sticky fingers and cheeks smudged with chocolate, too young to recognize danger when it was before him.

"Copter!" he shouted.

His Mom shushed him, instantly sensing the coldness emanating from The Mercenary. "Hush baby. Let's just get to the car and clean those hands of yours."

"But I wanna see 'copter!" He squirmed and tried to get down, but Mom clung to him tightly. Dad patted his son's shoulder, steering the shopping cart away.

"Last in the car doesn't get any ice cream!" At that, the two other kids made a mad dash away. The Mercenary tossed a disdainful glance their way as he stepped beneath the glowing Walmart sign.

77

THE MERCENARY

It was a good thing Walmart had security cameras that his geeks could hack into, or The Mercenary might have missed this very important stop.

After he'd located the salesboy who had advised the girl on her recent purchase, The Mercenary left the store with his own bag of goodies. Once again, he ignored the incredulous looks thrown his way, striding back to the waiting bird. Jumping in, he slid the door closed, banging on it two times to signal the pilot. The two had worked together on many missions and developed a streamlined method of communication.

The blades quickly whipped to life, and within seconds, they were airborne. The Mercenary leaned back and allowed the tiniest of smiles. While others hated the rocky motion of the aircraft, The Mercenary thrilled in it. He loved anything that resembled danger and had since he was a child. He remembered it was something his mother had worried about, this constant attraction to danger, but his father, a strict and successful corporate lawyer, had praised what he had considered his son's edge. Of course, this very edge would turn out to be their family downfall. The Mercenary frowned, snapping back to the present, surprised at the visit down memory lane.

Somewhat angrily, he removed the iPad from the shopping bag and turned it on. Cross-referencing a handwritten list of apps that the salesboy had scrawled down for him, The Mercenary began downloading the listed apps. It took only minutes to install them all. When the first app opened, he felt his stomach plummet as the welcome greeting flashed onto the screen.

Hello! Welcome to Speak, Spell, and Read, your one-stop app to teach your child how to speak, read, and write in two easy steps!

The Mercenary's breath hissed out of his lips. They were teaching the dog to communicate.

78

CHASE

O pen green expanses passed by as the truck rolled past with a comforting motion. We'd been going for a couple of hours now, and Sully hadn't spoken a word. Suppose I shouldn't have teased him about Sam, but honestly, if you'd seen the way he was ogling her. He was like the drooling cat in those cartoons, watching and waiting until the oblivious mouse went scrambling past.

Bandit lay next to me, snoring softly, the iPad nestled under his chin like some kind of high-tech security blanket. Earlier, he had told me how he's waited a very long time for people to understand him. Now that we had a system going, he didn't want to leave anything to chance and made sure the iPad was always in reach — just in case. The smooth rocking suddenly made way for a bumpier ride as Sully swung a left. I looked out across the dense forest around us and frowned.

"Er, you sure I shouldn't consult a map or something? Pretty sure, if it came down to it, we're not going to win a fight with a giant tree." Sully gave a snort which I took for his shortened version of "trust me". *Honestly, is it so hard to speak the words?*

He expertly maneuvered the truck onto a muddy path which I could only just see now that we were on it. We hit several bumps, one big enough to jolt Bandit from sleep. He raised sleepy eyes at me and yawned. I got a big hit of dog breath and tried not to gag (he is so sensitive after all).

Suddenly, the trees cleared, and we were at the edge of a ranch. It was a one-story building with a wraparound porch to one side. A stable stood to the far left of it that must house a couple of horses as I could hear a whinny in the distance. Just in front of the porch, a large plot of land had been turned into a thriving vegetable garden.

Sully stopped the truck, and we got out. Bandit and I were both taken aback by the lush fruits and vegetables being grown. A strawberry patch stood next to pears and apple trees. Thick vines, sagging from the weight of plump purple grapes, wove around a pergola. Vegetables of all shapes and colors decorated the area, including exotic-sounding ones like Kohlrabi and Daikon (thanks to my photographic memory and a school project on home-grown produce, I knew the names of most, though I had hardly tasted any of them). All I could think about was how one of these plots would have fed me for life on the streets. *Mental note to self: in the future, if still homeless, live on open land and learn how to farm.*

Bandit was sniffing around a tomato when a GUN SHOT thundered by, so close, it must have narrowly missed our heads. Sully immediately threw himself on top of us, sheltering us with his body. Bandit whined, scared and confused, but kept still.

"Who the heck's firing at us?" I hissed.

Sully's eyes swept the place quickly before finding their mark standing on the porch. I followed his eye-line to see a guy, a little older than me, pointing a lethal looking shotgun at us. He had shoulder length hair that would be girly if it wasn't for the square cut of his jaw. He was dressed in jeans and a flannel shirt, but even from here I could tell he was all muscle. Ridiculously, though we were in a pretty dangerous predicament, I found myself wondering what his eyes looked like close up. Apparently, I was about to get my wish as he called out to us.

"I'm going to count to three, and if you don't state what it is you're doing, my friend here (he gestured to his gun) will be only too happy to see you off."

Sully stuck both hands in the air. "I'm here to see my dad."

The boy lowered his gun. "You're Jake?" Amazingly, he managed to make this sound loaded with accusation. Sully didn't have a clue what his problem was, but his priority was to not get killed.

Sully nodded. "Is he here?"

The boy inclined his head *inside,* then disappeared into the ranch. I found the whole encounter weird. "Is this how they normally greet strangers in these parts?"

Sully helped me up to my feet. "Not usually, no."

"So we're really going into the house after the mad boy with the gun who just shot at us?"

Sully didn't reply but started walking in after him. I shared a perplexed look with Bandit before we followed hesitantly after him.

"Well, I hope your dad's going to be happier to see us."

79

SULLY

I stepped through the double doors and into the house.

Several rooms led off from the large entryway. To the left, there was a large, open-plan living area. Through the right doorway stood a well-stocked library and home office. I caught a glimpse of the kitchen where Zeb's prized moonshine rack stood. Ever since I was a kid, Zeb had been distilling his own moonshine using a still he'd found antiquing in New England. It was a dangerous hobby, and as a young boy, I had been warned to keep a wide berth. Not that I was ever curious enough to investigate — the white whiskey stank as far as I was concerned, and I never knew how anyone could stand to be near it, much less drink it. Zeb himself only ever drank them on special occasions, which were few and far between. The sight of them was at once familiar yet painful — there wasn't much happiness that I could remember, only anger and crushing disappointment.

Though this wasn't my childhood home — I had grown up in Burlington — I was familiar with the ranch as we had spent many a summer here when Zeb's friend, Roberts, had owned it. The last eight years or so hadn't been kind to the ranch though, which was finally showing its age. Paint peeled from the windows and worm-like threads dangled from curtains that hadn't been washed in what must have been a decade. I was surprised. When had the man turned into such a slob?

I stepped through into the lounge and gazed down at the floor where a myriad of scratches were now gouged into the floorboards. *Strange.* I didn't remember those.

Chase stared at me, frowning. *What's up with you,* her eyes all but said. I shook my head, *nothing. Everything's fine. Even though my insides are flip flopping around.*

As I began to wonder when Zeb would make an appearance, there came the unmistakable sound of powered wheels. Even before the old man in the wheelchair approached, I had found the answer to the scratches.

I looked down at my father and spoke one word in greeting.

"Zebediah."

80

CHASE

The old man in the wheelchair was the spitting image of Sully — if Sully were *old*.

Instead of brown, Sully's dad's hair was a shocking white. He had a beard too, but I don't think he'd ever be mistaken for Santa — his eyes lacked the twinkle. Those gray eyes pinned on Sully with an unreadable expression. There was a pregnant pause as both men stared each other down. Finally, when Sully's dad spoke, his voice was loaded with an unexpected hardness. "I was wondering when you would show your face."

Of all the things I had expected him to say, that wasn't one of them. Sully seemed to take it in his stride however, and didn't react to his less-than-welcoming tone.

"You knew I was coming?"

Zeb stared up at him, managing to look stern and disapproving in one go. "Insurance company called with some story about your clinic burning down, and you having pulled a runner. Told them the truth: that I hadn't seen you in almost ten years." He stopped, assessing Sully with those knowing eyes. "So it's bad then, whatever you've gotten yourself into?"

Sully's silence was answer enough. Zeb shook his head, as if he should be surprised by this, but wasn't. Watching him, watching his treatment of Sully, I felt an indignant rage building up inside me. *What was this guy's problem? How could he talk to Sully like this?!* As my mouth was about to shoot off with something I knew I'd regret later, Zeb's posture suddenly relaxed as some rigidness left his back.

"Sorry to hear about your loss. She seemed like a nice girl."

As Sully stared back, I saw his expression harden. "She was, which you would've known if you'd bothered to come to the wedding."

The sympathy in Sully's dad's eyes faded then, like a switch had been thrown. One minute he seemed kind, the next, I found myself taking a step back from the force of his anger.

"You threw your life away, turned your back on your mother and me, God rest her soul. After everything we had done for you, that was how you repaid us."

Sully's shoulders tensed, and he took a big breath before replying. "Everything you had done? You were my parents! You didn't do anything special. Far from it, in fact."

As Sully's Dad glared, a twitch formed in one of his eyes. "I got you into the best medical school in the country, but you wanted to toss away a career as a promising surgeon to cut into animals!"

I felt Bandit flinch then. He whined unhappily, not liking this turn of events. Couldn't say I blamed him, this was not my idea of a successful reunion. Standing behind Zeb, shooter boy seemed uneasy too.

"That's what I wanted to do, and I'm good at it," Sully seethed, hands clenched into fists by his side. "But you didn't care about that. All you cared about was your own reputation and carrying the family line".

"Your mother and I would've given anything to have half the talent you had, Jake! We never made it as surgeons, but you could have made something of yourself! Your decision didn't just make us a laughingstock, it was a criminal waste of your ability."

"It's not a waste to the families of the animals I save every day. Just because my patients can't say the words doesn't mean they're any less thankful for their lives."

At this, Bandit woofed. I guess, like me, he couldn't bear seeing Sully being taken down like this. The old man caught himself, suddenly remembering our existence.

"Who are they?"

"Chase and Bandit. They need our help."

Sully's dad laughed humorlessly. "So that's why you came back."

I'd been standing here, trying to pretend it wasn't awkward as all hell (which I think shooter boy was doing also, judging by the weird shuffle he'd been doing with his feet), but enough was enough. This wasn't going to get us anywhere. I took out Bandit's iPad. Before I continued with my plan, however, I needed to know one thing. I pointed at shooter boy.

"Who is he and can he be trusted?"

The boy snorted, insulted, but I didn't care. Clearly, the time for niceties had long gone. He looked me straight in the face.

"I live here with Zeb. Help him run the ranch."

Is this a weird time to notice his eyes were a frosty blue? Though they currently exuded hostility, I couldn't help but think how pretty they were. Zeb, Sully's dad, glared at me.

"Gideon is like my son. The son I never had."

The last sentence was said for Sully's benefit and it did the job; he looked like he had been punched in the gut. To his credit, he recovered quickly. He turned to stare Gideon down.

"This isn't a game. They burned down my home, we barely made it out alive. If you don't want to be a part of this, you're free to leave now."

Hearing the words, the antagonism left Zeb's face. He took in our haggard state, Bandit's wound, and the light way we were traveling. His expression turned serious.

"What's going on?"

"It's easier if we show you."

81

CHASE

The small group relocated into the parlor where a fire was already burning. Out here in the sticks, despite the sunshine outside, there was a chill that ran through my bones. Not used to the cold, I wasn't able to hide my shivering. I watched as Bandit walked over to the fireplace and sat, tongue hanging out with pleasure. He stared into the dancing flames, watching them with a childlike delight. I kneeled on the floor next to him, placing the iPad between his paws.

Gideon wheeled Zeb into the room, positioning him opposite Bandit. From his impatient expression, I could see he didn't care for all the theatrics. He wasn't happy with Sully's return, and he certainly didn't care for me, but, out of respect for Zeb, he was keeping a lid on his feelings. At least, I was hoping he would. I'm not a girl who likes confrontations, and we'd already had a few today.

Sully looked at us. "How about you guys show them why you're so special." Bandit turned from the fire to gaze at Sully. I handed him the stylus, and Bandit bent down and started to type...

"Hello. I am Bandit. Chase and Sully are my best friends."

The words were spoken from the app, but Bandit had clearly chosen them. Zeb and Gideon couldn't hide their shock. I was kinda amused, having gone through this exact moment myself, though obviously these were nicer surroundings. *Take it all in fellas.*

Zeb cleared his throat. "That's some trick."

In answer, Bandit typed anther sentence. *"No trick. I am special."* And there was that tongue again, lolling out in a grin. I wrapped my arms around him, resting my chin on his head.

"Yes, you are."

Gideon snapped his mouth closed. "How is he doing that?"

"*I read,*" came the reply. "*Chase got iPad. Now I can speak.*"

Somewhat skeptical, Zeb wheeled close to the dog. "Can you do anything else?"

Bandit tilted his head to one side, considering the question in such a human gesture, I thought there'd be no question whether we were telling the truth or not.

"*I am smart.*"

Zeb raised his eyes to Sully, frowning as his scientific mind struggled to comprehend what he was witnessing. "But how is this even possible?"

At that, Bandit lowered his chin to his paws, exhaling gravely.

"*They made me like this.*"

82

CHASE

Sully and his dad had been talking for some time now.

Well, some of it was talking.

Some was outright shouting as one or the other brought up past grievances. Bandit, Gideon, and I were in the kitchen where we'd moved to give them privacy, as it really was awkward having to watch them fight it out, but even here, we could hear their raised voices.

Zeb had a ton of questions; some of which I actually understood, but most contained words far too scientific for even my photographic brain to have come across. I sat with Bandit by the table, while the boy, Gideon, kept watching us from across the room. Always with those eyes. I'm not sure what it was about him, but he made me so nervous, my hands kept getting sweaty. Bandit must have noticed (he probably smelled the sweat), as his tongue kept snaking out to lick them. I moved them away from him and wiped them on my jeans, hoping he wouldn't notice. After a while, he came over from his position by the door and sat by us.

"Is he friendly to strangers?" he asked.

Bandit barked once, but it only caused him to flinch back. "One bark for yes, two for no," I explained. "And you can speak to him directly, you know. I mean, he's right there."

Gideon gave me a look but didn't reply. It was funny: he seemed to care so much about Zeb, but that concern stopped right there. There was an air of disdain around him, a deep mistrust for anyone else... and that included dogs, intelligent or otherwise.

He stared over at Bandit, frowning, as he wrestled with some thought or another. Finally, he must have decided that Bandit wasn't a threat after all, as he moved closer to him.

Tentatively, he reached out a hand, leaned across, and stroked him. Bandit sighed happily and nuzzled him with his nose. At this very normal response, Gideon couldn't help but smile... and my breath caught in my throat.

Turns out, his face was quite nice. Especially when he wasn't threatening anyone with a shotgun. There were dimples on his cheeks that made him look suddenly younger. Briefly, the thought flashed across my mind that he must have been a cute baby, before I shoved it aside, annoyed. *Why was I acting like some swooning teenage girl?* The kind of girl I'd seen at the mall, giggling and batting their lashes at some guy always made me want to hurl.

"When I was young, I always wanted a dog," he finally volunteered. I was so deep in my mental examination of his face that his voice startled me.

"Yeah? Your folks didn't let you get one?" Figured I'd make an effort at conversation since that's what we were apparently doing now. If I was honest, I didn't really mind.

"They weren't the giving type," he replied. His expression never changed, but I could hear the bitterness in his voice.

"Well, guess we have that in common," I responded before I could help myself. I'm usually very good at keeping things to myself, so this was unusual. It must've been those dimples. They were bizarrely distracting. "How did you come to live with Zeb? Are you related?"

He shook his head. "He took me in after my folks threw me out. Never liked them much anyway, so it wasn't a big deal. I moved around until I came across the ranch. I'd steal from Zeb's vegetable garden and sleep in the barn. Didn't think he knew, 'cept one day I woke to find a plate of hot food next to me." His eyes took on a faraway look. "I took the plate back to him after I had washed it. He told me I could stay so long as I helped around the ranch. I've been doing that since." He focused on me then. "How did you come to be on the streets?"

He asked so easily, so matter of fact, but I still wouldn't, *couldn't*, talk about it in any great detail. "Similar story, not very interesting." His eyes turned knowing, and he nodded, accepting this small explanation. I was grateful he wasn't going to pry. *There are some things a girl needs to keep to herself.*

Bandit laid down suddenly and lifted his leg, baring his stomach. Without thinking, I reached down to stroke the soft fur on his tummy, like every other time I did this, only this time, Gideon did exactly the same. Our hands touched, and I felt a brief shock of electricity before we both snatched our hands away. To my horror, I felt my cheeks redden.

"I need food," he said suddenly, shrinking back from me like I had the plague. Now, an ordinary girl might've had some issue with this, but me? My thoughts had already settled elsewhere.

"I could eat," I answered quickly, while my stomach had already begun a dance in anticipation. Bandit woofed once too, equally keen for provisions.

He stood up, somewhat peeved by how we had hijacked the situation and made his way to the fridge.

And with that, we hurried after Gideon, whether he wanted us to or not.

83

SULLY

I'd been talking to Zeb some three hours now, yet the old man showed no sign of fatigue. Fact was, he seemed more energetic than ever.

It took a while, but I had brought him up to date. During the long train ride, while Chase was fooling around with Bandit, I had worried how I would be able to recruit Zeb's help. A researcher in the medical field, Zeb was a smart man, but he hadn't had the acumen necessary to become a surgeon. What he lacked in physicality, however, he more than made up for in knowledge. More importantly, along with general antiquing, Zeb was a collector of old medical equipment, and amongst the odd assortment of machines and fixtures, I knew Zeb had in his possession, a refurbished 2004 CT scanner. Exactly what I needed to see into Bandit's body.

If it wasn't for this, I wouldn't have come back, tail between my legs. While I had expected my old man's hostility, what I hadn't counted on was how much frailer he now looked. And it wasn't just the wheelchair — something that had happened after I left. He just seemed *old*. A decade could really change a person.

The room fell silent as both of us contemplated our thoughts. I asked the question, pressing on my mind since I first arrived.

"What happened?" I gestured at the wheelchair.

The old man's face tensed. "An accident."

I waited for more, but it seemed nothing else would be forthcoming. I tried again. "But what caused it?"

A hiss of annoyance escaped Zeb's lips. He wheeled away, turning to face the window that looked out over the green fields beyond.

"That was always your problem, Jake. Never knew when to leave the past in the past." He wasn't referring to Emma, I knew, but I couldn't stop the raw ache that appeared in my heart at his words, nonetheless.

Taking a breath, I spoke. "You don't want to talk about it, fine, but let's set up some ground rules here. I don't ask about your accident, and you never bring up Emma. Agreed?"

If Zeb was surprised by the ultimatum, he didn't show it. Without blinking, Zeb issued a curt nod. "Now the dog. He needs a full workup: x-rays, blood tests, the works, right?"

I nodded in agreement.

"Tell me you still have the scanner?"

84

SULLY

I followed behind as Zeb took me through the ranch. Gideon and Chase appeared alongside, wolfing down the remnants of a sandwich. A few crumbs clung to Bandit's fur, the only sign of his own recent snack. I made a mental note to get Bandit more dog food, unhappy with the amount of human food the dog was consuming.

As we passed by the rooms, I was struck by the familiarity I felt, though I had never lived here myself. I recognized odd bits of furniture, and the patterned curtains my mom had struggled for an age to make.

Zeb arrived at the back of the ranch and proceeded to go outside. A path had been cleared on the lawn, laid over with smoothed out timber so that the wheelchair could glide over it without issue. I followed as my father lead me towards the barn out back. The building had changed some since I was last here. A fresh coat of paint covered the building, and old siding had been replaced with new. Even the roof had been renovated.

Reaching a double height set of sliding doors, Zeb gestured at Gideon to open them. I watched as Gideon wrapped his hands around the door handle — an iron lever — and tugged it down. The doors slid open effortlessly as strip lights flashed on inside. I gasped. Instead of the messy, hay-filled barn I expected, all manner of scientific apparatus lay neatly before me, separated into types: there were medical monitors designed to measure vital signs; physical therapy machines to help rehabilitate injured patients; and life support equipment, like the defibrillator, commonly seen on every medical show known to man. I, however, was only interested in the diagnostic section of gear. Striding quickly across the room, I zeroed in on a large donut shaped contraption in a corner of the barn.

"That GE Lightspeed 16. You've had it what, twelve years now? Does it still work?"

Zeb looked at me.

"Guess it's time we find out."

85

CHASE

Bandit whined unhappily.

Though Sully had explained what he wanted to do, just walking into the barn with all that medical equipment had made him anxious. He couldn't stop himself from panting, and I saw him walking behind me on shaking legs.

I kept turning to look at him, speaking encouragingly the whole time, but Bandit could sense my fear; it was impossible to miss, being almost as great as his. My concern only made Bandit's worse. He pressed close to me for reassurance.

I looked up at Sully, standing by the strange machine. "You're sure this won't hurt him?" I asked. My voice wobbled on the last word, and I hated myself for it. I wanted to be strong for Bandit.

"It's just an X-Ray machine, Chase. He won't feel a thing, but this will give us an insight into what's going on inside. With this, we should be able to see what might be causing the fits..." He trailed off, stopping himself from saying what was on his mind.

Bandit tugged on my sleeve to get my attention. When I looked down, Bandit pressed the home button on the iPad.

"What will it do?"

Activating the machine, Zeb looked straight at him. "You will lie here as several harmless beams will come from the machine. They will scan you and form several two-dimensional images that are then put into this," he pointed at another machine, a few feet away. "Once the images are inside the computer, the computer will layer them together to make a three-dimensional image that will clearly show us what is going on inside you. Does that make sense?"

Bandit barked twice. *No.* "*What is number die-men-son-all?*"

Sully grabbed a sheet of paper from the counter and drew onto it before showing it to him. "Do you see this test tube I just drew?"

One bark.

"This is two dimensional, as it is a flat picture, an image of the actual test tube." Bandit watched solemnly as Sully then picked up an actual test tube from the counter. "See this test tube, however, it's real. I can hold it in my hand. This is three dimensional. A three- dimensional picture, would be a picture that is made in such a way that it seems real. That's all that means."

"By doing this, we'll get a good image of your insides."

Bandit chuffed, but none of us understood his response. Seeing our confusion, he typed into the iPad.

"*OK.*"

Moments later, Bandit lay under the machine as Zeb nodded to Gideon, who flipped a switch. The CT scanner powered into life. Feeling the hum of electricity, Bandit's body shook with terror and unbidden, a yelp escaped. Having not left his side, I immediately touched him.

"What's wrong, Boy?"

Bandit whimpered and then seemed to calm. Laying his head down, he focused on a spotlight on the machine...

86

SULLY

I saw the way Bandit's body tensed as soon as the scanner switched on. Chase immediately offered what comfort she could, but it hurt me, all the same, to think what was done to him that simply turning on a machine could cause fear to grip him so entirely. I knew the scans wouldn't hurt him, though convincing the dog of this was another matter. At least the scanner looked like it was working. *If we had come all this way to find it wasn't...*

"Stand back," came Zeb's command.

Chase looked as if she were going to argue. "Just for a second, Chase. Just while the rays get to work," I said.

Chewing anxiously on her lip, Chase took a few steps back, but her eyes never left the dog. Wheeling back, Zeb settled a few feet away before picking up a remote switch lying on his lap. Giving one last look around the group to make sure the table was clear, he pressed the button.

Bars of light danced across Bandit's body as radiographic images began to appear on the computer by Zeb. While it was an old system, having come off the line somewhere around 2002, it had been refurbished to a good standard, and though it could only provide a 16-slice measurement (top-of-the-line ones could now manage 320), it should — provided it still worked properly — give us a decent look inside Bandit's body.

I watched as the cross-sectional images came together to form a three-dimensional map of Bandit's body. Even though I had seen CT scans throughout my career, I never stopped marveling at the technology being displayed before me. This simple but miraculous machine had saved count-less lives.

"Almost there," Zeb spoke reassuringly. To Bandit or Chase, I wasn't sure, but the kindness in his voice surprised me. I couldn't remember a time when Zeb had addressed me in such a manner.

Bandit was proving to be a trooper. Aside from his initial discomfort, he lay there calmly, but I could tell the dog was still anxious. Bandit was trying to steel his nerves but couldn't quite control his panting. His chest was rising and falling a little too fast. I kept this information to myself. No point stressing the girl or dog out further.

Within a few moments, the scanner fell silent and Bandit was pulled out. He immediately leaped off the gurney and shook himself as if to rid himself of that unpleasant experience and made his way to Chase's side.

"Good boy. You did so well," she said as she stroked the sweet spot behind his ears. I moved over to the computer and stood by my father, already reviewing the information on the screen.

"You see that?" Zeb asked solemnly.

He pointed at a mass, around the size of a quarter, that was growing on Bandit's brain. I nodded, unable to stop the sudden sinking feeling in my stomach.

"Yeah."

Chase came over, shoving me aside.

"What is it? What've you found?"

87

CHASE

The black-and-white image didn't make much sense to me, but I knew it wasn't good news. Sully's eyes looked haunted.

"What is it?" I asked again. More urgently this time.

When Sully's answer came, it was small. Defeated. "He has a tumor growing on his brain."

Somewhere in the back of my mind, I distantly remembered that that was what had killed Emma. A part of me felt deep sorrow for him that he would have to go through this again with someone else he cared about. Then I caught myself. *Wasn't tumor another word for cancer? My Muttface had cancer?*

"But it's fixable, right? You can get rid of it?" My voice came out a lot more panicked than I intended. Neither man spoke, just looked down at Bandit and me. "You're a vet, Sully! You must be able to help!"

Sully looked at me, concern radiating from him. "It isn't as simple as that. The tumor is aggressive; see how it's pressing on the normal brain tissue? It looks as if it's been there for some time, which doesn't make much sense. If Bandit escaped from a lab, there's no way a mass that size would have gone unnoticed. Frankly, it's a miracle he is able to function as well as he has."

"That's just science talk for you're not going to help him, isn't it?" I couldn't keep the accusatory tone from my voice, and *frankly*, I didn't care.

"It means I'm not sure I know how to. If I go in blind, I could do irreparable damage. This isn't my area of expertize. It's not something I've done or even know how to do."

I breathed in sharply. "Look, your dad's an expert researcher, and you're a vet. Putting the two together, surely that means you'll be able to help him?"

Sully and Zeb stared at each other. Sully looked aghast, but Zeb seemed to be considering my words. "It's incredibly risky."

I looked him straight in the eye. "If you don't help him, he's going to die, anyway." At this, Bandit's whole body shook. I hated myself for scaring him like that, but the others needed a push. Zeb paused, considering my words. When he finally spoke, his tone was reluctant.

"I need to think. Let's all rest and talk about this tomorrow."

I opened my mouth to argue, but Gideon shot me a look. "Enough already. He said he'll talk about this tomorrow." Without another word, he steered Zeb out of the barn and back into the ranch. I turned to Sully, faking a confidence that wasn't there.

"This is going to work. I know it."

He didn't reply.

88

CHASE

Sully showed me to a guest room overlooking the vegetable garden. The room was basic, containing only a double bed, a chest of drawers, and a side table, but to me, it was heaven and a serious step up from Motel Gross in Atlantic City. It made me wonder what Sully's room was like growing up. Even though he and Zeb didn't seem like they had had a great relationship, I'd bet the house that it's still better than what mine was like. Bet Sully had more than a bug-ridden mattress on the floor.

An old patchwork quilt lay over the bed. I sat down on it and ran my hand over the stitched squares. The handiwork was a little rough: some threads could've been better trimmed, and if I looked closely, I could see the squares weren't all the exact same size, but whatever; it was clean and comforting.

Seeing me studying the quilt, Sully stopped beside me. "My mom made that," he said. "Had a period where she tried to be crafty. Some mom's at school kept giving her grief because she was a career woman, and I guess they were threatened by that. One summer she decided to give them a run for their money. Didn't last long, though. She wasn't very good."

"Still, nice that she tried. The only thing my mom made was me and look how that turned out." I meant it flippantly, but Sully seemed upset by my words. I really have to watch this mouth of mine. Not everyone wants to hear my tale of woe. I looked to change the subject. "You haven't spoken about your mom before. What happened to her?"

Sully's eyes took on a distant look as he turned to stare out of the window at the vegetable garden. "She had the same line of work as my dad.

They were both workaholics. She was more patient, though, and kind. When I was young, she was my world, but when I got older and told them I wasn't going into the family business, they didn't take kindly to that. Things got worse when they learned I wanted to be a vet. Neither of them cared much for animals; they both considered it a waste, especially considering my pedigree. Far as they were concerned, I was a disappointment."

His voice broke a little at that word. He stopped, clearing his throat before continuing. "Ten years ago, out of nowhere, she suffered a heart attack and died. Just like that. No warning, no sign anything was wrong. Two world-class medical researchers living in the same house and neither of them had a clue."

Bandit left my side to press against Sully, offering his support. Sully gave him a grateful smile, bending down to stroke him. "After that, things changed. My dad, while never soft and cuddly, turned into an outright jerk. He retired, left the city and moved to the ranch here. I got a job in town working at the local garage. Saved every cent I earned, then went off to study. I met Emma at college. Knew from day one she would be my wife. We were happy and in love, but my dad refused to come to the wedding. Blamed her for not talking me out of this lowly career. After that, I decided he wasn't worth having in my life."

He tried to sound pragmatic, but I could see he was still hurting. It made me uncomfortable. This kind of raw emotion, I didn't know how to handle it. It actually made me regret ever asking, so I stayed silent. Sully must have picked up on my unease, as after a few moments, he asked, "What do you make of Gideon?"

To my horror, I felt my cheeks flush again. "Nothing," I managed to mumble.

He stared at me funny. "You spent a good while with him; you must have an opinion?"

"I don't know. He's just normal, I guess." I shrugged, hoping the ground would open up and swallow me whole.

"You think he can be trusted?"

My only answer was another shrug. By now Sully's brow was furrowed in an expression I can only describe as "perplexed". Probably wondering where the mouthy girl he'd gotten to know had disappeared to. I was wondering that myself. He must've finally sensed my discomfort as he headed to the door.

"Get some rest. I'll be in the room down the hall."

With that, he was gone.

89

SULLY

Something was clearly up with Chase.

While I knew she was stressed about Bandit's condition, what I hadn't bargained on was this bizarre crush she had obviously just developed on the boy, Gideon. Teenage hormones. I remembered them with the fondness of a rash I couldn't scratch.

I headed down the hall to the second guest bedroom. The sun had set by now, and my room on the East side of the ranch was pitch black. Flipping the lights on, I saw it had almost the same layout as Chase's room. There was a double bed in the center of the room, a closet, and a desk by the window. This bed was also covered with one of my mom's quilts; one of her earlier efforts. It had a marine theme with pictures of sailboats and seashells. I remembered how I had loved it as a kid.

Somehow, seeing that quilt brought her to the forefront of my mind. Whatever my issues with my dad, Zeb had truly loved my mother. Despite never having lived in this house, her little touches were everywhere. Feeling a deep ache, I turned away, shrugging out of my jacket, when footsteps sounded outside. I looked at the door to find Gideon standing with a tray of food in his hands. There was a sandwich, some vegetables freshly dug from the garden, and a glass of water.

"That for me? Thanks." I reached for the tray, but Gideon didn't move. Just stood there staring at me.

"Zeb asked me to put this together for you. If it were up to me, I'd tell you to do it yourself."

It was impossible to miss the hostility in his voice. With plenty on my mind already, I really didn't need an angry teenager to contend with, so I decided to tackle the issue head on. "You don't like me much, do you?"

"Why whatever gave you that idea?" came Gideon's snarky reply.

"I don't know what he's told you, but I can almost guarantee it's revisionist history." I didn't know why I was explaining myself, especially since I didn't care what this kid thought of me. His attitude galled me all the same.

Gideon came into the room, crossed over to the desk and dropped the tray onto it with enough violence that half the water spilled out of the glass. "That's where you're wrong, *Jake*." The way he said my name made it sound like a dirty word. "He hasn't said anything. What I know about you, I figured out myself."

I knew I could correct him if I wanted to, but I was over my daily limit of teenage angst. Seeing my dad was causing enough negative emotions, and that was without venturing into the minefield that was the brain tumor territory — which alone was enough to drain my energy. I just wanted to lie down and sleep.

So instead of correcting him, I said nothing. I sat on the bed and very deliberately pulled my boots off, preparing to sleep. As I had hoped, Gideon took this as a sign to leave, though he couldn't hide his disappointment. This kid was giddy for a fight.

Spinning on his heel, he marched out of the room. I wondered what Chase saw in him.

Kids.

90

CHASE

Bandit had already jumped onto the bed, iPad on and waiting to communicate when I heard footsteps stomping outside. Tip-toeing to the door, I peeked through the keyhole to see who it was.

It was Gideon. And he looked furious.

He was coming back from Sully's room. By the looks of things, whatever had gone on between them hadn't ended well. *What exactly was Gideon's problem with Sully? The two had never met before now, so what was with his salty attitude?*

He stormed past my room, disappearing down the hall. Even angered, there was something about the way he looked that drew me. I watched until he was gone.

Bandit woofed softly at me.

"What? I'm not doing anything." Caught, I answered automatically. In hindsight, he probably wasn't asking why I was staring after Gideon, but that's the first thing that crossed my mind. Moving guiltily from the door, I climbed onto the bed beside him where he was already busy typing.

"What is tumor?"

The official explanation was "a swelling of a part of the body, generally without inflammation, caused by an abnormal growth of tissue, whether benign or malignant." I knew this as I'd come across the explanation in a scientific journal once, back when I was studying and tossing around the idea of being a doctor (yes, I had dreams too - though I did also consider being a space cadet when I was young, so...). There was no way Bandit would understand *that* though, so we searched YouTube for videos that might make it clearer.

We watched a couple of videos put out by the American Cancer Society, followed by clips of past sufferers who were now cancer free. They had happy demeanors, but their eyes looked haunted. By the end of our research, I had almost convinced myself of a positive outcome.

God wouldn't make Bandit special just to kill him off.

That would make no sense whatsoever. Then again, I used to wonder why I was created if this miserable existence was going to be my life.

Clearly, God didn't exist.

We were screwed.

91

SULLY

An owl hooted outside my window. As it was an unseasonably warm night, I'd flung the window open to let the breeze in, but I now couldn't sleep due to the cacophony of sounds outside. In addition to the owl, a choir of crickets chirped incessantly as the occasional bat swooped across the dark sky. It had been so long since I had heard this much nature that, despite my fatigue, I was having a hard time sleeping.

Then again, I could only ever sleep next to Emma.

There was an old radio alarm clock plugged into the wall. Probably one of Zeb's "collectibles", as the red digits were stuck at 12:03 and had been that way since I'd first come into the room. I had no idea what time it really was, but it was long past midnight.

Sighing, I rolled out of bed and headed out into the night wearing just my shorts. The air was cooler out here, and a blessed relief from the cloying stuffiness of my room. Zeb was old school and had never believed in air conditioning. Said a man wasn't a man unless he could brave the climate naturally. I used to argue that his logic was asinine since we relied very much on heating during the long and brutal Vermont winters, but all that had done was to enrage my old man to the point my mom would have to step in to diffuse the situation.

The owl hooted again. I looked up into a cluster of trees to find him silhouetted against the round moon. He blinked at me, wide yellow eyes alert and watchful but showing no fear. Folk around here tended to leave the animals alone, so unlike in the city, they had not grown to fear man.

The moon shone over the ranch, granting enough light for me to see some distance ahead. Enjoying the moment, I started walking when a whinny caught my attention. I smiled, suddenly excited, and made my way to the stables.

Sliding the door open, my eyes picked out a group of thoroughbred horses. The gray, Derby, was a two-time state champion of Vermont. She'd ran for most of her life until skeletal fractures had cut her career short. Her owners — a pair of mercenary scumbags I had wanted banned from owning any animal — hadn't wanted to stump up the small fortune it would take to fix her injuries, so Derby was heading for the butcher's block when eight-year-old me had stepped in.

My mom and I had been visiting a local food market when I overheard Derby's owners haggling with the butcher. Appalled that this magnificent animal would see such a sorry end, I had pleaded with my mom to save her. My tears and compassion had moved her into action. Within a few hours, Zeb had come home to find himself the surprised owner of a retired racehorse. My philanthropist ways didn't stop there. Over the next ten or so years, I saved several more horses from the slaughterhouse. The ones I could rehabilitate were given to families to live out their days on green pastures and sunshine. The ones who couldn't were sent to Roberts' ranch, as there wasn't space for them in our townhouse in Burlington. I had spent every school vacation caring for my horse. Derby was my first rescue and my fondest.

I made a clicking sound in my throat. Derby looked up and snickered back a greeting, prancing on her legs. She remembered who I was. With a few strides, I reached her and threw my arms around her neck. Derby lowered her mouth to my shoulder and nibbled my shirt in that comforting way she did when I was just a kid.

"Hey old girl, how've you been?" She whinnied, pawing the ground. "I know, it's been a while. A lot's happened, but I've never forgotten you. You've always been my favorite girl." The horse seemed to calm at my words. She blew into my face, sniffing at me. As I stroked her I took in the other horses. There was one other familiar face, but I was surprised to see new inhabitants in the stables.

Leaving Derby was the hardest thing I had had to do, but there was just no way my new life in New York would allow for a horse. Before I had left, I only asked one thing of Zeb; that he care for Derby with the grace and compassion she was owed. While Zeb had never been an animal person, he still respected their right to a happy and safe life. I was inordinately grateful now to see how well Derby looked. In my absence, she had been well cared for. Having spent years resting, even her fractures had healed.

Two brushes still hung on the wall where I had left them: a curry comb and a hard brush, designed for use after the curry comb. I took the comb and started grooming the horse using circular motions, beginning from her neck, then to the barrel and all the way down to her rump, removing any loose hair, dirt, and mud. Derby's tail flicked from side to side, enjoying the pampering. When I was done with both sides, I took the hard bristle brush and went over Derby's coat again until it was gleaming and free of dirt. She was a whole new filly by the time I was done with her.

Hanging up my tools, I promised to see her again and was heading back to the ranch when I saw a crack of light spilling out from the barn.

Frowning at the lateness of the hour, I headed toward it. When I reached the door, I found Zeb inside, typing busily on the computer. Scans littered the counters around me as the printer hummed loudly, spouting reams of information.

"You're working late?" I said.

Zeb looked over at me, surprised by the visit, rubbing his red-rimmed eyes. "There's so much to consider. We can't miss anything."

I walked over to him, taking in the charts and diagrams, only some of which made any sense to me. "You honestly think we can do this?"

Zeb peered at me over the top of his glasses. "What choice do we have? That dog is a miracle, a scientific breakthrough." He laughed suddenly, at something only he could hear.

"Care to share the joke?" I asked.

"Your mother and I spent thirty years studying and learning, but here you are with the kind of breakthrough we always hoped to find."

It was meant as a compliment, but the way he said the word "breakthrough" had me on edge. "Bandit's family; he's not an experiment to us."

Zeb had the decency to look embarrassed. "I didn't mean it the way it sounded."

I nodded that I understood, though I couldn't find the words to say it. Like so many times before, when I had entered into Zeb's work zone uninvited, Zeb turned his attention back to the work at hand. As far as he was concerned, the conversation was over. However, unlike all those other times, I wasn't a kid, and I didn't accept the dismissal. Instead, I picked up a sheet of Zeb's findings, frowning as I tried to make sense of it.

"This tumor isn't like any I've seen."

Zeb looked up again, surprised I was still there. As if he suddenly realized I could be an asset, he opened up. "It's almost as if it's man made. Look at the placement. It's perfect."

A chill ran through me that had nothing to do with the night air. "You think they gave Bandit a tumor intentionally? Why would anyone do that?"

"I don't know. Maybe his intelligence has something to do with it."

"I know there have been cases where people were seeing things or became smarter than they were originally due to a tumor growing on the brain in just the right place, but this would be crazy. How would they know where to put it, for a start?"

We both looked at each other as the same thought crossed our minds.

"How many more dogs have they done this to?"

92

THE MERCENARY

I t was a bright and beautiful fall morning. Green fields flashed by in a blur as the train thundered down the tracks.

The Mercenary ignored them, having no interest in the scenery, pushing past passengers as he made his way to a specific carriage. He checked the log on his phone: Carriage C. Finally locating it, he moved inside, only to find a middle-aged couple in "his" seats. At The Mercenary's approach, the husband, a balding man in his forties with a protruding stomach, looked up from a half-completed crossword puzzle.

Though he was no longer dressed in police uniform, there was no denying The Mercenary's commanding presence. He leaned over them, letting his shadow fall over their faces.

"Sir, Ma'am, I'd greatly appreciate if you would move to a different carriage." He flashed open his wallet. The fake ID showed his unsmiling face and the logo of the FBI. "I'm investigating a possible crime that took place where you are sitting right now."

The woman recoiled with horror, clutching at her husband, who was already gathering up their things. "What happened? Did someone *die*?"

The Mercenary kept his face impassive. "I'm not at liberty to disclose that, Ma'am."

She sighed, shocked, reading into his reply. By now, the husband had their things loaded in his arms and was tugging her towards the door. "Margaret, come," he hissed, eager to get away. To The Mercenary, he said, "No problem Officer, we'll be moving right along."

The Mercenary watched impatiently. As soon as they had gone, he leaped into action. Sliding on a pair of glasses, The Mercenary waited and watched. An ordinary person wouldn't have spotted the difference between these and his image enhancement glasses, but The Mercenary could tell. These held a thicker lens and weighed more to accommodate the extra tech.

Within a few moments, a hum sounded between his ears as the glasses powered on. Suddenly, the carriage looked very different as the marks and lint, invisible to the naked eye, appeared. Staring at the multitude of sweat stains that now covered the seats, The Mercenary restrained a grimace. This was one of the reasons he preferred to travel in his own vehicles. People were nasty creatures.

Code flashed on the lens as the glasses filtered through their findings, listing every recognized item and discarding them as anything of note. The Mercenary scanned the room slowly, giving them a chance to work their magic. Eventually, they hit the jackpot as cross hairs zeroed in on a tiny speck. The Mercenary lowered into a crouch, moving his face in close.

It was a hair.

The fiber was tough and short. And brown. The Mercenary waited impatiently for the glasses to confirm their findings. Finally, a single word flashed up.

** MATCH **

It was Alpha's fur.

93

***

THE MERCENARY

Within seconds, the findings had been uploaded to the Facilities computers, with Dr. Robins, hard at work, examining the fur. The Mercenary didn't know what it was she was doing — he never knew the ins and outs of her work. He was a simple man with a simple job and operated on a need-to-know basis. And what she did with those animals, what she did *to* them? Some things were better left unsaid.

Finding nothing else of interest, The Mercenary left the carriage and moved along the rest of the train. It was a warm day, and The Mercenary had dressed accordingly, though the muggy air clung uncomfortably close. A trickle of sweat formed at the base of his neck. He ignored it, focusing on surveying his immediate surroundings. Passengers were dotted around the carriage. Most, he noted, were elderly or poorly dressed. He assumed anyone with the means would prefer to drive rather than travel in this suffocating hellhole.

A sign ahead caught his eye. The Mercenary already knew Sullivan's destination — it was stamped across his ticket. That meant a seven-hour train ride. It was doubtful they had the foresight to purchase provisions ahead of the journey. The Mercenary was hoping to find more information up ahead.

With that in mind, he entered the catering car.

94

THE MERCENARY

S econds later, The Mercenary strolled up to the counter where a twenty-something guy leaned against the refrigerator with an expression of utter boredom. Going by the droop of his shoulders, The Mercenary didn't think he'd be lasting long in this job. He glanced up at his approach. "Can I help you?" he asked.

"I need to know who was working this carriage yesterday, on this same train," The Mercenary said.

The server's face grew guarded. "Why? Did she do something?"

The Mercenary smiled reassuringly. "No, she's not in any trouble. I just need to speak to her."

He could see he wasn't getting anywhere, however, as the server just grew more suspicious. Seeing the Paranoia magazine peeking out from his bag on the floor, a publication read by conspiracy theorists, The Mercenary — an expert at profiling — made a snap decision.

"Look, I shouldn't be telling you this, but I'm with the FBI. We're looking for a criminal who we believe traveled on this very train yesterday. It's a long journey. I expect our suspect wouldn't have had the foresight to bring provisions, in which case they would have visited the catering car. I only want to speak to her, see if she can confirm a sighting." The Mercenary flashed his trusted FBI badge at the guy who leaned closer to The Mercenary, eyes wide with interest, though he still seemed reluctant to part with any information.

"I could get fired for giving out personal information..." He said, hesitantly.

The Mercenary nodded. "And I'm not asking you for any. You obviously know the girl who worked here yesterday." The Server nodded. "Can you just call her and let me speak to her now?" he asked. The Server hesitated, worried over any possible work ramifications. Suddenly, he shrugged. He wasn't doing anything wrong. Taking a phone out of his pocket, he tapped through several screens. Within seconds, the words "Calling Janet Home" flashed up and was answered after a few rings. The Server quickly explained why he was calling, then handed the phone to The Mercenary.

"I'm looking for some people who were on this train yesterday. A thirty-something guy traveling with a teenage girl and a dog. I think you might've seen them."

An excited female voice came on the line. The Mercenary guessed she was somewhere in her early twenties. "Haven't seen any guys with that description. People traveling on the train are usually older than that. I did serve a young girl yesterday, though. Come to think of it, she said she was buying food for her dog!" Janet said.

The Mercenary kept his face calm, though he was starting to feel a surge of excitement race through him. "Did she talk about it at all?"

The girl sounded confused. "Who, the dog? Not really. Just said she was buying some food for him."

The Mercenary took note of her use of the word "him." "Can you remember what she bought?"

Again, a confused silence came on the line. "Just some sandwiches and she took a whole tray of meats. Said I didn't need to bother wrapping them, just to dump them in a bag since they were for her dog."

The Mercenary nodding, mentally filing the information away. "We're almost done here. Can you give me a detailed description of what she looked like?"

The girl hesitated then. The Mercenary could almost see the questions racing through her mind before she voiced them. "Well, if you're looking for her, shouldn't you know what she looks like?"

The Mercenary smiled, though it didn't quite reach his eyes. "I need to establish whether we are talking about the same person, and any informa-tion I give out to you could sway your memory. It's better if you speak freely without any interference from me."

Her voice softened. The Mercenary could hear the moment she accepted his response. Even the Server bought his story, hanging onto every word.

"She was around five-foot-four. Short dark hair, kind of messy cut actu-ally, but it suited her. She was pretty, but a bit heavy-handed with the eyeliner if you know what I mean?" He didn't, but let her continue. "Think she was wearing a hoodie and jeans. They could've done with a wash. I remember thinking for a pretty girl, she sure didn't know how to dress to her advantage. And that's about it."

Nodding, The Mercenary slipped a business card onto the counter. "Thank you. You've both been a great help. If you think of anything else that might be useful, please contact my office."

With that, The Mercenary left. He'd gotten what he needed and didn't want to spend a second longer talking with these two idiots.

95

CHASE

A bright stream of sunlight landed on my face, waking me.

I yawned, stretching before noticing how *comfortable* I was. Suddenly, my eyes flew open as I remembered where I was. Bandit — who had still been sleeping — snapped his eyes open. He chuffed softly, which I took as his morning greeting. I scratched him under the chin.

"Morning Muttface."

He grinned at me; I guess he got the joke. I lay there for a blissful second, Bandit curled up by my side. Other than Motel Horror, it had been almost a year since I'd slept in a bed, and I'd totally forgotten how nice they were. Honestly, just wait until you've been sleeping on the sidewalk with nothing other than a newspaper to cushion you against the cold. Then you'll know what discomfort is.

BANG! A thundering crack sounded from outside.

"STAY DOWN," I yelled to Bandit. Rolling out of bed, I crouch-walked to the window, keeping my head as low as I could. My heart was racing so much I thought it would leap out of my chest. Rising slowly, I peeked out, sure I would see one of those SWAT-like guys who attacked Sully's clinic. But instead of the mass of black-clad figures I expected, there was only one. And he wore jeans and a tight shirt that showed off even tighter abs. Gideon.

He was aiming a pistol at a row of cans perched on a fence some distance away. As I watched, he pulled on the trigger. BOOM! A can danced off the fence and fell to the ground. He paused for the slightest second before letting off another shot. A second can tumbled down. Then another and

another until all the cans lay on the ground. I was impressed but didn't want
to show it. Instead, I opened the window and stuck my head outside.

"You can't use an alarm like normal people? What's with the gunshots so
early in the morning?"

He spun around and found me framed in the window. "There's two
things wrong with that sentence: one, it's after twelve, so morning has long
gone, and two, what makes you think I want to be like normal people?"

I frowned. "Well, what time is it?"

"Time you made yourself useful. This isn't a hotel, it's a working ranch."
He turned back to the fence and walked away from me, apparently done
with me right now.

I'll be honest. The guy might be cute, but he sure lacked in the affability
department. I looked at Bandit, who was staring at me, head tilted questioningly.

"Yeah. I don't know what I see in him either."

96

CHASE

Moments later, we were invading the kitchen.

The fridge had a bunch of meats and cheeses in it. I grabbed some of each and a jug of juice and was heading to the dining table before I saw a neatly stacked mound of canned dog food and biscuits. Someone had already been up and shopping that morning.

Grinning, I grabbed a can that was flavored with turkey apparently and dished it onto one of the two brand new metal bowls that was lying on the counter. Bandit couldn't keep still. He was literally doing circles around me. I'm guessing the smell of the food was driving him mad.

He whined, nuzzling my side impatiently.

"OK, OK, hold your horses, dog."

A confused sound came out of him, a cross between a moan and a sigh.

"It's just a saying. No need to get all literal," I explained as I placed the bowl onto the ground. He dived into the bowl, chomping and slurping with gusto. Remember how daintily he took that fritter from me back when we first met? Yeah, that dog was long gone. Apparently, he totally dug the food choice.

Smiling, I slapped some meat and pre-sliced cheese between two slices of bread and was chomping away at it when Sully appeared in the doorway. He was dressed in clothes I hadn't seen before. Zeb must have loaned them from his own collection, judging by the faded flannel shirt he was wearing.

"I was coming to wake you, but I see you already found the food," Sully said wryly.

I nodded, mouth too full to speak.

Bandit barked once, happily, his bowl already empty. He was licking it so much, the bowl was being pushed across the floor. I tore open the large bag of doggy biscuits and started pouring some into the bowl for him. Bandit didn't even wait for me to finish, just stuck his snout in there and started woofing down chow at a rate that was akin to the speed of light.

Sully grabbed a glass from the cupboard and poured himself a glass of OJ. Sipping it, he lifted Bandit's bandage and inspected the wound.

"A scab is forming. That's good news; it's healing nicely."

"That's one down," I said. It was meant to sound optimistic, but somehow came out a little desperate. Sully must've been able to hear it in my voice but chose to ignore it.

"I'll take it. I'll take anything I can get right now," he replied. He sounded weary. It was only when I took a closer look at him that I saw the dark rings under his eyes.

"You didn't sleep?"

"I was up most of the night. Zeb and I were trying to see what we could do."

He spoke without thinking, I don't think he realized he called his father by name, but I caught the use. Sully's issues with Zeb must run deep if he can't even call him "dad."

"And? What did you find?"

"Not much yet. We need to keep looking." He reached down to stroke Bandit, who had long finished his food and was now sitting there, watching us solemnly. I could feel myself wanting to ask if he could look a little faster, but another look at the bags under his eyes and I bit my tongue. Sully was trying his best. No need to beat him over the head with it. He gulped down the juice and took his glass over to the sink where he rinsed it before setting it upside down on a dish rack. He did this in one quick motion, like he'd done it a million times before, which I guess he probably had. I wondered whether this was something Emma had drilled into him. Somehow, I couldn't picture Sully being this domesticated without help.

"Will you guys be OK while I get to work in the barn?"

"Sure. We'll find something to do to occupy ourselves," I said. He nodded, eyes distant, thoughts already drifting away to the enormous task at hand. Within a few beats, the doorway was empty. I turned to Bandit.

"So... What do you fancy doing?"

97

CHASE

Turns out, Bandit just wanted to play outside in the sun.

He was running around, chasing and barking at anything that moved — being a goofball, basically. I was kinda surprised he didn't want to watch YouTube or read, but he'd said something about loving the smell of grass. I think where he was from, they probably didn't let him out much. If at all.

A brightly colored orange and black butterfly flew by. A Monarch. Bandit barked at it then chased it until it disappeared into the sky. He watched from below, tongue hanging out to one side, having the time of his life.

"He doesn't look *that* bright," came Gideon's voice from behind me. I forced myself not to turn, despite all my senses screaming at me to look at him. *Be cool.*

"He might be clever, but he's still a dog." I gave myself an internal pat on the back. Gideon stopped beside me, and we watched Bandit play. As the silence grew, I could feel myself tensing up. What was it about him that made me feel so awkward? I cleared my throat and gestured across the grass to Gideon's gun range.

"Where did you learn to shoot like that?"

"Here. Zeb thinks it's important to be able to protect your own."

"This doesn't look like the kind of place that needs protecting," I said. He turned to face me. The sun was behind him, casting his face in shadow. I tried not to focus on his chiseled cheekbones.

"It's not like we're back in New York. Can't imagine crime gets any tougher than a rabbit stealing from the vegetable garden."

He looked at me curiously. It was probably the first time I'd seen his brow unfurled. "That where you're from? New York?"

I nodded. "Not originally. But I've been living on the streets a year now. It's tough, but at least I'm my own person, you know? No one tells me what I can or can't do. And if anyone touches me, they get a taste of my fist."

Oh wow, I was mortified. I'd turned into Chatty McChatty. Flinching, I mentally chided myself for my behavior, hoping he couldn't hear my inner dialogue. All the while, he kept watching me with those intense blue eyes. I had to look away, worried they would see straight into my soul. "Bandit's the only friend I had until Sully came along."

Gideon kicked at a blade of grass. "That's like me and Zeb. He helped me out when I was in a bind."

Looks like neither of us wanted to mention our family or parents, and I was totally fine with that.

"So you're good in a fight?" he asked.

I stood taller. "I can hold my own. I've been learning the Israeli self-defense form of martial arts."

"You know Krav Maga?" He couldn't hide his surprise.

"You know what that is?" I couldn't hide mine either. Most people had never heard of it.

"I've seen Taken. We're not all complete hicks out here." His voice was empty of humor. There was the very real possibility that I had insulted him.

"I didn't mean you were. It's just not a common thing to know is all." I went to bite my tongue again before I caught the glint in his eyes. He was teasing me! A warm feeling flooded my body. I hoped to God my cheeks weren't as red as they felt. Luckily, he gave me the out I needed.

"You ever wanted to shoot a gun?" he asked.

98

CHASE

I watched as Gideon balanced five cans along the fence. The labels on the cans were bleached by the sun and riddled with bullet holes, but I could see enough to make out the pictures of coffee beans and peas. He scanned the ground quickly and found Bandit a few meters away.

"Hey," he called out tentatively to him, still not used to addressing a super intelligent dog. Immediately, Bandit stopped playing and trotted over to him. "This is dangerous work we're about to do. Can you go on back up to the ranch and wait by the porch?"

"*WOOF*," came the reply, then Bandit was off, running back to the ranch, tail in the air. Gideon waited until Bandit was a safe distance behind us before walking over to me. He held a small gun in each hand, which he showed me now.

"There are two types of handguns, a revolver and a semi-automatic pistol. Typically, the ones you see in cowboy movies are revolvers — they're the ones with a cylinder in the middle of the frame of the gun that's loaded with cartridges. Usually, these hold six bullets, but some hold five: those are made for smaller hands, like yours."

He showed me the revolver and gestured at my apparently small hands (I'd never given much thought to their size before, so it was news to me that they fell in the petite range).

"Revolvers have a revolving cylinder for holding ammo. You load it up and it's ready to go. As the trigger is pulled, the cylinder rotates, and the hammer pulls back. Like this, see?" He aimed into the distance and fired off a shot. Once again, a can danced on the fence before tumbling to the ground. "See how the cylinder rotates and lines up the next cartridge? When the trigger is pulled back far enough, that releases and strikes the round, firing the bullet. When all five shots are fired, you remove the empty casings and reload the cylinder." Done with the revolver demo, he slid it into his belt.

"Now, the other gun, a semi-automatic pistol, has a sliding mechanism at the top and a mag of pre-loaded ammo in the handle. When you pull the slide, a semi advances the cartridge into the chamber from the mag. As the first round is fired, part of the force of the shot pushes back on the side, ejecting the casing and chambering the next round in a fraction of a second. This makes for a faster and deadlier weapon." He held the semi closer to me to inspect. "That's pretty much it. There's the safety here. I've had it locked in place so we can't accidentally fire it. To turn it off, flip it up. There's a bit more to it than that, but that's probably all you need to know."

I raised a brow at him. "Why, because I'm a silly girl?"

He shot me a level stare. "Because I can't think of a situation where you'd need to know anymore."

"Oh." I did my best not to sound chastised, but failed miserably. I held out my hand. "Can I try the semi?"

He tried to restrain a smile. "Going for the heavy artillery. I like it." He handed it to me, muzzle down. "Take it from me gently, be careful not to touch the trigger until I say so."

I took the gun into my hands. The metal was cold and hard and heavy. My hands shook when I thought of how this was a weapon designed for killing. Weirdly, I found myself breaking out into a sweat. I felt slightly nauseous, and I was pretty sure it wasn't Gideon who was causing this reaction in me.

Gideon moved behind me so that his face was over my left shoulder. "Hold the gun, keeping your trigger finger outside the trigger guard."

I did as he instructed, trying to block out the strange feeling inside me.

"That's good. Now, keep the barrel pointed straight downrange, never up. A bullet fired up by accident will come down at some point and could hurt someone." He leaned in close until I could feel his breath on my shoulder. "Hold the gun in the firing-ready position."

He showed me what he meant with the revolver. I matched his finger work perfectly, so why did I still feel like throwing up?

"Good, steady the gun with the other hand like so."

Again, I matched him, move for move.

"Now stand in the proper firing stance. Your feet shoulder-width apart, one foot slightly in front of the other for balance." When he was happy with my form, he continued. "Line up the front sight on a can, and center it with the back sight."

"OK." As I said the words, they seemed to stick in my throat. I focused on the first can, keeping my hand as steady as I could.

"When you're ready, pull the trigger," he said.

I slowed my breathing then held it. Counting in my head. *One... two...* On *three* I pulled the trigger, but flinched as I did it. The bullet shot out of the gun, its recoil slamming down my arm and knocking me back a full step. The world slowed to a crawl as the bullet flew way past the target, impaling itself harmlessly into the trunk of a tree. Lowering the gun "downrange," I turned to Gideon, feeling sheepish. "Sorry. I didn't realize it would feel like that."

He shrugged, fine. "It's not as easy as it looks. You'd have more luck hitting the can if you don't flinch when you pull the trigger."

"Yeah. I know," I said. Ignoring the sick feeling in my stomach, I positioned myself to try again. *Ready... aim... and FIRE!* Again, I felt myself flinch when the bullet shot out of the chamber. This time, the bullet swerved left, missing the cans by an even wider margin. He frowned at me.

"Try again."

We went several more rounds. Each time, I kept flinching and kept missing my mark. Gideon grew more and more impatient until he snapped at me. "Look, you'll never hit anyone if you're scared of using a gun!"

I was already berating myself internally, so I really didn't need him to do the same. I felt stupid and weak enough as it was. He obviously didn't read the signs though as he continued. "These men coming after you are dangerous. The only chance you'll have against them is if you can use a gun."

"You think I don't know that?! I've already gone up against them! I saw what they can do, so I don't need you telling me!" I snapped back.

He glared at me, suddenly angry himself. "I'm just trying to help you!"

"Well don't!" I shouted back. Handing him the gun, I spun around and stomped back into the ranch, fuming.

99

CHASE

few snacks later, and even food wasn't soothing my bristling self. Poor Bandit had been trying to comfort me, nudging me with his nose and trying to engage me in conversation, but I was *mad*. For some reason, Gideon had rubbed me up the wrong way, and try as I might, I hadn't been able to shake my anger.

Sully and Zeb were locked in the barn researching. Luckily, Gideon had taken off somewhere in the truck, so I didn't have to deal with him again for now. Bandit and I had been wandering aimlessly through the house when we had stumbled upon a computer in the den. I fired it up, and we fooled around on a few quiz sites. Even though my heart wasn't in it, I wanted to keep up the pretense for Bandit's sake.

It was while we were messing around on the internet that I realized maybe I could help with the research. While we were doing the last quiz, pop-up windows advertising VPN's had flooded the screen. A VPN, in case you didn't know, stood for Virtual Private Network. Every computer that connects online has an IP address, basically a unique chain of numbers that identifies every computer. Of course, sometimes you might not want people to know where you are, like when you're doing things for nefarious reasons, or in my case, when you're trying to find out where Bandit came from, and that was where the VPN came in.

Accessing one was easy. You can literally subscribe to a service for a few bucks. Still, I hadn't lasted so long out here by using my money when I didn't have to. I signed up to a service that offered a free one month trial. Then I created an anonymous email address that wouldn't be traceable.

Using the VPN was as simple as downloading the application and turning it on. So now we were in stealth mode, I took a big gamble.

I went to the national missing animals database and input the numbers tattooed into Bandit's ear. Yes, I know this is probably what caused the SWAT team to arrive at the clinic, but they wouldn't be able to trace us this time, especially since I wasn't going to be dumb enough to call them on a landline.

Sorry, Sul, but that wasn't the smartest move you could've made.

The missing animal database seemed normal enough. It was a pretty active site, with some several thousand animals being reported every day. I figured it must be legit, though I wasn't about to take any risks. I set up a profile, calling myself Jane Doe who lived at 0800 Bite-Me Lane, Neverland, California. Luckily, it wasn't one of those sites that cross-checked your address against real data, so it accepted my details just fine.

A tingle of apprehension went through me as I called up the window to input the serial number from Bandit's ear. I typed the numbers in carefully, but I stopped short of hitting enter as a wave of doubt flooded over me.

What if I was wrong?

What if they could trace this?

I stared at Bandit, looking up at me with those soulful blue eyes. Then, in my mind, his eyes rolled back into his head as I watched him suffering through his first convulsion at the buffet.

My mouth filled with bitterness. So this is what fear tastes like. Remembering what I'd said to Sully last night, that Bandit would die if we didn't try...

I hit enter.

100

CHASE

I don't know what I was expecting. Maybe an explosion across the screen. Or for those black-clad SWAT guys to burst through the roof. None of these things happened. Instead, another window flashed up with a warning. This said the dog had escaped from a research lab. The dog was carrying a virus, but they made sure to state that it wasn't contagious. It made several mentions not to approach or communicate with the dog.

That's how it kept referring to Bandit. The dog. Jerks couldn't even give him a name. I studied the window, careful not to press anything that would make it go away, but there was no identifying information. Disappointed, I sat there, stumped, when a ping sounded — the alert that usually accompanied a new email. Clicking off the window, I went into the tab that still had my email mailbox loaded. There was one new message.

SENDER: Sunshine Research Laboratory.
SUBJECT: WARNING!
VIRUS CARRYING DOG ALERT!

I read the sender name and snorted.
Sunshine Research.
Who did they think they were kidding with that name? Might as well call themselves KILLERS R US!
The message of the email was pretty much a repeat of the warning. I couldn't see anything useful. When I hit reply however, the To: subject line automatically replied with the sender's email address, and something else...

A series of numbers separated by dots inside two rectangular brackets. I wouldn't normally have known what that was, except for the samples I was shown while setting up the VPN.

I grinned, thrilled by the finding — an IP address — and felt a moment of smugness. Googling the numbers, it gave me the location of Maryland, but nothing else. Still, determined to give Sherlock Holmes a run for his money, I input the same location into Google Maps.

Bingo.

I was in satellite view, so the building that appeared could easily be seen. It was long and low with a connecting maze of wings. The only windows were high up, presumably so prying people wouldn't get much of an eyeful. A discreet sign was mounted by the entrance.

I hit zoom to read the words inscribed there.

PLATINUM INDUSTRIES.

101

CHASE

I had a real lead!

I turned to Bandit and pointed at the sign.

"Does this mean anything to you, Boy?"

He woofed twice. *No.*

I was disappointed, but I should've guessed that would be the case. They probably never referred to the name of the company that was keeping him prisoner. Wouldn't make sense for them to be using personalized stationery or something. I spent a while more Googling before I finally hit pay-dirt.

Platinum Industries was the name of a group of commercial companies owned by billionaire Sebastien Forbes. A self-made millionaire by the time he turned twenty, Forbes was considered one of the world's wealthiest businessmen. Literally everything he touched turned to gold.

Apparently he was raised by a single mom working three jobs and never knew his dad. Wanting to help his mom, who was suffering from some kind of illness (I couldn't find any reference as to what it was), Forbes won his first job working in the mailroom of a prestigious real estate firm. Within a year he was promoted to office assistant.

Another year and he had his own office. By the time he'd been at the company five years, he'd become the majority shareholder. After this, he bought company after company, for such obscene sums of money that it made my eyes water. How was it possible for someone to have this much, when others — like me — had so little? It was insane.

I tried to find useful details on the actual building, but information wasn't forthcoming. It was listed as a lab, but that was about it. Looks like

Forbes didn't want anyone to know what kind of experiments might be going on inside.

I pulled up a picture of the man. As soon as his face flashed on screen, Bandit whimpered, his whole body shaking from fear. There was no need to ask if he knew who he was. The answer was clear. Seeing his terror only made me more determined.

"He won't hurt you anymore, Boy, I promise. He won't get away with this."

I made the promise before I even knew what to do. But it didn't matter. I would stop this man, billionaire or not. He wouldn't hurt Bandit ever again.

Cross my heart and hope to die.

102

SULLY

I rubbed tired eyes, blinking when I realized how dry they were. I had been staring at the scans for so long that their images were seared into my brain.

A man-made tumor.

It was impossible to fathom what twisted mind would create something as horrific as this, and I should know. I'd been trying all day only to keep coming up empty-handed.

Surrounded by papers himself, Zeb sighed, coming up for air. "I don't know what to tell you."

I tried not to let despair wash over me. "I know. It was a stupid idea. We can't go into his head like this. We'll kill him."

Zeb started organizing his papers into a neat file when Chase and Bandit burst into the barn. She held a printout in her hands and was out of breath from sprinting there.

"Sully! I know who's after Bandit! Look!" She thrust the piece of paper at me. It was a profile on secretive billionaire Sebastien Forbes. I was aware of him due to the man owning half of New York. It was one of the reasons the rent was so high that Emma and I were driven out of the housing market and had to settle outside.

I frowned. "Why would it be him?"

Chase gave an exasperated breath. "I did some detective work OK. I used a VPN, then put Bandit's serial number into that missing animal database." Seeing my alarmed expression, she raised a hand in my face. "It's fine, don't worry. The VPN hides our location. I'm not stupid OK? Anyway,

I didn't get anything on the database, but they sent an email to the anonymous account I set up. And the identifying information lead me to Platinum Industries, which is owned by Sebastien Forbes." She pointed at the printout where Forbes's unsmiling face looked back at me. "It's him, Sully. Just ask Bandit."

I looked over at Bandit, who pawed the ground, agitated, as Chase set up the iPad.

"Bad man. Bad man. Bad man."

Chase threw her arms around him, holding him tight. I was about to ask some questions when Bandit's eyes rolled into the back of his head. His little body tensed as I sprinted forward, hoping to catch him before he fell, but I wasn't fast enough.

Bandit dropped to the ground as his body shook violently.

103

———

CHASE

Oh God, not again.

That was the only thing running through my mind as I held Bandit's face in my hands. A loud buzz sounded between my ears. Somewhere, in the distance, I could hear Sully calling out instructions, but my mind couldn't make sense of his words. Terror was taking over, and all I could do was watch my best friend, hurting.

Bandit's tongue hung out. But what I usually found endearing now filled me with fear. Were the edges of his tongue turning black? I couldn't be sure, but in the weird monochrome that the world had suddenly faded to, it seemed like the color was draining from him.

Someone appeared behind me.

It must have been Zeb. He was talking heatedly with Sully. The two were trying to figure out how to help Bandit. An alarming keening sound rose from the ground. Like a banshee wailing in the wind.

It was a few moments before I realized it was coming from me.

I rocked back and forth on my knees, focused on Bandit. "Please... please... please..."

The words came out of my mouth but failed to form a sentence. My mind was blank. Unable to make sense of anything.

Suddenly, the door to the barn slid open. Gideon had returned, a large bag of groceries in his arms. Hearing the commotion, he had come straight to the barn instead of the house. He stood there now, framed in the doorway, mouth agape, face reflecting the shock all of us were feeling. He took a step towards us when the bag in his arms EXPLODED.

White liquid spurted out in a thick stream, soaking his boots, as the remnants of a milk carton drifted slowly to the ground. Gideon looked down, confused. Everyone else froze. *What had just happened?* It was Sully who realized it first.

"GET DOWN! WE'RE UNDER FIRE!" he screamed.

Gideon dropped the groceries and dived behind a steel cabinet as Zeb wheeled into a corner. Sully just had time to fly on top of me, shielding Bandit and me with his own body, before the room erupted in gunfire.

104

CHASE

Bullets tore through the barn, riddling the walls with holes, eating everything in their path.

Gone were the strip lights that were previously suspended from the ceiling. Cables severed by the incoming shots, the bulbs smashed down, plunging the room into near darkness. The light-box containing Bandit's scans exploded as shards of glass and metal flew every which way. A particularly nasty looking spear of steel whistled past my ear, impaling the ground inches from my head like it was nothing more than a marshmallow. My eyes went wide. That was way too close for comfort. Sully pressed down on us.

"Don't move!"

More bullets sprayed into the barn, devouring everything in their wake. Beams of light shone through the bullet holes, illuminating just enough of Zeb's barn to show it now resembled a set from an apocalyptic Hollywood movie production. I doubted that the remaining pieces would still work.

The onslaught had shaken me out of my daze. Heart racing, I could feel the adrenaline pumping. Every one of my senses were on fire, ready for action. One wrong move and we could be dead. I quickly checked on Bandit; he had stopped convulsing but was still unconscious. His breathing labored. *Why would they risk killing Bandit if they wanted him so badly?*

As if they knew what I was thinking, the gun fire ceased. Silence blanketed the room. We waited, but after several more seconds of inaction, Sully rolled cautiously onto his feet. Gesturing for the rest of us to stay down, he crept over to the wall and peeked out of a bullet hole.

"What do you see?" I whispered hoarsely.

"Those same SWAT guys who destroyed my clinic. But there are more of them. Three dozen or so."

Taking advantage of the moment's calm, Gideon hurried to Zeb, while I took stock of the damage done to the barn and noticed that the holes in the walls were a lot higher up than I had first realized.

"They're not trying to kill us."

Sully snorted, "Could've fooled me."

But I pointed at the walls. "Look. That's at least several feet over any of us. They're just trying to scare us. Bandit is too valuable for them to risk anything happening to him."

Knowing this, I felt a little safer. Not much, but enough to make my own way to Sully. Staring outside, I got my first look at the killers who were after us.

They littered the scenery, an abomination of nature. Each of the men was dressed the same: black pants and a tight fitting top that showed off how lethally fit they all were. Over their sweaters, they wore some kind of rubbery-looking vest; three guesses they were going to be bulletproof. Their faces were hidden under helmets with shiny visors. That figures.

Of course, this kind of scum wouldn't want to show their faces.

Each of the men held some kind of weapon. I knew enough from Gideon's lesson to know those weren't handguns, more likely some kind of automatic rifle. They probably weren't even legal. *But that's the great thing about America, our constitutional right to bear arms, right?*

Some distance away, a helicopter waited. I blinked, not believing my eyes. How could one have landed so close without any of us hearing it? Like the men, it was black, with tinted windows that obscured the interior. It didn't look like any I had seen in movies before, which might go some way to explaining its stealthy capabilities. This must be a toy Forbes had bought for clandestine operations. The more I knew about that guy, the more I knew he was never getting on my Christmas card list.

The blades of the helicopter were spinning and showed no sign of slowing down. Guess they didn't think they'd be here long. Sully pulled back the lids on Bandit's eyes. There were beginning to focus. "He'll come to soon."

Checking that Zeb was fine, Gideon glanced over at him. "Yeah, then what?"

Sully looked at me. There was no question in my mind — we would fight to the death. But before I could reply, a voice called out from outside.

"Mr. Sullivan and friends. We're not here for you. We just want the dog, so if you would be so kind as to step aside, you will not be harmed."

I looked outside again. Standing in front of the men was the leader, the guy Sully called Military Man. His skin was tanned, and aviator glasses wrapped around his face — not the face-obscuring helmet the others wore, but hiding all the same. He spoke through the helicopter's loudspeaker, his voice blaring out into the wind. He couldn't have looked shadier if he had tried. There was no way we could trust him.

Sully must have thought the same, as he yelled out, "Get lost!"

Military Man frowned, not liking his response. His army advanced several more feet, but at a signal from him, they stopped as one. Like eerie stone statues, they didn't move a whisker. Strangely, this frightened me more than the weapons in their hands. Anyone who could stop dead like that meant business.

"The dog will die if you don't listen to me!" said Military Man. "He's having fits, yes? Increasing in frequency? That's because he needs weekly medication that he can only get from the lab."

Sully and I exchanged looks, the same question mirrored in our eyes. *If he wasn't telling the truth, how would he know about the fits? There was no way he could see into the barn.*

"The dog escaped two months ago. That's two months he hasn't had his meds. I'm not a doctor, but we have one in our lab. She raised him and knows what he needs. If he doesn't get his meds soon, the next fit could kill him."

Everything he was saying sounded plausible, but I also knew there was no way Bandit would be safe if we just handed him over.

"Gideon and I can draw their attention. Buy you enough time to escape from here," Zeb offered. Sully looked surprised. I don't think he was used to seeing this side of his father. Zeb gave him a small smile. "I haven't been here much for you, but this I can do." Gideon obviously didn't agree with his decision though, going by the frown he failed to mask.

"I appreciate the sentiment, but they must have the place surrounded," Sully said.

"Whatever you decide, we can't stay here. There's next to no cover in this barn," Gideon was quick to point out. "We need to get back inside the ranch."

Zeb pointed to the tarp that had been covering the CT scanner. "Here. We'll use that as a stretcher to carry Bandit inside." Sully and Gideon hurried in the direction he pointed while I continued checking on Bandit. He lifted his head gingerly, slowly coming to, but he was weak and groggy and confused. I stroked his nose.

"Don't move, Bandit. You had another attack, but you'll be fine in a minute. We're just getting you back inside the house."

He laid his head back down in relief. He must've understood me, even if he was unable to respond. Sully kicked at the glass and metal now covering the ground, clearing a space while Gideon laid the tarp beside Bandit.

"Get his back end. Careful now," Sully instructed as he gently slid his hands beneath Bandit's head. Gideon took hold of Bandit's flank, and together they half lifted, half slid him onto the tarp.

"Good. Now grab the ends and stretch them taut. We want to make it as flat as possible," Sully said. They pulled in unison until the tarp stretched tight.

Zeb gestured to the west side of the barn, at a door I hadn't noticed before. "Quickly, there's a smaller exit on that side. It's closer to the ranch." He went ahead, the rest of us following close behind.

"On three... ready?" Sully asked. We all nodded. *"One... two... three!"*

On three, Gideon ripped open the door and the three of us bolted outside.

105

CHASE

Bright sunlight blinded me for a moment, my eyes having gotten used to the dimness of the barn. I must have stopped as someone kicked my ankle.

"Get moving!" came Gideon's voice.

I snapped to it, sprinting into the house as fast as my legs would carry me. Sully and Gideon came next, carrying Bandit between them. Zeb took up the rear, his wheelchair slow on the dirt path. I watched, gesturing crazily. "Hurry up, Zeb!"

He was moving as fast as he could when a wheel got caught in the gap between planks. Zeb tugged on the wheels, but the chair wasn't shifting.

Sully didn't think twice. He raced out into the open, reaching Zeb in seconds. Grabbing the handlebars, he shoved *hard* until the wheel came free. Pushing Zeb, Sully was running the last few feet to safety when shots blasted through the air. Sully hesitated only a second as the surrounding flowerbeds exploded before charging into the house with Zeb.

I slammed the door shut and bolted it, then turned to find Sully sliding down the wall to the ground. His face was pale. A dark red stain blossomed on his pant leg.

"You've been shot!" I gasped.

Zeb spun around, shocked, not having realized Sully had been hit. Sully examined his own leg, grimacing through the pain.

"I'll be fine, there's an exit wound," he said. His voice was relieved.

Gideon raced into the next room. I was so shell-shocked by Sully's injury, I didn't react. All I could think was that he was running away, and I couldn't really blame him. But seconds later, Gideon returned, the two handguns tucked into his belt and a shotgun in either hand. He gave me the semi, then handed a shotgun to Zeb. Seeing the gun in my shaking hands and my less than confidence stance, Sully shook his head in protest.

"She can't use that."

"She can, and she will," came Gideon's terse response.

Gideon raced to a window and drew the curtains across it. Zeb wheeled to the remaining window and did the same. I grabbed a tea towel from the counter and pressed it against Sully's leg.

"Press tight," I said. Sully grunted but did as instructed. Sweat beaded across his brow. It was horrible to think how much pain he must be in. By now, Bandit was on his feet. He must have gotten the lay of the land as he moved over to Sully and kept licking the hand that wasn't pressed against his leg.

Zeb peeked out from his window, immediately ducking back. "Here they come."

I knocked a table over and shoved it in front of us. It wasn't much, but it would give some cover so we weren't just sitting ducks.

And suddenly the door blew inward, splintering into a thousand pieces.

Gideon and Zeb opened fire.

106

CHASE

Shots rang out, ringing my ears.

I was expecting the horde of men to swarm inside, but there was only a robotic mechanism with a metal battering ram for a face. It had smashed the door with enough force that the entire thing imploded. Now it retreated as the black-clad men advanced.

Bandit whined, terrified, as Gideon and Zeb let off more shots. Bullets rocketed towards them but ricocheted harmlessly off their vests. Even Gideon, who I knew had great aim, wasn't making much of a dent against them. Having played enough The Last of Us at a friend's house, I screamed at them from behind the table.

"Shoot their legs!" They adjusted their aim and let off another round. Suddenly, screams filled the air as the men started falling, one by one. Reacting on pure instinct, they started firing back. Zeb wheeled out of the way as Gideon dived behind the fridge, opening it so the door could give more cover. Outside, the guy in charge yelled at his men.

"Cease fire! Cease fire!" But they were trained killers and our guys had shot at them. No longer holding back, they let rip with the full force of their arsenal.

I watched as Gideon and Zeb fought back. Sully was still bleeding, his color fading with every second. And I realized something then. These men, they would all die fighting for us. For Bandit and I. Unless I did something.

And just like that, the answer came to me.

I leaned in close to Sully and whispered in his ear. "I'm so sorry. I'll make this right."

He looked at me, confused.

"What're you talking about?"

I didn't answer, instead placing a hand on Bandit's neck. "Can you run?" I asked him.

Bandit's woof was drowned out by the gunfire, but I saw his jaws moving.

"Come. Heel, Boy!"

And with that, we took off through the house as I tried to drown out Sully's voice, calling out after me.

107

CHASE

W e ran, ducking and weaving beneath the windows, keeping out of sight.

Bandit was still a little wobbly on his feet, but he was doing better than I was. I had a plan. It filled me with terror, but it was the only one I could think of that would stop the others from getting killed, and it would give Bandit the best chance of survival.

We ran to the far side of the house, but even here, there were a few men blocking our escape. I felt the world spin as my breath caught in my throat and panic started setting in. *How would we get out of here without them seeing?* Suddenly, Bandit barked. And just like the first time we met, he ran off a few feet in front, stopped, then turned back to look at me.

So, of course, I followed.

Bandit ran through the ranch, towards the west wing. Reaching a door, he jumped up, grasping the handle with his teeth, turning his head until I heard an audible click and the door opened to reveal a flight of steps leading into darkness.

"A basement! How did you know this was here?!" I asked.

Bandit woofed then pawed his nose. I got his drift immediately. *He had smelled it. Didn't I say what amazing senses they had?*

With Bandit leading the way, I followed him down the stairs. Light shone through several small egress windows. I zeroed in on one in particular where a cabinet and chairs were already stacked in front of it.

"Over here," I called to Bandit. We hurried to the window where I scrambled onto the chair, then the cabinet. I had to keep my head down so I wouldn't hit it on the ceiling. With Bandit watching from the ground, I quietly opened the window. At a gesture from me, Bandit climbed up beside me and we both crawled outside.

A wall of ground greeted us, but it was only a few feet high, and there were staggered inset foot holdings in place — I'm guessing this was in case of fire. I climbed the steps quickly and took an 180-degree review of our surroundings where, as I'd hoped, it was clear. All the action was taking place by the kitchen. They weren't paying attention to this section.

Bandit ran up beside me, and together we stole across the grass, thankful it hadn't been cut in quite some time. The helicopter sat ahead of us. Aside from the pilot, there was only one other man guarding it. I gestured for Bandit to be quiet now. We would only get one chance at this.

Hunkered down, we crept towards the guard. When I got close to him, I didn't stop to think about what I was doing, just swung the gun on the guard's head, but a branch snapped underfoot, and he spun around to face me at the last moment. Startled, I flinched and only managed to hit him lightly. It wasn't enough to knock him out as I was intending, but he lost his balance, tumbling backward where he smacked his head hard against the helicopter. He dropped to the ground, out cold with barely a sound.

Well, that works too, I thought to myself.

Creeping to the back of the helicopter, I opened the door and had the gun touching the pilot's head before he even saw me.

"Don't do anything stupid. The gun's loaded." I hoped I sounded confident because I sure as heck didn't feel it.

"Don't shoot. I'm just a hired pilot. I'm not a soldier," came his fast reply.

"So don't do anything stupid, and I won't have to." That was actually a line from a movie I saw once, and if we ever get out of this alive, remind me to thank the screenwriter.

I checked out the interior of the aircraft, but the weapons were stored on the passenger side. The pilot had nothing on him; he was unarmed. Hopefully, he was telling the truth, but I wasn't taking any chances. Bandit and I climbed on board. I kept the gun trained on him the entire time.

"What do you want?" he asked.

I gestured at the controls with the gun. "What you're paid to do. Start flying."

"Where to?" he said.

I took a deep breath before answering.

"Platinum Industries. We're going to pay your boss a visit."

108

SULLY

I t was a war zone.

Shots rang out in every direction. I was painfully aware that I was injured, that Chase had probably gone off to do something stupid, and that we would all die if I didn't think of something quick. We were fast running out of ammo and options.

Gideon popped out from cover and fired at Military Man. With unnervingly good aim, he caught the jerk on the shoulder. I took immense pleasure watching the guy stagger back, blood pouring from a wound, but that feeling was short-lived, as three men came within fifteen yards of the house.

The two fell back as I scanned the kitchen, frantic for ideas, trying to blot out the screaming in my mind that I had to go after Chase when my eyes fell on Zeb's prized moonshine rack. Suddenly, inspiration hit. I half crawled, half dragged my way to the kitchen counter, calling out to Gideon, "Gideon! The moonshine!"

Gideon glanced over, confused, "What?" he said, as he fired another shot.

I pointed. "The moonshine rack! Get me the rack!" I yelled.

Seeing me fumbling in a drawer for a lighter, Gideon suddenly got it. Keeping low, he darted for the rack, carrying it back, where he plopped it down with a thud in front of me. Quickly, Gideon found a corkscrew and started unscrewing the bottle, but I frowned.

"That'll take all day! We don't have time!" I yelled. Snatching a bottle from him, I smashed the head of the bottle against the counter. It came away, raining glass onto the ground. Some clear white moonshine spilled out, filling my nostrils with its strong alcoholic scent. I set the opened bottle onto the ground, as Gideon hurriedly copied my messy, but fast technique. Grabbing a dish towel from the cabinet handle it was slung across, I used a knife from the drawer to slash the fabric, tearing it into strips as Zeb called over from his position by the door.

"The two of you need to hurry that up! I'm almost out!"

Nodding, I stuffed the end of a fabric strip into the first bottle of moonshine. Gideon and I worked frantically, adding more strips to more bottles until a row of the bottles sat waiting. Glancing outside, Zeb saw that the men were just three yards away now. I pushed myself onto my feet and in complete agony, hopped over to flank the other side of the door.

Gideon snatched two bottles and ran to my side as I sparked up the lighter. Gideon dangled a bottle over the flame.

"Come on, come on," I said impatiently, waiting for the flame to catch on the strip of fabric as Zeb continued shooting at our attackers.

Suddenly, with a fizzle, the strip caught fire. I grabbed the bottle from Gideon and HURLED the Molotov cocktail into the crowd of fast-approaching men. The bottle hit the ground, showering the men in liquid. A wall of flame ignited, engulfing the men in fire. Their anguished screams pealed out. I didn't wait to listen.

As Gideon handed a second lit bottle to me, I threw it at another group. More flames danced along the ground, followed by more cries. By now, Gideon had fetched two more lit bottles and was passing them to me, wordlessly. I threw missile after missile until the grounds were a cauldron of fire. What men survived were running for their lives as their vests melted into their skin. Only Military Man stood firm, a black shadow in the distance, just beyond the reach of the flames.

He would not run.

109

THE MERCENARY

The Mercenary was filled with an icy fury.

His cowardly men had taken off, running blindly through the flames in a mad panic and ignoring his command. The Mercenary glowered at their retreating backs, his eyes narrowing into thin slits. Imbeciles. If any of them survived this, they'd have him to contend with, and he was far more lethal than any fire.

Through the orange wall of flame, The Mercenary could make out Sullivan watching him from the door. He'd stopped throwing Molotovs. The Mercenary assumed they must be out. The two faced each other in a two-man stand-off. Then the boy started raising his handgun at The Mercenary. The Mercenary ducked, but the shot never came. Sullivan had stopped him.

What was this?

The Mercenary had his own weapon aimed at them and wasn't concerned that they would hit him first. He'd trained with the best and hadn't missed a headshot in over a decade. He watched as Sullivan took the handgun from the boy and gestured for him to take cover before he faced The Mercenary head on. His injured leg was giving him trouble. Even from here, The Mercenary could see Sullivan favored his left leg. He smiled to himself. *This fool thought he would outshoot him? Well, he was game.*

The Mercenary pulled the trigger of his semi.

It clicked, but nothing happened. *It was out of bullets.* Sullivan must have realized this, as he suddenly looked confident, while The Mercenary himself was filled with an awful apprehension. A million possible escape notions ran through his mind, but The Mercenary was rooted to the spot.

He would not run.

It was while he was thinking this that Sullivan took aim and fired.

The shot flew from the barrel and flew into his body. Pain exploded in his chest. The Mercenary staggered back, stunned, as he touched a hand to his now bloody chest. He looked across at Sullivan with unblinking, unbelievable eyes.

Then suddenly, the ground came rushing up to meet him.

And all was silent.

110

CHASE

The helicopter lifted into the air.

As soon as we took off, Bandit darted between my legs. Poor guy. I had tried to explain to him what was about to happen, but I guess I didn't do a good job of it. He sat there, huddled against me, nose shoved under my armpit. If we weren't about to do the most insane, most dangerous, there's-no-turning-back-from-here thing we'd ever done in our lives, I'd probably find that funny. As it was, I wished I had someone's armpit to stick my own face into.

Scratch that. That didn't sound right *at all*.

As the helicopter rose, and the ranch came into full view, I felt a sinking feeling in my stomach at the devastation before me. The barn was now punctured with so many holes; it was a miracle the entire thing didn't collapse in on itself. As I had experienced more times in the last half an hour than in my whole life, another wave of fear shot through me. Sully and the others were in danger, yet here I was running away. *What if they couldn't defend themselves? What if it was all too late?*

I shook my head to clear away the doubts. Only fools play the what-if game. I'd learned that the hard way when I was just a kid, wondering what if she wasn't my real mom? What if, somewhere out there, my real mom was a wonderful woman who loved to bake cookies and was desperately searching for me, her darling baby who was snatched from her during Christmas Mass? See? Even as a kid, I had a vivid imagination.

I stuck my face to the window, craning my neck to see below. The black-clad figures were advancing, but just when it seemed all was lost, a burst of flame engulfed the men! Sully was tossing some kind of homemade fireball at the attackers and it was stopping them dead! Go, Sully!

I watched as more and more rows of flame appeared on the ground. The men started running. It was hard to make out everything from up here, but it seemed Sully had won the fight. I sagged back against my seat as the relief poured through me. They were safe. Now it was just me and Bandit.

I kept my eyes and gun trained on the pilot. Now and then, he'd peer at me through a strategically placed mirror, but I met his gaze each time. If he even stared at me a little too long, I waved the gun at him. I think he got the message.

Fields of green passed below us as we hurtled toward Forbes and the place Bandit had originally called home. I stroked Bandit continuously, blocking out the negative thoughts that flittered at the edge of my mind. The ones that devilishly whispered things like *keep stroking. After all, you may not get to do that for much longer.*

You know, unhelpful stuff like that.

They must be related to the *what-ifs.*

Bandit trembled in my arms, and I found myself making soothing sounds of comfort. "It'll be OK," I told him. "We'll find a way to heal you. Nothing will happen to you."

I was really hoping it wasn't a lie.

111

THE CEO

His head was pounding.

Forbes rubbed at his temple and swallowed some aspirin. The headaches were getting worse. Last night, he could barely sleep due to the throbbing in his head, and the stress of Alpha's escape certainly wasn't helping matters.

He looked away from the computer screen in his office. The numbers he so loved watching rise blurred into each other today. Well, it was time for a break; The Mercenary was due to check in any moment now. In anticipation of good news, Forbes pressed the intercom.

"Yes, sir?" came the voice of his assistant over the line.

"I'd like a tea," he instructed.

"I'll bring your usual, sir," she responded. Moments later, his assistant entered carrying a delicate jade teapot and a matching cup. A pair of dragons were engraved onto the jade, swimming through the air, talons engaged. The powerful fabled creatures were something Forbes had taken a liking to as a young child.

His assistant, a neat brunette who wore the same uniform of shirt and skirt every day, picked up the pot and poured. Dark oolong tea swirled into the cup. Forbes breathed in the exotic aroma, feeling the tension leave his body.

Da Hong Pao was a rock tea grown in the Wuyi Mountains of China. A heavily oxidized oolong tea, according to legend, the mother of a Ming dynasty emperor was cured of an illness by it. Only six of the bushes where the tea originated were thought to remain. Ridiculously expensive, the tea cost more than gold and could sell for up to US$1,025,000 per kilogram.

Forbes had developed a taste for it after a business visit to China. The tea — traditionally only given to honored guests — had been used as a symbol to seal the deal.

Picking up the cup, Forbes took a sip, letting the warm liquid slide down his throat. His assistant left quietly. She knew the drill, knew he didn't like anyone to hover, particularly during this daily, sacred tea time.

The telephone rang, cutting into his moment of calm. Forbes reached over and pressed the answer button. "Yes?"

The voice that came on the line wasn't one he recognized. "I'm afraid I have some bad news."

Forbes closed his eyes, already predicting what the caller would say next. "The dog escaped."

"Yes, sir."

It took every ounce of willpower not to scream at the caller. He was lucky his head was pounding so much.

"Um, sir? There's something else. Hector's dead. They killed him."

A tidal wave of fury coursed through him. Unable to restrain himself any further, Forbes hurled the cup of tea against the wall where it smashed to smithereens. His head threatened to explode from the sound, but he was beyond caring now.

He shot up to his feet, grabbed the teapot and flung that too. Next came the computer, then the phone, whose cable he ripped out of the socket. All went flying against the wall.

The door opened a crack. His assistant, hearing the commotion, was back again to check up on him. Seeing his rage, she waited. Forbes searched for more items to destroy, but there was nothing. His desk was minimally decorated as he abhorred clutter.

Suddenly deflated, he sank back into his chair. Immediately, his assistant entered, a dustpan and brush in her hands as she went to work cleaning up the mess he had made.

Within minutes, a new phone was installed, and a new computer on his desk. His people knew the drill.

"I'll bring you more tea, sir," his assistant said.

Forbes didn't reply.

112

SULLY

With that one bullet, the man who had destroyed my home and cherished memories of Emma was dead.

I had thought that killing him would magically make me feel better. Instead, the hollowness inside stubbornly refused to fill. It seemed nothing would heal me but time.

As the initial madness subsided, I froze, a cold feeling in the pit of my stomach. "Chase! She's gone!"

Zeb, who had been tending to my wound by tying a towel around it, looked up. "What do you mean, she's gone?"

I took a deep breath. "She said she was sorry for everything, but she would fix this." I shook my head, barely able to comprehend my words.

"But how could they have gone?"

From my position, I had a clear view of the grounds. I could clearly see the vehicles belonging to the ranch and my own recently purchased truck. They were all accounted for. It was as I turned to stare at Military Man's downed body that the answer came to me.

"The helicopter. She must have hijacked the helicopter!"

"She did what?!" came Gideon's shocked question as he returned to the room.

I could punch myself for my stupidity. "He said Bandit needed meds, or he'd die. Oh, God."

Gideon couldn't take it in. "She wouldn't risk her life on a foolish thought like that."

I whirled on him, heart in my throat. "She wouldn't? You've known her two days! That dog was the only friend, the only family she has. Sure, she talks tough, but Chase is just a girl who has grown up without anyone caring for her. Do you know what that does to a person? Bandit is the only one who has shown her any love, so yeah, she would do exactly something as foolish as this."

Silence fell on the room, my outburst causing us all to take stock. Surprising us all, Zeb spoke.

"Then we'll go after her."

Of all the things I had expected my father to say, that was not it. I shook my head, but when I spoke again, there was a gruffness in my voice.

"We can't."

I didn't elaborate. Zeb opened his mouth, preparing to argue, but Gideon jumped in to finish what I hadn't been able to. "Your wheelchair, Zeb. You would only slow him down."

Zeb didn't like it, but he knew the truth when it was smacking him in the face. Another unwanted truth surfaced, however. "I hate to be the bearer of bad news, but you can't go after her either, Jake. Not with your leg like that. You can barely walk."

My mouth fell open in shock. My concern for Chase and Bandit were so great, I hadn't even considered my own injury.

It was Gideon who finally came up with a solution. "He can if I go with him. Zeb, you'll be OK on your own?"

Zeb nodded, even as I started to protest. He held up his hand, stopping any further objection from me. "Gid already called the cavalry, and they're on their way. There's no more danger for me here, so the two of you can keep wasting time, or you can go after that girl and bring them home."

And with that simple truth, our minds were made up. There was just one problem.

"Well, we know they've gone to... what was that name again?" I racked my brain, trying to think through the pain. *What had she said yesterday?* I pictured Chase flying into the room, waving her computer printout. Finally, it came to me.

"Platinum Industries! That was it, that's what she said!"

My euphoria was quickly dashed as Gideon looked at me, frowning.

"But where the hell is it?"

WHILE GIDEON DID his best to help, I — under my own father's insistence — was currently in the office, hoping to find a trace of Chase's whereabouts. I knew where she had gone — the lab Bandit escaped from — but nothing about its actual whereabouts. Scratching at the day's growth on my chin, I perched onto the edge of the chair in front of the computer. Moving the mouse, the screen blinked on. Pulling up the search bar history, I moved through it quickly, hoping to find some information here.

I got more than I bargained for.

The last search was the Wiki entry for one Sebastien Forbes. I scanned through the billionaire's biography, hoping for something to leap out at me. The man was richer than God — and had an ego to match — judging by the way he bought and sold companies on a whim.

Going backward through the results, I read through Chase's previous search on Platinum Industries. There wasn't much information on the business, just a building listed out in Rochester, which, if memory serves, was East of Niagara Falls. I could find nothing on what "industry" the company dabbled in.

So far, so nothing.

It wasn't until I got to Chase's email — and thank God she was still logged on — that everything fell into place.

And Chase was rushing into the Lion's den armed with only a sick dog and a gun.

TIME WAS OF THE ESSENCE.

Every second we wasted, the likelihood of saving both Chase and Bandit grew sparser. Those men hadn't hesitated to shoot. Once Bandit set foot on their premises, Chase's usefulness — and her life — were as good as gone. I tried not to let that terrifying thought debilitate me.

It was Gideon who came up with the idea.

The kid seemed to have gotten over his initial hatred of me, and for that, I was grateful. The last thing I needed was an angry teenager riding shotgun. We set up Zeb in the living room so he could see down the hill. If there was any sign of trouble, more unwanted visitors, he would notice them right away. I left him with food, water, and the phone within arm's reach.

Despite our history, I hesitated to leave. So much was left unsaid between us. So many years of resentment. As if he knew what I was thinking, Zeb laid a rough hand on my arm and uttered one simple word. "Go."

I nodded gruffly and turned to Gideon. "You have everything?"

He handed me a rucksack. Inside were the remnants of any ammo we could salvage. The shotguns were out completely, so there was no point in taking them. All we had was Gideon's trusty revolver, a swiss army knife Zeb once found at an antique fair, and a few thousand bucks that Zeb had stashed in the safe for a rainy day. In the cold light of day, our arsenal didn't look like much, and we both knew it.

"Maybe we'll get lucky and find a wine cellar there," Gideon grinned suddenly. "I brought a lighter, just in case."

My opinion of the kid rose up a notch after that. Despite the life or death situation we had on our hands, here was this kid quipping like he was from a Marvel movie. Gideon moved over to Zeb. "The Sheriff said they'd be here in less than ten minutes. It's been eight already."

Zeb nodded. "I'll be fine. I was just thinking life had been a little dull lately. This excitement came in the nick of time."

With a nod, I turned away from my father, forcing down the lump that suddenly appeared in my throat. I was surprised to feel tears pricking at the corners of my eyes. Not since Emma was diagnosed with terminal cancer had I felt this level of fear. Not only for Chase and Bandit, but as I realized now, for my father too.

"Don't die," I said to him.

Zeb snorted. "It'll take more than bullets to dispose of me."

Despite the gravity of the situation, a small smile broke out over my face as Gideon slid himself under my arm, taking the weight off of my injured leg.

Together, we hurried from the ranch.

MOMENTS LATER, however, we hadn't gone anywhere.

We stood, staring in shock at the sight before us. My truck, while it had been some time since it had come off the line, was now riddled with bullets. Oil spilled out from a gaping hole in the gas tank. I looked at Gideon. "What about the 4x4?"

Gideon was already moving, running to the side of the ranch.

"Well, damn," were the only words he uttered when he saw Zeb's car. All four wheels were punctured, and the hood popped up. He went to look under it when I stopped him. "Don't bother. They made sure we wouldn't be going anywhere."

"Well, what're we going to do? It's not like there are any taxis around here." Gideon said. I thought for a moment, lost, then looked towards the stables. Following my gaze, Gideon shook his head incredulously.

"Are you crazy? Those horses haven't been ridden in years! How do you know they still work?"

I stared at him evenly. "Horses don't lose the ability to run unless they're injured, and that bunch has had years to recover. Come on, help me there."

Moments later, we were each perched on top of a horse. I stroked Derby, my mount. She trotted friskily, seemingly excited by being taken out. I studied Gideon's ride critically; his horse was less eager for the exercise ahead but was otherwise fine. The short journey wouldn't do any damage to the two of them. Having ridden since I was a kid, I felt entirely comfortable up there, though I could see the same couldn't be said of Gideon, whose horse pranced nervously, feeling the boy's tension.

"He can feel your uncertainty. You need to take control."

"Well, it's a little hard to fake that when the thing weighs nine thousand pounds more than me," Gideon complained, tugging on the reins.

"Yeah, but *he* doesn't know that," I replied. "Use your legs."

With that, I kicked at my horse with my good leg and took off, galloping across the field, a trail of dust in my wake. Determined not to be left behind, Gideon yelled, "Giddy up," like he'd seen in the Westerns. His horse, Spirit, shot after me, leaving Gideon holding onto the reins for dear life.

AFTER WE'D LEFT the ranch, we rode some eight miles over several fields of corn, with Gideon calling out directions as we went. I was relieved that the area around here was flat, and from my position on the horse, I could see for miles. Several times, I glanced behind me to see if Gideon was keeping up, and he was, though his riding skills could do with some finesse. If these weren't such desperate times, and if my leg didn't have a bullet-sized hole in it, I would be enjoying this ride. I'd forgotten how great it could feel to be on top of a horse, wind whipping against a man's face.

Within some ten or so miles, the fields turned into a gravel drive. "Take the turn here," Gideon instructed.

I swung my horse around as a runway appeared before us. Situated at the end of it was an airplane with the slogan "I love a good crop dusting" sprayed onto its side. The plane was rusty and small and made me — not the greatest flyer in the first place — feel sick to my stomach.

"That's the plane? That rust bucket? Does it even fly?" I asked, an incredulous look on my face. Gideon seemed amused by my question. Probably payback for me dismissing the boy's horse-riding fear earlier, but I was saved from answering, as a bald man covered in grease stains approached, eyes bulging out at the sight of us.

"Someone shooting a Western I don't know about?" the man asked. I climbed awkwardly off Derby, my leg hampering progress, and landed on my feet much harder than I expected. Pain shot up my leg, leaving me momentarily breathless.

"We suffered some transportation hiccups," came my only explanation.

The man studied my wound where the blood was already seeping through the makeshift bandage. "What happened to your leg?" he asked.

I replied instantly. "Caught it on a sharp edge."

The man waited for more of an explanation, but I stayed silent until he finally took the hint and turned to Gideon, nodding at him. "Gideon. How's Zeb?"

Without missing a beat, Gideon responded. "Fine, Frank. He's staying home today. We have need of your services, however."

"Yeah, you want I should spray the lawn again? I keep telling you to chop some of those trees down, they're drowning the property in shadow." Frank said.

I stepped forward. "The lawn's fine. We need a ride."

Frank looked more interested in the conversation suddenly. He must've seen dollar signs in his near future. "Where to?"

I showed him a map where I'd circled our destination. Frank covered his eyes, shielding them from the sun, and looked down at his marker. "Rochester. That's some two, three hours flight from here."

I gestured at the plane. "Can it make it?"

Frank's face twisted into annoyance that he didn't bother to hide. "Of course it can. But I can't do it for a day or two. Mrs. Deloris wants me to spray her cornfields. Been having a problem with pests lately, so I told her—"

I held up my hand, interrupting. "It has to be now."

Frank stared at me bug-eyed. "But, Mrs. Deloris..." He never finished saying what Mrs. Deloris wanted, however, as I took a wad of bills out of my bag.

"Well... that's some nice change you got there, not enough for me to drop a regular client, however," said Frank, hedging his bets.

"I'll throw in some horses. Thoroughbreds," I replied.

Frank looked over my shoulders, at Derby and Spirit, and frowned. "That gray one doesn't look like there's much life in her."

"She's not for sale, but you can have your pick from Zeb's stables," I countered.

Frank studied me with a calculating eye. "And why would Zeb agree to that?"

I stared right on back. "Because he's my dad." Behind him, Gideon nodded confirmation.

A smile broke out over Frank's face. "Well, why don't you hop on in and we'll be on our way."

With that, Frank hurried to the plane, seemingly having forgotten Mrs. Deloris altogether.

113

CHASE

Just as I was beginning to doubt whether our pilot was actually taking me to Platinum Industries and not the ends of the Earth (it felt like we'd been in the helicopter some three weeks already), a building appeared, nestled amongst the green.

It wasn't a tall building, just two stories high, but what it lacked in height it made up for in length. The place must've been two city blocks wide. A modern (read: ugly) structure, blending steel and brick. The first thing I noticed was all those high-up windows we'd seen in satellite view earlier.

Can you say suspicious?

The pilot nudged the joystick (at least that's what it looked like), and the aircraft responded by tilting forward as we started our descent, but I tapped him on the shoulder with the gun.

"No. Don't land here," I said. I pointed to a field close by where a cluster of overgrown trees and bushes lived. "There."

He didn't respond, but shifted the controls accordingly. A few moments later, we landed neatly behind the trees, where I was hoping the helicopter would be shielded from sight. The pilot killed the engine. The sudden silence hung heavy in the air.

"We're here. What now?" he asked, challenging me with a glare. I got the distinct feeling he didn't like being bossed around by a kid. Well, tough.

"Get out, slowly," I said. I paid attention to his body language, bracing myself should he suddenly decide to do something stupid like run away. He climbed out, and I followed behind, close enough to do damage but not close enough for him to take me down if he chose to go that route. Then I walked around to face him.

"Good. Now get down on your knees."

He glared at me but sank to his knees. I looked over the top of his head, back into the helicopter, hoping to find something I could tie him up with, but other than a few headsets whose cords weren't even a foot long, there were just some seat belts, which if I had a knife on me, I could do something with, but of course, I didn't, which left me with only one option. Despite not liking the pilot, I gave him an apologetic smile as I swung the gun at the side of his head. This time, my technique was better. The gun connected with his head. He fell onto his side, out for the count.

"Is he really unconscious?" I asked. Bandit tilted his head at him, sniffed, then woofed. *Great.* I slid my hands into his pockets and came up with a leather wallet, a phone, and some keys. Tossing the phone on the ground, I stamped on it, HARD, until I felt the metal give way and heard the distinct *snap* of breakage. I've seen the movies, I know how cell phones are basically personal tracking devices and I wasn't about to take any further risks. Besides, look where my VPN trick had gotten us.

Flipping open the wallet, I saw a photograph of our pilot with his wife and two kids. They were smiling into the camera, looking like any other happy American family.

Wonder if his wife knew what line of work her husband was really into?

I scanned through the bills, some three hundred or so, resisting the urge to take them, and finally came upon a strange-looking swipe card.

It was strange in that other the name "Joe Kramer," who I guessed was our pilot, there was only a barcode beneath and a discreet logo on the top right corner.

I stared at that logo, recognizing it from my Google research.

Platinum Industries.

Bulls-eye.

BANDIT and I were outside Platinum Industries.

We were crouched beside a van in the busy parking lot. I kept my eyes peeled for security cameras, but unless they were camouflaged, I didn't see any.

From our position, I could see the main entrance, where a set of double doors separated us from the secrets within. Occasionally, a person passed by behind the doors, but it was relatively quiet — which was bad news for us. If we walked straight in through the entrance, they'd spot us immediately. We had to find another way in.

As I was contemplating our options, a car pulled into the parking lot. Some kind of weirdo pop music in another language played from the radio. As the engine died, an Asian lady got out. She wore white shoes and the overalls of a cleaner. Locking her car, she started walking towards the building, but instead of the main entrance, she steered left, taking a discrete path set into the manicured lawn that I had missed before.

Feeling a tingle all over, I whispered to Bandit, "Follow her."

We kept low as we followed the cleaner to the side of the building where she came upon a door. This one wasn't glass, and it wasn't see-through, but it was locked. The cleaner took out a card and swiped it on the door. I heard a few beeps before the door swung open and she stepped inside as the door swung automatically closed behind her.

Bandit looked at me and whined. He knew what was coming next.

We hurried to the door, then, before I could second guess myself, I took out Pilot Kramer's card and swiped it.

The door swung open, revealing a long, dark corridor ahead. Swallowing my fear, I looked down at Bandit.

"Stay behind me at all times."

And with that simple instruction, I stepped inside.

* * *

We'd been swallowed up by the corridor.

Or at least that's how it seemed.

Light fell in slants through those weird upper windows, leaving the bottom half of the corridor covered with shadows. I was filled with a sense of foreboding so great; it took all my willpower not to turn and run back outside. Hysteria was bubbling under the surface, and I had to bite down on my lip to keep from giving in to it.

I looked to Bandit for strength and saw that he was sticking to those shadows, blending in like a ninja. I was surprised at how good he was at this, then remembered that this was the dog who had broken out of here not that long ago. He had experience with this place.

The cleaner was nowhere in sight, apparently in a hurry to do her job. And who could blame her? This place was so damn jolly. We followed the corridor, past closed doors and offices — all blessedly empty — and down to a main hall. Discrete signs hung from the ceiling announcing boring departments like HR, Admin, and Research.

Nowhere was there a sign with "Unethical Secret Lab That Tortures Dogs." Hitting a dead end, I frowned.

What to do? It wasn't like we could just ask someone?

The answer that came was unexpected.

Bandit, who had been standing by my side while I studied the signs, suddenly shook with fear. His mouth opened and his tongue fell out, panting loudly before whining, a high-pitched, pathetic sound that stabbed at my heart.

Then, shockingly, he peed himself.

Right there in the middle of the hall. I grabbed him and we ducked behind a giant cheese plant, seemingly growing out of the marble ground.

"What is it?" I asked quietly, holding up the iPad. Bandit tapped quickly.

"I smell him. The Bad Man."

I hated myself for what I was going to do next, but I knew there was no other choice. "Take me to him, Bandit. It's the only way."

He whined again, circling in agitation. I stroked him, trying desperately to calm him down. It took several counts before the panting died down, but the trembling continued.

On shaky legs, Bandit started leading me towards the department labeled "Research."

WE HEADED DOWN MORE CORRIDORS, all gloomily lit like they couldn't afford the electricity here, which, very clearly, they could. I wouldn't be surprised if Forbes owned all the electricity in America. Judging by what I had read of him, he seemed the type.

We went past a door. Closed, with only a small window containing glass that couldn't have been bigger than a ten-inch square to see through. They were all like this, the doors. All hiding the experiments that must be being conducted on the other side. I would never have thought I'd be thankful for this, but as it was, it made being stealthy a whole lot easier.

We were approaching a doorway up ahead now. Beyond this, the corridor divided into two. I couldn't see past it, but I trusted Bandit, and right now he was my eyes. But as we crossed through the doorway, disaster struck.

An alarm SCREAMED overhead.

Too late, I looked up to discover we had just walked under a security camera. As we hadn't seen any before now, I had gotten complacent, and it was our downfall. I guess Forbes only put cameras in the ultra-secret areas.

We froze.

As I tried frantically to figure out an escape plan, a guard rounded the corner at a sprint.

"You there, STOP!" he called out.

Of course we didn't. We spun around and started sprinting back the way we had come, only to find one — make that — TWO guards flanking us from behind. Bandit barked loudly in warning. I was pretty sure he was telling them to back up, but either the guards didn't speak dog or they just weren't scared.

They advanced in unison. The guard who had spoken marched up to me.

"Hands up," he commanded.

Bandit bared his teeth at the guy, growling fiercely in response. I'd never seen him look so feral before. I totally bought his act, if that's what it was. The guard didn't consider either of us a risk, however, as he went to grab my shoulder. And that's when I didn't even think. Just reacted.

I jabbed him hard in the Adam's Apple. He choked, staggering back at his suddenly crushed windpipe. Feeling a sense of power, I spun around to face the remaining two guards. One kept his focus on Bandit, but the other's attention was on me. Roaring, I charged forward, meaning to destabilize him. My foot lashed out, and I kicked behind his knee.

Nothing happened.

He didn't fall like those YouTube videos had shown. Undaunted, I went for him again, but he was ready for me. At the exact moment my foot should have sent him tumbling, he bent his knee and caught my foot in it, vice-like. I was left hopping on one foot, trying frantically to disengage, but he wasn't letting go. He laughed at me.

"Someone's been learning self-defense, I see," he taunted.

I've gotta say, that was the last thing I expected or wanted him to say. Not wanting to show he had the upper hand, my mouth ran off as per usual. "Amazing what you learn on YouTube," I snapped back.

In hindsight, that probably wasn't a smart move.

He smiled menacingly, then punched me in the stomach. It happened so fast I wasn't prepared for it. Pain EXPLODED in my stomach, bringing tears to my eyes. I doubled over. I was fully focused on breathing, so my mind didn't make the connection of what was about to happen. In a very deliberate move, he round-housed kicked the back of my knee and that was it.

I went tumbling to the ground.

Bandit LAUNCHED himself at the guy but was tasered with a baton-like stick. Electricity sparked and hummed as Bandit hit the ground, unconscious. I screamed, crawling towards him. Before I could touch him, the other two guards hauled me onto my feet.

The guard who had struck me laughed again.

"Now that's how you do a Krav Maga takedown, girlie."

114

CHASE

The next few minutes passed by in a blur.

Holding my throbbing stomach, I could only watch helplessly as Bandit was laid onto a stretcher and carried beside us through the building. In the back of my mind, I knew I should be paying attention to our surroundings, that I should be memorizing the route so we knew how to break out, but the only thing running through my mind were the words, *please don't die, please don't die...*

The guards ushered me to the second floor and into an office. At least, it was adorned like one, with a giant glass desk and black couches arranged artfully around a coffee table. It was furnished like an office, but one entire wall was made out of glass, and this glass wall looked down over the entire building. From where I was standing, I could see just how gigantic this place was.

Hundreds of white lab-coated minions toiled away at stations, working on scientific equipment I had never seen before. In one direction, I caught a glimpse of a room that was dark, with what looked like thousands of cages in it. I couldn't see what was inside them from here, but I had an inkling. Everywhere, as far as the eye could see, experiments were being conducted. The scope of the operation took my breath away and caused my heart to thump wildly in my chest.

How would we have any chance of beating this? The man owned an entire universe!

And as that thought entered my mind, the man in question strolled in.

"So you're the girl who's been giving me so much trouble?"

I looked over at the sharply dressed man standing in front of me. He wore an immaculate suit of steel gray. Everything about it was precise, including the purple handkerchief folded into the upper left pocket. He had a commanding presence and walked like he owned the world, which probably wasn't too far from the truth. I was surprised to see he was bald and younger than I imagined him to be. He didn't look much older than Sully. But then I noticed how his cheeks were too smooth, how his forehead was empty of lines. Forbes wasn't averse to cosmetic enhancements, it seemed. His voice was soft, cloyingly gentle, and there was something about it that set my teeth on edge. I glared at him defiantly.

"And you're the jerk who put a tumor in Bandit's brain."

I wasn't sure what I was hoping for by antagonizing him like that, but it wasn't the small arch of his brow.

"Bandit? How quaint." He managed to make it sound like the worse insult in the world. "But, cute as your display of bravado is, it's time for you to leave. Alpha — my apologies — *Bandit*, is back where he belongs, in the lab that created him."

While Forbes was talking (*don't the bad guys always have to spout some spiel?*), I had been reaching my right hand behind my back. It was a slow movement. I was counting on the fact that neither Forbes nor his men would notice, their attention, as it was, drawn to Forbes and his rant.

Feeling my fingers tighten around the base of the gun I had taken from the ranch, I swung my hand in front of me now. Before any of them could move, Forbes found himself staring down the barrel of a Beretta 92. His men froze, not expecting this. Forbes's eyebrow twitched, the only outward sign of his disapproval. He looked at his men like they were something he had just scraped from the bottom of his designer shoes.

"Why does she have a gun?" he asked, his voice unnervingly soft.

The guard who had taken me down flinched, embarrassed... but there was something else in his expression... fear. "We didn't think to search her. She's just a girl after all..."

"A girl who has traveled across the country and broken into my building," Forbes replied, still softly, but now with a chill in his voice.

From the corner of my eye, I saw one guy try a flanking move. "Freeze, or your boss is going to eat a bullet."

He stopped immediately. My eyes darted from guard to guard, hyper aware of their positions. My finger was tensed on the trigger. I was prepared to use it and they knew it. What they didn't know, was how utterly terrified I was, and I was desperate not to show it. Willing my hand not to shake, I started backing towards the door.

"Let go of Bandit," I ordered.

The two men holding him in place released their grip on him. Bandit started moving over to me. Hope was beginning to rise up in me. *We can do this! I can get him safe!* Bandit was three steps from me and freedom when he dropped to the ground, shaking violently, head knocking against the floor.

It happened way faster than his other fits and was ten times as fierce. Losing it completely, I screamed, "Help him!"

The men didn't move, waiting for Forbes to respond. Forbes merely smiled at me before pressing a button on the intercom. "Please ask Dr. Robins to step in with Alpha's meds."

I ran towards Bandit, heedless of my own safety. Gathering his head in my lap the way Sully had shown me, I tried to stop him from hurting himself, all as I kept the gun trained on Forbes.

After what seemed an eternity, but was, in fact, only seconds, a woman rushed in holding a syringe. She wore one of the same white lab coats I had seen others wearing, but unlike the emotionless robots working for Forbes, there was panic all over her face.

"Alpha?!" she cried. Seeing him convulsing, her eyes flared open in alarm, and she darted towards us with the needle.

"Stop Elora." Forbes's command was chilling in its authority.

The woman, Elora, looked over at him, confused. "But he needs his meds. I've never seen a convulsion as strong as this. He was never supposed to survive this long without them. He might have only seconds before irreparable damage is done to his brain," she cried.

Forbes looked down at me. "Well, that depends on our young friend here. Kick over the gun and Dr. Robins will save Alpha. Or you can watch your friend die."

Every nerve in my body was screaming at me to do as he said, but I knew this was the only bargaining chip I had. I had to try one last time. "After everything you've done to get him back, you wouldn't risk his life any more than I would," I said.

Forbes just looked at me, a half-smile playing on his lips as if this whole thing were just a slight inconvenience. "What I need from him I can get whether he is alive or not. Can you say the same?"

I'd called his bluff, but he'd called mine, and as we all know, I'm a terrible gambler. Laying the gun down, I slid it over to him. One of his guards picked up the gun as Forbes nodded to Dr. Robins. She ran over and injected the contents of the syringe into Bandit's flank. I found myself counting in my head as I watched his small body convulse. *One, two, three, four...* by the time I reached five, the fit had stopped. Bandit's chest was rising and falling at its regular speed. Another two seconds and he opened his eyes. This time, there wasn't any of the confusion that had preceded his previous episodes.

Dr. Robins let out a relieved breath. I was surprised that she actually seemed to care for Bandit. It made her decision to work for Forbes even more baffling. I shot her a grateful look, regardless. She had just saved my best friend, after all.

"Thanks."

She took me in, blinking behind her glasses. I guess she hadn't really noticed me until now. Since her arrival, her attention was only on Bandit. Now, she saw the way we cuddled, how Bandit pressed up against me. Her eyes softened.

"Alpha, you made a friend," she said.

Bandit *woofed* in response. "One bark for yes, two for no," I explained. At this, her eyes teared up. So she wasn't a monster. Maybe Forbes wasn't either? Could I try appealing to his nice side? I looked back at him.

"I'm sorry I pointed the gun at you, but I was desperate. Bandit's not just my friend, he's family. He's all I've got. Can we figure out a way for you to get what you want while keeping him safe? Then we'll get out of your hair and you'll never have to see us again. We just want to live a normal life."

My voice cracked with emotion. I was on the verge of tears, but for the first time, I didn't care who saw it. I meant every word I said. Bandit's tongue snaked over and licked me across the face.

Forbes watched us emotionlessly.

"That was a lovely speech, and I truly feel your pain, but unfortunately, the answer is no. I will never let Alpha go."

115

SULLY

While I didn't think much of Frank's integrity, I had to hand it to the man; the guy could fly a plane. We landed an hour later in a field near Platinum Industries, a good hour ahead of his initial estimation. We were still a good football field away, but I figured this was far enough that we shouldn't be spotted unless someone was looking out for us, in which case, nowhere would be far enough.

As Gideon helped me off the plane, Frank tipped an invisible cap. "Good doing business with you."

"Give me a day or two. We'll be by to pick up Derby and Spirit, and we'll arrange the rest of your payment then," I said.

Frank nodded. "Fine. The Missus will take care of your horses until you return." And with that, he took off.

Gideon pulled a face at me. "Shouldn't we have kept him here for our escape?"

"We could have asked, though he didn't seem all that trustworthy, and I wasn't inclined to explain what it is we're doing here."

Gideon shielded his eyes and stared across to the building on the horizon. "It's still a ways away. We'd better get started."

Ordinarily, I would have run the distance in a minute flat, no sweat. As it was, all we could manage was a slow, limping shuffle. I've always hated having to depend on someone else, particularly someone who had had an issue with me, so I was grateful for Gideon's matter-of-fact help and attitude.

Especially as on the inside, I felt like I was falling apart all over again.

116

SULLY

Some ten minutes later, having crossed the fields, as I was approaching Platinum Industries, a glint of sunlight bouncing off of metal caught my eye. I stopped, staring into a dense crop of trees.

There was something behind them.

Going on nothing but gut instinct, I motioned to Gideon and reeled at our discovery when we got there. A jet-black, military-looking helicopter sat before me, a man on the ground next to it. He was wearing the dark uniform of the men who had attacked the ranch. I would bet the house that he was the pilot, and that this was the helicopter Chase had hijacked for a ride. *Clever girl*, I thought, smiling grimly. The man on the ground moaned, trying to sit up. Seeing us (and clearly not recognizing us), he touched the back of his head gingerly.

I took the moment to take stock of the situation. "Is Chase OK? The girl?"

The pilot blinked at me, confused, as his thoughts tried to collect themselves. "That goddamn brat. She hit me on the head."

"Yes. But is she OK?" I had no sympathy for him. Suddenly, the pilot must have realized who he was talking to, as his face turned spiteful. "You killed our men."

I glared down at the man, heaping as much heat into the look as I could muster. "You shouldn't have attacked us first. We won't go down without a fight."

The pilot smiled unpleasantly. "If she's still alive, she won't be for much longer. She's as good as dead."

I wasn't sure if it was the pilot's smug face or his words that did it. All I knew was that a deep rage was building inside. Seemingly of its own accord, my hand formed into a tight fist that swung at the pilot's face, full throttle. On connection, the pilot's head snapped back, smashing into the side of the helicopter with such force that his cheek would be fractured for sure. He fell back, unconscious again. I glowered down at him.

"No one talks trash about my family. No one."

117

CHASE

It was all starting to sink in. Forbes had no intention of letting Bandit go. Ever. And I had just walked him straight into his arms.
I could kill myself.
How stupid could I be that I trusted they would help? Didn't I know better by now? How many more times did the universe need to show me that PEOPLE WERE BAD?

I looked into Bandit's intelligent blue eyes, the world crashing down around me.

"Take them away," Forbes instructed his men. And just like that, he was done with us. His men advanced towards us, all eyes focused on Bandit. I was merely an irritation, a fly to be swatted away. I didn't even merit any thought from these men. Forbes turned away, about to leave, when the rage, pain, and confusion burst out from me.

"But why?!" I yelled after him. Forbes and his men stopped in their tracks. It seemed they had already forgotten about me. Forbes turned to look at me, confusion etched across his features.

"Why what?" he said.

"Why are you doing this? You can't take Bandit away from me without even telling me what this is all for?!" I cried. "That's not fair!" I knew my last comment sounded like a whiney kid, but that's all I had right now. I needed to know and wasn't thinking about my language. Forbes considered my question, then waved at his men to stop. He walked back to me.

"I've spent a lot of money and effort on Alpha. I can't just give him to you," he said, sounding almost reasonable. I wanted to kill him.

"How much money? If you just give us time, Bandit and I can make your money back, I know we can." I was willing to try anything. Pride was a long, distant memory.

Forbes hesitated as if reconsidering. "I've not seen this level of devotion before. It's really quite touching. Unfortunately, my life is worth more than this dog's."

I frowned, not understanding. "What do you mean, your life?"

Forbes opened his mouth to reply, but suddenly his eyes glazed over. One minute, they shone cold and calculating, the next they softened. He blinked in confusion, staring around the room as if he was seeing us for the first time.

"Do you know where my mom is? She's supposed to take me to school, but I haven't seen her? She told me to wait right here."

Forbes' voice came out like a child. The change was so startling, so sudden, that I found the whole thing super eerie. Then the moment was over. He shook his head as if mentally clearing away a fog.

"I've not seen this level of devotion before. It's really quite touching. Unfortunately, my life is worth more than this dog's," he said. Again.

"You said that already. Literally word for word. It's pretty disgusting that you're going to mock me when you've won already. I mean, who does that?" My mouth shot off before I could stop it. I steeled myself, waiting for the slap I could feel was coming. Except it never came. Forbes looked to Dr. Robins.

"It happened again?" he asked her, quietly — and something else I didn't expect to hear in his voice — resigned. She nodded. He turned back to me then.

"Well, yes. I do believe you deserve an explanation. You see, I am sick. A particularly nasty strain of Alzheimer's runs in my family. You know the disease? It is a progressive mental deterioration that can occur in middle or old age, due to generalized degeneration of the brain, and it is the most common cause of premature senility," Forbes said. He gestured out of the wrap-around window at the experiments below. "Everything I have built, all the billions I have earned, it is because of my mind. I clawed my way up from the bottom, from humble beginnings, but at the moment of my greatest success, I was informed of my condition. Since then, I have dedicated my enormous wealth to finding a cure. Everything you see here, this lab? It was created solely for this purpose."

As he spoke, pieces started falling into place. "And Bandit? How is he involved with this?" I asked. Although I was terrified by what the answer could be, I had to know.

"Alpha is the key. Within his brain lies the potential for a cure... except he ran away."

Dr. Robins had been listening quietly, but now stepped forward. "There are many, many cases throughout history of people having suffered head trauma who suddenly became incredibly gifted. Such was the case of one Texan man, who hit his head while diving, and subsequently lost thirty percent of his hearing. However, he also became an astonishing piano player overnight — when he had never even touched one before or learned to read music. It seems the head trauma caused his brain to reorganize itself in such a way that it could now do — at a mastery level — what it had never been able to do before."

She gestured with her hands while speaking. This was something she believed in absolutely. Seemingly not picking up any of my wariness, she continued.

"Another case study involved a high-school dropout brutally beaten by muggers that left him in a coma. When he awoke, he became the only known person in the world able to draw complex geometric patterns called fractals, which is, in layman terms, a never-ending pattern."

"I don't understand how any of this helps your situation." I directed my question at Forbes.

"Current treatment for Alzheimer's involves drugs that may help with both cognitive and behavioral symptoms. Researchers have spent years looking for new treatments to alter the course of the disease, but *what if it is the brain itself that should be altered?*" he said, eyes feverish with conviction.

You see how *What-If* questions are bad, bad, bad?

I stared at them both. "So this tumor Bandit has you gave it to him to simulate brain trauma?" Even as the words left my mouth, I understood the insanity of them.

"Yes," said Forbes. "We believe that once the brain suffers from trauma — that we control — it will reorganize itself and ultimately defeat Alzheimer's." His voice was triumphant, as if just stating this point meant it was a success. I realized in that moment that the man was completely and utterly insane.

"But that's crazy! You have no way of knowing this will work, and in the meantime, you're torturing all those poor animals!" I said, unable to stop myself.

Forbes's eyes narrowed into slits at the word "crazy." Thinking about it, I must've touched a nerve.

"I know a simpleton like you won't understand, however, what I do, I do for the good of all mankind."

I ignored the slur he directed at me, desperately hoping that if I could keep him talking, I would be buying Bandit time for a miracle.

"Well, why can't you wait a while, make sure that this will actually work?" I pleaded.

Forbes said, "I have begun to experience the latter effects that my mother experienced, prior to her losing her mind completely. We can't delay this any longer. We must operate now."

"*Operate*?" The word stuck in my throat, along with the fear. Forbes was already losing interest in me, keen to move things along, so I turned to the Doc for help. For someone who was on the brink of a medical breakthrough, she didn't look too happy.

"Mr. Forbes, I can't guarantee this will work, and operating on Alpha will most likely cause him to lose his intelligence. At worst, it could kill him," she warned, wringing her hands.

Forbes sighed. "That is something I will have to live with." At that, his men started towards us again. Bandit bared his teeth, growling fiercely, ears flattened to his head. He pressed urgently at my side, determined to protect me. But it wasn't me they were after. There were only three feet away from us now and approaching fast.

Suddenly, Bandit FLEW at one of the guards, savagely sinking his teeth into his arm. The guard screamed, flinging his arm about, trying to loosen Bandit's jaws from his flesh. Taking his cue, I launched myself at another guard, plunging my fingers into his eyes. He shrieked, staggering back. The tiniest flicker of hope rose in me. Maybe, just maybe, we could get out of this alive...

But then the guards trained tranquilizer guns at Bandit and fired. Darts stabbed into his flank. He yelped and dropped to the ground. Shaking his head to clear the fast rising fog, he tried to get up onto his paws, but whatever was in the darts was already taking effect. Within seconds, Bandit blacked out. I watched, helpless, as he was carried out, struggling against the guards who now held me captive.

Forbes frowned at me. "Despite what you may think, I am not a complete monster. I will allow you to watch Alpha's last moments." He left, and I found myself escorted into a viewing room overlooking an operating theater.

The guards shoved me against the window, and then I was suddenly alone. I ran to the door and tugged at the handle, but it was locked. I pounded my fists on the door, banging and screaming until my hands were throbbing with pain, but it was no use.

The hopelessness of it all overwhelmed me.

I sank to the floor, hugging my knees to my chest, and cried as I waited for them to kill my best friend.

118

SULLY

We finally arrived at the infamous building.

Seeing the glass-fronted entrance, I knew we couldn't just walk in, not without consequences, so we performed a quick reconnaissance around the building. It was Gideon who had spotted the staff entrance, which, hiding behind a dumpster, we were scrutinizing right then. An old man in blue overalls, a janitor, was leaning against the wall, smoking a cigarette. He must have been pushing seventy; what hair he had left was thin and gray, and skin sagged from his arms. Judging by the butt, which was almost done, he'd already been out there awhile. I knew if we were going to act, it would have to be fast.

"When he goes back in, we need to follow quickly behind. As soon as he turns, we move, got it?" I said. "We've got to be quiet. We can't give him cause for concern."

Gideon nodded, unfazed, which I suddenly realized was a curious thing. How was this kid so cool about breaking into this place? I was about to question the boy on it when the janitor threw the cigarette to the ground, stamping it out.

"As soon as he turns... now!" Gideon darted forward lightly on his feet, sticking close to the janitor, but I had momentarily forgotten about my injury, which slowed me down something awful. Thankfully, the janitor moved slowly with age. We were standing behind him when the janitor swiped his card, but when he looked up from swiping the device, my reflection appeared on the glass in the door. Startled, the janitor stopped short of fully stepping inside, the door held open in his hands. He turned to me, wary of seeing someone so close to him. I didn't think, but reacted instinctively. Leaning forward, I held the door open for the janitor, smiling in a friendly manner.

"Here, let me get that for you."

The janitor was pleasantly surprised. He smiled at us both, showing large gaps in his crooked, yellow teeth. "Not many youngsters with manners nowadays. Thank you, young man." He shuffled inside, not the least bit concerned he had allowed two strangers into the building. Even I was taken aback at how easy it was to break in. *Just goes to show, a little courtesy goes a long way in this world,* I thought to myself.

We followed the janitor inside, watching as the old man disappeared obliviously down a long corridor. I took in my immediate surroundings. No cameras. That was good. No guards either. Either Forbes wasn't concerned with break-ins or he wasn't hiding anything. Knowing the answer to that, I almost snorted out loud. Astonished by the arrogance of a man who would conduct unethical experiments out in the relative open like this, I limped along the corridor, keeping my eyes peeled for anything that might help.

We hadn't gone far when Gideon whispered to me. "Sully, quick, over here." I turned to find him standing in front of a closed door. A discreet sign on it said "changing room." Gideon opened the door cautiously. Once he was sure the way was clear, we snuck inside.

We were in a large changing room. A row of lockers took up an entire wall. Shower cubicles stood side by side, their glass still fogged from recent use. Beyond those, I could see spotless restrooms. These janitors really earned their keep. Gideon sprinted up to the lockers, tugging on several of their handles, but all were locked.

"What're you doing?" I asked.

Gideon slipped a hand into his pocket, retrieving a lock pick set. "I'm going to help us go incognito," came Gideon's reply. I watched in fascination as Gideon slipped the tools into a padlock, twisting them confidently until the lock suddenly dropped open — like my mouth.

"How the hell did you do that?" I demanded to know.

Gideon opened the locker. Inside, there was a pile of magazines, some pairs of socks, and a few granola bars. Nothing of interest really, so he moved to the next.

"Before I lived with Zeb, I, er... learned a few things."

"I see," came my response. I stared at the boy anew, seeing him with different eyes. Feeling my stare, Gideon sighed.

"Oh, come on, like Chase hasn't done worse living on the streets? Not everyone had a home like yours, OK? You should count yourself lucky." Gideon continued breaking open the lockers, so he didn't see my face reflect the shame I now felt. I had never considered myself lucky, not with the way my relationship with Zeb had deteriorated after mom's death, but seeing how Chase was living, what she had to put up with, and now hearing from Gideon a similar tale, I vowed never to feel sorry for myself again. From here on, I would be grateful for all I received.

"Bingo," Gideon said suddenly, having found what he was looking for — two white lab coats complete with ID's clipped onto their pockets. He handed the larger of the coats to me. My eyes fell on the ID now pinned to my lapel.

"So we'll be fine as long as no one looks down at the thing and sees I'm not Chinese," I said. I flashed the card at Gideon, who glanced down at the picture of an Asian man in his forties, a Dr. Lim.

"If anyone gets close enough to read them, we'll be toast anyway, so I wouldn't worry about that," was Gideon's only reply.

I had to hand it to him. The kid had a way with words.

We left the changing room and headed down the same path as the janitor. Rooms veered off now and then. I caught glimpses of expensive lab gear, steel tables, and high-tech computers. Everywhere I looked, my surroundings reeked of money. Forbes had spent a small fortune on this place. *He must mean business*, I thought to myself. The thought wasn't very reassuring.

We hurried through twisting corridors, going more on instinct than anything else. Every now and then, we would pass a PI employee. It took every ounce of willpower in those moments not to dart away. Forcing myself to continue as if it were my right to be here, I carried on, Gideon by my side. The staff seemed oblivious, focused on their own jobs at hand.

After some fruitless searching, I was beginning to panic when a sign caught my eye. It wasn't much, but the single word caused a chill to race down my spine. I pointed at the sign.

GENESIS.

119

SULLY

Gideon looked at me funny. "What about it?"

"Genesis. You know what that means? The origin of something. In the Bible, it literally means "In the beginning.""

Apparently not feeling any of the apprehension that had suddenly flooded my body, Gideon marched towards the door. "Then what are we waiting for?" And with that, he opened it and stepped through.

I was so unprepared for the move, I froze. When I finally recovered, I limped after him. "Of all the stupid…"

… And stepped into a giant room.

There were cages, seemingly hundreds of them. Inside each was a young dog. The dogs consisted of all breeds and sizes, nothing connecting them except their species. A tablet was attached to each cage with information on it, but I couldn't see what it said from here. I moved closer to one cage.

The dog inside, a German Shepherd, was spinning round and round without stopping. An outsider might think this was a trick or cute behavior, but I knew better. It was a sign that the dog was suffering from a compulsive disorder, most probably caused by living in such a confined space. This was a condition most often seen in shelter animals who had been stuck there for some time and was essentially a sign of severe distress. A wave of compassion swept over me. I clicked at the dog, making soothing sounds.

"Hey, Fella, you OK in there? It's going to be alright." The dog didn't react at all. It was as if he couldn't hear me. He just continued spinning, round and round and round. It hurt to watch him, so I turned my focus across to the next cage only to find that the Terrier in there wasn't faring much better. He sat in the corner, staring blankly at the wall. It was his way of tuning out his fears. If he couldn't see the scary things, then they weren't really happening. The Terrier was behaving like a terrified young child. Pain stabbed in my chest. *These poor animals, what were they doing to them?*

Across from me, Gideon was staring into the cage of a Bull Mastiff who had licked his paw so much, it had caused an open wound. "What's wrong with him? Why is he doing that?" he asked me.

But I couldn't speak for fear I would explode with rage. I looked at the information on the tablet of the German Shepherd's cage. There was a video file. I hit play.

Video footage flashed up on the tablet. The German Shepherd was chained up in a room. There was no give to his chain, so he couldn't move and was forced to stare at a screen. In front of the screen were five large numbers. As I watched, the number 4 appeared on the screen. The German Shepherd was panting, showing clear agitation. He whined, but couldn't get free. Suddenly, a jolt of electricity shot up from the chain to hit the dog. He yelped and pressed a paw onto a button, button two. The screen made an "error" sound, and a jolt of electricity zapped into the dog again. As the dog stood quaking in terror, the screen reset and the number one appeared. The dog got it wrong again and was punished for his mistake. I stopped the video, unable to watch anymore, but to my horror, I noted the clip was thirty minutes long.

Why were they torturing these poor dogs?

Closing the video, I was automatically taken to a live scan of the dog's brain, but there was something wrong with it. There was a mass, a tumor growing on it.

Just like Bandit.

"No..." Trying to curb the rising horror in me, I sprinted to the next cage and examined the tablet for the Terrier. There was more footage of the torture experiments that I had to click through before I located the live scan. It was the same, though the Terrier's tumor was in a different position. Gideon watched me, confused and concerned.

"What is it?" he asked again.

I went past several more cages, each time finding the same results. Finally, unable to take any more, I stopped at the sixth cage, shock radiating from me. "The dogs have all been given tumors in their brains."

"But why?" Gideon asked, utterly baffled.

Seeing an office across the way, my eyes hardened.

"I don't know, but we're going to find out."

120

ELORA

The mask on her face was irritating her today.

Elora looked down at Alpha's brain, which now lay open before her, like a work of biological art. She checked his vitals, liking what she could see. He was doing better than expected, which was something she had learned to expect of him.

Although she had voiced her concerns to Forbes, as usual, he hadn't been willing to listen. The thought that Alpha would lose his intelligence pained her more than she was able to admit. He was always her favorite, and after seeing him with the girl, she felt awful that she was going to sever their relationship with one cut of the scalpel, however, as always, Forbes was watching, and if she didn't do this, didn't do what he commanded, her family would be in danger. He had made that threat clear enough.

She glanced over at the girl, Chase, secured in the viewing room. She was sobbing and banging her fists on the glass. Elora wished she could reassure her, let her know that if nothing else, once the tumor was removed, Alpha could have a chance at living a long and normal life, even if he lost the personality that she had obviously fallen in love with.

She refocused on the brain now. Missing all those weeks of meds had taken a huge toll. Had they waited any longer to remove the tumor, Alpha's next seizure would most likely have killed him. Despite how she might feel about the situation by bringing him home, Chase had saved him. Elora worked swiftly, nimble fingers skimming across the brain.

With one final cut, the tumor was free, and with it, Elora was finally able to pinpoint the exact placement and position of the tumor that had caused

Alpha's intelligence. This was the missing key they had been searching for. Elora shot a silent prayer of thanks to Alpha. If she were able to use this knowledge to help Forbes, maybe they would all be free of him.

Elora placed the tumor into a steel tray and moved to seal Alpha's brain when Forbes's voice came over the loudspeaker.

"There's no time for that."

She stopped, shocked. *What did he mean?* Her unspoken question was answered as Forbes entered the operating theater.

"Stop! His head is open. You can't just come in like that. Do you know how many germs you could infect him with right now?" She leaned over Alpha, hoping to protect him, but Forbes merely took hold of her arm.

"You are going to put his tumor into my brain," he said, eyes gleaming with madness. "This tumor, pressing in such a way on the dog's brain, caused his intelligence. Don't you understand, Elora? *It caused his brain to reorganize itself.* This is what you've been working for!"

Elora gaped at him in astonishment. "But there's no guarantee it will work. There are too many unknowns..."

Forbes glared at her suddenly. Elora could feel his infamous rage simmering at the edges. "Is that a refusal, Elora? Are you saying no?"

She snapped her mouth shut, not trusting herself to speak. She just stood there, scared, shaking her head mutely.

"Good," he said simply, calmly, as his voice dropped back into its normal, soft tone. As he marched her from the room, Elora only had time to glance at Alpha, head lying open on the operating table, before he was out of sight.

121

SULLY

The office was neat and tidy — and unlocked, which surprised me. Then again, I imagined everyone who worked here already knew what experiments they were conducting and mostly likely condoned them, so there was no need for secrecy.

A small plaque on the neat desk said this was the office of one Dr. Elora Robins. Aside from a computer, there were a few medical journals stacked neatly on the desk and a pot of identical pens. Dr. Robins wasn't one for collecting, it seemed. Only dogs.

I pulled open a filing cabinet. Inside were hundreds of suspension files, labeled with a mixture of letters and numbers. Some sort of reference system. I ground the back of my teeth, overwhelmed by feeling. The dogs meant nothing to these people. They didn't even deserve a name. I opened a file and took out the paperwork. There was a picture on the front page, a Golden Retriever. Her stats were listed beside the headshot: weight, height, size — the usual. There was nothing of interest until the next page, which detailed her tumor extensively.

While I read, Gideon turned on the computer. He launched the mailbox, sifting through emails, looking for anything that might point them to Bandit and Chase's whereabouts. There were plenty to go through, and I could tell Gideon was beginning to feel the fruitlessness of our search.

Eye's skimming across the file, I suddenly found the answer I had been looking for.

"They're not trying to make super intelligent dogs! Forbes has Alzheimer's, and he's throwing all his billions into finding a cure!"

Gideon looked at him, not understanding. "But Bandit's intelligence, how does that factor into anything?"

"It doesn't. It's a miracle, a once-in-a-million side effect," I answered.

Thoughts raced through Gideon's mind, one in particular, something he had read. "But, I'm sure I've read that there are other animals that are a better genetic match to us than dogs."

"Yeah. Monkeys and pigs are typically closer to humans, but they require more care, and are harder to source, unlike stray dogs they could literally snatch off the streets." I waved the file at Gideon. "There were plans to roll the experiments out to other animals, but Forbes started deteriorating much faster than expected."

Still searching the mailbox, one suddenly caught Gideon's eye. He clicked it open. "Oh no," was all he could manage to say.

Dropping the file, I leaned over the boy's shoulder. The message on the screen was short.

Alpha is back in the building. Extraction will commence. Report to the Nursery.

I GLANCED down at my watch. "Dammit! This email was sent an hour ago! We've got to find this Nursery."

Gideon moved the mouse offscreen, bringing up a 3D image of the entire complex with every section helpfully labeled. He pointed to the one marked "Nursery." I blinked, not sure what just happened.

"How did you do that?"

Gideon grinned.

"The map is her desktop wallpaper."

122

CHASE

I couldn't believe it!

After everything he had gone through to get Bandit back, all the people and buildings he had destroyed, he was going to leave him there to die?! I felt a fury so strong; I thought I would explode!

Throughout the whole operation, I was helpless to do anything. I just sat and watched as she cut into his head. I will never forget the sound of that blade sawing into his skull for as long as I live. It felt like it was hammering into my own head.

At first, when Forbes explained what this was about, all I could think was how devastating it would be if Bandit lost his intelligence — if he couldn't talk to me anymore, or answer any pop quizzes. Then I realized I loved him. He was my family, and if that meant he was "just" a normal dog, he would be *my* normal dog.

The screens monitoring Bandit's vitals continued to beep, but I could see a clear decline in the figures. I didn't know what they meant exactly, but I was pretty sure a drop was BAD news. I had no idea how I would save him, I just knew I had to be in there with him. I couldn't stay locked in here apart from him any longer.

There was nothing in the room with me except for a desk and a couple of chairs. I grabbed hold of a chair now, and with all my might, I SWUNG it at the glass. The chair hit the window with a gigantic THUD, and the glass cracked but held. I backed up another step and took another swing, this one harder than the first. The glass started spider webbing as cracks began forming everywhere. Pumped by my progress, I hit the window.

Bang, bang, bang...

And suddenly, glass erupted everywhere. As Bandit was some ways away, no shards landed on him. I jumped through the hole I had created and scrambled to his side, fully expecting guards to stop me at any moment.

Seeing his head open like that, being able to see his actual brain, was *terrifying*. And the *smell*. I can't even begin to describe it. But even more frightening was the thought he might die. I looked for a phone, hoping to call someone for help, even though in the back of my mind, I knew it was hopeless. Who would I call? A newspaper? How would that help him? But in that moment of utter panic, fear, and desperation, I couldn't get my head to think straight. I needn't have bothered, however. There was no phone.

No help was coming.

He was doomed.

123

CHASE

I wasn't in the theater long when I heard some kind of a scuffle outside. I figured I had only seconds before the guards busted in and finished us off. I took hold of Bandit's paw, defiant to the end. So be it. If this was it, at least we'd be together.

Briefly, I wondered how Sully and the others were doing. Now that the end was near, I felt enormous guilt at the pain I had caused him. First, he lost everything he had of his wife and the clinic. Now his father's home was also destroyed, and who knew if Sully's gunshot was fatal or not. I wasn't normally a praying girl, but even I was willing to give it a go now.

Please God, please save Sully. Don't let him die too.

The noise from outside intensified. Something smashed. I stood in front of Bandit and planted my feet, determined to buy him more time.

Suddenly, the door crashed open, and in ran Sully and Gideon! I was so stunned I didn't move, just stood there, gaping stupidly at them. Was this a mirage? Was this wishful thinking?

Or was I just dead already?

Sully took in the scene before him and uttered one word, "Jesus."

It was that one word, spoken in typical Sully fashion, that cut through my shock. I ran over to him and threw my arms around him.

"You're here?! You're really here?!" I sobbed into his chest, not the least bit ashamed of how happy I was to see him. I felt his arms tighten securely around me. "You've got to help him Sully! Forbes made the doc leave before she could close him up!"

Sully quickly detangled himself from me. "Block that door," he instructed Gideon. "They'll probably try to come through once they know we're here. I need you to buy me as much time as possible."

Gideon nodded and grabbed an unused metal stand in the corner. I'd seen those on TV before, they were usually used to hang IV's or blood packs. Gideon slid the pole under the door handle, wedging it in place. Then he ran for some steel cabinets, pushing them towards the hole in the window I had created. Realizing what he was doing, I sprang forward to help.

Sully rolled up his sleeves and rinsed his hands in a sink. Tossing us some facemasks, he told us to put them on, then took position by Bandit. Even though half of his face was obscured by the mask, I could see the tension there. Remembering what he had said back at the ranch, about how brain surgery wasn't exactly his thing, I knew he must be doubting himself. So I spoke.

"Sully, you've got this. She's already taken the tumor. You just need to close him up. You've got this."

He glanced over at me, grateful for the encouragement.

Then, with Gideon and I watching out for Forbes's men, Sully operated.

124

ELORA

lora watched as Forbes laid the tray containing the tumor next to the operating table. This room was smaller than the one Alpha was in and more private. There was no window, no viewing room overlooking this. She noticed that everything was already in place for the operation. Forbes must have planned this all along to have it ready, which made her feel like an idiot. She should have known.

Forbes laid down on the table and waited impatiently for Elora to start. Elora glanced at the two armed guards who had marched her in and were now standing before her.

"I can't work with them here like this. It's too much pressure, not to mention, unsanitary."

Forbes scrutinized her face as if to assess her honesty. He must've decided she was telling the truth, however, as he nodded for the guards to leave. Elora moved to his side and began fastening the arm restraints around him when he stopped her.

"What are you doing?" he demanded.

"Securing your arms. It's standard procedure," she replied. His eyes narrowed suspiciously. Elora stopped, but went on to explain patiently. "In the event, the drugs wear off, which can happen one in five hundred thousand cases, any movement from you could have devastating consequences while I am operating. You know it's a delicate procedure. We can't afford to have anything go wrong."

She stood there, waiting for his answer. Finally, after what seemed like hours, he nodded. Elora reached over and secured the restraints around him. Then she picked up a syringe, depressing the needle until the air was squeezed out. As she approached, Forbes frowned. "Aren't you going to anesthetize me?"

"This will do the job," Elora explained, already sinking the needle into his arm. Forbes's brow creased with worry. "That isn't procedure. What is it?" he asked, trying unsuccessfully to mask his fast rising fear.

Elora smiled. "Ketamine. We usually use it on the dogs. I thought this would be apt."

Forbes' eyes flared open with alarm as he realized she wasn't abiding by protocol. He made a move to shout for help, but Elora was one step ahead of him. Covering his mouth with her hand, she spoke.

"I'm sorry, Mr. Forbes. This brings me no joy, but you have clearly lost your mind, and I can't stand idly by as you destroy any more lives."

Feeling a calm she didn't know she possessed, Elora watched the clock and started counting the strokes of the needle. When she reached nine, Forbes was out for the count.

125

CHASE

I watched Sully like a hawk.

His hands moved quickly and surely. They didn't show the doubt he had felt just minutes ago when I had to cheer him on, but he was having obvious trouble standing. He kept stopping, kept shifting his weight. The whole thing was mesmerizing, yet terrifying. He moved the flaps of Bandit's skull, repositioning them, ready to close him up when there came a pounding on the door.

Gideon shot towards it, gun held in his hands, aimed in case the people outside somehow got through. He looked to Sully for guidance, but Sully kept his focus on Bandit. I grabbed a metal clamp in my hands and went to wait beside Gideon. I figured I could get at least one good hit with the thing before I went down. I was hoping I would get someone's soft head with it. I was getting really good at that.

"Let me in, I need to save Alpha," came a frantic female voice from the other side of the door. Sully was so surprised, he stopped working.

"Who's there?" he called out.

"Dr. Robins," came the reply. "Forbes forced me away before I could finish closing him up, but he needs my help or he'll die!" she called. Sully and I looked at each other. Her voice sounded desperate enough, she *seemed* sincere, but what if it was a trick? In the end, I went with what my gut was telling me.

"It's true," I said. "She wanted to help him, but Forbes wouldn't let her."

Sully listened to my words and made a snap decision. "Open the door carefully. If anyone other than the doc comes in, Gideon, you shoot."

"Got it," Gideon said grimly. I took hold of the metal stand and pulled it away. Grabbing the door handle, I cranked it open a tiny notch. The doc's fearful face filled the gap.

"Hurry, let me in before the guards know what I've done," she said. I opened the door, steeling myself for something to go wrong. Beside me, I saw Gideon's whole body tense as he also prepared to fight, but the Doc darted inside and quickly shoved the door back closed. I jammed the rod beneath the handle again, locking us in.

The doc took in Sully's actions with horror. "Get away from him, you don't know what you're doing!" she cried.

Sully's voice was calm but firm. Professional. "I'm a vet, but I could do with your help. This is more than I'm used to." Reassured by his manner, the Doc rushed over, pulled on a pair of gloves and proceeded to help. Safe for now, I made my way back to Gideon's side. He looked at me, frowning as if he were struggling to find the right words to say to me.

"You think Bandit will be OK?" he finally asked.

I could feel the tears welling in my eyes again and fought to keep them down.

"He has to be."

126

SULLY

I couldn't begin to describe the relief I had felt when the good doctor stormed inside. Craniology wasn't my area of specialty, and though I didn't want Chase to know, the entire time I was working on Bandit, my heart wasn't just in my throat but dancing a fandango.

With Dr. Robins on the scene, I was able to take a backseat and assist with the closing. It was a marvel really, the way her fingers stitched so quickly yet neatly. The needle darted in, then out, with seemingly no effort at all. From the moment she took over, things went so fast, it wasn't long before we were done. The second she made the final cut of the stitches, Chase hustled over, fists gripped tightly by her side.

"Is he OK?" She had obviously been waiting this whole time just to ask.

Robins answered. "We won't know until he wakes up."

I had already rinsed my hands and was now wiping them on my jeans. "We need to get out of here pronto before Forbes comes back."

"I bought you some time, but he'll be discovered soon," Dr. Robins said. Off my questioning look, she explained, "I shot him up with ketamine. He'll be down for a while, though the guards might check up on him."

Remembering how the SWAT team had first arrived at my clinic with tranquilizers armed with that very drug, I felt a faint sense of justice. *Good, let's see how he likes it.* Chase shot a grateful look at her.

"Thank you," she said simply, but with meaning.

The Doctor flushed with something like shame, hanging her head low. "I'm so sorry about all this. Alpha was always special. I should've stopped Forbes sooner, but he'd made threats to my family..."

Seeing how distressed she was, I reached out and squeezed her shoulder, offering what little comfort I could. "When push came to shove, you helped. That's what counts."

She straightened up, resolved. "In the basement, there is a network of corridors. They're only ever used by my team. You can sneak out that way," she said.

Chase frowned. "Won't the guards know about them too?"

Robins shook her head. "No. My team are the only ones. We... use them to sneak in dogs for testing." As soon as she said the words, her eyes filled with tears. I was torn. On one hand, I wanted to alleviate her guilt. On the other, well, she had been torturing those poor animals for years. As if she knew what I was thinking, Robins straightened up suddenly. Probably realizing her feelings weren't important when there was so much more at stake.

"You'll show us the way out?" Gideon asked.

Robins looked at us. "Yes, but I need you to do something for me first."

I looked at her, suddenly apprehensive. "What?"

"I need you to help me free all the other dogs."

127

CHASE

My first instinct was to run.

Bandit was stable, and I knew the guards and Forbes would soon be hunting us down. It was on the tip of my tongue to say no when an image of thousands of Bandits trapped in cages flashed across my mind. I looked down at his unconscious face, at the ugly vivid scar on his head, which only minutes ago had been opened because of the experiments they conduct here. And I knew, without a doubt, they had to be saved.

Every last one of them.

"Sully... you take care of Bandit. I'll go with her and help the dogs." If Sully were surprised by my decision, he didn't show it. Instead, a look of pride came over his face. Then Gideon spoke.

"Me too. They're not keeping another one in those cages." He sounded real mad. The Doc smiled at us, grateful, then looked at Sully.

"Follow me, hurry," she said, already darting away. Sully grabbed hold of the gurney Bandit lay on, steering it after her. Gideon and I took up the rear. We hurried through winding corridors as the Doc led us to the west side of the building. I knew it was west, as the sun was beginning to set, casting a golden hue all around us. I kept an eye out for those cameras that had caught me out before, but the Doc knew her way and avoided anything that would alert them to our presence. Finally, we arrived outside a door marked "Genesis." Sully and Gideon looked grim.

"We're here," Sully said. It was clear by the expressions on their faces that they must have already been through here on the way to save Bandit.

The Doc came to the same conclusion, I think as she didn't bother to ask how he knew. She opened the door, then propped it open with a chair.

"Any sign of them, you shout and we'll go," she said.

Sully nodded. "Just be quick." To my and Sully's surprise, Gideon handed him his gun. Sully didn't make a big deal of it, but he knew this was a big move on Gideon's part; it wasn't that long ago that Sully was Public Enemy Number One. Gideon must've known that Sully hadn't forgotten his early treatment of him, as his cheeks were starting to flush with embarrassment.

In typical Sully fashion, however, he simply stated, "Thanks."

I snuck Bandit one last look, then followed Gideon into Genesis... and was immediately, painfully, struck by how many trapped dogs there were. I saw the tablets attached to each cage, but there wasn't time for me to explore. Gideon and the Doc were already sprinting to the far end of the room. I guess we were starting there first.

I reached a cage where a tiny Pomeranian was trembling. It ran to the back of the cage, obviously terrified of human contact. I had to grit my teeth to stop the wave of rage building in me. The cage had a simple bolt on it. No lock. I drew the bolt back and flung open the door. The dog whimpered, staring at me with fear-filled eyes, trying desperately to back herself further into the cage.

"It's OK pup, I'm here to save you," I said. It still wouldn't leave, not used to being offered freedom. I reached my hand in, meaning to take her by the scruff of her neck, but something amazing happened. As my hand came near her nose, she sniffed and suddenly, she licked my hand as the fear vanished. At first, I couldn't understand it, but then I realized what it was - she could smell Bandit on it! She could smell a happy dog and knew I couldn't be bad! I called out to her again.

"Come, heel." Hearing the encouragement in my voice, the dog ran out of the cage. Triumphant, I started on the next cage where a giant Doberman sat. This time when I went to persuade him to leave, I had assistance. The Pomeranian barked short, clipped barks at him. He pricked up his ears, listening, then came out without any urging from me. I was amazed but had no time to marvel at this display of communication, having already made my way to the next cage. From the corner of my eye, I could see Gideon and the Doc frantically doing the same.

"It's taking too long," Sully called suddenly from the hallway. I could hear the frustration in his voice. It must have been awful, him standing there watching us but not able to help. Abruptly, he wheeled the gurney into the room — but only just past the door, in case he needed to leave quickly — and limped into the room with us. By now there were some thirty dogs running loose as Sully started flinging open the cages. It was total chaos.

I was breathless, my lungs taking a pounding from the franticness of it all. My fingers were starting to feel sore where they were being rubbed by the metal of the locks, but I soldiered on — thinking of the dogs, yes, but if I were honest, mostly of Bandit. The longer we took in here, the more danger he was in. We had to do this quickly so we could get out of there.

We worked fast as a team. In no time at all, I glanced up to see we already had most of the cages opened. There were dogs EVERYWHERE, but noticeably, after their initial communication, they were now silent. It was like they knew we needed to be quiet. I wondered if any of these dogs were as intelligent as Bandit, but then I remembered they couldn't be, otherwise, Forbes would have cut their heads open too.

That one thought gave me a second wind. I worked faster.

As we were reaching the finish line, alarms suddenly peeled overhead. The Doc called out, panicked.

"They found Forbes! Hurry!" she yelled.

Instinctively, I started running for Bandit while the others continued freeing the last of the dogs. Grabbing the gurney, I started steering him back into the hallway, but suddenly guards appeared, blocking my path!

"SULLY!" I screamed.

128

CHASE

The guards rushed towards me. All eight of them.

The others looked over and froze across the room from me.

Sully had the gun, but he couldn't take out all of them at once, and stupidly, I was so panicked, I couldn't think straight. There was nothing I could do to stop them.

Then something miraculous happened.

The freed dogs bounded over, forming a barrier between the guards, Bandit, and me. Baring their teeth, the dogs — who were previously so scared, they wouldn't leave their cages — now turned into vicious animals. Snarling, saliva dripped from their jaws as they growled at the guards warningly. The guards stopped dead in their tracks. Though each had a weapon, there were far too many dogs for them to take on. They were at a complete standstill.

Not so, us. "Chase, this way!" The good doc called. I spun the gurney around and sprinted for her. She was standing by another door, Gideon beside her. Sully rushed up to greet me and took over the handling of the gurney. Together we ran for the door the Doc now held open. Seeing us escaping, however, one of the guards took aim at us.

SSSSSSsssnap.

A bullet shot towards me, whistling through the air, narrowly missing the top of my head to impale itself into the wall which exploded behind me. Before I had time to react, the dogs flew at the guards. Round after round of panicked shots were fired. A dog whined, then fell down, blood pouring from a gaping wound, but was immediately replaced by another dog, now savagely attacking the guard who had killed his fellow canine. It was carnage. I wanted to help, but there was nothing much I could do.

But then I saw the gas canisters. They were dotted around the room, used for some horrible purpose or another.

I pointed at them. Sully caught my gesture. It didn't take him any time to know what I was thinking. He nodded.

"Gideon," he called out. "Take over Bandit!"

Gideon shot him a questioning look but ran to replace Sully all the same. We split up to gather as many of the canisters as we could. Sully pointed to a point in the center of the room and dumped his canisters there. I followed suit as Sully threw the lab coat he was still wearing on top of the mound.

By now, the dogs had torn their way through several of the guards. Only two were still standing, still fighting, but it was a losing battle. The second from last guard was suddenly overcome by dogs, disappearing beneath them. Seeing this, the last guard turned abruptly and ran away. I took a grim comfort in this small victory.

"Dogs!" I called out, "Well done. This way!" I urged them through the door where Gideon and the Doc were waiting on the other side.

Sully found a bottle of isopropyl alcohol, which he poured onto the material. I remembered from chem class that isopropyl alcohol was flammable and could be used as an accelerant.

Holding the bottle, he ran through the room, making his way to the fire alarm, where he smashed the safety glass and pulled the lever. I was momentarily confused by his actions. Why was he warning them what we were about to do? As if he heard my unasked question, he explained. "They don't all deserve to die..."

As alarms shrieked overhead, I saw them now. Hundreds of people. Lab coats and cleaners and office staff, all racing for safety.

Sully removed a lighter from his pocket and spoke fast.

"When I light this thing, we may have only seconds before it blows," he said. "The three of you need to leave now to get a head start. I'll catch up with you."

I shook my head at him. "But Sully, you can't."

"I'm the fastest runner, Chase. Go, I'll be fine," he said. His expression was soft, but I could see resignation there too. Somewhere in the back of his mind, he knew the odds weren't good.

"No, you're not. Not with that leg." I pointed to his gunshot wound, which he had obviously forgotten about. He blinked at me, uncomprehending. "You can barely walk without help, much less run."

Sully opened his mouth, but couldn't come up with a logical argument. I spoke quickly before he could stop me. "You have to stay alive. Bandit still needs your help. And Zeb needs Gideon. And the dogs need the doc. I'm the only one who's dispensable." Even as I said the words, a gnawing hole opened up in my stomach when I realized the truth of them.

But Sully took me by the shoulders suddenly. "No, you're not Chase! Don't you ever say that again!" As if to prove how much he meant it, he crushed me to his chest. I could feel another sob rise up in my throat and had to pull myself away before I gave in to it completely.

"Guys… we need to move!" came Gideon's panicked voice. He looked equally unhappy by this new plan, but there wasn't any other choice. It made no sense for us all to risk our lives. Reluctantly, Sully handed me the lighter.

"You don't stop for anyone, understand? Once you light this, you run like the wind," Sully commanded. "I mean it, Chase. I've lost enough family this year, I'm not losing another one."

I nodded, not trusting myself to speak. Sully dropped a kiss on the top of my head and tore himself away. I swore there were tears in his eyes.

Then, despite the fact that my heart felt like it was being broken in two, I watched as they all left me behind.

129

SULLY

The Doc took us down into a basement where rusty pipes lined a maze of corridors.

The place was dark and dingy, lit only by aged lamps spaced at three-foot intervals. All the money Forbes spent didn't reach down here it seemed. We hurried after the Doc, running for what seemed like days but was probably only seconds. I couldn't stop seeing Chase in my head.

We shouldn't have left her!

The thought screamed in my mind until my ears pounded. There was a crushing tightness in my chest that had been there since the second I'd had to force myself to leave Chase. She'd looked so lost, so small, standing there.

It was a ridiculous plan. Why did they ever think it would work?! A few times, I turned to go back, but as if sensing my turmoil, Gideon had grabbed me by the arm and dragged me away.

I lost all sense of time. I shuffled after the others with only the pain in my leg keeping me grounded. After what seemed an eternity in the darkness, I saw a dim opening of light up ahead. We burst through into the fresh air with renewed rigor where I was struck by how dark it had gotten. The tip of the sun was barely visible on the horizon, the encroaching night approaching fast.

We had made it.

But no time to celebrate. We ran with the dogs to a safe distance away and waited.

Why hadn't Chase set the thing off yet?

What if something had gone wrong?

What if that last guard had brought more thugs back with him? What if Chase was lying dead and I would never see her again...

It felt like I was in the midst of a heart attack. Gideon paced as the Doc checked on Bandit, who still hadn't woken up. She pressed a finger high on the inner side of his thigh and felt for a pulse, nodding, happy with whatever she found. I felt a small fraction of my tension lessen. At least that was something. I was just wondering what the hold up was, when an almighty explosion went off, shaking the very ground we were standing on.

That was it. Chase had set the canisters off. A bright orange plume of fire sprang up into the night, illuminating the area for what seemed like miles. Windows shattered, destroyed by the soaring heat. I stared into the dark tunnel, straining my eyes, willing with every ounce of my being for Chase to appear.

"Come on, come on..." I mumbled.

After the longest time, something moved in the tunnel. A dark shape. It was so slight, I thought my eyes were deceiving me. But then a figure appeared, lurching forward, coughing up lungfuls of smoke. The face was blackened with soot, but I recognized her anyway. Sprinting forward, ignoring the pain that shot up my leg, I crossed the distance between us and hugged Chase tight.

"What, you wait for a bus to get here?" I said.

She coughed again in answer but grinned at me. "Just keeping you on your toes."

"What now?" Gideon asked. The Doc hesitated, thinking fast.

"We can't take my car, they'll have it surrounded by now," she said.

"Is there anything else around here?" Chase asked, gulping in large mouthfuls of air. The Doc nodded and pointed.

"There's a gas station and a drive-in burger place around two blocks away. There should be cars you can acquire."

I wasn't the only one who noticed the way she said "you". We turned to her, concerned.

"You're not coming with us?" I asked.

She shook her head, eyes shining with regret. "I need to see these dogs are safe. They can't go with you, so I'll have to lead them away."

"But where will you go?" Chase asked.

"I have friends, organizations I can contact who will help. I'll see to it that these dogs are rounded up and adopted into good families. It's the least I owe them." She stopped, her voice cracking. "Thank you for your help. I hope... I hope Bandit is OK."

Chase and I both took in her use of the name Bandit. With a small smile, she spun on her heel and ran the opposite way to them, calling out to the dogs. Some of them followed her, but others cocked their heads at us as if confused.

Chase pointed after her.

"Go with her. She'll keep you safe," she told them.

I didn't know if they really understood her or not, but they ran after her.

And then, for the third time that day, we found ourselves running for our lives.

130

CHASE

My lungs felt like they were drowning in smoke, but otherwise, I felt pretty great. Platinum Industries was burning to the ground, the dogs were free, and we were on our way home. Not a bad day's work.

The gas station and drive-in Dr. Robins mentioned loomed up ahead. I spotted it easily since there wasn't much around these parts. Sully was weary, sure that the drive-in and gas station served PI staff more than anyone else. We had to be careful. It wouldn't do to get caught now when we were so close to freedom.

Approaching the parking lot, Sully scanned the area until his eyes fell upon an old — and to my eyes — barely standing Range Rover. It was empty. Its owner probably inside, feasting on a happy meal.

"That one," Sully pointed at the car.

I frowned at his choice. "You don't think maybe something more new and comfortable?"

But Sully shook his head. "Too conspicuous. Besides, the owner is likely to care less about a rust bucket like this."

Gideon and I nodded and followed him there. Sully tried the doors — locked. He started searching the ground for a rock to smash the window with when Gideon stopped him.

"I've still got my lock picks," he said. I was confused, not understanding this exchange, but Sully stepped back to let him do his thing. He slipped the tools inside the lock, twisting it in a series of directions, feeling for the right moment. The lock sprung open, much to my astonishment.

"You have got to teach me that," I said.

Sully knew, as the adult, he really should dissuade them from such criminal activities, but the usefulness of the skill couldn't be denied. And truth be known, he wanted to learn how to do it too. Only for emergencies, though, of course.

Gideon opened the door and climbed inside. A jacket had been dumped carelessly on the backseat and there were a few cans of coke in the footwell, but the car was otherwise empty. In the trunk, Gideon came up with a toolbox, blankets, and the usual car maintenance items one found in a vehicle. But what he couldn't find were the keys.

I folded a blanket and laid it over the backseat. Sully carefully lifted Bandit from the gurney and set him on top of the blanket.

"So, you know how to hot-wire the thing too?" Sully asked hopefully. Gideon shook his head, however.

"I just broke into vehicles, I never stole them," came his reply. My ears pricked up at this bit of information, a fact Sully seemed to notice with some discomfort. I was searching the car for something, anything that would help, when opening the glove compartment, I suddenly grinned.

"Jackpot." I sat back, a cell phone in my hand.

"What're you going to do, call AAA for help? Couldn't we just use Bandit's iPad for that?" said Gideon.

I was already busy pressing buttons.

"No stupid, it's out of charge."

"So what're you doing with the phone?" he asked again.

"I'm going to show you how this is done," I replied, confident. Moments later, I held up the phone.

"Look, here's a video showing you exactly how to hot-wire an old car."

Sully looked down at the phone's screen and goddamn if I wasn't right. YouTube.

What an invention.

131

CHASE

We drove through the night.

I kept watch by Bandit's side, hoping he would wake, but Sully had said it was a big operation and he needed rest. He said I shouldn't worry. The length of time he was sleeping meant nothing.

I wasn't sure I believed him.

Gideon drove while Sully sat shotgun. It wasn't until we got into the car that Sully had collapsed, unable to move. He'd been forcing himself to continue despite his injury, but now that we were safe, he just sat, keeping watch in case our stolen vehicle was flagged up. There didn't seem to be much crime in these parts to generate any concern, however, or the cops were all asleep. Either way, our drive passed in relative calm. I, however, had had two cans of coke on an empty stomach, so I was on a nervous buzz from the caffeine high.

Sully kept the radio tuned to a news station. We figured if there was an arrest warrant out for our motley crew, we'd soon be hearing about it over the airwaves. I was starting to feel the beginnings of my sugar crash when we finally arrived back in Montpelier. And with a pang of deep shame, I remembered about Sully's dad. I'd been so consumed with fear for Bandit that I'd completely forgotten about his dad and the condition we'd left his house in.

We drove up to the ranch. Police tape formed the morbid outline of deceased people on the ground, though the bodies themselves had been moved. The bullet-riddled vehicles had been towed, and a tent now enshrouded the barn to contain DNA and forensics. Gideon parked the car and turned off the ignition. Sully took one end of the blanket, and Gideon the other. Stretching it taunt, they lifted Bandit out of the car. I hurried on ahead.

"Zeb? Are you here?!" I called out without thinking.

"Chase?" came his relieved voice, answering from his bedroom.

I ran in to find him propped up in bed. And he wasn't alone. Sam, our singing, hitch-hike driver, sat next to him wearing a Sheriff's outfit. Seeing me, her mouth fell open.

"Why, Bella. Hello again."

132

SULLY

earing voices, I hurried to my father's room, but the last thing I expected to see was Sam again. I blinked at her stupidly, gaping at the outfit she now wore.

"You're a Sheriff?" I asked.

Sam nodded, tipping an invisible hat. Seeing Bandit held between them, Sam rose out of her chair.

"Why do I get the feeling I haven't been given the whole story?" she said. Zeb stared at the two of them, frowning.

"You know each other?"

"I gave them a ride on their way here." She looked at me. "You're Zeb's son?"

Gently, I laid Bandit onto a couch, throwing cushions to the ground in front of him in case the dog rolled off in his sleep.

"Yeah." I didn't trust myself to speak further, unsure what was happening right now, of what Zeb might have told her.

"So your father isn't dead after all," she said this wryly, with an arch of an eyebrow. I had the decency to look embarrassed off Zeb's glare.

"Zeb here explained about the attack, but he hasn't said who they were or why they came after you. Apparently, he doesn't know. I'm inclined to believe differently."

"You hear that, Jake? She's calling me a liar to my face." Zeb's words were fighting, but there was a sparkle in his eyes. He liked her, I could tell. Still unsure what to reveal, I tried for distraction.

"What happened to the men who attacked us?"

"Dead. All of them. Damndest thing too, none of them carrying any ID. It's gonna be awhile till we can find out who they were." She studied our faces, one by one, trying to get to the truth, but neither I nor the kids would cave. Eventually, Sam settled her gaze on Chase.

"So what's your real name when you're not plagiarizing Twilight characters?" she asked. Chase flushed, called out. Sam went on, "I have nieces. They've made me watch that trash some six or seven times."

Chase hesitated as if wanting to lie, but must have sensed it wouldn't do any good. "Chase," she finally answered.

Sam nodded thanks and turned her attention to Bandit. "What happened there? That's a real nasty wound on his head."

As Chase plugged in the depleted iPad, preparing for a possible test of Bandit's skills, I was trying to think of a believable explanation, when two things happened simultaneously.

One, Bandit stirred, waking up.

And two, Forbes appeared in the doorway.

133

CHASE

I didn't know where to look first.

Bandit was finally waking up, but there was Forbes, pointing some kind of a military rifle at us, eyes bright with madness.

"You escaped," was all I managed to say.

Forbes glared at me, triumphant.

"You thought your little fire would kill me? Think again," he said.

Sully made a move towards him, but Forbes immediately swung his gun at him.

"Do not move, Mr. Sullivan. One more step and it will be your last," he warned.

Throughout the exchange, Sam had been watching the whole time, keen eyes assessing the situation. Her hand moved slowly towards the gun clipped onto her belt, but Forbes must have seen the motion.

"I wouldn't do that, Sheriff. Not unless you are prepared for the aftermath," he warned.

Sam stopped immediately, raising both hands over her head. "Sir, I don't know what any of this is about, but if you lower your weapon, we can discuss whatever it is that's bothering you." Her voice was calm, almost pleasant, though I heard the underlying steel there.

Forbes looked at her, expression scathing.

"Oh stop. Your tactics won't work with me. These people destroyed my life's work and stole my future! Now I'm going to take back what's mine, and there's nothing any of you can do to stop it." As he spoke, he waved the rifle around, not a care in the world that it could go off. Like he was playing eeny, meenie, he pointed the gun at each of us, finally settling the sights back on Sam. "Very slowly now Sheriff, I would like you to kick your gun away from you."

Sam nodded and slowly removed the gun from her belt. Bending down, she set the gun on the ground, then kicked it away from her, into the center of the room.

Forbes swung the gun very deliberately to Bandit, who sat up now, shaking his head groggily. I don't know if he meant him any harm or was just getting used to aiming with that gun, but I didn't think at all. I dived for Bandit, shielding his body with my own.

"Bandit, get down!" I cried.

But Bandit didn't move. I landed beside him, fully expecting my insides to be blown apart any minute. However, Forbes didn't shoot, focused intently instead on Bandit's face. He was waiting for his reaction. I rose onto my knees, staring into his eyes.

"Boy. Do you know who I am?" I asked, unable to stop the tremor in my voice. He stared at me blankly. There was no sign of intelligence in those eyes. No hint at all that he recognized me.

With horror, I realized that the Bandit I knew and loved was gone.

134

CHASE

My heart exploded painfully in my chest. At least, that's what it felt like. Bandit looked at me, but there was nothing there that showed he was the same dog I had gone through so much with.

"Bandit?" I cried, broken. He didn't even look at me, gazing around the room in confusion, then at Forbes. Directly at Forbes. It hit me like a sucker punch right then - Bandit wasn't afraid of Forbes. Forbes noticed the same thing as he suddenly started to laugh.

"All that wasted effort, when it seems he's nothing but a dumb dog after all," he guffawed, lowering his gun. Sam was staring at him hard, unmoving, trying to piece everything together, but there wasn't a single one of us who were able to explain. We were all too busy grieving. I reached out gently and took Bandit's face in my hands.

"Hey, Fella. It's OK. All that's important is now that the tumor's gone, you won't get sick again. I love you. You're my best friend."

Realizing he had won, that there was nothing worse he could do to us, Forbes turned away, leaving, uninterested in us any longer.

Bandit barked once.

I froze as that simple sound caused hope to flare inside. By the door, Forbes stopped dead. He turned slowly around, a frown beginning to appear over his features.

My bag was lying beside me, I took out the stylus and handed it to Bandit who took it gently in his mouth. Then, as we all watched, he very deliberately typed out the words *I LOVE YOU CHASE.*

Overwhelmed with relief and love, I flung my arms around him as Sam looked on, shocked. Gideon was grinning stupidly, Sully had tears in his eyes. Even Zeb was smiling. The only one not happy was Forbes. He stood there, shaking his head. "No... how can this be?"

Sully looked at him, triumphant.

"I'm guessing even without the tumor, his brain re-organized itself so he could stay intelligent. Nature is nothing but prolific when it comes to adapting. Funny how a simple dog can do what you can't, not even with all the billions you own."

"*WOOF!*" Came Bandit's timely response. His tongue was hanging out goofily again, and he couldn't stop licking my face. Having twisted in the knife, Sully turned his back on Forbes to fuss Bandit... which is how he didn't see the other man looking suddenly enraged. He didn't see Forbes raise his gun and point it at Sully's back.

But I did.

The world slowed to a crawl as adrenaline kicked in. I saw his fingers close in on the trigger. Without thinking, I dived for Sam's gun - on the floor in front of me - took aim, and fired. The recoil almost snapped my arm off. I was flung backward, but as I hit my head on the floor, I saw the muzzle flash tear out of the chamber as the bullet tore into Forbes' chest. A look of astonishment appeared on his face. He staggered back, blinking in disbelief, as blood blossomed over his shirt. Falling against the wall, he touched his chest. Seeing the blood on his fingertips, he slid down, unable to breathe, unable to take it all in.

Sam jumped into action, bounding over to snatch his rifle, which had clattered to the ground. She pressed her hand onto his chest.

"Don't you dare die. I want to see you do time for your crimes," she said grimly, but it was a losing fight. The color had already drained from his face, now encased in a sheen of sweat.

At the sound of the gunshot, Sully had looked over at me, at the gun in my trembling hands, still pointed at Forbes. It took a moment, but then it must have sunk in, how close he had come to meeting the reaper. He rushed over to me, holding me tight.

"It's alright now baby girl, everything is alright now."

I dropped the gun and wrapped my arms around him, bawling like a baby.

135

SULLY

The following hours passed by in a blur.

After Chase had saved my life, Sam had called in the cavalry, who arrived just in time to witness Forbes's demise. I didn't have faith in the system like Sam did and was mightily relieved when the paramedics announced his time of death.

Justice had prevailed.

Sam assured us that Chase would not be facing any charges. There were five allowable witnesses to testify that it was self-defense.

The coroner removed Forbes's body, and we were left to recover while Sam personally oversaw our statements. Still, it took a while to corroborate our reports, seeing as the words "super-intelligent dog" couldn't make it onto the document.

So much had happened in the last few hours, but one thing was startling: I was surprised how happy I was to see Sam again. As she worked at collating our reports, as she was told the whole story, I was taken by her confident yet compassionate attitude. She was a trooper too. After Bandit's initial words, he came right up to her and introduced himself. Bandit shocked us by telling her he liked her as she was *a good person.* Sam had seemed tickled pink by this.

I found myself in the kitchen next, setting the table while Gideon cooked, assisted by Sam. People were hungry, and it seemed natural for us to eat together. Chase sat with Bandit on the floor. She hadn't left his side since his return, and I couldn't really blame her. The two had been conversing furiously since Forbes's death as Chase explained everything that had happened following his capture.

Sam's laughter suddenly cut through my thoughts. It was warm and bubbly, and I wanted to hear that sound over and over.

"Soup's up," Gideon called out, carrying a pan of meatballs in tomato sauce to the table. I headed to the cooker where Sam lifted the lid off a pot of spaghetti.

"Here, let me," I offered and drained the water into the sink as Sam held back the spaghetti with a wooden fork.

"It's all about the teamwork," she said as she winked. I found myself noticing her dimples for the first time. *Cute*, I thought to myself. *Very cute.*

As we sat around the table, I saw how happy Chase looked. Surrounded by people who cared about her, Chase looked like the kid who'd woken up on Christmas morning and found the tree surrounded by presents. It brought a lump to my throat when I realized she'd likely never experienced that before.

I made a mental note to get the biggest Christmas tree I could find that year and to flood it with presents.

136

CHASE

Sitting around that table, stuffing our faces with the best spaghetti and meatballs I'd ever tasted in my life, I was feeling pretty amazing. Everyone was laughing and joking, and I noticed the way Sully kept sneaking looks at Sam. It made me feel warm inside. He'd been in such a bad way over Emma when I'd met him, but now it looked like he was finally coming out of it. And you know, Bandit's just the best judge of character, and he liked her a whole ton.

I had a feeling we'd be seeing a lot more of Sam in the future.

Since we'd arrived back, Gideon seemed different too. He wasn't argumentative or angry anymore. In fact, it seemed like he had something he wanted to say to me because I kept catching him watching me with this serious look on his face. Course, it could've been the way I was stuffing those meatballs into my face, but I'm telling you, they were so good!

When we were done eating, Zeb took off for a nap. His body had gone through a war and he needed rest in order to recover. Sully's leg had been patched up by the paramedics. Apparently, he'd been lucky as no major damage was done. It would hurt like crazy for a while, though. And he'd likely need further checkups and maybe some rehabilitation.

Sully and Sam went outside for a beer on the porch while Gideon and I cleaned up the kitchen. I didn't mind in the least. Here's a little-known secret: I like housework. I know that's not exactly exciting, is it? But housework is calming, and you get to see instant results. I don't know, guess I'm just weird.

I was washing up while Gideon took up drying duty since he knew where everything lived (although the place was still pretty shot up, so it'd need a heap more work to get it resembling anything like normal again). I caught Gideon looking at me strangely again, but this time I decided to call him out on it.

"What?" I demanded, throwing the sponge into the sink. "Why do you keep looking at me funny?"

He blinked, taken aback by my question, then a slow flush crept onto his cheeks and down his neck. It was quite adorable, to be honest, not that I'd ever admit it.

"I just er... wanted to apologize. For my behavior before," he began. I don't know what I expected him to say, but that wasn't it. I stared at him blankly as he continued.

"When you first got here, I was pretty rude. And then the thing with the shooting. I'd put two and two together about Sully and came up with five. You were just collateral damage."

"Collateral damage?" I said. "Wow, you sure know how to make a girl feel special." It was a few beats before my words sank in. I sighed, exasperated. "I already knew all of that on account of me not being brain-damaged, but thanks for the apology."

He shrugged awkwardly, shuffling on his feet. I could see his embarrassment as clearly as if he had a neon sign flashing over his head.

"I'm not a jerk, that's all," he finished.

Two barks sounded below us.

We both looked down to find Bandit at our feet, watching us. We burst out laughing as Bandit asked, *"What is so funny?"*

137

CHASE

The days following Forbes's death went past in a blur.

Using her influence, Sam had spun the truth until it became a simple story of how one billionaire, who had lost his mind to dementia, had attacked an innocent family in their home. She kept my name out of it (to protect the child witnesses), and of course, there was no mention of super-intelligent dogs, which suited us just fine.

The report also detailed how Forbes had burned down his own building in an effort to hide the cruel experiments he had been performing on animals. That last bit of information had hit a little too close for comfort, but Sam had said it was there to dissuade any of Forbes's former employees from continuing with the work if they should decide to do so.

While he recovered, Sully had received word from Doc Robins, who had managed to round up the escaped dogs, but now needed help to remove the tumors. The Doc turned up with a team of people who fixed up the barn overnight, converting it into a giant operating theater. They did such a great job that it looked better now than it had originally. With Sully's help, they worked tirelessly to remove the tumors as the dogs were then ferried away to a secret location where they could rehabilitate.

Apparently, the Doc had found many loving families willing to adopt the dogs. I was thrilled for them.

When they'd worked their magic on the last dog, Sully and the Doc came out of the barn. They found us on the porch swing, watching the sunset. This had become a ritual for Bandit and me. He loved the peace and quiet while I just loved being with my best friend. At their approach, we looked up at them.

"All done?" I asked.

Sully nodded, rubbing red-rimmed eyes, tired, but happy.

"That's it. That's the last one," Sully said.

Bandit jumped off the swing onto the ground, tail wagging, as he licked Sully's hand. The Doc bent down to look Bandit in the eyes. Sensing she wanted to speak with him, Bandit forced himself to sit, waiting.

"I'm so sorry for everything you went through. I never wanted that for you. I should've done something sooner. I hope you can forgive me," she said tearfully. Bandit stared at her solemnly, then barked once. "*Woof.*" Her face broke into a smile as she stroked him on the head.

"Now that we're done here, what's next for you, Elora?" Sully asked.

She straightened up, turning to face him.

"I'm going traveling. Somewhere I can do some actual good for a change. I'm thinking Africa. They need all the help they can get with the crisis over there," she replied. "Of course, it won't be the same. I'll miss this little guy here, for one."

"He'll be fine," I said. "He has us now."

The Doc smiled. "Yes, he does."

138

SULLY

I saw Elora off, wishing her well on her future travels, and went to talk to Zeb. I'd been doing this for several days now, working on the dogs then popping in to spend time with the old man.

Entering his room, I found Zeb in a recliner, engrossed in the latest James Patterson thriller. My brow raised of its own accord.

"Never thought I'd catch you reading something so mainstream."

"There's only so much Shakespeare one can stomach. Besides, this is good, solid fun," Zeb replied as he stared at me critically.

"How's the wound today?" he asked, already leaning forward to examine it. I turned to give him better access, knowing from experience any refusal would just be ignored.

"Itchy, but it doesn't hurt much anymore."

"Good. That means it's healing," Zeb leaned back, satisfied with my progress. Folding my arms across my chest, I went to study the titles on a stocked bookshelf. "Wow. You've certainly gotten through a lot of his books. Must be what, several hundred of them here?"

"I was stuck in bed for a while after the accident. Amazing how literary one can get when they can't move from their bed," came Zeb's reply. There wasn't a hint of bitterness in his voice, only sadness. I caught it, and for the first time, braved the question that had been playing on my mind now for a while.

"What happened, Dad? How did you end up in a wheelchair?"

Zeb stared out of the window, mind deep in his thoughts. I thought the old coot would ignore the subject as he had so many times before, but then Zeb continued.

"I was drunk. I was furious and broken, and one night, I drowned myself in my sorrows. It was shortly after you left, back in our old townhouse, after many heated words were said. I was so angry at you, but I was also crushed. When I came to my senses, I decided to come after you, but a bottle of vodka and two rums later... Funny how I'd been running up and down those stairs with no trouble at all for some twenty years, except that one night. I missed the top few steps and fell. When I woke up, I was paralyzed."

I was stunned, having never imagined I was the cause of Zeb's accident. And now things fell into place.

"This is why Gideon hated me. He blamed me," I said.

Zeb nodded. "I told him it wasn't your fault, but he never saw it that way. Kid's loyal to the bone. He didn't mean nothing by it."

A thousand thoughts flashed through my mind. All that time I'd spent hating my father when the truth was, we were both as stubborn as each other.

"I'm just glad you're home now, son," Zeb said finally.

I smiled. "I'm glad to be back."

139

SULLY

The sky shone like a dark sapphire.

I lay on my bed, staring out at the sky, thoughts tumbling through my head but at long last, feeling the peace.

Hearing nothing but crickets, I thought about how much my life had changed this past year. Yes, losing Emma was the most bitter blow and something that would probably take years to fully recover from, but being here now, back under my father's roof, knowing both Chase and Bandit were safe, I felt a calm that I hadn't felt since Emma was lying by my side.

I pictured her now, twirling in our yellow living room, paint splattered on her nose and laughing as she chased me with the loaded brush. And for the first time since her death, instead of gnawing grief, I felt only a deep sense of love.

I was still feeling this love when I fell asleep.

140

CHASE

I t was a bright and sunny fall day.

Zeb sat on the porch swing, a blanket covering his lap, playing chess with Sully. It looked serious, both of them focused with furrowed foreheads. They'd been at it an hour already. Sully had promised he'd teach me how to play in due course, but seeing how much concentration was needed, I wasn't sure it was something I wanted to try. I'd had just about all the excitement I could take.

Earlier, I overheard Sully make a phone call. And before you say anything, I wasn't snooping. I was getting something from my room when I heard his voice. He was talking to a buddy named Mark. Sounded like they'd had a falling out, but they were patching things up. I was relieved. Sully couldn't have had that many friends to begin with or he wouldn't have thrown everything away for us. Sully had told his friend that he was happy now that he was with his *family*. Isn't it funny how one small word can make you feel so many things? He promised Mark he'd get to meet us all one day. I didn't hear the rest of the conversation, as I'd already headed back outside, feeling guilty at what I'd overheard.

Gideon was tossing a frisbee with Bandit, whose wounds were healing nicely. Ever since our chat, Bandit had taken Gideon under his wing, so to speak. It was like he was waiting for Gideon to come to his senses about me before he would be his friend. It wasn't the same as us, however — Bandit and I were inseparable — but the two were definitely buddies. I appeared on the porch carrying a tray of cookies I'd just baked. The delicious smell of chocolaty goodness wafted over to them as they all turned to stare at me, astonished.

Annoyingly, I could feel my cheeks turning pink.

"What? They're just cookies. No need to make a big deal out of it," I said, embarrassed. Gideon jogged over and grabbed one off the plate. Sniffing it suspiciously, he took a tentative bite.

"It's good. Really good," he confirmed, and suddenly Sully and Zeb wanted one. *Men, right? Jeez.*

"Not you, Fella," I said to Bandit, sniffing around me hopefully. "You get these special non-chocolate ones," I said, sliding a plate of plain cookies under his nose. Note to reader: in case you didn't know, chocolate is super poisonous to dogs, so don't ever give them any. Bandit took one delicately into his mouth, reminding me again of that fateful first day when we met. I sat on the floor beside him, munching away, admiring my own baking skills.

"So buddy, now that we can do anything we want, what do you want to do next? We have the whole world in front of us, so go crazy," I asked him.

He cocked his head at me and typed into the iPad.

"A quiz!!! Oh boy, oh boy, oh boy!"

Anything in the world and *that's* what he wanted to do?

Stupid Muttface.

Thank you for reading WANTED.

If you loved this book, then please leave a review to help keep a roof over Jo's head, and also so other readers know to check out Jo's work!

The more reviews she gets for a book, the faster she prioritises writing more books in that series.

Keep reading for a look at HAUNTED,
the Chase Ryder series Book 2
AND
a special preview of her new series which also features an adorable dog!

THE CHASE RYDER SERIES BOOK 2
HAUNTED
JO HO
AWARD-WINNING SCREENWRITER

HAUNTED

BOOK 2

1

PROLOGUE

Acrid smoke filled the air, burning the back of his throat and stinging his eyes.

The Scientist swallowed uncomfortably, pressing a tissue against his nose, though it offered only the faintest respite. Firefighters littered the devastation before him, having battled the blaze long through the night. It had taken a small village to control the fire, and though it would never rage again, there wasn't much left of Sebastien's pride and joy.

The roof of the building that was home to Platinum Industries had collapsed and now lay in a pile of rubble. The once spotless glass windows (which Sebastien, ever the neat freak, had cleaned on a weekly basis) had exploded outward when the temperature had proved too much to bear, showering the ground with their remains.

His loafers kicked at a charred shard, the metal glinting in the afternoon sun.

Stupid fool. All those experiments, all that knowledge. Everything was now lost to the wind.

He had warned him, warned Sebastien that pursuing a selfish goal would be the end of him. Science — especially a breakthrough like the one his team had discovered — was meant for the world, not just one man, but as usual, Sebastien did as he wanted... and now the world was paying the price.

Having seen enough, he started moving towards his car. Amongst the fire trucks, police vehicles and corporate cars favored by the executives who formed Sebastien's legal representatives, The Scientist's own small hatchback seemed out of place, but he himself did not notice, not having a materialistic bone in his body. It was one of the things Sebastien, who had spent money like it was going out of fashion, liked to mock him for.

Last night, as he was getting ready for bed, he had received news of Sebastien's demise from his assistant Suzanne. Forever paranoid, Sebastien had his men regularly scouring police networks for news, particularly while they were on the hunt for Alpha. It was because of this that they were able to pick up the news of his death long before the police stepped in. The Scientist had gotten dressed and immediately made his way to Platinum Industries, hoping vainly that he would be able to salvage some of Forbes' work. Though he himself was never employed there (The Scientist kept his own lab), he had visited a number of times, so he knew what to expect. Still, it had hurt to see years of research and the billions invested into Sebastien's experiment going up in flames.

Luckily, none of it was his money.

Sebastien had been addicted to fame, luxuriating in the spotlight while The Scientist, a quiet man, was interested in only one thing — to make his mark in history by bringing man the most precious gift of all.

And he was very close to achieving it.

Sebastien's thugs' failure to retrieve Alpha was a terrible setback to his work.

Having seen what damage Alpha's new family had wreaked, The Scientist knew he had to rethink his plan, particularly as he didn't have vast wealth or cronies of his own to fall back on. Though Sebastien had been funding his secret research, his untimely death ensured his money would now be tied up in legalities. He would have no access to it and as the small-minded bureaucrats holding the public purse had no vision and would deem his work unethical — no matter how important it would be — it meant he could not go that route.

Despite these new setbacks, The Scientist knew this would only be a blip in his plans. Activating his phone, he called up live footage of his lab. The picture was grainy and in black and white, but he could easily make out the large steel tank inside which his experiment grew.

He would wait until his creation was born.

Then nowhere would be safe for Alpha to run.

2

———

CHASE

I stared out over the green horizon wondering how, even after six months of living here at the ranch, I hadn't tired of the view yet.

Thrushes flew across the early morning sky, chirping and singing a song that I had grown accustomed to in my time here. Zeb, Sully's dad, was quite the bird watcher, and it turns out, so was I. We had spent many evenings on the porch identifying our feathered friends while Bandit tried to memorize them. If you had told me a year ago, back when I had just left home to take my chances on the streets, that this would be my life, I'd have laughed in your face and called the Po Po to come take you away.

But you know what? I was kinda loving it.

I felt a warm breath on the back of my hand and immediately knew Bandit was with me.

"Hey, Buddy."

He woofed and pawed the ground in his usual greeting to me. Then he took my sleeve in his mouth and started leading me into the kitchen. I laughed.

"Wow, OK. I see we're hungry this morning."

He took the iPad that hung around his neck in the pouch Gideon had custom-made for him, set it gently on the ground and proceeded to "speak" using the Speak, Spell and Read app I had downloaded for him. Gingerly taking up the modified stylus into his mouth, he tapped out the words while the app spoke them to me.

"I am hungry every morning."

"We're so alike," I said.

"Like peas in a feather."

"What?" I said, momentarily confused before it sank in. "You mean peas in a pod. The other saying is "birds of a feather."

Bandit's mouth fell open as he tried to understand it all. He shook his head, looking perplexed.

"Your sayings are confusing."

"Yeah. Must be hard trying to remember them all." I scooped some doggie chow into his bowl and set it before him as I poured myself a giant bowl of cereal.

"Isn't it time you got a job or something before you eat us out of house and home?" came Sully's voice from the doorway. He came in, dressed in the jeans and checked flannel shirt that seemed to form the staple of his wardrobe here. I thought it made him look like a hick but Sam seemed to like it, which I guess was all he cared about.

"You mean, like you?" I shot back, knowing that Sully hadn't worked since we'd been here. Back in Greenwich, Sully had been a veterinarian, but that was before Bandit and I had turned up on his doorstep and changed his life forever.

"Least I have an expertize," he replied. "So do I... professional bum," I retorted. Bandit's tongue hung out of the corner of his mouth in what I now knew was his way of laughing. We did this kind of thing every day. After all, I'm the girl who calls Bandit "Muttface" as a term of endearment. Sully and I taking shots at each other? This was our version of "good morning".

Sully poured himself a cup of coffee and sat by the table as Sam came into the room. She was dressed in her Sheriff's uniform and the ends of her hair were still wet from a recent shower. The two of them had been inseparable since Forbes' death. It was Sam who had made sure no trace of Bandit was mentioned on the paperwork that was filed. It was because of her that we were safe and together today. She smiled at us over the top of Sully's head.

"Hey, you two."

Bandit woofed a greeting as Sam grabbed a donut from the counter and poured coffee into the steel thermos Sully had gotten her as a present. She whistled cheerfully, seemingly super happy. Sam was always chirpy, but she positively glowed this morning. I looked at Sully then back at Sam, staring suspiciously, but Sully flipped open a newspaper, hiding from sight.

"Where's Gideon and Zeb?" Sam asked.

"Gid had to be at work early today, he's already gone," I volunteered. "And Zeb's in the barn, getting things set-up." Sam looked suddenly disappointed. It wasn't a big change — she was still smiling — but some of her earlier brightness had faded.

"What's up?" I asked, wondering what had caused the change in her expression. She didn't answer straight away but looked at Sully who shook his head in the tiniest of motions.

"Oh, nothing. Just asking."

If I knew one thing about Sam, it's that she doesn't ask anything without a reason. She wasn't the kind of woman who spoke just to fill in the space (unlike my mom, who would only shut up when she was drunk and passed out on the couch). The hairs raised on the back of my neck, and I felt a tingle of apprehension.

"Seriously, something's up. What is it?" I asked, unable to keep my mouth shut. Sully obviously decided that now wasn't the time to talk about whatever it was they had to say, as he turned a page on his paper. Apparently, it was a riveting read as he wouldn't peel his eyes away from it. "Nothing's up, Chase. You don't have to worry."

He had always been a terrible liar, and this time wasn't any different. Seeing their expressions, however, I knew I wouldn't be getting anything out of them. Narrowing my eyes at them, I took my phone out of my pocket. By now, Bandit had woofed down his meal and was circling around me. Whatever was going on with them didn't seem to have affected him any. I took comfort in that, knowing that if it were terrible news, Bandit would have sensed it. As it was, he was almost tripping me up in his excitement.

"Dude, you need to chill out before you knock me over." He snorted, correcting me. As if I'd do that. He might not have said those words, but I heard it in his response. Sam grabbed a paper towel, dabbing the sugar from her mouth, then hurried out to work.

"Y'all be good now, I'll see you later."

"Bye, Hon," Sully said. And with that, she was gone. I shot a look at Sully, but he couldn't see my ire behind the newspaper. Annoyed, Bandit and I headed out to the porch where I settled on the swing. Bandit sat on the floor next to me. After everything that's happened, Sully insisted on getting me a phone, even though — outside of the random attack by those soldier types and Forbes — this was literally the safest place on Earth. Here, people didn't lock their doors. Sometimes they didn't even close them. Having lived in NYC for a while, I found this faith in humanity crazy bizarre.

Propping my phone onto a table, I started up a Jeopardy app that we'd discovered a few weeks ago. As soon as I laid my eyes on it, I knew we had to have it. As the intro music sounded, Bandit's tail swished back and forth across the porch floor in excitement. He set his iPad on the ground and took up the modified stylus into his mouth, primed and ready for action. As the voice of the host of the show came on, Bandit and I battled each other in what had become our post-breakfast ritual. Despite how it might seem frivolous, this actually served two purposes: one, it was Bandit's most favorite thing in the world to do, and two, it was a way for us to monitor his brain, something which Sully insisted upon as a precaution against future issues.

Though the operation at Platinum Industries had been successful, there wasn't any precedent for this and Sully did not want any more surprises; the two of us were still haunted by the fits Bandit had previously suffered. Sometimes, I'd wake up in the middle of the night, desperately afraid that Bandit would be dead. Whenever that happened, Bandit would wake too and come lie by my side, putting his head on my chest. He'd chuff at me, letting me know all was OK, and I'd stroke him until I finally fell asleep again.

Every morning, Bandit and I would go head-to-head at the game, and I'd only have to report to Sully if anything seemed off. So far (touch wood), I'd never had to tell him anything other than I was pretty sure Bandit cheated. He read voraciously and retained all the knowledge, so much so that despite my own photographic memory, most days he won.

It was a strange feeling to know that you were constantly being bested by a dog.

We did a couple of rounds of questioning when Sully popped his head out the door at us. "It's time, Fella."

Bandit slid the stylus and iPad into his pouch and went with Sully to the barn. I watched Sully, noticing he still walked with a limp. Zeb had been making him do these dance-like exercises every day. They were supposed to rehab his leg, but Sully always complained that he was "no damn ballerina." Gid and I were banned from ever going into the barn where he did them, however, because of how we'd reacted the first time we had snuck in. Let's just say you could hear us laughing clear across the state. Bandit always joined Sully in these sessions, though not to dance, that would be stupid. While Sully worked his muscles, the two of them would do physical checks on Bandit. I watched them go through them all once but they weren't very exciting to see so I usually just left them to it.

As they disappeared into the barn together, I cleared up the dishes in the kitchen, then went back to my room.

3

CHASE

After Bandit's physical, we headed into town.

Sully and Sam had been talking about the possibility of me going back to school for a while now, but I really, really didn't want to go. Just picturing myself in a classroom *every day* caused me to panic.

I knew it was stupid, I mean, look what we had gone through already. I'd taken out Forbes and his men. What the heck were teenagers going to do to me?

But I've seen Mean Girls.

I knew I wouldn't fit in. I never have, and the thought of having to try five days a week was getting me down, not least because I'd be away from Bandit so much — it was unthinkable. But whenever I said no, Sam would talk about how important an education was to get further in life. She'd bring up what I wanted to do in the future, asking difficult questions like that.

The reality was, I'd never given any of it any thought.

So much of my life before was just about surviving. I didn't know if I'd see another day. Who had time to worry about the future? I never got further than wondering where my next meal would come from, or if after I went to sleep in someone's doorway, whether I'd wake up again the next day.

I hoped to God that wasn't what the two wanted to discuss this morning. That would suck big time.

Since I was still too young to drive, Sully had gotten me a bicycle. I moaned about it a bit — didn't want him to think I was easy — but secretly; I was thrilled. I'd never had one as a kid and the luxury I felt now, in being able to get about so much further and faster than if I'd been walking was an independence I loved.

Bandit too, adored running beside me, but like most dogs, he never seemed to know how much was too much, so Gideon had built a special dog seat for him that we had attached to the back of the bike. It was Sully who had warned me about this.

Apparently, dogs were so thrilled to play and be with their owners that they wouldn't stop running beside them, but their little bodies weren't built for distance. Some get so overexcited that they won't stop until they become weak and collapse! This is an actual condition!

I figured Bandit to be smarter than that, but even then, I didn't want to risk it. So I always set a timer on my phone when we headed out. I let him run for up to fifteen minutes straight, but then he needs to ride behind me. Bandit had no problem with this and treated it like car rides. His tongue would hang out and he'd look positively blissful. When I'd asked about it before, about what it was that made him so happy, he said it felt like he was swimming in air.

My dog, the poet. *Who'd have thought it?*

We arrived at a garage on the outskirts of town. It wasn't a big production, but Warrey always seemed to have six or so vehicles being worked on. It was one of the reasons he'd hired Gid. Business had been picking up, and he wasn't able to manage on his own. Gid happened to call on him at the right time and when he showed Warrey how handy he was, he was hired on the spot. Rock blasted out from a stereo — not Gideon's choice I know, since he preferred alternative styles.

Warrey came over from the truck he was inspecting. Grease stains covered his T-shirt, and he had a bandana tied around his head. Sam had commented before on how good-looking Warrey was, I remembered as Sully had scowled for the rest of the day. Seeing me, he waved a wrench in greeting.

"Chase. How's it going?"

"Oh, you know. Boring. How about you?" I asked.

"I could regale you with the excellent work I'm doing on this engine right here, but I figure that's not going to help your mood any."

"You'd be right."

Bandit trotted up to him and gave him a small lick on the hand. Warrey patted him absently on the head as he called out over the music. "Gid, visitors for you."

There was a clang as tools were dropped, then Gideon slid out from beneath the car he was working on. Like Warrey, his shirt was also covered with stains, but where the older man wore a T-shirt, Gideon had only a sleeveless vest, one that showed off his toned arms... which I'd noticed quite a lot recently. He came towards me, one brow raised in question.

"Everything all right?"

"Yeah, we're just visiting. I took Bandit out for a run and we just found ourselves here."

I was about to say something else just as lame when I caught a figure moving from the corner of my eye. It was a guy, older than Sully but younger than Zeb. His long gray hair fell into his face as he struggled to maneuver a removal box up the fire escape outside using a pulley system that Warrey must have rigged up some time ago, judging by the screech that now sounded.

"Who's that?" I asked.

"Erik someone. Warrey finally found a replacement for his old tenant. He works in IT."

"What's an IT guy doing in the middle of nowhere? This town barely has wifi."

Gideon shrugged. "I don't know, didn't ask."

"How come?"

"He doesn't look that exciting to me. If you have questions, you can bother him yourself."

He just finished talking when Erik lost his handhold on the box and its contents crashed down the fire escape causing an almighty ruckus. I went to help him. "You OK up there?"

Erik stared down at me, embarrassed. "I'm all fingers and thumbs today."

I gathered up Erik's belongings, which mostly consisted of computery things as far as I could make out. "Interesting er, stuff," I began. "Gideon said you're into IT."

Erik nodded, wiping sweat from his brow.

"So what are you doing in the middle of nowhere? Most of the folks around here don't even use email." The question popped out before I realized it could be construed as rude. I hoped he would know I was just making conversation, shooting the breeze as Sully would say.

Erik smiled, looking at me with his piercing blue eyes.

"That's actually why I'm here. I lived in the city for twenty years and I'm sick of it now. The slow pace and fresh air will do me the world of good. Besides, city people aren't very friendly. I wanted to be in a place where everyone knew one another."

"Well, you've found it then," Gideon said, having joined us on the fire escape. "I'm Gideon, this is Chase."

"Ah, nice to meet you. Are you two together?" Erik asked. It was an innocent enough question, but I suddenly felt my cheeks turn red.

"No," Gideon replied, "but we do live together."

"As a family," I supplied quickly, "with my dog and some others."

Erik turned his attention to Bandit on the ground, watching up at us.

"That's your dog, I take it? He's a pretty thing."

I nodded. "His name's Bandit. Bandit, say hi," I called down to him, but Bandit made an agitated move and barked. "He's usually pretty friendly, he doesn't like it because he can't come up the ladder."

"Understandable," Erik replied. "Well, thank you both for helping me but I've got quite a bit more to move into the apartment so I should get to it."

"I work in the garage below but if you need a hand with anything, just let me know," Gideon offered.

"Why thank you, young man. So nice to see not all of your generation have lost their manners."

I climbed back down the ladder to Bandit's joy. He bounced up and down like he hadn't seen me in years — the dufus.

"That was nice of you, offering to help him," I said to Gideon.

"Are you kidding? Did you see the way he used that cinch? The guy's going to wreck it then who's Warrey going to get to fix it? Me. I just did that to save myself hassle in the future."

"Smart move."

"Right? They don't call me Three-Steps-Ahead-Dion for nothing."

"No one calls you that, you idiot," I laughed. Bandit barked twice — one bark for yes, two for no — making us both laugh even more.

4

CHASE

W e hung around until Gideon's shift was over and the three of us picked up the list of ingredients he and Sam had prepared last night.

Now that our motley family consisted of six, we took turns at cooking, but while I was the clear winner in the baking department, Gideon and Sam proved themselves amazing cooks. Literally, anything they put on the table was TO DIE FOR, which is why shopping for groceries had become the highlight of my day. I loved to see how these seemingly unrelated ingredients would come together to form a party in my mouth.

"What is all this?" I asked, looking at the endless list I had just unfolded.

"Don't know. Sam's cooking, but she said it's a surprise."

"But look at this. There's bacon, marrow bones — that's got to be for Bandit — shrimp, steak, and scallops. Scallops, Gid!"

"What about it?"

I shoved the list into his face.

"Don't you see? These are all our favorite things! Why is Sam cooking this?"

Gideon looked at me as if I was crazy.

"You just said they're our favorite... why wouldn't she, would be a better question."

"You weren't there this morning, but there was something fishy going on. Sully wouldn't look me in the eye and Sam was being cagey... They're up to something, I'm telling you."

Gideon gestured to the shopping cart laden with food. "Well, if they're going to feed me like this, then I'm a hundred percent behind them."

He took the list out of my hands and moved on, whistling happily as he pulled items off the shelf, but I couldn't shake the hollow feeling in my stomach. I hated surprises, and I knew they were going to spring one on us tonight. The food was clearly being used to butter us up.

I looked down at Bandit, who sat, head tilted up at me in question.

"I've got a bad feeling about this, Boy. I really have."

Feeling my anxiety, he whined at me.

5

CHASE

I stared at the spread before me.

Our usual — simple — dining table was covered with a decorative tablecloth that had delicately embroidered flowers on the corners. I'm not sure why, but the sight of them had me gaping. I didn't know things like this existed. Why would anyone think covering a table with a pretty cloth would be a good idea — it was only going to get splattered with food, especially if I got anywhere near it?

The soft light from candles set around the table cast a dreamy glow about the place. *Candles and table cloths? Were we trying to burn the place down?* I took a seat at the table, staring miserably at Sam and Sully in the kitchen as they finished preparing our meal. Bandit sat as he always did, by my feet, as Gideon strolled in pushing Zeb in his wheelchair.

"Wow, what's the occasion?" Gideon said.

I could have kicked him, tried in fact, but couldn't reach him, my legs having become tangled with that stupid tablecloth.

"All in good time," Sully said.

I knew it! They were up to something! But now I had proof, I didn't feel the least bit vindicated. There was just a hollow ache in the pit of my stomach. I glanced at Zeb to see if I could gather any hints from him, but he looked as clueless as I felt.

"What's this all about?" he asked, however, Sully and Sam continued as if neither of them heard him.

"Dinner's ready!" Sam called out suddenly.

She and Sully carried over plates of food for us, but I saw, with some confusion, that each plate contained a different meal. Zeb was served a steak, mashed potatoes, and broccoli. Gideon was given Shrimp Alfredo, a pasta dish. For me, Sam set down a plate of mac and cheese with bacon bits (made from real bacon, not that soy trash you get in a tub) and a burger oozing with cheese. As I'd guessed earlier, Bandit got his marrow bones, which he was already happily chomping away on. Sully's scallops were in another pasta dish, while Sam had made herself a chicken stir fry. Through my misery, even I could see that the two had put an enormous amount of effort into the meal.

It made me sick to my stomach.

They sat down, Sam staring at us expectantly. Sully, I don't know. He looked kinda nervous. He poured himself a glass of water, but some of it splashed out of the glass soiling the tablecloth. *Good! Stupid tablecloth.*

"Well, I know you're all wondering what's going on," she began. "We thought long and hard about what we're going to say and..."

But I couldn't wait to hear any more. Shoving my chair back so that it scraped across the floor, I shot to my feet.

"What is it? What is going on?! Can you stop drawing this out and just spit it out?!"

Four human faces and one canine one all turned to me in shock.

"Stop buttering us up with the food. If you've got something bad to say, just say it!"

My heart was racing and I could hear thumping in my head. It was like someone was pounding on it with a hammer. It was a miracle really that it didn't explode. As my words sank in, the shock suddenly disappeared from Sully's face and his expression turned contrite.

"Oh hell, Chase, I'm sorry. It never crossed my mind you'd be thinking this was something bad."

And now Sam looked apologetic.

"Hon, this isn't bad news. It's good news."

"It is?" I managed to get out.

Sam smiled over at Sully and reached for his hand. "Yes. Sully and I have decided... we're getting married."

Zeb and Gideon must have cheered or something, but I wasn't really sure as the blood was still pounding in my head. I was waiting for the other shoe to drop.

"Wait... that's it?"

Sam shot me a reproachful look. "Well gee Chase, I'd have thought you could show a little more enthusiasm..."

I turned to Sully to get confirmation. "Seriously, that's all you wanted to say?"

Even he seemed put out by my response. "Well, it's a pretty big deal to us."

"I thought you two were going to take off on us or something."

Sully's mouth fell open. "Why on Earth would you think..."

I gestured at the table. "Well, you made all our favorite food. Who does that unless it's an apology or a bribe?"

He trailed off suddenly, understanding shining in his eyes.

"Chase, I told you. We're family. Nothing will ever change that."

I felt the tears pricking at the corners of my eyes. Despite all the time we had been together, a part of me still believed that it was fleeting. That it would go away in a moment and my life would revert back to awful. I guess it would be awhile before I'd feel totally at ease.

Suddenly, the shock wore off and my eyes went wide.

"Wait. So, we're having a wedding?"

Sam nodded, smiling as Sully took her in his arms.

I looked down at Bandit, grabbing his head in my hands. "We're having a wedding Boy!"

He barked and danced around me, picking up on my delight. "There's going to be a white dress and flowers and cake! Oh man, there's going to be so much food! When is it?"

Sully stared across the table at us.

"We're thinking the end of summer. I have a few things I need to sort out before we can get married. That should give me enough time to do them."

Zeb spoke up now, hearing something in his voice. "What things?"

Sully looked at Sam, waiting until she nodded in encouragement before continuing.

"I need to go back to Connecticut. See Florence and Mark. Sort out paperwork..."

And make peace with the dead.

Although Sully didn't say those words, his intention was clear. But me, well now that I knew it wasn't anything to worry about, all I could feel was excitement.

"WE'RE GOING ON A ROAD TRIP!"

Sam smiled at me. "Yes, this way, we'll get it over with before school starts."

And just like that, they managed to put a pin in the bubble of my excitement.

Thanks a lot, guys.

6

———

CHASE

We set off against the rising sun.

I'm not sure what it was about early mornings, but Sully seemed to think it fitting. He said it was a psychological thing: new morning, new beginnings. There was only the faintest hint of sadness when he'd said it, but I knew better than to make a thing of it.

Since our family had grown in the last six months from three to six, transport had become a bit of a problem for us — it wasn't like we could just hitch a ride in the back of Sam's truck (though Gid thought that sounded like fun, and so did Bandit). One of the first things Sully did after Sam moved in was to buy a minivan. No, it wasn't glamorous, but it sure was comfortable. If I'd had one of these when I was on the streets, you would not have heard me complaining.

The greens of Montpelier soon morphed into the grays of the highway as we shot towards Connecticut. I was so excited at the prospect of a road trip that I had hardly slept last night, so I was paying for that this morning. We'd barely been on the road an hour when the rocking motion lulled me to sleep.

When I woke up later, it was to find us passing through New Hampshire. Having read about the place before, I decided some showing off was in order (I had a vain hope that if Sam could see how much knowledge I had up in my head already, she'd drop this whole going-to-school thing).

"Hey, did you guys know that the very first free library was funded right here, in New Hampshire? In a place called Peterborough in 1833. And, the first potato planted in America was also planted in this state."

Sully nodded absently while Sam actually listened to me. "I didn't know either of those things," she said, impressed. Buoyed by this, I continued.

"They also don't have to wear seat belts here, so we could legally remove ours and it wouldn't be a problem, just while we're in this state..."

"Absolutely not," Sam replied quickly. "Law or not, some things are better left to common sense, Chase."

"I was just saying we could, not that we should." But she didn't seem the least bit amused by this. I looked at Gideon hoping for some backup but he had earbuds in and was listening to a loud, emo track by the sounds of it, and Zeb was dozing in his chair, out for the count.

Of course, Bandit was captivated by my random facts. He pressed a paw onto my foot to let me know he wanted me to continue. He loved trivia almost as much as I did. "Let me think, what else do I know about New Hampshire... It holds the first presidential primary election as part of the process to choose a new president every four years."

"Who is a president?"

"Not a, the president. He or she, though it's always been a he so far, is the most powerful person in America. He lives in a famous building called The White House and gets to make laws and stuff."

I could have been a little more eloquent with my explanation, but it probably wouldn't have mattered, Bandit couldn't seem to wrap his head around the fact.

"He controls everything?"

"Yeah."

"Like how much food we eat? And when we eat it?"

"Well, no."

"Does he say when you have to sleep?"

"No, he doesn't do that either."

"What about playtime? Does he say how much you get to play?"

"Er... no."

"Then he isn't in charge. Sully is."

I had to hand it to him. You couldn't fault his logic.

We drove through a drive-in burger joint for lunch. Although there was a banner advertising it as the "Best Burger In Town", it wasn't a patch on the ones Gideon makes so either someone was lying or they didn't have very high standards in this place.

We drove for a few more hours. Zeb continued to snooze while Gideon went through the entire music collection on his phone. Bandit and I entertained ourselves playing I Spy, which he proved to be pretty ingenious at, noticing things the average person wouldn't. When we'd finally exhausted all the possibilities, I pointed at his iPad.

"Wanna watch something?"

"*Stranger Things! Oh boy, oh boy, oh boy!*"

"We just finished it the other day? Don't you want to try something else?"

"*Please, Chase. Stranger Things!*"

"OK, OK, but one day you'll have to tell me why you like it so much. I mean, it's a great show and all, but what exactly's your deal with it?"

"*Eleven and I are peas in a pod.*"

I heard the words as his Speak, Spell and Read app voice spoke them, but I wasn't quite sure what he meant. He must have sensed my confusion as he went on to explain.

"*I was made in a lab. Bad men wanted me to do things. Then I ran away. Mike saved Eleven, you saved me. And now we are a family.*"

I felt my heart melt. He leaned into me and I wrapped my arms around him, resting my chin on his head. "Yeah, we are."

Usually, this would be all the comfort he needed, but today, Bandit had something else on his mind. His little body was still tensed. He shifted his weight on his paws, battling with whatever was going on inside him.

"What is it, boy?"

"*I do not want to go back. I do not like the cage.*"

He turned his head to stare at me with those brilliant green eyes of his. I could almost feel the intensity of his words in them.

"*We stay together, Chase. We always stay together.*"

A lump formed in my throat and I found myself unable to answer him with words right away, so I just nodded as I hugged him harder. We'd been separated once before, and that almost killed us both. I was determined that no one would ever get between us again.

"I promise, boy. You'll never spend another day in a cage again."

I had no idea just how badly I would be breaking my promise.

7

THE SCIENTIST

The Scientist neared his target with the ease of one who was practiced in such maneuvers, though this couldn't be further from the truth.

Like the dog, he had spent most of his life in a lab, but unlike the dog, he had been on the other side of the glass. Where the dog had been the specimen, The Scientist would have been the one to study him had he been privy to Forbes' experiments at the time. Thinking this, a surge of red-hot rage coursed through him.

Once again, he lamented his partner's selfish quest. Science should be available to all, not only the select few.

The front door was in his sights. He crossed the few remaining yards and let himself in with the key he had swiped from the dumb mechanic. Why anyone would trust him with their keys was beyond him. He had kept them in a cabinet with a coded label that even a child could have deciphered.

There was no concern that he would be seen — the family were gone for a few days, on a trip back East. The Scientist knew all about it, actually... people around here really loved to talk. Sullivan was getting remarried and wanted to go to his previous home to bury his past. Of course, no one else knew what had gone on there, how Forbes' men had almost burned the clinic down. They didn't know about the dog or the science he carried within. No, despite all the talking, they knew only the surface story.

Which suited him just fine.

He entered the ranch, closing the door behind him. It looked much as expected. A mediocre home for a mediocre family. He felt a burst of anger that these people were the only thing stopping him from his scientific breakthrough. He missed his work, wanted nothing more than to get back to his lab where he could immerse himself in his experiment, but... his pet project was not finished yet. There was one last thing he needed, and the key lay within the dog. Having seen what was left of Forbes' personal army, however, The Scientist knew he had to be patient, but what he lacked in physicality, he more than made up for in intellect.

When he was a child, he was an avid chess player. It was one of the few things that had brought joy to his life. He was made the captain of the chess team within a month of joining it, angering the other members and their parents, but despite their vocal complaints there was something about his brain, about the way it was always thinking several steps ahead, that meant he was unbeatable at the game. His opponents learned to fear him as would this family, though by the time they would learn of his plan, it would be far too late for any of them.

He was in the girl's room now. Her disgusting clothes were everywhere. Empty food and drink cartons littered the table and floor. It was as if a pig lived here. Though The Scientist wasn't particularly clean himself, even he was taken aback by the mess. Beside the bed, there was a basket for the dog. His hairs covered the cushion, and there were dog toys lying beside it. The Scientist stared at a battered soft toy of a rabbit with half its ear hanging loose. These people were ridiculous to treat him like a child.

He climbed onto the girl's bed and found a perfect place on the book shelves to hide his camera. He angled it away from the bed — he wasn't a creep, after all; he had no interest or intention on spying on the girl that way — no; he was only interested in the dog. The camera was a slight thing, so small you really had to be searching for it to find it and looking at the state of the room, the girl would not notice it even if it were staring her right in the face.

Satisfied with the placement, he moved into the other rooms, hiding cameras in discreet places until the ranch was full of them. When that was done, he took out a spray bottle filled with a solution that he had created to mask his own scent. Given that dogs have such an acute sense of smell, it wouldn't do for Alpha to learn of his presence before he wanted him to. The Scientist went through the house, spraying every room until the solution was used up.

Satisfied with his mission, he smiled to himself.

The second move was completed.

Check.

8

―――――

SULLY

The drive East went by all too soon.

Sure, I had joked with the kids on the journey here, but my heart wasn't in it, my mind on other things. Well, one in particular. My deceased wife, Emma.

Just before Chase had appeared on my doorstep, Bandit near death on that shopping cart, his blood all over her, I had felt as if my world had ended. It was a slog just to get through the day, and let's face it, I hadn't been doing a great job of that as my buddy Mark — who I had flung a lasagna at — would testify. But opening that door to her had opened up a new life for me, one where I found myself in the unlikely position of being in love again.

I glanced at Sam. Her spiral red curls were being blown by the wind. This was not a woman who fussed over having immaculate hair. She wore it loose and natural, and it framed her beautiful face perfectly. An annoyingly upbeat song was playing on the radio and as usual, she sang along with it heartily. The woman was full of life. In the time I had been with her, I had never seen her broken or down. Her sunny personality was what had attracted me to her. It had been the same with Emma until those dark days that had drained any life she'd had left.

I hadn't meant to start a relationship with Sam — as far as I was concerned I wasn't in that place at all, hell, I couldn't even sleep in bed on my own until I tired my body out with my late night runs — but we had hit it off from the moment we met. We just... fit. And the kids loved her, even Zeb. It wasn't easy to leave Emma behind, but I knew it was time. Life had moved on, and she would want me to be happy, but before I could make the final step, there was something I needed to do.

So here we were.

As we turned a corner into my old neighborhood of Ellington, familiar sights came into view. I saw the giant Oak that was so strictly protected from harm that Old Mr. Felner's house had had to be built around it. The car passed by a playground where a group of young preschoolers were up to mischief as their parents watched on, chatting over cups of coffee. A slight pressure built up in my chest as a memory of Emma and me flashed up in my mind.

We used to sit on the swings, chatting about how many kids we were going to have. The number changed on a weekly basis, and the only thing we ever agreed on was that we wanted more than two. I mentally shoved the image away as I always did when Emma's face flashed up in my mind, unable to handle the conflicting emotions. Mentally, I knew I was ready for this next step, though I guess my heart was still confused, having loved only one woman for all those years to suddenly have it replaced with another.

We rounded another corner and suddenly I saw it. The site where my clinic stood before Forbes' mercenaries had set fire to it.

I was relieved to see that much of the ground floor — which still housed a veterinary clinic — remained. Upstairs, however, that was a different matter. My eyes grew wide as I took in how much it had changed. When I lived there, when I had called it home, upstairs was a simple apartment of four rooms, but it had now expanded across one side of the building and the exterior was painted a pale green. No hint of damage from the blaze remained. The entire place had been redecorated. It looked... nice, but it wasn't the home I remembered.

As I slowed the car, the noise died down as the others realized we had arrived at our destination. Seeing the changes, Chase looked as astonished as I. "Wow. They fixed it up a bunch, huh?"

"Well, last time you saw it, it was burning to the ground," I said, wryly, though my heart had started pounding inside my chest. I hoped Sam couldn't hear it. She was staring at the clinic, assessing it with her cool, calm eyes. She didn't say anything but turned to give me an encouraging smile.

"Looks nice. They did a good job," Zeb said. "Nice shingles."

I knew Zeb wasn't interested in buildings, shingles or otherwise, so this last was said for my benefit. The old man was trying to help the turmoil he knew I was going through. I killed the engine and in the silence that suddenly surrounded us, we piled out of the car when a woman in her sixties came hurrying out of the building. As usual, she wore one of the floral dresses that apparently formed the sole contents of her wardrobe.

"Sully?! Oh My God, it's really you?!"

Hearing that familiar voice and all she had meant to Emma and I, I suddenly found myself bounding the few yards to her. Grabbing her in a bear hug, I lifted her clear off her feet. She squealed in delight, though I noticed she seemed much frailer now. Had she always been this thin? I couldn't remember.

Moments later, we followed Florence inside.

9
─────

SULLY

Inside, the clinic looked much the same as it always had.

The same chairs sat in the waiting area, Florence stood behind the same counter where she greeted all new patients and filed their details into the computer. Fact was, there was only one discernible difference to my eyes, and I moved towards the giant pinboard now.

Where once the photographs and postcards littering the board were addressed to me, these now thanked Matt and Izzy, the two vets who had taken over from me. Judging by how many there were, they were doing a better job than I had ever done too. There was a lump in my throat. Since the night when I was forced to flee my own clinic, I hadn't had the luxury of giving this place and my work much thought. Now I found myself missing that simple life and the joy of saving a family's beloved pet.

As if she could sense what I was feeling, Florence's voice came from behind my shoulders. "They're great, but they are not you."

I turned to find her behind me. Tears misted up in her eyes that she didn't bother to hide. "I'm so happy to see you again." She turned to the others, who had followed her into the room. "And it's wonderful to finally meet all of you. I've heard so much about you."

Chase gave her a shy smile as Sam went to introduce herself.

"Hi Florence, I'm Sam."

Unwittingly, I held my breath. In the absence of our own family, Florence had been like a mom to Emma and me, so I found myself nervous of what she would think of Sam. Would she think I was betraying Emma's memory, that I was replacing her too soon? But I shouldn't have worried. Florence gave her a warm smile and cupped her face in her hands.

"So you're the one who has stolen my Sully's heart. I can certainly see why."

Sam smiled and some tension left her shoulders. I hadn't noticed until now, but she must have been feeling some pressure herself. After Forbes' men had attacked the clinic, I had fabricated a story about Chase getting into trouble with a gang while she was living on the streets. They attacked Bandit and when Chase came to me for help, she unwittingly led them to us. When I refused to pay them off, they attacked us and set fire to the clinic as a lesson. I'd explained to Florence that I was going to help Chase and wouldn't be back for a while and that a change of scenery would do me good. She'd bought that part of the story more, but she'd never asked any questions of me. That was the thing about Florence. Even if she knew you weren't telling her the truth, she respected your wishes.

Almost unconsciously, I moved outside the waiting room, to the bottom of the stairs that lead to the private quarters above. The chatter behind me faded as I took in the walls — no longer that sunshine yellow Em had painted them, now replaced with a pale blue. Through the pounding that sounded in my heart, I vaguely heard Florence invite the others to the kitchen for coffee. I knew her well enough to know she wasn't just being a good host — she was giving me time. Before she joined them, however, she came up to me.

"Matt and Izzy knew you'd want to see your old home, so they told me to tell you it's fine. Go ahead." She shot me a supportive smile before disappearing to the kitchen.

I took the stairs slowly, one at a time.

When I reached the top, what I saw before me was nothing like the home I remembered. Instead of the small kitchen/lounge I expected to see, I found myself in a large living area. Couches lined a whole wall in front of a flat-screen TV. There was a games console, a Playstation. Its controllers sat neatly beside a tower of video games. It seemed that outside of saving animals, the vets here liked to save the world too, judging by the titles of the games. I recognized a few of the names, having heard Chase and Gideon talk about them (they'd been bugging me about getting a console for a while now but I had resisted — call me old-fashioned but I'd had enough of Chase shooting guns, real or otherwise).

Where the kitchen had been, a long dining table now stood. Exotic flowers grew in pots along the window ledge, giving the air a spicy aroma. Several doors lead from the living room, through one, I could see the new, much-expanded kitchen. I wasn't much of a cook — that had been Emma's wheelhouse — so our quaint setup had suited me fine, but this new number came with marble islands and chrome fittings that even I could appreciate. I stopped myself from going inside, however, feeling drawn to the one room that had been our haven.

I stepped into the main bedroom now. A king size bed stood in place of where ours had been, but other than that, the room was unrecognizable. There were plush new carpets and furnishings, even the cream curtains we had made from fabric we had picked up at the local flea market had been replaced with something much more upscale.

With a fresh coat of paint and a drape of designer fabrics, our life had been completely erased.

It was painful and yet a relief at the same time. I couldn't see us in here anymore. This wasn't my home.

And with that realization, there came a sudden lifting of my heart.

10
————

SULLY

I rejoined the others to find them sitting around the kitchen table in the clinic below, drinking cups of coffee and nibbling at what looked to be a delicious homemade carrot cake. I was touched by how much effort Florence had made ahead of our return and mentally affirmed to eat a slice despite how little appetite I had.

Florence stood up the second she saw me, inclining her head to the office next door. I shot Sam a smile, letting her know everything was fine, and followed her to the other room. She greeted me with a pile of correspondence.

"These came for you after you left. I tossed out the obvious trash, leaflets and such, but these looked personal so I left them here for you."

"Thanks." I took the pile from her, quickly sorting through the envelopes. Most were letters from medical suppliers or final bills from the electric company. Nothing of any interest. I contemplated just throwing the whole pile into the bin when one envelope caught my eye.

It was plain but made from a good quality paper. And unlike the others, my details were handwritten in a neat, flowing script. I frowned, trying to place the familiar handwriting, but it escaped me so I tore the envelope open. Inside, there was a simple note made of the same stock and weight of the envelope. Only three words were written on it in that same familiar script.

"Always and forever."

THOSE WERE the three words that had been inscribed on our wedding rings. And suddenly, I recognized the writing.

It was Emma's.

11

SULLY

I looked up at Florence.

"What is this? Why is this here?" I demanded.

Startled, she leaned across so she could see the note. The color drained from her face as her eyes became muddled. "I'm sorry, I should have checked first."

"Where did this come from?"

She twisted her hands in apology. "I don't know. I thought it came in the mail with the rest of the letters…"

"Well, that's not possible, is it? That's Emma's writing, so you must've gotten this mixed in with the mail." I couldn't keep the anger from my voice. Those written words had hit like a truck, making me feel suddenly guilty over what I was here to do — and that was the last thing I needed. I knew my anger was irrational. It was obviously a simple mistake, but I was unable to rein my feelings in. Florence took the note from my hands.

"Yes, I know. There isn't a stamp on it, so I must have picked this up elsewhere. Let me get rid of it for you… unless you want to keep it?"

Her question hung in the air.

Every muscle in my body was tense. It wasn't that long ago when I couldn't throw a thing of Emma's away, but then that choice was taken from me when her things went up in a cloud of smoke. Now here was something tangible, a physical link to our past. I could feel my hands moving towards the note of their own accord.

"No. I don't want it."

Even as the words came out, I felt sick to my stomach. A part of me wanted to scream at her, that, of course, I wanted to keep it, but it took every ounce of my willpower to let it go.

Maybe this was a test. If so, I was determined to beat it. I pictured Sam's smiling face and forced myself to look away from the note.

"Get rid of it."

She nodded and hurried out of the room with the note.

And I let out the breath I had been holding.

12

CHASE

Something was happening.

One minute we were laughing, drinking coffee, and hearing stories of Sully's animal patient escapades, and the next Sully had returned to the room looking pale and subdued.

Sam had gone to him immediately, but Sully just shook his head. Whatever it was, he wasn't ready to talk about it in front of all of us. Recognizing this, Sam just kissed him on the cheek and gave him a supportive smile. But me, I wasn't respectful like that. I went over to him, Bandit by my side. He must have picked up on my concern as he whined softly at me.

"What happened?" I asked Sully.

He looked at me, weighing up whether he would tell me the truth, but he must have realized it wouldn't do any good to keep things from me, I'd get it out of him, eventually. He filled me in briefly. His voice was flat as if he didn't feel any emotion about the subject, which I knew was just his way of deflecting pain.

"Well, that sucks," was my eloquent answer. "Good job on letting it go though. Must have been tough."

He didn't answer. Finally, Florence came back into the room. She came up to Sully hesitantly, afraid to make any further mistakes. "We were hoping to surprise you, but under the circumstances, I think it's probably best if I run our plans by you."

"What plans?" Sully said, unable to hide the concern in his eyes.

"Mark is coming by tonight, to surprise you. We're going to throw a barbecue. Matt and Izzy will be joining us too after the clinic closes, but if you want us to cancel, we still have time."

Sully opened his mouth to answer, but then he hesitated. His eyes flicked over to Sam, watching him quietly from a few feet away. She didn't move or say anything, but her presence alone seemed to be enough for Sully to make up his mind. "No, that's fine. Keep it. It'll be fun."

Forgetting himself, Bandit barked once. He *adored* a good barbecue. We all knew he was agreeing with Sully, but Florence didn't. She just thought he was being cute. She bent down to stroke him. "Who's a good doggy? Would you like a treat? I think I've got some in my jar over there?"

It took a moment before I remembered that Florence had no idea how intelligent Bandit was, hence the way she was speaking to him. I could see that the last thing on Bandit's mind was food, but we needed to keep up his cover of "normal dog" so I nodded, silently telling him he should go with her. Faking enthusiasm, his tail swished back and forth as he allowed Florence to lead him away. Sam slipped her hand in Sully's. "So Mark's coming over? That's good, I've been wanting to meet this old friend of yours. The stories he must have..."

"Don't believe everything he says. Guy has a way of exaggerating," Sully said, looking alarmed now that he realized the two would be meeting.

Catching his expression, Sam became amused. "Got some stories you don't want me to know about, huh?"

"There's no need for you to know *everything,* is there? A little mystery is sexy," Sully said, a little desperately, I thought.

Sam laughed. "You're cute when you panic."

And that was my cue to leave. Sully being upset I could handle, but flirting with Sam?

That was just gross.

13

——————

CHASE

The party was happening in the backyard.

A bank of outdoor kennels stood on one side, but they were empty right now, their inhabitants having been moved inside so that the noise and smoke from the grill wouldn't bother them. We sat on a pretty terrace where roses climbed across a trellis and the outdoor grill glowed a cheery orange as the coals heated up.

Sully's friend Mark had arrived with a giant bowl of potato salad and some beef skewer things that had Bandit salivating at the smell. Before Sully could get excited at the prospect of Mark learning how to cook, however, Mark revealed that he had picked up both at his favorite deli. Sully made a joke about that being a first since he usually just got whichever poor soul he was dating to do all the cooking.

I had to admit, Mark wasn't what I was expecting at all. He had slicked back hair that shone from the amount of product he had up in there, thick black-rimmed glasses that I wasn't convinced weren't just for show and was the kind of guy who wore shoes with no socks. He was a hipster and unapologetic about it. He seemed like a nice enough guy, but I find it hard to trust any man whose nails were so neat. After some badgering, he finally admitted that he had regular manicures. He literally had nothing in common with Sully, but you wouldn't know it to see the two of them laughing and joking around. Sam must have thought their relationship curious too as she asked how they had met. Turns out, it wasn't long after the clinic had opened.

Mark had been dating this girl who had a cat with a sensitive tummy.

Unfortunately, he didn't know about that, or how to treat cats in general and had been feeding her milk and all sorts of human food — both of which are no no's since cats are lactose intolerant and human food contains too much salt, something which caused kidney problems in cats. After weeks of toiletry issues, the cat finally decided she'd had enough as she left several protest poops around their bed. When Mark's girlfriend found out he was the cause of her cat's distress, she dumped him, but he became friends with Sully in the process.

He and Sully were knocking back beers now, talking about things I didn't understand, like stock markets and bonds. The current vets, Matt and Izzy, had also joined us. Matt smiled a lot and had a booming and infectious laugh while his girlfriend Izzy was a dainty thing with a wicked sense of humor. They seemed like really good people and I was glad they were the ones running this place now.

Gideon, Zeb, Sam and I sat around the garden table as Florence brought out an old file of hers. "I thought you might like to see some pictures," she began as she showed us a leaflet of Sully opening the clinic to a crowd of well-wishers. "This was our first day here. It was a very proud moment for us," she said.

"You've worked with him since the clinic started?" Zeb asked, surprised.

"Oh yes. I had known the two of them a while. Well, I actually knew Emma first. She was my friend Irene's granddaughter. When they decided to open the clinic, I had recently lost my job to a younger, prettier model. When Irene mentioned this to Emma, she forced Sully to hire me. I suspect I wouldn't have been his first choice for the job, but she just wouldn't hear of it. She was quite the campaigner for justice. Couldn't bear any wrongdoing."

Zeb fell quiet. I suddenly realized how much of Sully's life he had missed since the two had fallen out. He'd never met Emma, so it must be hard to be faced with her memory like this. I remembered how, when we'd first turned up at the ranch, Zeb had blown up at Sully, letting him know that he didn't care to meet her or go to their wedding, as he was angry at Sully for tossing away his promising career as a surgeon. I think he somehow thought she influenced him on this, though anyone who knew him now could see that Sully loved saving animals. I couldn't imagine him doing anything else.

Sam stared at the leaflet. I realized then that this might be the first time she'd ever seen Emma's face. Her expression was stoic so I couldn't tell what she was thinking. She just stared at Emma, taking it all in.

Florence looked up at Sam suddenly, smiling. "I'm so happy Sully found you, my dear. It wasn't that long ago when I thought he would never get over losing her. I'm just so relieved he has found happiness again."

Sam gave her a warm smile. "I'm sure he would have moved on eventually, even if he hadn't met me."

"I don't know about that. Sully couldn't even get rid of Emma's things. Why, it was just before he left when Mark and I tried to help him, that their big fight happened. I felt it was unhealthy to be surrounded by memories of his dead wife like that, so we tried to force his hand. It wasn't just her pictures, you understand? Sully had kept her clothes, toiletries, everything... for a year. We'd tried unsuccessfully many times to help him rid them to no avail when we finally decided enough was enough. But when Sully saw Mark packing up Emma's things, he attacked him and wouldn't speak to him for a long time."

Something about her comment caused Sam's smile to waiver. I saw it, but, caught up in memory lane, the older woman didn't pick up on Sam's emotions. "Wasn't that only six months ago? "

"Why, yes. I guess it was."

"I didn't know that," Sam replied quietly. Her eyes turned thoughtful, but she didn't say anything else. Zeb, too, looked as if he were struggling with his own feelings. He'd lost his wife himself so he, better than anyone, should know what Sully had gone through. I thought about how much time the two had wasted through being mad at each other. If they had both gotten over their issues, they could have supported each other through those painful times. Hindsight, right?

Florence rifled through the file until she came up with another image. It was a newspaper article about a dog Sully had saved from death.

"And this is Sully with the first puppy he delivered. The mom was found dumped in an alley. She had been someone's pet until they decided they didn't want the puppies — probably didn't want the added cost of feeding them — so they just left her to fend for herself instead. Poor thing was starving when a local found her and brought her to us."

I felt anger at the people who could do this to her. "When there are so many shelters and charities that will take your dog for free, why do people still do this?"

Florence sighed. "Because many people are cowards, Chase and they don't want to face up to their responsibilities."

Bandit barked *yes,* but I gave him a sharp look, silently warning him not to do anything else that might reveal his specialness. Despite how Sully felt about Florence and Mark, despite how he trusted them, it was safer all around if we didn't tell them about his abilities. Catching my warning, Bandit lowered onto all fours before settling back down. To anyone else, it might have looked as if he were simply stretching, but I knew he was being submissive and saying sorry.

"Well, people who do that shouldn't be allowed pets in the future,"

Gideon said. His face was firm, and he had one hand on Bandit. It made me think how much he had changed during our time together. When he had first met Bandit, Gideon hadn't seemed all that interested in him. Then again, he hadn't seemed interested in anything other than Zeb. Florence pulled out some other newspaper clippings now but her face fell and she hesitated, not sure whether she should show them to us.

"What is it?" Zeb asked.

Finally, Florence took out the clipping. I looked down to see images of the nearly destroyed clinic on that fateful night when I had turned up unannounced on Sully's doorstep. The fire had fizzled out, but smoke still curled in the air. The picture must have been taken just hours after the blaze. Gideon had heard the story before, but faced with the pictures, he looked shocked.

"It probably looks worse than it is. I mean, the building didn't fall down and what could be fixed has been rebuilt." I don't know why I said that or why I was trying to make him feel better. It wasn't like he had any experience of it. He wasn't there that night.

"I didn't know it was that bad. I know you told me, but, I didn't really know..." He trailed off. "It must have been terrifying."

"Oh you know, I've been through worse," I shrugged, trying to play it off.

"I sincerely hope not!' Florence said, cutting into our conversation.

Of course, I wasn't going to explain what I had meant by that, but my own words got me thinking of a time I chose to forget. My thoughts went to a place they seldom visited, and a familiar face I tried not to think about flashed up in my mind. I shook my head, trying to erase the picture, but it was no use. Once it was there, it refused to go away.

Mom.

14

———

CHASE

Things had gotten heavy there for a moment.

As usual, whenever a situation became uncomfortable, I would get out of there, so I excused myself and made a break for the restroom. I splashed cold water on my face, hoping to feel refreshed, but I couldn't shake the black cloud that now hovered over me.

It was weird. When I usually thought about my mom, I felt only anger. I was mad at how she'd let Tubs into our lives, how she didn't protect me from him, and how she had let that jerk dictate how we lived. Although our lives were far from perfect before him, we had always had each other, but, as soon as she had let him in, it was like this giant Tub-sized wedge had pried us apart.

And suddenly, everything had changed.

I'd thought about leaving for at least a year, but I didn't have any money and there was no one I could run to. And while the beatings at home were bad, he'd mostly left me with only bruises or some missing hair — I'd suffered no broken bones, so I figured I could tolerate it. But then my appearance started to change, and I found myself growing in places that had been previously flat. When Tubs started noticing me in a different way, I knew I had to get out of there. He loved to drink, and I knew I was one drunken session away from something that would scar me forever.

Maybe it was all the revisiting and talk of old days, but I found myself with the sudden urge to hear my mom's voice. Since I had left home, I hadn't spoken to her, not even once. Hadn't really wanted to either, so this took me by surprise. I wanted to know if she regretted not standing up for me. Was she missing me now I was gone? There was a time — a long time ago, yes, but it happened all the same — when she put ribbons in my hair and bought me ice-cream along the beach. Was there any part of that mom left?

I thought about the many beatings I had endured, all while I waited in vain for her to put a stop to it... and suddenly a new thought occurred. I wondered who he was using as a punching bag if I wasn't there to take the blows. The thought stunned me until I found myself frozen to the spot. I couldn't believe I hadn't thought of this before. What if Tubs was hurting her now he couldn't hurt me?

Part of me was thinking, good, let's see how she liked to be pummeled for no reason, but another part of me, the part that was kind and loved by my new family, felt pity.

Eight months on the street had taught me not to be a rash person, but I shoved away my doubts and found myself wandering the clinic until I reached Sully's old office. A buzz had begun to sound inside my head. I figured it was nerves or a giant alarm, screeching at me to stop what I was about to do, but I ignored it. Like I was experiencing an outer-body moment, I watched myself pick up the phone and dial home.

The call rang and rang and rang.

With every unanswered ring, a coldness grew inside of me. What if she wasn't living there anymore? Maybe she had changed her phone number or moved, in which case I would never be able to find her again. Then my thoughts took a dark turn. What if she wasn't answering because she wasn't *alive* anymore... I was turning numb at the possibility. I ran through the possible places I could check for information when the call was answered by a familiar male voice that instantly caused my body to be flooded with anger and fear.

"Hello?"

It was Tubs, but I could barely hear him over the noise. Trashy music played in the background, and I heard laughing. I recognized the song that was playing as one of Mom's favorites. A crazy thought entered my mind.

Were they having a party?

"Hello? Speak up! I can't hear you!" Tubs yelled into the phone. Unable to help myself, I flinched like I always did when he yelled. Even now, with the many months and miles between us, I hated that he could still have that effect on me.

And suddenly, above the merriment, I heard Mom's voice calling out to him.

"Is it Renny? Tell her she's late and we're still waiting on the pasta bowl!"

My hand tightened into a claw around the phone. I felt like I had been run over by a truck. Not only was she alive, she was *thriving* without me. She didn't care at all that I was gone.

Tears welling in my eyes, I slammed the phone down.

I DIDN'T KNOW how long I had been standing there, but Gideon's voice shocked me from my dark place.

"What're you doing?"

I wiped the tears from my eyes and spun around to face him. He stood there, drinking a glass of lemonade with a paper umbrella in it. Seeing the ridiculous decoration, a bubble of hysterical laughter burst out of me. The ludicrousness of it, coupled with my experience of just moments ago, had me laughing in disbelief.

"OK," he answered, looking at me as if I needed help.

"There's an umbrella in your drink," I gasped, holding my sides.

"Yeah, it came with it," he replied, still not understanding why it was so funny, which of course, just made me laugh all the harder. He frowned at me and took another sip of his drink while he waited for me to regain my composure. "The others were wondering where you'd gotten to."

I took a deep breath. "I'll be there in a minute."

He continued looking at me, his brilliant eyes scrutinizing my strange behavior. He must have seen through my insane laughter as he suddenly asked, "Is everything OK?"

I bit my lip, wondering if I should tell him. We talked a lot, the two of us, and we were pretty close — at least, I thought we were — but I just wasn't comfortable talking about this. I didn't want him to think I was an idiot for calling her. When he'd learned of my past, he'd had a lot to say about what kind of people he thought they were. I knew his opinion on them, as he'd dubbed them trailer trash. I didn't want him to think less of me now so I figured it'd be best to just keep quiet about my call.

"I'm fine. Just hungry is all."

"Tell me something I don't know. Well, come on, the food's almost done. Those skewer things are amazing by the way, I've already had three. Bandit's been begging Sully, but he won't cave so you'll have to sneak him some." He waited for me to go. I moved past him and lead the way back outside.

"Mark must have stocks in hair gel, don't you think? And who doesn't wear socks in their shoes? Freaking hipsters," he lamented.

I burst out laughing again, but this time it was for real.

Trust Gideon.

He could always make me feel better.

15

SULLY

W e chowed down the delicious food and were spread around the terrace now, chatting in groups.

I finished my beer as Mark came up to me brandishing another one that he shook in front of my face. Good with the few I'd already had, I declined.

"Come on, Sul, loosen up."

"I'm not the one who wears suits for a living OK. I'm plenty loose," I retorted. "Anyhow, I don't drink as much as I used to now. My tolerance seems to have lowered as a result."

Mark looked over at Sam, talking to Florence and Zeb. "I'm guessing that's a good woman's influence on you?"

I smiled. "She's the best."

"Very different from Emma, though. She's tougher, though she's no less feminine for it. "

I fake glared at him. "Will you stop checking out my bride-to-be? She's off-bounds."

He rolled his eyes at me. "As if I would go for your seconds. She's not my type, anyway."

"Yeah, nowhere near submissive enough for you," I said.

"There's nothing wrong with an easy life, friend. I get enough excitement with the job as it is, and that was without all your shenanigans."

We stopped ribbing each other, both of us staring at this group of people I called family. Chase laughed at something Gideon had said, while Bandit watched the two of them, his tail wagging. Sam nibbled on a piece of pie as she chatted with Florence, Zeb, and the vets. Mark shook his head, struggling to take it all in. "I can't believe how much your life has changed."

"You and me both. I wouldn't have it any other way now." Even as I said the words, I knew that I meant them. It was a cliche, but time had healed all wounds. Like she could sense what we were talking about, Sam looked over at me and smiled, lighting up the place. God, she was an amazing woman. That I had won this lottery not once, but twice — I knew I was luckier than I had reason to be.

"She'd be happy for you, you know. Emma," Mark said softly. "She wanted you to remarry again."

I looked away from Sam to stare at my friend, startled by this bit of news. "She did? How do you know that?"

"She told me. During one of my last visits with her, back at the hospital." His eyes turned serious as he recalled the moment. "She made me promise that when the time was right, she wanted me to give you her blessing."

Tears pricked at the corners of my eyelids. I felt a huge sense of relief at his words, but there was also confusion. "Why didn't she say any of this to me?"

"Are you serious? You were insane with grief, Sul, and mad at the world. You were in no condition to think about the future, much less the possibility of another woman. She knew that too, which is why she left it to me."

Overwhelmed with feeling, I snatched the bottle from his hand. "You're right, this is a celebration so I should have another."

He slapped me on the shoulder, grinning. "Knock yourself out. Not literally though, I don't want Sam coming after me with her gun."

I laughed, feeling like a weight had been lifted off my shoulders.

16

SULLY

awn broke, bringing along with it birdsong that lit up the morning. We had camped out last night in my old apartment above the clinic. Matt and Izzy, the new vets — and a couple like Emma and I had been — were warm and welcoming hosts, graciously opening their home to us. Mark had said we could stay at his place, a penthouse apartment in the Chelsea district of New York, but we'd already traveled so much, the last thing any of us wanted was to feel the floor moving beneath our feet, even if it would have been the priciest floor the kids would ever have seen.

Despite this, I was surprised by their unwillingness to move until I found them on the Playstation, Chase and Gideon played on that thing well into the night.

Sam hasn't said much to me last night, just that she now knew why leaving here was an even bigger deal than she had imagined — she liked Florence and Mark well enough, but it was their loyalty to me that had brought tears to her eyes. After she had kissed me goodnight, she didn't say anything else. I knew she was giving me space, letting me process my own thoughts back under this roof where I had called home before we had met. I was grateful for her understanding.

I moved out of the bed carefully, not wanting to wake her. Her hair fell in wild abandon over her shoulders as she slept, and she was making that funny little sound she always did, the one that I now couldn't sleep without hearing. I squinted into the still dark room as I climbed over suitcases and shoes to find my workout clothes.

Tugging on a pair of jogging pants and a sweatshirt, I opened the door slowly and snuck outside, stepping over Gideon, sleeping on the floor by Chase. Seeing me, Bandit's ears pricked up as he chuffed in greeting and thumped his tail, but I put a finger to my mouth.

"Shush, don't wake them," I said to him. "Let them sleep." To my surprise, he nodded. I probably shouldn't have been shocked by this, but Bandit's intelligence still caught me off-guard at times. Patting him on the head, I made my way outside.

The air was crisp with the taste that always seemed to follow a recent sunrise. I jogged slowly, enjoying the simple sensation of tarmac beneath my feet. Though my gunshot wound meant I couldn't run like I used to, jogging still brought relief. This was still where I did my best thinking. Alone, out here in the streets, my thoughts could untangle themselves and any pressing concerns usually resolved themselves by the time I returned home.

I took in the familiar streets, drinking in the sight of them as I made my way to my destination. The neighborhood hadn't changed much: immaculate lawns and brightly painted houses with overflowing flower baskets hanging from front porches still greeted me from every angle. The place still looked as if it were straight out of a spread in Better Homes and Gardens. I'm not sure why I thought coming back things would be different. I had changed so much in the last year, I naturally assumed the same would be said of Ellington. Instead, I had to contend with seeing the ghost of Emma around every corner.

My thoughts drifted to Chase, who I noticed was also quiet last night. Several times I had tried to reach her, but whenever I caught her eye, she would give me a small smile and look away. It wasn't until then that I remembered she had her own memories of this place, and none of them good. I planned on talking to her after my run. Until then, she always had Bandit to confide in — many's the night I've walked past her room to hear the two of them conversing fiercely. A kid and their dog was a bond that could never be broken or replicated.

The hard ground changed to grass as I turned a corner into an area of brilliant green. I jogged past two six foot wrought-iron gates into the manicured lawns surrounding neat rows of headstones. Some were elaborate effigies of angels, while others were basic domes of stone. Emma and I had always found the statues too ostentatious and had promised each other that our own would be simple but solid, like our relationship.

When I had lived here, I came to this cemetery once a week, but it had now been half a year since my last visit. I knew it couldn't be helped, but I couldn't stop the sudden pain in my heart all the same.

Never forgotten, always and forever.

Those were the words I had decided for Emma's tombstone. A mix of

my feelings and our vows. I took the paths automatically, not paying attention to them. It was as if my feet knew exactly how to get there, and my
brain didn't have to do anything at all. I passed by a grove of trees shaped in
an arc and steeled myself, knowing I was approaching her resting place. As I
grew closer and finally caught sight of her tombstone, I blinked and slowed
to a walk, uncertain if what I was seeing was real.

Instead of the neat patch of grass I expected to see, the dirt
had *shifted* and clumps of grass lay on top of the grave. I barely processed
the idea that it could not have been an Earthquake, not unless they were
now a possibility in New England. So this meant only one thing.

Someone had vandalized Emma's grave.

17

SULLY

I was rooted to the spot, unable to take in the sight before me.

There were the remnants of a hole that went down a ways though thankfully not far enough for me to see down to her coffin.

Bile crept up in my throat, but I forced myself to keep it down.

What the hell was going on around here?

I looked around, eyes scanning the scenery to see if I could spot the culprit of the grave desecrater lurking around, but at this time of the morning, outside of the birds, I was the only visitor.

I didn't know what to do.

Part of me wanted to throw that dirt back and cover up the hole so Emma was safely tucked away beneath... But another part of me, the angry, twisted part was picturing what I would do to the person if I ever discovered who the hateful jerk was. Flushed with rage, I allowed myself the luxury of pummeling him in my head.

I was still picturing myself smashing his head into the dirt when I caught sight of something on the ground. It was small, with a dull brown pattern on it. As I got closer, I realized it was a hair clip, the kind Emma wore every day to keep her hair out of her face. I remembered she called it a banana clip. It stood out in my mind as I had always considered it a ludicrous name, for a ridiculous-looking object. This clip looked exactly like the ones she wore. Bending down, I picked it up to examine it and saw that I was mistaken. That splash of dull color wasn't a brown pattern at all.

It was blood.

My eyes flew open, startled by my discovery. I had never been one to believe in coincidences, but the odds were stacking up. I contemplated calling Sam with my discovery. If there were a logical explanation, Sam would find it. She would be able to make sense of this. Retrieving my phone from my back pocket, I unlocked the home screen when a chime sounded. It was a text message, but it came from a number I never expected to see again. The message flashed up on my screen, bright as day.

"Help me."

It was from Emma's phone.

Blood rushed into my head. I felt hysteria building up inside of me and my breathing begin to constrict. Gasping for air, I clawed at my throat but couldn't get my anxiety to die down. As panic took over, the world spun.

I felt the ground rushing up to meet me until my face landed in the dirt and I was blessedly out for the count.

18

CHASE

I knew something was up the instant I woke.

Bandit was prodding my shoulder with his nose, trying to get me to wake. When I asked him what was wrong, he just said, "Sully," with his iPad and circled the floor in agitation. It only took a few minutes for me to realize he wasn't here. I woke Gideon, but we decided against worrying Zeb or Sam — last night had been tough on them, and I didn't get the feeling from Bandit that Sully was in danger. Still, Bandit said he'd been gone a while, and he wasn't particularly happy.

"Can you find him, boy?" Gideon asked.

"Woof." Bandit took off so fast, we had to run to keep up with him. We ran past Sully's old neighborhood. I couldn't help but remember how, on that night we had met Sully, we had run through these streets then, though those circumstances had been life and death. In the bright light of day, I could see it was a decent place. There wasn't a single lawn that wasn't cared for, or a car illegally parked. Not for the first time, I felt bad that I had made him leave his perfect life here.

After a while, I realized Bandit was leading us to the cemetery when I saw the sign looming overhead. I wondered if we shouldn't respect Sully's wish to be alone, but then again, he had been gone a while... I figured he'd just have to be mad at us. We rounded a bend when Bandit barked a warning before tearing off towards something in the distance. I squinted into the horizon before I realized what the slumped mound on the ground was.

"Sully!" I screamed.

We hurried to his side. My heart was racing as I fell to my knees. Bandit was darting around him, sniffing in agitation as Gideon felt for a pulse.

"Is he OK? What's wrong with him?" I cried.

"He has a pulse. It's strong." Gideon examined Sully, checking for obvious wounds. "I can't find anything immediately wrong with him." He was still looking for injuries when Sully groaned and slowly opened his eyes. He looked up at us, glazed and groggy.

"What's going on?"

"We just found you passed out on the ground. Are you OK? What happened?" I couldn't stop the shrillness in my voice, this being the last thing I expected to find. Sully blinked at us, taking in his surroundings. His eyes grew suddenly weary.

"I'm OK. Let's talk about it when we get back."

"What? No! Just tell me, right now!" I demanded.

A haunted expression came over his eyes. He hesitated, whatever it was, bothered him deeply, but he also knew neither Gideon nor I would be dropping this anytime soon.   He reached into his pockets but couldn't find what it was he was looking for. Moving quickly onto his knees, he searched the ground around him.

"My phone... can you see my phone?" he asked, his voice unable to mask his panic at being unable to find it. Bandit barked, then came over, carrying the phone gingerly in his mouth. It had been lying a few feet away. Sully took it from him gratefully. "Thanks, boy. It's... the text is in there."

He didn't explain what he meant by that, but I figured it would make sense soon enough. Sully turned the phone over, but we all saw that several cracks now crisscrossed the screen. Concerned, he pressed the home button on his phone, but nothing happened. "Come on... come on..." Sully said, beginning to fall apart. "I need to show you what she said..."

He pressed the button, getting increasingly more desperate until he finally yelled at the thing. "Work Goddamnit!"

Gideon and I said nothing, but shared a look over the top of Sully's head. The guy was falling to pieces, and we had no idea why. Bandit whined unhappily as Sully suddenly took in his immediate surroundings. He was staring in disbelief at the grave. "But... I don't understand, it was disturbed..."

I followed his eye-line to study the grave. Some dirt looked like it was loose, like someone had been digging around but then had put the soil back in place but there wasn't enough to make me think anything in particular. Plus, Sully himself had been lying on it. I'm not saying he dug some of the grave up with his bare hands — that would be loopy — but a quick glance at his fingers and I saw that there was some dirt under his nails. I literally had no idea what was going on.

I looked to Gideon for help. He nodded briefly at me, then took Sully firmly by the arm. "Let's get you up. The others will be getting up soon. Why don't we go back and you can tell us what happened over breakfast?"

His voice was calm and reasonable, like finding Sully freaking out on his dead wife's grave was a regular part of our morning. Glazed, Sully nodded and allowed us to lead him away.

As we left the cemetery, I couldn't help tossing looks over my shoulder. By now, the sun was already shining brightly, casting long black shadows onto the ground. Though I couldn't see anything in those shadows, my senses were in overdrive. Despite all evidence to the contrary, it felt like we were being watched.

Chilled by the thought, I urged the others out of there.

By the time we got back to the clinic, everyone was up.

Sully wouldn't talk about what happened at the cemetery, despite my hounding him with questions. All he would say was that I needed to wait until he could speak to Sam first. I knew it shouldn't have, but the fact he was shutting me out like this, that he was picking Sam over me, it really hurt. Although I was super concerned about him, it was possible that I may have sulked some on the way back.

Florence had already set the table for breakfast with a spread so lavish, it looked like it had come out of a movie. There were plates of Danish pastries (I only knew what they were as Sully had taught me about them a while back — said New Yorkers were particularly keen on them) and jelly doughnuts. There were also waffles and pancakes and a fruit bowl that was the one concession to health.

I noticed no one touched it. Wasn't that always the case?

We made small talk, even though our hearts weren't in it. We had to keep up the pretense or Florence might notice something was up. When I saw that she had made everything but the Danishes and doughnuts from scratch, I asked why she didn't take shortcuts. Microwaves were invented for a reason after all, but she waved off the appliance like it was the devil and ranted about how bad they were for not just our health, but also the environment.

She was very proud of the fact that in sixty plus years she had cooked all her meals and would never touch that microwave trash. Sully tried to make a joke of it by saying look what he's had to put up with all these years, but it fell pretty flat. Luckily, busy with the food, Florence didn't notice.

Despite the effort she had put into the meal, the knot in my stomach wouldn't allow me to eat, which was totally unlike me. I picked at the food, feigning interest, impatiently waiting until Florence went downstairs to open the clinic. As soon as she was gone, Sully finally spoke.

"I know how this is going to sound so I need you all to promise that you won't say anything until I finish talking." He looked at me then, somewhat sternly. "Promise me, Chase."

My mouth fell open. "Why am I being singled out?"

Sam would have laughed but for the serious expression on his face. Suddenly concerned, she shot him a curious smile. "What's going on?" she asked quietly.

Zeb lowered the coffee he had been sipping and looked at us. "Speak up, son."

Sully clasped his hands together in front of him, taking a deep breath. "I went to the grave this morning, but it had been disturbed."

Gasps sounded around the room.

"I know how crazy this sounds. I searched the area but couldn't see anyone, but then I found this hair clip, it's exactly the same as the ones Emma used to wear. And it looks like there's blood on it."

He showed us a simple clip. While he was right — that dull red stain did look like dried blood — there wasn't anything else on that clip that would warrant special treatment. Sam must have thought the same as she spoke up.

"That doesn't really mean anything, Sul. Those clips are very common — heck, I've a few at home myself," she said, trying to placate him. "And the blood, well, first of all, we don't know that it is blood. That would need to be confirmed, and if it turned out that it was, it's still not enough to warrant an investigation unless a person has been reported as missing who wore clips like this."

Sully turned his attention to her. I could see he was struggling with his next words.

"That's not everything, Sam. After I found the clip, I was just about to call you when I received a text message... from Emma's phone."

At that, we all gasped. Gideon's eyes were as wide as mine were I'm sure, but somehow, Sam kept her cool. "Can I see the text?"

Sully paused then, looking trapped. "Well, that's the thing. My phone isn't working now. I think it broke when I fell on it."

She frowned, picking up on the one thing that concerned her the most. "You fell? Are you alright?"

Sully shrugged her question off, uncomfortable. "Yeah. It's nothing."

"That's not true though, is it?" Gideon said softly. "When we found him, he was lying on the ground... unconscious."

Sam's eyes flared open in alarm. "What happened?" she demanded. Zeb too couldn't hide his sudden agitation. "Do we need to get you to a doctor?"

"No, I don't need a doctor. I'm fine," Sully replied firmly. "I'd just had a shock is all... I had a panic attack and passed out."

Sam didn't speak for a moment, her mind ticking over everything she had been told. "You panicked because of the grave and the text message?"

"And the blood on the clip," Sully reminded her.

"You're sure that text was from her number? You couldn't be mistaken?" She spoke carefully, like she was treating him with kid gloves. Sully picked up on her tone and replied, his voice peeved.

"I know her number, Sam. She had the same number for ten years. It's not like I'm going to forget it."

Silence blanketed the room. No one wanted to doubt him, no matter how crazy he was sounding.

"I'm sure there's a reasonable explanation for this," came Sam's steady voice. Though she must be shaken, she kept whatever she was feeling out of her voice. It was one of the reasons she made an awesome Sheriff. Nothing seemed to faze her, ever. Not even the return of Sully's dead wife, apparently.

I knew Sully was going through hell. He spoke in clipped sentences and his eyes were glazed over in shock. This trip was meant to be for him to move on, yet how was he going to do that now Emma was back and hanging over his head. I really felt for him, for the two of them.

"We only had friends in this area, at least, I thought we did. It doesn't make sense for anyone to do this to me."

"Unless your trip home fell on someone's radar and they decided to screw with you. Do you have any enemies here? Anyone sick enough to do this?" Sam asked.

Sully shook his head. "I just saved animals, Sam. No one was interested in me until Bandit came along."

The sudden silence suffocated the room. I had been so focused on Sully that the possibility that this could be linked to Bandit hadn't even crossed my mind. I dropped my gaze to look at him now. He came to my side and pressed against me, worried.

"Not even Florence and Mark know about him?" Sam asked.

"Yeah, I didn't want to get them involved, so I left them out of it," Sully replied.

The implication of his answer filled me with terror. While I knew there could be a simple — if twisted — reason for this, we had been through enough that I didn't like loose endings. Especially when they involved someone who was dead and buried for over a year.

"Emma's phone... what did you do with it after she died?" Sam asked, mind already working through this like it was one of her cases.

"Well, that's the thing... After she died, I kept going through her phone just to read her messages. But one night, I'd had too much to drink and must have fallen asleep on the couch. When I woke up, the phone was crushed. I probably trod on it during my stupor. I threw it away months ago before Chase ever turned up at the clinic."

He paused then, for his next words to sink in.

"The phone doesn't exist."

19

SULLY

The second the words left my mouth, I knew there was a simple way to clear this up.

"Sam, let me use your phone."

She handed me her cell even as her eyes grew wide, knowing what I was about to do. I dialed the digits from memory, fully expecting there to be a logical explanation to all this... like I was having a breakdown. Something. I hit enter and waited, gripping the phone so hard, I thought it might shatter in my hand. Sam pinned her eyes on me, love and concern radiating from her. Chase and Gideon flanked my side while Zeb sat by Bandit, neither of them moving. It was as if they thought their proximity would protect me from whatever was happening.

Musical tones sounded from the phone, followed by an automated voice notifying us that this phone number was no longer in use. I couldn't move. Couldn't do anything but stare at the phone. How was this possible when I had only recently received a message from this line?

Sam frowned, but I couldn't tell if it was from concern for me or herself. Somewhere in the back of her mind, she must be doubting my sanity. I couldn't say I wouldn't be doing the same if the shoe were on the other foot. The dead dial tone echoed around the room, loud and ominous.

"What kind of dick pretends to be someone's dead wife?" Gideon finally said, breaking the silence. While the rest of the group seemed stricken by events, Gideon was taking it in his stride. He didn't believe anything out-of-the-norm was happening. He probably thought it was a bunch of basement-dwelling teenagers out for kicks. I still didn't have an answer about what was happening, but I knew one thing, and one thing only.

It wasn't safe to be here anymore.

Whether a simple prank or something more nefarious, I couldn't risk Florence or this clinic again. We had to leave immediately.

"Pack your things, we're going home."

I didn't bother explaining why, and I was relieved when no one questioned my decision. Chase, in particular, had grown pale, probably remembering what happened the last time we were here. I gave her shoulder a squeeze, and she leaped quickly into action, gathering her things. For someone who loved Twenty Questions, she knew when keeping silent was the better course of action. I gave Sam back her phone. She took it, looking contemplative. The others disbanded to prepare for our journey home, but Sam had a thoughtful expression on her face.

"What is it?" I asked.

"Can you pack? I think I'd like to check out the grave site."

My instant reaction was to say no — I didn't like the thought of her being out there alone. As if she sensed my objection, she reached for my hand.

"You know I can handle myself. I'll be careful."

"Still, I'd be happier if you took someone with you."

"That's not necessary, Sully. I won't be long, I promise."

With that she kissed me on the mouth then headed off before I could argue. I knew Sam could take care of herself better than most people, but I wasn't particularly happy about her visiting the grave without me. However, I also knew I was in no fit state to return there.

Looking at the clock, I decided I'd give her twenty minutes then call to check her progress. I was hoping she would find something that would corroborate my story at the very least, something that would make me sound less like a madman.

20

SAM

S am drove the short distance to the cemetery.

When she had asked Izzy, the vet, if she could borrow her car, the other woman didn't look remotely concerned by the request at all, she only asked if she was going far. It was a testament to the stories Florence must have told about Sully that Sam was immediately deemed trustworthy by extension. When she had revealed that she wanted to pay her respects to Emma, Izzy's eyes had softened, thinking what a wonderful thing she was doing. She even insisted that Sam take the flowers that had just come in from a grateful patient with her. Sam had tried to refuse, but despite her diminutive frame, Izzy was incredibly strong-willed.

So now Sam drove towards the cemetery, a bunch of flowers hastily wrapped in a plastic bag lying on the passenger seat next to her.

Although she hadn't been there before, it wasn't hard to find. Just a few short turns with the car and she was practically there. She probably would have found it even without using Izzy's GPS.

Parking, Sam grabbed the flowers and got out of the car. A breeze whistled through the trees, providing a pleasant soundtrack as she navigated to Emma's grave. A few early morning visitors were dotted around. One elderly couple even nodded to her as she went past. Their eyes were red from tears that they didn't bother to hide. Sam guessed they must have lost a dear one quite recently and lowered her head, respectfully.

She had been going maybe five minutes when she saw the arc of trees that signaled she was approaching her destination. Her pulse sped up even as Sam didn't expect to find anything. If things were as Sully had described,

Chase and Gideon would have noticed. As it was, they had been noticeably silent when Sully had explained his sequence of events. Still, Sam had to give him the benefit of doubt.

She knew she had the right tombstone even as her eyes recognized the name inscribed on it. Seeing the words Sully had chosen, conflicting emotions coursed through her: sorrow for the pain Sully had gone through, and though she wasn't proud of it, she also felt envy for the dead woman who still commanded so much of his heart. Yet Sam would never reveal that to Sully, knowing he could never be expected to take on board her own feelings on the subject.

Her eyes traveled down the headstone, to the patch of grass surrounding it. She could see that some of the earth here had been disturbed as Sully had described, but what she saw would be consistent with say a squirrel who decided to dig around while he searched for nuts. Or maybe some maintenance work had gone on in the cemetery.

Either way, it should not have caused Sully to have reacted the way he had.

Trying to quell the anxiousness that was starting to churn in her stomach, Sam bent down to examine one of the spots with her finger. The earth was only loose on the very surface, about two inches deep, adding weight to her squirrel theory. Brow lined with concern, Sam surveyed the area to see if anything suspicious caught her eye, but there were only the rows of tombstones, marking the resting places of other past souls.

What on earth had made Sully react the way he had?

21

SULLY

W hile I packed, I tried to wrap my head around the phone message. I was sure I had canceled Emma's phone contract shortly after her death, but those were dark days and I had muddled through them medicated by beer and sleeping pills. It was possible, I knew, that I had missed it somehow — I was the man who had been hoarding her things, after all, maybe I had left it deliberately so I could always hear her voicemail.

Sam returned from the cemetery just as we started loading the car. We couldn't talk with others there, not with Florence hovering around us, so the two of us stepped aside. Under the shadow of a tree, several cars away, Sam revealed what she had found.

"I'm sorry, hon. I just didn't find anything that seemed out of place." She had explained her animal theory to me, but that didn't jibe with what I had seen. I didn't understand how this could be. It wasn't in my mind, the message and the holes on the grave, they were real.

"You're sure? Did you check the other graves? If it were an animal, they wouldn't have just hit Emma's."

"I did... there just wasn't anything there." She looked pained, like she wanted to be on my side, but couldn't. A rush of disappointment flooded over me. None of it made any sense.

"We can talk about this later, Sul, once we're home."

I nodded mutely, unable to collect my thoughts. It was almost a relief that I could focus on the manual task of packing. Soon after, everything was together. I made our excuses as Florence stared at me. The women in my life had always been able to see through whatever I was hiding from them, and Florence was no exception. Despite the fact that we were cutting our trip short by several days, she didn't complain, just gave me a hug and asked if she had to worry about me. I said no. To her credit, she didn't even flinch, but we both knew I was lying.

As we piled into the car, Florence slipped her hand through the window and gave mine a squeeze. Her eyes shone with tears as she shot me a small smile.

"Try not to get into any more trouble. My heart can't take another incident."

I kissed her hand and started the engine. As we pulled away, I saw her watching me from the curb, her figure growing smaller and smaller until I could barely make her out anymore.

22

——————

CHASE

For someone who had been initially so excited by the possibility of a road trip, I was so relieved when we pulled up outside the ranch just over four hours later.

Sam and Gideon had taken shifts driving while Sully rested. No one had really discussed doing that, but I guess we decided he needed a break. There wasn't much talk of what had happened at the cemetery and the missing text.

Sam said she'd run the number through the system, but for now, we just had to assume that someone knew Sully would be going home, someone who had something against him and who decided now was the time to get back at him. Sam was absolutely firm in this, refusing to consider any other scenario, but I knew Sully wasn't convinced. I could see it in the way he didn't meet her eyes when he agreed with her. I had a horrible feeling that maybe; he wasn't quite as ready to let Emma go as we had thought.

Sam parked the car as we piled out. Sully went to help Zeb while Gideon flung open the front door and we started trooping inside when Bandit suddenly froze, his ears pricked high. He whimpered and spun around, searching for whatever it was that had gotten his attention. Then he pawed the ground and looked at us. I'd known him long enough to know what he wanted even without the iPad which was still packed in one of our cases.

Follow me.

Confused, I went with him as he led me to the back door. "What is it?" I asked.

He whined at me, pawing at the door. Whatever was going on, Bandit didn't have time to wait for his tablet. He shoved his nose at us urgently, hurrying us to open the door. Frowning, Gideon unlocked the door as Bandit tore off into the long grass, barking and whining until he reached a particular spot and stopped, circling the area, barking at us.

"He's found something," Gideon said concerned, as we hurried out there. He had much longer legs than me plus he could run faster so he got to Bandit before I did. When I finally reached them, panting from the sudden exertion, he waved at me to hang back.

There was a shadow in the long grass.

A shape that was low and *moving*. As Gideon got closer, it whimpered, and I recognized that sound immediately.

It was a dog.

Some kind of mongrel mix. It had the face of a German Shepherd, but its short legs resembled those of a Corgi. I remembered seeing them once and finding them kind of comical looking — I'd read somewhere that the Queen of England had an entire tribe of them.

This dog was short but painfully slim. Her brown eyes were pinned on us in alarm. Her tongue hung out as she panted, terrified.

"Back up," Gideon said. I did as he commanded, gesturing at the others who, having realized something was up, were now coming up behind me, to stay back. Bandit darted around the dog, sniffing like crazy. He whined as if what he could smell concerned him, then he dashed to my side. Seeing how scared the other dog was, however, I figured he wanted us to give her space.

Gideon lowered into a crouch, making himself smaller, then he shuffled closer, making soothing sounds. "Hey, girl. I'm not going to hurt you. I just want to help."

The dog's eyes darted wildly as she took in all of us before settling on him. She bared her teeth in a snarl but couldn't stop the trembling in her body. I knew it was bravado, a show she was putting on to try to warn Gideon away. Still, scared dogs acted irrationally sometimes, attacking without warning, so he had to be careful.

He stopped, reaching slowly into a pocket where he took out the remnants of a Nutter Butter pack. The dog's nose wrinkled as she smelled the cookie. She kept looking at Gideon, but some of her suspicion became overridden by hunger as a great blob of drool suddenly fell from her mouth. Gideon saw this as he snapped a cookie in half and tossed it to her. It landed between her paws, right under her nose. Her jaws lunged forward, and she snapped up the cookie, never taking her eyes off of him. He threw the other half at her. Again, she ate it up. She looked at him, eyes begging for more. Gideon gave her the rest of the pack, which she hovered up in no time.

"I'm sorry girl, if you want more, you'll have to come inside with me. I'm all out," he said, showing her his bare hands and the empty wrapper. The dog looked at him, then his hands, then the empty wrapper. A whine of fear escaped her lips as she tossed a nervous glance at the rest of us, though we were rapidly backing away.

Gideon moved slowly towards her. She whined again but didn't move. Slowly, slowly, he stretched out a hand to touch her. She trembled under his touch but allowed him to pet her. He fussed her for several moments just letting her get used to him when finally her tongue snaked out to lick him. Gideon smiled.

"See, that's not so bad now, is it?"

He stayed with her until he could stand up without her cowering behind him.

"Come on, girl, follow me. We've got lots of food inside."

I wasn't sure whether she understood him or not, but the dog wouldn't move. Gideon tried again.

"No one is going to hurt you. We just want to see if you're alright," he pleaded. Still she wouldn't move. Gideon stopped, not knowing what else to do when Bandit barked beside me. I don't know what he said, but her ears pricked up and she started towards the ranch of her own accord. I stroked the top of his head, marveling once again at him.

"Thanks, boy," I said to him gratefully.

"Woof."

23

SULLY

Gideon fed the dog, who wolfed down the food like she hadn't eaten in days.

I hadn't been able to get too close to her — she growled every time anyone who wasn't Gideon approached her. I was glad she trusted him, though it made examining her a bit of a pain.

I could see her ribs clearly showing against her side. Her coat was encrusted with dirt and I was pretty sure those black spots were mites in her ears. I'd instructed Bandit to stay away from her until I could clean her up, as I didn't want him to catch anything from her. Bandit seemed all too pleased to comply, which surprised me. I thought he'd like another dog around, but she seemed to put him on edge. He kept sniffing her and staying behind Chase. I'd seen him with dogs before, back at the clinic when Forbes' men had attacked us. Bandit had asked the other dogs for help, so I knew he wasn't afraid of dogs — far from it — so this behavior was a little puzzling. It could just be he was protecting his territory. However, as clever as he was, Bandit was still just a dog.

"Since she trusts you, I'll need you to hold her head and talk to her calmly while I try to get a look at her," I told Gideon. "Now, she may get frightened. The key are her ears. If she lays them flat on her head, she's going to attack, in which case, you back up immediately."

"Got it," Gideon answered.

"Sam, Chase, you guys have this sheet ready. If it looks like she's going to attack, the two of you throw this sheet over her and we'll trap her in it. If she can't see, she won't be able to attack. We use this technique all the time so you should be fine," I said.

I caught Chase staring at me funny. "What?"

"Isn't that only used on cats?" she asked.

"How do you know that?" I said. "Wait, let me guess, you read it somewhere and your brain filed it away for exactly this moment?"

She nodded.

"It'll work on her too." I nodded to them all. "Ready?"

Gideon started stroking the dog as I approached from her side — not her back — I wanted her to see me coming so she wouldn't be startled. At my first touch, her legs shook, and she tossed a few nervous looks at me, but Gideon's voice seemed to have a calming effect on her. She pressed her head into his hands as if she was afraid to look at what was about to happen.

I felt around her torso. Though her ribs were prominent, I couldn't feel any breaks. It was the same for her legs. Looking into her ears, I confirmed my early suspicion — they were plagued by the little suckers. If she'd let me, I could clean out the majority of them, but I'd need drops to get rid of the rest and to deter them from coming back. I'd try that later when she was more at ease with us, but right now, I just wanted to make sure there wasn't anything pressing to contend with.

Bandit whined by Chase, hyper concerned. Hearing him, the dog shook with fright. We all knew Bandit would never harm her but it seemed she wasn't so sure. I didn't think she would hurt any of us, but I also didn't want to run the risk of her flipping out.

"Bandit, could you stay outside? Your being here seems to be scaring her."

Bandit whined unhappily and shook himself as if to say there was nothing to fear from him, but he trotted out, tossing us a longing look over his shoulders as he went.

"Thanks boy."

Sighing deeply, he left the room. Carefully, I took hold of the dog's mouth, mindful that even in her weakened state, those teeth could do plenty of damage, and what with my face being so close to those jaws... Well, I was being vigilant.

I pried her mouth open. Her teeth weren't too bad — she was younger than I had first thought. Breath was as expected (bad), tongue a decent color. Next, I examined her legs where I could see thick scars that had healed around the bottom of her legs, close to the paws. There was a matching scar around her neck. A red-hot burn of rage started building inside me. These scars were consistent with being chained against her will for an extended period. Shifting her fur, I saw other scars and bruises, some only days old, while others had clearly been there much longer. Unable to hide my feelings, Chase picked up on my anger immediately.

"What's wrong?"

I looked at her. "She's been badly beaten, chained and starved, up until the moment she probably escaped."

Chase drew in her breath sharply while Gideon gripped his fists into balls.

"You think someone did this to her recently?" he asked.

I nodded. "Yeah, but they've had a while, judging by the scars and bruises I've found. Might be that she's always been tortured. We could be the first nice people she's met."

Gideon looked at the dog, with her head in his hands, hiding from the sorry world that had broken her. "I'm sorry, girl, but whoever they were, they won't hurt you again. You're safe now."

She looked up at him with large brown eyes and whimpered.

24

SULLY

I t wasn't until I sat on the edge of our bed that I realized how weary I was feeling.

I tugged off my boots, letting them drop to the floor with a thud. Sam moved past into the ensuite bathroom. Moments later, I heard the sound of running water. Steam curled out from the bathroom, fogging the air. I was surprised to see Sam return fully dressed.

"You're not getting in the bath?"

"No, I'm drawing it for you. It's been a long day, figured you could do with some relaxing."

I normally only ever showered, preferring the pounding water to beat down on my body, but the idea of lying in a hot bath didn't seem too bad right now. Maybe a soak would clear the tension from my mind and shoulders. She looked at me and dropped a kiss on my head. If I were a smart man, I would've just gone into that bathroom and let the hot water do its thing, but I wasn't. Frowning, I took her hand.

"You've known me what, six months now. If I'm not sure about something, I don't bring it up, true?" I asked. She looked down at me and nodded.

"I'm not saying you're lying, Sul, it's just... you've been under a lot of stress. I knew going back wouldn't be easy for you, seeing your friends and previous life. I don't even know if you've had time to grieve properly..."

"That's not what this is. I am not making this up because I miss my wife, besides the timing doesn't make sense. Why would I suddenly be doing this?"

She didn't say anything, just continued to look at me with those piercing eyes of hers.

"We have just decided to do something big, Sully, maybe deep down, you're not ready for the changes that might bring about."

I realized then what she was thinking. "This hasn't got anything to do with us getting married. I don't have a problem with that, with moving on."

"I know," she said. "Listen, don't worry about it tonight. I'll look into the calls in the morning when I'm back at work. I'll run a trace, see what I can find out."

Relief surged out of me. Despite how she had said she would do this before, I guess there was a part of me that doubted she would, but if she was going to do that, it meant she was willing to believe me. She didn't think I was the mad man I was beginning to sound like.

She nodded in the direction of the bathroom. "Go on before it gets cold."

She shot me a smile as she opened the suitcase and started to unpack our things from the trip. I gave her shoulder a squeeze as I headed into the ensuite.

"Thanks hon."

25

SAM

S am focused on the clothes in front of her, taking out several armfuls and dumping them onto the bed. The everyday action of folding clothes was bringing a small sense of peace. If she could just sort the mound in front of her, maybe her mind would stop shrieking and sending out its distress signal.

She saw Sully drop his clothes on the floor (something that usually drove her mad, but today the normality of it gave some relief) and lower into the bath. From her position opposite the ensuite, Sully would not be able to see her as he had his back to her.

Exactly the way she wanted it.

Keeping a watchful eye on him, Sam moved to his side of the bed, to where Sully had left his cell phone. Watching to make sure Sully wasn't going to see what she was doing, Sam picked up his phone, unclipped the battery and slipped out the SIM card which she quickly put into her own phone.

When Sully had been giving his explanation of events at the cemetery, he had caught her off-guard and Sam had not remembered that a phone's log wasn't actually saved on the device itself, but on the phone's SIM card. It wasn't until they were on the drive home that this had come to her attention. Sam knew she could have mentioned this to Sully earlier, but the truth was, she wanted to check this out herself.

She turned her phone on and waited impatiently, tossing a look at Sully to make sure he couldn't see what she was up to. Sam wasn't an insecure person and had never had reason to go through her man's phone before.

The boyfriends she'd had before Sully had all been decent guys, but the relationships had ended when the romance had fizzled out. She was still friends with a few of them, though their new wives weren't that keen on Sam being in the picture, so she had respected their wishes and disappeared out of their lives. Having to deploy this duplicity now hurt Sam almost as much as it would Sully, but she had to know.

The logo for the phone appeared, followed by Sully's home screen, and Sam was in!

Scrolling quickly through the menu, she came to the text message log, but she could find no mention of the text Sully claimed to have received — there were just the usual texts sent from each of them.

She swiped through until she reached his text messages. Nothing seemed out of the ordinary, just the usual texts sent from each of them. There was one from Sam, asking when they wanted to do their big reveal dinner, a few from Gideon with basic housekeeping questions. Chase had sent Sully some funny memes. The sight of them made Sam's lips curve into a smile. What was it about Chase and memes? The kid was always trawling through the net to find them, or she'd be laughing at her phone reading 9Gag. Trying to explain the joke to Bandit usually resulted in more laughter, as the dog just did not understand the concept of humor. Thinking of them, of her family, the smile left her face as Sam felt another pang of unease that she couldn't shake. They were so happy before this trip. Why did this have to happen?

Finding nothing in the inbox, Sam clicked on the sent folder. There were only three texts, but what she read was enough to send chills down her spine.

"Who is this?" read the first text. The next asked, "Why are you doing this?" The last text, consisting of only one word, had the biggest impact on Sam.

"Emma?"

Sam looked over at the man she loved, relaxing in the bath.

Her eyes dark with worry.

26

CHASE

I t took a while, but Sully was finally happy that he'd done all he could for the dog.

Not that he expected to find a missing report on her, but Sully ran through the usual sites all the same. She wasn't an expensive dog, wasn't used for breeding. It looked like it was a clear case of neglect and abuse. Though I wasn't happy about this, I had to admit it was easier to focus on her, rather than what had happened with Sully at the cemetery. We'd retreated into our own rooms, but I was sure Sam and Sully were having more conversations about it all.

Bandit and I were having a big discussion of our own. He sat with me on the bed, asking questions about the other dog. I was trying my best to explain, but it wasn't like I had many answers myself.

"She doesn't like me."

Hearing his iPad say those words, I shook my head and scratched behind his ears on the favorite spot of his. "Not true, Muttface. She doesn't know you is all. She needs time before she'll trust us."

"Except Gideon. She likes Gideon."

"Well, yeah, she does seem to be into him."

An image of him flashed up in my mind. Gideon, making comforting sounds as the dog shivered in his hands. I hadn't wanted to make a big deal of it at the time, or even now I guess, but something about the way he took care of her, how he was genuinely concerned for her... it had made me feel kinda warm inside. Like I'd drank a mug of coffee or something, but then my thoughts drifted to Sully's predicament and I found myself turning cold.

"Chase what is wrong?"

"This whole Emma thing is freaking me out. Why would Sully think she texted him?"

"Maybe it is a mistake?"

"Has to be, right? Sully can't really be thinking that his wife is back from the dead, not after all this time. Things like that don't happen."

A knock sounded on my door. I looked up to see Gideon, the other dog trailing behind him like his shadow. Seeing us, she stopped dead.

"Hey girl," I called out to her. "Do you want to come inside?"

The dog whimpered and backed up until her rump was against the far wall, very clearly not wanting to come in. Gideon reached down and patted her on the head, trying to reassure her. I was surprised to see that she didn't cringe away from him.

"Wow, she's really taken to you," I said.

"I've been bribing her with food for hours, so yeah, it hasn't gone to waste," he replied. "Can't get her to go near anyone else though, even Sully, and you know animals usually love him."

"She just needs time. Of course, now she's decided to adopt you, you know you're responsible for her," I grinned, liking his trapped expression.

"She follows me everywhere. Even to the bathroom. I was taking a leak when I realized she was standing between my feet. It was pretty disconcerting."

I laughed, "I'd love to have seen that." I said it without thinking, but the minute the words were out of my mouth, I blushed furiously. Idiot! I wanted the floor to open up and swallow me whole. "What I meant was..." I didn't need to finish though as Gideon was shaking his head.

"Yeah, I know. Let's forget you said anything and move on."

"Please."

Bandit walked up to Gideon and nuzzled his hand, but as soon as he got to him, we heard growling from the door. The dog was watching us and didn't like Gideon petting another dog. Bandit stopped, tilting his head to listen to her.

"She does not like me."

"No boy, she's just jealous and insecure. And you're another dog, I'm sure this is normal behavior," Gideon explained. "But since she is so flighty and attached to me, maybe it's best if I stay away from you for a while. Just so she feels a little more at ease around here."

Bandit sighed, green eyes looking impossibly sad as he moved away from Gideon and came to sit beside me. I tried to placate him with a hug and felt him lick my ear in return, which felt totally gross but, not wanting to upset him any further, I took it like a trooper. *The things we do for our dogs.*

"Have you come up with a name?" I asked.

"I have, just not sure whether I should name her yet..." He trailed off, looking uncertain.

"You're worried you'll name her then her real owners will find her?"

He nodded.

"You saw the condition she was in. Look at her, she won't even come into the room when Bandit and I are clearly nice. No one is looking for her. If anything, they're probably running scared that we'll find out who they are and sue the living crap out of them — which would be totally worth it. We should so do that."

A smile flashed over his face. I tried not to think about how that made me feel and stuck my face in Bandit's fur. "So what is it, what's her name?"

"Pixie," he said.

I grinned at him. "That suits her perfectly."

I turned to Bandit. "What do you say, can you introduce yourself to Pixie nicely? Maybe you could loan her one of your toys? She's probably never had one."

Bandit barked, then trotted over to his bed where several toys sat around it. His nose hovered over his Frumpy Rabbit soft toy, but I knew Pixie would never get that. It was his absolute favorite thing outside of his iPad. He nudged Frumpy out of the way, then picked up another soft toy — a cat with a long tail — and moving to the doorway, he stopped a few feet from Pixie. A low, warning growl rumbled in the back of her throat. She might only be a tiny thing, but she sure didn't seem to know it.

Respecting her wishes, Bandit laid the toy on the floor gently. Pixie kept growling even as she tried to meld herself further into the wall. It upset me, if I'm honest. Here was Bandit, literally the nicest, smartest dog in the world, offering her one of his toys, and she was just going to yell at him.

Bandit took a step back, watching her. Pixie stared back at him, eyes wide, ears turned towards the back but not yet flattened onto her head. Gently, gently, he nudged the toy. It rolled towards her until it bumped against her paws. Still, she didn't move, didn't even glance down at her feet.

"She's really scared of Bandit for some reason," Gideon said. Hearing this, Bandit whined, then backed all the way back into the room. When he was back with me, Pixie suddenly leaped forward and snatched the toy into her mouth.

"One small step for dogkind I guess. I'd better take her to her room, get her settled."

"She's not staying with you?" I asked, surprised.

"Sully doesn't think that's smart since we've only just met her. He's not sure she won't harm me yet, so she's going to be spending the night in the den."

"Right. Sensible plan."

Gideon clicked his tongue at Pixie and started walking away when I stopped him with a call. "Gid...?"

He turned back to me.

"What do you think is going on with Sully?"

His brow creased with concern as his eyes grew dark with worry. "I don't know, but Sam will figure it out." With that, he went away, Pixie following close behind as she tossed Bandit one last look.

27

THE SCIENTIST

Staring into the live feed of the ranch, The Scientist watched the proceedings in the girl's room with interest. So the boy was bonding with the new dog while Sullivan was showing signs of post-traumatic stress disorder.

People were so predictable, it was boring.

Take the girl. Despite all that had happened to her — and The Scientist had managed to find out quite a bit about her life thanks to Forbes' soldier monkey — she was ordinary street scum, trailer trash. To think this was the girl who had wrecked his partner's life... It was unfathomable.

And the vet... so he'd received a text message from his dead wife's phone, and that was enough to unravel him. The Scientist almost felt sorry for the Sheriff, if that were an emotion he allowed himself to feel. Here she was, thinking that she was going to get married soon when clearly her husband-to-be hadn't gotten over his previous wife. He mulled over the complexity of feelings and how they were the downfall of man — he himself had learned this the hard way. He tensed as a memory clawed its way up from the darkest pit of his mind.

He saw himself as a young boy, a talented boy who wanted nothing but for his parents to acknowledge him, however, they were too busy with their work and social lives, and he was nothing more than a nuisance they kept fed. Occasionally, they would trot him out like a pet to showcase. Their friends loved to see how bright, yet how deeply awkward he was. They would coo at his brain, then laugh when they saw him trip over his own clumsy feet. In their eyes, he was nothing but a clown. But he would show them.

He would show them all.

Looking at the girl now, at how she conversed with the dog over her concerns for Sullivan, he saw she was just a child and a very insecure one at that. The dog, however... he was such a specimen! And it wasn't only his intellect or the way his brain had physically altered itself... the dog seemed like he had genuine feelings.

Human emotions.

It would be almost a shame to do what he had to, but that was the way of science. The groundbreakers were the ones who took risks — even unpleasant ones — in order to get the result they needed. What was that saying he was so fond of?

A genius is one who shoots for something others can't see... and hits it.

Well, he was already a genius, that much was obvious. He only had to wait for the world to see it.

He looked down at his experiment, at the rise and fall of its chest, and smiled.

Soon, my lovely. Soon.

28

CHASE

The sun streamed in, bathing my face in warm light.

I woke and stretched as Bandit snuck a morning lick at me. I'd told him a million times to leave my face alone, but he seemed to think I didn't mean it, plus I got the feeling it amused him. I suppose there were worse things to wake up to, so I usually tried not to make a deal of it.

"Hey, we should go check on Pixie. See how she's doing this morning."

"I hope she liked my cat."

I climbed off my bed, tugging on a thin sweater. Fall was still a month or so away, but there was a definite chill in the air when I woke now. I flung open the curtains, enjoying the scenery outside. Trees stretched out across the horizon as far as the eye could see. It's funny how I didn't miss the busyness of New York one bit. Yeah, it was laid back and quiet here, but I'd had enough excitement to last me a lifetime already. I was looking forward to the day I could sit on the porch and yell at kids to get off my lawn.

Yes, I know I sound old, but I don't care.

We went down the hall, towards the den where I knew Gid had set up a private corner for Pixie. He'd pushed a few tables onto their side and created a sort of table fort for her that he'd covered with blankets for privacy. We had tried to keep her contained in a room at first, but she'd panicked like crazy when we'd shut the door on her. Sully thought this way was better. She'd be contained but wouldn't feel like she was being caged.

Pixie seemed a tiny bit happier this morning, though the blanket we had given her to sleep on was ripped and bitten to shreds, as were the ones we'd used to drape over the tables. Bite marks punctured what was left of

Bandit's cat — chunks of it were spread all around her like roadkill. She must have been gnawing at the thing most the night to kill it like this. Horrified, Bandit took in the sight of his mutilated friend and tried to paw all the pieces into a pile that he picked up gently into his mouth. I felt like a total heel since it had been my suggestion to loan the toy to her. I shot Bandit an apologetic look.

"Sorry, boy, I didn't know she'd do that. We'll try to fix this one OK, and if I can't, I'll get you a replacement cat, an even better one!"

He woofed in agreement, but hung his head sadly. Those big green eyes of his looked almost as if they were tearing up. Then again, he was always very sensitive. I guess it would be awhile before he'd get over his loss. Feeling awful, I focused my attention on Pixie, hoping she would distract me from my guilty conscience.

"Hey, girl. How're you this morning?"

She looked at me, eyes wide. Her legs shook a bit, but she didn't otherwise move or growl. Well, this was progress. I smiled at her. Bandit came closer for his own look, but as soon as she saw him, she bared her teeth and whimpered at the same time.

"Sully's never seen that reaction before," came Sam's voice from behind me.

I looked over my shoulder to find her there. She was already dressed for work but seemed a little down this morning. Dark shadows rimmed her eyes, and her smile wasn't as bright as it usually was.

"He checked on her last night, when he couldn't sleep. Bandit must've heard him as he went to join him, but Pixie did the same thing then when she saw him. Sully said it's a double reaction that he's never seen before — usually it's one or the other — but not both. He's pretty confused by it."

"She is strange."

The words came from Bandit. We looked at him.

"Well, she's had a tough life. She's bound to have some scars," Sam explained. But Bandit whined and continued.

"She killed my cat."

Sam laughed then and scratched his ears.

"Oh buddy, we'll get you another one."

"But it won't smell the same."

Gideon came up from behind us, looking bright-eyed and well, completely put together. I tugged my sweater down self-consciously, wishing I'd showered before I left my room. Why did he always look like he'd just stepped out of a catalog?

"How's she doing?" he asked.

"Better, I think, though she killed Felix and the blankets, and she still doesn't seem keen on Bandit," I answered, watching as he went over to her slowly, offering his hand so she could sniff him first. Amazingly, she stopped trembling and allowed him to pet her.

"She really does like you." I was super impressed by how she trusted him.

"Got good taste obviously," he replied, smug.

"Or she's been so badly tortured, she's lost all sense," I retorted, rolling my eyes.

Sam had been listening to us, but now her face became serious. "Guys, I need to speak to you about something, but not here. I need Zeb as well. Sully's going to pick some things up for Pixie after breakfast, so can you stick around? I won't be long, but it's important I speak with you all."

She said all, but I noticed she was omitting Sully.

"Sure," I answered, while Gideon just nodded, his eyes mirroring my concern.

BREAKFAST WAS A TENSE AFFAIR.

Gideon had cooked bacon and eggs but hardly anyone ate. Sully just drank coffee while he checked over Pixie. She seemed a little happier with us today and had yet to growl at anyone, though she watched us like a hawk, only stopping when Gid put a bowl heaped with doggie chow in front of her face. She wolfed down the lot of it like how Bandit used to when we'd first had him. I knew how she felt. I knew what it was to be starving with hunger. I made a mental note to get her some extra treats when I popped into town later.

Since Sam had mentioned that she wanted to speak to us without Sully, the whole thing had been hanging over my head. It must have been bothering Gid too, as he was unusually quiet. Thoughts on his own mind, Sully didn't seem to notice how troubled we were all feeling today. Only Zeb seemed oblivious, doing a crossword while Bandit watched, fascinated. Though he was pretty hot stuff with the Jeopardy app, crosswords he just couldn't get his head around. Something to do with the phrasing of the questions had him super confused. He couldn't answer even the simplest ones, so he thought Zeb was a God whenever he finished one. I pushed cereal around in my bowl until Sully left.

Pouring a glass of OJ, Sam sat in her usual seat beside Sully's empty chair, at the head of the table. She cleared her throat and looked at us.

"I know none of us want to be talking without Sully here, but there are some things I feel it's important for us to discuss, particularly after recent events," she began. Gideon put his fork on the table while Zeb, who never ate much in the morning anyway, watched her, eyes dark and inscrutable.

"I've been looking into grief counseling. I think Sully's stressed and the trip East raised unresolved issues that he still has regarding Emma's death."

"It's been a year and a half though," Gideon said. "Surely he's moved on by now."

Sam shrugged. "It takes some people longer to get over the death of their partner. There is no time limit to this."

"I'm not over losing my wife, and it's been quite a bit longer for me," Zeb said, backing her up, his brows furrowed with concern.

I looked at Sam, not wanting to say anything yet feeling compelled to. "But, you guys are getting married..." I let my sentence trail off, not sure how to finish.

Sam nodded and gave me a reassuring smile that didn't quite manage to reach her eyes. "Yes, we are. But I think the thought of a wedding — no matter how small — is causing memories of his previous wedding with Emma to surface, and with that, his mind is panicking."

"You think he's cracking up?" Gideon asked, worry emanating from him in spades.

"I don't think it's helpful to label it," Sam said, a little sternly.

"I agree," Zeb said. "Probably best just to keep an eye on him, make sure he's looking after himself."

"Yes, we need to look after him. And it isn't helpful to doubt what he thinks."

"You mean the text?" I asked.

"The thing is, whatever is going on, Sully believes it, so we just have to stand by him for now. Let's just give him some time. I'm sure he'll sort himself out."

Bandit pawed the ground and shook himself, which actually meant he was in fierce agreement.

"But you're going to look into it, right? Just in case?" I said.

"You betcha," Sam said, her eyes turning hard.

Relief flooded through me. If someone was messing with Sully, Sam would find them. Sam wouldn't let them get away with it.

29

CHASE

I went through the rest of the morning aimlessly.

After Sam and Gid went to work, Zeb retreated to his room to read. He said it was a perk of being old that he could just laze away his time, but I was young and needed a schedule. It was partly his insistence that made me the de facto grocery shopper for our clan. Carrying an empty shopping basket, I stared up at the endless shelves, mind blank by the options available to me. Who were the people who decided we needed so many versions of the same thing? How different could canned tuna taste? They were even priced the same. I wasn't sure how long I'd been looking at a brand of beans when Bandit's wet nose touched my hand. I shook my head, clearing myself from my daze, and looked down at him.

"Sorry, bud, just have a lot on my mind, you know?"

He woofed once. *Yes, I know* I translated his answer, sure that was what he meant even without the iPad. One of the perks of living in a small town was how everyone knew one another. At first, this had made me super nervous of being here. I just wasn't used to people knowing my name or my business but, it did have its positives, like being allowed to bring Bandit inside the grocery store, even though the owners knew he wasn't a service dog. Zeb had been shopping here close to forty years now, and the owners were old friends. I was pretty relieved. The last few times I'd had to fake anything, it hadn't gone down too well.

Unbidden, a painful memory surfaced from six months ago.

It was during our visit to Atlantic City when Sully was treating us to the biggest feast I'd ever had at Caesar's Palace. It was a buffet about a block long and would have been the best day in my life if Bandit hadn't suffered his first seizure there. Seeing his eyes roll into the back of his head and his mouth foaming, I had to fight to stave off a shudder. Even though I knew he was fine now, just remembering that moment had me feeling all kinds of terror.

As if he could feel it (which, I'm sure he could — probably smelled it on me or something), Bandit took hold of my sleeve in his mouth and gingerly started leading me to the bread aisle. *That's right, we needed bread.* I found a loaf, then scanned through my list and started grabbing the items. Ten or so minutes and a bagful of groceries later, I checked out and was walking towards the exit when one of the owners, a man with a bad comb-over and puffy cheeks, stopped me. Despite his lack of a clue on all things concerning appearance, Mr. Wellis was a nice guy and never had a bad word to say about anyone.

"Hey, Chase." He stooped down to pat Bandit on the head before slipping him a dog biscuit that he kept in his pocket for such occasions. Bandit took it gratefully and gave him a lick of thanks.

"Hi, Mr. Wellis." I hoisted the heavy shopping bag up against my stomach, wondering briefly if I'd maybe bought too much to fit onto my bike.

"Did you manage to find your friend?" he asked.

I blinked at him, confused. "No, what friend?"

"Oh. A lady. She was asking about you. You must have just missed her."

My mind was a jumble of confusion. I couldn't think who he meant.

"You're sure she was asking for me and not someone else?" I asked. We pretty much knew the same people, so this was pretty weird. I felt a slight twinge of apprehension but quickly shook it off. Mr. Wellis wasn't exactly great at getting facts right. Trying to get him to pass on a message was like playing Chinese Whispers. A couple of weeks ago, I'd asked him to let me know when the chorizo was back in stock (Sully was a big fan), but when he'd finally found me to let me know, he'd lead me to avocado section. Not sure how chorizo had become avocado in his head, but there you go.

Mr. Wellis shook his head. "No, she was definitely asking for you. Wonder where she could have gotten to?" He stared out the window, out into the street, but couldn't find her. My apprehension suddenly grew into the beginnings of panic. Who could be looking for me when no one knew I was here?

"I gotta get going, this bag's getting kinda heavy." I wasn't exactly lying either, the bag had suddenly become a dead weight in my arms. Beside me, Bandit didn't make a sound, but he shifted his weight between his legs back and forth, a clear sign of his agitation.

Mr. Wellis stepped out of my way. "Sure. If I see her again, I'll let her know I spoke to you. You want me to give her Zeb's number?"

"Um, no, can you just take down hers? I can always call her back." Once a suspicious New Yorker, always a suspicious New Yorker, even if I had lived there less than a year.

"No problem, see you tomorrow. You too, Bandit." He patted him on the head once more, then went back to work. I shot Bandit a look and inclined my head to him, telling him to follow me outside. He came immediately, staying close, intelligent eyes scanning the street for signs of this mysterious woman. We arrived at my bike. I swung the bag up, trying to set it into the front basket when someone CRASHED into me. The bag was knocked clean from my hands and food went rolling every which way.

"Oh jeez," I said, looking at the loaf of fresh bread, now lying dirty on the ground.

"Chase! I didn't see you there," came a voice from behind me. It was a familiar voice, made husky from the many cigarettes she smoked on a daily basis, and one I didn't think I'd ever hear again in my life.

I spun around to see the woman standing before me.

"Mom," I gasped, unable to believe my eyes.

30

CHASE

She hadn't changed at all.

Her bleached blonde hair was still dry and tucked into an untidy ponytail, and her eyes were heavy with the thick layers of mascara she liked to wear. She was dressed in jeans and a cheap blouse that she had buttoned up wrong. I wasn't sure what it was about that fact that almost undid me.

How had she found me?

"What're you doing here?" I gasped. Hearing the shakiness in my voice, Bandit pressed against me, looking at her, not understanding the situation but prepared to support me all the same.

"I came to find you," she said. Her eyes started watering with tears and she reached out to hug me, but I stepped away from her. Bandit whined, unsure what to do.

"But how did you know where I was?"

"Does it matter, Chase? Don't you care how far I've come to find you?" she asked, somewhat desperately.

"I don't know why you're here or who told you, but I don't want anything to do with you," I said harshly. "Go home." She flinched, but I didn't care.

"Come on, can't we just talk? Let me buy you a root beer float. They have them in the diner across the road. I know how much you love them." She touched my arm, but I shook her off.

"That's where you're wrong. I hate root beer, mom. Always have. It's coke floats I like."

She blinked, confused for a moment. I could see her literally racking her brain.

"You're sure? Could have sworn that's what you liked..."

"I guess that's too much for you to remember isn't it, what with you always so focused on pleasing Tubs." I spat the words out, relieved I was finally able to say the things to her that I never could before. Not if I didn't want to be beaten for it. Saying his name caused a flicker of fear to rise through me. I suddenly realized she might not have come alone. My eyes scanned the street left and right, looking for any sign of his hulking shape. Bandit moved in front of me, ready to protect me from the danger he could sense I was fearing. Despite everything else, I felt a surge of love towards him. My buddy would never let me down. Not like Mom.

Realizing I was looking for him, she spoke. "I came alone. He doesn't know I'm here."

"Well, that's one smart thing you've managed to do in your life. Congratulations."

I didn't care that I might sound like a jerk right now to anyone passing by. They had no idea what life was like with this woman. What I'd had to put up with in the last few years. Shooting her a look of disgust, I picked up whatever groceries I could salvage off the ground. Sensing I wasn't in any immediate danger, Bandit grabbed a can of soup, carrying it gently between his teeth. His action caught her attention and she must have finally noticed him as she gave him a look of disgust.

"You got a dog."

She'd never liked animals, and I'd only been lucky enough to get a baby duckling from her after she'd been given it from a neighbor who worked on a farm. I figured I didn't have to answer to her anymore, so I chose not to answer that question. She didn't deserve to know anything about me, and I was furious that she was even here.

"It's none of your business, what I do and don't have. Just go away and leave me alone." I shoved the groceries into the basket, taking the can from Bandit. She grabbed my arm, trying to get my attention.

"Please, let's just talk..." she began, but I'd already had enough of her being here. I shook her off again and grabbed hold of my bike.

"GO AWAY!" I yelled, suddenly having lost all control. My voice carried out into the street, causing startled faces to look my way in concern. Mr. Wellis came out of the store then, and for the first time since I've known him, he wasn't smiling. He called over to me.

"You OK, Chase? Is there a problem here?"

Though his words were directed at me, he was looking at her, and by his stance, I could see that he just needed the word and he would come deal with her himself. I felt so overwhelmed by his support, I felt tears prick at the edges of my eyes.

Mom must have seen he meant business too as she raised both hands in front of her and backed off. "No, no. No problem here. I'm going," she said, walking briskly away.

Angrily, I wiped the tears from my eyes as Mr. Wellis' expression turned sympathetic. "You want to come inside, tell me what she wanted? I can call Sully or Sam for you?"

I shook my head, mad at myself for letting her get to me. "No, I'm good. I'm just going to head to Warrey's to see Gideon. Thanks, Mr. Wellis, thanks for helping."

"You're welcome, Chase. You take care now."

I took off on my bike, Bandit following close behind. Once I was a little distance away, I tossed a look over my shoulder, but she was long gone.

31

CHASE

I reached Warrey's in five minutes flat.

I knew I could have gone home, but it was a longer ride and I felt I would be safer in town, with Gid, rather than out in the fields on my own. I didn't know what my mom wanted, or whether it was true that she was here without Tubs. The whole thing was bizarre and not in a fun way.

Luckily Warrey wasn't around, but I could see Gideon's head peeking out from behind the wheel of a 4x4. Without Warrey around, the radio was tuned to a local station, and the volume was low as Gid didn't really have it on to listen to. He was just never able to deal with silence despite living in the middle of nowhere.

Hearing my tires crunch onto the gravel drive, he looked up, surprised to see me. I guess I wasn't able to hide how I was feeling as he knew immediately that something had gone down. Throwing down a wrench, he marched towards me.

"What's wrong?"

I told him quickly, trying all the while not to give in to my panic. When I was done, his eyes looked as wide as mine. Wiping the grease stains onto his jeans, he took out his phone.

"We need to tell Sully."

I nodded in agreement. I'd actually wanted to call Sully immediately, but I couldn't do it in front of Mr. Wellis or my mom. Now we were safely away from prying eyes, I was desperate to hear Sully's take on it. He would know what to do. I rested my hand on Bandit's head, getting comfort from the feel of him there. He leaned against me, tongue snaking out to lick my hand now and then.

Gideon put his phone on speaker and he called Sully. The call rang and rang, but he didn't pick up. When it cut to voicemail, Gideon spoke into the phone. "Sul, it's Gid. We've got a big problem. Can you call me when you get this?" He hung up and looked at me. "How did she find you? Did she say?"

"No," I replied miserably. An unwanted thought was beginning to creep up on me and it was one I didn't want to face or own up to, but I knew I had to. "But... I did call her."

"What? When?" he demanded, arms folded across his chest.

I stared down at the ground. "When we were in Connecticut. But I called them from Sully's clinic and I didn't say a word! So she can't have known it was me, can she?" My eyes grew round at the possibility.

"That doesn't make any sense. Even if she figured out it was you and looked up the area code, it would have led her there, not here. She must've found you another way, but how?"

"I don't know."

"Did she say what she wanted?"

"To talk. But I didn't give her a chance," I said. And suddenly I felt so stupid. Here we were, trying to second guess her appearance when if I hadn't been acting like an emo kid, I could have just asked her what she wanted. Neither of us had the answers, but one thing was clear: I wasn't getting a good feeling about any of this.

Where was Sully?

Why didn't he call us back?

32

___

SULLY

I could see my destination just ahead of me.

All morning I had run around town, grabbing basic items we'd need for Pixie. It was clear that her distrust of Bandit wasn't going to go anytime soon, so it was double of everything. Not just food bowls and a bed, but also brushes and blankets. Pixie wouldn't like anything that would smell of him.

As I sped through my to-do list eager to have it done with so I could get onto what I really came out here for, I realized it felt good to be on my own. All night, I had struggled with my "problem" as I was fast calling it. Sam was a trooper, but she clearly didn't believe me and I honestly couldn't blame her. I'd racked my brain until it was ready to explode, but I was still to find a logical explanation; how had that text vanished into thin air? While the others thought I was suffering from stress — and it was entirely possible that I was — I was convinced that the message had been real. I knew I had received it, which meant *someone had sent it to me*.

And I was determined to find out who.

I pulled into the parking lot of the wood-clad building and killed the engine. As I climbed out of the truck, my phone started vibrating in my pocket, but I had already drawn the attention of the man in front of me, who was approaching with a friendly wave. Around my age and fit from the many days spent patrolling the area on foot, he wore an olive green shirt, the same style as Sam's though, being a higher rank, her uniform usually consisted of a white shirt — which she was happy about since the green clashed with her hair apparently (I wouldn't know as she looked pretty fantastic in anything, but I had it on her good authority that was the case and I had learned long ago not to argue with the women in my life).

I glanced down at the phone to see "Gideon calling" flashing up on the display. If I answered, I'd run the risk that he'd hear Brad's greeting. It was best if I just called him back later so he couldn't figure out where I was. The last thing I needed were more skeptical faces staring at me. I flipped the phone to silent, slipped it back into my pocket, and forced a smile.

"Hey, Brad, how're you?"

"Good, good. Wife tried a new recipe last night, her Asian style, secret recipe beef. No idea what was in it, if that's the real name or just something she made up, but that may have been the best steak I've ever had in my life." He patted his stomach fondly, happy from the memory of his dinner.

"Nice. Sam'll have to see if she can pry it from your wife," I said, only half my attention on the conversation. Though I knew what I was about to do wasn't bad per se, my heart raced and I felt like I was going behind Sam's back.

"She can try, but I'm guessing she'll get no joy. Woman seems to think she's going to bottle and sell it." He inclined his head inside. "Sam's out on patrol right now, you want me to radio her?"

I already knew she was out, having discreetly enquired as to her schedule today. It wasn't Sam I needed to see.

What I was about to do, I didn't want her to know about.

"Actually, Brad, I'm hoping you might be able to help me out with something."

33

SULLY

Brad looked at me curiously.

"Sure thing, Sully. You want to go inside?" he asked.

I nodded and followed him into the reception area. Lana, a blonde with a neat updo, smiled at me over her glasses as she tapped into a computer with brightly painted nails.

"Hey, Sul," she greeted me.

"Lana," I nodded at her, careful not to ask how she was. Lana loved to talk and needed only the slightest encouragement before torturing her victim with an intricate blow-by-blow of her day, which usually began with a description of her latest ailment. As I didn't want to run the risk of Sam getting back while I was still here, I averted my eyes and walked quickly past her station. Even without looking at her directly, I could sense her shoulders slump in disappointment and knew I had made a quick escape.

Brad walked over to a drinks station and grabbed a mug. "Coffee?" he asked, but I shook my head, keen to get moving. He must have sensed this as he set the mug down and moved into his office. I followed him inside.

I'd been here a few times before, though always while Sam was around. Usually, we'd shoot the breeze while I waited for her to finish her shift. Today was different, however, and I found myself taking in the room with new eyes. Framed photographs lined every surface. There was Brad with his missus and their five kids, ranging from toddler to surly teenager. And another of their wedding day. Then one of each kid as they went through kindergarten through to middle school where the oldest ones now were.

Brad was quite the family man, it seemed. I wasn't sure if that bode well for me.

"Brad, this is a bit of a delicate matter, so I would appreciate it if you wouldn't talk about this to anyone else, not even Sam," I began. What the hell, might as well go in guns blazing.

His eyes went a little wider, but other than that, he kept his face stoic, though I noticed he now clasped his hands on the desk in front of him. It was probably a position he took when dealing with the public, and it was very possible he didn't realize he had subtly shifted his stance with me. "Oh," he said. "How can I help?"

"Are you able to track a phone number for me?"

Whatever Brad had been steeling himself for, that wasn't it. His shoulders visibly relaxed.

"Do you know whose number it is?"

I had known this question was coming and had toyed with several possible answers. Had even considered telling the truth, but I knew that would open up a whole kettle of fish that would end badly for me.

"No," I replied as I shifted uncomfortably in my seat. The lie stuck in my throat, and it was all I could do not to clear it. "I need to know who messaged me from this number and if you pinpoint their location. I've been getting abusive messages from them, and I need to know if I should be taking them seriously. "

"Alright." He slid a notebook to me. "Write down the phone number and I'll see what I can do."

I scrawled Emma's number onto his pad but didn't give it back to him. He studied me, a questioning expression on his face.

"Is there anything else?"

"I also found something and I want it examined."

Carefully, I took out the banana clip which I had placed into a plastic bag. I knew my fingerprints were already on it, but I was hopeful that by doing so I would preserve any other identifying information.

"I found this near... my ex-wife's place. There's blood on it, I want to know if it's hers," I replied. It took a few moments for the words to sink in. When they did, he couldn't hide his shock.

"I apologize if what I'm about to ask sounds indelicate, but, I was under the impression that your ex had passed away?"

I cringed inwardly. *Damn these small towns.* Somehow, I had thought I'd get a break, that Brad wouldn't know about Emma, but of course, I wasn't that lucky. "She has, but I still need to know about this."

His eyes suddenly widened. "You're suspecting foul play?"

I didn't know how I could answer his question without going into the whole sordid thing so I lied again, then waited for lightning to strike me down. "Yeah. But don't bring this up with Sam, please. It's a touchy subject between us."

"No kidding," Brad replied.

I had to hand it to him. He was taking this far better than I thought he would.

"Is it possible? Can you identify her using dried blood?"

Brad shrugged. "I have a friend who works in forensics. She was just telling me the other day that researchers for a new study have developed a way of determining a person's age range from blood samples left at a crime scene. The test works by measuring levels of an enzyme called alkaline phosphatase, which change in the body between childhood and adulthood. Other than that, the blood should be able to give an indication to sex and race, but I'm not sure it can identify her completely, however."

"Why not?" I asked.

"We'd have to compare the DNA profile we come up with what exists of your ex. We can only conclude it is her blood if the profiles match," he explained patiently.

"So, you'd need a pre-existing profile of my ex?"

Brad nodded. "Yes. We might be able to compare the findings with medical records, I'm assuming she had those?"

Memories of numerous hospital visits and treatments flashed up in my mind, more than I ever cared to remember. I tried to push the unwanted thoughts away.

"Yes."

"Go ahead and write down her name, date of birth and place of birth. I'll look into it."

I scribbled down the information and handed the notebook back to him.

"Thanks for doing this, Brad. I know I've put you in a difficult position."

Brad studied me silently, thoughts going back and forth in his head. Then he sighed.

"Yeah, but this sounds serious so I'll do it."

He took the bag with the clip inside and called up a form on his computer. Realizing he meant to get to it now, I pushed back my chair and stood up.

"Thank you," I said simply.

"I'll call you when the results come back."

I left quickly before he could reconsider.

34

———

SULLY

I drove home in a daze.

while I had succeeded in getting Brad's help, I now had the added concern that maybe he wouldn't keep his promise to me. Sam was his boss, after all. It was very possible that she would find out. My hands tightened on the wheel. *Dammit, Sully!* I should have thought this through, but what with last night's restlessness, coupled with the stress of the past few days... I wasn't firing on all cylinders. I tortured myself, going back and forth with my thoughts until I pulled up outside the ranch. Grabbing the items I had purchased for Pixie, I barely made it to the door before it was thrown open by Chase, looking wild and upset.

"You didn't call us back!" Chase cried.

I was momentarily thrown before I remembered Gideon's missed call.

"I was in the middle of something. What's going on?" Even as I said the words, I noticed that the room was heavy with tension. Gideon sat by Zeb, the two looking like they'd just had a serious discussion. A ways away, Pixie lay on a mat. She seemed to be resting, but her eyes kept searching for Gideon, reassured by his presence. Bandit kept darting towards me, then Chase, not sure who to go to. I went inside, closing the door behind me and dumped the bags onto a table.

"I think we may have a problem," came my dad's voice. I was about to ask him what when the front door opened and in came Sam. Seeing us congregated there with our serious expressions, the smile of greeting froze on her face.

"Is something wrong?" she asked.

"The two of you need to take a seat," Zeb said seriously. Sam looked firstly at me, then the others, before coming to settle by my side. We sat on the sofa, waiting expectantly.

Moments later, we'd been given the whole story. I looked at my dad, trying to keep my face bland even as my stomach began to churn. "But how could she know that Chase was here?"

I felt Sam tense beside me and turned to her, surprised to find a guilty expression on her face.

"I think... that might be down to me," she said hesitantly.

Shocked, four faces turned to look at her.

"I'm sorry. I never thought she would come here in a million years." She turned to Chase, eyes pleading. "I'd have warned you if that was the case, Chase. You know I would."

"You called her?" Chase said in disbelief. "Why would you do that?" She didn't bother to hide the accusation from her voice.

"I knew you wouldn't like it, but I'm a sheriff. I have to uphold the law. Although she was terrible to you, you are still a minor and I am legally bound to inform your parent that you are safe. I only called to tell her that you were with us so she wouldn't worry. I was trying to protect us," Sam said, a touch desperately.

Though her words made sense, I was feeling betrayed, so I couldn't imagine how Chase was feeling right now.

"And you kept this from me?" I asked her. She looked at me, eyes pained.

"I didn't want to, but I also didn't want you to have to keep this from Chase. I thought it was better if it was on my shoulders. If you want to blame anyone, then you should blame me."

"Oh don't worry, I will!" Chase cried before storming off to her room. Bandit whined, running after her. Gideon and Zeb sat there, shocked, neither of them knowing what to do. Torn up inside, Sam made a move to follow Chase, but I stopped her.

"Don't. I'll go. You've done enough."

She flinched at my words, and though I felt a jerk for saying them, my mind was on Chase. I hurried after her, ignoring Sam, calling my name.

35

CHASE

Tears pricked at my eyes as I stormed into my room.

I let Bandit in, then slammed the door behind me, every cell in my body raging. I couldn't believe Sam had betrayed my trust like that. This whole time we'd been living together, and she had kept this from me. How could she do that? And now Mom was here to do God knows what. A chill ran through me as I realized that legally, she could take this to the courts if she wanted. If she were twisted enough, she could try to get me back.

I sat on the bed, the room swimming before me as images flashed up in my mind. Images of court cases and interviews and being dragged away from Bandit (she'd never allow me to keep him). And Sully, staring at my empty room.

A whimper sounded.

I thought it was Bandit before I realized it had come from me. Bandit jumped up, placing his paws on my knees, and tucked his head under my chin, trying to comfort me. I wrapped my arms around him and buried my face in his fur.

"No matter what happens Bandit, we'll never be separated, OK? We'll always be together."

He woofed into my armpit, which ordinarily would make me laugh, but today, I just felt like crying. A knock sounded on my door. Angrily, I grabbed a pillow and flung it at the door.

"Go away, Sam! I don't want to talk to you!" I cried.

But the door opened anyway. Sully stuck his face in the gap, concern marring his features. "It's me."

Seeing him, I sniffed and nodded, letting him know it was OK to enter. He came in, shutting the door behind him. Silently, he sat beside me on the bed. We stared straight ahead, neither of us knowing what to say.

"I didn't know, kiddo. Sam didn't tell me," he began.

"I figured. There's no way you would have kept this from me."

"Yeah," he replied dully, looking as shocked as I felt. "What did she want, your mom?"

I stared blankly ahead. "I don't know. Forgiveness? She said she was sorry."

"And did you... forgive her?" he asked tentatively.

My head spun around to him. "Of course not! I told her to go away! I don't want anything to do with her. There's no apology big enough in the world that will make me forget all the crap they put me through."

He nodded, accepting my answer. I wasn't sure, but I thought he looked relieved. "We need to think about what to do if she comes here," Sully began. "What do you want us to do?"

I blinked, startled. "Why would she come here?"

"She's already turned up in town, and it's not difficult to find out where we live. I'm sorry, Chase. I know it's hard, but you have to face up to the fact that she'll probably turn up on our doorstep at some point."

"She can say whatever she wants to, but there's no way I'm going back, that's all I know." I expected Sully to back me up on this, but he stayed silent. Another chill ran through me as a different, far more worrying thought took hold. "She can't *make* me go back... *can she?*"

Sully stared me dead in the eyes. "Let's not worry about maybes... We'll get Sam to look into the legalities and go from there."

He threw his arm over my shoulders and drew me close. I stared down at Bandit's face, even as my vision blurred over with tears.

It was a while before I was able to leave my room.

I knew Sam wanted to talk to me, but I just couldn't face her. Sully must've said as much as she gave me a wide berth. Zeb came by a while ago with a tray of food for Bandit and I. He'd brought a bone for Bandit and a bowl of chili with some crusty bread (someone must have made an additional shopping trip since my bread was still lying out on the street). He looked like he wanted to say something to me, but then thought better of it. Patting my hand, he gave me the food and left. One thing I was learning about Zeb, he wasn't one for empty words. It was one of the things I loved most about him.

Hearing a sound outside, I looked out of the window to see Gideon and Pixie outside. He was rolling a ball by his feet. Pixie watched his every move but didn't chase after the ball. She sat on her haunches, looking like she wanted to pounce each time the ball rolled past her nose, but something stopped her. I was amazed to see how patient he was with her. He never badgered her or forced her to do anything. He just sat there, rolling and re-rolling that ball.

A few minutes later, I went outside to join them, Bandit by my side. Gideon looked up on our approach. Because of this, he missed catching the ball, and it flew past Pixie. Bandit ran after it, caught it in his mouth, then brought it back to Gideon. As soon as he got to him, however, Pixie growled at him.

"Bandit's our friend, Pixie. We don't growl at friends," Gideon told her patiently but firmly. It was like Pixie didn't understand him, however (which she probably didn't). The growling slid low down her throat until it turned into a fierce rumble. Bandit whined, trying to let her know he wasn't a threat, but that just seemed to egg her on as she went CRAZY. She started barking, dancing behind Gideon for safety.

"Shh… it's OK girl…" He called out, trying to calm her, but Pixie continued. Bandit whined again and backed behind me. Unable to calm her, Gideon shot Bandit a pleading look.

"Can you go back inside? I'm sorry, boy, but she is just too scared of you."

Bandit looked at me, asking for my command. I nodded apologetically. "It's only until she gets used to you. It won't be long, I'm sure."

Bandit woofed unhappily but started back inside. When he was a few yards from the house, I saw him toss a sad look over his shoulder, but he continued to go. He cut such a lonely figure, I felt awful for him. In the entire time we'd been together, we'd barely been separated, yet here I was, sending him away every time I decided to spend some time with Pixie.

As soon as he was out of sight, Pixie stopped barking and her breathing returned to normal. It really made no sense why she was so scared of him. Bandit was the gentlest dog in the world. "You think another dog attacked her before? One that reminds her of Bandit? Her reaction to him just isn't normal," I said.

"Maybe? I don't know, but she does only freak out when he's here. It's probably best that we keep him away from her until she gets over whatever it is."

I nodded, agreeing as I lowered down to my knees. Sully had told me a while ago that when a dog is threatened, it helps to make yourself as physically small as possible. Pixie hadn't shown any animosity towards me, but I didn't want anything else to set her off, so I moved slowly, trying to be as dainty as possible.

Then something amazing happened.

Pixie came over and gave me an all over cautious sniff. Suddenly, without warning, she laid down next to me and put her head on my knee. Gideon's mouth fell open. I had to force myself not to laugh at his expression.

"She hasn't even done that to me yet," he said, unable to hide his annoyance. I know I shouldn't have, but I shot him a smug grin.

"Clearly, I've got the magic touch."

I lowered my hand to her head and started to pet her, cautious that she could decide she didn't like me again at any moment. But she just closed her eyes, enjoying the fuss. Gideon blinked at me.

"OK. I don't feel the least betrayed. Thanks, Pixie."

We both watched as she relaxed and started falling asleep. Gideon sat down beside me, still playing with the ball absently. We stared out at the field, watching trees sway in the breeze.

"Sam's feeling awful," he began. "She wants to apologize to you."

I'd had some time to deal with my anger now, which wasn't the red hot burn it had been earlier. Now there was just a dullness. "I know. I'll talk to her later."

He nodded. We sat there quietly, when we heard the front door slam and a car roar away, burning rubber, leaving a cloud of dust in its wake. It was Sam's truck.

"I'm guessing they must've had words," Gideon said.

I nodded, feeling torn. On the one hand, I was glad Sully had spoken to her. On the other, Sam had meant well, and I really liked her. I liked how they were together.

I wasn't to know that things would only get worse from here on in.

36

CHASE

Seems none of us slept great last night.

Dark shadows ringed Sully and Sam's eyes. I knew mine hadn't fared much better. Their body language wasn't as easy as it usually was either. They kept avoiding each other, dancing around each other in the kitchen as they got their breakfast ready. I fed Bandit, but even he didn't seem interested in his food, pushing it around the plate with his nose. Poor guy really wasn't happy with the way Pixie was with him. We'd talked about it last night. I'd told him that it wasn't anything he had done, but he didn't believe me. He genuinely believed the dog had something against him.

Who'd have thought Bandit would be so sensitive? I guess he'd never experienced being unliked before. Even back in the lab where he escaped from, they had celebrated his cleverness, so he wasn't tortured like the rest of the dogs were. But Bandit heard their cries, watched them trembling in their cages. Though he himself hadn't been hurt, he had hurt for them, so whatever Pixie had gone through, Bandit would get it. Of all dogs, he would understand. I told him that when she finally was able to be calm in his presence, he should just tell her all that. He seemed happier after our talk now that we had a plan.

Sam was in civilian clothes this morning, which meant she wasn't working today. She stood by the toaster, waiting for her toast to be done, but I saw how she purposely didn't look my way — giving me the space I had asked for yesterday. I felt like a heel suddenly, for causing all the tension around the place, so I poured a glass of juice and looked at her.

"You want some OJ?" I asked. She looked up at me, surprised, then her eyes softened gratefully.

"Yeah. That'd be great, thanks, Chase."

I poured her a glass, handing it to her and suddenly we were friends again. I knew I could have done a whole big spiel, but truth was, I'd missed talking to her, and avoiding her was both awkward and impractical. The toast finally popped up from the toaster. She took two of the slices, put them on a plate and offered them to me. I took the plate and dumped a great glob of peanut butter onto it when there came a knock on the front door. Immediately Bandit started whining and pawing at me. We'd left his iPad in my room so I couldn't figure out what he wanted. Moments later, Gideon came inside, a sick look on his face.

"Chase... your mom's at the door."

And just like that, the relief I was feeling was ripped out of me.

"WHAT DO you want me to tell her?" asked Gideon.

When the rushing sound faded from my ears, I looked at Sully, speechless. His brow had creased into a worried line, but his expression was resolute.

"I guess she's not going away, so we'll have to deal with this sometime. Might as well be now." He looked at me as he spoke, waiting for my response. Despite his words, if I disagreed and said I wasn't ready, I knew he would have told her to go away, but seeing Sam's guilty expression, I knew my small family couldn't keep going through this every day, so I steeled myself.

"It's fine. Let her in."

Moments later, we were all in the living room, watching as my mom came in. She'd changed her clothes since yesterday and was now wearing a yellow skirt, white t-shirt and flip-flops that showed the chipped blue polish on her toes. Despite that, and the stain on her shirt, she looked more presentable than she'd been throughout my life, when her outfits usually consisted of the skimpy leopard-print mini-skirts Tubs liked her to wear.

I didn't know what to think. This mom clashed so much with the one I remembered. Even her hair was clean, as if she were truly making an effort. For some reason, this made me super uncomfortable. I would actually have preferred it if she looked the way I expected her to.

Across the room, Sully stared at her. He had yet to speak, but I could see he was thinking the same things I was. Having heard all the stories about what she was really like, I'll bet he was wondering how that monster could be hiding under such a boring appearance.

Mom tossed a quick look around the room, giving them all a timid smile before she focused her attention on me. I watched the corners of her mouth turn up even more as she took a hesitant step towards me.

"Chase..." Her voice cracked, and she seemed to struggle for words. She reached out a hand towards me, but I took a step back. It wasn't even conscious. I just didn't understand what she was doing here, and being so close to her physically was filling me with all kinds of unpleasant emotions. Picking up on my feelings, Sully moved to stand in front of me. He was being protective. Bandit must have picked up on our vibes too as he went to join his side.

"I'm Sully. Chase has been living with me for these past six months."

Mom's hands fidgeted by her side. I think she was debating whether to offer it to Sully to shake, but she must have decided against it. They stayed clenched down by her side.

"I'm Tracey. Tracey Blueman. Thanks for looking after Chase for me."

Sully didn't reply, not knowing what to say. An awkward silence blanketed the room until Zeb wheeled forward, offering his hand.

"I'm Sully's father, Zebediah. It's good to meet you, would you like a drink?" He was being purposely pleasant, like this was a normal visit from a friend, popping in from out of town.

"Have you got soda? Something sweet?"

"Yeah, we have it." This was from Gideon. He was staring at her with eyes that were hard with hate, unable to hide his loathing for this woman. Seeing him come to my defense like that filled my heart with love. Gideon didn't always show what he was really feeling, so this was a bit of a surprise. Zeb frowned at Gideon, shaking his head reproachfully.

"Gideon," he said. "That's not how we treat guests."

"Well, she hasn't exactly been invited, has she? Let's not pretend anyone wants her here."

"Gideon!" Zeb snapped sharply. His angry tone shocked me. I had never heard Zeb reprimand anyone before.

"I don't wanna cause any trouble," Mom said. "He's right. You must be hella surprised, but I swear I don't mean any harm. I just wanted to see my little girl."

"Why don't we sit down in the living room. There's a lot to catch up on. Come on through," said Sam, surprising everyone. No one moved. Sam sighed. "Look, clearly there is a lot to talk about, it's silly for us all to stand here. Go inside and sit."

Realizing no one would move before I did, I nodded and let Sully lead the way. I sat on the couch, Sully and Gideon flanking my side as Bandit sat in front of my feet. I was in a triangle of protection, yet despite being surrounded on all sides, I was still feeling super vulnerable and this made me mad. She couldn't do anything to hurt me now. She was just one person and Tubs wasn't anywhere in sight. So why was I feeling so scared? Why was there a chill in the pit of my stomach?

Sam pulled out a chair and Mom perched on it. She sat opposite me, clasping her hands in her lap. "You're Sam?" Mom asked. "You're the one who called?"

Sam nodded. "It wasn't my intention that you come here like this. I only called you, woman-to-woman, to let you know your child was safe with us. I had no idea you would come here like this. I really wish you had phoned first and given us a heads up."

A flush crept up across Mom's face. "I was afraid none of you would be here if I called first."

"Well, we are," said Sully. "So what is it that you want exactly? What's your purpose for turning up like this?" Now Zeb turned his frown on Sully, but Sully just ignored him. "You may be her legal parent but you are no longer her guardian."

It was impossible to miss the challenge in his voice. He was daring my mom to say something different.

"I only want to spend time with her. I wanted to see her face myself is all, not just take a stranger's word for it."

After she spoke, the relief from Sully was palpable. I myself felt the tension leave my shoulders and Bandit relaxed against my legs. She wasn't here to drag me back home. There would be no court case. Zeb smiled.

"Well, let's get Tracey a drink and we can catch her up on the last year or so of Chase's life."

37

CHASE

After we had gotten over the shock of my mom's appearance, we spoke for a while, letting her know how Sully, Bandit, and I had first met. Of course, we left out any reference to Bandit's super intelligence, and we changed Forbes' men to criminals, but we kept most of the story the same.

Mom had listened to it all without saying a word, letting out just the occasional gasp or so. I left out our whole confrontation with Forbes and anything about Platinum Industries and ended simply by saying that Sam and Sully had met and now we all lived together. Mom had asked a few questions here and there, like where did Gideon come in? But that was about it. Occasionally I caught her staring at Bandit but she'd never been very keen on animals so I figured she was just keeping a wary eye out on him.

Once Sully and the others realized that she really was just here to talk, they relaxed and left us alone. We now sat on the porch while Bandit snored softly by my feet. There were things I wanted to say but hadn't yet broached. I stared out into the distant green horizon, letting the sounds I loved wash over me. When I finally worked up the nerve, I voiced the question I'd been meaning to ask since her arrival here.

"Where's Tubs?" I asked, deliberately keeping my voice as emotionless as possible.

"Home. He... he doesn't know I'm here," she replied.

"He doesn't?"

"No. I didn't say where I was going, he would only have stopped me. He hasn't gotten over all the money you took."

I looked at her and saw the way her hands tightened in her lap and lines creased her forehead. She was worried, thinking of the reception she might receive when she finally went home.

"If he doesn't know you're here, where does he think you are?"

"I didn't tell him. I left a note and said I was going out of town but would call when I could." A normal person might think she was being respectful to my wishes to stay here anonymously, but I knew she was too scared to tell him the truth — that she was coming to find me. Although Tubs had never liked me, I think he liked having power over me, liked having his own personal punchbag, but after I had taken off, the only one left for him to rule was my mom, so her disappearing like this? He must be furious.

We sat there silently for a while, neither of us saying anything. My mind was a mess of emotions and I just didn't know what to think. One thing struck me about her being here, though — I had never seen her so calm. Then again, I had never seen her without Tubs all these years. He had always been by her side or behind her, towering over her like an immovable mountain. Without him, she seemed almost happier. It made me wonder for the millionth time why she didn't just leave him, but I wasn't going to say anything about that. I didn't want her to think that I cared.

"You really ate food from the trash?" She frowned, unable to comprehend it all.

I nodded and shrugged. "The first weeks were the hardest. It takes a while before you get used to sleeping on hard ground and the first few times you look for food in a dumpster, the smells make you vomit, but after a while, the hunger takes over everything else so you don't even smell the rottenness or taste it anymore."

She looked down at the ground at my words. "It's good you have these people now, they seem like good folk."

"They're the best," I said.

She looked down at Bandit. "And you have a dog too. You've always wanted a pet."

At the word pet, Bandit pricked his ears towards her even as he kept his eyes closed, snoozing. "Yeah, he's much more than a pet though. He's my best friend and family."

"Well," she said. "He's just an animal, don't go humanizing him."

It was on the tip of my tongue to correct her but I knew there wasn't anything I could say that wouldn't reveal Bandit's secret so I bit down on my tongue and refrained from replying.

We'd been out there on the porch for a while before I was suddenly aware of noises coming from inside the ranch. The others were getting ready to go out. Sully suddenly popped his head around the door.

"We're going into town. You wanna come with us or stay talking with your mom?" Though it was a question, Sully didn't look too comfortable asking it. I was pretty sure Sam had put him up to it. My mom shot me a hopeful look, but I really didn't want to be left alone with her. Despite how much nicer she seemed suddenly, there was a wall around my heart and it wasn't coming down anytime soon. I jumped up to my feet.

"I'm coming with. We're done here."

Sully nodded, looking relieved. Mom got to her feet awkwardly, knowing that she was being dismissed.

"I'm only here a few days. Can I come back to see you?" This, she directed at me. I couldn't answer. My throat constricted, and it felt dry and uncomfortable. They both waited for an answer, but all I could manage was a shrug. She smiled, grateful for the crumb I had given her.

"Thanks, Chase." She turned to Sully next. "You too. For all you've done for her."

As Sully escorted her to the door, I didn't move. I stood there watching until she disappeared out of sight.

A LITTLE WHILE LATER, Sully, Sam, Bandit, and I were at the Four Seasons Mall. It was an hour out of town, and we generally only came here on special occasions, when we couldn't pick up what we wanted in our local stores. Sam and I liked to do our clothes shopping here as there was so much more variety. Also bonus, there was a Starbucks! I guess this trip was her way of apologizing to me because it certainly hadn't been planned.

On the drive here, Sam had tried to make basic chitchat, and I had responded, not because I was particularly interested in what she had to say but because I wanted her to know that I wasn't mad at her anymore. I had gotten over the initial shock of seeing my mom, and though we'd only spoken a little on the porch, some of my bitterness had faded. I was relieved to see that she and Sully also seemed to have fixed whatever issue had been going on between them, or at least they were pretending to in front of me. They seemed almost normal. I say seemed because it was all a little forced.

The bright colors and sounds of the mall were blinding. I couldn't get used to the sudden noise as chatter and music exploded in my ears. Although I had come from New York, which was so much louder with its sirens and traffic, Montpelier was only a small town with just 10 or so shops on its high street. Noise to me nowadays was an owl hooting outside my window at night.

We made a beeline for the pet store, which was around ten times bigger than the one back home. We always came here first, to allow Bandit to choose a toy for himself. It was here where he had picked up his Frumpy Rabbit. Sully went to the same section where we had found Bandit's though all the rabbits were sold out, there were only cats and fish left. He picked up a cat to show Bandit.

"This is to replace the one Pixie destroyed. And let's get her a fish so she can have one of her own," he said to him. He probably expected Bandit to agree, but he only whined instead. We grabbed basic provisions for the dogs before the three of us went into a J. C. Penney. Fall was approaching and with it, the air had become distinctively cooler. I needed a few sweaters, so I grabbed some that were on sale and paid for them with my allowance. Sully and Sam had gone off to get him a new phone since his old one was still not working. It was hugely frustrating for him, as he was desperate to show us that phone message.

When I was done, I finally found them wandering around in the baby section. Holding onto a baby grow, Sam's eyes had misted over and she was smiling at Sully. The weariness he had been wearing for days left and he too seemed suddenly wistful. And the thought hit me like a punch in the gut.

They wanted a baby.

I felt shaken to the core. Why had I never considered this before? Now that they were getting married, a baby was obviously in their future. For some reason, the thought filled me with dread. I was happy with the way things were, I didn't need a screaming baby in the picture, and I was ashamed to admit that I was afraid. If they had their own child, would they still want me? Especially now my mom had turned up.

I must have moved and caught Sam's attention because her eyes suddenly drifted over to me. She set down the baby growth and smiled at me. "Hey Chase, you done?"

"Yeah," I said. "What're you guys looking at?"

"Nothing," Sully said. "Just looking."

He tried not to make a thing of it, but I could see he was caught out. "I'm parched, let's go get a Frappuccino."

Ordinarily, I would have whooped at the thought of that sweet and creamy coffee goodness.

As it was, I silently followed them as I felt like my whole world was falling down.

38

SULLY

We came back from the shopping trip with Sam happy, feeling that she had mended some of her issues with Chase, but I still had residual issues I needed to face. The visit from Chase's mom had left me on an uneven keel that even now, hours later, I was still reeling from.

Alone in our bedroom, I could hear Sam and the others cooking in the kitchen. They had only just started, but Sam was determined to make her infamous lasagna tonight. It was a favorite of all of ours; she had gotten it from a celebrity chef's recipe book. From start to finish, the entire process took three-and-a-half hours, but it was well worth it. I excused myself from kitchen duty, but the others didn't seem to mind, knowing I had things on my mind.

I shut the door. My laptop sat as it always did on a small desk by the window with a view looking out across the fields of green. I pulled the chair away from the desk, sat down, and turned on the laptop. Since my visit to the deputy's office, I had tried my best to not think about the messages I had received from beyond the grave. Though I had done a pretty good job not speaking about it to anyone, every night when my head hit that pillow and I closed my eyes, the words would appear one-by-one searing into my eyelids, followed by an image of that hair clip.

I was back to not sleeping again.

More than anything, I wished I could go for a night run, but I knew Sam would know what was bothering me if I did, and I couldn't stomach another fight with her. I'd been wanting some time when I could collate my thoughts, but now that I was finally alone, I found they were a mess.

Sighing, I activated Google. Almost without my meaning to, I typed in "possible reasons for a disturbed grave". I wasn't expecting to find much, but several hits came up. There was a report from the UK of badgers, digging around a cemetery who accidentally unearthed human remains. I guess an animal could have dislodged dirt on Emma's grave, like Sam had mentioned, but that wouldn't explain the clip or the text. Other reports talked of grave robbing and superstitious beliefs. Another mentioned the retrieval of mementos buried with the body. Frankly, the longer I read, the more the possibilities grew even more far-fetched. I probably should have stopped when a related article of people seemingly coming back from the dead was suggested to me, but I was too far gone and had to see this thing through. Of course, I knew how crazy that sounded, but I was living with a super intelligent dog so I was willing to suspend some disbelief.

I found some fifty or so cases of people who were declared dead only to spring back to life — sometimes in their own graves, other times in the morgue — the stories were unbelievable but apparently true. I found myself rereading one account in particular, of a woman who had died of cancer only to come back to life inside her coffin after being buried. Passer-bys had heard her screams, but by the time she was rescued, she had died of suffocation. Every case had a similar fact, one that I couldn't hide away from — the survivors were all recently declared dead. Unsurprisingly, I could not find stories of people waking up from the dead a year later.

I could see in Sam's eyes, in the way that she had become so gentle with me of late, that she was treating me with kid gloves and it infuriated me. I wasn't going insane, and I was determined to prove it. For the millionth time, I glanced at my new phone, hoping for a missed call or message from Brad — who I'd given my new number to almost the second that I'd activated the phone — but the screen stayed stubbornly blank. I carried on with my research, finding more and more elaborate tales of ordinary people coming back from the dead.

I had no idea how long I had been reading. My mind was agog with facts and possibilities, but I hadn't come up with any concrete evidence that would help explain my situation. I was still researching when there came a knock on the door, followed by Sam's appearance. Seeing that I was hunched over the computer, Sam looked surprised.

"I thought you were napping?"

Quickly, I exited Google and closed the laptop. "No, just needed some alone time. Wanted to process today is all."

She looked over my shoulder at the laptop. "What have you been up to?"

I ran my hand through my hair, trying to keep as natural as possible. "Nothing much, just seeing what I could find out about Chase's mom."

Sam looked surprised. "You know I ran a check on her before I called, right? But there was nothing of interest, nothing that we didn't already know."

"I figured as much still, no harm in trying."

I stood up and tucked the chair back under the desk, then made my way over to her, sniffing the air appreciatively. "Thanks for cooking tonight."

"Sure. Dinner is ready."

"Okay," I agreed and went past her to the kitchen, relieved that she wasn't going to plague me with many more questions.

39

SAM

Sam watched Sully walk down the hall, but she didn't follow him. Despite how the air smelled so tantalizingly of her food, Sam found herself without much appetite and wasn't in any hurry to eat. She waited until he disappeared around a corner before going into the bedroom.

When Sam had appeared at the door, she'd seen how quickly Sully had snapped the laptop shut. She recognized that guilty expression on his face; it was the same one her perps wore whenever she'd catch them in an embarrassing act. All Sam wanted now was to see what Sully had been up to for the past few hours.

She opened his laptop and looked through the recent hits. Seeing the hundreds of searches he had made in the past few hours, Sam felt a mixture of fear and anger. They had talked about this. She thought he was over the Emma-texting-from-the-grave-scenario, but clearly, he had been lying to her.

Feeling duped but knowing now wasn't the time to bring this up, Sam went to the kitchen where she sat down at her place at the table. She tried her best to seem normal, especially for Chase's sake — God knows the girl had been through enough today — but the only way she could get through the meal without exploding was by not looking at Sully. She felt so betrayed, so hurt, she could not look him in the face.

Sully, for his part, didn't notice or was dealing with unresolved issues of his own. He made appreciative sounds over his food but didn't say much otherwise. In fact, they were all quieter than usual.

Looking at Sully over the top of her glass of water, Sam steeled herself for what was to come.

Tonight, Sam thought.

Tonight she would resolve this once and for all.

40

SULLY

Dinner went down like a pile of rocks.

Despite this being a favorite meal, the pasta clung to my throat, and I found it difficult to swallow. Even the spicy tomato sauce that usually had my tastebuds doing a dance seemed overly sweet tonight, giving it a sickly taste. As Sam had spent three hours in the kitchen making this, I did my best for her benefit, but I was pretty sure she could see through my act. Even Chase, who was usually able to eat anything, spent most of the meal pushing the food around her plate.

To think it was only three days ago when everything was fine.

If Zeb noticed our moods, he didn't show it, keeping up a decent level of conversation. He even mentioned Chase's mom. While he didn't go as far as to say she seemed nice, he managed to convey that he didn't find her a monster either. Gideon, however, could not be swayed. He didn't like her and made no qualms about it. He didn't believe people could change, and there was nothing any of us could say that would make him think differently.

Picking up on our vibes, Bandit had spent the entire meal under the dining table running between each of us, pressing his nose into our hands. He was doing the rounds to check on us, making sure we were all okay. Poor thing was working overtime. Pixie, who had still not warmed to him, stayed in the den while we ate. Gideon wasn't happy with this arrangement as he wanted Pixie with us at all times, but I explained that it was better to let her have some space so she could come to us of her own accord.

I took a sip of my water and noticed that Sam was watching me. When I

caught her eyes, however, she looked away from me. I knew from experience this wasn't a good sign. Something was up and I didn't think it was the
visit we had had from Chase's mom.

When the meal was finally, blessedly over, I went to do the dishes as was
normal whenever Sam cooked, however, tonight she came up beside me as I
was setting the dishes in the sink.

"Hey, you think we could chat about something?" It wasn't really a question, and her tone implied that.

"Sure," I said. I tapped Gideon on the shoulder. "Can you guys finish up
here?"

Gideon shot me a long-suffering look. "Oh, I see what's going on here.
Eat and run. That's nice."

I gave him a distracted smile. "You know me." But my eyes were already
following Sam, who was heading into our bedroom. I went after her, dragging my feet a little. A sixth sense told me I was about to get a scalding and I
wasn't looking forward to it.

A few seconds later, I joined her in the room. "What's up?" I asked.

"Can you close the door behind you?" she replied.

I did as requested and went to join her on the bed where she was sitting.
She turned to me, eyes searching my face.

"Sully, I'm not sure how else to say this so I'm just going to come out and
say it. I need you to be silent and just listen to me, okay?"

Baffled by what was happening, I nodded.

"I know you've been keeping things from me. Ever since the day you
visited Emma's grave, you have not been the same. Now, I know you said
you received a text message from her phone but there isn't any proof of that,
however, despite how you were behaving I was willing to let things lie, but
you're still fixated on this thing and I think it's a really big problem."

I was actually relieved she was bringing this up. The two of us had been
tiptoeing around each other for days now and the pressure had been mounting. Now at least we could talk about this.

"I didn't mean to keep things from you, but I know how crazy it sounds. I
knew you didn't believe me. I was just trying to find some proof that I could
show you, or at least an explanation for what might have happened."

She didn't answer, moving instead to her bag, which hung on a hook on
the wall. She took something out of it, a sheet of paper.

"The thing is, I know that's not all you did. You went behind my back
and asked my deputy for help."

"Well, he wasn't supposed to tell you that." I couldn't help feeling
angered by Brad's betrayal. So this was why he hadn't called back, the little
snitch.

"He didn't. He covered for you, but I figured things out when Lana mentioned you had dropped by."

Of course, Lana and her big mouth. I should have known.

"What were you thinking Sully, dragging them into your madness?"

My eyes hardened. "So you finally admit you don't believe me?"

She threw up her hands, exasperated. "How am I supposed to believe you, do you know how this sounds? You passed out on her grave, Sully! She's dead! How can you keep ignoring this fact? Have you any idea how scared Chase was when she found you?"

"You don't get to ask me that. I know better than anyone how Chase feels."

"That's crap and you know it. You've been so fixated on that supposed text you've barely been there for her at all."

"What about that clip then? That's something, but you keep conveniently ignoring that!" I didn't want to sound like a jerk, but she was getting me riled up something fierce.

She laid the piece of paper she had fished out of her bag onto the bed. The logo across the header announced it as a forensics lab in Baltimore. Brad's friend must have come good after all. I raked my eyes over the page, but the results were as good as gobbledygook. It made no sense at all.

"What does it say?"

"It says that the blood is inconclusive as it is more than two days old," Sam replied. "For the study Brad mentioned to work, the blood needs to be fresh. What it did reveal is that the owner of the blood was a woman with an 'O' blood type."

"That was Emma's blood type!" I said excitedly, more loudly than I had intended to.

"So does something like forty-seven percent of the world, Sully. It's the most common blood-type there is," she answered warily.

"You're going to find fault with whatever I say, aren't you?" I shot at her at my wit's end. "Fine, the clip is inconclusive. I don't know how many times I have to explain it to you, but that text was real. The message was real. I actually think the bigger problem is how you won't believe me."

Sam opened her mouth to argue, then must have thought better of it as she stayed quiet. Suddenly her eyes teared up, and she looked at me, broken.

"The problem isn't whether the text is real. The problem is you're still hung up over your dead wife and you are not ready to marry me."

I scowled, wondering where she was getting this from. ""No, that's not what's happening here."

She nodded fiercely. "Yes, it is. You think it's a coincidence that this all started after we decided to get married? We were fine, then you proposed, and I said yes. All this started happening immediately after."

"It started happening because we went back so I could tell my friends of our good news. I went back to make peace with the dead, as you damn well know. If anything, this should prove how much I love you, how ready I am to get married."

She shook her head at me sadly. "I really think you believe that."

"I do," I said emphatically.

"Then you need to do something for me. You need to see someone."

"You mean, like a shrink?" I asked, incredulous. She nodded. "No way am I seeing some quack."

Sam jumped onto her feet, suddenly furious. "Then you obviously don't care about this as much as you say you do."

With that, she stormed out of the room, slamming the door behind her.

41

CHASE

I had just finished the dishes and was going to my room when I saw Sam heading out of their bedroom and into the back porch. She sat on the swing, looking lost and alone, while Sully sat on the edge of the bed, not faring much better.

I'd been meaning to talk to him all day, but there never seemed to be a chance. My head was a whirlwind of emotions and I didn't know what to do with my mom. I really needed Sully's help, so I was relieved to find him finally alone. I went up to him and knocked on the door.

"Sul?" I said.

He looked up at me but didn't say anything, so I continued. "I kind of need to talk to you." But Sully wasn't really looking at me. He stared past me, his eyes dazed.

"Sully?" I asked again.

"Yeah," he answered distracted. "What did you want to talk about?"

Although he had asked me the question, I could see his heart and attention wasn't in it. Whatever was going on between him and Sam had taken everything he had. There was no point talking to him now, that much was obvious, so I just shrugged. "You know what? It can wait."

He finally looked at me. "You sure?" He couldn't hide the hopefulness in his voice. Knowing he couldn't wait to get rid of me, I felt an insecure pang in my chest.

"Yeah. I'll find you later," I said, already backing away. Sully didn't even respond, thoughts already somewhere else.

I went out to the front yard and found myself walking towards the vegetable plot. Tending to it had become one of my responsibilities since Gideon now worked at Warrey's most of the time. Originally Zeb's pride and joy, he now relied on us to look after the upkeep as he couldn't do it easily from his wheelchair. We had planted some cool weather loving veggies a little while back, so now our patch was thriving with kale, spinach, peas, and beets. Seeing some weeds sprouting up between the radishes, I kneeled down onto the grass and absently began to pluck them. I was so focused on the task at hand, I didn't hear the whir of Zeb's wheelchair until he was almost upon me.

"I was just coming out here to check on the plot myself. How is it looking?"

"Good. I'm getting rid of the few weeds that seemed to have grown overnight."

He wheeled to a stop opposite me. "That's the thing with weeds, leave them alone for just a second and they grow back, bigger and stronger than ever. It's the way with most unwanted things, unfortunately. That is why it is best to cull them before the unwanted effect takes root."

I stopped to look at him, wondering if he had a second meaning, but I couldn't tell by his face.

"How are you coping anyway, Chase? Lots going on today."

I nodded, not trusting myself to speak straight away. With horror, I found that my eyes were tearing up, and I had no idea why. I focused on the weeds as if there were suddenly something of the utmost importance tangled inside them. I took a breath, then when I spoke again, I was relieved to find my voice held steady.

"I don't know how to feel. I've been so angry with my mom, you know? But then she turns up, looking so unthreatening, so pathetic that I almost feel sorry for her, which then makes me furious! I mean, how can I feel sorry for her after all the things she's done? The things she allowed Tubs to do?"

I fell silent then, done with my enraged outburst. Zeb surprised me by taking it all in his stride. "You feel sorry for her precisely because she is a pathetic person. She has been with an abusive drunk for years, letting him berate not only you but her. All that time spent with him would have eroded any confidence that she had. She is only a husk of a person now, but you, you are kind and strong and loving, despite what she has done to you. You should feel proud of yourself for being that way, Chase. You know better even when your own mother doesn't. That takes real character."

I blinked back my tears, touched by his words.

"You shouldn't worry about how you are feeling. It is what it is. You are going through what you need to in order to get to the other side. The only thing you need to remember is that you are not alone. We are all here for you. Got that?" he grinned, suddenly.

I smiled, unable to be miserable any longer.

"There you go, there's that smile. Gideon thinks you're pretty when you smile, did you know that?"

"What?" I managed to blurt out ungraciously.

"It's true, he told me," Zeb said. Smiling wickedly, he winked at me then headed back into the ranch, leaving me wondering at what he meant by that last comment.

42

BANDIT

No matter where he went, the air was filled with tension.

Dinner was usually the happiest time for Bandit, but tonight he had exhausted himself from constantly having to check up on everyone. Though nobody said anything, Bandit knew they were all desperately unhappy. He could smell their misery like it was a dirty pair of Gideon's socks.

Chase had been very quiet since the visit from her mother. She had already explained about her past, so Bandit knew Chase was very confused over her mother's appearance. Wanting to cheer her up, Bandit went to his bed and fetched Frumpy Rabbit, meaning to give it to Chase to cuddle. Maybe if she had Frumpy, she wouldn't be so sad. He had it in his mouth when he suddenly smelled Pixie's undeniable scent behind him. He spun around to find the other dog standing in the doorway. She didn't do anything, just stared at him in that unnerving way of hers. Bandit sniffed the air once again, not liking her smell. He didn't know what it was that disturbed him, but something about it wasn't right. He wished that the others would believe him, even though Bandit wasn't able to explain it himself.

He whined at the other dog now hoping that she would speak to him. Back where he was from, he was always able to get along with the other dogs. They knew he was special, and though he hardly ever saw them, on the odd occasion when he did, they would clamor around him, wanting his favor, so Pixie's dislike of him was extreme. The other dog kept staring at him eerily. She didn't blink or move until Bandit found himself suddenly afraid. If she didn't move away from the doorway, he was trapped in this room.

He whined, wagging his tail at her in a show of friendship. He was hoping the gesture would be echoed, but Pixie's tail stayed frozen like the rest of her. Suddenly there came a low growl in her throat. Pixie flattened her ears on top of her head and bared her teeth at him. She took one step towards him into the room.

Bandit stopped wagging his tail. He stood frozen, worried, and concerned, as Pixie advanced, snarling and growling threateningly. Bandit dropped his toy and braced himself. Everything about her screamed danger. Though he hadn't done anything to cause her to become so angry, Bandit knew that Pixie was seconds away from attacking him.

The other dog advanced, getting closer and closer, until she was within leaping distance of Bandit. Feeling suddenly territorial, Bandit bared his own teeth in warning. Though he didn't like to fight, it didn't mean he wouldn't protect his home if push came to shove. This was his special space that he shared with Chase, and Pixie had to learn that she couldn't bully him away from it.

Like he had fired a starter's pistol, Pixie flew towards Bandit, snapping her jaws at his face. Bandit spun so that her jaws narrowly missed him, chewing only on air. He twisted his body, throwing it at her using the full weight of himself to knock her off balance. She fell down, but sprung back onto her paws almost immediately. Circling him, Pixie tried to find a vulnerable spot.

Sensing her tactic, Bandit spun around, but he was slower than the smaller dog. Pixie sank her teeth into his rump, causing pain to explode in his body. Howling with rage, and driven only by the animal instinct to survive, Bandit bit her on the only place he could reach — her neck. Pixie screamed as Bandit held on to her neck. She let go of his rump, unable to focus on her own attack now that she was hurting.

Through the commotion, Bandit suddenly heard Chase's voice. She had arrived in the doorway, eyes wide with horror at the sight before her. Bandit was thrilled! Now Pixie would learn that she couldn't attack him without consequence. Chase ran into the room, but instead of dragging Pixie away as he expected, she pulled *him* off the other dog!

"Bandit, NO! What are you doing?" she yelled at him.

Bandit was so shocked his jaws loosened around Pixie and he backed away. No one had ever yelled at him before, especially not Chase. As soon as she had appeared, Pixie stopped fighting and now she curled into a ball and whimpered pathetically. Bandit was stunned by the change in her. A minute ago she had been willing to tear him to pieces, but in one breath she had changed into this cowering, pitiful pup. Bandit wished he had his iPad so he could explain, but he had left it outside in the living room. He moved to Chase now, but she waved him away angrily.

"No, boy! Bad dog! I can't believe you would fight Pixie! She's so much smaller than you. You should know better!"

Bandit whined, desperate to explain himself, but Chase was furious with him. "No! I don't want to hear it. Get out! I don't want you in here!"

Bandit was heartbroken. But they were best friends. How could she tell him to go? Couldn't she see that Pixie was pretending? Even now, as Chase fussed over the other dog, Bandit could see Pixie throwing evil looks his way when Chase wasn't watching. Bandit was terrified of leaving Chase alone with her. What if Pixie hurt Chase while Bandit wasn't here? He barked, trying to warn Chase of this, but she misunderstood his intention.

"Are you arguing with me? Get out, Bandit, I mean it! You are not sleeping here tonight!"

With that, Chase slammed the door in Bandit's face. The last thing he saw was Chase comforting Pixie in her arms, like she usually fussed him.

Desperately unhappy, Bandit whined at the closed door, hoping Chase would open it again. She must have heard him, however, as she shouted through it. "Go away, Bandit! I mean it! You don't fight other dogs, especially ones smaller than you!"

Full of despair, Bandit turned around and slunk away to spend his first night without Chase.

Unfortunately, it would not be his last.

43

BANDIT

It had been a terrible night.

Doing as Chase had commanded, Bandit had stayed in the living room while she and Pixie slept in the bedroom. After the fight, Pixie hadn't wanted to leave Chase's side, so being kind, she had decided to let her stay in their room.

It was every dog's worst nightmare.

Since the day Bandit had met Chase, they had spent every single night together, so it had taken him a very long time before he could fall asleep without her. And even then, he kept waking up throughout the night, concerned about her well-being until eventually he had given up and gone outside her room. There, outside the closed door, he had lain on the ground with his nose in the gap between the floor and the door. By doing this, he was able to smell Chase and reassure himself of her safety. He tried to ignore Pixie's scent every time it wafted into his nose. Knowing that the other dog was so close to Chase filled Bandit with anxiety. He knew the others thought he was just jealous, but that wasn't it at all. Bandit knew Pixie was dangerous, and he was determined to prove it to the others until then, however, he would keep a watchful eye on her. He had to protect his family.

At exactly seven 'o'clock Chase woke up. Bandit knew because she woke at this time every day. Chase had taught him the meaning of time so Bandit understood that this was no coincidence. He heard her rustling in her bed and petting Pixie. He whined and scratched at the door, unhappy that he wasn't in there with her. She must have heard him as she got off the bed and padded barefoot to the door. Suddenly the door opened and Chase was standing there. Unable to quell the surge of joy Bandit felt at seeing her, he launched himself at her, bathing her face with his tongue.

"Ew," she exclaimed. "What do I say about licking my face?"

Bandit jumped down, tail wagging from side to side with such ferocity that it almost threw him off balance. He followed her into the room, happy that he was allowed back in only to find Pixie still sitting on Chase's bed. Bandit stopped dead. As the other dog started shaking with fright again, Bandit sniffed and scanned the room to make sure everything was as it should be. Other than Pixie's strange smell, everything seemed the same until his eyes fell on his bed, which lay beside Chase's. There, torn into a million pieces, was Bandit's beloved Frumpy Rabbit. Pixie had mauled him to death.

Bandit was horrified.

He ran to the basket, to his rabbit, lifted his snout to the ceiling and howled in despair. Startled by his reaction, Chase ran over to see what was wrong. When she saw what was left of the rabbit, she bent down and threw her arms around Bandit, hugging him close.

"I'm so sorry. She must have done that while I was sleeping."

Footsteps thundered down the hallway as Gideon ran inside, clutching a baseball bat. "What is it, what's wrong?" he demanded.

Chase pointed to the rabbit as Bandit's howl receded into a whimper.

"Damn, Pixie did that?"

Bandit barked once, strongly and accusingly.

"Don't worry Boy, we'll get you another."

However, Bandit knew no other toy would ever be the same again.

44

CHASE

I felt so bad about Bandit's rabbit.

It was the first toy I'd gotten him, and it was his favorite. He's slept with that thing every night since I've known him, so I can't believe Pixie did that. She must have destroyed it while I was fast asleep because I didn't hear a thing. I can't believe I woke to find her sleeping at the end of my bed looking angelic when she had completely killed Bandit's rabbit. It made me feel even worse about asking him to sleep outside, but I had never seen Bandit fight a dog before. Maybe I was too hard on him — I never even gave him a chance to explain, just took Pixie's side because she wasn't as smart or as big as him.

I grabbed my bag, shoving Bandit's iPad inside (he obviously couldn't wear it when we went out, but I always kept it on me, in case he wanted to speak) and went to retrieve my phone but I was annoyed to find it wasn't plugged into the charger. I had definitely plugged it in last night when I had set my alarm clock, but the cable wasn't in the phone now, having fallen behind the bedside table. Looking at the battery icon, I could see that I only had a little charge left, but I didn't want to wait to head into town. I wanted to replace Bandit's toy so he could quit walking around like a lost puppy.

I was glad it was just the two of us as we headed out on our daily shopping trip. I had a lot to make up for and I was determined to do it, starting right now. What with Sully being preoccupied, Gideon spending so much time with Pixie, and Sam who seemed permanently angry lately, it made me realize just how much I needed my buddy. I couldn't take him for granted again.

We were approaching the grocery store when Bandit snapped to attention, sniffing the air with interest. He shot a look over his shoulder at me,
chuffed, then moved a few feet away.

"What is it, boy?"

Of course, he couldn't answer me out here, so I just followed him as he
obviously wanted me to. He led me to a battered old car parked by the side
of the road. I frowned, wondering what he was up to when something
moved inside the car. It was a person. They were huddled into a ball and
fast asleep. It took a few moments before I recognized the untidy brown
hair.

"Mom, what're you doing here?" I asked, tapping on the window.

The figure inside woke with a start, blinking confused eyes at me.
"Chase..." She seemed momentarily disoriented, looking around her until
she finally remembered what she was doing. "Sleeping, obviously."

"But, you can't just do that. There are laws about this kind of thing!"

"There are?" she replied, genuinely perplexed.

I didn't answer, too busy wondering why she didn't stay in a motel.
There was a Motel 6 only a few blocks away. She could hardly have missed
it. And then the answer came to me. "You don't have any money, do you?"

She didn't immediately reply, but a red flush appeared on her cheeks.
She looked caught out, embarrassed. "It's not like it's cheap coming all the
way here. Besides, it's free to sleep in the car."

I don't know why the thought of her sleeping in her car affected me like
it did, but I suddenly felt a pang of sympathy for her and it made me real
mad. I didn't care about her so I sure didn't care where she was sleeping. I
cycled quickly through my anger until I came to another emotion —
concern.

"I hope you're not here to ask us for money because that's not going to
happen," I warned, suddenly tense.

She blinked at me, her eyes growing hard. "I told you why I'm here
already! I don't need your money!" This, she snapped as I had obviously hit
upon a sore subject. I didn't reply. We stared at each other in silence, both
of us weighing the other one up. Finally, she sat up, pulling a cardigan
around her. "Where are you going?" she asked pleasantly, as if we did this
sort of thing all the time.

I gave her a look. "That's none of your business," I said sharply. If I were
back home, this kind of response would have gotten me a slap, as it was she
just looked at me evenly.

"You're right. I only asked to make conversation."

Her reasonable tone made me feel like a heel. What was going on
around here? How was I the one feeling bad? Deciding I didn't have
anything more to say to her this morning, I got back on my bike.

"You shouldn't park there like that, it's illegal in this state," I said before taking off with Bandit. I didn't give her another look as the two of us continued through town until we got to the pet store. Once inside, I let Bandit choose whatever he wanted. Though we searched the entire store, there wasn't a replacement for his rabbit — they only had a small selection of stock. In the end, Bandit picked a panda. He had told me before that he liked how round and happy they looked, like a ball made out of fluff. I went to the checkout, paid, and put panda in my basket. I was deliberating over whether I should stop for some flowers, maybe surprise the others with fresh pastries when I heard a shout. Turning, I saw my mom jump out of her car. She was yelling at a guy, running fast into the distance.

"Someone help me! He just stole my bag!"

Stunned, I didn't immediately react, but Bandit started barking as he bolted after the thief. Concerned for him, I went after him on my bike. No way was I going to let Bandit deal with this guy alone.

Bandit swerved around the corner as I pedaled after him. He was going so fast I had to force myself to keep up. My legs were already screaming with pain, but I kept up the momentum and shot after him, navigating past the back alleys that we now found ourselves in. He ran left then right, following smells or sounds that my human nose and ears could not make out.

Finally, I caught sight of the thief in front of us. He was a skinny guy with mousy- colored hair and an awkward manner about him. He ran up to a waiting vehicle — a black Prius — and jumped into the car. I couldn't make out the driver except to see that he had hair that he wore in a ponytail. As Bandit and I neared them, the driver gunned the engine, and the car took off, leaving a cloud of dust in its wake.

There was no way I would be able to catch up to that car now. I stopped, summoning Bandit to my side. "Bandit! Heel!"

He came back to me after tossing a longing look over his shoulder at the fast retreating car. His body language seemed to say that he thought he could catch them, but I knew it was fruitless and I didn't want him to exhaust himself; he was already panting heavily. We returned to the main street to find my mom waiting for us.

She hurried over, concern etched over her face. "Why did you do that? You shouldn't have chased him! What if he was dangerous?"

I was surprised to see how worried she seemed to be. It was almost as if she were truly afraid that I had almost caught that guy.

"I can handle myself and so can Bandit," I said more harshly than I intended. I don't know what it was but I couldn't seem to be my usual cheerful self around her.

"I know, you scared me is all."

I looked into her car, into her home-away-from-home, and saw how sparse it was. Other than a few empty cartons of food, there was just a blanket and a hairbrush. "What was in the bag?" I asked.

"My purse, some make-up. All my cards." She raked her hand through her hair, the only outward sign of her turmoil. I sighed inwardly. I wanted to leave, but I knew it was the wrong thing to do. Despite everything that had happened between us, I couldn't just leave her stranded with no money. Of all people, I knew how that felt.

"I guess you'd better come with me to Sam," I said reluctantly.

"Sam? Sully's girlfriend? Why?" she asked.

"You don't know? I thought we'd told you. Sam's a sheriff."

For a brief second, I thought she looked alarmed before her expression quickly changed to one of surprise. "No, none of you mentioned that. She doesn't look anything like one."

"Sheriffs only look like sheriffs when they're wearing the uniform and when you turned up yesterday, it was her day off." Seeing the strange expression on her face again, I wondered what was up with her. "Why, you have a problem with sheriffs?"

She shook her head quickly. "I've never much believed in the law is all."

I thought about the times the neighbors had called the cops on her and Tubs after another one of their epic drunken fights. The cops had never liked either of them and had made it obvious how little they thought of them both, so it made sense why she wasn't particularly keen on them back. "Well, Sam is different. She will be able to help you."

But Mom shook her head. "I don't wanna drag her into this. I've already barged into her private life, how about we leave the professional one alone?"

I frowned in consternation, putting my hands on either side of my hips. "So you're just going to let that guy get away with stealing your purse?"

"Of course not. I'll report him, just not to your substitute mom. I don't wanna ask for her help."

"So this is a pride thing?" I asked, shaking my head in disbelief.

"Look, can we not do this? I've been awake less than five minutes. Most of my money's gone and I don't know what I'm going to do about that. How about you give me a break?" she said this a little desperately causing me to feel suddenly ashamed. I fell silent, kicking at a stone on the street. Bandit looked at her, then me, waiting patiently for me to decide our next course of action. Looking over her shoulder at Denny's Diner, I came up with an idea begrudgingly.

"Denny's has a phone you can use to report the robbery. We can grab some drinks there too... I have enough to cover us for those," I offered.

She smiled at me gratefully. "Sounds like a plan."

I crossed over the street to Denny's and chained up my bike outside. Zeb had laughed before, when he saw me do this once. Crime wasn't rife in

Montpelier, he'd said. Apparently the last time an incident had occurred was several years ago, and that had involved some out-of-towners, but I'd rather be cautious and not sorry even if it meant incurring ridicule, especially after what had just happened to my mom.

I looped the lock around a lamppost, and the three of us headed inside.

45

CHASE

Denny's was a simple place without any airs or graces. The only decoration they utilized were the cheerful checked curtains hanging on the front window, but other than that the place was, as Sully liked to call it, utilitarian. For my own personal taste, I had always liked how honest they seemed in here — it was the same with the food. Nothing fancy, just good simple comfort food. I lead Mom and Bandit to my favorite corner booth, where Bandit jumped up onto the seat next to me. Like the grocery store, they were used to seeing us together, and no one minded his presence.

Although it was breakfast time, neither one of us wanted to eat much, so I ordered two Coke floats. Our waitress, a slim woman in her 30s who had served me many times before, set the drinks down in front of us with a smile. "Let me know if there's anything else I can get you." She patted Bandit, then left, leaving us to our business.

Mom stood up. "Guess I should make that call."

I pointed across the room. "The payphone is over there. I'd let you use mine, but it's almost out of charge."

She nodded and disappeared to use the phone. I took a sip of my drink, letting the sweet liquid slide down my throat. Bandit nosed forward, sniffing hopefully at my glass, but I shook my head. "Sorry bud, but this isn't for you. Sully would have a fit if you had this much sugar."

He looked at me in disappointment but backed away from the glass. I stared outside blankly, draining my soda until Mom returned moments later.

"That was quick," I said.

She slid back into her seat. "Wasn't much I could tell them. They said they'd get back if they had any news."

I frowned at her. "That's it? What're you supposed to do in the meantime?"

She shrugged thin shoulders. "Wait, they said."

I pushed my empty drink away, annoyed. "What're you supposed to do for money until then?"

Mom played with the straw on her own drink but didn't drink any of it. "Don't think they care. Not like they have a pot of cash that they give out to callers."

I knew she was right, but it just seemed unhelpful.

"Thanks for trying to catch that guy," she said, giving me a grateful smile.

I shrugged like it was no big deal. "You should thank Bandit, he was the one who went after him. I just followed to make sure he was safe."

Hearing his name, Bandit's tail thumped on the seat next to me. His tongue was hanging out in that goofy grin of his. Mom looked at him uncertainly.

"Right. Thanks, Bandit."

He woofed, pleased with himself. Though she gave him a small smile, I could see it didn't quite reach her eyes. Even though she could see how good he was, she still didn't like him. I would never in a million years understand how that could be, how some folks just didn't like animals. People who were allergic or scared because they had been attacked by a dog when they were a kid? That I understood, but not liking them without a reason? That made about as much sense as a vegetarian who ate fish.

We sat there for a while as she continued to play with her drink. I watched as the ice cream melted into a layer of vanilla foam, fidgeting in my seat. The silence made me uncomfortable — we weren't just a normal mother and daughter after all — so I forced myself to break it.

"So, what's new back home?"

She looked at me over the top of her glass. "I'm still working part time in the bar, and Tubs is still driving trucks. A bunch of new people moved into the park, but I haven't met any of them yet. Let me think, what else... oh, I did see Miss. Hannah, a while back, bumped into her at Subway. She asked about you."

Miss. Hannah was my head teacher. She was a tiny thing and had to wear crazy high heels just to reach my chest, but she made up for that with her booming voice. She was a stern woman who had a habit of sneaking up on you when you least expected it: most of the kids were scared of her. I always thought I got on her nerves because I messed around a lot in class, so this was a surprise. "What did she say?"

"She just wanted to know if I had heard from you."

"That's nice. I thought she hated me."

"Well, she doesn't."

This was certainly stimulating conversation, not. I figured we could sit here making awkward chit chat all day or I could just say the things that have been on my mind for so long. With nothing left to lose, I decided to bite the bullet.

"Why are you still with him?" she blinked, taken aback by my direct question. Hesitating, she fumbled for an answer.

"It's complicated..." She finally began, but I interrupted her.

"No, it's not. He's an abusive jerk and you should have left him long ago." I retorted angrily.

She lay her hands palm down on either side of the glass, pushing down on the table for strength. "It's not that simple, I can't just leave. That's my home."

"It's a tin can. It's worthless and you can get another — equally worthless — someplace else. Someplace where he isn't there." My words were becoming clipped the angrier I got. Concerned for my spiraling mood, Bandit snuck his head onto my lap to comfort me. He sighed a big, long doggie sigh.

"And who's gonna take care of me if I did that? If I left him, who's gonna pay my bills or the rent, you tell me that?"

She was getting angry now too. Her mouth was set into a tight line, and she folded her arms across her chest.

"What are you talking about? Why does somebody have to look after you? You're a grown woman, why can't you look after yourself? Look at me! I spent eight months by myself on the streets and I was fine... and I'm fourteen!"

She looked at me, shaking her head sadly.

"You don't get it, do you? I'm not like you. You've always been able to take care of yourself, but I can't do that. I'm not built that way."

I was stunned.

I couldn't believe she actually believed that. Is this why she had never looked after me when I was growing up? Had she always thought I was so capable that she just never bothered to be my mother? My heart ached as I felt suddenly deeply sad for the little girl I had been, the one who had needed her mother to protect her from harm. After all this time, I finally understood why my life had been the way it was.

She couldn't stop thinking about herself, not even for one minute.

"Other people deal with crap everyday Mom, and yet they manage fine. You need to stop feeling sorry for yourself. Stop being a victim."

I thought my words would put her on the defensive. Instead, her eyes turned bright. She sat up a little taller and her arms unfolded. "Actually, I have something planned and when it works out, I'll be able to get myself straight."

"Good," I replied, "but is this something you can still have if Tubs is in the picture?"

"No," she said quietly, looking down into her drink. Her shoulders drooped, and she looked suddenly resigned. "It's been so long, I don't know who I am anymore..." She looked up at me, but now I saw something other than the despair she wore around her — it was hope. "But these few days without him, even though I've been sleeping in my car, I've felt better than I have in years."

She smiled then. "I'd forgotten what it feels like when you don't have to answer to anyone but yourself." She looked almost young again when she smiled like that. "I like it."

"So you know what to do," I said.

She nodded, suddenly vulnerable. "Will you help me?"

I started, startled by her request. "Help you, how?"

"Well, that guy took off with my bag. Everything I had was in there..."

My eyes hardened. "I already told you, if you're asking for money..."

She raised her hands at me. "No, no. I'll still have a little on me. I'm saying if I went for help, would you come with me?"

I didn't answer straight away, not knowing what it was that she wanted. I snuck a sideways look at Bandit, but he seemed as confused as I was. "Come with you where, exactly?"

She took out a printout of a website from her pocket to show me. It was a place called Pinewood and was some sort of woman's charity from what I could make out. "There's a shelter for women like me. It's about an hours drive from here. I found the information yesterday and have been thinking about it ever since."

My eyes narrowed. "Wait, you found this out yesterday? But you let me go on about leaving Tubs when you've already half decided to?"

She sighed at me to stop. "It gets a lot easier to realize what you should do when you're away, Chase. But just because I know what I should do, it doesn't make it any easier for me."

I bit my lip to stop from telling her off any further. She was right. Since I'd been away from them, my head had gotten much clearer and I had certainly become happier.

"Please? Would you just come with me for support? It shouldn't take long."

She seemed so desperate that against my better judgment I found myself caving. "Let me call Sully and tell him where we're going."

She nodded. "I'll use the restroom while you call."

She got up and left the table. I took out my cell and dialed his number. It rang for five rings, but he didn't pick up. I let out an exasperated breath. What was with Sully and his inability to pick up the phone these days? I left a quick voicemail telling him that I was going to accompany my mom to the women's shelter in Pinewood, then stroked Bandit.

"You think I'm doing the right thing?" I asked him. He made a sound that was half whine, half chuff. I figured he agreed although, like me, he wasn't particularly happy about it. We sat for what must have been five minutes before mom returned to the table. She had a paper bag in her hands and I could smell the undeniable scent of sausage and egg muffins wafting up.

"Splashed out on breakfast with the last of the cash I had on me. My way of saying thanks. Why don't you guys eat on the way? I want to make sure we get there early, I've heard they give out beds on a first-come basis."

She left the diner as Bandit and I followed her outside. I went to grab my bike, but she stopped me.

"That's not going to fit in my car."

I looked at her small car, then my bike, and I knew she was right. I felt my forehead crease into a frown. I wanted to bring it with me, just in case something happened and I needed to find my own way home, but I could see that it just wasn't going to happen.

"Ok," I said reluctantly. Making sure the bike was securely locked, we got into her car. I took the passenger seat while Bandit climbed into the back. He was already looking out of the window, excited by the idea of a ride. Like other dogs, he loved to hang his head out of it, while his tongue lapped up bugs, air, and dirt. Not for the first time, I wondered why this was a thing with them: you'd never catch a cat doing that. Mom handed us the muffins.

"Thanks," I said as I unwrapped mine, but I stopped her when she went to help Bandit with his. "That much salt isn't good for him," I said.

She shook her head and laughed. "Come on, one isn't going to hurt is it?"

Bandit paced the seat, anxious for the food. He was practically drooling by this point, so I figured it would be really cruel if he wasn't allowed one. "Fine," I said to him. "But we can't tell Sully, okay?"

Bandit woofed, yes.

I noticed that she wasn't eating. "You're not having one?"

"You know I can't eat in the morning," she replied, which was true. All the time growing up, I maybe saw her eat breakfast only a few times. "Besides, it means they're more for you two." She shook the bag and I could see that there were still some muffins left inside.

Happily, the two of us chowed down on our muffins as my mom started the engine and drove us out of town.

46

SULLY

fter our fight last night, Sam and I had barely spoken and when I woke this morning, it was to find a note on the bedside table asking me to meet her at "our place."

This was a secluded spot in the nearby woods where Sam and I loved to hike along the nature trail. We'd had many a picnic there, and this was the one place we retreated to when we needed a timeout from the rest of the clan, much as we could get to within ten minutes, anyway.

The sun shone brightly, though it wasn't enough to compete with the morning cold. Buttoning up my flannel shirt, I jumped out of my truck and grabbed Sam's thermos, which I had found draining on the sink. She'd forgotten to take it, so I filled it up with coffee. I'd brought mugs and donuts with me too, as food always seemed much nicer when enjoyed outdoors. I was trying to make amends, and this seemed the least I could do for the woman I loved.

Leaves and twigs snapped underfoot as I hiked briskly, enjoying the crisp air. These hikes were the one thing I had missed when I lived in Ellington. Deep down, I wasn't a city person, and the lack of greenery and mountains had hit me hard, but it was what Em had wanted. She'd had friends and family there, and it didn't make sense for us to be anywhere else.

I had only been going a few minutes when I saw Sam's figure ahead of me. She was sitting on the grass, her back against a towering oak. Although she wasn't wearing anything fancy — just jeans and a sweater — my breath caught at the sight of her. Her cheeks were red from the cold and her eyes bright. Her glossy curls spilled down her back like a velvet curtain. Thoughts of our fight last night flew straight out of my mind.

At my arrival, she stood up. I leaned forward to kiss her, but she ducked out of the way. Seeing her serious expression, butterflies did a dance inside my stomach.

"Hey."

"Hey," she answered softly, keeping her eyes on the ground.

This definitely wasn't good. She couldn't smile at me, could barely look at me. And her confident, normal manner was nowhere to be found.

"Thanks for joining me up here," she started. "I know we didn't have a restful night."

"Do you want to sit down? I brought us breakfast..."

I held up the food, but she shook her head, disinterested. "Sully, look. I need you to listen to me without interruption."

An alarm sounded deep within my head as a thousand objections flooded my mind. However, respectful of her wishes, I nodded. She shoved her hands into her pockets and continued.

"This isn't working for me. I was ready to move ahead with you, but it's become clear to me now that you're not in the same place, and as much as I hate to say this, as much as I hate to do this to you, Chase and the others, I think it's best if we took a break."

Of all the things I expected her to say, that wasn't it. I felt the smile freeze on my face as I stood there, motionless. "I know I've been distracted with everything that's happened, but don't you think this is extreme?"

She shook her head sadly. "No, I don't. You asked me to marry you, and then you freaked out as soon as you saw your ex-wife's grave. I don't need to be a shrink to see that this is a big, big problem."

I set down the food and grabbed her hands. "I didn't freak out when I saw her grave, Sam, I freaked out when I saw that it had been disturbed, and then there was the comb and the phone message. Please don't make this out to be something it's not."

She pulled away from me. "I'm not going to talk about all that again — we just keep going round in circles when, the truth is, we might not ever know where the message came from, if it came at all. I did run a trace on that number, Sully, but it came back with nothing. There has been no activity on that line since Emma's death. And the contract ended a few months after she died. You canceled it yourself."

I tried to hide my feelings on the subject, but I was reeling from her revelations. "Well, I said, I probably had... I just didn't remember. You can't hold that against me, I was dealing with the loss of my wife!"

Sam paused, taking a breath. "It's not just that... when we met, you gave me the impression that you were long over Emma, but when we were at the clinic, Florence told me how you were holding onto Emma's things for a year Sully - you couldn't even get rid of her toiletries. We only got together a month or two later. How could you have gone from one extreme to the other?"

"Because I did!" I yelled, unable to help myself. "I fell in love with you, and I moved on."

Sam shook her head sadly. "No. You're not over her. In fact, I think you haven't grieved properly and you may be suffering from a form of depression that can cause hallucinations. Which means you really did see that message, if only in your head."

I blinked, unbelievably. "Are you serious?"

Her voice became earnest. "Yes. I've been looking into the different forms of grief and your symptoms fit. It's why I wanted you to get help. Think about everything you've gone through, Sully. Emma's cancer, her death. Then, while you were clinging onto whatever you could of hers, you were attacked by Forbes' men who destroyed everything you had — they essentially destroyed her all over again for you."

I heard her words, but I couldn't take them in. She was wrong. "That's not what happened. I'm fine, dammit! The only thing that would cause me to feel grief again is you breaking up with me!"

Her eyes filled with tears. "I don't want to, but I can't stand by and watch you get worse. I've waited a long time to find my husband, and I'm not about to rush that now, especially if you're not ready. I care about you too much to do this to you."

"That doesn't even make sense. You care about me too much to marry me?"

Among the thick cloud of confusion and panic that had fallen over me, I realized that my pocket was vibrating. Someone was calling me, but I ignored it.

"One day you'll understand, Sully. When this is all over, and you are finally over your ex, you will know why I did this."

And with that, she ran off.

I wanted to chase after her. Wanted to grab her by the shoulders and shake her until sense returned, but I remained frozen, rooted to the spot.

I could do nothing but watch the woman I loved walk out of my life.

47

CHASE

I inhaled that muffin and the next like my life depended on it.

Since I'd lived here, I'd gotten used to having breakfast, so today when I skipped it, it had seemed like a really big deal. Usually, we had toast or cereal, though occasionally Gid would whip up some eggs and bacon. Those times didn't happen as much, now that he was a working man, so those muffins felt like a real treat. Bandit had chowed his down in two bites and was now licking his chops and making happy noises in the backseat.

I wiped my mouth on a napkin and looked out at the scenery. Trees and buildings blurred past as we drove away from the town, hitting country within moments. Fields of wheat and barley shimmered under the morning sun. The sky was a brilliant blue, and it was only the slight chill in the air that revealed summer had passed. I shot a sideways look at my mom, but she seemed intensely focused on driving. She sat stiffly and her hands gripped the steering wheel real tight. I guessed she was nervous about what we would find ahead of us.

I checked my phone to see if Sully had messaged — he hadn't and I was annoyed to find that the battery was now blinking at me. Figures that the moment I left town, my phone would be dying.

"Do you have a car charger?" I asked my Mom.

She shot me an apologetic look. "Yes, but it was in my bag."

Of course it was. Just my luck.

I fell silent as we continued on our journey. We didn't talk, which was good in a way, as now we were in this small confined space, I found I didn't know what to say. If I were honest, we never really spoke much to each other before either. Mom was always preoccupied with her latest boyfriend, and when there wasn't one in the picture, she'd spend all her time going out while she tried to find a new one. From the age of ten, she'd frequently left me alone in that trailer while she trawled the local bars for her latest victim, but I had never minded as it meant I could stay up late and watch whatever I wanted to on the TV. I also learned how to make a mean mac and cheese in the microwave.

To fill in the silence, Mom had tuned into a radio station. The music played now, a pop number that was really familiar, but for some reason, I couldn't think what it was. I had a photographic memory so forgetting song lyrics happened to me literally never. I frowned, trying to concentrate.

What the heck was this song?

I leaned back into my seat when I noticed that I was feeling drowsy, which was weird as I had only recently got up. My head started feeling heavy, like it was too big for my neck. I glanced behind me to see that Bandit was nodding off too.

And suddenly I felt a cold feeling in my stomach.

Sweat broke across my brow as the fear hit. I looked at my mom and saw the way her hands gripped the wheel. Her shoulders were tense, and she kept her eyes on the road ahead as if she was determined not to look at me.

I knew without a shadow of a doubt that she had drugged us.

"What did you put in the food?" I managed to exclaim, even as my tongue felt like it was pinned to the roof of my mouth.

She looked at me then, guilt all over her face.

"I'm sorry. I had to do it."

Anything else she said I couldn't hear.

Blackness took over, and I felt myself sinking into oblivion.

48

THE SCIENTIST

The call came right on cue.

The woman, Tracey Blueman, phoned to say the girl and dog were leaving with her as planned. She would drug them and meet us at the arranged location. The Scientist felt his excitement build as he waited for her car to arrive. For more than six months he had carefully set out his chess pieces, planning for this moment, and now that it was almost here, a warm feeling spread through his body.

"This is so exciting, Xavier!" Dick said.

He tried to hide his flicker of annoyance. Dick was Xavier's assistant, a student he had picked up in his science class. There was one like him every year. Quiet, shy, and lonely, he sat at the back of the class, never raised his hand, ate alone in the canteen, and had no friends to speak of. He had noticed him straight away. Every time he had seen him in passing, the boy had had a nose in a textbook. It was his armor against a world that had yet to notice him.

But notice him it hadn't.

And that wasn't really surprising. Of medium height, he had a slim build. His hair was not quite blond yet not dark enough to be brown. He wore thick glasses to correct heavy short-sightedness, but the lenses enlarged his eyes to comical effect, making him seem like an owl in appearance.

It hadn't taken much to turn him. All Xavier had to do was notice him and toss out a kind word here or there. Within a few months of Xavier implementing his plan, Dick had become his willing accomplice.

Raised by a family who didn't understand him, Dick wasn't close to his parents, who seemed happy that their son was now across the country at college. They were so far away that it made no economic sense for Dick to go home, even for the vacation season. It was during the summer vacation when Xavier began his plan in earnest. Throughout the semester, he had invited Dick into his home under the guise of helping with his science experiments, but the reality was, Xavier was grooming him. But Dick was too stupid, too desperate for approval to notice. He started lightly, using hypothetical questions to see how far he could push the boy, and Dick had lapped it up like a dog, never suspecting a thing.

It was Dick who had sent Sullivan that message on his phone using an application that made it look as if it had come from his dead wife's phone, and Dick who had disturbed the grave. This part of the plan was actually Dick's idea, and Xavier had found it quite devious and brilliant. He would never tell him that, however. To keep Dick under his control, Xavier only ever complimented him when absolutely necessary; it was part of the brainwashing process. Dick was so starving for approval he would do all that Xavier wanted without complaint.

Dick smiled at Xavier now, causing splotches of red to appear across his neck and cheeks, which only made his acne seem ten times worse. Xavier tried not to let the sight of them disgust him as they always did. *Had the boy never heard of Proactiv?* He nodded. "Let's not get too excited until she actually gets here."

They waited in his Prius, in the car park of a Walmart, as Xavier thought back to his first visit with Tracey Blueman.

He had initially learned of her identity through the reports Forbes' mercenary had compiled. Though Hector wasn't someone he liked or ever had dealings with himself, he had to admit the man excelled at his job — up until the very end, anyway.

In Hector's files, Xavier had learned who the girl Chase was, who her parents were and what kind of life she had lived. Her mother was a person of low moral fiber. Reading about her relationship with the alcoholic and seeing how cheaply they lived, Xavier knew she could be bought, so he wasn't at all surprised when she had agreed to his deal so willingly... Some people just didn't make good parents. He himself knew that better than most. His own had never wanted a child. They were partygoers, selfish to the core and only ever wheeled him out as a freak to be admired or feared. They couldn't wait to send him away to boarding school, where they no longer had to deal with the inconvenience of his being there.

Xavier hated them with a vengeance.

The plan had come together quite simply with the only hiccup appearing when Tracey Blueman had called, worrying over how she would be able to separate the girl and the dog away from the rest of the family. Again, it was Dick who had come up with the idea for the fake robbery. He felt that for Chase to help her mother — who she was clearly resentful of — something bad would need to happen to her. There was too much history between them, but having studied footage of the girl at home, Dick had seen that the girl was inherently kind, and they had quickly used that failing against her. If Xavier actually cared one bit for the Dick, he would have encouraged him into the field of psychology, as science was very clearly wasted on him. As it was, Xavier didn't waste energy on simple emotions such as like or dislike.

A car turned into the parking lot. A beaten up Toyota with a woman behind the wheel. Xavier sat up a little taller.

"Is that her?" Dick asked in his nasal voice.

Xavier leaned forward in his seat, straining to get a better look. "I don't know."

The car parked, and the woman got out. Xavier recognized her cheap clothes and desperation immediately. "That's her."

They got out of the car and crossed the parking lot to meet her. She tossed a nervous look in the direction of her car where they could now see the dog and girl sleeping soundly. Wringing her hands, she greeted them. "I did my part, now where's the money?"

Though this was the agreement, her lack of concern for her own child disgusted him. Xavier's gaze hardened as he gestured to Dick. "Please hand Ms. Blueman her payment."

Dick went to the trunk of Xavier's car, opened it and took out a large canvas sports bag. Inside, divided into blocks of five hundred, was one hundred thousand dollars in cash; Xavier had counted it all himself. It had taken a lifetime to save up that much money. Despite his parents' wealth, they had never shared any of their fortune with him, neither had Forbes, and Xavier had always been too proud to ask either for help. And now, here was this trailer trash, selling off her child for only one hundred thousand dollars. His mouth curled into a sneer that he didn't bother to hide.

Tracey Blueman snatched the bag out of Dick's hands. She yanked down the zip to check the contents inside. When she saw the bills, her eyes went wide with greed. "It's all here?" she asked.

"Of course it is," Xavier replied, annoyed. "I do not go back on my word."

She took the hefty bag from them and tossed it into the boot of her car. Then she opened the door to the back seat.

"Dick, if you would be so kind..." Xavier said.

Dick jumped to attention. Leaning in, he slid his arms under the unconscious dog and carried him to Xavier's car where he set him down inside a cage on the backseat. Next Dick went over to the girl and carried her to the car where he positioned her next to the cage. The woman looked at her daughter, her guilt and shame obvious to see.

"She's going to be okay, right? You said she wouldn't be harmed?"

"Now you are concerned for her well-being?" Xavier asked, one brow arched in question.

"You told me she wouldn't be hurt. You said you just wanted the dog for your science experiment," she replied.

"And I meant it. The girl will be returned to her family." Xavier put an emphasis on the word "family."

The woman flinched as Xavier intended for her to. She bit her lip, unsure then and looked at the girl again. Her hesitation and mistrust began to grate on him. He'd had enough of this woman now and was itching to get away.

"We had a deal, Ms. Blueman. You have your money now, so please leave or we will be forced to take it all back."

The threat worked as expected. She recoiled physically from him, moving quickly to the driver's seat. Climbing in, she put her hand on the key in the ignition.

"I'm sorry, Chase," she whispered.

Casting one last look at the daughter that she was leaving behind, she turned the key. And as the engine roared into life, she pressed down on the gas and drove away.

THEY HEADED WEST, away from this Godforsaken pathetic town.

Xavier had already packed away Erik-the-IT-man's things, leaving no trace of him behind. For several weeks before his initial "move" here, he had scoped out the town, making copious notes as to the family's routine. As he had hoped, it was fairly consistent. The Sheriff worked eight to five on weekdays most weeks, doing the occasional weekend shift as and when it was required. The young boy — a new hire to the town's garage — worked nine to six. Sullivan seemed to spend a majority of his time just doing things around the ranch, or rehabbing his leg under his father's watchful eye. Which left Chase, who came into the town daily with the dog to pick up the day's groceries. It was all so mundane, so uninspired, Xavier wondered how they didn't all kill themselves from boredom.

When the mechanic's previous tenant moved out during his stakeout, he knew it was a blessing in disguise. While he had no desire to live here, he knew he would never have a better opportunity to get so up close and personal. So, with just a handshake and a few hundred dollars cash deposit,

Xavier had found himself living above the mechanic's garage, where he could observe Chase and Gideon's daily comings and goings.

It was masterful, really. He had been right under their noses, but they never suspected a thing. A laugh bubbled up in his mouth, which he tried to hide under a cough. He preferred that Dick never knew his true feelings. It kept the boy on edge, which is how he wanted it.

To truly control someone. It was best to keep them on an uneven footing. They should never feel comfortable or be able to predict your reactions. Like chess, this was another game Xavier excelled in.

While Dick drove, Xavier climbed into the back of the car and performed his inspection of the specimen.

Even to his naked eye, he could see the dog was in excellent health. His coat gleamed and his eyes — well, what he could see of them — were bright. Clearly, this dog was not lacking in any physical comforts. The girl and her friends had served him well.

Xavier moved the fur around the dog's head until he felt the raised scar behind his skull. This was where Forbes' doctor had opened him up. When she had removed the tumor that had originally been placed inside his brain to stimulate trauma.

When Xavier had first learned of this plan, he had thought it ludicrous, but it amused him now that his own breakthrough required the use of this one small dog. He needed what the dog had to complete his own experiment.

He was so close to making history he could barely contain himself. All he needed was to see how the dog's brain had reorganized itself, how it had healed itself, and he could get his experiment to do the same. In addition to seeing into his brain, he wanted to investigate the dog's DNA helix and find what code might be added or missing in order for his body to be as it was.

If what he was proposing worked, he would become the most famous man in history.

Not that fame was what he was after, of course. He only wanted the world to recognize his genius and treat him accordingly. Once he made history, he knew his parents would come crawling back to him — and he couldn't wait to tell them where to go.

If it wasn't for their precious cargo, he would instruct the hapless Dick to drive faster. As it was, Xavier willed the boy to drive more carefully than he had done in his entire life.

49

SULLY

I don't know how long I stood there under that damn tree.

Sam had said her piece and just like that, she was gone. I was left reeling. Despite my turmoil of the last few days, I was in love with Sam and had planned on our future together. Now, not only had that future vanished in a cloud of dust, it looked like I wouldn't even have her in my life. I couldn't collate what had just happened with my life. Only yesterday we were looking at baby clothes, but Sully Jr was now a distant dream.

I forced my feet to move. On autopilot, I walked back to my car and climbed in. Somewhere in the back of my mind, I remembered my phone had rung during our conversation. I took out my cell to see a missed call from Chase. She had left a voicemail. Numbly, I listened as her voice came over the line. She was saying something about going with her mom to a woman's shelter. If this was any other day, I would have called right back and said exactly why that might not be a good idea, but I could barely get the fog that was clouding my mind to lift long enough for coherent thoughts to surface. Bandit was with her and I was sure they were fine. All I could think about was getting home. What if Sam were packing right now? Maybe I could persuade her not to leave.

Energized by the thought, I gunned the engine and drove home as fast as I could.

When I got to the ranch, I couldn't see Sam's car, but she parked it around the back at times so it didn't necessarily mean she wasn't here. I knew my brain was in complete denial of events, but I didn't care. I was holding onto whatever thought I could to get by. Getting out of the car, I didn't bother shutting the door. I just bolted inside.

The ranch was deathly silent. I listened for signs of any movement, but all was suffocatingly still. "Pixie?" I called out. My voice echoed around, sounding strange and desperate to my own ears. I had no idea what I was doing. Even if the dog knew her name, it wasn't as if she would answer me. She wasn't Bandit.

With a sinking heart, I turned towards our room. From the corner of my eye, my mind registered a fact that seemed a little odd. I glanced into the living room to find dad's wheelchair in the corner of the room. Of the man himself, he was nowhere to be seen.

Strange.

Frowning, I changed course and headed into the living room. As I grew closer, I saw the glass on the floor.

The decorative bowl that usually sat on the table had smashed and now lay in several pieces on the scratched floorboards. The coffee table that previously housed the bowl was askew, like someone had bumped it. My heart started to race as it suddenly came to me that something was terribly wrong. I fished out my phone, preparing to call the others when I saw a boot sticking out from behind the sofa. Made of a tan leather, it had the mismatched laces that Chase often laughed about.

It was my dad's boot.

50

SULLY

S printing forward, I finally saw him. He was lying on the ground. Unconscious.

"Dad!" I cried.

He didn't move.

There was an angry gash on the side of his head where I suspected it had hit the floor. I felt for a pulse and was relieved to find one. Quickly, I ran my hands over his body to see if I could find anything broken or out of alignment. As far as I could tell, the only injury he had was the one to his head.

Unless of course there was something wrong with him on the inside.

The thought filled me with dread.

I was wondering if it would be safe to move him when I saw there was something gripped in his hand. Prying it open, I found some kind of gadget inside. It took a while before I realized I was looking at a spy cam, the kind people put inside toy bears when they left their child at home with a new babysitter.

What the hell? Where had he gotten that from?

I didn't have time to worry over the spy cam, however, I needed to get him help.

"Gideon? Sam? Are you here?" I yelled out, hoping desperately that one of them would answer my call. Only silence greeted me.

Carefully, I picked him up and carried him to the back of my truck. I didn't put him in the passenger seat as I had no idea what damage he might have inside of him. I couldn't risk there being an issue with his neck or his unconscious body falling forward and hitting the dashboard.

Running back inside, I grabbed several of the quilts my mom had made when I was a kid and ran back out with them. Rolling them into tight rolls, I wedged them securely around him as best I could.

I could call for an ambulance, but the nearest hospital was a forty minute drive away, and I knew I could get him there faster if I drove myself.

Forgetting all about Sam and Chase, I shot off to Memorial Hospital.

51

SULLY

I sat in the waiting room anxiously tapping my foot on the ground. It had been at least an hour since I'd arrived at the hospital and the doctors had taken over. I watched as they placed my dad onto a gurney and wheeled him away. Although I had checked with the front desk multiple times, there was nothing to report. The receptionist, a woman with unruly hair and eyes that looked too big for her face, assured me that as soon as there was any news, I would be given it. I knew that was crap. It was the line they gave people to keep them away. Florence had used it herself back at the clinic to spare me having to deal with concerned parents. There was nothing I could do but wait.

Suddenly the doors crashed open as Gideon thundered through the entrance. Spotting me in the waiting area, he ran to my side. "Where is he?"

The kid was still in his work clothes and hadn't even bothered to wipe the grease stains from his hands. He must have come straight from the garage when he picked up my message. I shrugged helplessly.

"Still being checked out by the doctors. They haven't told me anything."

Gideon marched straight up to the front desk and demanded to be given a status update on Dad's health. Despite his aggressive stance, the receptionist was calm and comforting, having faced endless desperate and frightened family members before. She fed him the same line she had given me and gestured that he should wait by my side.

Defeated, he came back over and sat down. "What the heck is taking them so long?"

I shook my head, not really wanting to think about what the reasons might be. In my experience as a vet, the faster you knew what the problem was, the less serious it was. Gideon's eyes searched the area, looking for something to focus on until they landed on a vending machine. "You want a drink?" he asked.

"I'm fine, thanks," I replied, though the reality was far from the truth. My throat felt dry and thick with mucus from not having drunk anything all day. Sam's thermos with the coffee was still in the truck untouched though I couldn't summon up the energy to get it. Despite feeling like I'd spent a week in a desert, I didn't want anything. The only way I would feel any better was to know what was going on with Dad.

The doors ahead of us opened and the doctor who had assisted my dad came over to us. His expression was grave, but I couldn't tell anything else by his demeanor.

Gideon and I both jumped to our feet. The doctor, whose name was Dr. Edmund Lyman according to the name badge on his shirt, offered a small smile.

"Your father has received a serious head trauma and is still unconscious. At this point, I can't tell if he will come out of it or not, so, unfortunately, all we can do is wait. All other vital signs are good. It's just the head wound that seems to be the issue. Do either of you know what might have caused it?" he asked.

I shook my head. "No. I was out with my... with Sam, but when I came home, I found him on the ground like that. I have no idea what happened. And Gideon was still at work, so he doesn't know either."

"Zeb was home with one of our dogs, Pixie," Gideon offered. "I left the two of them alone when I went to work."

A puzzling thought occurred to me. "Thinking about it, I didn't see Pixie when I got back. The house was silent, I didn't see her anywhere at all."

The doctor tried to piece the puzzle together. "If something scared her, she might have run off. We'll keep a close watch over your father. I'll let you know if anything changes. Obviously, if you find out any information in the meantime, please call and let me know immediately as it might help solve the mystery of what's happened to him. Other than that, you might as well go home as there is nothing you can do here."

Gideon and I looked at each other, both of us wanting to argue our reasons to stay, but the Doctor was obviously prepared for this.

"Fella's, even if you stay, he won't know you're here. I suggest you go home, get some rest, and wait for my call."

His tone brokered no argument. Having instructed us, he went to the receptionist to check for messages and then was gone.

"I know he's treating Zeb and all, but I don't care what he says. I'm not going home. Where're Sam and Chase?"

His innocent question hit me like a knife to the heart. With all that had happened, I had forgotten my conversation with Sam this morning, but now her words and actions invaded my head. "Sam and I are taking a break," I said slowly.

Gideon couldn't have looked more incredulous. He almost laughed, thinking my words ludicrous until he saw that I was serious. The shock left his face to be replaced by concern.

"This is for real? What the hell happened?"

I shrugged. What could I say when I didn't understand it myself? I bit down on my lip, not trusting myself to speak any further. Seeing that I wasn't willing to discuss the subject any longer, Gideon dropped his line of questioning and moved to another.

"Does Chase know?"

"No. I need to call her back, actually. She's gone with her mom to some woman's shelter."

Gideon froze at my words. "What are you talking about? She didn't say anything about that this morning?"

"I gather it's something that only came up today. I was with Sam when she called, so I didn't actually speak to her."

Taking out my phone, I dialed Chase's number. Instead of the ringtone I expected, however, the call went straight to voicemail. There wasn't even the few seconds delay that would signify bad reception. For the call to go through to voicemail so quickly, it meant only one thing.

The phone was turned off.

An uncomfortable feeling started inside my stomach. Seeing my face, Gideon spoke. "What is it?"

"Her phone's off."

CHASE

Darkness surrounded me.

My head felt foggy and my mouth was parched. I felt like I hadn't had a drink in days. I must have had the worst sleep of my life to be feeling like this. My body ached, and I shivered, unexpectedly cold. I reached over to stroke Bandit, but instead of his soft fur, my hand touched something cold and damp. It took a few moments for me to realize what it was.

Dirt.

Confused, my eyes flicked open. Instead of the ceiling I expected to see, there were a canopy of leaves suspended above me. Beams of light struggled through the dense foliage, but they had such a long way to go that the area immediately around me was dark and unwelcoming.

Where the heck was I?

I pushed myself to my knees and looked around me. There was nothing but endless trees as far as my eyes could see. Straining my ears, I listened for sounds of civilization. Voices, a car, anything that would signify I wasn't a million miles away from people, but there were just the birds screeching over me, and the wind rustling through the bank of trees. This was like a terrifying dream that I hadn't woken up from.

What was I doing in the middle of a forest?

Where was Bandit?

I tried to call for him, but the words stuck in my throat. I swallowed painfully and tried again. This time I was able to yell out his name, although my voice sounded weak and fearful.

There was no response.

I screamed his name, louder this time, more desperate, but still, there was nothing. No answering bark or the joyful sound of him crashing through the forest towards me. Wherever he was, it wasn't here.

I stood up, frantically trying to remember where I had been before I woke up here. I was in a car, wasn't I? I remembered watching mom drive to the shelter. Bandit was in the backseat, and we were both eating breakfast.

The muffins.

It all came suddenly crashing back to me. We were both eating the muffins mom had given us, and that was the last thing I remembered. Was there a car crash? Had we been in a crash and I somehow crawled here to safety?

I looked down at myself but couldn't find signs of any injuries and my clothes were undamaged, so my theory had to be wrong. Had Mom taken off with Bandit? But she didn't know anything about him. She had no idea he was special, so that made no sense either.

My heart was beating in my chest and I felt hysteria rise up inside me. Where was he?

Suddenly I remembered my phone. I just had to call Sully, and he'd find me. Sam used phones to locate people all the time, I knew that from experience. I reached into my pocket only to find that my phone wasn't there. Growing increasingly desperate, I patted my pockets, but it was no use, my phone was gone.

And then the panic really took hold.

SULLY

Gideon and I rushed home to the ranch.

We were hoping desperately that when we got there, we'd find Chase and Bandit in the kitchen eating us out of house and home, but only oppressive silence greeted us. We searched the place but couldn't find signs of them or Pixie. I had drilled into them the importance of being contactable at all times, so this vanishing act was a bad sign.

A really bad sign.

I punched in a number on my phone. It ran countless times without being answered. Just as I was beginning to think it never would, Sam's voice came on the line.

"Sully, I don't think we should be talking right now."

Hearing her voice almost broke me, but I forced myself to focus, my concern over Chase and Bandit overriding even my own turmoil. "I'm not calling about us. Listen, some things have happened: Dad had an accident, he's unconscious and in the hospital, and Chase and Bandit are gone."

"Wait, what did you say?" Her concern and confusion radiated down the line.

"I got home after our talk and found Zeb on the floor unconscious. And there's something else — he had a spy cam in his hand. It looks like he found it under that glass bowl in the living room. I think he was attacked because he found that camera. There's a nasty bump on his head and he hasn't come to yet. I tried calling Chase after I got to the hospital but her phone went straight to voicemail and she knows better than to turn it off."

"That's... OK. When did you last hear from her?" Sam asked, her voice suddenly taking on a professional tone as the sheriff in her kicked in.

"Not since this morning when she left. She left me a voicemail, which I only picked up after we spoke this morning. She said she'd gone with her mom to a woman's shelter. She wanted to help get her checked in. Her mom said she was going to leave that guy she's with, so I guess Chase thought it was her duty to go with her."

"Duty? Chase doesn't owe her a thing." Sam said firmly.

"You and I know that, but Chase, despite everything she's been through, she's a sweet girl. She cares about people even when she shouldn't."

"I know, it's one of her best and worst qualities," Sam said immediately concerned. "I'm assuming Bandit is with her?"

"Yeah," I replied.

"Come to my office, I'll see what we can do to find her."

"Thanks," I said relieved and grateful for her help.

"Of course," Sam said. "Whatever is happening between us, she's still my family, Sully. You both are."

There was a lump in my throat the size of Texas, so I didn't trust myself to answer. I nodded, even though she couldn't see the gesture.

"We'll be there in ten minutes."

54

SULLY

Less than thirty minutes later we were pacing Sam's office.

Brad, her deputy, was putting a trace on Chase's phone. At my appearance, he had given me an apologetic smile, knowing that Sam had found out about my personal request. He even apologized before I shrugged it off. The man hadn't done a thing wrong. Besides we had something much more worrying to contend with right now.

I wasn't sure how the trace worked exactly, but it wasn't anything near as exciting as they made it seem in the movies. The process was long and laborious, and as yet we had come up with nothing.

"We're not getting a read on her phone, but that's because it's off. We'll only be able to get a hit once it's turned back on again. Unfortunately, the last known location was here. We have to wait to see if the trace picks up anything again."

"I can't believe she's gone off with her, what could she be thinking?" Gideon exclaimed, fury masking his concern. "I knew we shouldn't have let her into the house that first time. We're stupid for trusting her!"

"What's done is done, let's not torture ourselves over things we can't change," Sam said evenly. "We don't know that her mom has done anything. There could be a simple solution to this, like her phone has run out of charge. Still, I've put out an alert, just in case. If she hasn't gone far, we'll find her."

I couldn't help but hear the disclaimer in her sentence. "If she hasn't gone far?" I looked at the clock, then checked my phone for the time of the voicemail message. It was at least six hours since any of us had spoken to Chase. Six hours could give someone quite the head start. "What about that spy cam, can you get anything out of it?"

"I don't know. I've given it to our tech guys. They've already explained that it's an internet IP wireless camera, which basically means that it broadcasts what it sees to an online storage facility. They're going to see if they can find out where that is. If we can get in, we'll be able to see what they've seen. If we get really lucky and they haven't decrypted their IP address, we may be able to find them that way."

"But we're never lucky though, are we? If they're smart enough to get into our home and wire it up without any of us knowing, they've probably got that area covered." I didn't like how I was channeling Negative Nancy, but the odds seemed so against us.

"What about Bandit?" Gideon said. "What about the tracker you put into him?"

Sam frowned at me. "What tracker?"

"After what happened with Forbes, I put a tracker inside Bandit!" I had completely forgotten about the thing. "Gid, I could kiss you right now!"

He grinned at me, suddenly relieved. "Please, don't. Just find them that'll be good enough for me."

I ran to the computer and called up a website. It was a network that we vets used when we were trying to trace missing animals. It was a little like having a microchip that also functioned in a similar manner to the locate your iPhone facility Apple provided its products. I opened a second window and logged into my email, scrolling through the messages until I came to the one I wanted. When I had put the tracker inside Bandit, I had registered it with this website. As part of the service, the website had emailed me Bandit's reference number, the one I would need if he ever went missing. I typed in that number now and hit enter.

We waited anxiously as a timer spun around on the screen. Finally, a map loaded with a beeping icon. "That's it!" I said. "That's Bandit!" I hugged Gideon, yelling into his ear. "Well done!"

After our brief celebratory moment, I leaned in closer to see where he was and heard Sam gasp over my shoulder.

"Back there, that's Harrisburg in Pennsylvania. This means he's past it already. That can't be right, can it?"

I had no answer for her question. Instead, I listened to Chase's voicemail again. Paused, then rewound the part where she mentioned the name of the women's shelter.

Without my even asking her, Sam opened another window on the computer, searching for a woman's shelter in Pinewood, which was just over an hour's drive from here, but Google returned an error. There was no such place in Pinewood.

The shelter didn't exist, which meant Chase was being lied to.

Sam and I looked at each other, horrified.

55

CHASE

The facts were undeniable.

I had blacked out only to wake up in the middle of a forest with no dog and no phone. None of that was good news or an accident, *and we already knew what I thought of coincidences...* While I had no idea how I came to be here like this, I did know one thing — I had to get out of here; I had to find Bandit. My Muttface was likely in danger.

With an aim in place, I scanned the area around me. There really was nothing but trees and leaves and dirt. A hysterical laugh threatened to make its way out before I choked it back down.

No, you will not panic. Get a grip.

Then I saw a dark shape on the ground around ten feet away from me. It was too small to be Bandit — thank God — still; I approached cautiously. I was alone and defenseless so I felt vulnerable; even the least threatening forest creature had the potential to be dangerous if disturbed. When I drew close, I realized it was a bag, the kind you wear over both shoulders. It was navy in color, with a bright orange label that I would have noticed right away if there was a bit more light around it, and there was something else about it that was odd... it looked brand new. I reached for the bag, noticing that it was made of a cheap polyester fabric. It actually reminded me of the ones Sully had gotten excited over in the Dollar Store. This thing wasn't exactly built to last. I pulled open the drawstring holding it closed, then tipped the contents of the bag onto the ground.

A bottle of water fell out, followed by three bargain basement energy bars and a torch. I inspected the side pockets hoping for more, but that was all there was... basic supplies that would only last me a day, possibly two. Looking at items, I came to two immediate conclusions. One, whoever had dumped me out here — and it was clear now that I had been put here on purpose — they didn't want me to die. And two, let me revise what I had thought just moments ago... Muttface was *definitely* in danger.

I shoved the items back into the bag and stood up, determined to get out of here so I could find my buddy.

Think Chase, what do you know about navigation?

I turned around slowly until my eyes settled onto a light in the distance. The sun! I could use that to work out my location. It hung low in the sky, which I knew meant I didn't have long before night fell. I had to get out of this dense forest before it got dark or I would be screwed.

Positioning the sun so that it was directly in front of me, I started walking.

Please, please let me get out of here before it gets dark.

56

SULLY

By now it had become clear to us, Chase's mom had kidnapped them both. I had no doubt in my mind. Though I desperately hoped it was just a case of her wanting Chase back, her disappearance added with the discovery of the spy cam made me suspect that it had something to do with Bandit.

And that terrified me.

If her mom knew he was special that opened up a whole host of questions I did not want to ask. Was it possible that someone else out there knew about him?

I focused on Bandit being the reason for the kidnapping rather than Chase, as there was a large part of me that refused to believe her own mother would hurt her. In all the stories Chase had told about her childhood, her mother was selfish and not particularly nice, but she had never hurt her. She seemed a victim herself. I desperately hoped Chase was okay. She had to be.

Sam yelled down the phone. She was trying to secure a helicopter that we could use to get to Bandit's location faster, but unfortunately, this required some red tape and her hands were tied. She couldn't reveal the helicopter would be to rescue a minor as that would instantly become an FBI issue, or mention anything about a super-smart-dog-that-had-been-created-in-a-lab either. It was looking more and more like we were on our own. We'd have to jump in the car and go after them.

It was a terrible idea, and we all knew it.

As they had a six or seven hour head start, we could be playing catch-up forever. Unable to get anywhere, Sam slammed the phone down and marched over to me.

"I tried, but there's nothing I can get us. There isn't a way to get help without telling anyone what we are doing." She sounded as desperate as I felt.

While Sam had been on the phone, Gideon had been impatiently watching over my shoulder while I kept my eye on the beacon announcing Bandit's current location. He grabbed my arm and started pulling me away from the desk.

"We're wasting time! Let's just go after them ourselves." He looked at the two of us, pleadingly. Sam grabbed her gun and slid it into its holster securely as she nodded in agreement.

"You're coming with us?" I asked her, shocked.

"I told you, you're family," she said.

I was so relieved by her answer that I almost broke down.

The three of us rushed outside and started after them.

57

CHASE

I had been walking now for what seemed like hours.

My feet screamed from pain and I was sure I had developed blisters the size of ping-pong balls. Branches tore at my arms, covering me with scratches that itched one minute, then stung like crazy the next. Wind whistled through the tears in my thin cardigan, and I knew it was only the exertion from the exercise that kept me from feeling the cold. I could still see the faraway sun, but it was barely a dot on the horizon. Night was fast approaching, and I had made no headway out of the forest.

Knowing it was highly unlikely that I was going to be rescued anytime soon, I had to seriously consider my options for camping down for the night. There was a part of me that wondered if I'd be able to navigate by torchlight, but twisted tree roots shot up from the ground all around me, not forgetting those freaking branches. If I tried walking at night without being able to see much around me, I would run the risk of hurting myself — and that was the best-case scenario. I was pretty convinced that, knowing my luck, I would end up dead in a ravine or blunder my way into the path of a bear, which they probably had in these parts, if only I knew where these parts were.

So no exploring in the dark. I would be sleeping here tonight.

I found myself a tree, one with a thick trunk, and started gathering leaves beside it. It wasn't much, but that trunk would offer some shelter in case of rain or wind. From my time on the streets I knew when sleeping rough, one of the worst things you had to deal with was the ground. If you didn't insulate yourself from it, the cold would creep into your bones causing a restless night so my priority was to find whatever I could to create a layer between myself and it, but seeing as there were only leaves and dirt and twigs, I didn't have much to work with.

Back at the ranch, one of my favorite hobbies was watching survival shows on television. You know, the ones where they left celebrities on an uninhabited island for a couple of days or weeks where they have to survive with nothing but a knife? Those were one of the few shows I loved to watch so I knew that finding water was of uber importance, as was creating shelter, and if I was going to be here more than one or two days, making a fire could be the difference in saving my life. While whoever it was had left me here with a bottle of water, a fire would give me the light and heat that I would most likely need to see me through the night. I also knew that a fire helped psychologically, lifting the spirit so you wouldn't give into despair.

I went through all the ways I knew of starting a fire without matches or a lighter. I could use the sun if I had a magnifying piece of glass of some kind, which of course, I didn't. Trust me to be in the one wood where nobody littered. But when I glanced back at the sinking sun, I realized that even if I had a magnifying glass, the sun wouldn't last long enough for me to get something started. I knew I could use batteries and aluminum foil or a cell phone and steel wool. While I was thinking along those lines, the right chemicals could also work, but I had none of those either. In the end, I realized my only possible option would be friction-based fire starting, in other words, rubbing some sticks or stones together which — going by what I remembered from those shows — was also the hardest way to do it, which was just great. I needed another challenge.

Feeling sorry for myself, I dug around the ground looking for a couple of sticks that might work.

If you're wondering how I knew all of this, I've that enormous photographic memory, remember? After searching for a while, I finally found two sticks that seemed like they would do the job. I was intending to use a technique called a Friction Drill where you have one stick standing vertically in the other stick, which would lay horizontally and have a groove cut inside. I was going to use my shoelaces to wrap around the vertical stick, which I would use as a spindle. As the spindle rotates under the correct speed and friction, it should cause embers to appear. Feeling hopeful, I started rotating the spindle, but within seconds, the thing kept sliding out of place or the shoelaces would slip off. I reset it time and time again, but I couldn't even get it to stay in place long enough to get any friction going.

It was hopeless.

Rage surged through me as I flung my hard-found sticks away. Inky blackness inched towards me as the sun began to set. I fixed my eyes on that sun, memorizing that glowing image, hoping that that would be enough to get me through the night. As it finally dipped out of sight, I found myself in a well of terrifying darkness. I fumbled for the torch, fingers sliding blindly around it until I was finally able to flip the switch on, but the beam that appeared was weak and only lit the area immediately before me.

By now, I was shivering from the cold, but that wasn't why I was scared. Now that the sun had gone, it seemed the forest was *alive*. All around me I could hear rustling as creatures trod over leaves. Invisible things stirred in the branches overhead, causing the hair to stay permanently raised on the back of my neck. I was terrified that at any moment a scorpion or snake might drop down on me. Briefly, the thought that scorpions provided a decent amount of calories entered my head before I almost retched. I'd die first.

I emptied out the bag and folded it before setting it down on the ground. Sitting on it, with my back against the tree trunk, I wrapped my arms around my legs and rested my chin on top of my knees. Only my butt touched the ground, so I hoped the rest of me would stay warm.

As I fought to fight the panic creeping along the edge of my mind, my thoughts drifted back to Bandit as a desperate gnawing ache appeared in my stomach.

Where was he?

Were they hurting him?

58

BANDIT

C old.

Why was it so cold?

Bandit opened his eyes to find he was in a place he had never been before. There were vertical lines in front of his eyes that he didn't understand, and the air smelled dusty. And old. Like this place, wherever it was, had not been cleaned in a century or more. His tongue felt thick with dryness and he smacked his lips together, looking for a water bowl. He shook his head, trying to clear away the fog that clung there.

He sniffed the air anxiously, desperate to locate Chase's smell, but there was just that dust. It was so thick that he could not find his friend. Forcing himself onto his trembling paws, he tried to make out where he was. As he examined his surroundings more, he came to a terrible conclusion. The vertical lines in front of his eyes were bars.

He was trapped in a cage.

Bandit began to pant heavily as memories surfaced of his time spent before in places like this, and with them came the fear. How had this happened? How was he back in a cage?

He backed away from the bars but took only a few steps before his rear hit the back of his prison. This was a small cage, smaller than any he had been in before, back where he was from.

Unable to control himself, he whined, a sound of pure fear as he turned around and pushed at the bars with his forehead.

"Now, now, none of that," came an annoyed voice.

Bandit looked up to see a man in front of him. He was not interesting to look at and he smelled like the liquids Sully liked to clean the bathroom with. It wasn't a nice smell and irritated his nose. Bandit pawed at it, disgusted when he suddenly realized that he had seen this man before, at Gideon's workplace — and he hadn't liked him much then. He had tried to warn Chase that something about him was *wrong*, when she and Gideon had been on the fire escape helping him move into the apartment above the garage, but as they had been out in public, he didn't have his iPad on him at the time. And as the two had left the man soon after, Bandit had forgotten to tell them. Bandit whined now, feeling bad. Maybe if he had remembered to warn them, he and Chase would still be together now.

Wanting to speak, Bandit went for his iPad before he remembered it wasn't in the pouch he wore around his neck: it was in Chase's bag. He barked, deeply unhappy by this turn of events.

The man watched him in fascination. "My name is Xavier. You are probably wondering what you are doing here, yes? I am a scientist, a world-class scientist if you must know, and you are the key to my greatest experiment."

Bandit had heard this kind of talk before. Where he was from, people often spoke of him like he was a thing to be used, so this did not frighten him. No, what frightened him was the manic gleam in the strange man's eyes. Bandit barked at him, frustrated that the man could not understand him. *Maybe if he could speak to him, the man would let him out?* However, Xavier shrugged, unconcerned.

"I'm sorry, I do not understand what you are saying."

Bandit's eyes scanned the room until they found his iPad lying on a table in the far side. It wasn't in Chase's bag after all! He barked again, pawing in the direction of his iPad. Xavier saw the motion with interest and smiled.

"You want your iPad? You want to communicate with me?"

Bandit barked once for yes, but Xavier shook his head. "Despite how intelligent you are, I don't care what you have to say. I am only interested in what lies inside your head. I believe you knew my old partner, Sebastien Forbes?

Hearing his name caused frightening memories to assault him. Bandit saw Forbes command the white-coats to do terrible things to his friends, things that had them foaming at the mouth and wetting themselves. Sometimes, after a Forbes visit, his friends wouldn't be able to stand for several days and had to crawl around on their tummies.

Bad man. Bad man. Bad man.

Bandit shook, unable to stop the chill that raced through his body at the mere mention of the man who had tortured him for most of his life.

"I see that you do. Don't worry, he and I are very different people. Sebastien was obsessed with healing his own illness and cared nothing of the world, unlike me. What I do will change humanity forever. What I do, I do for all of mankind. So you see, Alpha, I'm not like him at all."

A sound came from the next room and with it, the smell of burgers and the sweet drink Chase liked called Coke. A young man came into the room. He was thin and there was a nervous air about him. Bandit could see he was younger than Xavier, and he seemed excited. He bounded over to the cage and stared at Bandit.

"He's awake! He doesn't look that smart, does he?" he said to Xavier.

"And how is a smart dog supposed to look, Dick?" Xavier said, barely able to contain his patience. Dick shrugged.

"I don't know, I just thought he would look more special." He wandered towards Xavier and stopped at the bench where the iPad sat. "Pretty clever of them to teach him how to speak using an iPad." He stared at the tablet as if it were a mythical creature that would come alive at any moment.

Frowning, Xavier crossed the distance to him, snatched a heavy metal bar from the bench, then violently smashed it onto the iPad. One, two, three times! The glass screen cracked and smoke rose from the destroyed tablet. Dick jumped back, startled... and a little afraid.

"Why did you do that? I was looking forward to using it with him!"

Xavier fixed cold eyes on him. "The last thing I need is for you to be communicating with this dog. I don't want him filling your little head with any of his big ideas."

Bandit had watched the two in silence, but now he barked louder and louder, until Dick covered his ears, cringing. "Why is he doing that! Stop it!"

Xavier studied Bandit shrewdly. "He is probably concerned for the girl, Chase?"

"Woof!"

"The girl is fine. We dumped her in a forest, but she'll be OK so long as she figures out how to get out of there. We weren't going to harm her. She was collateral damage, and we needed her out of the way."

Hearing this, Bandit felt some of the panic lessen. She was safe! Chase was fine. Or at least, she would be. Squashing himself into a corner of his prison, Bandit sat and tried not to let the fear overwhelm him.

Chase would come for him.

He knew she would.

59

SULLY

Hands gripped on the wheel, Sully watched the needle flirt dangerously towards eighty. It was against the law to drive any faster, but Sully wondered if that still applied when one of its own representatives were in the car.

Gideon had fallen into an exhausted sleep on the backseat. When they had first left, Gideon had insisted upon driving. Wired with all that had happened, he'd had no other outlet, so Sully had stepped aside. He'd let the younger guy drive for several hours until they stopped for a restroom break. It was Sam's idea to switch drivers then, as she had seen the younger boy's eyelids drooping from weariness, now that his initial adrenaline had faded.

The three of them didn't know what they were more concerned about. Having to leave Zeb while he was in intensive care at a hospital almost caused Gideon to break. The kid considered the old man his own father, and in the six months that they had lived together as a family, Sully thought of him as a younger brother though Sully wasn't quite as ready to adopt him like he had Chase and Bandit. Although Bandit was only a year or two old, his brain and intellect were on par with those of a teenager. Sully was only in his thirties and didn't feel old enough to be a father of three grown kids. He felt a sudden sob rise in his throat and had to force himself not to give in to it. His own panic would not help the situation. He looked over at Sam, sitting stoically in the passenger seat, and shot a prayer of thanks that her calming presence was here for this.

Her eyes were fixed on the screen on her phone, which was tapped into the tracking website. The entire time we had driven, Sam called out instructions although as they had gotten quite far ahead of us, the directions mostly consisted along the lines of "stay on this road for another four hours."

It was impossible to believe that, even with all her contacts, there was no legal way for us to catch up to them any faster. Every option we brainstormed led to alerting the authorities, which was just too dangerous. I even toyed with the idea of stealing a helicopter like Chase had, but Sam had put an end to that fast enough. Licensed helicopters needed to file flight plans and get clearance, all of which took time that we didn't have. Sam warned us that if we tried to fly without them, we'd be caught soon enough. Chase had gotten lucky that the one aircraft she hijacked had been a stealth machine that didn't play by the rules. Unfortunately, we couldn't rely on the same good fortune.

Sam looked up from her phone and I could feel her eyes fix on me.

"You want me to take over?" she asked softly.

I shook my head. I needed the physicality of driving. Going through the motions grounded me and made me feel like I was doing something to save them.

She accepted my response but kept staring at me, something clearly on her mind. "Since we're stuck here anyway, I suppose we should talk about us?" she began.

Before she could say anything else, I stopped her with a hand. "I don't want to be a jerk, but I can't do this right now. There's only so much I can take, so can we drop this for another day when my family aren't in danger?" I probably sounded more bitter than I wanted to, but to hell with it. My heart was already broken. She didn't need to stampede all over it too.

She nodded and fell silent.

I continued to drive.

60

CHASE

I was up by the crack of dawn.

Even with all my preparations, I had barely slept at all. I hadn't felt that icy, deep-in-my-bones-cold since when I had first left home. It was just after winter then and I had survived by sleeping huddled in archways and doorways, burning fires in trash cans to keep warm. But last night there was no fire or shelter from the cold, and the sounds of the forest woke me every time I had almost drifted off to sleep. I was exhausted and felt like the dead, but I knew I had to push on.

I reached up and felt my lips with my fingertips. They were dry and peeling, which seemed astonishing considering it hadn't been that long since I had last had a drink. Despite my best intentions, I had finished that bottle of water a few hours ago. I still had an energy bar left, but the stuff was cloying and made me even more thirsty than I already was. A picture of a cool, refreshing glass of water invaded my mind. I could almost feel the liquid moving down my throat. My mouth even made the motion of swallowing before a sob escaped.

I shook myself. Get a grip, Chase. Bandit needs you, so stop crying over no water.

I got up and stretched my weary body before I started moving once again using the sun as my navigation tool. At some point, if I just went far enough, it should lead me somewhere different. That's what always happened on those shows, anyway.

I walked, barely feeling the branches now as they scratched against me. In the back of my mind, it was yelling at me that my body could be going into shock, but as there wasn't much I could do about it, I pushed the warning aside.

It wasn't important, only Bandit was.

I conjured up an image of him in my mind and held it there as I continued forward.

61

———

BANDIT

Bandit woke to feel cold steel beneath his paws.

He had barely slept all night and had only finally managed it when he collapsed out of pure exhaustion. The man, Xavier, had gone, but Bandit could still smell him. He knew he was never too far away. There was another room close by that he liked to stay in. Bandit didn't know what he did in there, but he heard Xavier talking to himself sometimes. Bandit didn't like him. He frightened him almost as much as the bad man had.

The other boy, the younger one who smelled of burgers, was closer. Bandit could hear him now approaching softly. His footsteps were quiet and considered... Bandit knew from experience that people only walked that way when they were being sneaky. Chase did this sometimes when they played hide and seek. He could always hear her breathing or her footsteps, but he never told her. It amused him not to. Thinking about her now, a whine escaped his lips.

He missed her so much!

He was thinking this, wondering if she were safe when Dick came in. He was holding a blanket as he approached the cage.

"I thought you might like this to sleep on. That cell must be cold."

Bandit barked once, softly. He didn't want the other man to think that he wasn't grateful for his kindness, he wanted him to know.

"Now I'm going to open the door, but please don't attack me or try to escape. Xavier has this place rigged with cameras and you wouldn't get far."

Reaching the cell, he pressed a button on a remote that he found on the workbench, then as the door unlatched, in one quick movement he tossed the blanket inside before slamming the door shut again. Bandit grabbed at the blanket and spread it out as best he could. He stood on it, feeling relief from the cold metal on the pads of his paws. He circled the blanket before sitting down. For this one little moment, Bandit felt a little less terrified than he had been since he had first woken up in this prison.

But that all changed with the sound of hard shoes pounding the hallway outside, followed by a strange clinking sound.

Whimpering, Bandit moved to the back of his cell as Xavier stormed into the room carrying a giant syringe and some heavy looking chains. Seeing Dick, however, Xavier stopped dead.

"What is that? A blanket? The animal will probably soil it and then there will be germs. What were you thinking! He could catch something from the filthy thing. Get it out of his cell!"

Dick shot Bandit an apologetic look as he opened the cage door and pulled the blanket out, dislodging Bandit — who still stood on it — in the process. Bandit made a sound of pure desperation as Dick whispered *"Sorry."*

Xavier pulled on a pair of rubber gloves as he picked up that wickedly long syringe with a giant needle attached and approached the cell.

"Now Dog, this will hurt far less if you don't struggle."

Bandit looked up at the roof of his prison and howled.

62

CHASE

I had been walking now forever, it seemed.

My head thumped with a headache caused by both tiredness and lack of water. The world spun around me at times, which I knew was another symptom of dehydration. It didn't matter how fast or slow I went; the forest was ever looming and there was nothing on the horizon but those trees and branches. I started to wonder how long a person could survive without water, food or sleep. I was pretty sure the figure was a couple of days so I had a good twenty-hours or so left inside me. Whatever happened, I knew that I would find Bandit or I would die trying. My buddy needed me.

I know that my need to save him — which overrode my concern for my own well-being — might seem impressive, but if I were being honest, I was also driven by overwhelming guilt. The fact that this happened at all was my fault.

If I hadn't been stupid enough to trust her, Bandit and I would be together, in our room right now playing our Jeopardy game and eating junk food.

Last night, while I had been trying to sleep but couldn't, my brain had kept going back to all the things that had happened, until it became clear as glass that this was my mom's doing. Somehow she had planned this and had separated us on purpose.

But why? For what reason?

Tears pricked at the corners of my eyes, which caused a disbelieving laugh to escape. How could there be enough liquid inside of me to cry when my mouth felt like there was a desert inside of it? It made no sense at all. As my vision misted over with tears, I heard a sound coming from ahead of me. And for once it wasn't a bird or a squirrel or those possible snakes. I stopped dead and listened to something that bubbled and moved. I blinked, dazed but suddenly hopeful.

Was that the sound of running water?

I picked up my pace and started running towards it. As I got closer, the sound of water became louder until I broke through a bank of trees to find a small river in front of me.

I sobbed with relief, yet still felt half terrified that this was a mirage. Falling down into it, the water seeped in through my clothes, soaking me as I laughed in delight. It was real! The water was so clear I could see the stones lying on the riverbed. Cupping my hands, I scooped up water and drank blissfully. It was the best thing I'd ever tasted in my whole life. Impatient with the small amount I was able to scoop up, I shoved my whole face into the river and gulped it down like a fish.

When I had drank at least a gallon and my tummy felt swollen, I stood back up. Now that I had quenched my thirst, I felt so much better. The headache that had been plaguing me the last few hours vanished almost instantly and energy surged through me. Staring at the river as the fog started lifting from my mind, I realized something else: I could just follow the river now instead of wandering aimlessly in the forest.

Rejuvenated, I started downstream.

I'm coming, Bandit. I'm coming.

63

SULLY

We didn't stop all night.

When I got tired Sam took over and when she was too tired to continue, she swapped with Gideon. We drove that way until the blinking lights of Pittsburgh were behind us. Sam hadn't tried to talk about our relationship again. The rational part of me knew I had been harsh by cutting her off as I had done, but I was barely holding on. I could not think about our broken relationship on top of everything else.

Gideon had barely spoken since he had been up. It was like he didn't know what to do without the other two around him. As soon as he woke, he called the hospital to check up on dad, but there had been no change — he was still out for the count. At least his vitals were stable. The doctor had every hope of a recovery. We still didn't know what had caused his accident, but I was pretty sure that someone had attacked him and frightened Pixie off. That little dog would not have run otherwise. I was terrified to think that it might have scared her away.

"You think Pixie is okay?" Gideon asked, his voice cutting the silence like a knife. I glanced at him in the rearview mirror.

"I'm sure she's fine. She's managed to get away before, I'm sure she didn't go far. When we get back, we'll probably find her waiting for us on the porch." I didn't really believe this, but I wanted the boy to stop hurting. There was enough pain in our hearts without him worrying about the dog, too.

Sam shot a look at me from the corner of her eye. She saw straight through me but didn't say anything. She knew, as well as I, the unlikelihood of my words. Rummaging through her bag, she pulled out two bottles of water.

"Here, drink, the two of you." She handed the bottles to us. I declined, despite how thirsty I was. "You're tired and stressed. If you don't drink, you'll pass out and that won't help any of us, it certainly won't help Chase or Bandit any."

It was difficult to argue with her logic.

Like a pair of schoolboys that had just been chastised by their teacher, Gideon and I took the water she offered. I opened the bottle, gulping it down greedily, then felt immediately guilty.

What if Chase and Bandit were thirsty? They'd been gone almost twenty-four hours now. What if they were hungry?

Putting the cap back onto the bottle, I sat the bottle in the drinks holder, deciding that I wouldn't eat or drink another thing until I had them both back in my sights, no matter how ridiculous that sounded.

Sam would just have to deal with that.

64
____

CHASE

The river twisted and turned as it made its way downstream.
I followed the water, taking care not to slip on the moss-covered rocks and stones that littered my path. Buoyed from escaping the woods and re-energized by my drink, I moved quickly and it wasn't long until I saw the gray line that signaled a road was ahead of me.

Relief washed over me so fiercely, I broke into sobs again. I had done it. I had hit civilization.

Not until that very moment had I really believed that I was going to get out of this alive. But now that I could see the road, I knew I was safe. Using the last of my energy, I ran for the road and reached it within minutes. Turning back, I marveled at the distance I had crossed — sports had never been my thing and I had never run that fast before in my life. But like the woman who finds herself suddenly able to lift a burning car to save her baby, it was amazing what you could do when the ones you loved were in danger. Looking at the empty road, I knew I just had to wait for a car to pass.

I was planning on flagging it down. Ordinarily, I wouldn't recommend hitch-hiking. The world was filled with weirdos and it was my motto never to be trapped in a confined space with one, but it wasn't like I had a choice. I had to get to a phone to call Sully and warn them. By now they must have realized that the two of us were missing, but only I knew we weren't together.

As my feet pounded the road, I looked at the sky, still pink from its recent sunrise. Besides my footsteps, the only occasional sound came from a bird flying overhead. This wasn't a main road, and it seemed I was in the middle of nowhere. With a sinking heart, I realized that it might be some time before a vehicle turned up, and even then there was no guarantee that they would stop. Steeling myself for more walking, I squared my shoulders, trying to ignore my screaming feet.

I hadn't been going long when I suddenly heard the welcome sound of an approaching vehicle. I spun around to find a lone car turning the corner. It was pretty old looking. As it approached, I saw that there were many scratches to the paint job and several dents that it had accrued over its lifetime. An old man sat behind the wheel, a woman — his wife, I guessed — beside him. They must have both been in their seventies as to my eyes, they looked older than Zeb. I started jumping up and down, waving my arms. The car came to a stop a few feet in front of me.

I bolted to the driver's door.

He wound down the window, looking startled to see me. "What is a young girl like you doing out here at this time of the morning by yourself?" he exclaimed.

"I need your help. Do you have a phone I can use?" I looked at him and his wife pleadingly. The woman, whose face was made up immaculately with tightly wound curls piled neatly on top of her head, nodded.

"Why yes, of course," she said, elbowing her husband. "Harold, what are you waiting for, give the girl your phone!"

Harold reached into his pocket and took out a Samsung phone that he handed to me. It was the sort of basic phone that Gideon would have mocked. No frills or internet access, I took it gratefully and was punching in Sully's number before they could change their minds. After a few seconds, it started to ring and Sully's wary voice came on the line. "Hello?"

"Sully! It's me!" I cried, almost bursting into tears right there.

"Chase?" He sounded so relieved that my eyes started to tear up. "Where are you?"

I looked at Harold. "Where are we?"

He blinked, confused by my question, but answered it anyway. "You're right outside Dresden, Ohio."

I repeated the location to Sully. I heard him repeat that to someone, probably Sam. "What happened, Chase? What are you doing there?" he asked, concern making his voice harder than normal.

I stared at the old couple, watching me wide-eyed. "I can't talk about it right now, but she lied Sully. My mom lied. I'm not exactly sure what happened, I must have blacked out because I woke up in the middle of the woods on my own."

"You're not together?" Sully asked, incredulous. I heard him curse then, several words I'd never heard him say before.

"You need to find Bandit, I think she took him," I said this softly, hoping Harold and his wife wouldn't hear.

"We're on our way to him. We have his tracker, so we're trying to get to him now. Wait, whose phone is this?" Sully demanded suddenly. He must have seen the number on his phone and not recognized it.

"I flagged down a car. It belongs to this old couple who were driving."

"Let me speak to the driver," Sully said. I didn't even question his command, just did as he requested. I handed the phone to the old man. He took it without question.

"Hello?" he said to Sully. I couldn't hear what Sully was saying, but the old man's expression changed from questioning to surprise. "Why yes, it's MAJ-124. My full name is Harold Benjamin Bartlet and my wife and I live in Wilmington, Delaware, around two hours south west of here." The whole time he was speaking, his wife watched him with varying degrees of perplexity on her face. Eventually, she just snatched the phone from him and started yelling into it.

"Who are you that you would leave your daughter in such a state? How dare you ask us all these questions when we have nothing but concern for her? Why, she's not any older than my grandchild! The nerve!"

Hearing her outrage must have put Sully's mind at rest. I guess he rationalized that they weren't anything other than they seemed. It wasn't likely that they were in on some evil plan with my mom. Gently, Harold took the phone back from his wife. Sully said something to Harold that got the old man nodding in agreement.

"Yes, I can take her to Red's place. It's an eatery a few miles from here. She'll be safe with us until you can come and pick her up." He listened as Sully said something else to him. "Why yes," Harold answered sounding surprised. "That's the address, that's the one. How did you know?"

Whatever Sully said next caused Harold's eyebrows to raise. His face turned stern, as did his manner. "Young man, I know you are concerned about your daughter but there is no need to make threats at me. We will take her to Red's diner and wait for you there. I'm giving your daughter the phone back now, I assume you won't be making threats at her too?"

I took it from him. "What's happening?" I asked.

"We're going to come and get you and then we can all go after Bandit," Sully said.

"No. You've got to get to him now! You don't know what they might be doing to him!" I had to fight the urge to scream the words at him.

"Well, I'm not leaving you with two strangers in the middle of nowhere," said Sully, his voice brokering no room for argument. I was surprised, having never heard Sully use that tone with me before.

"I'll be fine. I just found my way out of a forest, didn't I?" I replied, somewhat testily. I didn't want to be a brat, but I could handle myself. Bandit, however... I couldn't bear it if anything happened to him.

Sully didn't respond straight away. I heard Sam and Gideon speak heatedly with him but couldn't make out what they were saying. When he came back on the line, he sounded resigned.

"New plan. Gideon is coming to get you while Sam and I go after Bandit. When Gideon arrives, the two of you will meet us at whatever location we find Bandit. I'll send you the details, but Chase, you have to promise not to go anywhere. Do not go off with anyone, understand? And when you get to this pit stop, you call me from a landline there. Sam will run a trace so we can see exactly where you are. I don't think Harold or his wife are lying, but let's be cautious all the same."

"Okay," I said. "I'll call you soon as we get there. You just make sure you find him, Sully."

"I will," Sully said. I expected him to hang up then, but he didn't. "Be careful. I can't have anything else happen, okay?" He sounded so wary, so broken, that I picked up on it immediately.

"What else has happened?" I asked, scared at what he might say next. There was a moment's pause.

"Don't worry about it now. Let's just get you back to us." He tried to sound reassuring, but I could hear the strain in his voice.

"Sully, is everyone OK?"

"We're fine. You just make sure you're safe, you got that?"

"I promise," I said and hung up.

65

SULLY

I handed the phone to Sam to find her watching me with a funny look on her face.

"What?" I asked.

"I'm impressed with the way you handled that. You sounded... well, you sounded like her dad."

I felt myself get a little embarrassed. "Yeah, well, I'm nowhere near old enough." She didn't respond, but kept on looking at me with that funny expression.

Now that we knew what we had to do, we had a new problem — we were missing one car. Seeing that we were nearing a gas station, I pulled in. "We need to acquire an extra vehicle," I said.

Gideon nodded, and as soon as I stopped the car, he jumped out. Sam frowned, staring at the cars. A young family sat waiting for their dad in one, but the other two were empty, their drivers inside the gas store.

"How is he going to get us a car? It seems unlikely that anyone would be willing to sell one to us, even if we had the cash. They'd be stranded here if they did and there doesn't look like there's going to be a taxi firm for miles?"

I avoided her gaze, feeling suddenly uncomfortable. "I don't think that's what he has planned." She frowned at me, unhappy with my response, then spun around in her seat to see what he was up to. I cringed inwardly, guessing what her next reaction was going to be.

"Oh my God, is Gideon breaking into that car?"

Before I could reply, she jumped out of the car and marched over to him. Feeling helpless at what was coming next, I quickly followed her.

"What do you think you are doing?" she hissed at Gideon over his shoulder. He froze, a lock pick already jabbed into the car lock. Apparently, he always kept some with him for just such an occasion.

"It's okay, I've done this before," the hapless boy responded. Her eyes flashed dangerously, but he didn't see it. Focused as he was on the car, he also didn't see me shaking my head behind her.

"When?" she demanded, hands on her hips. "When have you done this before?"

Gideon gestured behind her at me before I could stop him. "When we were escaping Platinum Industries. We didn't have a vehicle, so I stole one. Sully said it was fine."

Sam's eyes hardened as she spun around to glare at me. "Oh he did, did he?"

I felt it might be time I spoke up for myself. "Well, I did that one time on account of the fact that I had just been shot and Bandit was almost dead. We sort of had more pressing things to contend with. And the truck we took was a rust bucket. No one would miss it. The owner probably made more out of the insurance than he would have done the actual car." The more I spoke, the bigger the grave I was digging for myself. I forced my mouth shut, knowing that Sam would have a lot more to say to me about this later.

"Gideon, please remove that lock pick and step away from the car. I will acquire one for us myself, except I will do it legally." With that, she stormed into the gas station. I heard her make some sort of announcement, then she waved her sheriff's badge in front of a guy's stunned face. Moments later she came out with a set of keys and pointed at the car Gideon had been trying to steal.

"Not everything has to be a crime," she said somewhat testily.

"We don't all have a badge we can wave around," I replied, "so I wouldn't get too high and mighty over this."

She gave me a withering look that had me wishing I had kept my mouth shut.

66

CHASE

I got into the car with the elderly couple.

They let me hang onto the phone, which I found comforting. If anything happened, I just had to hit redial and Sully would know.

We drove for another five minutes or so before the eatery appeared. Despite how early in the day it was, cars packed the parking lot. The diner was made to look like it was made in the 50s or 60s and was quaint and charming.

"Margaret and I eat here all the time," Harold offered. "They do great pancakes."

At the word pancakes, my stomach suddenly growled. Hearing it, Margaret laughed. "I guess we'd better get some food into you, when was the last time you ate?"

"I had a couple of energy bars through the night" I responded. "Before that..." I trailed off as my thoughts returned to those muffins and Mom. I couldn't believe that it had only been 24 hours since I was in her car with Bandit. So much had happened, it felt like weeks had already passed. An image of Bandit doing his version of a smile as he stared out of the window on the back seat flashed up in my mind. Seeing his face, I felt a stabbing pain in my heart and my arms ached to feel his furry body in them. Harold saw my expression and mistook my need for hunger.

"Let's get you warm and fed while we wait for your dad," he said.

Inside, country music played on the radio, though it wasn't loud enough that I could make out the song. The place was heaving with customers, most of whom I noticed were around the same age as my hosts. Apparently, this place was a major hit with the oldies. The smell of coffee and freshly baked waffles hit my nostrils, causing saliva to flood my mouth. Although I wanted nothing more than to sink my teeth into doughy, sugary layers of goodness, there was something I had promised to do first. My eyes swept the area until they found a phone along the bar area — but it wasn't a payphone. Margaret saw my consternation and spoke. "I'm sure they'll let you use their phone. Go ahead and ask nicely."

I nodded and approached the man who stood behind the counter managing orders. He looked up at me when I neared, even as he barked out an order to the cook behind him in a steamy kitchen. "Haven't seen you before, young lady?"

I climbed up onto a stool. "No. I'm from out-of-town. Um... I need to use your phone. Margaret said it would probably be OK to ask?"

He scanned through several receipts, mind already elsewhere. "Sure. Go ahead. Just no international calls, please. Some of you kids seem to think it's funny when I get my phone bill."

He turned away from me, setting down the receipts onto a spike that was already a third full, and focused on refilling the coffee machine. Picking up the phone, I dialed Sully again. He answered straight away. "That you, Chase?"

"Yeah. I'm here," I replied.

"She's there. You want to run the trace, or are you happy with just the number? It's come up on my phone?" His voice was further away, as he spoke with Sam. "Hang on, Chase. We're just checking to see where you are."

It went quiet as Sam did whatever she needed to do. Moments later, Sully came back on the line. "Got it. We know where you are. You think you'll be OK to wait with these people?"

I looked across the room at Harold and Margaret. He had pulled out a chair for her and was now tucking her under the table and laying a napkin across her lap. It was clear that he loved her very much and that he took very good care of her. "I'm safe here, Sully, don't worry. Harold and his wife seem like nice people."

I heard him let out a long breath. "Excellent," he said. "Gideon is getting ready now to come and get you."

"Okay. Did Zeb and Pixie stay at home, I haven't heard them in the car with you," I asked.

There was a long, long silence. When Sully spoke again, his voice was strained. "Zeb is in the hospital. He had an accident. He's unconscious."

"What?" I cried out, shocked. "What happened?"

"We don't know. I found him unconscious and Pixie was gone. Zeb had a spy cam in his hand... I think someone rigged up the ranch and has been spying on us for a while." He fell silent as the full force of his words came to me.

"But that means they know about Bandit," I said, unable to keep the fear at bay.

"Yeah," was all he could say.

I swayed on my feet, reeling. Who were these people? I felt totally unsafe suddenly and stared at the sea of faces surrounding me, realizing that any one of them could be behind Zeb's attack and the cameras in our home.

"Chase, we have your location now. So I am going to get off the phone and send Gideon to you. Anything happens, or even if you just want to talk, you call me okay? I'm right at the end of the phone."

"I will," I replied. "Just bring him back to us so we can go home."

"I'm working on it, Chase. I'm working on it."

67

CHASE

I made my way back to the couple.

On my approach, Harold gestured at a chair opposite him. I sat down as Margaret handed me a menu.

"Thanks," I said. Although I was relieved that Sully was on his way to Bandit, I couldn't shake the numbing fear that had flooded me since the moment Sully had told me about the cameras in our home. I felt so hopeless here, being so far away from him.

"Since your dad won't be here for a few hours yet, you should order whatever you'd like. You must be starving if you spent the night in the forest by yourself."

"I am, but I don't really have any money on me," I replied hesitantly. I wasn't fishing, but I didn't want them to think I could pay for a meal either. These people had already been so nice to me, the last thing I was going to do was eat and run.

Margaret gave her husband a look as her eyes softened. "Well, of course, we're paying child, what kind of people would we be if we didn't help you after your horrific ordeal?"

I looked at them gratefully and saw the kindness in their eyes. I gave them a smile, my first in forever it seemed.

"Oh, Harold, look. Isn't she pretty when she isn't scowling?" Margaret said, eyes twinkling. My smile grew a little wider at her comment.

A waitress came and poured coffee in our cups. She obviously recognized them both by the welcome she gave them, but didn't know them well enough to address them by name. I filed this away in my head, adding it to the pile of evidence I was accruing that the Bartlet's were good, honest folk.

I grabbed my cup and started gulping the scalding liquid down. It burned my mouth, but I didn't mind, desperately craving its heat in my stomach. I glanced down at the menu, which had all the usual items you'd expect in a place like this.

"Can I have the stack of pancakes with bacon and eggs? And some toast, too. And orange juice?" I said this to the waitress but my eyes were on my breakfast mates as it would be they who would be paying for the meal. Harold nodded as if he were happy with my choice.

"Margaret and I will just have some scrambled eggs, I think. We don't usually eat much in the morning, but we'll keep you company."

The waitress nodded and went off quickly. She was nice enough, but seemed rushed off her feet. Looking around the place, I could only spot two waitresses, which seemed silly given how busy they were. *Must be short-staffed.* I gulped down the rest of my coffee quickly when I suddenly noticed how filthy my hands were. I didn't want to think about how the rest of me must have looked. Embarrassed, I stood up. "I should probably go wash up."

Margaret pointed to the restroom. "Last door on your right past the counter." I nodded my thanks and followed her directions.

The restroom was like the rest of the place, quaint and clean. Catching sight of my reflection, I was shocked to see how crazed I looked. It wasn't just the streaks of dirt over my forehead either which added to that illusion, but I found not one, but two leaves in my hair, not to mention I looked as if I were back to my dumpster diving days. Taken as a whole, I was amazed Harold and Margaret hadn't thought I was a feral beast. Pretty sure I wouldn't have let myself into my car if I had one. I pumped a handful of soap from the dispenser and started scrubbing. It took a while, but after several rounds of washing and rinsing, I almost resembled myself again. Realizing this was about the best I could do without an actual shower, I went back to join the others.

The food had arrived and now covered the table. The smell of buttery pancakes wafted into my nose as the sight of the crispy bacon caused my stomach to clench in anticipation. I sat down quickly and grabbed a piece of bacon, meaning to shove it in my mouth when I suddenly remembered what had happened the last time I had eaten. I hesitated, lowering the hand holding the piece of meat.

"I know this is going to sound strange, but, could you eat a mouthful of all the food on my plate first?" Harold's eyebrows raised in question while Margaret just looked confused. "Please," I continued. "I can't eat until you've had some first."

They looked at me funny before giving each other a perplexed look, however, they each grabbed a fork and took a nibble of everything.

Relieved that the food wasn't drugged, I crammed the piece of bacon into my mouth, forgetting all about utensils. Although Harold and Margaret seemed a little taken aback by my lack of etiquette, neither of them said anything. I chewed fast, inhaling everything in sight while they picked at their eggs with a fork. In no time at all, my plate was empty. Harold must have sensed I could still eat as he signaled the waitress. "Tess, can we have the same again? Thank you."

With horror, I heard myself making a strangled sob and had to physically choke it down. I would not break down in here, not in this nice place with these nice people. I would not repay their kindness by embarrassing them like that. Harold looked away respectfully while Margaret's own eyes crinkled over with sympathy as she stretched out her hand and patted me on the arm.

They sat silently across from me, sipping out of their cups of coffee while I demolished the second round of food. Finally, I leaned back against my seat, hands across my swollen stomach. I had expected to feel satiated, but instead, I just felt sick. Turns out sleeplessness and exhaustion coupled with worry and food don't mix.

"Can you tell us what happened to you?" Margaret asked, concern etched over her face. "Do we need to call the police?"

I shook my head warily. "Trust me, there's nothing they can do. I just need to regroup with my dad and we'll be able to sort this out. But thank you," I said, finally remembering my manners. I took a gulp of OJ and waited for the waitress, who came back and cleared the table. After she filled up our drinks once again, she disappeared off.

"If you don't want us to call them, you're going to have to explain why that is," Harold said kindly but firmly. "I don't want to intrude, but these are not normal circumstances and I need to know that we are doing the right thing by you."

I looked at them, knowing that I owed some sort of explanation, even if it couldn't be the real story.

"My mom and dad have been fighting for years. They've never gotten along, but dad had finally decided to get a divorce, only my mom wasn't happy about it as dad pays for everything. So, anyway, one thing led to another and when she found out that I didn't want to live with her she went crazy. She got drunk and must have drugged my food because when I woke up, I was in that forest. Our court day is today, so I think she had this crazy idea inside her head that if I couldn't make it there to stand against her that she would win somehow. I don't know. It's messy."

Normally I can lie without blinking, but I felt bad about doing it to

them. Still, it wasn't like I could tell them what was really going on.
Margaret squeezed my hand.

"That's a terrible thing your mother did, I'm so sorry dear." Harold
nodded in agreement, but he looked more stern about it. "Are you sure we
shouldn't tell the police? I would have thought this would help your father's
court case?"

I shook my head. "No. Despite what it looks like, we have it under
control now."

"And what about Bandit?" Harold asked. "I heard you mention his
name a few times."

I looked him square in the face and hoped that he was buying my story.
"He's my dad's dog. She knows he loves him — he's had him for years — so
she took him out of spite."

Margaret shook her head, making clucking noises even as her eyes
turned hard. "Some people just shouldn't be allowed to have children or
pets."

She would get no disagreement from me.

68

SULLY

The tracker had finally stopped moving a few hours ago and was fixed at a location just outside of Cleveland, Ohio.

Google maps showed that it was a disused school. I suppose as evil headquarters went; it was a pretty clever choice. No one would be poking around, and they — whoever our enemy was — would be free to do whatever it was they were doing.

The building flashed up before us as I slowed the car to a crawl, coming to a stop by a dense bank of trees. I didn't want whoever was inside to be notified of our arrival. I was getting a sense of déjà vu except the last time I had hidden a vehicle behind trees; it was a crop-duster, and Gideon and I had just arrived by Platinum Industries. This deserted place was a far cry from that high-tech behemoth, however.

The school was old and sprawling and made up of several one-story buildings. At some point, this must have been a fun learning establishment going by the faded painted calculations and symbols that I could still make out beneath a blanket of ivy. A good number of the buildings were boarded up, but that still left five or six possible buildings where Bandit could be housed, which seemed a lot of ground for the two of us to cover.

"We need to get to him quickly since they've already had him for some time. God knows what they're doing to him. We should split up."

Sam gave me a look that showed she clearly disagreed with my suggestion. "Nope. We stay together." Her voice had no room for argument, but I tried anyway.

"Come on, Sam, I know how to take care of myself." I knew she wasn't worried about herself, so her insistence on staying together must be out of her concerns for me, and my ego didn't like this one bit.

"Yeah, well, last time you thought that you were shot so..." She left it hanging, but I filled in the dots.

"I wish Chase hadn't told you that," I grumbled under my breath. "Not everything needs to be shared."

Although the place wasn't being used (other than by these bad guys), it was still owned by the government or some such entity as they had done a decent job of keeping the school free of vandals, although they didn't go as far as to fork out for wired security alarms — I could find none of the usual blue and white signage that signaled an ADT presence. It looked like the buildings had basic water and power supplies, however, as I couldn't see a generator anywhere, unless one was tucked away around the back.

Huddled together, we approached the first building. A giant rusty chain wrapped around the handles on the front door. Even if we could get the door open, we would never get through that chain. I looked over the brick-work until I came to a window, almost hidden behind a curtain of ivy. "We get in through there."

Sam nodded and pulled her gun from its holster. As I parted the ivy, Sam held her gun by the handle and smashed it against the glass. The window cracked, then broke into a thousand pieces, raining glass around us. I cringed at the sound, impossibly loud in the near silence.

"I hope they didn't hear that."

Sam shrugged. "If they did it's too late, and if they didn't, we have the upper hand."

"I like how you think, even if it is strange logic that got you there," I replied.

Sam shot a smile at me, eyes flashing with life. It was at that moment that I realized how she thrived on this kind of excitement. Seeing how bright her eyes were and how red her flushed cheeks were, I realized just how much I loved this woman. When we got through whatever this was, I was determined to win her back.

Climbing through the window, we found ourselves in a dark corridor. Light slanted in at angles that illuminated patches of ground ahead of us, but left the rest of the corridor shrouded in darkness. Dust covered every inch of surface, giving the place a musty, unpleasant scent that had me scratching my nose. Unperturbed by any of this, however, Sam put her analytical eyes to work.

"The dust hasn't been disturbed, I don't think anyone's been in this wing for a while," Sam said.

"Yeah," I agreed. "Let's see where it takes us though, hopefully, it connects to one of the other buildings. It'll be a lot quieter than trying to smash through another window."

I turned on the flashlight on my phone, using it to highlight the way ahead. Sam went to walk before me, but I pushed her behind. "Single file. Me first, you after. Got it?"

She looked at me, unimpressed with my bravado. "Really? We're doing this now?"

I nodded, not messing around. Whatever she thought of my capabilities, I was going to do my damnedest to protect her. I expected her to put up more resistance, but her eyes suddenly softened.

"Okay, tough guy. Lead the way."

We walked down the corridor, eyes and ears peeled for any movement or sound, but other than a mouse scrabbling past when it saw us, all was silent. We walked until we reached a set of double doors. Grabbing the handle, I turned and pushed, but there was something on the other side of the door, wedging it closed. "Give me a hand with this," I said.

Sam came up behind me, put her shoulder to the door and waited for my count.

"Ready?" I asked. She nodded. "Three, two, one... push!"

Together we shoved the door hard and got it open about a foot before we stopped, unable to move it any further. I could see the corner of what looked like a steel cabinet lying horizontally behind the door. Either it had fallen down of its own accord or someone had put it there to dissuade visitors. I was pretty sure I knew what the answer might be.

We squeezed through the gap and found ourselves in a gymnasium. Empty bleachers loomed eerily, the ghost of past crowds haunting the place. Although the room can't have been used in years, I could almost hear the sound of a whistle blowing followed by a stampeding team as it raced up and down the court. It'd had been over a decade since I'd last stepped foot in a place like this, and truth was, I hadn't missed it, never having been a fan of school, remembering how stressful it was when I realized early on that I wouldn't become the surgeon my parents had expected of me. This had eventually led to our estrangement. So much time wasted because the two of us were too stubborn to pick up the phone. Thinking of my dad now, lying in the hospital bed alone, I felt the guilt torment me, even as my head knew that he would want me to save Chase and Bandit first.

Hold on, dad. Be the usual stubborn goat you are, and just hang on...

We moved through the sports hall towards another set of double doors at the opposite end when I heard a sound. I stopped as hope flared up in me. The sound was small but distinctive, and one I recognized immediately.

It was the sound of paws.

"Bandit?" I asked softly.

Sam stared at me quizzically. "You heard him?"

"I think so," I said.

Re-energized, I sprinted towards the double doors and pushed them open to find myself in another endless corridor. This one wasn't as dark as the last, however, so I could see very clearly the dog standing in front of me.

It wasn't Bandit, but it was a dog I recognized.

Pixie.

69

SULLY

Shock and disappointment tore through me.

I couldn't believe my eyes. "Pixie?" She tilted her head at me and listened as if she was trying to understand what I was asking of her.

"You think whoever took Bandit and hurt Zeb, kidnapped Pixie?" Sam asked.

"It seems likely though I've no idea what they would want with her?"

Sam looked thoughtful as she studied the dog. "Maybe they were just told to grab a dog and didn't know what Bandit looks like?" Sam offered. "Until we found her, we only had the one dog."

"They had a camera in the ranch though? Shouldn't they have seen her through that?"

"I don't think we ever had Pixie in the living room. She stayed mostly in the den or with Gideon. And you know she didn't like Bandit, so if he was around, she usually wasn't."

"But why is she roaming around on her own?" I wondered aloud.

"Maybe she snuck out from wherever they had her contained. She's done it before, after all," Sam replied logically.

Her explanation made sense. I crouched down until I was eye-level with the dog. "Pixie, do you remember me? I got you that nice food and toys. Gideon would be really excited to know that you're okay." The little dog didn't react until I mentioned Gideon. At his name, her ears pricked up.

"That's right. Gideon's your friend." Pixie did a little dance with her paws that let me know she had understood at least some of what I had said. "You know who else is your friend? Bandit. Can you take us to him, Pixie?

Can you take us to Bandit?" She tilted her head the other way. For a moment, I thought she didn't understand, but then she barked three times and started moving away. She stopped a few feet away, then turned back to look at me.

"She's going to take us to him!" I said excitedly.

"Good girl Pixie, good girl!" said Sam.

We took off after the little dog. She led us through twisting corridors and empty classrooms, never hesitating in her direction. She barely even sniffed at her surroundings, so I knew there was no doubt that she knew where she was going. I could feel the edge of my panic lessen, knowing that any minute we would be reunited with Bandit. I hoped to God he wouldn't be in the same condition as the last time I had found him when he was lying across the operating table with his head cut open. The Doc wasn't with us this time and I wasn't sure I would be able to save him without her help.

We must have been going for some ten or so minutes when Pixie turned to look at us, barked three more times and then started racing forward.

"This must be it!" I sprinted after her as she ran through a doorway, Sam following close behind. We were still running when I found myself skidding to a halt. There was a barrel of a shotgun in front of me and it was pointed right at my head.

A man in a white lab coat with long hair and a younger guy, who looked just a year or two older than Gideon, stood ahead of us. They both had shotguns that were trained on us. In that brief first moment of seeing him, the man in the lab coat reminded me of those scientists we had seen at Platinum Industries, except this man didn't bustle about like those did. He was calm and considered, clearly in control. Despite our circumstances, he had a mild-mannered air about him. He seemed perfectly ordinary, like someone you would never give a second glance at. It was either a cunning disguise or something that he'd need to spend a lifetime discussing with a shrink.

I looked past them to see a cell — and trapped inside was Bandit. Seeing me, he jumped to his feet and barked excitedly.

The scientist looked down at Pixie. "Well done, Dog. You brought them right to me."

Shocked by her betrayal, I could only stare as the scared and sweet little dog I had come to know suddenly changed demeanor completely. Her eyes turned cold as she bared her teeth at me, snarling viciously. She looked wild and ferocious and utterly terrifying.

I could have kicked myself. We should have listened to Bandit when he had warned us she was strange. Looking at her and the man, the truth came to me. "You're a spy. You were working for him the whole time," I said to the dog.

"You're not as dumb as you look," the scientist said to me.

"Oh I don't know, I'm feeling pretty stupid right now," I replied.

I stared around our surroundings, hoping to find something to help us out of our predicament. There were a row of windows set high into the wall but they were tiny, put there just to let more light in. An odd assortment of scientific apparatus covered the benches — I had no idea what they were used for. The young guy who I guessed must be his assistant, came at us with cable ties that he tied around our wrists.

"Not so tight unless you're deliberately trying to stop the blood flow," Sam said through clenched teeth. Immediately the boy looked apologetic.

"Sorry, I've never done this before."

"You don't say," Sam said, peeved at being caught.

After he had restrained us, he started backing away when the scientist stopped him. "Aren't you forgetting something, Dick?" He stared pointedly at the gun still in its holster around Sam's shoulder.

"Right," Dick said as he relieved Sam of her weapon. "Do you want me to put them in the utility room?"

The Scientist shot him a withering look. "I don't want them in the same room as the dog, so what do you think?" It wasn't really a question if his scathing tone was anything to go by. Dick flushed, embarrassed, then gestured with the gun at us. "Follow me, please."

I gave Bandit one last look as we were lead away from him, into another area that contained several small metal tanks — around the size of a dog I realized — that were connected up to a complicated system of liquids and gases. The tanks had long been empty, however, and I couldn't see any signs of what they might have once contained. My mind flicked back to Pixie suddenly, who had stayed in the room with the Scientist. For her to be as deceptive as she was, required abnormally high intellect... of Bandit proportions, essentially. But that wasn't all she would need. Despite Bandit's cleverness, like all dogs, he was a straight shooter. The kind of deviousness Pixie displayed was alien to their kind.

I had been silent a while now, and Dick finally noticed. Worried that I might be up to something, he stopped suddenly and looked at me. "Whatever you're thinking, it won't work. Xavier would have already thought of it before you."

"Xavier? That's his name?" I asked. Dick nodded, not the least bit concerned that we now knew his boss's identity.

"I was thinking about Pixie. How she behaves isn't normal for a dog," I began.

"That's because she isn't a normal dog," Dick replied. "She was created, right here."

"Created?"

Dick hesitated, possibly wondering if he should let me in on the big secret, but then he shrugged. "Well, I guess it doesn't matter if I tell you now since neither of you will be getting out of here. Pixie was genetically grown, cloned from the DNA of a regular dog but then adapted into the creature you know now. Xavier created her out of nothing but a few minuscule cells. When she became fully grown, and Forbes was making headway with his Alzheimer's research, Xavier copied the placement of the tumor that is inside Bandit and put it into Pixie. It's why she's as clever as he is."

Sam and I looked at each other, reeling by what we were being told. "But that's not all he did, is it? He did something else to make her so devious?"

A grudging respect grew over his face. "Yes. During Forbes' research with the tumors, they found that if they placed the tumors on different parts of the brain, there were differing results. For example, placed in one area, the tumor made the dog very aggressive, in another, the dog became very controllable."

I pictured Pixie changing her personality like Jekyll and Hyde, and the horrific answer came flooding to me at once. "He put multiple tumors inside her brain, didn't he? That's why Pixie is the way she is?"

Dick nodded. "Yes. Her head's riddled with the things. We think that the many tumors might also be tampering with her personality, causing her mood to swing, but that suits his purpose so they have been left as they are."

Sam had been watching the two of us closely while we spoke. I knew she was looking for the right moment to stage an attack, but before she could do anything, we arrived at a metal door. The old metal sign on it had lost a screw and now hung precariously on one end. The writing was faded, but I could make out the words "Utility Room". Dick opened the door and moved us inside ahead of him.

Barring a few boxes of old files with past school kid's names that someone had forgotten to deal with. It was empty.

"But Bandit was suffering from convulsions with just the one tumor, Pixie must have physical side effects?" I asked, unable to stop feeling concern for the dog, particularly now that I knew her behavior was through no fault of her own.

"Oh, she's dying for sure. Probably doesn't have more than a few weeks left, but she's already served her purpose so it isn't a great loss to Xavier, especially now that he has Alpha back."

Sam suddenly spoke up, her voice filled with concern. "Has him back... he had him before?"

"Oh, sorry, I thought I'd already explained that. Alpha was created here too via the same cloning process. He was actually Xavier's greatest success until Forbes took him away when he was barely a pup. Xavier's thrilled to have him home."

The boy's eyes turned bright thinking of the scientist's happiness, and I realized at that moment, just how much Xavier controlled this kid.

"Xavier is a lunatic. I've met his partner and Forbes was no better. Do you have any idea how brainwashed you are?"

Dick's eyes glittered angrily. "Don't you dare talk about him like that! Xavier is a God amongst men. You have no idea how important his work is!"

"So important that he kidnaps little girls and conducts unethical experiments on the powerless? Don't be so stupid." I didn't bother to hide my disgust. He needed to hear the truth, no matter how much it hurt.

"Stupid?" Dick said. "You're the one who thought his wife was messaging him from the grave. If anyone's stupid, it's you!" He stopped, waiting for my reaction, convinced that he had won over me. And he was right. I felt like I'd been punched in the gut.

"That was you?" I asked, my voice barely above a whisper.

"Xavier wanted you preoccupied, so I came up with the idea to mess with you. I knew you were going back to visit your wife's grave — hell, the whole town knew — so I dug it up a bit, and left that hair clip for you to find. Then I messaged you using an app that makes it seem like the message came from a particular phone line. You were so hung up over your wife that you lost your mind over it completely. So who's the stupid one now, huh?" Dick gloated. He turned to Sam next, determined to stick the knife in. "If I were you, I certainly wouldn't be marrying this guy, not when he's still so in love with his wife."

I couldn't breathe, knowing what this idiot child had done to me. It was all I could do not to kill him: my hands might be bound, but I could still wrap them around his scrawny neck. I counted to three in my head, desperate for the rage to quieten. I had to keep reminding myself that this boy was under the thumb, that he didn't know any better. I couldn't take it out on him, no matter how badly I wanted to. Through the haze of red, I saw Sam looking at me, her face filled with sorrow, regretful now that she knew I hadn't made up the message.

Dick marched us to the corner of the room, then backed away. He kept looking at me, hoping that I would say something he could use against me, but I was numb. Disappointed, he left. Moments later the door closed in front of us and I heard it lock.

We were trapped.

Silence enveloped us. Trying desperately to regain a small sense of myself, I turned to Sam. "Told you we should have split up."

She shot me a withering look.

70

BANDIT

Sully was here! Oh boy oh boy oh boy!

Bandit knew he would come. He knew they wouldn't leave him here like this. But seeing them, Bandit was also worried now. Dick had taken Sully and Sam away with a gun pointing right at them, which Bandit knew were terrible things. He was there when Chase had used one on the bad man. After the loud sound when Bandit thought his ears had exploded, the bad man had died and Chase had cried. They could not die — not only did he and Chase love them, Sully was also their pack leader.

Fueled by the knowledge that they needed his help, Bandit ignored his own fears and threw himself at the cell door. He slammed against the metal, using the full force of his body. The doors rattled — they did not seem to be that well made — but the door remained firmly closed. Ignoring the pain that shot through his body, Bandit moved to the back of the cell to get a running start and *HURLED* himself at the door again.

The cold metal hit him like a wall but stayed locked. He landed hard on his feet. Whimpering, Bandit held up an injured paw and licked it when a sound from across the room caught his attention. He turned to find Pixie staring at him. Her eyes glittered as she flattened her ears onto the back of her head. Prancing up to the cell, Pixie nudged the door with her nose.

Bandit barked, yes! She was helping him!

Though they had never liked each other before, Bandit was thrilled that Pixie was now his friend. Excited, he chuffed in encouragement and lowered down onto his stomach. He barked instructions at her, letting her know that the way to open the cell was on the bench. He described the object as best he could as Pixie went over to investigate. She jumped up onto her two front paws so she could see onto the counter.

Daintily, she picked up the metal bar Xavier had used to destroy Bandit's iPad. Bandit barked twice. No *that isn't right*. She dropped it down with a clang, then nosed around the bench with Bandit barking more. The closer she got in their version of "hot and cold". Finally, she picked up the remote Bandit had seen the others use to open his cell. He bounced up and down on his paws, ignoring the pain that shot up his right front leg.

Yes! That was it!

Pixie moved her nose over the button but stopped short of pressing it.

Bandit barked at her to do it, but she deliberately set the remote back on the bench and made a noise that sounded like laughing.

Bandit froze, shocked to the core. She was taunting him! She had no intention of helping him at all!

Hurt and confusion flooded through him. What was wrong with her? Why was she such a bad dog? He never got the answer to his question, however, as Xavier came into the room. Seeing Bandit limping in his cage, he frowned, displeased.

"What have you done to yourself, Dog? Have you been trying to get out? I hope not. I can't have you hurting yourself — I need my specimen undamaged."

Seeing Pixie across the room, Xavier shot her a look. "You best not have been upsetting him, or it's back into the tank for you."

At his words, Pixie cowered and shook, backing away from him. She seemed genuinely scared, causing Bandit to feel even more confused. *Why did she help him if she was scared of him?* Nothing about her actions made any sense.

Xavier scanned the room until his eyes settled on those heavy chains he had brought in with him before. Grabbing them now, he came towards Bandit with them.

Moments later, Bandit found himself with one heavy chain around his neck and four around each of his paws, each of which were now secured to the ground. Bandit could only stand, sit, or lay down, but other than that he could not move. Whimpering, he hung his head in misery.

Xavier nodded, satisfied with his work. "There. You can't move, therefore you cannot hurt yourself."

Dick came into the room carrying the drink called coffee that Bandit knew Sully liked, but he stopped when he saw him. Seeing that he looked uncomfortable with what he had done, Xavier took the coffee from him and took a sip before speaking. "He's fine, besides it's the only way to make sure he won't hurt himself. It looks far worse than it is. I did the same to Pixie for years while I was training her and look how well she turned out."

Bandit suddenly realized that these were the very chains that had caused the scars on Pixie's body. Even in his despair, he felt sympathy for her. No dog should ever be chained up like this, no matter how bad they were.

Xavier drank more of the coffee as he studied scans and charts as Dick watched Bandit from across the room guiltily. Having seemingly forgotten his threat of only moments ago, Pixie now wove herself between Xavier's legs, desperate for affection, but the older man grew tired of this very quickly and kicked her out of his way.

Hurt, Pixie slunk off into a dark corner as she watched Bandit with those angry black eyes.

71

SULLY

Well, on the plus side, Bandit was safe. In a big cage, essentially, but safe.

Sam and I were stuck in our own prison, with those cable ties that were clasped pretty tight around our wrists. Thankfully Dick had left our hands bound in front of us so it wasn't as uncomfortable as it could have been. Still, we were in quite the predicament and I wasn't sure how we were going to get out of this.

I had been trying to wrap my head around what we'd been told. Not the Emma thing — that I had bolted down and filed away for another time. I knew if I focused on what Dick had done, the anger and resentment would bubble over and consume me. I could not afford for that to happen, so I willed myself to move past it. I would deal with that when I had the luxury to.

And so it was that I now found the vet in me taking over. What Xavier had done to Pixie defied all natural laws and was madness at best. In spite of Dick's grand talk, Xavier wasn't any better than his old partner had been. As far as I was concerned, they were both as deluded as each other, though Xavier was worse in my book. At least Forbes had been suffering from a disease which would have soon debilitated him. From what I could see, Xavier was wrecking lives and torturing animals for his own ego... he had to be taken down.

There was a pipe in the room Sam had been staring at for close to a minute now. I tried to think how it could possibly help our situation, but failed completely. After Dick had left, she had sat quietly beside me. I figured she must be pissed at being caught out like this, what with being a sheriff and all.

"Don't be so hard on yourself, you didn't know this would happen," I said, I thought, helpfully. She looked at me, an exasperated expression on her face.

"You think I'm concerned about our situation here?" she said.

"Well, sure. We're tied up and locked in a room. They took your gun and everything else we had of use. I don't see how anything short of a miracle will get us out of this."

She moved on to her knees and stood up gracefully, one brow arched in challenge.

"A miracle, huh? How's this for a miracle?"

With that she raised her clasped hands high over her head, then she swung down fast and forcefully... With a snap, the cable ties broke loose and clattered to the ground. And just like that, Sam's hands were freed. I gaped at her, astonished.

"How the hell did you do that?"

Sam shot me a triumphant grin. "Gravity and physics, my friend. When you swing your hands down with so much force and pull them apart on the downswing, the cable ties can't take the force and snap. This is survival 101 training. Haven't you seen the Youtube videos?"

"Like you ever watched Youtube until Chase got you doing that." A thought occurred to me next, causing me to frown at her. "So the whole time he was tying us up, you knew you could get out of it. No wonder you didn't seem afraid."

She gestured at me. "You try. Just get them as high above your head as possible and swing down fast and furiously while trying to pull your hands apart."

I tried to get up onto my feet, but I wasn't half as graceful as she was when she had done it. I staggered to my feet clumsily was probably a better description of what I did. Once I was up, however, I did as she instructed and goddamn if it didn't work.

I was amazed.

"It's lucky he didn't tie our hands behind our backs. Then we would have been in trouble," she said.

"We're not out of the woods yet," I replied. "We still need to find a way out of this room."

"Well, let's get searching."

72

CHASE

After we'd eaten, we sat there at the table drinking coffee and chatting.

Once I had given them my creative explanation of events, Harold and Margaret hadn't bothered me with any more questions about my life. Instead, they seemed happy to just talk about theirs.

They were childhood sweethearts, I learned, having met at high school. They were married young and had five kids by the time they were in their 30s. Sadly, one of the kids had died at a young age. Some horrible illness, they had said. They explained that their son, Stephen had been sick his whole life forcing them to spend their entire fortune on his medical bills, as they desperately tried to find something that would help him. A cure never materialized, however, and eventually they lost that nice big home they had saved their entire lives for.

After Stephen had died, they downsized and moved to Wilmington, where it was cheaper — though far less safe — to raise their other kids. They were heartbroken and had never really recovered from it. It wasn't the physical bricks and mortar aspect of losing their house that they missed, but the memories they had shared with him there. They could never be replaced and this being before the time of phones with video cameras, they only had pictures of him. I remembered how Sully had been when I had met him. He had been clinging on to his wife's memory by hoarding her things. I can't imagine how it must have felt for Harold and Margaret to have let go of the only home they had known with their son.

Seeing as I had started to feel down by their story, they quickly explained that though their funds had diminished greatly, they considered themselves blessed to have seen their remaining kids grow into happy and healthy people who went on to have kids of their own. Margaret had been so proud when she took out her purse and showed me several photos of their whole family that she kept in her purse.

I was amazed not just by the sheer number — there must have been at least forty of them — but by how close they all were. Here they were at Thanksgiving, then Christmas, then at one of their grandkid's birthday parties. The family even threw summer get-togethers at a campsite where folk flew in from all across the country. These were highly organized affairs that included scheduled events like a performance show and sports. They even made itineraries for them. *I mean, who were these people?*

I'd never met my dad or anyone from his side of the family. My mom didn't get on well with her family either, so I had only really met one aunt a few times. She lived in Arizona and had a lot of pets, was all Mom would tell me. She didn't mention her often, but whenever she did, she had this look on her face. I knew what it was straight away, even if she could never admit it — she was jealous of her sister. From what I knew of her, she had a happy life and a loving husband. Apparently that was all my mom needed to know to be envious of her enough to cut her out of our lives.

I had looked down at Margaret's family, at the army of people that she called family, and wondered what it must be like to be surrounded by people who loved you.

Suddenly I realized what I was thinking and felt immediately awful. Sully loved me and Bandit too. Even Gideon... probably. And of course, Sam and Zeb. I felt bad for my moment of ungratefulness. You know how they say if you are never grateful for what you have, you will never have enough? I saw it on an Oprah rerun once, and it had stayed with me ever since. I mentally reminded myself that my life was very different now, and that I should be grateful every day for that.

We'd been in that diner for hours now. I had told them I didn't need a babysitter, but they refused to leave until my family got here. Harold said they had been coming back from visiting their daughter who only lived a couple of hours drive away near Cleveland, so they were in no hurry to get home. Her oldest was just heading off to college and they had gone to give him money towards his tuition. They had just sold Margaret's car — which was much nicer and newer than Harold's — to pay towards his school costs. As they had told me this, I regretted all the food I had put away. I took in their appearance, finally able to see how their clothes were patched several times over. Here I was eating like crazy when money was a concern for them.

Although the time passed as pleasantly as it could under the conditions, my mind kept drifting to Bandit. Until he was safe, I couldn't relax. I found myself drumming my fingers on the table in agitation.

When both the breakfast and lunch shift had gone to be replaced by the evening staff, the door finally opened as Gideon came rushing in. I shot to my feet, so ridiculously happy to see him. I leaped up from the table and threw myself at him before I even realized what I was doing. His arms went to encircle me and he squeezed me right back. We were holding each other for a few seconds before I suddenly got all embarrassed. Gideon and I hung out all the time, but we didn't really touch, so this was kind of a big deal. We stepped away from each other; me blushing furiously while he looked suddenly awkward.

"And this must be your brother then, as it obviously isn't your father," came Harold's voice. It sounded like he was trying hard not to laugh.

"No, I am her... brother," Gideon said unconvincingly. "Our dad couldn't get here because of..." He stopped suddenly, looking at me for help, not knowing what cover story I had given them. I rushed in to fill in the gaps.

"Court. Dad's in court. That's why he couldn't make it, but my brother is here now so that's great and we should get going."

I turned to Harold and Margaret then, suddenly feeling desperately sad that I would never see them again. They really were decent people in the world I was learning this every day. I threw my arms around the two of them, much to their shock, but they hugged me right back. "Thank you so much," I whispered to the two of them. Margaret had tears in her eyes as she patted me on the shoulder and smiled.

"You get on back to your family, dear. I'm sure your dad, or whoever he is, is looking forward to having you back." She had a twinkle in her eye. It was the first time I realized that neither of them had been buying my story, yet still they had sat with me and paid for all that food, even though they knew I was lying the whole time.

My mind was literally blown.

I turned to Gideon. "Do you have any money? I ate a ton of food so we need to pay them back."

Harold and Margaret shook their heads, aghast. "Oh no, dear, we don't need your money. You keep it. It was a pleasure to help you."

"But," I argued, "what about your grandson? You just said you sold your car to pay for his schooling."

"We'll be fine Sweetheart, we always have been, and we will again. The Lord has a way of providing. Bless you for offering though, child. Tell your dad he raised you well."

I smiled at them, feeling myself tear up. If only they knew.

"We better go," Gideon said.

I nodded. "Thank you again, for everything. Bye."

I followed Gideon out the door when I suddenly turned back around. "Wait, what's your surname again?" I asked.

Harold looked surprised and curious, but he answered. "Bartlet. Why?"

I shook my head. "No reason, I just wanted to know who I owed this kindness to."

And with a last smile that I flashed at them, Gideon and I left the diner.

73

CHASE

The car Gideon had brought with him was in better condition than the Bartlet's. It had leather seats and AC, something I usually adored but barely appreciated right now. I wanted to know everything that had happened since I had left that morning.

Gideon explained what they knew, but it wasn't until he came to Zeb that I started asking questions. I was stunned by what had happened to him, but most of all I felt guilt, guilt that I wasn't there in his time of need. Since I had arrived at his ranch, Zeb had been there for me the whole time. From Forbes' death, Zeb had never complained about Bandit and I suddenly living in his home, not once. Instead, he had become the grandfather I'd never had so the fact he was in a hospital unconscious with none of us by his side, that killed me. I tried to be strong, however, because despite how awful I was feeling, it couldn't compare with Gideon's pain. His initial relief at seeing me had faded somewhat. Now I could see just how stressed and tense he really was.

I borrowed his phone and called the hospital to check on Zeb's progress, but nothing had changed. It took some convincing to get them to give me any updates since they said family only and I had no proof that I was until I described Sully and Gideon to them.

After I finished with the hospital, I tried calling Sully, but his phone went straight to voicemail. I felt a moment of panic as this wasn't usual. What if the bad guys had gotten to them? I was about to say just as much to Gideon when I realized that it was more likely that Sully had turned his phone off so it wouldn't ring if the bad guys were searching for them. You always saw this in the movies when people were trying to be stealthy, but suddenly their phone would start ringing at just the worst time possible. I knew Sully and Sam were smarter than that, however. At the first sign of danger, they would have switched it off. Still, I wanted to get a message to them to let them know I was safe, so I sent Sully a text message that simply said, "left the diner."

I figured, worst-case scenario if someone had gotten hold of their phone that message wouldn't mean very much to them and it would not warn them that we were on our way.

Having done as much as I could with the phone, I studied Gideon's profile. His jaw was clenched tightly, and I was getting really concerned that he would literally bust a gut or something. "You want me to drive?" I offered. He looked at me skeptically.

"I didn't drive 5 hours to save you only to die now, so no thank you."

"If we crashed it wouldn't be my driving but your teaching that would have done it," I retorted. It felt good to bicker. It felt normal, like we weren't driving towards our impending doom. But the conversation died down as quickly as it started. It was too much effort to joke around, especially when we were both so concerned for our family.

Turning to the window, I stared at the scenery blurring past, praying silently in my mind that we would get there in time.

74

CHASE

We pulled up at the rundown school a few hours later.

I saw Sully's car parked by some trees and we pulled up alongside. There was no sign of either him or Sam, not that I really expected one. I stared out at the sprawling buildings, suddenly overwhelmed by the scope of our search. *How were we going to find them? How were we going to get to them before the bad guys?* Gideon must have thought the same as me as he stopped dead in his tracks, his eyes surveying the scene around us.

"Where do we start?" he asked me. I was about to hazard a guess when something glinted in front of me. I zeroed in on some pieces of glass on the ground and continued up until I found the window that had recently housed them. I pointed. "There. That's where Sully and Sam got into the building. That glass looks freshly broken. And look how clean the frame is: they knocked all the glass out of it so it wouldn't cut them when they climbed inside."

Gideon studied the window and nodded, agreeing with my assessment. "Before we go," he leaned into the trunk of the car and retrieved a flashlight and a wrench.

I stared at the items in his hands, unimpressed. "What, no gun?"

"Sam already has one, plus she figured this would be enough."

"But she isn't with us," I pointed out.

He looked at me exasperated and rolled his eyes in that way that always half irritated and half amused me. "Thanks, Captain Obvious."

"You didn't tell her you're a crack-shot? Doesn't she know what you did before when Forbes' men attacked us?" I asked, unable to get my head around it all. Gideon was the best shot out of all of us. It seemed stupid not to arm him to the gills.

"Sam feels very strongly against us using weapons of any kind. I think she still considers us kids."

"One day, we need to sit her down and tell her every little detail, even if it means getting Sully in trouble," I replied glumly.

We headed over to the window and climbed inside, careful not to cut ourselves on the remaining bits of glass that the others had missed in the frame. Gideon switched on the flashlight as the beam spotlighted the way ahead. He swung the flashlight around, searching for any signs of them when the light picked up some footprints on the ground. "One big set and one smaller one," I said studying the imprints in the dust.

With their trail set easily in front of us, we followed their footsteps down the corridor and into a sports hall. Here the dust wasn't as bad as in the corridors, so the footprints trailed off, but Gideon spotted doors at the end of the room. One was slightly ajar, as if someone had gone through but hadn't closed the door completely behind them. "They must have gone through those doors," he said. I nodded and the two of us moved quickly through until we found ourselves in another corridor. Here the torch picked up another set of prints, but these were smaller and distinctively doglike. My eyes flared open in hope.

"Bandit's paw prints?" I asked.

Gideon lowered into a crouch to study them. He frowned, uncertain. "I'm not sure, I can't really tell, but it seems likely."

I moved beside him to examine the prints myself when we heard a sound from down the hall.

Panting.

I was so familiar with that sound, I knew instantly that it was caused by a dog breathing through it's open mouth. I looked at Gideon, meaning to tell him when Pixie rounded the corner.

I blinked, my shock mirroring Gideon's own.

"Pixie? What on Earth?" Gideon asked. Seeing him, Pixie froze for a few moments before her tail started to wag vigorously back and forth. She ran up to Gideon and jumped up against him as she squirmed and barked with delight at seeing her long-lost friend. Gideon was thrilled to see her safe and bent down to pet her. But I didn't move, thoughts racing through my mind.

Something was very wrong with this picture.

She was the last to have seen Zeb before he was injured, but she had disappeared only to reappear here now. At the location where Bandit had been taken to. Now, I'm not a girl who believes in coincidences at the best of times, so I figured the bad guys must have brought her here. But why wasn't she locked up somewhere, like I assumed Bandit was?

Gideon must have sensed my hesitation as he stopped to look at me, but before he could voice anything, I shook my head at him. I bent down and gestured at Pixie. "Hey girl, do you know where Bandit is?" I asked her.

She cocked her head and considered my question. Then she spun on her heels and did several loops in a circle with excitement. She barked three times, darted away, then came back again, paws dancing across the ground with impatience.

"She wants us to follow her! She's going to take us to him!" Gideon said, pride and excitement in his voice. "Lead the way, girl," he said and started after her.

I didn't move, thinking about the things that had been happening lately, and a niggling doubt went through my mind. Bandit — wonderful, loving Bandit — could not get along with this dog and I hadn't listened to his reasons why, but I'd always trusted my Muttface before, and even though this might be too late in the day, I decided to trust him once again. Instead of following Pixie, I lunged forward and picked her up in my arms.

Immediately her head snapped around as she snarled and barked viciously at me. The change in her was absolute and terrifying. It was all I could do not to let go of her. I moved my head away from those snapping jaws.

"Chase, what are you doing?" Gideon asked. But even as he asked, his expression went from bewildered to concerned as he saw how violently Pixie was reacting. Quickly, he clamped his hand around her mouth, squeezing her jaws together so she couldn't hurt me. "I've never seen her like this, it's like she's turned feral."

I looked at him, shaken, straining to hold her still. "Or maybe this is who she really is," I said quietly. "Bandit kept trying to tell us about her but we wouldn't listen. And the thing with Zeb, you know Pixie was probably the last person or animal that saw him before he went unconscious, right? What if she had something to do with it? What if she's working for the bad guys? It would explain why she's running around this place on her own."

Gideon frowned, trying to take it all in. "But how is that possible? She's just a dog, what would be the purpose of leaving her with us?"

I shrugged. "I don't know, but everything started to happen around the time she turned up. All I know is, Bandit didn't trust her and he must have a reason for that, and now we find her here where it's all happening. Yeah, we can't trust her."

As I said this Pixie bucked wildly in my arms, trying frantically to get away. It was getting harder and harder to restrain her. My muscles spasmed, having to fight against the dog. "We need to put her somewhere, I can't keep holding on to her." Gideon looked around, then nodded towards a room at the end of the hall.

"In there," he said. Together, we moved towards the room as fast as we could, while we held tight to Pixie who still hadn't stopped thrashing in my arms. I had no idea how she had any energy left.

Gideon kicked open a door and we went through into a small restroom and placed pixie into a cubicle as Gideon quickly shut the door behind her. Then he took out a coin and flipped the lock closed from the outside. Trapped, Pixie went *insane*. Growling and snarling, she started flinging herself at the door.

Smack! Her whole body connected with the door with a loud crash. I had no idea how she didn't break all the bones in her body, but Pixie fell down to the ground then launched herself at the door again. She was making such a horrendous noise that even though it seemed obvious, she was working for the other side, I was still concerned about her hurting herself, but we had no choice. There was nothing we could do for her so we left her there and hoped that the others — the bad guys — were too far away to hear the racket she was causing.

We moved away until her barking was a faint sound in the distance. "Give me your phone," I said to Gideon. He handed it to me without question. Although I didn't expect him to answer, I called Sully's phone again, but this time the phone was on. My heart flared up with hope. After a few rings, it was answered by a man's voice that I did not recognize. And with that, my hope was quashed.

"Where's Sully?" I demanded of the unknown answerer.

The man's voice came down the line, weedy yet triumphant. "Would that be Chase by any chance? I'm impressed, I never thought you would find your way out of the woods so quickly." His words made me think about my mother as another jolt of fear raced through my body.

"That was you? Is my mom with you?"

He laughed, although it was without any mirth. "She's probably drinking away the money I gave her. You really have been very unlucky with your parents. Absolute trash, the two of them."

Although I had suspected that she was in on whatever this plot was. To hear it straight from his mouth hurt like hell. I didn't reply immediately, not wanting him to hear my pain.

"I take it you are here to save the dog, Sullivan and Sam? Well, I will make it easy for you, if you come to me now I will spare their lives."

I don't know what possessed me to do what I did next, but I didn't think about it — I just reacted. I ended the call and switched off the phone.

Gideon looked at me aghast.

"Why did you do that? What have you done?"

XAVIER

The dead dial tone sounded in his ear.

Xavier stared at the cell phone in his hand, shocked. "I think she hung up on me," he said to Dick. His assistant's face became concerned. "Well, that seems a stupid thing to do, doesn't she want to see her family alive?"

"I guess not," Xavier replied. "Bring them to me. Now that the girl is here, I'm not happy knowing that our two captives are in the other room. Bring them here so we are all in the same place. And do it quickly before the girl gets here."

Dick nodded and rushed to do his bidding.

In his cage the dog suddenly shot up, having heard the conversation. Although he couldn't speak, Xavier had no problem understanding the hope that now shone from his eyes.

"Yes, your friend Chase is here, but she is walking into a trap and there is nothing you can do to save her."

Furious at him, the dog howled in desperation even as the chains kept him immovable.

SULLY

We'd been searching the room for anything that would aid our escape, but other than those ring binders which contained some very boring reports, the room yielded no treasures. It looked like the only way out was the way we had come in. As luck would have it, though the buildings were worn around the edges, this door was solid and nothing was breaking through that lock short of a bullet. Unfortunately, as Sam's gun had been taken along with the rest of our personal items, I couldn't see a way out of this room. There would be no miracle a second time around. I was about to admit as much when I heard footsteps approaching.

"Quick," I whispered. "Get on the other side of the door, someone's coming!" Without a word, Sam darted to the other side while I waited with my back pressed against the wall, trying to make myself as inconspicuous as possible. Seconds later, a key slid into the lock and the handle turned until the door was cautiously opened, but when the person — I couldn't tell yet whether it was the assistant or the scientist — saw that the room was seemingly empty, he threw open the door and marched inside, pointing a shotgun ahead of him.

Immediately, I jumped on him, wrapping my arms around him, dragging him into the room. The assistant — I recognized it as him now — struggled against me until Sam pressed some fingers into the back of his neck. Presumably, he didn't know that she didn't have another weapon on her. He froze as Sam took the weapon off of him and patted him down, searching for anything we could use, but on his entire person, he seemed to only have the keys to this room, some cable ties, and his phone.

"Tie him up over there," Sam said as she pointed to a thick column holding up the ceiling when the hapless assistant spoke. "You're too late, you know. Even if you leave now, you won't be able to save her."

I stopped dead. "What are you talking about?"

"The girl, Chase? She's here. And my boss is going to get rid of her."

The blood started rushing through my head and I took great pleasure in punching him in the face. The boy's head snapped back as the shock of the blow sent him reeling. As I waited for him to regain his faculties, his future use of the sentence sank into the furious fog in my brain. "She's too smart for him."

He swung his head around to refocus on me. Blood dripped from a cut on his lip, but his fevered eyes showed no pain, such was the force of Xavier's hold on him. "I doubt it," he said. "Xavier's the smartest man I've ever met."

I thought quickly, trying to come up with a plan. "If that's the case then I guess you're coming with us."

Sam shot me a startled look, obviously wondering if I'd lost my mind.

"If he does have Chase, then we're going to need a bargaining chip."

"Right," she replied. "I guess we don't have a choice."

"Nope," I said pushing Dick ahead of me as we followed him.

I wasn't ashamed to admit that I felt some vindication in using Dick against his beloved boss. *Karma always comes round to bite you in the ass.*

CHASE

Okay, so I had no real plan.

I just knew that if I had stayed on the phone, he would have said something and I wouldn't have been able to get out of there and then we would all be screwed so basically I panicked and hung up the phone. I rage-quit as Gideon, who played a lot of video games, would say. All I knew was that we wanted to avoid that guy. If he really did have the others, then we had to make sure we didn't add to his little arsenal.

"We need to call the police," Gideon said to me, but I shook my head violently against the idea.

"No. We need to find Bandit first. We can't involve the police until we get him safely out of here." Gideon looked like he wanted to argue, but he knew I was right. We hadn't come this far to wreck it all now.

We were about to turn down a new corridor when we heard someone quickly approaching. We tried to go the other way, but we ended up at a dead-end, and the footsteps were getting closer. Suddenly Gideon grabbed me by the shoulders. "I'll lead him away, but when I do, you get out of here. You find Bandit and the two of you get out of here and then you call the police to save the rest of us."

Every nerve in my body shrieked no. There was no way I was doing this. Who knew what they would do to him once they caught him? Not to say the idea of being alone in this place didn't thrill me in the least. "There must be another way," I began, but Gideon shook his head.

"We don't have time for this Chase, we have no idea how many of them there are. Just do as I tell you. Go!" He handed me the torch and before I could say anything else, he took off towards the footsteps.

And as he vanished around a corner, I found myself alone.

I felt small and suddenly very, very scared.

78

CHASE

After Gideon left, it took a few moments before I could move. The silence was overwhelming and I could suddenly hear every tiny bit of sound. It was like my senses were in overdrive, heightened as they were for any sounds of danger. I had been the same way before that night in the forest. I couldn't believe I was feeling like that again, and so soon after.

I waited forever it seemed, but there were no footsteps coming my way so Gideon must have successfully lured whoever it was away from here. I was hoping desperately that he was safe. But I knew I didn't have the luxury of worrying about him.

I had to find Bandit.

Backtracking through the one-way system I soon found myself at a cross-roads, but I took the one path we hadn't taken before. I moved swiftly, light on my feet, a skill that I had learned during my time on the streets. I wasn't a big girl and although I liked to think I could handle myself: flight was always better than fight, and better than all that was if they never saw you in the first place.

I followed the network of twisting corridors until I passed through old classrooms and the cafeteria. I almost missed the door set way at the back of the room, but what I noticed was the dust was disturbed on the ground by it. And it hadn't been kicked up by just one person. There was a definite arc left in the dust that suggested that the door swung back and forth on a regular basis. Feeling excited, I hugged the walls and kept myself low to the ground as I moved behind tables and chairs, just in case someone came through the door — if they did they might miss seeing me so long as I didn't move.

Reaching the door, I pushed it open just a gap so that I could see through to the room beyond. It looked like it used to be an office in here, a pretty big office but an office all the same. A wooden bench wrapped around the room hugging the wall and there was a bank of flat-screen monitors on one side. Some of the screens showed different areas around the school, but with horror, I realized that the rest were inside our ranch. I even recognized my own room. From the vantage point on screen, I worked out that the camera would have been on my shelf, which was covered with all sorts of junk, so it wasn't surprising that I had never noticed it before. There was a crudely drawn poster on the wall. I ran my eyes over it to discover it was a map of the school and on it, someone had noted down every trip wire, alarm and camera that was in this place. I was horrified to see that there were quite a few. It made it seem very unlikely that Gideon had gotten away.

Feeling sick to my stomach, I tore my gaze away from the monitors to see a room beyond. From a small porthole window, I could see what looked like scientific apparatus, but my eyes weren't interested in any experiments being conducted. They were focused on a cell in the back of the room where inside, standing up, his tail whipping back-and-forth was my best friend, my Muttface and he could barely contain himself from seeing me. I wondered why he wasn't moving, however. Usually, you couldn't keep him still, especially if he was excited. I snuck over to the window and peeked through.

It was then I saw the chains.

Bandit had been chained in place! Fury burned through me. How dare they do that to him! Seeing his reaction, I knew that there was no danger in the room so I rushed inside. Bandit whined and tried to shove his nose through the bars of his cell, but he couldn't reach.

"What have they done to you!" I cried, reaching through the bars to stroke his head. His tongue snaked out, and he managed to lick my hand.

"We need to go now OK, how many guys are we up against?" Bandit barked at me twice. I blinked, surprised by the low number.

"Two, just two guys?" Bandit barked once for yes. I suddenly felt much more hopeful. Two guys we could handle. We'd taken out an army before, so yeah, I was liking the odds.

I fumbled around the outside of the cell looking for a latch or something where I could open it, but there was nothing. Instead, there was this weird automated lock on the door, but unlike the rest of the place, this lock looked high tech. Whatever the guy was spending money on, this was it. Bandit whined and pawed on the ground. I turned around, worried that maybe someone had snuck up behind me, but there was no one.

"How do I get this open?" I asked. Bandit pawed the ground again.

I scanned the room quickly, trying to figure out what had caused this reaction in him. Across the way, lying on a bench, I could see the remains of what was probably Bandit's iPad but even from here the cracked screen was obvious. I looked back at Bandit who was still doing his funny paw movement, almost like he was pointing.

Wait, that's what he was doing, he was pointing!

I ran over to the bench to investigate. All manner of scientific stuff was spread over the bench. There were documents and x-rays and scans and graphs and I didn't know what any of it meant, but I knew they wouldn't be helpful for opening Bandit's cell. Grabbing the papers, I started shoving them out of the way when I suddenly found a little remote control. There were only two buttons on it, but Bandit suddenly started shaking with excitement. Bingo. Grabbing the remote, I pointed it towards the cell and pressed both buttons.

The doors swung open! But he was still chained up inside. I ran into the cell to find that the chains were clipped together using carabiner clips, the kind that rock climbers use. It consisted of a simple D shape but instead of a spring-opening gate — which would have been quite easy to open — it had a screw-lock, something which Bandit's paws and jaws would not be able to work.

Luckily, I had my hands.

Quickly, I unscrewed each of the carabiners that were keeping the chains in place until I had him free. He leaped up and wrapped his paws around either side of my neck and then licked my face all over. I stumbled back from the weight of him and would have fallen if it wasn't for the cell wall behind me. Hugging him close, I lay my face against his fur as I listened to his heartbeat, thankful that my friend was back with me again.

"We're not safe yet. Do you know the way out of here?" I asked him. He barked once again and started moving away. I followed, quickly.

79

XAVIER

While his hapless assistant went to secure the prisoners, Xavier went hunting on his own. Though he didn't have the kind of money and manpower that Forbes had had at his disposal, Xavier knew enough to place alarms around key points at the school. This was how he had known Sullivan and his girlfriend had arrived, and how he knew to send Pixie to lure them into the trap.

It was this same alarm that allowed him to know that they now had two extra visitors. It was a simple system, consisting of an invisible beam that ran across the floor of the corridor. He was notified each time someone broke the beam as a silent alarm would flash by the monitors. One of these alarms had been tripped just minutes before.

His hand twitched down by his side, the hand that held the sheriff's gun. He didn't like weapons as he found them Neanderthal, but it would not do to go up against these children alone — he had read the reports and knew that at least the boy was good with firearms. Xavier wasn't worried about his own life, however, knowing that they would not hurt him until they secured the dog and their adoptive parents.

Xavier knew he had the upper hand, so the gun was for show more than anything else.

Once the children had tripped the alarm, Xavier had sent Pixie to trick them as she had the others, however, she still wasn't back and it had been a while now. Xavier knew something had gone wrong, though his security system would not show him what that might be. He walked now, towards the spot where he had last seen Pixie on the monitors.

He hadn't gone far when he heard them close by. Hugging the wall, he shrank into the shadows until he was completely hidden from sight. Holding his breath, he waited. A figure materialized in front of him. It was the boy, Gideon. Xavier didn't move, expecting Chase to also appear, however, it seemed the two had gone their separate ways. Not a problem, Xavier thought to himself. One was better than none. Pointing the gun in front of him, he took a step out of the shadows.

The boy must have sensed him before he saw him as he spun around, but he had no weapon and Xavier had the advantage of surprise.

"Whatever you are thinking, stop. There is nothing you can do that will be faster than my finger pulling on the trigger of this gun."

Gideon stared, recognizing him immediately. "You're Erik, the IT man. You were there, the whole time?"

Xavier smiled. "Yes, right under your noses. It is amazing how complacent people can be once they believe themselves out of danger."

"You won't get away with this, we'll stop you!" The boy couldn't help but make the threat.

"Oh, I highly doubt that. Now, I do not want to hurt you so just tell me where the girl is."

Gideon glared at him, defiant to the end, and almost spat the words out. "I don't know. She went another way."

"Well, she won't go far, not once she knows that we have you all."

Carefully, keeping his eyes pinned on Gideon, Xavier took out his cell phone and hit one on the speed-dial. The phone rang and rang and was finally answered just as Xavier began to feel a hint of concern.

"You have something more pressing to do than to answer the phone?" Xavier asked testily.

"Well," came a voice that was clearly not Dick. "That depends on whether you consider being tied up and gagged more pressing."

Xavier felt a moment of shock before it faded into grudging respect. "Mr. Sullivan. I see you have managed to escape, how commendable."

"Yeah, well, I was getting pretty bored in that room, wanted to stretch my legs. Now, much as I don't want to sound rude, I make it a habit never to speak to people I don't like so how about we cut to the chase and strike a deal. Release Bandit and in exchange, you will get your assistant back?"

Xavier didn't answer straight away as his mind furiously calculated several possible outcomes. Finally, he decided on one. "Follow the signs to the science lab. I will meet you there."

Before Sully could respond, Xavier disconnected the call.

Xavier knew Sullivan thought he had the upper hand... and he was happy to let him think that.

80

SULLY

I turned to Sam, a triumphant smile on my face.

"Well, that was easier than I thought it would be."

She gave me a look that revealed she wasn't quite as convinced of our success as I was. "I wouldn't be counting your chickens yet," she said.

Despite what I had said to Xavier, his assistant Dick wasn't gagged, but I did find some twisted pleasure in binding his own wrists together with some spare cable ties that we had found in his pocket. It was the least I could do to repay what he had done to us. It was nice, a full circle moment, as Tony Robbins would say.

I pointed the shotgun at the kid, who was only a couple of years older than Gideon. I wondered how a boy like him got involved with this kind of thing but knew it all boiled down to bad parenting; nearly everything did. He was probably missing a father figure, which is how he fell under Xavier's grooming. I realized how easily Gideon could have become this boy. As the thought played on my mind, I determined that I would do better by him. Gideon would not end up like this.

With Dick leading the way, we reached the science block in just a few minutes. The dark and twisting corridors of this place were a lot easier to navigate when you had a guide. I pushed open the door, gesturing for Dick to enter first. While I didn't think there were any traps, I wasn't taking any risks. Dick strode confidently in, Sam and I following close behind.

The room we found ourselves in used to be an office but had now been equipped with a bank of monitors lining one wall. The first nine monitors seemed to display areas around the school, but the last nine were focused on an entirely different location.

It took a moment before I recognized the ranch, at which point the puzzle came crashing together.

The camera I had found in Zeb's hand — they were hooked up to the monitors here! With growing horror, I took in the familiar sight of our home. When I realized that there was a camera in Chase's room, however, a white-hot fury rose inside of me. Sam must have reached the same conclusion as I felt her suddenly tense beside me. What sick animals were they that they would spy on a teenaged girl's room? And then another thought came to me, of my dad, lying unconscious in the hospital. It seemed likely now that Pixie had attacked him after he had stumbled upon one of their hidden spy cams. The only time they would have had the chance to bug the place was during our trip back East... I couldn't believe their plan to unhinge me and split us apart worked so well. Even Chase's Mom, they had bought her assistance somehow. My mind felt like it was going to explode.

We moved past the office, into what was once a large science lab, but now housed research more than anything else. The walls were covered with diagrams and notes that I could not make out from my position by the door. I suspected even if I could read them I wouldn't understand a thing they said. There were many complex symbols and what looked like code. Amongst the scribblings, I caught a glimpse of diagrams of an oblong tank. It looked a lot like something you'd find in an X-Men movie.

Across the room, there was a sound as a second pair of doors that were nearly hidden in shadow, opened. The two of us tensed as I aimed the weapon on the two figures coming inside. As they stepped out of the blackness and into the light, my world spun. It was Gideon, and he was being marched inside at gunpoint by Xavier. Seeing me, Gideon's face turned apologetic. "Sorry Sully, he came at me from nowhere..." He trailed off, mad at himself for being captured.

"It's fine, we have his assistant so we're one-for-one right now."

The scientist looked at me. "I suppose I should introduce myself as it would be rude not to. My name is Xavier. You've already met my assistant Dick there."

I held my hand up, cutting off any further conversation. "We don't have to do the evil-man-explains-his-grand-plan thing. I just want my family back. I'll give you your assistant, you give me Gideon and Bandit, and we will go on our merry way."

The half smile that had been on Xavier's lips suddenly hardened. It was the smallest change, barely perceivable, but I saw it. In one instant, he turned from mild-mannered scientist to cunning nemesis.

"Unfortunately, you have made a mistake in your calculations. Dick knows what is at stake here. He knows how important my work is, as such, he wouldn't hesitate to give his life."

He looked to Dick for confirmation. Dick nodded, sticking out his chin proudly. "Xavier's work is all that matters."

Sam let out a hiss of breath. "You can't mean that. Neither of you." She turned to Dick. "You can't give up your life for this madman!"

But Dick shook his head at Sam sadly. "You just don't get it, do you?"

"And they never will," finished Xavier. "What I have created is something that could change humanity as we know it. I have spent my life working on this particular project and it is almost complete. What I do, I do for all of mankind and in the grand scheme of things, isn't that worth one boy's life?"

"You don't know that your experiment will work. There's no guarantee, an innocent being could be killed for nothing," Sam cried.

Xavier looked at us, almost apologetic. "I don't expect you to understand. Throughout history, the people with the greatest creations, the ones with the biggest effect on the human race, were always mocked and never believed. I have long accepted that this would be my fate."

"You're talking in riddles and haven't explained a thing!" I said. "Why can't you just leave Bandit alone? You already know about the tumor placement, what more could you need him for?"

Xavier explained patiently, as if to a child. "The tumors are nothing. Alpha has other properties which we don't yet understand. Have you ever seen him sick or hurt? If so, has it ever occurred to you that he recovers incredibly fast? That kind of accelerated healing is the final element I need for my project. Once I have that, there will be nothing in this world that I can't cure."

I wanted to tell him he was crazy, but a memory surfaced of the time I had operated on Bandit myself, only for him to come out of the anesthetic far faster than he should have done. Then there was the stab wound itself, which healed very quickly, even under conditions that would normally cause stitches to tear, or at the very least, an infection to occur. And then I thought of the head trauma caused by the Doc removing his tumor. Bandit's brain had rewired itself in record time afterward. We had been so relieved he was fine and hadn't lost his intelligence, none of us had really questioned it.

Xavier saw the look in my eyes and smiled. "I see that you do know what I am talking about. So you see, I am not quite the madman you first thought of me. Now, Mr. Sullivan, unless you are willing to kill Dick and risk Gideon's life, hand me the weapon please."

I looked at Sam, then Gideon, feeling helpless. Despite all that he had done, I couldn't harm Dick; the kid was under Xavier's twisted control after all, shooting him would be like shooting a person who was suffering from a mental illness. Sam gave me a small nod to let me know I had her support. Reluctantly, I handed the shotgun to Xavier.

"Regardless if Bandit has that ability or not, what you're doing is still wrong." I was determined to have my say, even if it proved detrimental to my health.

"At the end of the day, I do not care what you think, and while I don't like hurting people, I will if I deem it necessary."

"Like it was necessary to hurt my dad? It was Pixie, wasn't it?" I said. "You got her to attack him."

He nodded, emotionlessly. "When he found the bug, I instructed Pixie to take him out. I let her use her own creativity how. It was she who decided to do what she did. Speaking of the dog where is she?"

Gideon looked at him, hatred spilling out from his eyes. "Locked in a room where she can't hurt anyone anymore."

"What about Chase? You think I haven't noticed that she's not here. Where has the girl got to?"

Gideon glared at him. "You'll never find her. You can kill us all, but you'll never find her."

Xavier's eyes narrowed, the only sign of his displeasure. "Is that a challenge? Because I do love a good competition."

Keeping his eyes on Gideon, Xavier leaned over the bench and retrieved a familiar -looking phone. My phone. He scrolled through until he came to a listing that I couldn't see from over here. Pressing the button, he must have also hit speaker as the ring tone started echoing around the small room.

Moments later, Chase's desperate voice answered. "Sully, please tell me that's you?"

"No. This is Xavier. I have your whole family with me right now, Chase. If you do not come to the science lab within five minutes, I will kill them all, starting with Mr. Sullivan here."

81

CHASE

The call came just as Bandit and I were approaching the exit.
Light streamed in through the doors ahead. I actually had the phone in my hand, ready to call the police like Gideon and I had planned, when the phone rang.

Seeing Sully's name flash up on the screen, I hadn't hesitated at all. I just answered the call. Now I was wishing that I had thought twice about the call before answering it. It's true what they say about hindsight.

If I had ignored the call, I could pretend that I didn't know about his ultimatum, but now, we were in a bad way.

A really bad way.

I looked at Bandit, desperately wishing that we had his iPad so that he could communicate with me. I had around four minutes to come up with a plan that would save us all. What could I do? I looked at Bandit again, his furry face staring up at me, mirroring my concern in his green eyes.

What could we do?

82

CHASE

Think, Chase... think!

With every second that passed, I was horribly aware that it was another second closer to the death of my family. I had to come up with a way to save them, but how? Bandit whined beside me, feeling helpless. Even if he had an idea, he wouldn't be able to communicate it to me with our basic system of yes and no. While I tried to keep the overwhelming panic at bay, a mental clock ticked down inside my head, making me feel like the pressure would cause it to explode.

I shook my head to clear the fog. I couldn't let them down. I had to figure this out now but with millions of worse case scenarios flying at me from all angles; it was hard to focus, much less think of a doable plan.

Three minutes, Chase! THREE MINUTES!

OK... let's do this in steps.

The guy had the others trapped somewhere. I wouldn't be able to take the two of them on without any weapons... so my only option was to get them away from the others!

Thrilled, I now knew what I needed to do. My mind went through several possible options, but as they ranged from unlikely to impossible, I shot them down fast. I stared around the corridor I was desperate for something to jump out at me. But there was just the dust and dirt. Nothing tangible that I could use. I was about to give up when I saw it. The small red flower-like shape of a sprinkler attached to the ceiling... and with it, the bank of TV monitors and the map of the camera locations that I had seen in the office flashed up in my mind. With my photographic memory, I could see every single one of the locations.

And suddenly, I knew exactly what I needed to do.

"Bandit, I've got it!" He danced around me excitedly as I quickly explained my plan to him. After I had run through the details, I checked that he had understood them all.

"Woof."

He dashed down the corridor while I ran into each of the small rooms leading off from the corridor. The first was completely empty, but in the second, I found a few textbooks, covered with an inch of dust. *Perfect!* Grabbing them, I sprinted out of the room and went into the next. But this room had nothing I could use. Trying not to freak out over the time, I bolted into the next few rooms until I found myself in a classroom. And here, with relief, I saw some tables and chairs stacked in the corner.

Dropping the textbook, I grabbed a table and dragged it across the room until I could position it under one of those sprinklers. I stacked a chair on top of the table, then hurriedly tore pages out of the book. With the loose pages in my hand, I ran outside, almost colliding with Bandit, who returned with a rusty bin in his mouth.

"Good boy, that's exactly what we need!"

Taking it from him, I dropped the torn pages inside, set the bin on the ground, then we searched for the final missing piece. It was Bandit who saw the beer bottle first. He barked and grabbed it. Bringing it to me, I smashed the bottle on the ground, then grabbed a shard which I held over the bin.

It was the early afternoon, and a sunny day, so I was desperately hoping that it would be enough to start a fire. As I waited impatiently, I suddenly wondered how, for the second time in recent days, my life relied on my ability to start a fire. It would have been funny if it wasn't for the fact that a madman was about to start shooting my family down, one-by-one.

The two of us stared at the paper in the bin, silently willing for it to catch alight. I had lit fires using this method several times while I was on the street, but I had never been timed for it, plus it worked much better when it was a magnifying glass, but as I didn't have one on me, it was this or nothing.

Please, God. Please make this work.

By now, I'd lost any idea of time, but I knew we must be coming close to his deadline. Deathly afraid, I tensed, my body on full alert for the gunshot that would announce that all was lost when a black mark appeared on a piece of paper! It started to scorch then sizzle as the sun's ray focused through the glass to form concentrated light.

"It's working, boy!"

"Woof!" He cheered me on. And suddenly, the rest of the paper burst into flames! We'd done it! We sprinted back inside even as Gideon's phone started to ring again. I snatched it up without hesitation as we ran into the classroom. I set the bin on top of the chair, just beneath the sprinkler and the two of us immediately run back out into the corridor then answered the call, breathlessly. Before I could speak, the man's irritated voice came down the line.

"Time's up young lady, yet I don't see you here?"

"Wait!" I yelled desperately. "We're on our way! Don't hurt any of them! We got a bit lost, but we're almost there now!"

"If I don't see evidence of your imminent arrival, you can say goodbye to Sullivan."

He hung up, but I was beyond relieved that they were all still alive.

"Quickly, Boy, onto the next part of the plan!"

He took off fast as I prayed that my idea would work...

It just had to.

83

SULLY

I sat on the ground, in a line with the others.

Our hands were chained behind us, locked up tight and secured with padlocks. Having learned their lesson, there were no cable ties that we would be able to easily escape from this time. I looked at Sam to find her genuinely scared. Seeing the fear on her face made me realize that the danger was very real. Unless Chase could come up with a way to get us out of here safely, we were going to die.

When we were previously in danger, everything had happened so fast, I had no time to think of anything other than trying to survive, but now I found myself reflecting over everything that had happened. I ran my eyes over Sam's face, desperately trying to memorize every beautiful freckle and line. Even as fear would have crippled lesser people, her eyes never stopped working the room. She would be trying to find a way out of this for us until there was no time left.

I should have married her the instant we had met. What a fool I was for waiting this long.

An image of Zeb flew into my mind, pale and unconscious, lying there on his hospital bed.

I'm sorry I failed you.

Tears blurred the edge of my vision even as my eyes moved to rest on Gideon. The boy who had initially greeted us with a shotgun, so determined was he to protect my dad. Gideon sat there quietly — very unlike him — with a focused expression on his face. He kept his eyes pinned on Xavier and Dick, who had their eyes peeled to the monitors on the wall. Their weapons lay within reach, but neither had their hands on them. I tried to get his attention, to let him know my regret at failing him too, but Gideon never looked away from them. As I watched, he slowly changed positions, shifting his right leg and bending it back so that the heel of his boot was inching towards his hands.

What was the boy doing?

Slowly, carefully, I saw Gideon remove a thin piece of metal from the inside of his boot, and suddenly I realized what it was. His lock picks! My eyes flared open as I realized what he meant to do. I had to buy him time. Neither Dick nor Xavier could see what he was up to.

What could I do to help him?

84

SULLY

Getting up on my feet, I ignored the terrified looks Sam cast my way as I suddenly barreled into the two men. I smacked into Xavier, knocking him into the monitors where his head hit them with a satisfying thud. He stumbled back, stunned, touching his head where it must have been throbbing something bad.

"Sully! What're you doing?" I heard Sam scream in the background, but I didn't have a chance to answer. Furious that I had dared touch his idol, Dick roared as he came at me with his bare hands, too mad to even think about snatching up a weapon. With my hands bound behind me, I made an easy target so that even this weedy boy was able to sucker-punch me in the face. I dropped down, reeling from the blow. Dick shook his fist, hurt from hitting me, and grabbed one of the guns. As he pointed it at me, Sam suddenly darted forward, blocking his shot with her body.

"No! Please don't hurt him. You don't have to do this!" she cried.

"Sam! Get out of the way!" I shouted at her. This was disastrous and the last thing I wanted. I had wanted to buy Gideon some time and was willing to risk my life to do it, but Sam's actions had me facing the death of another woman I loved. The fear almost suffocated me.

Dick's finger hesitated on the trigger. Whatever he felt about me, he obviously didn't feel the same about Sam. "What do you want me to do?" he asked Xavier.

Still seething from the blow to his head, Xavier glared at me. He opened his mouth to give the command to end me, but then his eyes were drawn to the monitors as Bandit raced across one of the screens. On another screen,

Chase appeared, desperately chasing after him. A light blinked on a monitor, drawing his attention. Xavier smiled.

"It's too late, Sullivan. It seems the dog has made his decision to sacrifice himself for you."

Turning to study the chart on the wall, Xavier located Bandit's position. "He's by the junction between the library and the gym. He just tripped the alarm by the boy's locker room. Get there quickly before the girl does," he instructed Dick. The boy nodded, grabbing his shotgun. Shooting one last filthy look at me, he went to do his bidding. Holding onto the remaining shotgun, Xavier pointed the weapon at me.

"As soon as the dog gets here, you are a dead man, Mr. Sullivan."

And then a miracle happened.

He barely finished speaking when an alarm suddenly shrieked overhead and the heavens burst open.

Water rained down on us, pouring out from the sprinklers overhead. I realized in an instant that Chase must have set them off! *Clever girl!* Xavier froze, unsure what to do. He stood there, watching the water spray onto the paperwork pinned to the wall, turning the calculations into inky blobs. Then panic hit as he saw his life's work becoming ruined.

"No! My work!" he screamed.

Leaving the gun, he ran to the bench, pulling diagrams and calculations off the walls, trying frantically to protect them from the water. Pre-occupied, he never saw that Gideon had broken free of his restraints. Quickly, he unlocked my chains, then Sam's, as chaos and water showered down on us. With the three of us free, I picked up the chain and ran for Xavier.

Scrabbling around with an armful of his work, and with the alarm drowning out all sounds, he didn't see me coming until the chain lashed out at his head.

It hit him with a sickening thud. His eyes flew open in pain before they rolled into the back of his head. He fell down into a pool of water, out for the count.

85

CHASE

Huddled in the dark room, Bandit and I waited.

Having memorized the locations of the cameras and trip wires they had set around the place, my plan was for it to look as if Bandit had run off without me, to make it seem like he was sacrificing himself for the others. We tripped the wire that lead into this locker room here, and we were now waiting for them to leave the others to find us. Bandit hid behind the door while I waited in the shadows close by with Gideon's wrench and his flashlight.

It didn't take long.

Someone thundered down the hallway outside and crashed into the room. It was a young guy, not much older than Gideon and quite a bit weedier. He held a shotgun in his hand, so I knew we had to be careful. I waited until he approached me and I turned the flashlight on and aimed it at his face. Blinded, he instinctively went to cover his eyes when I hit him with the wrench using the full force of my body, and Bandit flew at him from the other side. The guy dropped onto the ground like we'd knocked him over with a demolition ball. Bandit stood over him, snarling into his face while I relieved him of his shotgun.

"Don't move, scumbag!" I hissed into his face.

The guy froze, eyes still glazed from the flashlight. Having scoped out the room before his arrival, I knew there was a small side room in here. Though it was empty, it still carried the scent of chemical cleaners. I prodded the gun at him.

"Get up. Slowly..." I commanded in a voice that was hard from the hatred I felt at this guy who had been threatening my family. I marched him into the side room, shut the door, and wedged the wrench under the handle so that he couldn't get out.

As we started out of the locker room, towards the others, the sprinklers and alarm turned on.

And with it, I knew we only had moments before the fire trucks would arrive.

"Hurry Bandit, we've got to free the others!"

86

SULLY

Xavier lay on the ground, unconscious.

My hand itched over the trigger of the shotgun, but Sam stopped me. "No. You do that, and you'll never come back from it."

I looked at her, torn. Though I heard the truth of her words, I wanted retribution for the pain this man had caused on so many others. In that moment, I didn't care about the future, whether I would regret this. I wanted nothing more than to blow this man off the face of the Earth.

My finger started moving of its own accord, but I stopped short of pulling it when two familiar beloved faces flew in through the doors.

Bandit barked joyously, while Chase ran in, stunned but relieved to find us safe and sound. "But, I came to rescue you," she said, confused yet happy.

"And you did an amazing job, hun, the sprinklers were genius," Sam said, smiling as she hugged her close. I didn't even blink. I ran over and grabbed the two of them, mashing their bodies against me until Chase's muffled voice sounded from within.

"Sully... I can't breathe..." she said.

Watching us from across the way, Gideon fussed Bandit, grinning. Chase pulled reluctantly away from me, brushing the wet hair from her eyes.

"This is him? This is the guy who's been after Bandit?" Chase looked down at Xavier's prone form. She rolled him over with a sneaker to see his face, but gasped when it flopped into view.

"This is the IT guy who's renting the apartment above Warrey's!"

Gideon nodded, mouth tight from the guilt of not knowing that this was the man who was out to ruin our family. "I had no idea… if only we'd known sooner, I could've done something. Maybe Zeb wouldn't be lying in the hospital now if I had…"

I shook my head at him. "You can't blame yourself, Gid. It happened, but now it's over."

"We're not out of it yet," Chase said suddenly. "The fire trucks will get here soon and there's still all this stuff everywhere." She pointed at the piles of Xavier's paperwork. Though some of it had been ruined, I could still make out his writing on the rest. "And what about him? We can't just leave him there. Remember what happened with Forbes…?"

It was Bandit who came up with the solution. Grabbing the chains Xavier had used on us, Bandit carried them over to Xavier and dropped them onto his prone body, his intention clear as day. Chase nodded and looked to Gideon for assistance. "Gid, help me get him into the cell. Let's see how he likes a taste of his own medicine."

"Woof!" Bandit barked solemnly.

While they dragged him into the cell and chained him up, I looked to Sam. "Quickly, we need to destroy anything that mentions canine anatomy or Bandit. If you're not sure, just tear it up." I led the way, ripping up whatever I could get my hands on.

We quickly destroyed all the evidence we could find that mentioned Bandit. Xavier had taken copious notes and pictures. Some of the notes I understood, but I had no idea what the end goal was. All I could fathom was he had some sort of living experiment that he was conducting, but it looked like something was wrong with it. He needed Bandit's brain's ability to remap itself and his super fast healing to essentially fix his experiment's damaged organs. In the brief amount of time I had to go through his notes, what I learned filled me with dread. The last time a scientist had played like this he created Frankenstein and we all know how that story turned out.

We got rid of most of his research, though I made sure to keep the most incriminating things I could find. These I stacked under a sheet of plastic where they would be protected from the water. We worked fast, together as a team. With the alarm screeching overhead, I knew we didn't have much time to get out of there before the fire trucks started turning up.

I found a vial of Telazol, a cocktail of two other drugs, which when used together resulted in the sedation of cats and dogs. Xavier had obviously been keeping it in case he needed to use it on Bandit, but I took it now. The plan was to use it on Pixie. I was ready to leave Pixie to the cops to deal with, but even after everything, Chase reminded me that it wasn't Pixie's fault. You don't get bad dogs, she had said. Only badly trained dogs, and that was on the owners. She had pleaded with me, letting me know that if anyone could help her, it would be me. I had mixed emotions knowing that she was the cause of my father lying in hospital, but in the end, I knew Chase was right. I had spent my life saving animals, and I couldn't turn my back on this one.

As we left to find her, we passed by the office Xavier had used as his control room.

"Hold up," I said to the others as I ran into the room. Searching around the monitors, I guess I was hoping for a simple way to disconnect the cameras that they had in our home. I couldn't find one, however. As the cameras were all inside the ranch, though, I hoped the authorities wouldn't be able to identify the location. In any case, there wasn't much I could do about that now. I turned to leave when a movement on one of the screens caught my eye. A figure had moved out of one of the school's corridors, through a door to the outside. I would have thought it a figment of my imagination, but for the fact that the door was closing slowly on itself now. I had no time to guess at who that might be, however, as Gideon called through the door at me.

"Sully, hurry up!"

Nodding, I sprinted out to join them. We found Pixie moments later. It took two of us to hold her down as she had worked herself into a frenzy by now. When the syringe finally sank into her, she yelped and twisted her head around, trying to snap at me with those jaws, but the drug was quick-acting and within seconds she was out for the count. I picked her up and followed Gideon as we met back up with the others. Securing her into the back of my car, we drove off, moments later passing by the fire trucks as they screamed past us on their way to the school.

With that chapter blessedly over, we sped back to Montpelier.

Back to my dad.

87

MR SMITH

He had been tipped off by a detective in the police department. The company that he worked for, a covert department of the government, had feelers everywhere. It was their job to investigate crimes that were considered unusual in nature, the sort of case Mulder and Scully would have looked into. He glanced into the rearview mirror to check his disguise once again. He had a nondescript face — perfect for this line of work — and was currently wearing the uniform of a forensic investigator. Not that anyone would check his credentials, but if they had, they would discover his name was Mr. John Smith. Good luck trying to identify him with the most common name in America. Grabbing his tool case, he cut through the cops littering the scene and followed the crime scene tape to the room that had gotten local uniforms so worked up.

On his way, he passed by what had been a science lab. The local police had been very disturbed when they had found the man who they now knew was one Xavier Williams, a science professor at a community college in Columbus, Ohio, strung up inside a jail-like cell. He had been chained so tight that he had not been able to move an inch. Despite this, however, when they had found him, all the man had cared about was his research. He was still screaming at them to protect it when they had dragged him and his assistant away.

Mr. Smith arrived in the basement of the derelict school. Water dripped from the sprinklers still. They had been turned off now, however, the occasional one still leaked. He followed the markers set by the police until he reached a strange contraption in front of him.

It was a steel tank shaped and sized like, well, like a coffin. The lid was made of glass and through it, he could see that the tank contained some kind of thick liquid. Lifting the lid, he tried to get a better look at the substance inside but was unable to determine what it could be using the naked eye alone. It had a faintly chemical smell, but he couldn't put a name to it. Opening his tool case, he took a sample of the liquid and bagged it up. It would be sent to their private laboratory, and the results given to him soon after. Focusing on the job at hand, he must have leaned against a switch of some kind as images suddenly appeared on the inside lid of the tank. Sound too came out of hidden speakers along the side of the tank. He stopped to watch the images, which appeared to be a collection of video footage that was somehow being projected onto the lid.

The footage all consisted of one man. He looked to be in his thirties. Athletic build, kind eyes. He smiled and laughed a lot. His voice boomed out from the speakers, saying nothing of interest from what Mr. Smith could gather. It was a jumble of nonsense video, the kind of thing you might find in someone's home video collection before they edited it down. No one else featured in the footage. Running his hands along the tank, he finally found the switch that had activated the footage and depressed it. The footage and sound blinked out.

Curious, he thought to himself. This would need further investigating into.

Until he had the tank drained, there was nothing else he could find inside it, so he turned his attention to a nearby table where a pile of paper-work sat. He went through the pile with gloved hands so as not to disturb any fingerprints. What he could initially decipher, he found of great interest.

It looked like Xavier might not be insane after all.

What he was looking at was a possible way to accelerate cloning. Whether or not Xavier was successful was another thing, but his work would have to be looked into for sure. This kind of discovery could not be allowed into the public eye if, in fact, he had been successful. He had knocked this kind of thing on its head before, and he would do so again. So long as his bosses kept him in employment, it wasn't for him to question their instructions.

He came to an X-ray and stopped, perplexed. While the rest of the documents had pertained to human elements, this scan showed a dog. As he studied the scan, he found more items of concern. He took the scan and slipped it into a protected envelope that he tucked inside a hidden pocket in his jacket. This wasn't for the local lab. His people would examine this in confidence.

It took hours to comb through everything else in that room. He found a few more references to a dog and took all of those. It wasn't until his eyes were becoming gritty and dry from staring so long that he stopped. Looking at his watch, he was surprised to find that so much time had passed. He'd order takeout tonight, so he could eat while he logged everything he had found into the system.

He stood up and stretched his aching muscles when something caught his eye. He crossed the room to the far side and saw a cell had been built there. It looked like the cell that was upstairs in the science lab, except this one had a bed in addition to a toilet and sink.

Turning on his flashlight to UV, he shined the torch under the bed, knowing that beds were a haven for forensics. Stains and lint, invisible to the eye, flared up. But there was something else, something golden. Moving in closer, he saw it was a long strand of blonde hair.

Carefully he picked it up with a pair of tweezers and slipped it into a bag.

What puzzles did this hair hold?

He couldn't wait to find out.

88

CHASE

We must have broken so many speeding laws to get back home as fast as we did.

Anytime we were stopped by police (which happened at least three times) however, Sam just flashed her badge and explained it was a matter of life and death. At one point of our journey back, we even got ourselves a police escort. If I weren't as tired as I was, I probably would have enjoyed it a lot more. As it was, I was too exhausted to take much of it in. I just wanted to get back to Zeb to make sure he was okay. I felt like every minute we weren't by his side, was a minute he might not make it.

Pixie had still not come to in the back of Sully's car. We had secured her in a blanket so when she did wake, she wouldn't be out to move or hurt herself. It was the best we could do with what we had. Sully said she'd be fine, so I took his word for it. While Sully drove (Sam was traveling with Gideon — they weren't more than a car or two behind us at all times), I called a friend who we thought might be able to help Pixie. Knowing that Xavier had messed with Pixie physically, we knew there was only one person we trusted who might be able to figure it out.

"Hello," she answered the phone sounding surprised. "Sully?" she asked.

"No, Doc, it's Chase. Sully's driving." I said.

"Chase! What a lovely surprise to hear from you. How are you all?" Doc Robins said.

I looked at Sully, then Bandit lying in the back seat and decided maybe now wasn't the time to get into everything. "I'll fill you in later, but Sully wanted to ask if you could do us a favor? We have another dog here. She's smart too, like Bandit, but not in the same way. Sully said she's got several of those tumors inside her and they're causing her to be mean and aggressive. He doesn't know what to do. Can you help?"

"There's a lot more to the story that you're not telling me isn't there?" came her voice over the line.

"Yeah. We'll tell you all about it in person. Can you get to our place? We should be there in a few hours. We're stopping off at the hospital first."

"Is everything okay? Who's been injured?"

I wasn't able to answer as I found myself suddenly listening to the dead dial tone. Frowning, I stared at the phone to see that it had died and there wasn't a charger in sight. Feeling my consternation, Sully looked at me.

"What happened, is she coming?"

"I think so. I didn't get to find out because your phone died." I started rummaging in the glove compartment, but other than gum and a sponge for the windscreen, I didn't find what I was looking for.

"I think I left it with Sam. We'll just have to make do until we meet up with them again."

89

SULLY

We arrived at the hospital after visiting hours. The nurse in charge wouldn't let us inside at first, especially when she caught sight of Bandit, but Sam used her authority to get onto the ward. That badge was like a magic wand: wherever she waved it, things always happened. I thought we would be meeting more resistance than the one nurse, but as we turned the corner that would lead to my dad's room, his doctor, who was going over a patient's file by the nurse's station, looked over at our motley crew in surprise.

"There you are. I've been waiting all afternoon for you to call me, why haven't you called back?" He demanded. I was taken aback by his tone.

"We were out of town and my phone died. Why, has something happened?" Even as the words left my mouth, I felt a cold hollow build in my stomach, but the doc smiled at me.

"Your father is awake Mr. Sullivan and has been waiting — very impatiently might I say — for you all to get here."

I heard the words, but I was too afraid to believe him, so I didn't move until I felt a tugging on my arm. It was Gideon.

"What are you waiting for?" He ran past me into dad's room. And suddenly, like my feet had a mind of their own, I found myself racing after him. By the time I got inside Gideon was already at dad's bedside holding onto his hand. The old man was propped up against the bed, but other than a bandage around his head, he seemed his usual self.

"Glad you could make it finally. Wouldn't want to interrupt whatever important thing you've got going on."

A smile broke out over my face. I crossed the room in three quick strides and hugged him. I was expecting him to push me away — we'd never been the touchy-feely type with each other. Instead, his arms came up around me and he patted my back before we let go of each other.

"You had us all scared there for a moment," I said.

"We've got the good doctor to thank for that." He gestured at him standing in the doorway. Seeing that we were all fine, the doc smiled.

"I suppose it wouldn't do any good to tell you all to leave because he needs his rest?"

"They just got here! Give them a moment, would you?" Zeb said, peeved.

The doctor smiled and nodded. "Half an hour and then I won't be able to stop the nurse from kicking you out." He left, smiling at us. I waited until he was out of earshot before I started speaking again. As soon as he was gone, Zeb's expression changed, and he became deadly serious.

"It was Pixie. Did you find her? She attacked me after I found a camera in the house. I was just going to call to warn you when she went crazy and started attacking me."

"Yeah. We know," I said. He looked at me in surprise.

"You do? How?"

We filled him in on everything that had happened since his accident. As we talked, his eyebrows raised higher and higher until at one point, I thought they would shoot clean off his head. When we were done, he let out a long, drawn breath.

"That's some excitement you all have gone through. Makes me glad that I was out for most of it."

"When are you coming home?" Gideon asked hopefully.

"I suspect they will want to keep him in for a day or two, to make sure he's in the clear, but he'll be back soon," said Sam.

"And when I do, I am ready for another round of your lasagna you hear? That bump on the head wasn't enough to kill me, but the hospital food might," he said with a glower.

Sometimes, he and Chase were so strikingly similar.

90

CHASE

Birds sang outside my window, signaling all was well with the world. I woke to a commotion outside.

Bandit wasn't in his usual place on my bed, but I could hear his excited barking outside. Moving to the window, I looked out to see Doc Robins had arrived, and she was playing with Bandit and talking to him. I couldn't hear what she was saying from here, but whatever it was, he liked it, as he started jumping up at her with delight.

When Bandit had been at Platinum Industries, it was the Doc who had taken care of him. Blackmailed into working for Forbes, the Doc was the only person to have ever showed kindness and affection to Bandit... until he met me, anyway. When it was all going down at PI, it was the Doc who helped to save the day. We owed her a lot.

I pulled a cardigan over my PJ's and went out to greet her. When she saw me, a big grin spread over her face.

"Chase! It's so good to see you again."

"Hi Doc, how was Africa?"

"Did you manage to help out there," asked Sully who had joined us. She turned to him and gave him a hug.

"A little, though it is never enough, is it? I'm glad to be back on US soil, though. It seems my work here isn't over with either." She stared past him into the house. "Where is she, the dog?"

"We've got her safely secured in the den. She's managed to exhaust herself after working into such a state yesterday. Now she's just cowering in the corner, although that could be an act. You can never tell with her. She is a very good actress."

The Doc stared at him, her eyes glittering with intrigue. "That is highly irregular for dogs. They usually show all their emotions. Subterfuge isn't common in the species, if at all."

I looked at her suddenly worried. "You are going to help her, right? You're not going to just be doing experiments?"

She looked at me. "Of course I'm not going to experiment on her. Nothing I do will hurt her, I promise. My days with those kinds of experiments are over. No, what I have planned for her is to remove those tumors. Then after that, it's lots of patience and love."

She looked nothing but sincere, and Bandit certainly wasn't acting like he was concerned. I hoped that maybe Pixie could be fixed.

Everyone deserved a second chance.

Bandit and I had gotten ours, so I hoped I could say the same for Pixie in the future.

91

SULLY

While Elora examined Pixie, I'd accepted a phone call from Dad. It seemed he was ready to come home that day. Hearing the news, a great weight lifted from my shoulders. Until he had been given the green light, I hadn't realized how concerned I was that something else would happen to him, but now that I knew he was coming home, there was something pressing I had to do.

I found Sam inside our room where she had spent the night — I had slept on the couch. We hadn't discussed our relationship since we'd gotten back and we were too tired to do anything but sleep last night, so I had taken the couch respectfully to give her space, but now it was time to talk. I was ready.

Sam had a suitcase on the bed and was packing her things when I came into the room. She looked up at me, hesitating for only a second.

"How's Pixie reacting to Elora?" She asked.

"Better than expected, actually. I don't know if it's just exhaustion or if she can sense the Doc means her no harm, but Pixie has calmed right down. When I left them, the Doc was feeding her some treats."

Sam picked up a work shirt and folded it neatly before setting it inside the suitcase. "That's good. Hopefully, she can give Pixie the help she needs." She reached out to pick up a sweater when I took her hand in mine. She stopped and looked at me.

"I know I haven't been myself since the visit East, but I need you to know that what happened was never an excuse. I never behaved that way because I wasn't ready to marry you. I am completely and wholeheartedly ready to be your husband. I love you Sam and I think I'm finally ready to let go of the past. I need you to trust me, to trust us. I need you to marry me."

Her eyes softened and I could see she wanted to believe me but there was that slight hesitation that hint of doubt in her eyes. I had hurt her with my actions, and this doubt was the result of it.

"I don't know, so much has happened..."

I entwined my fingers with hers and drew her in closer. "Exactly. It made me see sense. My life is with you and the kids. You are my family now so let's make it official. Let's go get married."

Her eyes widened as she suddenly understood what I was trying to say. "You mean now? Are you serious?"

"I mean this week. We don't need a crazy ceremony. We can do it in our local church."

She was caving now, I could see it, so I pushed harder. "You were right, I know that now. I was under a lot of stress and a part of me was still getting over Emma's death, but she's gone and you're here, and I'm not interested in waiting anymore. Lets just get on with our lives. So what do you say, Sam?"

She looked up at me, her big beautiful eyes spilling over with tears.

"I do."

92

CHASE

The time had come to say goodbye to Pixie.

The Doc had led her to her car and the rest of us had gathered around them. I immediately noticed that Sully and Sam were holding hands. I don't know what happened between them in the hour that the Doc was getting acquainted with Pixie, but I was so relieved. I loved the two of them together; they had felt right, right from the moment they had met, so when they separated, it felt like my parents had split up, which was crazy I know since I didn't know either of them a year ago.

Time changes so much.

The Doc helped Pixie into her car. She had some sort of grate in between the front and back seats, so if Pixie suddenly decided to Hulk out, she wouldn't be able to attack the Doc. I was surprised to find Bandit coming out to say goodbye, knowing how many issues he had with her. But I was even more surprised to find he had his new rabbit toy in his mouth. Even though Pixie had never been nice to him, Bandit knew it wasn't her fault. He jumped up onto the back seat and carefully laid his toy in front of her. When she didn't move, he nudged it towards her. Eyes wide, she grabbed the rabbit. I was half expecting her to lay into the thing like she had done with his other toys, but she just hugged it to herself for comfort. Satisfied that his gift had been accepted, Bandit jumped back down and came to my side.

"Good boy, Bandit. That was a super nice thing you just did."

He woofed, pleased with himself. Gideon stepped forward and fussed Pixie one last time. She pressed into him, seemingly scared of leaving. She had taken his love for granted and now it was going away. I knew how that felt, having come close to losing Bandit myself. I hugged him close to me as Doc got behind the driver's seat and gave us all a wave.

"I'll be in touch as soon as I have any updates but you can check up on her anytime, I started a private Facebook group for us."

Gideon and I shared an amused look, neither of us expecting the Doc to be a Facebook user. She gave us a quick smile over her shoulder and then they were gone. The others headed back into the house, but I hung back with Bandit. I crouched down until we were eye-level with each other.

"I'm so sorry that I didn't listen to you about Pixie. You tried to warn me but I had my own stuff going on and like Sully, I got caught up in it all. I promise I will never do that again, OK? I'm really sorry buddy."

Bandit leaned over to lick my face. And as the familiar smell of his dog breath washed over me, I figured all was right with the world.

93

CHASE

When the others left to bring Zeb home from the hospital, I decided to stay at the ranch with Bandit. I knew the staff wouldn't be keen on letting him in the hospital, and since I wasn't going to leave him ever again, staying home was the best solution. Besides, I had something I needed to do.

Bandit sat opposite me now, head cocked in question, as he could feel the nervous waves pouring out of me. Grabbing the phone, I dialed a number — careful this time to hide our caller ID — and waited, rubbing my sweaty palms over my jeans. The call was eventually answered by an angry male voice.

"What?" he demanded.

Though I had steeled myself for his voice, hearing it still caused negative emotions to flood my body. I shook them off, determined to see this through. "I'm calling for my mom," I answered, proud of the way my voice remained steady.

"Chase? You're too late," he said spitefully. "She's gone."

"Gone? Where?" I asked.

"Hell if I know. Her clothes are gone, and she took off without a word. Didn't even pay the rent so now I'm being tossed out, can you believe that?"

It was unbelievable that he thought I would feel sorry for him. I realized at that very moment that both Tubs and my mom were very similar people: they were both selfish and too involved with themselves to ever care about anybody else. Though I had a million things I had spent years storing up to say to him, I realized one simple word would convey them all.

"Good," I said, then I hung up.

So she had finally done it... she had finally left him. While I was furious at the way she had used and betrayed me, I had to admit that there was one small part of me that was happy she had finally left him behind.

Maybe now she could be a better person and can go for that life she had always wanted.

94

SULLY

Days later, I found myself tugging at the collar of my shirt, not used to wearing such confining clothes.

My hair had been newly cut, I'd even had a close shave. All in all, I was looking quite dapper, even if I said so myself.

I could hear a hum of anticipation from the church's reception hall outside. We didn't know that many people here, but it seemed the whole town had turned up, regardless. I hadn't realized how many people liked our small family, in particular, Sam. They had waited years to see her married off and today was the day. Earlier, I had caught a glimpse of Warrey outside, looking like he had stepped out of a copy of Mechanic GQ. A bevy of available women were trying to get his attention, but he scowled at them all. I felt secretly proud that the better man had won Sam's hand.

Take that, Warrey.

There was a knock at the door and in came my dad, looking quite the gentleman himself. I couldn't think when I had last seen him in a suit and was surprised to find he seemed more at ease in one than I.

"Hey," he said to me. "You almost done?"

"Yes," I said, without any hesitation in my voice.

"There's something missing though," he said as he gestured me closer. He held a simple white rose in his hand, which he now pinned to the lapel of my suit. It matched the one on his own.

"Thanks." I checked my reflection in the full-length mirror and caught the uncomfortable expression on his face. "What is it?"

Dad looked up at me, clearing his throat to speak when Gideon came into the room, followed by Chase and Bandit. Gideon wore a suit not dissimilar to my own, while even Bandit had a bowtie around his neck for the occasion, but it was Chase who stole the show. She was wearing a pretty peach dress that showed off her glossy chestnut hair and creamy complexion. She looked beautiful... and truly uncomfortable. I grinned, watching her pull on the dress, fidgeting.

"Do they make these unbearable for a reason? How do people wear these things? And my God, the shoes! I hope you're not expecting me to walk gracefully in them," she exclaimed. Gideon shared my amused smile, which only caused her to glare more.

"Stop being so smug just because you don't have to be strapped and cinched into submission," she complained grumpily.

"Well, you look very pretty if that's any consolation," said Gideon, causing Chase to shut up instantly and blush furiously. She didn't say anything else, but she stopped tugging at her skirt and stood up a little straighter.

"Just like the Princess in Bradley the bumblebee."

This had come from Bandit, who had been given a brand-new iPad. He was referring to the first picture book we had taught him to read. After reading the book, he had compared Chase to the Princess. It was the first time he had paid a compliment to Chase, and she had taken it about as well as she had taken this one. Some girls craved attention for their looks, but Chase wasn't one of them, preferring that people liked her for her smarts instead. It was one of the things I loved most about her. Despite her embarrassment, she bent down to stroke him.

"So, are you guys ready for this?" I asked them.

"Are you kidding me? I just want to know why you hadn't done this any sooner," Gideon exclaimed. By his feet, Bandit barked once in agreement while Chase nodded. Even Zeb agreed. Though he had fallen silent since the kids' appearance, he seemed very much on board with proceedings.

"It was obvious the two of you should be together even during that first meal we had together, you know, when you made spaghetti?" Chase said, cutting into my thoughts.

Her words struck a chord in me. If I were honest, that was the moment that had cemented the deal for me too. Seeing Sam's dimples and her smiling face, I was gone even then, but it was amazing to hear the kids had felt the same.

An usher knocked on the door. "We're just about to start. Can we have the groom's party outside?"

We all jumped to attention. I had been here before, but previously I had felt nervous and anxious. This time, I felt only peace and calm. We had already gone through so much together. What was a little wedding?

As Gideon opened the door, I followed them outside to meet my new wife.

I couldn't wait.

95

SULLY

The ceremony flew past.

Before I even knew it, we had exchanged our vows, and we were now standing on the steps of the church as confetti rained down on us. Through the colored rice, I could make out some familiar smiling faces, among them Florence and Mark, who had traveled here faster than a rocket when I had given them the news. I hadn't realized just how much they cared, or how desperate they were to see me happy again. To have them both here now made the moment complete. I was about as happy as a man could be.

We ran up to my truck, which someone had decorated with a "just married" sign. I helped Sam inside, hoisting up the long hem of her dress and tucking it around her then turned to find Zeb beside me. The bandage was gone from his head now, but he still looked a little pale. He swore sunshine was all he needed, that and good food. Throughout the ceremony, he had seemed a little subdued. While Sam busied herself with well-wishers, he looked at me a little awkwardly. Finally, he spoke.

"Son, I'm sorry I didn't support you in your first wedding. It's clear that Emma was a lovely person, and I'm sorry I never got the chance to meet her, but I'm here now, and I hope I can make it up to you this time around."

I knew how hard that was for him, and I was truly touched. With that simple apology, years of anger and resentment melted away. He reached out and offered me his hand. I shook it as he smiled at me.

"Congratulations Son, we all love her."

I shot him a grin, then searched for the kids. Chase seemed suddenly shy as she came up to me and gave me a big hug while Bandit pressed against me in his own version of an embrace.

"Enjoy your honeymoon," Chase said. "Bring me back something from Montréal."

"Woof!" Bandit agreed, making us all smile.

"I will," I promised. "You guys be good and stay out of trouble. We'll be Skyping you every day to check in, and remember, Montréal is only two and a half, three hours drive away, tops. We can come back in case of any emergencies."

Gideon rolled his eyes at me. "We'll be fine. Just leave already before Sam goes without you."

As if she heard him, Sam honked the horn impatiently.

"OK, OK," I said as I climbed into the truck beside her. She leaned against me, happily slipping her hand in mine. As I looked into the rearview mirror, at these people who had joined us on the happiest day of our lives, I saw a blonde figure hovering at the back of the crowd. I couldn't make out her face at first, through the waving hands and confetti, but then the crowd parted like a wave and her face stared directly at me.

Looking exactly the same as she had when I had last seen her alive.

It was my wife.

My other wife.

My dead wife.

I froze, but before I could react, a flash of light blinded me as Chase yelled out, "Say cheese!"

When the light died down, and I found my eyes readjusting, Emma had vanished.

I shook my head, knowing it was just my mind playing tricks on me… I had just spoken to my father about Emma, so it wasn't unreasonable that I would see her again now. Having been here before, I was determined not to fall for those tricks again. Smiling at Sam, I focused on my bride as I pulled the truck out of the driveway. She leaned out of the window, waving energetically and blowing kisses, happiness causing her cheeks to turn rosy.

As the crowd of loved ones cheered us on, I drove us towards our future.

Just my bride and me, knowing that whatever came next, the two of us would weather it all.

THE CHASE RYDER SERIES BOOK 3
HUNTED
JO HO
AWARD-WINNING SCREENWRITER

HUNTED

BOOK 3

1
———

CHASE

"And the first answer in this Double Jeopardy round... for $1,600, this 1972 novel is about a community of rabbits in Berkshire, England, who set out to find a new warren."

The sound of the announcer's cheerful voice sounded from the iPad that lay propped up on the floor of the wooden deck.

At first glance, the pattern that covered the tablet's foam case seemed an odd design choice. It was only on closer inspection that the millions of tiny depressions that covered the case could be identified as punctures caused by two rows of sharp canine teeth.

Seeing them, my lips curled into a grin as I pictured the much-loved culprit. No matter how carefully he tried carrying it, inevitably, Bandit would grip onto the thing with way too much enthusiasm.

Fact: iPad cases weren't designed to be handled by our four-legged friends.

Then again, I couldn't really blame Apple for the lack of insight: they couldn't know that in addition to regular people, their devices were also being used by a super intelligent, genetically modified dog.

As I stared down at the device, snatches of our eventful journey popped into my mind, filling me with a sense of wonder that still hadn't faded even now, almost seven months to the day since I'd first set foot on this ranch.

Everything that had come before seemed so long ago that the memories were fuzzy, as if they were hidden behind several sheets of material. You know the ones, those long white almost-see-through curtains they always use in trendy New York loft apartments in the movies.

From my time in the trailer park with Mom and Tubs, when I ran away, to the months of surviving by myself, homeless and alone... those memories had faded until they were tiny black and white snippets in my mind. Still, they were unpleasant enough that on the rare occasion when they did surface, I would bury them back in the far recesses of my mind.

I didn't like to focus on bad things... I couldn't see the point of deliberately making yourself feel bad.

Across the spectacular horizon that formed the Montpelier backdrop where Zeb, Sully's dad's ranch was based, red-gold leaves spoke of the approaching fall.

Though the sun still shone brightly in the sky, mornings now came with a chill, one that required a light cardigan over my usual sleepwear of an old tank top and shorts. I even had socks on my feet — reluctantly — as they were something I hated. I was a barefoot or flip-flop kind of girl, although, during my time on the streets, there were many nights where all I wanted was a pair of socks to warm my frozen toes.

My hands were wrapped around my favorite mug where only the top of the boldly printed slogan could be seen, yet I didn't need to see the words to know what they were: "ACHIEVEMENT UNLOCKED. Fifteen whole years of being awesome."

It was a present from Sully, something he had picked up on one of his trips out of town but which I loved to death. Call me sentimental, but I thought it was kind of wonderful — and true, obviously.

I sipped at my coffee as Bandit lay on the deck before me, his long pink tongue hanging out as his tail thumped an excited rhythm on the floor. The sun glinted off his glossy black, brown, and white coat, which was a far cry from the dirty, dull, and starving appearance he'd had when I'd first met him. Then again, having spent the morning dumpster diving, I probably wouldn't have won any beauty awards myself.

See how much fun it is to go down Memory Lane?

Delicately picking up one of the many stylus pens we had made for him, Bandit tapped "Watership Down" into the iPad. His answer was greeted by loud in-game applause and more tail thumping.

Over the last few months, Bandit had developed an insatiable appetite for books and had read through pretty much all the children's classics, sometimes several in a day. His tastes were broad, but he had a special place in his heart for stories that featured animals.

To the casual — and shocked — outsider, this would seem like he was just having fun, though this was an actual exercise Bandit went through every morning. It was how we regulated his brain to make sure all was working as it should be.

You'd never know it seeing him now, but Bandit had come very close to meeting the Reaper... and that hadn't been the end of our troubles. A pang of shame welled up inside my chest when I thought of how I had become so caught up in my own family drama, how I had believed all that rubbish my mom had spouted, that Bandit had been taken on my watch.

Of all people, I should have known better than to trust her.

She was gone now, having sold me off for one hundred thousand dollars.

Strangely, I didn't feel as bitter as I had expected. I knew I'd never see her again. That kind of money wasn't something she would ever have hoped to see in her lifetime. It afforded her the luxury of changing her miserable life and ditching Tubs, and she wouldn't risk losing any of it for sentimental reasons.

She was gone, and I was pretty OK with that.

I had my own family now, one who actually cared about me, and I would do anything to keep them safe.

Leaning forward, I stroked Bandit's head, mentally affirming that I would never take him for granted again. His eyes flicked up at me before settling back onto the screen. His tail swished a pattern back and forth across the wooden floor. Tails were ridiculous things if you thought about them. I mean, what was their purpose other than to knock things down?

A sound burst out from the iPad, a kind of hallelujah music blast signifying something important. I thought Bandit must have unlocked some kind of in-game trophy, but it was just an announcement that had just popped up on the tablet.

A giant red banner bisected the screen, letting us know that they were giving away tickets for a special charity edition of Jeopardy that would be broadcasting live. Bandit's hopeful eyes raised to my own, his tail thumping harder with excitement. I clicked on the banner only for the small print to appear.

"Sorry, boy. This is happening in Los Angeles. If it was in New York, where the normal shows are filmed, we might have been able to swing it, but that's way too far from us."

He sighed. A long sigh of disappointment that tugged at my heart. I hated to disappoint him, no matter how small. Not wanting to focus on what he would be missing, I pressed the button to start a new round. Bandit instantly perked up again.

"I love this game!" he typed into the tablet, grinning at me.

"We know," I said. "We would have moved onto something else by now if you'd let us."

"Has he ever lost an actual game?" Gideon asked, yawning, even though he'd been up at least an hour. He sat across from me, sleep still fogging his eyes. A tuft of his hair stood up awkwardly on his head, and I had to resist the ridiculous urge to smooth it down. We were close, but not *that* close.

"Not that I've seen." He was one of those people who needed *hours* to wake. While we could get him doing simple tasks like early morning pastry runs, his brain didn't really click in until halfway through the morning, usually around ten or eleven.

If only there was an app that could work on him, too.

"Are you going to eat that?" Gideon gestured to the last donut, a frosted cinnamon one that lay on the middle of the table. I stared at the sugary doughy ring of deliciousness.

"I hadn't decided to *not* eat it, but I guess you could have it, if you want. I mean, you did get them and all," I conceded reluctantly.

"Gee thanks, Chase," he said. "It's not like you haven't already had five. Oh wait, yes you have."

"You know I can't control my fast metabolism. Isn't that right, Zeb?"

I looked toward the end of the porch. Zeb sat in his wheelchair, head ducked low, reading the paper, sipping from a cup of coffee. For some reason, he always sat away from Gideon and me, especially in the morning.

"If there is any way I can get out of this by not answering, that would be ideal," Zeb responded without even looking up.

It was coming up to two weeks since Sully and Sam had gone on their honeymoon, during which time Zeb had been drawn into every single one of our disagreements. Judging by the surly tone in his voice, I think he was getting tired of being our referee.

"What time are they calling?" he asked, finally looking up at me over the top of the newspaper.

I glanced down at my watch — a gift from Sam who felt that phones didn't make a suitable equivalent — to check. "Any second now, actually."

As if Sully knew we had been talking about him, Bandit's iPad suddenly started ringing as the familiar Skype icon blinked on-screen.

Dropping his stylus pen onto the floor, Bandit set the iPad on the table. I tapped the answer icon, propping the tablet up against the juice jug so we could all get a good look at them. After a few seconds, the video call connected, and Sully and Sam's happy faces appeared.

"Hey! How's everyone doing?" Sully said, squinting into his phone.

As if he hadn't seen or spoken to him for years, Bandit's entire body shook with excitement as he shoved his face at the screen until his nose filled up the frame.

Chuffing into the iPad, he talked a mile a minute, though, of course, without the tablet to translate, it was pretty hard to know what he was saying. Laughing, I wrapped my arms around him, gently easing his face back so that we could all see Sully and Sam, and they could see more than a shiny, wet nose.

They were crammed into a packed restaurant. People feasted on giant plates piled high with French toast and waffles, fruit salad, sausages and bacon. It all looked so good that I felt a surge of envy even though I had only just eaten.

Outside, large crowds of people milled around, jazz music playing behind them. I tapped the screen's volume arrow, turning it up so we could hear them above the music.

"We're fine as you well know," said Zeb. "There really is no need for you to call every single day. Don't you have better things to do on your honeymoon?"

Beside Sully, Sam laughed. She wore a pretty halter dress with giant sunflowers printed onto the fabric. Her usually tied back blonde hair flowed loosely over her shoulders. There was even a touch of glossy lipstick on her lips. She looked so pretty and happy. Used to Sam in her role as the town's Sheriff, I had never really seen her so girly like this.

It was nice.

"Don't worry, we'll get back on that real soon," Sam laughed, causing a flush to color Sully's face. She pinched his cheeks, laughing. "Never noticed how cute you were when you blushed."

The screen suddenly turned away from her as Sully shifted the phone's perspective to him, pushing Sam offscreen.

"That's enough of that," he said, trying to regain control of the conversation. "Segueing into a topic that isn't going to make me uncomfortable... what's everyone doing today?" he asked.

Munching that last donut, Gideon leaned forward in his seat. "Oh, you know, the usual. I've decided not to fight crime today. Going to hang up the cape and rest my superhero self."

Sully answered without blinking. "Another day off from the garage? Is business that bad?"

Gideon shrugged. "I don't think it's ever really booming. This is Montpelier, after all."

Bandit made a sound between a snort and a chuff in his version of a laugh. Unable to speak since his iPad had been hijacked, he padded off to the grass, retrieving his favorite ball, then very deliberately, he set it onto the table in front of Sully. Sully looked at the red ball and laughed.

"I guess Bandit's day will consist mostly of fetch. What about the rest of you?"

I rolled my eyes.

"Why are you asking this boring question? We're obviously doing nothing exciting. Everything's fine. In fact, it's been boring as heck since you guys left. Can't we just talk about Montréal? Like, are Canadians really that weird? Do they really finish all sentences with "ey"?" Once I'd started, I wasn't able to stop the stream of questions.

"Yes and no," came Sully's short answer. "They're just people, Chase. There's nothing special about them and they don't have any distinguishable traits apart from how they like to speak French for some reason. Sorry to disappoint you."

I must have looked more disappointed than I realized, as he shot a reassuring grin at me. "Don't worry, we'll come here together one day."

"Not if they keep playing that terrible music we won't. What's wrong with actually carrying a tune?" This had come from Gideon.

A cluster of powdered sugar had caught on his upper lip giving him a comical sugar mustache that clashed with the serious expression on his face (Gideon had a love affair with music but hated anything he deemed pretentious, which apparently included this particular kind of jazz).

"Young people and their inability to appreciate the classics." Zeb shook his head sadly. "Right there is everything wrong with the world."

Sully looked at us, an eyebrow cocked crookedly in question. "We've barely been gone two weeks. What have you done to him?"

My face went immediately bland in that expression I always used whenever I didn't want to admit to causing trouble. Problem was, Sully knew me too well even if Bandit hadn't jumped up, placing his two front paws onto the table to bark at him.

I shot Bandit a dirty look. "You little snitch."

Bandit opened his mouth in a goofy grin that turned into a yawn, dropping back onto all fours. Sully crossed his arms, still waiting for an explanation — one that he could understand. Reluctantly, I translated what my dog had said.

"It's possible that we may have asked him to referee our debates a few more times than he wanted."

"It's important to know that by 'asked' she means 'hounded'," Zeb cut in.

Sully tried not to look amused by the resigned tone in his voice. "We'll be back tomorrow, Dad. Hang in there."

"I'll try, but I'm not promising anything," Zeb said grumpily.

Sam whispered something in Sully's ear that had him standing to attention. It wasn't only Bandit who had the goofy grin on his face now. I figured I would never want to know what it was she had said. Probably something disgustingly cute

"Looks like we should get going."

"Seriously Sully, we're fine. Nothing is going to happen between now and tomorrow. Go and enjoy the last day of your honeymoon. You'll see more than enough of us when you're back," Zeb said.

Sully's eyes roamed over each of us one last time, like he was doing some kind of mental check. Finally, he nodded. "You two behave. Try not to kill my father. We'll see you all tomorrow."

We shouted goodbye — even Bandit, who howled enthusiastically — and then the screen went blank. I got up from the table and went into the kitchen to see if there was any cereal left. Spying the Cheerios box, I picked it up and shook it, relieved to hear the rustling inside. I was pouring the last of it into what was probably a mixing bowl, judging by the size of it, when the doorbell rang.

"Chase, can you get that? I've got laundry to do."

I'd had the spoon in my hand ready to dive in when Gideon's voice called out to me. Sighing, I shot the cereal a sad look and went to answer the door.

Through the frosted glass I could make out the woman outside. She wasn't wearing a suit or carrying any products, so she wasn't a saleswoman of some kind.

I opened the door.

The woman was a little taller than me with a slim dancer's body, long blonde hair and delicate features. No make-up adorned her face yet even without any help, she was naturally pretty, but it was her sapphire eyes that caught my attention, staring at me as they were in utter confusion.

Though I had never met her before, she seemed somehow familiar. She opened her mouth to speak, but no sound came out of it. She only stood there, her birdlike hands gripping onto a rucksack as if they were a lifeline.

I was about to ask what she wanted when it suddenly hit me.

I *did* know who this woman was...

And yet... it couldn't be possible.

The world started spinning around me. My mouth fell open, my face turning slack-jawed. I could feel my heart begin to pound as the blood in my veins turned to ice.

From somewhere in the back of my mind, I heard Zeb call out. "Who's at the door?"

The woman in front of me didn't move or say a word. She only stood there staring beseechingly at me — as if I would be able to explain away this madness.

I didn't know how to respond.

"I think it's best if you come here," was all I managed before my voice died in my throat.

Hearing the shock in my voice, Zeb came over, lines creasing his face. When he arrived beside me, his hands froze on the wheels of his chair.

We stood side-by-side, staring at the visitor, unable to hide the shock from either of our faces.

2
───────

SULLY

At the crack of dawn, we drove the three or so hours back from Montréal in a state of bliss.

After the stress of the last few weeks when I had almost lost not only Sam, but my entire family, the trip away had been exactly what we'd needed.

The first few days of our honeymoon, we'd never even made it out of the hotel.

If it wasn't for the Godly room service — and man, did Montreal know how to make a great brunch — we probably would have starved, no joke.

Around the third day, when we realized we should actually experience the city so that we would have something to report back to the family, we took a lazy boat ride in the Old Port.

Technically, the correct name would be Le Vieux Port, but since I sound like Bandit when he tries to speak with a mouthful of ball whenever I attempt any French words, the world rested easier when I gave in to my native tongue.

After the blue waters had relaxed our souls, we took a leisurely stroll along the boutiques that lined quaint cobblestone streets, picking up the odd trinket or gift for the kids. I was particularly taken by an arts and crafts store where a rainbow of dream catchers hung in the window. Bandit still suffered from the odd nightmare, worrying that the Bad Men would be coming after him again. I got him one of the biggest on display, hoping it would help psychologically if not realistically.

When we'd exhausted the Old Port, we tried visiting RESO, the famous interconnected underground city downtown that ran for some thirty-two kilometers.

Montreal was known for its long and punishing winters, where, for six months of the year, the city would be barraged by icy winds that kept the temperature below freezing, while the streets above would be blanketed in a sea of snow. Its citizens had come up with a creative solution to keep their lives going despite the brutal weather by building an entire city underground, one that connected to their metro system — linking up to ten stations — so that a person could walk the entire length of downtown without ever having to go up to the surface.

Excited to experience this, we'd disembarked at Peel metro and started our shopping spree.

Two hours later, I was already regretting our decision.

While the subterranean mall did not disappoint, filled to the brim with household brands sitting side-by-side with their designer cousins, it turned out shopping was a lot more exhausting than either of us had prepared ourselves for.

Back home, our local shops consisted only of the essentials. With the one grocery store that also doubled as the post office, Warrey's garage, a Dollar General where we picked up most of our household items, and a handful of eateries, we'd had to drive almost an hour to get to the nearest mall, but that was nothing compared to this behemoth.

A kaleidoscope of color assaulted our eyes, while various styles of music boomed out from the store's speakers, clashing with each other in their haste to win the war of the noises.

Then there was the general sound of the people: parents fighting with young kids, and dogs who were much less behaved than Bandit. Even the smells that drifted up from the basement food courts turned my stomach.

It was all too much for us simple folk.

Barely making it to the next metro stop, we admitted defeat, packing it in for craft beer and smoked meat sandwiches at Schwartz's, a place so renowned that it was standing room only.

Sam had discovered it on a food blog during her research where the glowing reviews numbered in the thousands. She had bookmarked the eatery, letting me know that we *would* be stopping at it during our honeymoon. After tasting their food for myself, I could certainly see why it was so popular.

I was even giving serious consideration to franchising a branch back home — if only for myself to enjoy.

On hotter days, when the sun warmed the city enough that it seemed summer was lingering around, we strolled through the stunning Botanical

Garden with its themed gardens, enjoyed the many outdoor theaters that the city freely offered, and ate until we were fit to burst.

Happy as I was, in love with my new wife as I was, I couldn't help missing the kids back home.

When we passed by a Mclaren showroom, I felt a pang that Gid wasn't there to experience it, loving sports cars as much as he did. We certainly never got those back home where it was all four wheelers and trucks. I took as many pictures as I could, but when the manager started glaring our way; we knew it was time to beat a hasty exit.

Chase was a little tougher to buy for, but not in the usual difficult teenager sense; quite the opposite, in fact. The girl had been given so little that she was grateful for *everything*. No matter how small, or how ordinary, each gift had been so happily received that I had started to doubt if she really liked the presents, or was just so glad to get something. I couldn't tell the difference. And the thing of it was, I wanted her to like the gifts I got her.

I wanted her to be happy.

She'd had so little of it growing up. It felt right that I should spoil her now.

I guess that's what happens when you become a dad. Your life isn't your own anymore. Suddenly, everything has a richer meaning, and the world feels heightened.

At least, that's how it was to me. I knew I was a pretty decent parent, unlike Chase's real mom. To think I'd trusted her to be alone with Chase.

Even now, the anger burned, turning my heart to stone.

The less I thought about her, the better. That woman didn't deserve an ounce of sympathy from anyone.

Sam sang most of the way back in that rich voice of hers, while I joined in, harmonizing perfectly. We sounded good, maybe good enough to enter one of those televised singing competitions that the kids loved to watch if we had been so inclined.

Remembering the spring when Chase, Bandit, and I had to perform on the streets of Atlantic City, I thought about how much more money we would have made if Sam had been there to sing with us. It would be such a different experience if we went there now that we had each other... and money.

Money was king, unfortunately.

Everything that happened before the honeymoon seemed like a fading nightmare. The breakup that had left me reeling, Chase and Bandit being kidnapped, Dad falling into a coma... Through it all, one thing had become clear to me: I knew without a doubt that Sam was my person.

My eyes slid over to her, taking a moment to eat up the sight of her twinkling eyes as she sang a popular country song with gusto. The woman lived her life like that. She wasn't afraid of anything. Her vivacity filled up the holes that had been left in me when I had become a widower much too young.

I was a whole man again, and I liked it.

Fall was starting to encroach on this part of the world and as we drove through Montpelier towards the ranch, the trees had started to turn. Red and gold swallowed what was left of the green. The chill in the air grew more pronounced the closer we got to home.

A snow filled winter was something Bandit had not yet experienced, but it was something Montpelier excelled in. We had attempted to explain what snow was on several occasions, but it continued to perplex him. He couldn't wrap his big old dog head around it. Picturing Bandit careening down a hill on a toboggan while Chase raced after him, I laughed.

Sam looked over at me. "Care to share the joke?"

"It was nothing, just thinking something silly."

She smiled and rested her head on my shoulder.

The miles passed easily until the ranch finally appeared, looking exactly the same as when we had left it. There was something great about that. We were home, and within seconds, we would be surrounded by our loved ones.

I couldn't wait for us to start our new lives. Maybe, if we were lucky, there would be another kid to add to our mix soon...

A baby's face popped into my mind, round and chubby with a mix of our features. I was hit with a longing so strong that I had to hold my breath. We'd briefly discussed the possibility of having our own children, but I knew we were on the same page.

Sam was as keen as I was to get going on it. We'd have to be careful how we broke the news to Chase. Despite how much we loved her, Chase's old insecurities would surface now and then, and a new baby would probably cause some of that angst to surface, until she came around to the idea at least.

When the time came, we'd be treating her with kid gloves.

I parked the car then sprinted to Sam's side. Flinging open her door, I offered my hand.

"Here you go, my lady."

She was tickled pink by my gesture. Taking hold of my hand, she let me help her out of the car. Her feet barely touched the ground before I scooped her into my arms. Her peals of laughter floated into the sky.

"Put me down before you drop me!"

"What do you mean, drop you? Do you know how much I can bench-press?"

"No. Do you?"

"Of course not. I've never bench-pressed anything in my life. What is it anyway?"

She laughed again and flung her arms around my neck, probably concerned that I really would drop her. Truthfully, my arms were already starting to ache, but I was determined to carry my new bride over the threshold. Some traditions had to be upheld.

"OK, tough guy. Five bucks says you don't make it."

"If we're going to do this, let's make it interesting. Ten bucks... *and* you do my laundry for a week." Sam hated laundry at the best of times. I thought this was a suitable enough punishment for her lack of faith in my manhood.

"You're on." Her eyes breathed life, her lips parted in a big smile.

Digging deep into my core (despite what I'd said, I had known my way around a gym a time or two so the joke was about to be on her), I crossed the distance to the front door, maybe not as easily as I'd like, but at least I got us there.

Briefly, I wondered why the others weren't here to greet us. The way I had imagined our homecoming, Bandit and Chase would dash out of the door long before I even stopped the truck. We never had many visitors in these parts, and you could usually hear a vehicle approaching. They had to have known we were back.

Since no one opened the door for us and I couldn't get it with Sam in my arms, I leaned awkwardly toward it so she could reach over and grab the handle.

She threw open the door.

We saw directly through to the lounge, where Chase sat on the couch beside a blonde woman. The two had been chatting but stopped when the door burst open.

My face broke into a welcoming smile when the blonde woman turned from Chase to look at me... and my world imploded.

It was all I could do not to drop Sam.

I stood, rooted to the spot, my smile frozen on my face.

This couldn't be real.

This couldn't be happening.

Sensing my shock, Sam's eyes darted to me, unable to hide the concern in them. When she couldn't understand what was causing my distress, she twisted back to the blonde.

"What's going on?" She finally asked. "Who is that, Sully?"

I couldn't speak.

My mouth had turned sandpit dry. I wasn't in control over any part of my body. The blood pounded through my temple, threatening to pop a vein.

The blonde got up off the couch and took a step towards us.

"I'm Emma," she said, answering Sam.

"I'm Sully's wife."

3

———

SULLY

I couldn't move.

In the back of my mind, I could hear a voice speaking into my ear, asking what was going on, but I had shut down, unable to process what was standing in front of me.

The blonde approached us.

With every step, her familiar face assaulted my senses. Those beautiful gem-like eyes and sweet cherry lips were exactly as I had remembered them.

Even her movements were familiar: she'd always had the grace of a dancer, while I seemed as clumsy as an oaf in comparison. She glided toward me, an impossible apparition, and one which I had seen on multiple occasions after her death.

But this time, she was real.

Her chest moved as the breath went in and out of her body. Her golden hair glistened as the light bounced off the strands that tumbled over her shoulder. She was as familiar to me as the air.

The one thing that was odd — other than the fact that my dead wife was standing in front of me — was the confused expression in her eyes, which must have mirrored my own.

I was yet to say a word.

My arm muscles, aching at first, were now cramping up a storm. Unceremoniously — though completely by necessity — I had to set Sam down. She buckled a bit, not ready to be dumped onto the ground so abruptly.

Her eyes flared open, shock radiating through her.

"Emma? But that's not possible..." I barely recognized my voice, pushing toward hysteria as it was.

Was I experiencing a nervous breakdown as a delayed response to losing my wife? Had I imagined everything that had come to pass in the last six months?

And yet, there was Chase coming toward me, as real as anything I had ever seen. In her face shone the sympathy she directed not only at me, but Sam as well. As usual, Bandit was only a few steps behind, whining a greeting that carried his own confusion.

"Sully," Chase began, then broke off as she tried to find the words that were tripping over her tongue. "She turned up here yesterday, after our call..."

She fell silent again, her hands clasped together. Even from here, I could see how white they were. She must have been squeezing them so tight.

"Chase has been trying to explain everything that's happened in the last year and a half, but I can't remember any of it. I don't even remember you," the blonde said in Emma's voice.

My dead wife's voice.

"I need to sit down," Sam said suddenly.

Her eyes were glazed over, her lips had turned white. She was in shock and that scared me. For the time I'd known her, Sam always had her wits about her, so to see her like this...

This had to be real.

Somehow, my wife, the woman who had died some eighteen months ago, whose body had been ravaged by cancer and which I had watched be buried into the ground — was back.

Sam went to the couch.

Taking a seat at the end of the floral couch that my mom had loved, Chase sat beside her, reached over, and took her hand. Sam shot her a quick, grateful look, then flicked her eyes back to Emma.

Searching for something to say, anything I could grab a hold of, I finally addressed *her*. "If you don't remember me, how did you get here?"

"The pictures in the bag. I found them when I woke up," she answered cryptically.

I tried to focus on one thing at a time as everything seemed too difficult right now. What had she just said? "What pictures?"

Emma retrieved a bag that had been sitting on the floor. It was a cheap navy bag, the kind of thing you could pick up at a dollar store, with an orange label. She rummaged inside until she came up with a handful of photographs that she held out to me.

"Here," she said. "Look."

I looked down at the thirty or so pictures she held in her hand, unable to take them from her, as I was afraid to touch her. I didn't want to know how a dead wife — who had returned from the grave — would feel.

Turning my attention downward, the pictures swam into view.

Faces floated up at me, our faces. There Emma and I were on one of our first dates at a local drive-in theater. Taken by a helpful passer-by, the picture framed us in the seats of the battered Ford truck I had driven at the time.

While Zeb and I had patched up our differences now, back then, we hadn't been speaking. My parents were a renowned surgeon and respected medical researcher. With their support and backing, it was always decided that I would follow in their footsteps to become a surgeon myself, but my heart had been drawn to another path...

One that had led to Emma.

I waited for the thought to shift, trying to focus on the memories that sat in her hands. Whether we were in a far-flung location experiencing one of the many exotic vacations we loved to take, hosting barbecues at the clinic during our July 4th celebration, or doing something as humdrum as painting a room in our recently bought house: in all the pictures, we were laughing, blissfully happy and in love.

My head felt like it would explode.

It wasn't only Emma's presence here that was impossible. The very pictures themselves shouldn't have existed: they had turned to ashes in the fire that had consumed the clinic and our home.

But here they were, as solidly in her hand as the woman herself.

I looked up at this woman and saw she was exactly the same as my wife in the pictures.

My hands started shaking. Tears blurred my vision, though I wasn't sure why I was crying. I couldn't tell whether they were tears of happiness...

Or fear.

Chase, who had been respectfully and unusually quiet until now, suddenly spoke.

"Emma doesn't know what happened to her or where she came from. But she woke up not far from here with that bag beneath her head. Aside from those pictures, she had some water and some energy bars."

Her voice broke as if she were struggling to complete her sentence. Tearing my gaze from Emma, my eyes slid over to Chase. She had that grave expression I had only seen a few times before, the last being when her mom had turned up unexpectedly at the door.

"I recognize that bag, Sully," Chase began, her voice heavy with concern. "It was the same one I woke up with when I found myself in the woods."

Sam turned to Chase, her work self kicking in. "What're you saying, exactly?"

Chase's eyes grew round.

"Remember the big experiment Xavier boasted about? I think, somehow, he managed to bring Emma back."

$$4$$

SULLY

One year and two months, over ten thousand hours or some six hundred thousand minutes.

That's how long Emma had been dead for, how long she had been buried, six feet under the ground.

Depending on where you went to for your source of information, there were either four or five stages of decay for a body. Suffice to say, either way, there would not be much of my Emma left. My muddled mind clung to these facts, repeating them over and over inside my head.

"How did you know how to find us if you can't remember Sully?"

This had come from Sam.

Some color had come back into her cheeks as she fought to gain some manner of control. Despite the shock we were all feeling, Sam the Sheriff was about to take charge. I couldn't have been more relieved and didn't feel a lick of shame about it.

Emma turned to Sam, looking her up and down, biting her lip, uncomfortable by the question and the tone which came along with it.

"I followed the path, then the signs to the town and showed people the pictures. It wasn't until I came to one man that he told me where you were. He looked at me strangely, but I didn't know why. I didn't like him," she added, her lips pursing into a pout.

"It seems an unlikely thing for someone in town to give a complete stranger our home address." Sam didn't bother to hide the scepticism in her voice. Somewhere in the back of my mind, I felt myself wanting to laugh hysterically. Of all the things that had happened in the last five minutes, *this* is what she questioned?

"Well, he did," Emma said, somewhat petulantly. "He said something about not being surprised, then told me exactly where you would all be."

Through the fog of bewilderment I found myself in, I suddenly knew exactly who she was referring to. "Was he a mechanic? Owns a garage in town?"

Emma nodded. I looked over at Sam. "Warrey. He's never liked me. Probably hoped I lied to you about Emma. He doesn't know she is... about my situation." I finished quickly, not wanting to insult or scare her even though I understood how ludicrous that was, given how pretty damn scared I felt myself right now.

Emma eyed me with the open curiosity of a child, taking in my features. She leaned in so close to me that I felt myself flinching.

"Why can't I remember you? Shouldn't I be able to remember my husband?" she asked, as if I was still hers.

Reaching up, she traced a finger along my jawline, though there was nothing sexy or loving about the gesture. Then her head came up close to my neck as she started to *sniff me?*

A thought jolted through me, filling me with unease. I stepped back away from her. Her fingers fell away from my face.

Feeling suddenly unsteady, I moved away from her, stopping by Chase on the couch.

"What exactly have you explained to her... to Emma?" Her name stick in my throat, thick and cloying.

Chase's expression changed, her lips twisting into a nervous, apologetic smile. "Just that you *were* her husband, but that she's been... gone a while."

My heart sank.

As I suspected, Chase had left the tough talk to me.

"There's obviously some discussion that needs to happen. A lot has changed since you were last... here," Sam said quietly.

"I've been here before? I don't remember this house either?" Misunderstanding Sam's meaning, Emma's eyes swept the area, trying to place the house in her mind.

"That's not what I — Listen, I know this is going to be hard for you to understand, but you still need to hear it: I'm Sully's wife now. We actually just returned from our honeymoon."

Emma's face turned stricken. As the news sank in, another emotion took over. She spun to face me, eyes blazing with heat, crossing the room to me in several quick strides.

"You married another woman? What kind of man does that when his wife disappears? Did you even look for me?"

With every question, she jabbed her finger at my chest until I finally caught her hand in mine, not wanting her to hurt herself. Her hands felt cool to the touch, but they also felt *real*.

They felt alive.

I dropped them as if they were hot coals.

"That's not what happened... You don't understand. You're... You died."

"I'm obviously not dead, am I? I'm standing right here." Emma blinked at me, confusion turning her blue eyes hazy.

"But you did die, Emma. I watched it happen. Buried you myself."

She laughed at me, finding my words ludicrous, but when no one else joined in, her smile faded. I plowed on, knowing what needed to be said, however impossible this conversation might be.

"You had cancer. We couldn't cure it. When you finally passed, the disease had eaten away most of you."

Anger flashed across her face. She glared at each one of us. "This isn't funny. Why are you people doing this? This is cruel. Just because I don't remember anything doesn't mean you can make fun of me."

"We're not picking on you. He's telling the truth. I just didn't know how to tell you," Chase pointed out gently.

"I grieved for you a long time." I needed her to know that, whatever good that would do.

"Clearly not that long if you married someone else!"

"I didn't meet Sam until a year after you had died."

Tears misted in her eyes as she struggled to accept what I was saying. "So you're saying you thought I was dead for over a year?"

"It'll be two years in December. And you did die. You died right before Christmas."

A gasp came from Chase. I didn't realize she hadn't known this until now. Sympathy poured out of her as Bandit whined his own platitudes. Emma's head shook left and right, unable to accept the news.

"You're not making sense. I didn't die. I can't have died if I'm here."

"Well, we don't really know what you are right now," Sam answered in a gentle tone normally reserved for toddlers.

"*What* I am? So not only am I dead, now I'm not even human?"

Her voice went up a notch, hysteria not far behind.

"That's not what Sam's suggesting. None of us have any answers right now. I don't think we can jump to any conclusions. We all need time to get used to you being here again." Chase sounded far more mature than her years.

Emma's lower lip trembled, those glistening sapphire eyes of hers threatening to spill over with tears.

"I don't remember anything before I woke up, but I know I have feelings for you. You feel familiar to me."

She grabbed my hand, placing it against her heart. I could feel it beating beneath her chest. *Thump... thump... thump...*

And that terrified me.

Wrenching my hands away, I stepped back from her even as she stared at me with such betrayal that I almost fell. The world tilted on its axis. I felt as if the ground might come rushing up to me when I felt a strong presence by my side.

Sam.

She had left the couch and come to my side, where she was now silently giving me her moral and physical support. I sagged against her, taking in her strength as my own.

Bandit stood up and whined. Padding over to Emma, it seemed he wanted to offer some form of comfort, but as he came near her, his steps faltered. He stopped just short of touching her, his nose wrinkling as he sniffed the surrounding air cautiously. Taking out his iPad, he typed.

"She does not smell right."

Emma glared down at him, apparently unsurprised that the dog was communicating with them in such a manner. "Well, you don't exactly smell great either," she snapped before turning her eyes back to the rest of us.

"I came to you for help, not for all these questions or judgement. You need to help me because I've nowhere else to go."

Her eyes glittered with feeling. She was either the best actress I'd ever come across, or she truly was as scared and desperate as she seemed. Sam must have come to the same conclusion as she softened her voice.

"I can go to the office and see if I can dig anything up?" She offered, but I shook my head.

"We're not going to find anything about her. Whoever is behind this isn't going to register her."

The whir of Zeb's wheelchair interrupted our conversation. He came into the room, Gideon at his side.

"Welcome back," Gideon said. "I see you've met our predicament. Seems Zeb spoke too soon when he said nothing would come up before your return."

Gideon's flippant attitude might have raised a few eyebrows, but I didn't rise to it, knowing this was his way of dealing with a pressure filled environment.

My dad shot me a sympathetic smile. "I had hoped to welcome you with better news after your vacation. I'm sorry that this is what you had to come back to."

Hurt flashed over Emma's face as her eyes turned to flint. "You think I want to be here? You people could be crooks for all I know. I came to you for help, but if all you're going to do is stand there being mean to me, then I'm better off alone."

She shoved the photos back into her bag. She was walking toward the exit when the door exploded inward, sending her flying back. She fell onto the floor, her body landing with a thud as a high-pitched ringing sounded in my ears.

Smoke and debris filled the air. I found myself coughing after inhaling a lung full of smoke. "What the hell?"

After making sure that Bandit was safely behind the sofa where he had naturally darted to, Chase sprinted to Emma's side, tugging on her arm to help her up.

Her eyes were glazed over with shock. Other than that, she seemed unharmed, at least from what I could tell by a cursory glance.

Gideon had acted fast, shielding Zeb from the blast with his own body. Recovering faster than I could give him credit for, Gideon sprinted behind cover, pushing Zeb's wheelchair with him, while Sam had darted out of harm's way herself, flattening against the wall, keeping herself out of sight from the entrance where a gaping hole now stood.

All that was left of the front door were the shards of splintered wood that now littered the floor, and the blackened hinges, which swung at an angle, attached to the frame by a single, solitary screw.

Sam and I shared a tense look.

I signaled silently, letting her know that I would move forward to scope out the area. She nodded, though she didn't seem happy by my decision. Using the smoke for cover, I eased my way to the front in a crouch-walk, keeping myself low to the ground.

Through the clouds, I could see movement outside.

First, I could only spot the one figure, but as the smoke began to clear, the hazy figures multiplied at a rapid pace. Fear clutched at my heart when I saw our front yard littered with black-clad men.

And a flashback of my clinic crashed into my head.

In my mind's eye, I saw Forbes' men — led by that ruthless mercenary — come crashing into my clinic armed with shotguns.

Blinking, I forced the memory away, knowing I needed to deal with this new nightmare. Details flew at me. I took in their all-black military-like outfits. Belts made out of bullets and magazine clips were slung casually across their bodies as if they were some kind of utility fashion item. They stood stock still, several feet away, their eyes hidden behind yellow-lensed glasses that made them look like bugs.

Even as I realized this, I wondered why none of the men were moving.

Why would they break down our front door only to stand there? What were they waiting for?

Then my gaze lowered to the long range sniper rifles they each held in their hands.

Sniper rifles that they were now aiming into the house.

"Get away from the windows!" I yelled, waving at the others, frantically signaling for them to back away. "Get down!"

"What is it?" Gideon screamed out.

"They have snipers," I managed to warn before my voice gave way to the stark terror that rose up inside. Before, when Forbes's men had come, they had only the one objective — to take Bandit back.

My eyes flicked over to him betraying my thoughts, as Chase immediately sprinted to Bandit's side. Trouble may have loved company, but it seemed to love our beloved dog more. Pulling him behind the couch, they flattened against the floor when a hail of silenced bullets impaled the wall above them. Plaster fell off in chunks, leaving them wearing a coat of white dust.

"That's too close for a warning shot," Sam called over.

"Then what are they doing?" Chase cried, the whites of her eyes looking abnormally bright.

"I think they're trying to kill us," Sam finished.

The hairs on the back of my neck rose. I felt everything as if it were amplified. We were under attack *again*. Though this time, they didn't want Bandit alive.

This time, they wanted him dead.

"Well, let's not make it easy for them." I replied grimly.

Turning to Zeb and Gideon, I gestured to the far wall uttering the three words I had hoped never to say.

"Contingency Plan A!"

5

———

CHASE

H earing those words come out of Sully's mouth, I knew we were in trouble.

Big trouble.

The kind we might never be able to get out of.

We had been against this hard place before, and after that first time, then what happened with Mom and Xavier, Sully swore that we'd never be taken by surprise again.

Clearly, he had been wrong on that front.

This time, though, we were at least partially prepared for it.

Over by the west side of the room, Sam's hand was already reaching behind the bookshelf she was using as cover.

I didn't need to carry on watching to see what she would find: I knew the handgun that lived there, nestled in a holster that Sully had fastened to the bookshelf during one long weekend after Xavier had been caught. Before the wedding, when unhappy that he and Sam would be leaving us for their honeymoon, he had decided we would erect secret defenses around the place.

Of course, our weapons hadn't come to much use when Xavier had broken in, since none of us had been here to use them. Zeb had been alone when he had attacked, putting him into a coma that we'd thought he'd never come out of, which, luckily had only lasted a few days.

Tearing my thoughts from the past, I focused on what I needed to do. Bandit's stomach was pressed to the floor in the way Sully had taught him when we'd been going through our contingency plans. Gideon had mocked him at first, sure that our problems were over. Tossing him a look, I saw that he was as glad as I was that Sully had forced us to learn the drill.

We'd practiced only a handful of times, but we seemed to remember what was expected of us. *Only grab a weapon if you can*, came Sam's voice in my head. The safest way to survive an attack was to hide. I was only to fire a weapon if I was forced to fight.

Seeing those black-clad figures outside, the ones who I would still wake up in the middle of the night fearful of, I knew without a doubt that running wasn't an option.

I heard a whimper and thought that it had come from Bandit until his tongue snaked out to lick my hand, offering what comfort he could. There was no time for him to use his iPad. No time for anything other than to find the weapon that was closest to me.

But in the madness of the moment, my brain froze, and I found myself unable to remember where it was.

Snapping around to Sully, I saw he was busy locating his own gun, a rifle that stood upright, half-hidden in the umbrella stand. Gideon was scrambling to the kitchen, where several more handguns were hidden in various drawers and cupboards.

My hands felt like claws. I was so scared. The last time I had used a gun, I had killed a man. Though he had deserved it, the memory of it had haunted me for months after. I wasn't sure if I would be able to do it again.

Hearing the weakness in my thoughts, I clamped down on them.

My family needed me! This was no time to be scared. I had to fight for them. I had to protect them, the same way they protected me.

Knowing I'd get strength from Bandit, I turned to him, expecting to see those loving eyes of his on mine. Instead, his attention was on the space beneath the couch: specifically the floor, which he scratched at pretty frantically. I wasted a few precious seconds wondering what he was doing when it suddenly came to me.

Hunkering down, I reached beneath the couch, feeling around the wooden slats until my fingers closed around the Glock that was taped to the underside of the sofa.

This was what my Muttface had been trying to tell me if only I'd been listening.

Taking hold of the gun, I ripped it away. There was a thirty-round mag inserted into the gun. The metal felt cold in my hand and heavy with the weight of the world.

My fingers tightened around the metal. I got back onto my feet into a crouch.

"Stay low," I hissed at Bandit. He nodded, not wanting to make a sound in case it would give our hiding place away. The air was so thick with tension that I could feel it. Our group waited, each of us armed with a weapon except for Emma.

When the door had exploded, she hadn't moved. I hadn't even thought about what I was doing. I just found myself by her side, yanking her down since she seemed unable to do so on her own. She had yelped, startled by my forceful tug, but now that she was down, she had curled into a tight ball, her hands wrapped around her head.

A soft mewling sound came out of her. She sounded like a terrified child.

Silence had fallen in the house. You could hear a pin drop. During our drills, Sully had commanded us not to fire until either he or Sam gave the command. It was always best not to engage if there was any kind of chance that we could escape.

I clutched my weapon, biting my lip until I tasted the rusty iron of blood. I watched, holding my breath, as Sully hesitated. I could see his mind ticking over our options when— *pffffftttttttttt.*

A silenced bullet hit the television, causing it to explode in a burst of electricity.

More silenced bullets whistled through the air above my head. A lamp shattered, caught by one of the stray bullets. The sound as loud as a thunderclap.

Sully's eyes turned flat.

"Shoot them!"

And with that one command, I aimed my weapon outside and let rip.

6

SULLY

This was it.

This was the end.

The over-powering smell of gunpowder swamped the low-ceilinged room, filling my nose and making my eyes water.

Steel flashing from her eyes, Chase popped up from behind the couch, firing shots through the doorway, before ducking down again.

The extra large magazine she had taped next to her firearm ensured she wouldn't have to reload soon. We made sure that this was the case with every weapon we owned. Sam had taught us that ducking out of view would make it more difficult for any attackers to hit us with their shots. It was one of the first lessons in gun fighting we ever learned.

The longer you stayed in view, the more chance you had of getting hit.

A flash of blonde hair caught the corner of my eye, drawing my attention to the far side of the room where Sam took aim. Her lips were a thin, tight line. A frown creased her forehead, but other than that, she looked impossibly calm and composed.

I knew better than anyone that looks were deceiving.

The more stressed Sam became, the quieter and calmer she seemed. It was a tactic she had cultivated to throw criminals off the scent, and I was sure it was working now. If the men who hunted us outside could see her face, maybe they would be taken aback by her lack of fear.

Maybe they would back away.

Wishful thinking.

Through the chaos, I took in the faces of the people I loved, desperately wishing that we had more time together.

I saw my dad fighting so bravely from his wheelchair, Gideon by his side. He handed Gideon bullets while the boy aimed and took fire for all he was worth.

Bullets sprayed out of his gun and out of the window. Glass smashed, raining onto the floor around his booted feet, but Gideon kept his aim sharp, his eyes glued to the enemy outside.

When one gun was empty, he silently handed it to Zeb to refill while he picked up another of the several handguns he had taken from the kitchen. The old man's sight wasn't great, his aim was even worse, but even with those handicaps, he was making himself useful.

Sam, who was the next closest to the opening, fired again. I felt a grim satisfaction when I heard a man's grunt of pain, followed by the sight of his spray of blood that splashed onto the porch's faded floorboards.

I didn't know why these men wanted us dead, but that they were here at all meant we were enemies. Neanderthal as it may have seemed, it was us or them.

And it sure as hell would not be us.

Someone whimpered close by and I knew instinctively that it was Emma. I turned, searching across the war zone that our living room was fast turning into as plant pots and furniture exploded, showering debris all over the floor.

Emma had crawled behind a table where she huddled, her eyes wide and frightened like a child. While the rest of us defended our home with everything that we had, Emma only sat hunched over, arms wrapped around her knees, unable to move.

Her terror was palpable, yet I couldn't think about her — not with everything else that was happening. So, I tore my eyes away, to find the face of the woman I now called my wife.

She had stopped firing, realizing that our shorter ranged weapons weren't doing much against their snipers. In fact, it suddenly occurred to me it was stupid to even try.

One wrong move and they would have us in their crosshairs.

Sam suddenly darted to the nearest window and drew the curtains closed.

"Block the windows! They can't shoot us if they can't see us!" she instructed.

Moving as fast as I could, I closed the curtains around the windows on my side of the room while Gideon helped Sam with hers. In the murky half-light that remained, nothing felt real. I was in a nightmare that surely I would wake up from any second now.

A noise came from behind, raising the hackles on my neck.

Spinning around, I raised my gun, ready to blast the scumbag to kingdom come until I saw the two familiar figures sneaking around the kitchen.

Chase and Bandit.

They were scrambling across the kitchen floor, staying low to avoid getting hit. I watched as Chase grabbed a hand towel, shoved it into the sink, then turned the taps on full. The metal of the taps glistened, encased by the flowing water that now flowed around the worktop, soaking the floor tiles.

What was she doing?

Was she was trying to flood the house? What would that solve? The questions ran through my mind until it suddenly occurred to me — she wasn't trying to drown our home. She wanted to protect us in case the men tried to set the place ablaze. She was making sure we wouldn't be trapped inside a burning building.

This thought hadn't come out of nowhere, but from our previous defense of the ranch, when, with our backs up against the wall, we had improved Molotov cocktails using Zeb's prized moonshine.

But we had none of that now.

The moonshine — which had taken Zeb months to perfect — was long gone, but Chase, in her infinite wisdom, was covering the floor with water and giving us an extra chance at survival.

She was buying us time.

My heart swelled with pride even as I knew it was pointless to resist any more. What could we do against a skilled team of killers? We had been lucky to escape the last attack by Forbes's men, but we wouldn't be so fortunate a second time.

"Sam," I called out above the noise. "We need to get out. We'll never survive this."

"They have the front blocked. Pretty sure they'll be pushing us from the back if they haven't started to already," she said.

Bobbing and weaving, I ran to the other side of the room, keeping away from those windows as best I could, knowing that obscuring their vision might not be a foolproof way of protecting us since they could still shoot through the thin material.

The smell of powder hung in the air. Across the front yard, the shooters were moving with urgency, forming a tight semi-circle as they advanced toward us. In addition to their snipers, they now carried riot shields they held out before them in a defensive black wall. The shields were full length, covering them from head-to-toe. Their heads, along with their bodies, were completely hidden from view. With almost no place we could shoot them, things were looking really bad for us.

I racked my brain, trying to come up with a solution that would keep us alive when a hail of bullets tore through the walls and windows. Emma screamed, her cry piercing the air, cutting through my terror.

"Back up," I hissed at my family, reaching out to grab the handlebars of Zeb's wheelchair. He kept himself bent so low, his head almost touched his knees as I wrestled with his chair, trying to get him as far away from those shooters as possible.

I was almost to the kitchen before I noticed only Gideon and Sam still with me. Chase and Bandit had gone ahead, vanishing from view, but it was the figure crouching beneath a table that caused my heart to leap into my throat.

Emma hadn't moved.

I wasted a moment, scanning my eyes up and down her body, expecting to see blood blossoming from a gunshot wound, but there was no injury that I could find. She was just scared: too scared to come out from there.

Sam read the expression on my face. The blood left her face, leaving her white as a sheet. "No!" she uttered when I bolted toward Emma.

More shots flew in, ricocheting off the walls, eating up a path everywhere they hit. A bullet went past my head, so close that pain exploded in my right ear. All sound dulled in that ear as a high-pitched whine took over.

I knew I must have been hit, but assumed the bullet hadn't done too much damage as I was still standing. Keeping my eyes glued to Emma, I sprinted to her side, taking hold of her hand.

"Come on," I said urgently, tugging her along. But she resisted, using her body weight to pull away from me.

"Leave me alone!" she yelled. "This has nothing to do with me!"

I spared a quick glance at the open doorway. The row of men were seconds from breaching the house. We had to go... *now.*

"We don't have time for this," I hissed through gritted teeth. Hauling her onto her feet, I tossed her over my shoulder as if she wasn't more than a sack of potatoes.

She struggled against me, out of her mind with fear. Although she must have known that I was trying to keep her safe, she resisted every step of the way, pummelling my back with her small fists.

"Let me go!" she screamed until I set her down with the others.

I caught the furious look Sam shot me and turned away. I'd have to deal with her anger later — if there was a later. Looking through the small window in the kitchen, I saw another row of the shielded men.

Jesus.

They were everywhere.

We couldn't go out either end, and since we lived in a ranch, there was no upstairs we could flee to either, even if it would trap us on an upper floor.

We were out of options and time.

My tongue felt thick in my mouth. I was struggling to form the words to our predicament. While we could split up and hide, that would buy us mere seconds at best, and try as I might, I wasn't ready to separate the family. If we were going to die, then it would be together.

My eyes scanned the group, memorizing each beloved face, when I noticed two were still missing.

My heart near stopped by the realization.

"Where are Chase and Bandit?" I asked, a sick feeling in the pit of my stomach.

Shocked silence greeted me, only to be quickly replaced by a furious rumbling from outside.

The house seemed to quake from the ground up as something big and fast came hurtling toward the ranch. Before I had a chance to react, the western wall of the room disintegrated into rubble when an armored truck careened right through it, mowing down several armed men who had just stepped into the house.

Dust and rubble fogged the air, turning it thick and making it impossible to breathe without choking. I coughed, fear clouding my mind as I considered what fresh horror this could be when the driver's door flew open and a familiar - and beloved head - leaned out of it.

"What are you waiting for?" Chase cried. "Get in!"

I gaped at her in astonishment. How the heck had she gotten outside, and where had the truck come from?

"Come on idiots, get in before they come after us!"

Shooting to my feet, I grabbed Zeb's wheelchair and sprinted to her. "In the truck. Now!" I yelled at everyone else.

Despite the stunned faces, they all — even Emma — did as instructed.

We climbed into the truck as Chase slammed the door shut. Stepping on the gas, burning rubber so that the tires squealed, we tore out of the place we called home.

7

CHASE

I floored it.

My hands gripped the wheel so tightly I thought my fingers would snap off. I had only driven a few times before - thanks to some lessons with Gideon - so I wasn't entirely comfortable driving this humongous thing, but I was doing my best to keep my concerns to myself, what with the army of bad guys hot on our heels.

Bandit sat beside me, stomach pressed to his seat. He kept his head beneath the window, beneath the line of sight. His intelligent eyes fixed on me, silently urging me on as he pricked his ears and scanned the area, listening for any sign of approaching trouble.

The truck I had stolen was a bit of a beast, made from some kind of rein-forced metal that meant it wasn't even dented, not even after ramming into the side of a house. And it wasn't only the outside that was impressive: the inside was a thing of beauty too.

The interior walls were lined with custom shelves that were filled with ammo of all kinds. I recognized the .38 specials that Gideon used in his revolvers, mixed in with .45s, but some grew to wickedly big sizes, almost the same length as my phone. A chill went through me as I wondered why anyone would ever need bullets *that* big: they looked like they could take down an elephant.

Had they been meant for us?

Shoving the horrifying thought from my mind, I looked into the rearview mirror so I could see directly into the attached cabin where the others were doing their best to strap Zeb's wheelchair to one the steel benches, secured to the truck's sides. The benches had extendable seatbelts for extra security. Directly opposite from them was an office of sorts.

There was a metal table where a high-tech looking laptop, that was connected to several flat screen monitors, sat. From my quick glance, I also spotted a weird-looking phone and what seemed to be a map.

Lowering onto a bench, Sam was reaching for her own seatbelt when she saw Emma, struggling to stay upright in the middle of the cabin. There was a glazed look in her eyes, like she wasn't really seeing anything.

I knew she was in shock, though she seemed to have enough of her faculties around her to know that she didn't trust any of us. This apparently led her to the decision to stay as far away from us as she could.

Sam called over to her. "You need to sit down before you hurt yourself."

Emma tossed her a terrified look. "Who are those men? Why are you kidnapping me?!"

Sam's eyes turned bright with annoyance.

"We're trying to keep you safe! Sit down before you get yourself killed."

Emma looked as if she wanted to argue back. She chewed on her lower lip making no move to comply. It was only when the truck went over a rough part of the road, causing her to almost lose her balance, that she took a seat by Sam — though far enough away that there was an empty space between them.

Sam waited, but Emma made no move to secure herself. "You need to strap yourself in," she hissed.

Emma shot her a look of confusion..

"Strap myself into what?"

Gritting her teeth, Sam grabbed the seatbelt that was fixed onto the wall of the truck, wrapping it around the other woman and clipping it into place.

"You don't know how to use a seatbelt?" asked Sam.

Emma's only response was to look down at her hands. It seemed she really hadn't understood what Sam had instructed her to do. Bracing her hands on either side of her, Sam waited for someone to break the silence that smothered the truck.

"At least we can fight back. Should be a while before we run out of bullets," I said over my shoulder, hoping to break the tension between them. Of course, this was a mistake as the truck swerved beneath my hands. My heart plummeted to my stomach as I tried to straighten up. The truck felt so unwieldy, but we didn't have time to stop and change drivers: in the side mirrors, I could see the men piling into three identical trucks.

"Get ready, they're coming," I yelled. *Why couldn't they just leave us alone?*

A deathly silence greeted my warning until Gideon's voice broke it. There was a new stressed tone in it I didn't like.

"I don't have my guns," he admitted.

"Why not?" I cried out, flicking my eyes to him briefly, then wishing I hadn't when I saw the sick look on his face.

"I dropped them to help Zeb."

"I'm empty, too," Sully echoed his words, seeming to shrink before us. Sam was looking his way with a knowing expression.

"He had to drop it when he went to save Emma," she said. Her voice wasn't loud but carried the weight of an anvil that might as well be dropping on my head.

"Are you telling me Sam's the only one with a weapon?"

I pretty much shrieked out the question, but I couldn't help it, having to leave my gun behind when I crawled out of the basement window with Bandit in order to steal the truck.

They didn't bother to ask where mine was, having figured out that I didn't have it. What did it matter where it had gotten to? We had one weapon between the seven of us. Our chance of survival was less than zero at this point.

Suddenly, a barrage of hailstones pelted the truck, leaving crater-like dents in its metal frame. One after the other, they clattered against the vehicle. The awful noise reverberated around the truck, deafening us, causing Bandit to howl next to me. Dogs had much better hearing than we did, so if the noise was affecting me so badly, I can only imagine how painful it was for him.

Examining one dent, Gideon suddenly gasped. "The truck's bulletproof!" He yelled, his voice filled with a sudden excitement.

Sully reached out his hand to touch the wall when several more dents appeared right beneath his fingertips. He yanked his hand back, but it wasn't necessary — the bullets could not make it through the reinforced metal.

"He's right," Sully said, relief turning his face slack. His shoulders sagged, letting go of the tension that had kept his back ramrod straight. "They can't hit us through the truck."

"Then why are they shooting at us? Wouldn't they know that?" I asked.

A furrow creased Zeb's forehead as he studied the trajectory of the dents. "I think they're trying to get wheels. And maybe Chase too. It's possible the glass isn't bulletproof."

At this revelation, I felt super vulnerable sitting in-between several large panes of glass.

"Not that I want to be the bearer of more bad news," I began, "but we're driving across an open field right now. There aren't even trees that can hide us: there's no way I can lose them."

Sully glanced out of his nearest window, his eyes turning black with seriousness. "We need to stop them from following us."

"I'm not liking our chances of taking potshots at them with only the one gun," Gideon began.

Scanning the cabin, Sully's eyes alighted on a metal box that sat on the desk beside the laptop.

He suddenly smiled, eyes glinting with hardness. "We won't have to. I've a better idea."

8

———

SULLY

Sprinting to the box, I lifted it carefully from the desk, eyeing the small oval objects with a mix of fear and reverence.

"Chase, I'm going to need you to keep the truck as steady as you can, OK?"

Hearing the gravity in my voice, she tried to crane her head to me.

"No! Keep your eyes up front," I yelled at her. "Keep it steady and straight, you understand? Our lives depend on you doing that.

Chase gaped at me in the rearview mirror. "What's going on? What's happening?"

"Are you thinking what I think you're thinking?" Sam asked, her eyes wide and round as she stared at the box's contents.

"Son?" Zeb asked, a world of understatement in that one-worded question.

"Holy crap," Gideon exclaimed, sending Chase's hackles rising.

"Someone needs to explain what is going on before I totally lose it!" she yelled as Bandit barked in agreement, sounding as peeved as she was.

"Chase, I've found a box of grenades."

She didn't immediately answer. Needing a moment for my words to sink in. I grabbed the box of grenades, carefully handing them to Sam. "Hold on to these a sec."

Moving back to the table, I grabbed the laptop, sliding it to the back of the cabin as I tipped the table onto its side. It was wide enough that it came up to my shoulder. Grabbing onto the corner, I half pushed, half shoved the table across the floor until it was positioned in front of the gate. It wasn't much, but I hoped it would provide some form of protection.

"When I say ready, Gideon, I'm going to need you to slide up the back gate. Sam, keep yourself strapped in, but I need you to hold on tight to my belt, so I don't get tossed if we hit a bump or something."

Chase blinked several times, her face growing paler by the second.

"*That's the plan?* You're going to lob grenades at them? What is this, Call of Duty? What if you miss? What if one of them falls out of your hand and rolls back into the cab with us?"

She was voicing the concerns I had already run through my head, but I needed to keep them all calm — Chase most of all — since she was the one responsible for keeping the ride smooth.

"None of that will happen if you focus on the driving. This is all we have to fight back with Chase, so that's what it's got to be. Sam, Gid, get ready."

"No!" Emma shouted suddenly, sprinting back and forth like a trapped animal. "You're all crazy! I don't want to get blown up. Let me out!"

As if she was going to leap over the seats, she ran towards Chase, but Bandit snapped his head around to her, growling fiercely and baring his fangs in warning. Stopping her short. He was smart enough to know what Emma wasn't — that her panic could distract Chase into crashing the truck.

She shirked away from him, retreating to her corner, scared out of her mind, but at least, out of the way for the moment.

Gideon's fear was palpable as he moved away from Dad and towards the back of the truck. Sam sat back in her seat, her trembling hands indicating her anxiety about my plan; although she knew we had no alternatives, that didn't mean she wanted to do it. She fiddled with the belt buckle until it locked into place.

These men had forced us into a terrible position. They were forcing my hand.

Trying not to think about the devastation I was about to cause, I made my way to the gate. As I ducked behind the table shield, Sam looped her fingers through my belt until she had a strong grip on me. Raising her eyes to mine, she gave me a terse smile.

"Give them hell."

My heart swelled with so much love for her it almost brought tears to my eyes. What a woman.

I spared a look in Chase's direction. "Let me know when you're ready, Chase."

"Oh God, Oh God, Oh God," she chanted in a panic. "Wait! Give me a second."

I kept quiet, giving Chase a few seconds to think, although our time was limited. Our only hope was to take out these criminals as quickly as possible and make our escape. Finally, after what seemed like an eternity, Chase nodded.

"I'm as good as I'll ever be."

I turned my focus to Gideon. "Ready?"

Gideon nodding, not trusting himself to speak. His hands hovered over the switch that would raise the gate. Opening my legs wider, I bent my knees, taking a bigger stance, hoping it would help keep my balance should anything happen.

I took hold of the first grenade and carefully placed it into the pocket of my hoodie, making sure the pin couldn't accidentally be knocked out. The metal was bitingly cold, and the grenade felt a lot lighter than I thought it would.

I'd never had any dealings with these tiny instruments of death, so there was no way of knowing how heavy they were supposed to be, or even, preparing myself for the handling of them.

Everything I knew about them, I had learned from watching Gideon and Chase play those popular video games back when we had visited my old clinic. The new vets who had taken over the place enjoyed playing games, though I would never allow the kids to have a console. They'd had enough dealings with violence to last a lifetime.

Now, of course, I was kicking myself.

I would have put time into the games myself if it meant having a better handle on our current situation.

I loaded up each of my three other available pockets with grenades, then grabbed one in each hand. Nodding at Gideon, I gave the command.

"Now!"

Gideon slammed his hand on the switch. As the gate rose, I pulled the pin out of the first grenade, making sure that I had the safety lever firmly gripped and pressed down to the side. As long as I didn't let go, the grenade would not go off until a few seconds after I released the lever.

I could not afford any mistakes. I would blow us all to smithereens if I did.

A cloud of dust blew up, kicked up by the racing vehicles. The trucks weren't too far away from us, maybe only fifty feet or so, and closing rapidly. Sweat broke out across my forehead as I imagined their snipers focusing their sights on me.

If I were going to do this, I only had seconds before they would inevitably start firing. Seconds before I dropped to the ground with the armed grenade in my hand...

Aiming for the closest vehicle to us, I hurled the first grenade at it.

The world slowed right down. I held my breath, watching as the grenade sailed through the air in a perfect arc. When it started coming down, I knew I had mis-timed my throw as it landed to one side, far enough away that I wasn't sure it would do any damage to the truck behind us.

Was that enough?

Would it have any effect?

I was still wondering when KABOOM!

The grenade exploded, sending forth a wave of debris that fogged the air causing the trucks to swerve wildly to one side. A hole appeared on the road, cracks forming on the rough surface in an ad hoc pattern. They weren't large enough to be a problem for the truck's wheels, but they'd feel it.

Taking another grenade out of my pocket, I primed it when a glint of something moving caught my eye. Ice water filled my veins as I saw the point of one of their snipers sticking out of an open window. At the speed we were traveling, with the uneasiness of the road's surface, I wasn't so much worried over the unlikelihood of a bullet hitting me: I was concerned that it would miss me and get one of the others.

Knowing I couldn't waste another moment, I hurled the second grenade. It flew like a guided missile, twisting through the space between us until it landed a few feet in front of the truck's path.

The driver's expression changed the instant he knew there was no way to get away from the blast. His gaze dropped to the ground as his face filled with terror. His mouth hung open in a voiceless scream as the force of the explosion sent the truck toppling over, scraping several feet along the dirt until it finally came to a grinding stop. The truck behind it was going much too fast to stop. The driver tried to swerve away, but the bumper clipped the downed truck, causing his vehicle to fishtail. They careened into the last truck.

Then all was still.

Gideon whooped behind me as Chase tried desperately not to spin around in her seat.

"Did it work?" she all but cried out the question.

I didn't answer, watching as the men crawled out of the trucks. A few limped out, having to be helped by their friends. Their shirts were torn. I could see cuts and bruises, but the majority of them seemed unharmed.

Which meant I had only delayed them for a moment. As soon as they were able to fix up their vehicles or call in reinforcement, they would be after us again.

Unless I made sure I put a stop to them.

Taking out another grenade, I armed and threw it at the pile-up that now blocked the road. Before that could even detonate, I tossed out the last remaining grenade.

The explosion that came was several times the size of the others. The force was so great; it knocked me backward and onto my butt. The table slid aside. Pain flew up my tailbone.

Thick black smoke swallowed the world. I could barely see two feet in front of me.

"Is everyone OK?" I called into the cab.

A chorus of "yeses" rose in answer, including one very distinctive bark. Only Emma didn't speak, but she stood far enough back to be unaffected by the blast. I'd check on her as soon as I could, but right now, I needed to see what remained of the small army that had come after us.

"Can I stop now? Did you stop them?" Chase asked pretty desperately.

"I don't know. I can't see through the smoke. Keep going," I instructed. "We need to put as much distance away from home as possible. We can't stop and we can't go back."

As the words left my mouth, their message hit home like a ton of bricks. Our lives. Everything we had built over the last half a year, including my mom's little touches that she had imprinted on the ranch before she had passed away... We were leaving it all behind.

For the second time in my life, I was having to flee my home with no warning.

The truck hurtled along as Chase floored the gas. I signaled it was safe for Sam to let go of my belt. She loosened her hands, which had been gripped tightly onto me. With my hands now empty of grenades, I held onto one of the metal brackets that was welded onto the truck, my eyes straining to see behind us.

Finally, I spotted some shapes inside the cloud of black smoke. The trucks were burned out, hollowed husks of themselves. They looked like something out of a movie, their sides eaten away by the blast. I kept my eyes peeled for signs of movement, only to spot two shadowy figures crawling out from the wreckage.

From this distance away, even if the smoke wasn't an issue, I wouldn't have been able to make out their faces. But one man, the taller of the two, with a slimline shape, stood his ground, feet planted on either side of him, staring at us.

Reeking of animosity.

A chill went down my spine, spreading until it froze my feet to the floor. Call it intuition, but in that very moment, I knew without a doubt that we would see those men again.

Only this time, they would bring bigger guns and more manpower.

Needing to erase the image of that shadowy figure watching us, I strode over to Gideon and hit the switch. The gate shuttered down, providing a wall between us and them.

I couldn't see them anymore. Couldn't see the wreckage and destruction

I had caused. I had expected to feel vindicated. Instead, I felt sick to my stomach.

Having spent my entire life saving lives, I was horrified by the deaths I had likely caused, even if I had excellent reasons for my actions. I looked at Sam to see the same conflicted emotions across her face. When she caught my stare, she gave me a wobbly smile of support.

Turning, my eyes found Emma where she had slid along the bench until she was as far as possible from the rest of us. The whites of her eyes seemed brighter than they should be. She shivered, arms wrapped around herself.

"Are you okay?" I asked.

In response, she shot me a wild look. "You should have just left me there. You people are completely insane." Curling into a ball, she turned her back to us.

9

———

CHASE

My fingernails dug into the leather of the steering wheel, my knuckles turning white. The last minute felt like an eternity; as if time had slowed to a crawl, and any wrong move would lead us straight to hell. It was so much pressure that I just was not prepared for.

There was a massive tightness in my chest that wasn't a familiar sensation. I hadn't hit anything. I wasn't injured. Yet there it was, this rapidly rising pressure that threatened to crush me.

A hand fell onto my shoulder — Sully's. That was enough to help me release the breath I had been holding since he had shouted his crazy plan. He squeezed my shoulder, letting me know he was well, then climbed in next to me.

"In just a second, we're going to swap seats. Keep your feet on the gas. I'm going to put my foot on the pedal, then you're going to hop over me to the right while I slide left. Understand?"

The fact we couldn't even stop for a second to change drivers told me we weren't out of danger. My mouth went dry but I nodded. I couldn't wait to be relieved of driving duty — I was pretty sure I'd never volunteer again.

In fact, this entire experience had put me off driving for good.

I was done.

"OK... now!" he said, his foot having already stepped onto the gas. The second Sully grabbed hold of the wheel, I released my grip, hopping over him quickly while he took over the reins.

My legs, however, had a mind of their own. Frozen stiff from all the tension, they refused to cooperate. They tangled up with his until I managed to pull myself clear and stumbled, face-first, onto the seat beside Bandit. He lowered his nose to the back of my head, so close that I could feel his breath blowing into my neck.

"I'm fine, boy."

He woofed, satisfied with my answer, and raised his nose to the sky to take in all the scents that were like another language for him. Within those smells, he could determine a million factors that our human brains would never understand.

Sully checked each of the mirrors, making sure we weren't followed while I tried to regain my composure. My heart was still thumping a beat in my chest: I was hoping it would calm soon or I was pretty sure I'd be having a heart attack — at fifteen. I knew it was possible since I'd read it in a magazine once... and we all knew how my photographic memory had a habit of being right.

Bandit laid his head on my lap, his eyes rolling up to look at me. I stroked him, half to comfort him, half for myself. I couldn't believe what had just happened and wasn't ready to deal with any of it yet. I was just happy to sit there petting my dog, pretending that none of that madness had just occurred... but all the while, Sully's eyes burned into me. Even though I didn't want to. Even though I knew some kind of tirade was coming, my eyes slid over to him.

"Have you any idea how much danger you were in?"

He had his bug-eyed look, a look that I'd only seen a handful of times in all the time I'd known him. He wasn't kidding around. Sully was mad as all hell right now and that was on top of being scared for our lives.

"Pretty sure we were all in the same boat," I said, not meaning to sound flippant. My back was up, and truthfully, my pride was taking a beating too. I had got us out of the ranch, hadn't I? We had been sitting ducks in that place. "It wasn't looking particularly good for any of us."

Apparently, common sense had left the vehicle and taken a long trip away.

"So you thought you'd run out there *toward* the men with guns?" Sully demanded, gripping onto the dashboard so hard I thought he would rip it off. Unnerved by his anger, Bandit whined, then shifted his head to Sully's lap in an attempt to comfort him.

"Well, we'd managed to sneak out the last time someone attacked here us. I figured we might get lucky again if Bandit and I took the basement route out. And you know what? I was right. They didn't expect us to be going to them. No one was in the vehicles. No one paid any attention to us until it was too late."

Instead of being impressed by my explanation, Sully only grew angrier. A vein throbbed on his forehead, threatening to burst.

"You shouldn't have gone out there without me. I don't care that you were successful. You were lucky this time, Chase, like you were lucky when you stole the helicopter, but this luck is going to have to run out sometime!"

I was wounded to the quick. Wasn't he going to give me *any* credit for getting us out of there? He sat, a volcano about to blow, while I was burning up a decent rage too.

A hand came over the seat to rest on Sully's shoulder. Followed by dangling ends of blonde hair that crested over the back of the headrest. "It's OK, Sully. It's OK."

She said nothing more than that, but kept her hand on his shoulder. Like magic, Sully's heat faded. Sam was a calming breeze to his rage. When she saw that his anger had receded, she gave him a hug, then sat back down.

"You don't risk yourself, Chase. That's what I'm trying to say."

His voice cracked at the end of the sentence as a weariness came over him. Some of my bravado vanished. I knew he was right, but at the time, all I could think was that they were all in danger. I couldn't stand by and let them all die after everything our family had been through.

"I'm sorry. I didn't really think. I just wanted to get us out of there. We were trapped in that house, and we couldn't even shoot at them with our guns since they were too far away. I know I shouldn't have done it, but I would do it again if it would keep us safe."

I was as stubborn as they came. I also knew that no matter the danger, I would always risk my life for them. They were my people. My family. Bandit was my best friend, and no one was going to kill him. Not while I had anything to say about it.

His eyes became suddenly bright.

"Chase, you still don't get it. You're the kid. I'm the parent. It's on me to keep us safe. Not you."

"Aren't you the one who's always grumbling that you're too young to have all these teenagers?" I tried for brevity, knowing how desperately it was needed right now.

"I risk my life, Chase. Not you. Not ever you," Sully finished, looking stricken.

Feeling the love flow out of him, my lips curled into an apologetic smile. "Sorry."

He nodded. His gruff way of accepting my apology. The car sped along the winding road, the engine roaring like a lion as the wind whipped against my face. I sat in the passenger seat, staring blindly at the countryside rushing past us, reliving every moment of the attack like it was happening all over again. Even when I closed my eyes, I could still see the faces of the men, their eyes full of intention, as the lasers from their guns danced dangerously close to my loved ones.

I don't know how long I stayed motionless, my thoughts a jumble of confusion and distress. I was startled out of my reverie by the sound of a familiar whine. Bandit, my loyal companion, had come to my side, nudging me gently with his wet nose, his eyes filled with concern. He shoved his face into my hands. My fingers wove into his fur, craving the familiarity of his comforting presence.

"Does anyone know who they were?" Sully asked, only to be greeted with a wave of shaking heads. Seemed no one had a clue. Sully turned his attention to Emma — the new unknown in our group.

"But they have something to do with you."

From where she sat across from us, Emma looked at him. "I have never seen them before in my life. Then again, I've never seen any of *you* before in my life."

"But that doesn't change the fact that they turned up hours after you did," Gideon mused out loud, weighing up the facts. Of course, Emma took offense at his words.

"Those men were trying to kill *you*. Why are you trying to blame me? I have nothing to do with any of this. Can you just let me out? It was a big mistake coming to you for help."

"I can't do that. It's not safe." He didn't explain who it wasn't safe for.

"It does seem too big a coincidence that they arrived within a day of you," Sam said. "It seems likely that she led them to us."

"I told you I don't know who they are! I don't even know who I am! Why would I lead them to you when Sully is my only link to this world? How do you know they're not after me?"

The second the question left her lips, the blood drained from her face. "Could they be after me?"

Her only answer was the silence that blanketed the vehicle like a thick fog. The dull buzz of the engine and the occasional crunch of gravel under the tires were the only sounds that penetrated the silence. Twisting to face Sully, she pleaded, "You have to help me! You can't let them kill me. I need to find out who I am and why I'm here."

The poor guy was in complete torture, his gaze sliding between Sam, then Emma, then back to Sam.

I couldn't even begin to understand how he must be feeling. How could anyone have known that his dead wife would come back to life like this? Had this happened last year, when I had just met Sully, this would have been the miracle he had been praying for. But now... So much could change in a year.

"We need to stop. Come up with a plan. Let's pool our resources, see what we have with us," said Zeb, the voice of reason. He sounded calm, yet in control. He was the leader we needed right now.

"We can't go home. All we have is what's on us and what we can find in this truck."

Gideon left his seat, coming up behind. "At least they don't seem to be following us."

Sully wasn't doing a good job of pretending things were fine: I could feel the tension pouring off him in waves. The air inside the truck was thick with unspoken emotion, and each passing moment only seemed to exacerbate the stifling atmosphere. Several moments passed with only the sound of the road beneath our tires filling the space. When he finally spoke, it was with quiet resignation.

"Somehow, I don't think that's the last we'll see of them."

His words hung heavy in the air.

10

THE CLEANER

Black smoke billowed from the burning trucks, mixing with the heat of the flames. Their acrid dryness scratched at the back of his throat, making him thirst for water.

Having eaten through the fuel that had leaked from the trucks, the fire was finally beginning to die down. Trucks lay in ruins, their twisted metal frames still glowing from the intense heat that had engulfed them only moments earlier. Charred bodies littered the ground, some so badly burned that they were no longer recognizable.

His men — or what remained of them.

Some had been with him through hell and back. They'd met serving in the military, risking life and limb as they battled hostiles in foreign lands. What they'd shared hadn't been just friendship, but a sacred bond. A brotherhood that was sealed with their own blood.

Now his brothers lay in pieces.

He forced the rising grief away, knowing there wasn't time for that now. There was much cleaning to do, and it had to be done *fast*.

He made the call, hating the silence that came down the line when he was forced to request an additional crew to help with the mess. But, with time of the essence, it couldn't be helped.

Milton hunched over the still body, his six-four frame awkward with the strain of an injured right arm, sustained during the pursuit when an explosion had flung him out of a vehicle. Only his sheer size had saved him when he'd landed in a ditch. Though The Cleaner knew it to be pointless, he watched as Milton pressed his fingers to the body's neck.

The man was gone.

"We need to move the bodies out of sight," he instructed Milton and his other surviving man, Bond. "Help is on the way, but we can't take the chance of someone driving past, spotting them and asking questions."

Bond nodded, face and beard crusted with dirt, making it seem as if he had turned gray early. In his late forties, he might be the oldest, but a lifetime of working out meant he was the epitome of health. His body was a well-oiled machine, one the Cleaner knew he could count on.

The three got to their macabre work, carrying or dragging their former colleagues away, hiding them in the fields of corn that flanked the road. The blood stains they could do nothing about, and the trucks would have to be left as they were for now.

When the road was as clear as they could make it, the three sat and waited.

When the job had come down the line initially, he had studied the notes with the meticulous attention to detail that he used for everything. Didn't matter if he was at home, surrounded by three noisy children, cooking a simple meal in the apartment he stayed at whenever he was on a job, or fixing whatever needed fixing for his bosses, John Smith — as he was known — was a stickler for details, planning everything within an inch of its life.

Take the raid at the Montpelier ranch.

He had scouted the operation himself. During his recon, disguised as an electrician from the local utility company, working alone — which is how he preferred it — he had been parked in his van, logging the family's comings and goings for several weeks.

Ever since his discovery of Xavier's experiments.

Every morning, the boy would pick up fresh donuts and pastries from the local grocery store though the sheriff never had much time for breakfast. The girl would play some game on her phone with the dog, usually with the vet and old man joining in. It all seemed so wholesome. Just your typical American family with their genetically modified, unnatural experiment of a pet. They were as predictable as the sun rising at dawn.

Or so he'd thought.

The paperwork that lined the walls at the abandoned school was unsalvageable, destroyed by the sprinklers, as were the computers with nearly two decades worth of Xavier's research. If not for that single strand of blonde hair he had found, attached to that ominous-looking tank in the basement, Smith wouldn't have had much to report.

But in that single strand of hair lay an enormous threat to the future of mankind.

And that there was the problem.

It should have been a straightforward operation, but he'd never bargained on the arsenal of weapons inside the house or the family's relentless will to survive. Left with no choice, they'd had to return fire.

His thoughts were interrupted by a car appearing on the horizon. Peering through his binoculars, Smith could see there was only the one driver. He felt a pang of relief.

One person could be easily dealt with.

His nightmare scenario would be a family... *with children.* Though he didn't want to think about it, he knew that no matter what his feelings were, he would have to do his job.

When the driver finally pulled over, hurrying out of his car to assist them, Bond handled the matter in the way he would have done himself. He knocked the driver out with a simple blow to the back of the head. He'd been so efficient, Smith doubted the man would ever know what had happened.

Hiding his car behind the wreckage of the trucks, they continued to wait.

Two hours later, they were rewarded by the sight of what looked to be a first response unit for a natural disaster. There were several fire trucks, ambulances, and police vans among the procession. Only the police vans darkened windows hinted that they might not have been the real deal.

Smith got to his feet to greet them. He had only to give the briefest of instruction. The men — and they were all men — got to work setting up cones and road signs, implying a burst gas main had caused an explosion.

The bodies were quickly sealed into bags, then taken away by ambulance for disposal at a nearby hospital. Their families would be fed a story of their heroic deaths and receive more money than they could ever use under the guise of insurance policies.

Back at the ranch, the area was going through a similar process where all trace of the warfare would be erased. Not a single bullet hole or shell casing would be left. He wasn't sure what cover story would be created — there was a separate PR department to handle that — but it would have to be strong enough for the locals to believe.

Leaving the crew to finish up the task, Smith was examined by a doctor, deemed fit if bruised and battered, and left at a nearby motel. Milton had been whisked away for his arm shattered arm to be replaced, leaving him with only Bond in the next room.

He showered, washing away the grime of the attack. Later, Bond brought over food from the place next door. The burgers were greasy, the fries, limp, but Smith inhaled them as if it was his last meal.

He'd spent several hours on his satellite phone, answering questions about the day's travesty that had cost his department six figures to handle. His bosses were not happy and needed assurances that the job would be completed.

He swore that it would.

When the light started to fade, Smith called home, his lips curling into a big smile when his three young kids answered, clamoring over each other to talk to him.

He answered their questions as truthfully as he could — it was much easier to bend the truth rather than outright lie. They and everyone else, including his wife, thought he was a consultant for an oil company. The cover gave him the freedom to take off at a moment's notice. It also paid well, helping him to look after his family.

"When are you coming home?" His youngest asked.

"Hopefully soon. I don't think this job will take that much longer to finish."

"Don't forget my present, Daddy."

Smith laughed, picturing the pout on his four-year-old's face. "As if I ever would."

"I brushed my teeth by myself," he boasted, so proud of himself.

"Wow. What a good boy you are. If you put yourself to bed, Mommy will come and kiss you goodnight soon."

"'K. Byeeee!" Smith heard him yelling as he started running to his room. A moment later, his wife's concerned voice came over the line.

"Did you hear about that explosion? Something about a gas main. I saw it on the news. It's not far from where you are is it?"

No, honey. Not far at all.

"I heard, but I wasn't near it. Don't worry."

He heard her exhale, relieved.

They chatted about her day, what the kids had gotten up to, how the house down the street had finally sold. Inane, boring conversation. It was music to his ears.

All too soon, it was time to go. After promising he would be home soon, Smith hung up the phone, then went to sit by the desk. Opening his laptop, he hit the power button, but instead of coming on, the screen filled with static before blinking out entirely.

Smith rubbed his forehead, fighting the urge to toss the useless thing at the wall. Truth be told, he should have checked earlier that it was in working order, but with one thing after another, it had slipped his mind.

And now he would pay the price.

Sighing, he picked up the phone again, keying in the number for his boss.

11

SULLY

All around us the landscape was flat, with the occasional clump of trees and a clear stretch of road before us, lined with endless rows of corn. A sea of yellow stretching as far as the eye could see that we could have been in the plains of Iowa instead of a hundred or so miles west of Montpelier.

Ordinarily, this would have been of some comfort, but today, the openness, the wideness of the expanse, made me antsy. We were exposed to every passerby. It made us sitting ducks, though if those men were to turn up again, the one positive was we'd be able to spot them coming from a distance.

The road remained mostly empty, with only an occasional car motoring past. If more men were coming, they wouldn't catch up to us for a while — and that's even if they knew what direction we had traveled. Even I didn't know where we were, or where we were heading. It was disorienting. I felt like I had no control over anything.

I had to hope the uncertainty would buy us time to plan our next move.

As I drove, I found my eyes glancing over at the artillery strapped to the walls of the truck. I quickly scanned the ammunition, pushing away any memories of the men and their guns targeting my family. My gaze moved to that high-tech laptop that had been returned to the upright table (somewhere, in the midst of all the chaos, it had been thrown clear across the cab), but there wasn't a dent on it. With its gleaming metallic lid and one-inch thick molded casing, it looked like it had landed straight out of a sci-fi flick. I wondered if we could make use of it somehow.

Zeb, however, had his mind on matters other than our weaponry. Reaching into his pocket, he retrieved his wallet. "How much cash do you have?"

We pooled our resources, Chase laying everything out onto the seat beside me.

Sam had her purse, but mine was back in our truck, along with our suitcases. We hadn't managed to bring them inside the house before all hell had kicked off.

Chase threw down a twenty-dollar bill she found in a back pocket. But other than that, there was only Zeb's wallet, which contained mostly cards rather than cash. When she turned to Emma, Emma clutched her bag tighter to her chest.

"I don't have any money. Can't you just leave me alone?"

Her misery tugged at my heart as an overwhelming urge to protect her came over me. I had to stop myself from launching across the truck to gather her into my arms. Of course, that immediately led to a crushing wave of guilt. As if my mind was cheating on my new wife with my old one.

Chase backed away from her. Since we had checked the contents earlier and knew what was — and wasn't — in there, we left her alone, neither one of us comfortable enough to approach her.

Taking out the cash from the wallets, Chase counted out our funds, which came to a measly hundred bucks.

"We're not going far on this," Zeb finally said, wishing desperately that the opposite was true.

Silence fell like a cloud. Still on high alert, her body tensed for any sign of danger, Sam's voice cut through our rising panic. "We should sweep the truck for bugs, cameras, and trackers."

She crossed to the table and felt beneath the underside of it while the others fanned out and began their search. When she couldn't find anything, she ducked her head under it only to surface moments later empty-handed. Gideon squatted down to examine the wheel-wells while I poured over the cab, keeping one hand on the steering wheel.

Chase didn't move, her slender frame perched beside me. "Um. What exactly am I looking for? Like, is it really going to have a flashing red light or beep like they do in the movies?"

"Just see if you can spot anything suspicious or out of place," Sam answered.

In lieu of responding, Chase's rolled her eyes, waving her hands around. Her meaning was clear to us all: *everything was suspicious and out of place.*

"I've only ever seen the ones Xavier used, which I swear he picked up at Radio Shack," Gideon replied. "Doesn't seem like these guys would have shopped in the same place."

"Would do you suggest?" I asked.

"Gideon, take over for Sully a moment. We need to work over this truck."

After checking the way was clear, I stopped the truck. We swapped places, though Chase shot me a momentary look of outrage until I raised a brow at her. "You really want the responsibility of driving this thing again?"

"No," she answered with only a hint of sulkiness. "Just figured you could at least ask, since I did such a great job."

"Woof!"

Ever her biggest cheerleader, Bandit made his opinion clear. I crossed over to the table and picked up the laptop.

Encased in steel, possibly even titanium, the laptop was small but looked indestructible. On the screen, a detailed 3D map of the surrounding area was shown. The map revealed not only road names but also nearby terrain. There were also indications of other elements of the landscape that would probably be helpful if only we had any idea what they meant.

A blinking green dot represented our current position. I pressed down on a few keys, but nothing happened.

I moved my fingers to the screen, wanting to see if it was touch-screen. Unfortunately, it responded to my touch by shutting down and a window popped up, requesting a fingerprint ID or user code to unlock it.

I uttered a curse under my breath.

Of course, the thing would be security protected. We'd be getting no further use out of it. "Other than our own phones, our biggest threat is that laptop," Sam said. "If it's showing our location to us, presumably it could do the same for them."

Beside the laptop, there were flashlights that looked as if they doubled as UV lights. Chase rummaged through the glove compartment to see what she could dig up, but the thing was empty. Not even a stick of gum.

"I've got nothing."

She checked the sun visors next, flicking them down, hoping to find paperwork or something tucked up in there, but, again, she came up empty.

The truck was conspicuously absent of any identifying information, and that filled me with no end of dread.

Only people that didn't want to be found, who had experience of staying invisible, could hide their tracks so well.

"You think these guys are related to Forbes? Or Xavier?" Chase asked.

"I don't think Xavier's involved with them. He was a two-man band. They do seem to be more Forbes' type of accomplice, but he's dead," I mused out loud.

"Not that it seems much of a problem these days," Gideon said, low enough that Emma wouldn't have heard him from the back of the cab.

"Gid, stop the truck for a sec. Park it off the road. I want to talk outside." Sam instructed.

Finding a spot he favored, Gideon killed the engine. We piled out of the truck — Gideon and I helping my dad out — though Emma stayed huddled inside, refusing to have anything to do with us.

"Leave her be. She just needs time to come around," Zeb seemed sure, though I didn't know where his newfound faith had come from, particularly given that he'd never met Emma before she had died. When we were a small distance away, Sam stretched out her hand to us.

"Give me your phones."

The adults passed their phones to her without hesitation, but Chase and Gideon's faces were identical in their displeasure.

"Seriously?" Chase moaned.

"Yes. You know they can track us on these," she replied.

"Can't we just take out the sim cards or turn them off?" Gideon asked.

"Even if we turn them off, devices can still be tracked nowadays," Sam answered, killing the hope in their eyes.

Reluctantly, the kids handed over their phones. Taking out the sims, I crushed them in my hands, then tossed the phones to the ground, trampling on them with the heel of my boot until they were well and truly beyond repair.

"That hurt more than I thought it would," Gideon said.

"We'll get new ones when we come upon some cash. In the interim, you should think of the bright side," I offered.

"And that is?" Gideon asked.

"Since neither of you have any friends, anyone you would have called is already here." I was trying for a bit of lightheartedness, but it sank like a pound of rocks.

"So now I'm a loser with no friends *and* I'm being hunted by an army of killers? Great. Thanks."

I probably needed to practice my cheerleading skills and take a few lessons from Bandit.

"Now, the laptop."

Bandit bounded into the truck obediently, returning seconds later with it in his mouth, though he clearly struggled with the weight of the thing. Sam took it from him, ruffling his fur.

"Thanks, boy."

She threw it onto the ground. I stamped on it, hard as I could, digging in my heel, but I barely made a dent.

"Must be made of the same material as the truck," Gideon's mouth twitched, though he knew better than to outright laugh at me.

Moving to the truck, I positioned the laptop directly in front of one wheel and backed clear out of the way. On my signal, Gideon revved the engine and ran over it with the truck.

There was a popping sound as the laptop flattened into a thin disc. "Good luck tracing us with that," Chase commented.

"We need a place to stay, and supplies," Sam said. "And we need to get a move on. I'm not happy with us just being out in the open like this."

"I might know a place. Remember my friend Mark? He has a cabin on a lake in the middle of nowhere. He doesn't get out there very often and since he's got more money than sense, he refuses to rent it out, so it should be empty. He should be able to help us with money, too."

"Well, you can't call him with our phones," Gideon remarked unhelpfully, apparently still smarting.

"I wouldn't have used them, anyway. We need a public payphone."

We stared up and down the barren road. The only visible sign of human presence were the two sets of tire tracks that snaked down the center of the road from where we had come. Forget phones. There wasn't even a telephone pole in sight.

"What are we going to do until we find one?" Chase asked.

"The only thing we can do. Drive."

12

CHASE

With Sully now back in the driver's seat, he drove us onward. We kept our eyes peeled for anything to use to our advantage.

The fields of yellow were broken up by a house here or there, but with only a few sparse rows of trees popping up, it didn't seem like there was any place we could safely make camp. Nowhere we wouldn't be seen from the road.

Though the picturesque countryside rolled past our windows, we were still on edge from our narrow escape. With no idea where we were heading, we were just ambling along, hoping to find somewhere we could park for the night until Sully could make that call.

But, as if we didn't have enough to contend with, we had another problem within our ranks.

It had started innocently enough.

Shortly after we escaped, Emma had apparently gotten over her need for solace and had started hovering near Sully. Though it was Sam's natural place to be beside him, Emma stuck close to Sully, seeking the comfort she only found in his presence. He, in turn, seemed unable to ask her to leave.

And the thing was, he might not even want her to.

At times, I would catch him staring at Emma with this awed expression, like the one parents had for their newborn babies. When he realized I had noticed this, he'd hide it by coughing or turning away. But, if I had caught him doing it, I was sure Sam would too, which might go some way to explaining her rigid back. So straight and unyielding that it seemed like it might snap.

The result of all this was that Sam hadn't talked to her new husband since Emma's reappearance. While Zeb was zen-like about the whole thing, convinced that the situation would resolve itself given time, Gideon was doing his level best to avoid Emma. It was surprisingly easy since she ignored him completely.

Picking up on all the tension, Bandit tried to console Sam by placing his iPad into her lap, offering a quiz game for the two of them to play. Sam had tried, but her mind just wasn't on it. She gave up after only a few questions, pretending to have a headache. I couldn't stomach the disappointed sigh he gave, so we went a few rounds. He won every one, of course.

Having grown tired of watching Emma cling onto her man, Sam finally approached them, a determined expression across her face.

"Do you mind if I sit with Sully now?" Sam had asked, pointedly yet politely.

Apparently not valuing her newly granted lease of life, Emma responded, "You're not happy with taking my husband. You want this seat too?"

Sam's eyes had flashed dangerously, but she kept her voice even. "I just want to talk to him. We've had little opportunity."

"Still more than me, though, right? Since I've been dead for almost two years."

Not even Sam knew how to argue with that. "I'll check in with you later," Sully had pleaded with Sam then. Although I was pretty sure he would have preferred Sam's company, letting Emma sit with him seemed to keep her quiet. Since peace seemed as if it was going to be lacking in our near future, it was smart of him to take what he could.

This meant Sam was sitting with us. During the short time we had been traveling, she grew increasingly convinced that Emma was connected with those men.

"They only appeared when she did. We don't actually know if she's working for them."

"Maybe... but it doesn't make sense why she would lead them to us. She seemed genuinely shocked by it all." I was trying to see all sides, play Devil's advocate. Clearly, I must have hit my head during all the explosions. It was the only logical reason as to why I wasn't keeping my mouth shut.

"She might not have known that was what she was doing. I just think we need to be cautious around her."

"I've told you a million times already — I'm not working with them! Why won't you believe me?"

Emma's piping voice cut in behind us. We had been so lost in our conversation that we hadn't heard her approach.

Bandit shot me a woeful look, knowing he should have heard her first since dogs had much better hearing. I guess he must have been as caught up in the conversation as the rest of us.

Suffice to say, things had now soured between them to where they weren't speaking — to each other or anyone else.

I would catch Sam sending a hostile look Emma's way now and then, while Emma did her best to ignore her. It didn't help matters that Emma had those pictures of Sully in her lap and wouldn't quit studying them.

The tension in the truck was palpable, like a tangible force was keeping them apart. Every time Sam caught Emma looking at Sully — which in fairness was a lot — her fingers would curl a little tighter in her lap. Her hands resembled claws now she had been doing it for so long. I wanted to force them to relax.

But I wasn't stupid enough to get in their way. I hadn't survived this long without knowing which battles to avoid.

The rhythmic rocking of the truck soon lulled Zeb to sleep. His head relaxed against the back of his chair as a peaceful expression came over his face. He often napped in the afternoon, and even our current predicament couldn't stop the siren call of tiredness when it hit.

We'd been silent for a while when I soon felt a familiar rumble in my stomach, so loud it seemed to reverberate in the cab. My cheeks turned hot.

"We're way past our normal mealtime," was my only response.

Suddenly, Emma put down the photographs she had been studying intensely. Rummaging inside her bag, she retrieved an energy bar. She unwrapped it and immediately started eating it in front of my eyes. I was a little taken aback by the lack of consideration and could tell the others were, too. Sam's eyes burned a path toward her, but either Emma didn't notice or she genuinely didn't care.

Within three or four bites, she had almost eaten the whole thing.

"Aren't you going to share that with the rest of us?" Sam asked, sounding as incredulous as she looked.

"Why would I do that?" Emma replied, completely confused by the question. "I'm hungry too."

"But so is Chase — you just heard so yourself — and probably the rest of us by now. How can you hear her say she's hungry, then sit there eating that bar by yourself?"

Emma held onto the last bite of her bar, her voice surging into a plaintive wail.

"But it's my food. It was in my bag and I'm starving."

"So are the rest of us," was Sam's response.

The air was so thick with tension, you could have cut it with a knife. Not wanting this to become yet another thing between them, Sully finally spoke up. "It's all right. She can have it. We'll work out the food thing later."

Barely had the words left his mouth, then Emma shoved the remaining bite into her own, chewing so fast that I thought she'd choke. The fact that Sully was letting Emma get away with bad behavior *and* that he wasn't backing her up, didn't sit well with Sam. She sent a scathing look his way.

Sully was in for an uncomfortable conversation tonight. Of that I had no doubt.

Wondering if I should say something to break the tension, I was given the opportunity when a large shape outside caught my attention.

"Sully! Take us over there!"

My suggestion confused him, and he didn't initially see what I had seen until the barn came into clearer view.

A large hole had eaten away a third of the roof and it was overgrown with ivy and weeds. The place was unused and unloved, but what had gotten me excited was the sheer size of it: it looked big enough to hide our truck inside.

Sully beamed at me.

"Good spot, Chase. We'll camp here and move on tomorrow."

Swinging the truck off the road, we headed to inspect our home for the night.

13

SULLY

The ancient double-height barn had walls that might originally have been a rosy red, but time and weather had bleached the paneling dirty pink.

Where windows had once wrapped around the top level, only splintered holes remained. Wind whistled through the holes, growing gradually more intense as the sun began its descent in the mottled crimson sky.

I knew that we didn't have much time before darkness fell. If this was to be our camp, we needed to make it suitable as quickly as possible.

Behind the barn stood a few smaller buildings in even worse condition. One, a single storey residence, looked to have been a farmhouse once. Ghosts of its previous life were everywhere.

A wheelbarrow lay on its side in a ditch. A tractor missing its steering wheel and seat. A rusty weathervane — long fallen off its original perch — now lay half buried beneath layers of grass.

Another outbuilding contained piles of oily metal and machinery. I wasn't sure what any of it was for, only that they had to do with the large overgrown fields of wheat and barley that surrounded us.

I approached what was left of the farmhouse first, hoping to find something we could use. The front door was closed but when I twisted the door handle, it turned, if reluctantly. Stepping inside, I was immediately hit with a cloying, musty smell that scratched the back of my throat.

Coughing, I reeled back, needing a moment. I gestured to the others. "Stay back. There's mold. Let me check it out by myself."

"Be careful, son," Zeb instructed. He had woken from his nap and was now scoping out the area, his dark eyes taking stock of the place.

I stepped carefully inside, cupping a hand over my nose.

Dust and chaff danced in the half-light that barely passed through the dirt encrusted windows. Though its owners had long abandoned the house, some furniture remained.

A round wooden table and two chairs, both missing several legs. An oversized cupboard took up one wall. I approached the cupboard hopefully, opening its doors.

Inside, aged newspaper covered the bottom of the shelves, where a few chipped mugs and plates sat discarded. Unless we wanted to risk slicing open our mouths every time we took a drink, there was nothing we could use.

Moving to the kitchen, the source of the mold became clear. A sizeable area of black covered the ceiling. What wasn't black was brown with water stains, though there was no sign of the leak that had caused all the issues. Turning away, I scanned the rest of the room. Only the odd pot remained. There was no canned food. No hidden treasure.

I went through the rest of the house, but it was clear within moments of exploring that my search wouldn't reap any rewards.

I inhaled deeply as I stepped out of the house, relieved to no longer be breathing in the toxic fumes.

"I'm going to check over there." I pointed to a building containing the machinery.

Inside, it seemed in a better state than the house had been. My gaze went straight to a bucket containing a few discarded gardening tools. There was a trowel with a handle that had rotted away, but I struck gold with a pair of pruning shears that hadn't fallen apart. Picking them up, I rejoined the others by the barn.

"The good news *is* the barn is big enough for the truck," Gideon said. "But the bad news is we'll have to clear that vegetation growing over the doors before we can get inside."

I showed them the shears. "It's lucky I found these then."

"You think they'll do the job? They look in pretty bad shape." Chase eyed the shears in my hand, openly doubtful.

I ran my eyes over the weeds, relieved to see that they weren't too thick. "The worst of the culprits I can attack with the shears. You guys can probably get the rest off with just your hands. I don't see any thorns, so you should be fine. There are five of us, not including Bandit. I think we'll be able to clear most of it away before it gets dark if we get going now."

"I need to rest," said Emma from somewhere behind the group. "I've had a really trying day."

A bolt of guilt shot through me: I had actually forgotten she was here. I'd been so focused on the task at hand that she had gone clear out of my mind.

But with only the sound of her voice, everything came rushing back.

My thoughts were the only thing that was rushing, however, as Emma found a patch on the ground and went to sit on it. She curled up on the ground and closed her eyes, apparently going to sleep right there.

I was torn between two conflicting mindsets. On the one hand, I wanted to grab her and force her to stand up and help us, but on the other, I wanted to be understanding and give her anything she asked for. That devilish inner voice of mine reminded me that this wasn't something that ever happened — dead people did not come back — and that I should be thankful for every moment I got with her.

"Let's continue without her. No point forcing her to do anything. She'll likely be of little use to us," Zeb murmured.

He had been staring at me as if he knew exactly what I had been thinking. I shot him a grateful nod, happy not to have to consider Emma for the immediate future.

I made my way to the doors and started hacking away at the overgrown weeds with the shears, relieved when they started coming away from the doors. The kids went to work on my left, Sam and my dad on my right. Even Bandit tried to help, gathering what he could in his mouth, then backing away, swinging his head from side to side to tug it loose.

We went hard and fast, working up a quick sweat, though I didn't mind, finding the manual, thoughtless labor easier to deal with than the swirling mass of confusion that swam through my mind.

Sam hacked away at the weeds beside me but didn't say a word. That's not to say I couldn't feel her bristling. Her energy was wired like electricity and an explosion felt imminent.

All I could do for now was focus on clearing the weeds away so we could get inside. If I spent one second to consider all the things that happened since the morning, my brain would meltdown.

14

CHASE

W e were in a race against the declining light.

The sun was almost on the horizon, a visual ticking clock representing how much time we had before we'd have to use the truck's lights — defeating the purpose of hiding away out here in the first place.

Bandit ran between us, helping when he could. He had stopped trying to pull the ivy off by himself as he'd ended up tangled up with it, and was now picking up whatever we had freed, dragging it to a pile off-side.

Zeb hadn't said much since we'd gotten here. His silence unnerved me and I found myself keeping an eye on him... just in case something else was going on with him.

He never acted his age, though I wasn't actually sure how old he was — whenever I asked, he just replied that he was several hundred years old. I was acutely aware of not only the terror we'd just experienced, but that he had only come out of a coma a few weeks ago.

I was worried this would be too much for him.

His color seemed good though, and outside of being quiet, he looked okay. Then again, I had always looked pretty okay too when I had been on the streets, even when I was so weak with hunger that I could barely see straight. Back then, faking strength had been part of my strategy to stay alive. I knew that if I showed no weakness, I just might last another night. Shooting a sidelong glance at him, I moved closer.

"So, this is all pretty terrifying," I began.

He looked at me and nodded. "Have to say I didn't see any of this coming. I had thought my final act would consist of sitting on the porch and watching the sun go down, not running for my life."

I flinched inwardly. "I'm so sorry Zeb. I feel so guilty about making you lose your home. Especially as I'd already done that to Sully. I can't believe it's happened again."

His eyes turned hooded. "Dear girl, you weren't the one who attacked us. I don't hold you responsible for any of your actions. That was a gutsy move, what you did. And it saved us. Anyhow, a house doesn't make a home, Chase. You of all people know that. Family, loved ones, that's what makes a home. The rest of it is immaterial."

Despite his words, I knew he was just trying to put a brave face on it all. Noticing my lack of conviction, he took my hand and squeezed it.

We went back to working side-by-side in silence. Sam had moved away from us. She hadn't spoken to anyone, but now and then I could hear her mumble angrily to herself as she tugged hard at the ivy. I couldn't hear what she was saying, only picking up a word or two. Enough to know she wasn't happy that Sully had let Emma off the hook so easily. It was seriously eating her up.

Not wanting to stare, or get caught staring only to suffer her wrath, I turned and found myself looking at Gideon.

He tore at the ivy, the muscles in his arms flexing in a way that had me staring. Sweat glistened on his brow but instead of being grossed out, I found myself thinking how *hot* he looked. Catching me staring, Zeb smiled.

"He's the most loyal person I've ever known, you know." He stopped working, his eyes taking on a faraway look. "Did I ever tell you how we met?"

I shook my head — I didn't know this story.

"I found him in my stable one morning. He was fast asleep in an empty stall with only the hay to keep him warm. I had heard noises coming from there in the night, but had put it down to raccoons — they love to pillage my vegetable garden, so I assumed they were spreading their net further afield. I was tired that night and didn't bother to investigate."

His lips curled into a smile at the memory.

"When I woke in the morning, I brought my shotgun down with me only to find this skinny kid sleeping like a babe. He had little on him and his clothes were dirty. It was likely he hadn't washed in a while. I didn't have the heart to wake him, so I went back to the house and rustled up a large breakfast. Took it out there for him, half expecting him to have woken up by then, but he was still out to the world. He later revealed that he had traveled quite far on foot and was exhausted by the time he had turned up on my property. I set the plate of food and a jug of water and juice on the barrel next to him, and left him to it."

Oblivious to the two of us watching him, Gideon carried on working.

"I went about my day not hearing a peep from him. Just when I was beginning to think that he had probably eaten, then done a runner, there came a knock on the door. Gideon stood on my porch, my plate in his hands. He had eaten the food, but had also washed the plate and the cutlery outside before handing it back to me. It was that minor detail that told me everything I needed to know about him. He was a good kid who had hit on hard times, but his heart was solid."

I would have gasped, but I didn't want to break the spell. Our stories were so familiar, both of us living rough on the streets, then being rescued and cared for by two generations of the same family.

Zeb continued. "I told him right then and there that he could stay if he helped around the ranch. I would give him a roof over his head and feed him if he helped with the odd job around the place. He proved so useful that I started paying him. That was two years ago and the rest, as you know, is history."

Gideon and I had spent a lot of time together, but we had an unspoken agreement to never discuss our past lives, making all of this unfamiliar to me.

"Has he ever told you about his family?" I asked.

"A little," Zeb answered. "He has two older brothers, never got on with either of them or his parents. By the sounds of it, they weren't very good people. His parents made them all quit school as soon as possible, insisting that they get jobs — any job — and pay them for the roof over their heads. Gideon wanted a better life. He wanted to make something of himself, but they wouldn't even consider letting him continue school. He was the only smart one in the family, and they resented him for it, treating him like dirt.

When he tried to stick up for himself, they said he was too big for his boots and threw him out. It may well be that they didn't actually mean for him to go: they could have been trying to teach him a lesson, but you know Gideon. He left and never looked back. You and he both have that in common."

The world was such a strange place.

You had people out there so desperate to have kids they would go into debt and risk everything in order just to try. And then there were our parents, who gave birth to us but couldn't wait to toss us away.

My thoughts came to rest on Sully and his relationship with Zeb. Although I didn't want to stir up any painful memories, I wanted to know more about them, more about their life before I had met them.

"What about you and Sully's mom? I know nothing about her. Neither of you talk about her much."

Zeb smiled a bittersweet smile. He must have formed a picture of her in his mind as his eyes turned bright with emotion.

"It's cliche I know, but I believe that when you meet the person who is right for you, you know it. You feel it in your heart and your gut, but it's nothing like how it's represented in the movies. There's no explosion. No world spinning out of control. It's actually the opposite. It's feeling like you've come home, that this is where you are supposed to be. If the person that you are with makes you feel like home, then that's the one you should be with. That's how it was with us."

A whole host of emotions flew across his face. He missed her with an ache that was palpable, but there was also a great love radiating from him. Even now, so many years later, Zeb was still madly in love with his wife.

I looked back at Gideon helping Sully with that door, confused thoughts swirling through my mind. I felt at home with Gideon, but wasn't that because we lived together as a family? Wasn't he already part of my home?

Thankfully, a loud creak interrupted my tangled thoughts.

Sully, Gideon, and Sam had cleared enough of the vegetation away that they were now opening the door. The door protested loudly since it hadn't been opened in such a long time, but they were able to work it free with a carefully timed pull.

Dust particles floated, creating a hazy filter through which I took in the sights. Beams of light fell in through the holes in the roof. Giant cobwebs hung from the rafters, making me suppress a shudder at what might also lurk up there with them. I knew I should be more concerned about men with guns, but at least they would make some kind of noise before they attacked. Spiders were deadly, silent, and just plain gross.

Hay bales were scattered around. Empty food troughs sat in rows along the walls, remnants of half-rotten grain still lining them. An earthy smell came from those troughs, but nothing too unbearable. If we cleared them up, pushed them to one side and swept the floor a bit, we would confine most of the smell to the one area.

"This will be fine for tonight," said Sully. "We'll pile the bales around us to keep out the cold. They can also offer some protection if those men do find us."

Emma stirred, waking from her nap (how anyone could have gone to sleep like that was beyond me). She yawned, stretching like a cat, and went to stand beside Sully. As soon as she looked inside the barn, she shook her head.

"It's so dirty. I can't sleep in there."

"You just slept on the ground," Sam pointed out immediately.

"That was different. That was outside. This is dirty *inside*."

Though she answered Sam, she addressed all of her responses to Sully, as if he was the one who had made the point.

"Emma's always been a bit OCD about cleanliness," he said without thinking, only to be immediately hit by the full force of Sam's hurt. She dropped her gaze, not wanting him to see it, but I caught it. It made me feel terrible for her. Not only had Sully inadvertently taken Emma's side again, but his comment made it seem as if it was he and Emma who were the couple.

"That's no skin off my nose. If it were up to me, she would sleep outside on her own where anyone can see her for miles around." Sam styled it out smoothly, like she hadn't just been stabbed in the heart.

Suddenly, Emma didn't seem so sure of herself. Glancing around at the open expanse, she must have realized how vulnerable she would be out here. Hugging her bag to her chest as if she were afraid we would steal it from her, she went inside.

"Since you all already smell, I guess it doesn't matter if I get dirty too," she said.

The others followed her inside, though it was a while longer before Sam would join us.

15

CHASE

The atmosphere was getting suffocatingly intense.

It felt like we'd been in the barn for hours already, though according to my watch it had only been minutes.

We cleaned out the mess until the back of the barn was relatively decent — about as decent as a crumbling barn could be, anyway. Still, some people couldn't be pleased.

Using a few of the hay bales, Sully had created a corner for Emma, laying out a tarp that he'd found so that the hay wouldn't itch her skin. The second she had inspected her bed for the night, though, Emma complained, declaring she wasn't an animal, so how could they treat her like one?

Bandit, my lovable Muttface, attempted to ease the awkwardness by bounding onto the "bed" he had already circled several times. He gave a cute "woof" to let her know that it was plenty nice enough for him, and therefore should be good enough for her too.

Emma was completely unaware of what he was trying to communicate and distorted the entire story to make it seem like Bandit was on her side.

Words were spoken, from Sam mostly. By the time they had finished, Emma had retreated to her corner, but only after shooing Bandit away like he was nothing but a nuisance.

Sully attempted to make another corner for himself and Sam, but she stopped him with a death glare before snapping that she was quite capable of creating her own bunk for the night.

After that, Sully was completely lost.

He kept tossing looks between Sam and Emma, wondering who he should speak to. He would start walking to one, stop, turn around then head to the other, only to stop again. It was painful to watch.

Finally, realizing that whatever he did would be wrong, he mumbled something under his breath and went out to the truck.

16

SULLY

The night air wrapped around me, carrying the earthy aroma of the surrounding fields. The silence was broken only by the occasional chirping of crickets and the gentle rustle of leaves in the breeze. Above, the stars twinkled against the fast-approaching night sky. As the barn faded into a black silhouette, I soaked up the momentary calm. Out here, I could pretend that all was well with the world. That the relentless onslaught of wonder, confusion, and fear wasn't waiting for me inside.

Reluctantly, I tore my gaze from the sky and retraced my steps to the barn. A movement caught my attention even before I heard the sounds of my dad's wheelchair scraping across the dirt floor. Random strands of hay were caught in the wheels, creating a rhythmic whipping sound as he approached.

"I'm just taking a breather before I start on your bunk for the night."

"I can wait, son. I actually wanted to talk to you. See how you are. Hasn't been much time for that."

My gaze swept the room, automatically stopping at Emma's corner only to find it empty. A bolt of panic tore through me, shocking me with its intensity.

"She's only taking a restroom break. She's fine, son." His voice cut through my alarm as his cool eyes assessed me. "I imagine this has all been hard to handle."

"You always seem to understate the moment."

"Never seen the point of working myself into a frenzy. It's not exactly productive. Saying that, I wouldn't know how to feel in your shoes. Tell me what's been going through your mind."

I looked into his concerned eyes. "I guess I don't know how to feel. The honeymoon was about as perfect as it could be. Sam and I were so happy, but ever since Emma showed up, my head hasn't been on straight. I can't understand how she's here, how any of this is happening."

"None of us can. It defies all logic."

"But that's not even the worst of it. The worst was how, once the shock had faded some, I'd catch myself feeling thrilled." I lowered my gaze to the ground, ashamed of myself. "I'd be excited that she's back, but then I'll turn and see Sam and it feels like I'm cheating on her. I'm a wreck."

Zeb smiled sadly. "You need to give yourself a break. This only just happened. Your mind needs time to get over the shock before you can even begin to fathom how to feel."

"But that's just it. We don't know how much time we have. We're out here, being hunted, yet I can't get my head around my relationship issues. What kind of man lets that happen?

Zeb laid his hand on my shoulder. "The kind who cares about his family and puts them above his own feelings and fears. Trust yourself, Jake. You're a good man. You'll do the right thing."

He sounded so sure of himself that for a moment, I actually believed him.

The sound of footsteps crunching over the ground interrupted our conversation.

Chase, Bandit, Sam, and Gideon headed toward us in a group. "What're you two gossiping about?" Gideon asked.

"We were just discussing our strange predicament."

"You're talking about Emma, right? Thank God. My brain is about to implode if we don't figure out what she is." Chase plopped herself beside me, folding her legs beneath her. "I have several theories already."

Forgetting in that moment that she was angry at me, Sam sent an amused look my way. Chase's theories were usually pretty entertaining.

"First off, and least most likely to be honest, we have alien."

Gideon cocked a brow at her. "Why would an alien disguise themselves as Sully's dead wife? What purpose would that serve except to drive him crazy?"

"Exactly, which is why that was the *least* likely option. Next, I'm thinking she could be someone else, someone who's had tons of surgery to make her look like Emma."

"You mean like the real life, Barbie?" Gideon asked.

"Yep. Just like her."

"What on Earth is a real-life Barbie?" Zeb asked.

"Exactly what it sounds like: someone who has gone crazy with the plastic surgery to look like a human doll. When we get our phones back, we'll show you." Gideon promised.

"Say that were possible. It would cost an absolute fortune, not to mention how painful numerous surgeries would be. Why would someone go to all that effort?" Sam asked, putting a dampener on our discussion.

We were all stumped there.

"Moving on then. What about... robot? That might explain why she doesn't react the way we expect her to, why she has no memory before waking up. Maybe "waking up" is actually code for "turning on?"

"It's not actually that crazy. They've been making robots for years in Japan, creating not only household helpers but also sex bots," Gideon volunteered.

Sam shot him a level stare. "And you know this, how?"

A blush tinged his cheeks. "Reddit."

Sam's only response was to stare at him until he withered under her gaze.

"But what's the point of sending a robot only to attack us immediately after?" Zeb queried, not buying it.

"I don't know. But you've got to admit it would explain some of her quirks."

"Or perhaps somehow, Xavier really did bring her back from the dead." At this, all the air was sucked out of the place. As unlikely as it seemed, Gideon's point wasn't one any of us wanted to entertain.

"We can discuss this all we want but the fact of the matter is, we don't really know," Zeb commented. "When you get to my age, you learn that asking questions that you have no possible answer for, is a fruitless task. Better to put your energy elsewhere, into something practical like helping me to get a bed ready. I need to stretch and get out of this chair."

A flicker of exhaustion flashed over his face. His mouth was pressed into a thin line, his expression weary.

It suddenly dawned on me what a toll this must be taking on him, and guilt quickly overcame me. Here I was, consumed by my relationship problems, when my father was barely keeping it together.

"Sure. Let me get something sorted for you quick." Chase jumped up and started grabbing armfuls of hay, spreading it around, layering it until there was an inch of straw covering the ground.

Gideon and I helped lay Zeb onto his "bed" but I could see he wasn't comfortable: his head was bent at an awkward angle.

Chase removed her cardigan — leaving her with a long-sleeved T-shirt

—and folded it into a makeshift pillow which she placed under his head. His grateful eyes traveled over to hers.

"Thank you."

Not for the first time, I marveled at how sweet a kid she was.

17

CHASE

After making sure Zeb was settled, I went about creating a little section for Bandit and me, using whatever I could salvage. After I was satisfied, I laid down on our bed to test it... and immediately wished I could get back up.

Despite the layers between my bones and the ground, the cold seeped through, turning my blood to ice. Knowing it would only get worse throughout the night, I gritted my teeth and gestured for Bandit.

"Come closer, boy."

Padding to me, he circled the ground, kneading it with his paws before laying down, setting his head onto my thigh with an enormous sigh.

His warm body pressed against me, taking away some of the chill. I stroked his head, running my fingers through his silky fur. The ordinary act of petting my dog calmed me, slowing down my spinning thoughts until my head felt clear enough to think again. Stroking him, I could almost forget that we were being hunted — again.

Almost.

Bandit whined, blowing out a puff of breath. He could feel my tension. Could probably even smell it on me. Not wanting to move away from me, he pawed at the iPad around his neck. I obliged his unspoken request, taking it out and setting it on my lap just in front of his face.

His long pink tongue snaked out, licking my hand in thanks as he picked up the stylus-pen. I watched as he typed, reading the words before his iPad could speak his question.

"Why doesn't Emma like Sam?"

"I don't think she likes anyone too much."

"But Sam is nice."

I stole a quick glance at Sam, who was clearly having some kind of standoff with Sully and didn't seem quite as nice in this current moment. "Yeah. Then again, she doesn't seem to like you either."

"That is unfortunate."

"Right? Who doesn't like you?"

"The Bad Men," Bandit answered, managing to make the iPad sound solemn despite the naturally cheerful, youthful voice we had selected for him. *"They are back again. Why won't they leave us alone?"*

"I don't know." I wanted to say more, but my voice cracked. My eyes had begun to mist up which only made me angry on top of the fear. What would tears do for us? They wouldn't help us, they certainly wouldn't help Bandit. I had to be strong, especially with Sully's world spinning so far out of control that he couldn't see land. My family needed me to be brave.

Squeezing my eyes closed, I lowered my head, letting my hair hide my face as I fought to regain my emotions. Taking a few breaths, I didn't look up again until I was sure I had it together. I should have known that I couldn't fool him. Bandit stared at me with those beautiful, soulful eyes.

"Don't worry. It will be OK."

He woofed to let me know he really meant it. I didn't want to question his faith, but I had to ask.

"How do you know that? How are you so sure?"

"Because we are together. As long as we are all together, all will be OK."

I didn't answer him. I couldn't.

I didn't want to point out that the last time we had fought back together like this, Bandit had ended up on an operating table with his head open.

An icy shiver went up my spine as the horror of that memory refused to go away. Pushing it aside, I hugged Bandit, squeezing him with all of my might, when his head suddenly shot into the air. I froze instantly, tension flooding my body. Had they found us *already*?

"What is it?"

He typed quickly, making errors in his haste, though I could read his chilling message all too well.

"I cn snell blood."

"Whose blood?"

Instead of answering, he bounded to the far corner of the barn. I raced after him, senses firing.

"Bandit wait!"

My shout alerted the others. Out of the corner of my eyes I saw Sully's head pop up, but I didn't stop to explain. If there was blood, then I didn't want my dog anywhere near it, but Bandit kept on running, swerving around a wall of hay bales until he skidded to an abrupt stop, barking sharply.

I ran ahead of him, shielding him with my body. It was instinctual, and I had no real control of myself. If someone was going to get shot, it would be me first.

Instead of the bad guys I expected to see, however, there was only Emma.

She huddled on the ground, her back to us. When she heard our approach, she turned. I immediately saw how white her face was. She looked wan and scared. The patch of straw by her feet was dark and glistening wet. *Had she wet herself?* It wasn't until I took a step closer that I realized the hay was soaked in *blood*.

"Oh no." The metallic smell of the blood filled my nose, making my empty stomach flip-flop.

Emma turned toward me, leaving me with a clear view of her left arm which lay limply by her side. I could now see the deep and jagged cut running along it. The flesh was raw and the blood was still seeping from the wound, pooling onto the straw by her feet.

"I knew I wasn't a robot! See!" She showed me her arm, though her jubilation at proving us wrong lasted all but a second. Staring at her blood, her face grew even paler, if that was even possible.

"I didn't know there would be so much blood. I don't feel so good…"

She swayed and would have fallen if Sully hadn't leaped forward and caught her.

"For God's sake, what has she done now?" Sam gasped, rounding the corner with Gideon pushing Zeb in his wheelchair.

Emma flashed her an injured look beneath her lashes, but stubbornly refused to answer.

"She must have heard me talking. She was trying to prove she wasn't a robot," I explained, remembering all the things I'd said that were now making me feel very guilty.

Sam scanned the scene of the crime, taking in the jagged cut, then the rusty, blood-tipped nail that lay by Emma's feet.

"So you cut yourself open with a rusty nail? Of all the stupid…"

She stopped herself from whatever it was she wanted to say next. Taking a sharp breath, she commanded, "Stick your left hand in the air above your head and put pressure on the wound."

"Why?" Emma looked utterly baffled by this suggestion, as if Sam had just asked her to perform an Irish jig.

"It'll stop the bleeding until I can put something on it."

When Emma didn't move, Sully grabbed her arm and held it above her head while Sam looked for something she could use to dress the wound. Spotting Emma's bag, she opened it.

"That's mine!" Emma protested weakly, sagging against Sully.

Flashing her an incredulous look, Sam rifled in her bag until she found a small bottle of water. Unscrewing the cap, she lowered Emma's arm back down, pouring water over it.

"Ouch, that stings," Emma flinched, but Sam held onto her.

Gideon tore a strip from the denim over-shirt he wore. Sam wrapped the strip around Emma's arm securely. When she was done, she looked Emma in her face.

"Don't ever do anything that stupid again. You could have hit an artery, or that arm could become infected. You could have given yourself tetanus for all we know."

"What's that?"

"It's a serious disease that's caused by cuts or punctures from a contaminated object."

"Like the nail?"

"Yes. If that nail is infected, you could become sick."

Emma's eyes had become very wide. "How sick?"

"Very sick."

Her eyes grew even wider.

"We'll know if you suddenly start getting muscle contractions and can't breathe."

Suddenly, Emma starting hyperventilating, flailing her hands around. "But I can't breathe! I must have it!"

Sam shot her a level look. "It doesn't happen that fast. What you are experiencing, is a panic attack."

Taking pity on her, Zeb smiled gently. "I'm sure you don't have tetanus. It's very rare in the US."

"Almost as rare as coming back from the dead," Gideon quipped before he could stop himself.

"Let's leave her alone so she can get some rest. There's been quite enough excitement," Zeb commented firmly as Gideon wheeled him away. Giving Emma one last look, Sam followed after them.

"Was the old man telling the truth? Is it rare?" She'd addressed the question to Sully, but he didn't answer.

"I think so," I responded, since Sully had yet to say a word. He busied himself replacing the bloody straw with a fresh layer as Emma peered into his face, something other than her arm bothering her.

"Aren't you going to say something? I thought you'd be happy that I'm not a robot?"

But happy was the last thing Sully seemed to be feeling. If anything, he looked stricken.

"Try to get some sleep."

Then, instead of returning to Sam as I expected, Sully started for the front of the barn.

"Where are you going?" I asked.

"Someone needs to keep watch. I'm taking the first shift. Sam, the next. Then Gideon."

"Bandit and I can do one," I volunteered.

"We've got it covered. Go to sleep."

Without another word, he retreated to his post, leaving Emma staring after him like a lost puppy.

18

CHASE

The night enveloped us, pitch black, without a single star in the sky to illuminate the way.

Thigh high grass whipped against my legs as I ran, lashing against my bare flesh. The pain was biting, yet I knew what would become of us would be ten times worse if we were caught.

The night air whipped at my face as I ran faster than I ever had before. Bandit raced alongside, but try as I might, I couldn't see him. I couldn't see anything ahead of me, only the faintest outline of the distant horizon that I was using as a guide.

The footsteps thundered behind us, increasing in volume and speed. I glanced back and could just make out the silhouettes of several hulking figures. In the darkness, they seemed impossibly large and though their faces were indistinguishable, somehow, I knew exactly who they were.

They were catching up.

I wanted to scream at Bandit to hurry, but a cloying fog stopped me from forming the words. Though I was screaming, though I was raging inside, only the thinnest sound emerged.

My fear had reached a fever pitch. Forcing my feet to go faster, my breath was coming in short, sharp bursts. My pulse racing, I ran so fast that I couldn't even feel the ground beneath my feet anymore. Suddenly, I went flying as something tackled me.

I hit the ground with a thud; the air knocked out of me. I heard Bandit whining, but I couldn't focus on anything other than that great weight that had fallen on top of me. My heart, my airways were being crushed — and there was nothing I could do.

I was going to die.

Despite not being able to see anything, a giant shape blurred toward my face. I was hit by the smell next. But it wasn't the acrid smell of poison or death I expected. The scent that filled my nostrils was familiar. *Loved even.*

The whining came again, this time right in my ears. So loud that it made me flinch. Something soft rubbed against my face, starting on my chin, then moving up to my cheek. I was becoming aware of my aching body next. Of the cold, rigid hardness beneath my back. And that heavy, crushing weight on my chest.

My eyes flew open.

The black spots took a few moments to recede, and when they did, I found myself staring up at Bandit's concerned face, now only inches from my own. And that heavy, crushing weight was just his body lying on top of mine.

I blinked, relief washing over me, as I tried to force the nightmare away. My eyes rose past Bandit's head and I noticed the ceiling was much higher than I expected it to be. This ceiling wasn't my ceiling from home. This wasn't my ceiling from the ranch.

Suspended from *my* ceiling was a cute mobile that Gideon had made for me during the two months he had fancied himself a metal worker. The sun glinted off the tarnished steel in the morning, as the portrait of the dancing girl and her dog twirled round and around. It was a sight that I loved dearly, but with a crushing ache in my heart, it slowly dawned on me that I would never see again.

Where I was now, no mobile girl danced. And the early morning light that streamed in came not through the window, but a gaping hole in the roof.

And suddenly, everything that had come to pass in the last twenty-four hours came crashing into my mind.

Bandit, who must have sensed my distress while I was sleeping, chuffed a greeting at me. His breath warmed my face as the familiar weight of him kept the mounting panic at bay.

For a moment, I thought of how dogs are often suggested as emotional support companions. They can sense distress from their owners without any type of teaching; they usually know to pin them down if they were having a panic attack. This was similar to the effects of an weighted blanket: providing comfort and security to its user. It's one of the many reasons why dogs are advised for people with PTSD. After everything I had gone through, even before I met Bandit or Sully, I wouldn't be surprised if I suffered from it myself.

Intruding on that thought, Bandit's words from the night before echoed in my mind, and I was suddenly struck by their relevance.

He had been right.

As long as we were all together, we would weather whatever storm that came.

I turned my head to find Zeb sleeping soundly beside me. A shaft of the pre-dawn light spilled over his face and illuminated the myriad of lines that carved their way across his features. I was struck by how old he suddenly seemed. How frail and withered. Had he somehow shrunk in the night?

Bizarrely, I knew the reverse of this to be true. At school, I remembered reading a textbook that explained how people actually began the day an inch taller. It had something to do with how gravity would compress the cartilage in our spine when we stand, walk, or sit during the day. When we sleep, the spine lengthens, making us just that little taller in the morning. Looking at Zeb though, it seemed the opposite, and I didn't like how anxious that made me feel.

I propped myself up onto my elbow to see the area littered with sleeping bodies.

Sam still slept in her corner, while, curled in a fetal position across the room, Emma looked strikingly young and vulnerable.

When she was silent like this, when she wasn't moving, I felt almost protective of her. She was so childlike and simple in so many ways that even though she irritated the heck out of me, I also felt kind of sorry for her.

Bandit chuffed softly at my face, wondering where my mind had gone. I moved a hand up to scratch his nose.

"Hey, boy"

He chuffed again, quietly, so as not to wake the others. Though he seemed in a relatively good mood — did dogs have any other? — his movements were sluggish this morning: I knew I wasn't the only one who'd had a tough time sleeping through the night.

Glancing up through the hole in the barn, I saw the purple-pink sky outside. Thin clouds crawled slowly across the horizon, as if they had only just woken too. In the distance, there was the sound of birdsong, but it wasn't the rousing chorus that signified the break of a new day. It was one or two birds singing an early morning tune. Their sleepy voices were the only disruption to the serene silence...

Until I heard a sound from outside the barn and moved Bandit's head from my chest so I could sit up. Through a thin gap in the wall, I glimpsed Sully pacing outside.

We got up, moving carefully around Gideon, who lay protectively on Zeb's other side. As soon as I emerged from the barn I was hit by the brisk morning air. It sent such a chill straight into my chest that I had to stifle the urge to cough. Rubbing my hands together, I looked at Sully. "Did you manage to get any peace last night?"

Sully raised red-rimmed eyes toward me, shaking his head. He looked bad, like he hadn't slept at all. "If you mean, did Emma and Sam finally resolve their issues so that we could all move on, then the answer is no."

I wish I could have Bandit's positive attitude and reassure him that things would work out, but the words died in my throat. Over and over, the question ran through my mind: how was Emma here?

What even *was* she?

Every movement Sully made was agitated; I could almost see the tension roll off him like a wave. He had been such a shell of a man after Emma had died. It had actually taken losing everything he had been clinging onto to finally move on with his life, though it seemed life wasn't quite done toying with him yet.

The world could be so cruel.

"One good thing that comes from not sleeping, is that I was able to come up with a plan of sorts," Sully interrupted my thoughts.

A tiny glimmer of hope rose in my chest. "Oh yeah, what is it?"

"We need help to get away from these guys so I'm going back to the gas station we passed yesterday. They must have a phone there. I'll call Mark and pick up basic supplies while I'm there."

I didn't want to knock his plan, but I had been hoping for something bigger and grander. Still, it was practical and didn't sound like it would be too difficult or risky to execute.

"Let us visit the restroom, then we'll be ready." I was already turning away when he stopped me.

"No. It'll be less conspicuous if I'm alone. Now that my leg's better, I can run again. Maybe not as fast as before, but I can make decent time."

When I had met him, Sully could not sleep without his wife beside him. His only recourse were the punishing late night runs he ran to physically exhaust himself, though after he had been shot in the leg during our escape from Forbes' lab, we weren't sure if he'd ever run again. Sully had surprised us with his determination. The bullet had gone straight through leaving a clean wound. After months of rehab, he graduated from walking to a slow jog, but he had kept at it, determined that Forbes wouldn't take this from him.

The last time I saw Sully running, he had managed to out-pace me, which, technically wasn't a big deal since I wasn't ever going to win any race. But, he'd been able to keep going while I was wheezing and gasping for air after only a few minutes. I had faith he would be able to do this, though I didn't have to like it.

Sully must have felt my objections, as he gave me a small smile.

"I'll be fine. If anything happens, if I see any sign of those men, I can just disappear into the cornfields. You know it'll be easier to do that on my own. As much as I'd love for the two of you to go with me, I would have so much more to worry about. Alone, I can be in and out before anyone notices me."

"You're just going straight there. You're calling Mark, grabbing some food and then coming straight back?" I asked, reiterating the plan, hating how needy I sounded yet kind of not caring either. Sully nodded.

He looked past me, into the barn. I couldn't see where his eyes landed, but I had a pretty good guess what — or who — he was staring at. "Honestly... I could do with some alone time."

The weight of the world pressed onto his shoulders. He sagged in front of me, becoming smaller until he suddenly shook himself, straightening back to full height. "Let them sleep longer, but if they're not awake by the time the sun is up, get them ready in case we need to make a fast exit."

"Okay."

I wasn't able to say much else. Bandit pawed the ground, as alarmed by our imminent separation as much as I was. Sully wrapped me in a sudden, tight hug and stroked Bandit on the head.

"Don't you two worry about a thing. I'll be right back."

He took off at a slow pace, trying to shake his muscles awake. I twisted my fingers into Bandit's fur, watching as he grew smaller and smaller, until his figure was a black speck in the distance, desperate to ignore the hollow feeling in my stomach.

19
____

SULLY

Don't look back.

Forcing myself to place one foot after another, and despite my senses shrieking at me otherwise, I jogged away from my family. Away from my loved ones.

I was acutely aware that Chase and Bandit hadn't moved. I could feel their eyes boring into my back. Though my stomach churned like a river, it took every inch of willpower not to sprint back to them.

I knew what suffering was. I knew what it was to have loved and lost, to have your family ripped away from you, their lives hanging in the balance on the whim of a madman. So, their presence in my life wasn't something I ever took for granted.

I had made that particular mistake once, and it had almost cost us our lives. Nothing put things into perspective more than a near-miss with death.

It was for this very reason I had to do this alone.

I hadn't been lying when I'd said we'd draw too much attention if Chase and Bandit had come with me, but there was a darker thinking to my logic that I hadn't wanted to express.

If I ran into those men again, I didn't like my chances. Better that my family were hidden away with transport close to hand. If they needed to make a quick getaway, they could do so. I was learning the hard way that this is what fathers did.

They protected their kids against threats, and threw themselves into danger if that was what was required of them. Good fathers would at least not the garbage Chase and Gideon had the misfortune of growing up with.

Although, not all matters were so black and white.

Take my relationship with my father. There were years when we had never exchanged a single word. I was too busy feeling the righteous justice of my anger, while he had become so disappointed that I would never follow in his wife's footsteps — footsteps which he himself had never been able to fulfill — that he'd willingly cut himself out of our lives. Was there anything as dangerous or as self-serving as a parent who imposed their unfulfilled desires onto their child?

I was grateful we'd repaired our relationship now, though it had come at no small cost. If the stubborn fool had told me about the accident that had ultimately crippled him, I would have come home sooner, but pride had proven stronger than the fall.

I loved him, but I prayed I wouldn't make the same mistakes with my kids.

Unable to help myself, I tossed a quick look over my shoulder — and immediately wished I hadn't. As I had suspected, Chase hadn't moved an inch. Even with the distance beginning to separate us, I could see the miserable expression that clouded her features.

And I knew exactly what she was thinking.

There was still a large part of her that questioned if I was really going to return. She had learned growing up that nothing in life was ever certain, and it had become clear that this fear would persist even when we were together. Even if everything continued to go smoothly, there would always be that lingering doubt that our happy life together wouldn't last. But with the emergence of these men who were so intent on killing us, her worries proved true.

Have faith, Chase. I will be back and we'll climb our way out of this hellhole together.

My feet pounded the tarmac, the cramped tendons beginning to loosen up. My breath was beginning to catch as my pulse sped up. The crisp morning air swam into my lungs, shocking my system.

All night, my head had been filled with a manic clutter of questions, cycling from fears about the men and why they had shown up now, to Emma, sleeping less than fifty feet away from me.

Deep down, I knew it couldn't be my wife.

I knew she was dead.

But if you had asked me a year ago, I would have said dogs couldn't use iPads. The woman who had appeared in our house looked and sounded just like Emma, though the lack of memory was convenient. Chase was right: it wasn't beyond the realm of possibility that she was another woman who'd received extreme plastic surgery to look like my wife.

I had seen images of people who wanted to look like a movie star. No matter how many thousands of dollars they spent, the end result could never look quite like their idol; some features were too exaggerated, such as a nose or an eyebrow line that was slightly too perfect.

This Emma, however, was the spitting image of my own.

And that wasn't all.

I'd catch her with the same mannerisms as my late wife. It was never anything obvious, or something anyone else would notice, but I had lived with and loved her, and I knew her inside out. I knew how, whenever she was troubled, she tended to chew on the corner of her lip — just as this Emma did.

In the early hours of last night, I had found myself passing her corner more than once. Each time, she had been sleeping on her stomach, one hand beneath her face in exactly the way my Emma had always slept.

And when she had cut her arm yesterday, she had almost fainted from the sight of her own blood. It had been a running joke between us about how my Emma could work in a veterinary clinic yet be so irrationally scared of blood.

Each time I considered the possibilities, her frightened face would appear and my body would react. A protective surge would come over me, leading to a heavy sense of guilt that would leave me almost breathless.

It was enough to make a man's head explode.

Deciding it was safer to steer clear of those waters, I flipped my thoughts to the matter at hand. It wasn't safe to stay on the roads. I would feel much happier once we could ditch the truck for a different ride, even if those bullet-proof walls would be missed.

Picking up the pace, I pushed forward, the uncertainty and fear driving me toward the gas station we had passed yesterday, not long before we had found the barn.

Birds flew overhead while a light breeze rustled the stalks of corn on either side. As the sun crested over the horizon and painted the sky in wispy shades of blue, the turmoil brewing inside lent me the strength to keep going.

Eventually, I arrived at my destination and was relieved to see that my recollection of the place had been correct — the gas station was in an extremely isolated spot.

What I hadn't factored on was, given how off the beaten path it was, how popular the place would be, especially when the day had barely begun.

Five cars sat waiting beside a gleaming motorcycle, their owners inside grabbing gas or taking a leak. I spotted a pay phone but hesitated. From the direction I had come from, I could only see one side of the gas station. I would feel safer having scoped it out from all angles before using it.

With that in mind, I slowed my jog to a walk, crossing to the other side when my heart seized in my chest and I stopped dead.

Two large white trucks were parked in front of me.

I about had a seizure when I noticed the logo of a well-known oil company plastered to the side of one truck. Dried mud had baked onto the wheels of the other truck, which had no identifying features other than the two furry dice that hung off the rearview mirror. When I caught the California license plates, I felt my tension lessen.

The armored trucks that had come for us had been identical in their anonymity, but they were also brand new and so spotless that you could have eaten off them. It seemed unlikely that these trucks were owned by the same men who were after us.

Still, I felt uneasy. Keeping my eyes glued to the vehicles, I made my way to the phone. Rummaging in my pockets, I fished out a couple of coins, hoping they would be enough to cover it. I had no idea what it cost to make a phone call these days.

Holding my breath, I dialed Mark's number.

20

SULLY

Other than Sam, Dad, and the kids, Mark was the closest thing I had to family, even sticking with me during my year of bereavement when I'd acted like a clown.

A wave of shame came over me when I thought about how I'd behaved the time Mark had brought me a home-made lasagna that had been painstakingly prepared by his bedmate of the moment. We had a disagreement which culminated in my hurling it out of the window where it had shattered onto the sidewalk below.

Thankfully, we made our peace after that. He was even at the wedding, marveling at how the universe had let a schmuck like me get so lucky a second time.

Well, buddy, have I got news for you.

Mark worked on Wall Street, dealing with high-end accounts, making the kind of figures that made my eyes water. Irritatingly, he only worked a few days a week, spending the rest of his time golfing or entertaining his latest model conquest.

Despite how little he actually worked, Mark was the opposite of lazy and kept an early morning routine. Rising at five AM, he would hit his home gym so I knew he would be awake.

The phone started ringing. I held my breath in anticipation of him answering it on the other end. The phone rang once, twice, three times...

With each unanswered ring, my heart pounded faster.

I considered that Mark might be away on another one of his "work" trips, which seemed to consist of nothing more than going out with his firm's wealthiest clients for several days of debauchery, only to return nursing a hangover and an empty wallet. On one occasion, he'd returned looking like he'd been hit by a truck though he'd swore he'd had the wildest time of his life.

We both had a very different understanding of the word.

The phone continued to ring. I counted up to the seventh ring and was sure his voicemail would kick in when his pain laden voice finally sounded over the line, husky from sleep.

"Who in God's name is calling me so early?"

Hearing his familiar voice, my chest tightened with emotion. Uttering a quick prayer of thanks, I started talking. "Mark, it's me."

I made sure not to say my name. While I didn't know who these people were, I had already seen the kind of artillery they commanded. If they were anything like the mercenaries Forbes' had recruited, they likely had all kinds of gadgets at their disposal, so a trace on his phone didn't seem all that unlikely.

Mark gasped, his voice becoming quickly awake. "I've been trying to reach you! Where are you?"

The question seemed a bit much as he coughed, dry heaving coughs into the handset.

"I can't say. I'll explain in a minute, but... what's wrong? You sound like you're in pain."

Mark coughed again, a racking sound that rattled my own ribcage. "That's because I am. Hold on."

I heard him reach for a bottle of pills. He swallowed a couple, chasing them down with a mouthful of water. "That's better," he said.

"What happened?"

"I'm not sure where to begin."

"The beginning's usually a good place."

"I would if I could remember it. Thing is, I apparently had an accident."

Concern made me grip the telephone tighter. "An accident?"

"Well, they tell me it was an accident — but, I can't actually remember."

I tried to make sense of his words, but my brain was not yet firing on all cylinders. "I don't understand."

"I woke up in a ditch with two cracked ribs, a black eye, and a nasty concussion. My wallet and keys were gone, so they think I was mugged. Everything hurt like a bitch."

"Jesus. When did this happen?"

Mark didn't answer straight away. I heard him move, probably trying to get into a more comfortable position. When he came back, he sounded stressed.

"Yesterday. I knew I had been at work because my assistant confirmed that, but after I had a few drinks with a client, I was attacked and found in the park by my place."

Although the idea arose that this could be related to us, I said nothing of it — best not to tip off the bad guys if they were in fact, listening in on the call.

"That really stinks. I hope they catch the guy." My words sounded lame and would do little to console him though Mark didn't seem to mind. I said a lot about the guy but as a friend, he was as solid as they came, so solid that he didn't even notice I wasn't quite behaving as a caring friend should.

"Listen, I have more bad news. It's why I've been trying to reach you," he continued. "You need to steel yourself."

His tone had taken on a graveness I had only heard once before.

When the end was near, Mark had been waiting in the corridor outside Emma's hospital room. I had been holding onto her hand when she finally succumbed to the cancer she had valiantly fought for two years. I had been by her side every step of the way, encouraging her when she felt weak, and comforting her when she'd been afraid. But in the end, the cancer had taken its toll, slowly draining her life until she was nothing but a husk of her former self.

When her chest stopped moving, I had uttered a wail so full of despair that Mark had rushed into the room and held me like I was a baby. Over and over, he had said how sorry he was.

To hear that tone in his voice again, I knew that whatever was coming was going to be bad. Considering all that had happened recently, I squared my shoulders, preparing myself for the worst.

"It's Florence. She passed away. I'm sorry Sully, there was nothing anyone could do."

Of all the things I had expected, that hadn't been it. His words slammed into me with the finality of a ton of bricks. Only my hands gripping onto the phone stopped me from being leveled.

Florence.

Her lined face came into my mind. Since the opening of the clinic, she had seen me through the best and worst years of my life. In the absence of my mother, she had been, for all intents and purposes, my substitute one. She had been there to lend her shoulder after Emma had passed. She had been the one to plan and execute the funeral. In that initial, bleak week after my loss, when I couldn't move because of the grief, she had taken care of me.

But now she was gone and I would never speak to her again. Tears misted my eyes, despair welling up a storm inside. I felt myself crumpling, my body leaning against the walls of the phone box until it bore my full weight and was the only thing keeping me upright.

"How did she die?"

"She had a date to play bridge with a friend, but Florence never turned up or called. Her friend was concerned, so she went to her home. Florence had given her a set of keys on the rare occasion that she wasn't home and needed someone to feed her cat. She found Florence slumped in her favorite armchair. Her TV was on and there was a microwave meal on her lap. If it's any consolation, they don't think she suffered."

An icy cold stole over me.

Mark didn't know Florence like I did. He was unaware of her strange quirks, including her irrational fear of ballerinas. She believed they were emotionless and deliberately mangled their feet to balance in a way that was never meant for humans. Needless to say, she avoided ballet performances at all costs.

Mark didn't know that.

He also didn't know how much Florence abhorred microwaves.

She didn't believe in them and only had one in the house as it was gifted from her brother. She could not bear to part with it and disappoint him, so instead, the machine had sat on her side table, unplugged and unused because she could never accept that they used radiation to heat up food.

And it wasn't only her own use she was concerned with, frequently voicing her displeasure at me just for microwaving a burrito. Hell, the woman was such a purist, she wouldn't touch any food that couldn't be grown.

There was no way in hell that Florence would eat a microwave meal.

A lead weight dropped in the pit of my stomach as my thoughts took a darker turn. Had those same men gone after her? Had they killed her and tried to pass it off as a natural death?

It felt insane to even pose the question, yet I had already experienced what they were capable of.

"When did she die?" I asked, keeping my macabre thoughts to myself. I shouldn't say anything unless I had proof, and even then, I wasn't sure it would be a good idea. The less Mark knew, the safer he would be.

Except Florence hadn't known a thing, and she was dead now.

"Well, that's another bizarre coincidence," Mark continued. "It must have happened the same day that someone mugged me, if you can believe that."

My stomach sank all the way to the ground. I could believe it, and unfortunately, I now knew my suspicions were justified.

The men who had come after us had killed Florence and attacked Mark.

It took every inch of willpower not to blurt out the truth. What was the point in endangering him further? If I didn't reveal any of my predicament, maybe, just maybe, they would leave him alone. After all, if they had already gone after him once but left him alive, surely they must have concluded that he did not know anything.

"Anyway, you didn't know about any of this, so why are you calling so early?" Mark asked, suddenly concerned.

"I was actually calling for a favor. I figured your cabin would be empty this time of the year and wanted to ask if you'd mind us borrowing it. I was thinking of taking the family for a vacation, but it doesn't seem the right thing to do now, so scratch that idea."

I could almost hear him frowning down the phone line. I silently willed him to buy my excuse.

"Obviously, it's yours if you want it. There's nothing you can do to turn back time, so you shouldn't let what's happened spoil your time with the family. The keys are hidden in the flowerpot with a rose painted on it. The place is stocked with food too, so yeah, be my guest."

It sounded like the answer to our prayers so having to reject it felt like a physical blow.

"No," I answered, trying to keep my voice natural. "I'll figure something else out. Maybe we'll head back to Montreal. Sam and I just had a blast there for our honeymoon."

Mark went silent, and I felt myself grow wary. I was never able to hide anything from him and I worried he wouldn't buy my story. When he spoke again, a new awareness had crept in.

"What's going on? Is there something you need to tell me?"

It was on the tip of my tongue to spill my guts and receive his help, but I knew I couldn't risk it. He wasn't a part of this and he never could be. "I'm about as fine as I can be under the circumstances. Don't worry about me. I've got my family to pull me through. You just heal up."

I could hear the gears turning in his mind, but something in my voice must have told him to drop it.

"You know I'm here anytime you need me?"

"Yeah." I had to get off this call or I would blow it. "I'll call back in a few days to find out about the funeral. I assume her niece is organizing it?"

"Yeah, Paula's been a trooper. Even adopted the cat. That thing's going to be spoiled rotten."

Heavy silence came down the line. I cleared my throat, forcing my voice to sound neutral.

"I need to go. Take care of yourself, bud. Stay away from those parks and ditches."

Without waiting for a response, I hung up.

21

SULLY

Though the conversation with Mark had left me shaken, I couldn't allow myself the luxury of breaking down. I was only halfway through my task, and even then, I had struck out.

My head was spinning.

If they could kill an innocent elderly woman and leave a man half dead in a ditch, there would be no reasoning with them.

Faced with a relentless enemy, the stakes had never been higher. Their intentions were crystal clear –- total elimination. It was a chilling reality, one that set this conflict apart from anything we had encountered before. With Forbes' men — in the initial stages at least — there had been a glimmer of hope amidst the darkness: the enemy's desire to keep Bandit alive. It was a slender lifeline in the midst of chaos. Yet, as the battle raged on, even that flicker of hope faded. Now, the transition from wanting Bandit alive to the ruthless pursuit of total annihilation marked a turning point, forcing us to confront an enemy devoid of mercy.

I had to grab provisions and hurry back to the others to relay my discovery. We needed to formulate a new plan.

Crossing the threshold into the gas station, my senses heightened, acutely aware of the stakes that rested upon my shoulders. The hum of fluorescent lights above echoed in the sterile atmosphere. My gaze darted, scanning for any telltale signs of surveillance. There, behind the cashier's counter, I spotted the glint of a lens – a silent sentinel capturing the movements of unsuspecting customers. Another camera, strategically positioned, kept a watchful eye on the gas pumps, its unblinking gaze tracking every vehicle that pulled in.

With a calculated calmness that I didn't feel, I took swift action. My hand reached out, fingers grazing the fabric of a baseball cap displayed on a nearby stand. It was a stroke of luck, a conveniently placed accessory that now became my disguise. Pulling it from the rack, I slipped it onto my head, feeling the reassuring touch of the worn fabric against my skin. In one fluid motion, I tugged the cap low, its brim casting a shadow over my eyes, obscuring my features from prying lenses.

As I adjusted the cap, I made sure to fold and tuck the price tag beneath the fabric, erasing any trace of my impromptu disguise. I was uneasy with the act of stealing, but there was no other way. I had to stay incognito. My family's safety depended on it.

The cashier, a young guy in his twenties, nodded at me. I nodded back a greeting but didn't say a word. Turning my head from the cameras, I moved toward a refrigerated unit. The chilled air wrapped around me as I swiftly selected an array of sandwiches, bananas, candy bars, nuts, and as many bottles of water as I could carry.

My arms already half full, I stopped a shelf of dog food and loaded up on the cans. Balancing everything carefully, I made my way to the waiting line when Florence's face flew into my mind with a forcefulness that left me breathless. It was impossible to grasp that she was dead because of us.

Because of me.

I'm so sorry, Florence. This wasn't the ending you deserved.

"You ready?" The cashier asked, interrupting my guilt trip.

Jolted back to reality, I jumped. "Yeah, sorry."

Dumping the food onto the counter so he could reach them easier, I watched, a boot tapping an impatient beat on the floor as I waited for him to ring them up. With every chime of the till, my money seemed to diminish faster than I could count. I forked over the bills reluctantly. When the cashier handed me my change, I had to suppress a laugh — was it really worth the effort of giving me back two dimes?

Unbeknownst to the diligent cashier, my nerves were stretched thin, every muscle in my body wound tight with tension. He worked with methodical precision, bagging up the goods carefully, heaviest items first. Under ordinary circumstances, I might have appreciated his precision, but why did it have to be this, of all mornings, for me to meet the world's most conscientious — and slowest — cashier? As I silently urged him along, a flash of metal caught my eye.

I glanced over at the coffee machine, which looked to have been buffed within an inch of its life — from this same guy, no doubt. What was he going for? Employee of the year? When, suddenly, reflected in the shiny metal, I saw a truck approaching.

And it was *identical* to the one we had stolen.

My stomach lurched at the sight. My senses were on high alert as adrenaline coursed through my veins. They were here! How had they found me so quickly? Could they have traced the call *that* fast? It didn't seem possible.

I only had seconds, a minute at most, to make a getaway without them seeing me. Scooping up the bag of groceries, I raced out of there. There was no attempt to stay undercover this time.

Trying to stop the panic from taking hold, I scanned the area to see if there was anything I could use since jogging back would be out of the question.

I needed a ride.

Glancing across the lot, I assessed my options. One car had its driver already inside, while another's tyres were being checked over. The other two vehicles were nowhere to be seen, having presumably left already.

Spinning around, I searched for something, anything I could use when my gaze landed on the motorcycle I had seen on my way in. It was a nice-looking bike. A Harley Davidson with the American flag airbrushed onto its leather seat, but what I noticed more than its atheistic appeal, was the absence of its owner. Hopefully, he was in the john.

Hurrying to the bike, I dumped the bag into the luggage rack at the back of the bike and climbed on. To my enormous relief, the keys were still in the ignition.

Shooting a prayer to the heavens, I turned the key. The engine roared to life startling its owner who — it turned out — wasn't in the john at all, but hidden from my view behind a gas pump on a mobile call. The biker, a stocky guy with a large tattoo of an octopus wrapped around his neck, yelled over.

"What the... That's my bike!"

As multiple faces turned toward me, I gunned the engine and peeled off, leaving a cloud of smoke in my wake.

22

CHASE

Watching Sully take off like that was a little like I had agreed for him to walk out of my life forever, as if my lack of action could be taken as silent consent.

Technically, I know that's not what actually happened, but I still couldn't shake that nagging doubt that wrapped its dark fingers around my heart. That absolute fear shocked me to my core, but also made me feel furious with myself.

Throughout my childhood, I had looked after myself. When my mom wasn't locking me in our trailer so she could abandon me to her ongoing hunt for a man, she would drown her sorrows or veg out in front of the TV for days on end. Forget her being the parent, I was the one who took care of us.

I was the one who did the dishes and cooked boxed mac and cheese in the microwave. I washed the laundry in the tub whenever we were low on cash — which was basically all the time. I even had to get up throughout the night to check that her cigarette butts were actually out, as she had a habit of dozing off while smoking on the sofa.

Yet despite everything I did for her, I know she never loved me. I was never more than a slave she could boss around, her little caretaker. When Tubs came into the picture, things had grown ten times worse. Now she had a partner who drank even more than she did. Every one of their binge-drinking sessions ended in a violent fight with me somehow, always catching the worst of it.

But when Tubs started viewing me as more than just his punching bag, I knew I had to get out of there, but I didn't have a clue what I was really setting myself up for.

Living on the streets was a constant fight for survival, one you never got a break from. Finding food wasn't the only struggle — an empty stomach you quickly grew used to. The lethargy and weakness could be combated by carefully timed nibbles of an energy bar. No. The worst thing was never knowing where you were going to sleep that night... *and if you would ever wake again.*

The doorways and alleyways that were a typical homeless person's bedroom provided next to no security. Drunks and druggies often wandered too close for comfort. And sometimes, just the random creepy opportunist looking for a "good" time. I don't think I actually slept through an entire night while I was homeless. To think I only used to worry about my mom's cigarette butts; those had been the good old days.

Which is why, standing here now, I couldn't understand why I felt so helpless. I had been through hell and back, all on my own. It made no sense at all for me to feel like this.

A cold, wet nose nudged the back of my hand. In the depths of his green-eyed gaze, I saw a reflection of my own concerns mirrored back at me. Bandit's unspoken understanding bridged the gap between man and beast, a silent pact of loyalty and love that went beyond words. With a gentle touch, I scratched the top of his nose, his fur soft beneath my fingers, grounding me in the reality of his presence.

He nudged the iPad on the ground with his snout, a gesture both endearing and astute, and typed.

"Sully will be back."

Great. Now my dog was having to reassure me of my insecurities. Good job being the strong one, Chase.

"I know," I answered. "I just wish we could have gone with him. It doesn't feel right to have him out there alone without even a weapon or a way to reach us if something goes wrong."

Bandit lowered his head to the digital keyboard again.

"Sully is smart. He is our pack leader. He will be back soon and then we can leave together."

A sound came from behind us, the creek of the barn doors opening as someone stepped through. We looked over to find Emma staring at us in annoyance, running her fingers through her hair in an attempt to unravel the knots that tangled her blonde locks.

"It is too early for you to be making so much commotion," she said grumpily as she gave up on her hair, wrapping her arms around herself to ward off the chill.

We were barely a sound. I was just speaking to Bandit."

Her lips turned down with disapproval.

"The two of you don't know how noisy you are. You woke me from clear across the barn. It's not like I had much rest either, not with my arm hurting so much and all the snoring you did."

Was she on crack? I was incredulous and unable to hide it. "I don't snore!"

"Then what was that loud rumbling sound that came out of your mouth the whole night long. Him to." She pointed a skinny finger at Bandit, who shot me such a comical look of shock that a laugh almost burst out of me.

"For someone who has no idea what they're talking about, you sure do a lot of it," I shot back before I could stop myself. Her eyebrows rose a notch. I could feel my anger bubbling up.

"Well, you are a horrible little girl," she retorted.

I stared at her. "Seriously? That's all you've got?"

She glared at me then, stamping her foot. "And you smell! Both of you!"

With that, she turned around. With her nose in the air, she stormed back inside. Stomping every step of the way, she made as much noise as her ballet pumps would allow her.

"That's one way to wake up the rest of the clan, I guess."

"*Woof,*" came the answer by my side.

23
______

CHASE

Until Sully returned, breakfast was a pathetic affair.
All I had was some gum, warm from being in the back of my jeans. Sam fared a little better — she found a bag of peanut M&M's in her bag, which she divided between us. Well, between the rest of us, excluding Emma. She had retreated back into her corner, apparently not interested in anything to do with us now that Sully wasn't here.

The rest of us ate our candy quickly, eager for what little energy it would provide. Bandit had none since chocolate was poisonous to dogs. He said he was fine to wait for Sully, but Sam stopped herself from eating, staring at the meagre portion in her hand.

Observing Emma from across the room, a flicker of irritation marred her usually composed expression. She mumbled something; the words lost under her breath, but her tone was laced with frustration.

With a determined stride, Sam closed the distance between them. I watched as she split the meager portion, extending a peace offering toward the other woman. It was a testament to her kindness that she was willing to share, even in the face of her obvious annoyance. However, her attempt at goodwill was met with an unexpected reaction. Emma's eyes widened, a horrified gasp escaping her lips as if Sam had offered her something unimaginable.

"Are you kidding me right now?"

Sam's voice was hard and her eyes had turned flat. She snatched her hand back, withdrawing her offer of food. I moved towards them, unsure of what Emma had done that caused Sam to react in such a fashion. When I got there, however, I instantly saw what had drawn Sam's ire: Emma was halfway through another energy bar while an empty bottle of water lay between her feet.

"You drank the water too?"

She jumped guilty. "I only had the one bottle. My throat was feeling tight. I was worried I might have caught the Tetanus and wanted to make sure I could still drink..." she began, only for Sam to cut her off.

"You heard us over there. You know we barely have anything between us, yet here you are, hiding in this corner, so you still don't have to share your food with us. I can't believe how selfish you are!"

Shockingly, Emma's eyes brimmed with tears. "You're always yelling at me."

The tears took Sam by surprise, their sudden appearance like a crack in a dam that had been holding back a torrent of emotion. It was a vulnerability she hadn't expected, and she must have felt a pang of sympathy as she paused, softening her tone. "You need to think, Emma. We're all in this together. Everyone's hungry and thirsty, not only you. If you want us to treat you better, you need to think a little less about yourself and more about others. It's the only way we're going to get through this."

Emma fell silent. I actually thought Sam might get through to her for once.

"What does Sully say?"

Sam blinked, startled by the question. "What does it matter what he has to say?"

"He's my husband..."

"So you're only interested in what *he* thinks? Unbelievable!"

Emma didn't answer, looking trapped. Her lower lip trembled. I felt more tears might be coming. A low, drawn-out whistle emitted from Gideon's lips as he approached. I could tell he had woken recently as his clothes were rumpled and there was a smudge of dirt on his cheek. As tired as he looked, he had already helped Zeb into his wheelchair and was now pushing him toward the source of all the commotion. He ran a hand through his disheveled hair. "At least she's honest, right?"

A look of gratefulness came over Emma. "Thank you," she answered, as if Gideon had meant it as a compliment. "At least *he's* being nice to me."

Gideon's face turned surprised. "Just to clarify, I was being sarcastic."

Emma bit her lip, those tears finally spilling over. "So you're being mean, too. Yet somehow you're all shocked that I won't share my food with you. Why should I when none of you like me?"

"That hasn't got anything to do with this!" I burst out, unable to keep it together anymore.

"We're here as a team because someone is after us! We have to work together, and that means sharing what resources we have if we're going to have any chance of staying alive. You can't just do your own thing when you're with us. It doesn't work like that."

"We share whatever we have, Emma. It's what families do," Zeb agreed gently, but we may well have spoken to a brick wall for all the good it did. She retreated into a ball, hugging her bag to her chest.

"You can say whatever you want, but I know the truth. None of you are my friends. Only Sully cares about me."

I had half a mind to set her straight since I wasn't totally sure that was true. She made me so angry, especially when you factored in that she could be the very reason our lives were in danger. After all, we had been fine. Happily living our lives when she plowed into our home and ruined our lives.

What a selfish little—

Whatever curse word I was about to think was wiped clean from my mind at the sound of a motorcycle roaring toward us. Icy fingers of fear raced down my spine. My heart rate spiked, my stomach plummeted as I imagined those men to be back.

Sam waved at us frantically. "Back! Hide!"

I didn't need another warning.

Bandit and I sprinted behind a stack of hay bales while Gideon steered Zeb into a dark corner. Emma hadn't moved, her face white as a sheet. Like a rabbit in the headlights, she stood there until Sam pulled her down.

"Get down, idiot!" she hissed through her teeth.

For the first time since I'd known her, Emma didn't answer back. Cowering into a ball, Sam kept her hand pushed down against the back of her head, afraid that Emma would give us all away.

I stole a furtive glance at one of the many gaps that lay within the walls of the barn, but couldn't see the motorcycle or its rider outside. Bandit's nose twitched, trying to pick up a scent. I'd been with him long enough to recognize his warnings, so I steeled myself for his reaction.

He whined, a happy whine, then let out a bark. The tension that had flooded my body immediately left.

"It's Sully," I called out to the others.

Their faces came back into the light, reflecting the relief I was feeling. The bike was kept running though Sully appeared in the doorway, clutching a bag of what had to be food. Instead of the welcoming smile I was expected, his face was pale. The fear that was in his eyes was tangible.

"We need to get out of here. Now!"

We hurried over to him, talking over each other in our haste.

"What's going on?"

"Did they find us?"

Sully gestured for us to simmer down. "They're right behind me. I saw one of the armored trucks as I was coming out of the gas station. We need to leave."

Gideon's hands tightened into fists, unable to take in the news. "But we got rid of all electronic devices. Nobody has one they can trace, do they?"

A chorus of head shakes was his answer. Sam had already explained how they could be easily tracked. I hadn't known until she explained that if a cell phone that was turned on, even for a few seconds, it could give an indication of its location. It's how law enforcement officers caught criminals all the time, but we were smart enough to know better.

Well, except for one person, maybe.

Without meaning to, we all turned to Emma.

"You don't have anything in that bag that could have led them to us, do you?" Sam asked Emma in the voice she used at work, the one that reeked of authority and had lesser men quaking in their boots.

Not Emma, though, who wasn't smart enough to know better. "We already went through this! You saw what was in my bag. All I had were pictures and food. Why are you trying to blame this on me?"

"It's not about blame. It's about finding out how they got to us," Sam explained carefully.

Picking up on her tone, Emma glared. "You don't have to talk to me like that. I'm not an idiot."

The two women faced off against each other as the air grew heavy. From the corner of my eye, I saw Gideon move toward the truck we had stolen. Without warning, he suddenly dove beneath it. I wasn't sure what he was hoping to find, but within seconds, he emerged with a flashing, coin-sized device.

"They have been tracking us this whole time," Gideon explained, a sick look on his face.

Sully turned an even paler shade of white.

"I should have known. I can't believe I didn't check under the truck." He looked so mad at himself that Sam entwined her fingers with his. The simple gesture caused Emma to give them the side-eye.

"None of us thought to look there. Don't be so hard on yourself. Let's just get out of here before they arrive. We could just leave the tracker here to buy us time?" she mused.

"No," Sully responded. "The gas station is too close. It wouldn't be a long enough distraction."

I looked at him, mirroring the concern I saw in Sam's eyes. Some kind of plan was forming in his mind, yet I knew instinctively that I wouldn't like it. "What are you thinking?"

"I'm going to take the tracker with me on that motorcycle. We'll both take off at the same time, but I'll go in the opposite direction. I'll lead them away."

A frown creased Sam's forehead, ageing her by several years. "No. We shouldn't split up again. It's too risky."

Sully stared into her face, wavering. He didn't want to leave us either, but he pushed her toward the truck.

"We haven't got time to discuss this. Get in the truck, then take off down the road. We'll regroup after I've gotten rid of the tracker and lead them astray. I think that's our best bet."

I clung to the expectation that her sharp mind, the one we had come to rely on in our worst moments, would conjure an alternate plan. But as I scanned her expression, a sinking feeling settled in the pit of my stomach.

Sam's face, usually a study of determination, was now marred by a profound sense of defeat. I could see the gears turning in her mind in its desperate search to keep Sully with us, but the gutted expression that clouded her features told me she was coming up empty-handed.

"I don't like it, but I can't think of a better idea right now," she began hesitantly. Sully took that as the confirmation he needed. He kissed her quickly and steered her to the other side of the barn. He took out the map we had found with the truck.

"There," he pointed at a location on the map. "See this town up here. We'll meet there. It's several towns away, so in the event that they do find us, at least we won't be open targets. There will be civilians and witnesses. If the situation calls for it, we should be able to escape.

We nodded our agreement.

"Chase, you have the route memorized?" he asked me. "Because I don't have a photographic memory, I'm taking this map with me."

I tapped the side of my head, nodding. Sam went to hug her husband one last time when, with a speed that surprised everyone, Emma threw herself at him, jostling Sam out of the way. Her arms wrapped around Sully as if she believed she could physically anchor him in place.

"You can't leave me with them. You're the only one who likes me." Sully pulled her awkwardly off him, shooting Sam an apologetic look.

"That's not true. The others will look after you as well as I can. You all need to go now."

"But..."

Sully held up a hand to her face, stopping her protest. He dumped the bag of provisions on the floor of the truck and jumped back onto the bike — which I suddenly realized I had no idea how he had gotten it — and sped off down the road leaving us feeling hollow, overwhelmed with devastation.

24

SULLY

The Harley roared beneath me, vibrating through my entire being as I gripped the handles, my fingers white with tension. The powerful engine drowned out the world blurring past in streaks of yellow as I went at a breakneck speed.

Considering my limited experience with motorcycles, it was astonishing that I managed to keep the Harley upright. Until now, my interactions with bikes had been confined to the occasional joyride on the ones from Mark's extensive collection. I used to tease him relentlessly about his mid-life crisis machines, never truly understanding the allure of the open road and the freedom they offered.

However, in this moment of chaos and desperation, my perspective had shifted drastically. The skills I had learned, albeit begrudgingly, during those weekends, had become my lifeline. I clung to the handlebars, my knuckles aching, drawing on every bit of knowledge I had absorbed from those rides. Without the protection of a helmet, the wind howled in my ears.

As I sped away, the vivid, nightmarish images of the men attacking us back at the ranch replayed in my mind like a horror film, causing my chest to tighten with a mix of fear and anger. Each detail, every menacing face and hostile gesture, was etched into my memory, fueling my determination to escape their clutches. My grip on the bike's handles tightened involuntarily, my fingers pressing into the grips.

I stole a glance into the rearview mirrors, my eyes scanning the road behind me for what felt like the hundredth time since I had pulled away from the barn. Every nerve in my body was on edge, expecting to see those menacing trucks barreling down on me. Yet, for reasons unknown, there was no sign of them. Although it seemed impossible, my anxiety rose another notch as the thought that they could have seen through my plan and found my family already, snaked into my mind. I dug my fingers into the handles until I thought they would bleed.

I would know if something had happened to them. Somehow, I was sure I'd feel it in my gut.

The tracker was now securely tucked inside the luggage rack. I remembered the way it had blinked insistently when I closed the lid, a beacon of hope in the darkness.

Despite the adrenaline that pumped through my veins, an empty ache formed in the pit of my stomach. I wished desperately that I had had more time with them, that we hadn't been torn apart so abruptly. But in that split second when I had fled, with the threat closing in around us, this was all I could think to do. With the map tucked into my shirt, I focused my thoughts and energy on rallying with them at the designated meeting point.

I rode in silence, with nothing but the never-changing scenery to keep me company. The sun shone down, bathing the world in such glorious light that our desperate fight seemed almost like a dream. But whenever I tried to picture Sam behind the wheel and my family riding in the bed of the truck, a lone grenade would blast into the windshield.

Shaking my head, I fought the nightmare away. If I kept entertaining these worst-case scenarios, all that would happen is I'd crash this bike and be of no use to anyone.

Determined to draw the men away, I pushed on until some twenty minutes later, a large sign greeted me. It was another truck stop, this one much bigger than the last. I scanned the surroundings, taking in the gas station and a busy diner, advertising a $4.99 deal for breakfast that must have been popular judging by the cars that packed the parking lot. An idea came to mind, causing me to take better stock of the place. I slid the bike into a tiny space at the front.

Spotting a trashcan, I thought about simply dumping the tracker there, but I wasn't sure that a static signal would be the optimum option. Ideally, I needed to lead them as far out of the way as possible, and since I couldn't do it all by myself — not if I was going to meet back up with them again soon — my best bet would be to attach it to one of the vehicles that were already here.

Without warning, I felt the hairs on the back of my neck rise and turned to find a man openly staring at me. My first thought was that it was one of the bad guys.

My hand was reaching to turn the key in the ignition when I noticed that he was adorned with vivid tattoos that snaked across his arms and neck. His weathered face bore the marks of countless battles, with a rough beard framing a set of lips that seemed permanently etched in a scowl. His eyes, deep and cold, were like two smoldering embers, emanating a fierce intensity that seemed to challenge those who dared to meet his gaze.

Clad in worn leather, patches and insignias adorned his jacket, marking him as a person who thrived on rebellion and independence. The sound of heavy boots echoed with each step he took.

Those facts gave me pause.

Then I noticed the other tattooed guys surrounding him, sporting bald heads and beards, and oil-stained jeans, looking like they had all stepped out of a TV show. They either sat astride or stood beside various makes of Harleys. And as I took in that bit of information, my stomach sank.

They were all riding Harleys.

The biker who had been staring at me shouted over. "That's a nice bike."

I hoped we were just shooting the breeze, though I suspected we weren't.

"Yeah, I think so too," I answered, hoping that would be the last of our conversation. Of course, I wasn't so lucky.

"I'd be interested in knowing where you got that seat from. Haven't seen any of those around these parts."

Sensing trouble, his friends were starting to look my way. I tried to keep my voice natural under the increasing scrutiny, wondering about my bad luck. A confrontation with these wannabe Hells Angels was the last thing I needed.

Despite knowing his question could be a trap, I couldn't see a smart way to extract myself. Besides, I had an inkling he knew damn well where I had gotten the bike from or he wouldn't be asking.

"It's amazing what you can get on eBay these days," I replied as my eyes slid away from him, still looking for that suitable place for my tracker.

I didn't hear another question out of him, which I took as a hopeful sign. Climbing off the bike, I took a step toward the cars in front of the diner when I felt a tap on my shoulder. It was the tattooed biker. He had crossed the distance between us and was now standing right behind me.

"The thing is, friend," he said in the unfriendliest voice I'd ever heard. "That's not something you can buy off eBay. In fact, that particular seat is an original and handmade by my buddy Mike Sheldon. That there bike you're riding belongs to him, and since he is my friend, I know how much this baby means to him. I know he would sell his wife before he got rid of that bike. So, for you to be riding it means only one thing: you stole it."

I would have thought it admirable how he was sticking up for his friend, except there was a nasty air about him. Every word he spoke was laced with malice and came with a sneer. He was spoiling for a fight. This wasn't about being a Good Samaritan.

I sized him up. Beneath his shirt, his muscles rippled. He had bulging biceps that spoke of countless hours spent in the gym — and possibly steroids. He reeked of menace that was impossible to ignore.

I knew without a doubt my morning was about to take an even darker turn.

"This is not what you think," I began, trying to buy time. He cut me off with a wave of his abnormally large hand. What kind of protein shake was this guy on?

"Oh, this is exactly what I think," he said. "Which is why you're going to give the bike to me."

I took a step away from him, my muscles coiling with tension. The air crackled, heavy with the weight of anticipation. Every nerve in my body screamed caution, urging me to be vigilant, to watch for the subtlest of movements, the tiniest shifts in his expression that could betray his intentions.

His eyes, dark and inscrutable, bore into mine, holding my gaze with an intensity that sent a shiver down my spine. I felt like a cornered animal, aware of the danger but uncertain of how to escape. I clenched my fists, my palms moist with sweat, and tried to steady my breathing.

"Thing is, I would love to, but I actually can't."

"Well, that's a shame. And here I was thinking you were smart," he said, lying through his teeth.

Suddenly, he came at me — all two hundred pounds of him. Reeking of cigarettes and gasoline, he smashed a fist into my face. I saw it coming from a mile away, as though he was strong, he was also slow, signaling his intent clearly. I dodged, ducking my head to one side. But he knew the move was coming and adjusted himself accordingly.

His fist connected with my cheek as pain shot through my skull. I felt my teeth rattle and the bitter taste of blood flooded my mouth. My head snapped back as the world danced rings around me.

I barely had a second to breathe when the guy came barreling toward me again. I knew I couldn't outfight him — he was too strong. I would only get out of this with all my limbs intact if I used my head.

Knowing he had the advantage, he was expecting me to defend myself when I struck out, aiming a kick to the back of his knees that he wasn't prepared for. Losing his balance, he toppled to the ground, hard. Trunk-like arms flailing like a windmill. I even thought I heard something snap.

I felt a rush of euphoria, but that quickly subsided when his buddies started our way. My hand palmed the tracker and I feigned a stumble as I tossed the thing into the saddlebag on my opponent's bike. Feeling a grim sense of satisfaction, I shot him a look as I gunned the engine on my bike.

"Have fun, jerk."

Before his buddies could come after me, I peeled off, leaving a cloud of dust in my wake.

25

CHASE

We piled into the truck as fast as we could. Sam ran around to the driver's seat, climbing in.

"Do you want me to drive?" I heard Gideon ask as I bent down from the interior of the cab to help lift Zeb into the truck.

"No. I've got it," Sam replied.

Gideon grabbed hold of the wheelchair, then shot me a look. "Ready?"

Preparing myself, I planted my feet and nodded.

"Lift!"

I pulled with all my might, while Gideon groaned from the strain. He was doing most of the lifting since my muscles weren't exactly known for being strong.

"Bend your knees, son. Careful," came Zeb's urgent voice. He braced his hands on either side of his wheelchair, but could do nothing to help us other than to stay as still as possible.

Gideon's muscles strained as he hoisted Zeb's wheelchair up high enough to set it down inside the truck. After double-checking that Emma and Bandit were with us, I slammed the gate shut. Sam revved the engine and shot a glance in the rearview mirror as Gideon clambered into the passenger seat.

"Everyone belted in?"

There was a quick chorus of yes's, then we were off, bumping along the farmland until we swerved onto the road where the ride turned smoother.

I sat with my arms around Bandit, my face in his soft fur, though who was comforting who, I couldn't say. Thoughts flew through my mind. Terrible, dark thoughts that I didn't want to give any power to, but it was impossible not to worry about Sully.

Not that I didn't have faith in him — if anyone could do it, it would be him — but those men were armed to the gills. There were so many of them and they were trained. We'd defended ourselves against the first wave that had attacked us. I knew we'd caused some casualties, maybe even fatalities, but not even twenty-four hours later, they were back. Even if Sully could take care of a second group, wouldn't that just delay them? Wouldn't they just send more men after us?

I glanced over at Gideon, wishing I was sitting next to him so we could talk. We'd gotten pretty close lately, and even though we argued about stuff constantly — stupid stuff like who lost the remote this time — when it came to anything serious, we always had each other's backs. We weren't just family now. We were fast becoming best friends.

And maybe even something more.

He sat straight, his spine rigid as his eyes scanned first one direction, then the next, constantly keeping watch for danger.

I felt Sam's gaze on me. Her eyes, usually warm and lively were now hooded with concern, though she tried to hide her fear with the quick, small smile she flashed my way.

"Chase, you're on food duty. Why don't you see what Sully brought us?"

"I'm not really hungry," I said, realizing it was true the second the statement left my mouth.

Gideon spun around with absolute disbelief in his eyes. "Did you hit your head?"

Sam's smile turned understanding as she continued. "Sully went to all that trouble for us. It won't do him any good if we collapse from hunger, Chase. It's OK to eat something. We need to keep our strength up."

Bandit laid his head on my knee and woofed. I realized he must be starving, since he had missed at least two of his own meals. Feeling like the worst owner in the history of pet owners, I opened up the bag Sully had left for us.

There were enough sandwiches that we could have one each. I tossed them to the others, hesitating only when there were two left. One had obviously been meant for Sully, and the other, Emma. Sensing my hesitation, she stared at me with those unfathomable blue eyes. After the way she had behaved, she didn't deserve any charity or kindness, especially since she had already eaten.

I was expecting Emma to say something as she usually couldn't help herself, but she surprised me with her silence. Her eyes eating up the sight of the sandwich in my hands, however, communicated a world of longing.

Gritting my teeth so I wouldn't say anything, I tossed the sandwich over to her.

Finding several cans of dog food in the bag, I took one out, then stopped, having hit a snag. Watching me, Gideon pulled a face as he realized my predicament. "Don't suppose anyone has a can opener by any chance?"

Of course, no one did. "I don't need a can opener," I informed him. "I can get it open with a knife or a spoon, even a fork."

Gideon grinned suddenly, taking out a folding knife from his pocket. He often carried it around on his key chain in case of an emergency. He hopped over his seat, brandishing the knife as he came closer.

"You sure this is safe?"

"I've done it a million times. No one owns a can opener when they're living on the streets. You make do with whatever's around."

His eyes went a darker shade of green and seemed to hold a myriad of emotions. I felt a subtle shift in the air, as if the energy around us had changed. Gazing at me intently, he didn't speak, but his look made me self-conscious.

"Hand it over then," I said, reaching over and taking the knife from him. Setting the can vertically on the floor, I flicked the knife open.

"OK, stand back a bit, just in case. While I've done this before, I haven't actually opened a can in a moving vehicle. Best if we keep our fingers and paws a safe distance away."

Bandit and Gideon obediently shrunk away, giving me the space I needed. Lowering the point to the inner rim of the can, I wrapped one hand securely around the metal handle of the knife. The knife wasn't exactly easy to hold, especially while the floor kept shifting beneath my feet — but I had no other choice. My Muttface needed to eat. My right hand balled up into a tight fist

Keeping my body as still as possible, I brought my fist down onto the top of the knife handle, just above where my fingers gripped it. The point of the blade bit into the can, puncturing a tiny hole into the surface. Positioning the knife so that as much of its point sat in that hole, I repeated the same move, resulting in a slightly larger hole.

Behind me, Gideon gave me a supportive whoop. "Hey. That's pretty neat."

"Yeah, but now we've come to the hard part." This was where it could go horribly wrong.

I slid as much of the knife into the hole as I could, then angled the blade so that its sharpest edge aligned with the unopened part of the can. Taking hold of the can with my left hand, I gripped it tightly and starting working the blade in a forward-back motion, sawing at the can.

The metal started giving way, but not without a lot of pressure from me.

I blew out a breath of effort that lifted the hair out of my eyes before it fell down around me again. I found myself wishing I had something to tie it back with.

Gideon must have sensed my frustration as he leaned toward me and took up my hair in his hands. He was so close I could feel his breath on my face, warm puffs of air tinged with the familiar earthy scent that clung to him. It was a smell he always seemed to have, the one that came from his time spent working in Warrey's garage or tending to Zeb's vegetable garden. A subtle blend of motor oil and soil, the aroma wrapped around me. His very proximity made me lose myself momentarily. I had to stop sawing or risk losing the use of my hands completely.

"What's wrong?" he asked.

I searched my brain frantically for an answer that wouldn't reveal how mixed-up I was feeling. Why were my hormones going crazy? What terrible timing was this?

"Nothing. Just waiting for the truck to smooth out," I lied. We hadn't actually been hitting any bumps, so the fact he didn't question this was a minor miracle.

I went at the can, working the knife first one way, then another, twisting the can to follow my progression until I had finally cut away enough of the end. Still using the knife, I slid it beneath the opening then, flattening the blade against the lid, I bent the lid back.

I got a big whiff of meaty dog food for my efforts.

"Woof!" Bandit said happily. He did a happy little dance, four paws doing some version of a jig as his butt shock with excitement. Without meaning to, his tail whipped painfully against my arm as he typed into his iPad, impatient for his food to be served up. *I'm so hungry, Chase. Hurry please!"*

Even starving, my dog had better manners than me.

"You did it!" Gideon congratulated me, letting go of my hair. I felt a moment of disappointment that he didn't seem as affected as I had been by his closeness but I shoved the thought aside. Bandit needed to eat. I'd have to deal with my weirdness later.

"What're we going to dish it up with? I know he's super smart, but he still can't use a fork to eat out of a can."

"No. I haven't figured out how to do that yet," Bandit agreed.

Since none of us had the forethought to bring plates with us, I rummaged inside the plastic bag to see if there was something I could use. Other than the one uneaten sandwich — which I was determined to save for Sully — I found a bunch of bananas, bottles of water, a few bags of nuts, some more cans of dog food, and six bars of candy.

None of which was particularly helpful to us at this moment.

I turned my head from the floor, staring around the truck, but all I saw was ammo and more ammo until the bag under my fingers struck me with inspiration. I emptied it, turned it inside out, then smoothed it along the floor of the truck. Grabbing the can, I tipped it upside down, watching as the dog chow landed on the bag in one big plop.

"I know this isn't perfect, but it's the best I can do in a pinch," I apologized to Bandit. "You'll have to be careful that you don't bite through the plastic since it won't taste great and is probably really bad for you. I've heard plastic does terrible things to animals when it's ingested."

He nodded, his eyes shining at me with gratefulness. Then, with an enormous sigh, he dived into his food, eating it as daintily as I had warned him to. I swear his teeth never even touched the plastic: he used his tongue to flick the food into his mouth.

"That's disgusting."

It was Emma, of course. Hearing her voice, I was reminded how she was like an unwanted guest. One who would never go away.

"Do you have a better idea?"

"Just give him the other sandwich so he won't make such a mess. That stuff stinks."

"That's human food. Besides, it's also Sully's. We're saving it for him. He'll be hungry when we meet up with him."

"If we meet up with him," Emma grumbled.

I think it was meant to be under her breath, but she was like a child who didn't realize their whispering was as loud as their normal volume. We all heard her, even Sam. I saw her shoulders tense and her fingers grip the wheel more tightly. Her jaw clenched tightly. I think it took everything she had not to snap back a retort. Trying to smooth over the moment, it was Zeb who spoke.

"Sully will be there."

His voice had a finality to it that brokered no argument. Hearing the warning in his voice, Emma bit back whatever response she may have had. Not wanting to engage with the worrying thought that flitted in the corners of my mind, I waited for Bandit to finish.

When there was nothing left, and he had licked every inch of the gravy from the bag, I took it away from him, and hung it over the edge of the table, weighing it down with the other cans.

I wasn't sure of anything right now, but we could need the bag again, so it paid to be diligent.

As the miles flew by, we were left alone with our troubled thoughts, the rhythmic hum of the road beneath us, a steady reminder of our relentless drive forward. I gazed blindly out the window, watching the fields blur past in a hazy green and gold mosaic as the landscape transformed with every passing moment. The sky above was a canvas of shifting colors, from the soft pastel hues of dawn to the mid morning glare.

Despite the beauty that surrounded us, all I could do was to count the minutes since Sully had left us behind. I prayed desperately that we wouldn't run out of time.

26

———

CHASE

I don't know how long we had been driving, maybe a few hours, when a strange spluttering sound emitted from the truck's engine, startling Gideon awake.

It seemed strange that he could sleep at a time like this, but I remembered reading how stress could bring out different reactions in people. Some became hyper like they had drunk a gallon of caffeine, while others simply crashed out.

A curse shot out of Sam's lips as her eyes jerked to the dashboard meters — specifically at a needle that had slid past the letter E. Gideon blinked at her with groggy eyes.

"Is that saying what I think it's saying?"

Sam's lips were a thin, white line. "Yes."

Zeb called over to them. "What is it? Is something wrong with the truck?"

Sam looked over her shoulder at him. For someone who was usually so expressive, her face was strangely emotionless.

"We're out of gas."

As if to emphasize her point, the engine stuttered, then went out completely. The sudden silence was a shock to the system. We sat around, our faces looking equally stunned, when Sam suddenly punched the steering wheel.

"How could I have been so stupid?!"

I didn't want to say anything, but I actually agreed. The second the thought went through my mind, though, I felt a hot flush of shame. Sam was under a lot of pressure. She had made a mistake.

But this mistake could cost Sully his life.

Bandit whined at me, sensing my distress and feeling his own. Surprising me, he picked up one of the candy bars and left me to run over to Sam, where he laid the bar on her lap as an offering of comfort.

Sam reached up to pat him on his head. "Thank you, boy, but I'm good for now."

Bandit stayed with her, pushing his body against her as overcome by emotion, Sam's eyes began to glisten with tears. Her shoulders shook. I could see her fighting to gain control of herself.

Gideon smiled supportively. "Don't blame yourself. It could have happened to any of us."

"Of all people, I should have known better. I'm a Sheriff, for crying out loud!"

"Whose husband is off alone to deal with an army of dangerous men while his dead ex-wife sits not ten feet away. I think you've earned the right to slip up."

This had come from Zeb. Having detached himself from the seatbelt, he moved over to her. "Sully, wouldn't want you to feel this way."

"No one blames you, Sam." I felt like such a jerk for saying it, when in fact I had been blaming her only a few seconds ago. But, she needed my support, and I was fast getting over my disloyalty.

"Why doesn't she get told off when she makes a mistake?" piped up *that* voice from the corner. Three guesses who.

"Because it was an actual mistake, while yours wasn't," Gideon responded.

"But we're completely stuck. What are we supposed to do now?"

"Now we get out and walk," Sam said. She jumped out of the truck, slamming the door behind her.

"Not me. I'm staying right here until Sully finds me." Emma folded her arms across her chest.

I couldn't help the exasperated look I gave her. "The rest of us are leaving. You can't stay here alone."

"Yes, I can," Emma answered without even looking at me: her were eyes fixed at a point past my head.

"What's going on here now?" Zeb wanted to know.

I nodded my head at Emma, replying in a scathing voice. "*She* says she's not leaving. *She* thinks Sully's going to come and rescue her."

"Let's try to make this easier for everyone, shall we?" Zeb suggested in a gentle tone, far too kind for my liking. I wanted him to be more confrontational, but he was taking the part of mediator. "If you stay here, you risk being found by those men. Even if Sully could come back to you, what good do you think he could do against them all? If we stay together, we can keep each other safe."

Emma fixed her gaze on him, her eyes partially veiled by her long lashes as she carefully weighed his words. The air seemed to thicken with anticipation, the silence stretching as she pondered the implications of what he had said. Finally, after what felt like an eternity, she let out a sigh, a sound heavy with the burden of her thoughts. In a sudden burst of energy, she sprang up from her seat.

"Alright, I'm coming, but only because you're begging me to." Without a further glance at us, she marched out of the truck.

Zeb looked at me, one gray brow arched high. "Spirited, isn't she?"

"Not the word I would use," I said. We helped him off the truck and took stock of our surroundings.

The sun hung low in the sky, casting a warm golden glow across the vast fields of corn that flanked the empty road where we stood. The air was still, filled with the faint rustle of leaves and the distant calls of unseen birds.

With a sense of growing unease, I cupped a hand over my eyes, shielding them from the glare, and scanned the horizon. I strained my eyes, hoping to catch a glimpse of something — anything — that could provide a glimmer of hope or direction.

My gaze traveled along a distant tree line, followed the curve of the road ahead, and traced the outline of the sky, but there was nothing. No distant silhouette of a building, no hint of civilization on the horizon. Just an endless expanse of nature, untouched and undisturbed.

"You guys have everything you need?" Sam checked with us before we set off.

Gideon tossed a look inside the truck, his eyes straying to the ammo. "It feels wrong to leave all of that there, but since we don't have the right guns..."

"They would only weigh us down," Sam decided for him. "Come on. We've got a long way to go. I don't want us still out here when it starts getting dark."

We set off, leaving the truck where it stood. God knows what someone who came upon the bullet-dented vehicle was going to make of it.

We started walking along the country road. I offered to push Zeb, but Gideon wouldn't hear of it. Flexing his muscles at me, he assured me he was fine, though it wasn't long before his breathing became more labored. Not wanting to embarrass him, I decided it was best not to make a thing of it, trusting that he would let me know when he needed a break.

Bandit kept up with my pace, walking alongside. Every so often, his ears would perk up as if he heard something, and I'd feel a wave of anxiety until a rabbit or fox darted out of the cornfields.

The once-bright morning sun had disappeared behind thick gray clouds, leaving a chill in the air. I tightened my cardigan around me, knowing the others were feeling it too. Gideon had tucked his hands inside the sleeves of his jacket; he used one sleeve to grip Zeb's wheelchair handlebars so that not even metal could touch Zeb's skin. The blanket he had been using before we were forced to leave the ranch covered his legs, or else he would have suffered much more than he currently was.

As fast as we were going, our progress was slow, hindered by the wheelchair. When Gideon started stumbling, Sam swapped with him. And when her pace slowed, I took over.

Emma never volunteered to help.

She kept to herself at the back of the line. Occasionally, I could hear her muttering — it seemed a personal hobby of hers — but I could never make out what it was she was trying to say. Which was lucky, really, as I was pretty sure I wouldn't like it.

We'd been going less than an hour when Emma's mumbling grew progressively louder until Sam finally couldn't take it anymore. Turning, she shot her a glare that could have cut ice.

"Just spit it out! This incessant mumbling is driving me nuts!"

Emma seemed taken aback. She stuttered an unintelligible answer and had to try again. "We can't get anywhere like this, not when we're going so slowly."

"What would you suggest we do otherwise, genius?" Sam stopped walking, placing a hand on either hip.

"We're not going as fast as we can because of him." Her finger pointed at Zeb. "He's slowing us down. We should leave him and come back later. Without him slowing us down, we'd get to Sully much faster."

She finally stopped talking as the rest of us were looking at her in horror. Bandit broke the silence first, placing his paws on Zeb's knees and barking twice.

NO!

"Do you even hear how crazy you sound when you speak?" Gideon was seething, filled with disgust — mirroring how the rest of us felt. Bizarrely, instead of being ashamed of her suggestion, a look of utter confusion came over Emma's face.

"Why are you all looking at me like that? This is the only thing that makes sense. We can't get to Sully quickly with that wheelchair, slowing us down. I'm not saying we kill the old man or anything. I'm saying we just leave him here for now. How is that crazy?"

"His name is Zeb," Gideon replied, a chill in his voice.

"You're a monster, you know that?" Sam spat out the words, letting each one have full effect. "He's family. We don't leave family, so you need to shut up." A sudden surge of red-hot rage erupted from Sam. The sheer force of her anger hung in the air, so palpable and raw that it sent shivers down my spine.

Emma, caught in the torrent of Sam's fury, stood frozen, her eyes wide with shock and fear. The words she had been about to utter died on her lips, replaced by a stunned silence. It was as if the sheer intensity of Sam's rage had stolen her voice, leaving her unable to respond. I could see the confusion etched on her face, the innocence of her intentions clashing with the unforeseen ferocity of Sam's reaction.

In that moment, I knew that Emma truly did not understand the magnitude of what she had said, the impact of her words were lost on her. Her face was a mask of bewilderment. Her body language mirrored her confusion, her shoulders hunched, and her hands trembling.

Which really made me wonder.

What kind of person would not know how awful a suggestion that was? The answer would elude me for a while to come.

27

THE CLEANER

The cleaner, Smith, wasn't having a good week.

Ten hours had passed since anyone had laid eyes on Sullivan and his family. After a restless night on a mattress that seemed to defy the definition of comfort, Smith was relieved when his new crew had arrived. Their entrance brought not only some welcome fresh faces, but a shiny replacement laptop. By the time the signal from the tracker had flashed up, they were packed and preparing to leave the motel behind.

As Smith pushed forward on the road, his eyes caught a glint of metal up ahead. The source of the glimmer soon revealed itself: a speeding motorcycle, its exhaust pipe trailing a smoky haze in its wake. Out here, in the middle of nowhere, Smith felt his skin crawl. He much preferred the high rises and bustling anonymity of city life. The thought of residing in a close-knit community, where not only your name but also your secrets were common knowledge, petrified him.

Of course, maybe his line of work made him see things differently.

Smith's life was a delicate balancing act. His job, shrouded in secrecy and reliant on the cover of darkness, forced him to navigate the blurry lines of morality. Yet, he was a soldier, unswervingly loyal to his commanding officers. To him, their actions, no matter how dubious, were justified in the name of the greater good and the safety of his country. Following orders without questions had become an ingrained part of his existence. It was a mantra that allowed him to find peace amid the chaos.

This cloak of secrecy, however, while essential, cast a heavy veil over his existence. Smith's world was a grayscale, devoid of the vibrant hues of ordinary life. Few knew of his existence, and even fewer understood the weight he carried on his shoulders. Yet, it was precisely this anonymity that propelled him forward, shielding his family from the dangerous world he inhabited.

In the quiet moments between missions, when he could finally be the father his children needed, Smith found solace. Tucking his kids into bed was a scared ritual and a reminder of the life he was fighting to preserve.

Inside the van he had chosen for this mission, he and his crew remained hidden, faces obscured from prying eyes. Smith had learned to evade attention, realizing that the gleaming armored trucks he usually favored would stand out too conspicuously. They screamed of newness, drawing eyes and questions he preferred to avoid.

Adapting to his environment, Smith constantly switched vehicles, never opting for the same one twice if he could help it. A precautionary measure, this meticulous attention to detail was his way of ensuring that he and his crew remained ghosts in the shadows. It was a survival tactic that had kept him one step ahead for years.

Smith understood the messiness of humanity all too well. Even his highly trained men, skilled in the art of disappearing, left traces of their existence. A DNA sample here, a strand of hair there, remnants of their presence were scattered like breadcrumbs, potential hazards waiting to be discovered. In their line of work, invisibility was paramount, and any trace, no matter how minuscule, could compromise their mission.

"We're all set up," came Jackson's voice, breaking the tense silence inside the van.

With his nondescript appearance and forgettable face, Jackson was relatively new to him, having only served with him one time before. If Smith had his way, Jackson wouldn't even be on the mission, but their horrific disaster yesterday had cost him dearly, to the tune of eight men.

Smith's eyes flickered over the monitors, calculating their ETA.

"If we stay at this speed, our ETA is in three minutes," he announced, his voice firm and steady, betraying none of the lingering unease he had felt ever since he first discovered Xavier's perverse experiments.

Cracking his knuckles, Smith tried to quell the surge of adrenaline that started coursing in his veins. It wasn't the thrill of violence that fueled him, but the anticipation of closure. The knowledge that another mission was reaching its climax. Unlike some of his colleagues, Smith did not relish the act of taking a life. The aftermath weighed heavily on him, haunting his thoughts long after the job was done.

After each assignment, he retreated into seclusion, seeking refuge in the sanctuary of his apartment. Days were spent cocooned away, the outside world reduced to digital transactions and food deliveries. His connection to reality became tenuous, a deliberate act to shield himself from the memories of his victims.

The faces of those he had erased persisted in his mind, their silent specters haunting his every waking moment. Only when their ghostly presence faded could he muster the strength to return to his children, to don the mask of a loving father and shelter them from the darkness that defined his existence.

It was this streak of humanity that made him the best at what he did.

He was a master profiler, a cunning detective who could slip into the minds of his targets, anticipating their thoughts and predicting their next moves with unnerving accuracy. His ability to understand the psyche of his adversaries was uncanny; it was as if he could see the world through their eyes, mapping out their intentions and unraveling their secrets. Once he had a scent, a mere hint of his target, it was only a matter of time before they were ensnared, trapped by the web of his expertise and the relentless pursuit of his team.

In his two decades on the job, Smith had made remarkably few mistakes, a testament to his skill and experience. Yet, Sullivan's friend, Florence, had been an exception, a stain on his otherwise impeccable record.

A few nights ago, his team had descended upon her house under the cover of darkness, following orders to extract information about the elusive dog. They had applied their specialized concoction, a blend designed to loosen her tongue and wipe her memory clean of the night's events. It was a formula crafted by brilliant chemists, a tool in their arsenal meant to ensure their operations remained undetected.

But fate had other plans.

Florence's heart had given out unexpectedly, an outcome that no one, especially not Smith, had anticipated. She hadn't been on their list for elimination; her death was an unfortunate consequence of their well-practiced techniques gone awry.

Smith had been absent during the incident, engrossed in interrogating Sullivan's other associate, Mr. Wall Street. When news of Florence's untimely demise reached him, he had acted swiftly, issuing orders to his team to stage her death as natural. It was a desperate attempt to cover their tracks, to minimize the fallout from their unintended actions.

His phone buzzed, signaling the arrival of a message. The sender was simply named "Employer." Even if Smith had known his bosses' real names — and there were several, though he tended to have only the one point person — they were careful never to use any names in their exchanges.

Have you found them?

Smith typed into the phone quickly, his fingers flying over the keys.

Negative. Should have news by the end of the day.

The response was instant.

See that you do.

Smith put away his phone, knowing it was the end of their exchange. Glancing ahead, he saw the top of Sullivan's head, hidden beneath a helmet spray painted with the image of a sultry woman in a red dress. She pouted at him, blowing a kiss in an exaggerated sexual manner that reminded him of Marilyn Monroe.

Smith waited, biding his time until their van was only inches away.

"Now!" he shouted, bracing himself.

The screeching of tires filled the air as Jackson slammed his foot on the gas, propelling the van forward with a sudden burst of speed. The vehicle surged ahead and cut off Sullivan's path unexpectedly. Caught off guard, Sullivan lost control of his motorcycle, falling to the tarmac with the weight of his bike pinning his legs to the ground.

As the van came to a halt, Jackson killed the engine, plunging the scene into an eerie silence broken only by Sullivan's moans of pain. Smith sprang into action, bounding toward his target, a gun gripped firmly in his hands. He signaled his men, a silent command for them to cover the area, to keep their weapons ready but their trigger fingers disciplined.

"Where are the rest of them?" Smith demanded, cutting through his moans.

The helmet turned toward him, but the man didn't respond. Thinking he might be in shock, Smith nudged him with a boot.

"Your family, Sullivan. Where are they?"

Slowly, Sullivan raised his hand, a deliberate movement meant to show he was unarmed, and flipped up his visor. The eyes that stared up at him weren't the ones he was expecting. In fact, they were the eyes of a complete stranger.

Smith's gaze shifted from the unfamiliar eyes to the rest of the man's form. He took in the bald head, the tattoo creeping up his neck and disappearing beneath the collar of his leather jacket. Now that more of him was in view, Smith could see he was bigger than Sullivan, with a stockier build and an attitude to match.

"I don't know who this Sullivan is, but he isn't me," the biker growled, his words tinged with both pain and frustration. He spat out a mouthful of blood, defiance etched on his bruised face. "You've got the wrong guy."

And just like that, Smith's week had become ten times worse.

28

SULLY

Glendale was a little town off the highway.

Our chosen meeting point, I didn't know anything about the place — hadn't heard of it even — but it looked like the typical small-town you'd find dotted around the US. I knew the type, though I had never had much cause to visit, having stayed in Connecticut before I'd been forced to leave.

I tossed another look behind me, but the road was clear: the trucks were nowhere in sight. Unbelievably, I'd made it here in one piece.

The afternoon sun cast a warm glow over the quaint little town, making the green and white Welcome sign appear even more inviting. It was a typical American small town, the kind you see in movies and read about in books. The kind of place where life moved at a slower pace.

The population here was small — under five hundred — but as I crossed into it, I could see that what it lacked in people power, it more than made up for in businesses.

Main Street stretched out before me, lined with shops and eateries, each one telling a story of the town's history and character. The colonial-style buildings stood tall and proud, their painted shingles adding a touch of cheerfulness to the atmosphere.

My eyes were drawn to a charming restaurant that stood at the heart of the town. Its red and white striped awning and vibrant flower baskets gave it a welcoming feel. I could see families gathering inside, enjoying hearty meals and sharing laughter. It was a place that seemed to have a soul, a place where memories were made.

Beside the restaurant, a smaller ice-cream and dessert parlor beckoned to passersby. Though not as grand as its neighboring eatery, it had its own charm. The scent of freshly baked waffle cones wafted through the air, enticing anyone who walked by. Despite its size, the parlor seemed to hold a special place in the town's heart, offering sweet treats to both locals and visitors alike.

A few doors down was a brightly branded pizza joint. Then came several bars. Their windows were adorned with daily specials with the kind of prices that wouldn't have bought a coffee back home. Speaking of the devil, I suddenly caught the tantalising aroma of a rich, dark brew. My mouth watered, my cravings take over.

It had only been a day since I had my last cup of coffee, but it felt like a century. A grumbling sound emitting from my stomach reminded me that I hadn't eaten in a while, either. A car pulled up behind and honked at me, startling me out of my thoughts. I needed to get out of the middle of the street or I'd start annoying other drivers and causing more attention to be thrown my way. Spotting a parking lot outside a grocery store, I headed there when I stopped in my tracks.

If those other bikers came to this town, they'd spot the bike and would know I was here. It was too risky to leave it out in the open like this. Checking that no one was nearby, I maneuvered the bike to the alleyway behind a grocery store. The smell of days-old urine and rotten food filled my nose, reminding me that even in Nice-ville, people still treated alleyways like they were their personal public restroom.

Wheeling the bike behind a dumpster, I dug out a few flattened boxes from inside, arranging them over the bike, covering it the best I could. I was about to head back into the town when the ground suddenly shifted beneath my feet. I caught my breath until I realized it was just a sign of low blood sugar.

Having lived with Chase and her high metabolism long enough, I knew I needed energy or there would be a crash coming. I checked what money I had left — less than eighty bucks. I hesitated, not wanting to spend a dime of it, but I was struck by another wave of dizziness that left me nauseous.

I had to eat something or I wouldn't be of any use to anyone.

Scanning my options, my eyes lingered on the pizza place. Loaded pies with long strings of mozzarella cheese and glistening slices of pepperoni that would have given my favorite joint back home a run for its money. If only they sold by the slice.

Dragging my eyes away, I shuffled into the grocery store where I picked up another cheap sandwich and a candy bar. Not wanting to pay for water, I stopped by the drinks station, sighing with relief when I saw the jug of tap water provided for customers.

Filling a large paper cup, I gulped it down, then knocked back several more, stopping only when my stomach felt bloated.

I paid, headed back outside and took a walk around town while I ate my food, keeping my eyes peeled for any sign of the other truck. All things being equal, my family shouldn't be too far behind so I wouldn't venture far. Keeping my eyes down, I tried not to draw attention to myself.

As I passed the less frequented parts of town, the once-charming atmosphere began to fade away. The buildings lost their cheerful facade, replaced by a worn-out appearance. The motel on the Southside came into view, a stark contrast to the cozy businesses I had seen earlier. Its deteriorating siding whispered stories of neglect, and the creaky wooden sign, barely hanging on its rusty chains, seemed to groan in the wind.

The fading sign had almost completely scraped away the word "Glendale," so that all that remained was "lend al" from "Glendale Motel." The rundown motel consisted of two floors that housed twelve rooms if that. Each window looked like a blank stare, devoid of life and warmth.

My footsteps echoed on the sidewalk as I continued my vigil. I couldn't afford to let my guard down. The hollow feeling in my stomach persisted, intensifying with each passing moment. Despite my efforts to fill the void with food and water, the gnawing worry for my family overshadowed any physical discomfort.

I glanced back at the motel, a passing thought crossing my mind. It might have been a place to lay low, to regroup and plan my next move. But something about it felt off, the aura of neglect making it an unappealing option. Then there was that issue of cost...

I decided to press on.

After I had gone up and down the length of Main Street, I knew I had to find a better way to kill time or that unwanted attention would surely be heading my way.

Pushing open a door, I stepped into a bar. The dimness inside matched the heavy stench of cheap beer. The place was practically empty. A wino slumped over a pint in one corner looking as if he hadn't washed in a week. He probably smelled the same too, as the bartender — a guy who looked to be in his twenties, wearing hipster pants that sagged at his butt but clung to his skinny legs — was giving him a wide berth.

A girl in a miniskirt batted her eyelids at the bartender. The pimply-faced guy looked like he thought it was his lucky day. The two were so involved with each other, they didn't even look my way.

A glowing neon sign pointed the way to the men's room. As I stepped inside, darkness enveloped me momentarily until my fingers found the light switch.

The ceiling light flickered on, casting the room in a dingy yellow pallor.

Dust covered the rim of the light, not having been cleaned this side of the century. Luckily, the stalls looked decent enough: I was glad I couldn't smell anything other than the cheap floral dish soap in the dispenser by the sinks.

I crossed to the mirror where my wan face stared back at me.

The biker had done a real number on me. I had a cut above my right eye where the blood had now congealed. My cheek felt tender. Though the skin held only a hint of red now, I was sure it would turn a wicked purple by tomorrow.

I splashed cold water onto my face, gingerly washing around the swelling. Pumping a few pumps of that soap into my palm, I washed the back of my neck and under my arms. The cold water felt good against my tired body, and even though I wasn't able to get a proper scrub-down, I still felt better. Tearing off a few squares from the paper roll fixed to the wall, I dabbed myself dry, then gave myself a final once over.

It was still me who stared back from the mirror but at least I didn't look as haggard as when I had first arrived.

I headed to the bar, and waited for the barman to stop talking to Ms. Miniskirt long enough to serve me, but after a full minute, he hadn't even turned my way. I tapped my fingers impatiently on the bar top, the sound growing louder with each tap until he couldn't ignore me anymore.

Fixing me with a look that somehow seemed to convey he was more annoyed than I was, he asked, "What'll it be?"

"Coffee. Black."

The words were barely out of my mouth before the bartender gave me a look.

"Sorry. Kitchen's closed." Turning to his friend, he laughed, feigning a wide-eyed look. "Wait, what am I saying? We don't even have a kitchen."

On cue, the woman burst into giggles. Now that I could see her up close, I realized my mistake. She wasn't a woman at all, but a girl who couldn't have been more than eighteen, with a face that was plastered with make-up and thick, tarantula-like fake lashes.

I couldn't see what was so funny.

"I'll have a can of whatever is cheapest."

If the look he gave me before was bad, this made me feel like I was something he had to scrape off his shoe. Reaching under the bar, he retrieved a can of off-brand cola from a mini fridge, slamming it down onto the counter. The girl all but dismissed me with a fleeting glance.

"Do you need a glass with that too?" his tone dared me to answer.

"I think I can manage." There was a hint of danger in my reply. The punk was testing my last nerve and he needed to know it.

He looked me up and down, though he was shorter than me. The air turned heavy with tension before he came to his senses and shifted his focus back to the girl. His posture had changed in the last few seconds, his shoulders braced for impact. Knowing he had caught my drift was enough for me. Taking my drink and what was left of my ego, I sat down at a table with a decent view of the town.

Popping open the can, I took a small sip. Normally, I shied away from sugary drinks, so the intense sweetness hit me by surprise and made me long for water to wash it down. Trying for optimism, I comforted myself with the fact that it wouldn't be difficult to make the drink last. I would have at least an hour before that barman finally got bored with the girl and kicked me out.

Tossing another quick look at them, I mentally adjusted the time by another hour. They were giving off some serious heat. Hopefully, they would keep each other distracted for a good while. Shifting my attention back outside, I anxiously waited for my family to appear.

29

CHASE

You know when you're stuck doing something you don't want to? Well, that was me right now, down to a T.

Caught in a hard place between two women with some major issues with each other while a sinister SWAT team came after us. And then there was Sully, off playing chicken with the bad guys. I felt like I was suffocating under the weight of our predicament.

The more we had to walk, the more I could feel the resentment pouring off of Emma. One second she was a child, all vulnerable and wounded, and needing our protection, then the next, she was a powder keg ready to explode at a moment's notice. Her mumbling became a constant background drone with the only recognizable word being "Sully." Her fixation on him only added fuel to the already blazing fire, intensifying the strained atmosphere that surrounded us.

Despite harboring negative feelings toward her, I couldn't deny she had a real connection to him, though my mind refused to believe that she was actually his wife. I mean, it just wasn't possible. Even Bandit kept his distance from Emma, a feat made easy by her apparent dislike for him. Other than all the bad guys we'd ever come across, she was the only person in the world who didn't like him.

And you know what they say about people who don't like animals...

Sam had been leading the way for the last hour or so, Gideon and Zeb bringing up the rear. Emma was somewhere between us, but I hadn't bothered to check on her in a while. Where she was concerned, no news was good news.

After walking for so long, I could feel the cold seeping through the soles of my sneakers. It made me worry about Bandit's paws. If my feet, wrapped up in socks and cushioned by my shoes, felt like they were turning into blocks of ice, how were his paws doing? Staring down at him, I asked, "Are you okay? Is the road too cold for your paws?"

He nuzzled my hand as if to say he was grateful for my concern, then barked twice for no. He was a lot sturdier than me, it seemed, even with all my training on the streets. I've always suffered from cold feet, even as a kid. It was actually the one thing I inherited from my mom.

Thinking about her now, I recalled her face, but it was like reopening an old wound. Whenever her image came into my mind, it was accompanied by a pang in my chest, a visceral reminder of the complex feelings I harbored. Since she had taken off, I avoided thinking about what she had done. How she had betrayed me and sold me out. It just brought too many complicated emotions to the surface.

Emma's relentless mumbling jolted me from my thoughts. Tossing her an irritated look that she didn't catch, I sped up my pace — Bandit matching me stride for stride — until we caught up to Sam. She gave us a small smile that didn't quite reach her tired eyes.

"How are you guys doing?"

The normally cheerful demeanor, which had always been her trademark, was nowhere to be found. Lines of stress etched her face, replacing the usual softness with a weariness — and hurt — that was alien to me.

"Oh, you know. Tired, hungry, worried about Sully, but what else is new?"

Sam didn't answer, choosing to cast a glance at Emma instead. She opened her mouth as if to say something, but decided against it. I guess she didn't want to open up that can of worms, not that I could blame her.

"The town sure looked closer on the map," I said.

"You're telling me." Reaching up, she massaged the back of her neck, attempting to rub the day's tension away. "Isn't that always the way? Just when you think you've gone far enough, along comes something that makes you realize you haven't even scratched the surface."

I knew exactly what she was alluding to, though only a fool would continue down that treacherous path. Instead, I changed the subject and focused on the most pressing thing on our minds. "You think he's okay?"

"Look at everything that's happened to him. All that he's gone through and is *still* going through. If I'm sure of one thing, it's that Sully can take care of himself, even if he has a hard time believing it. We just have to stick with the plan and keep going."

Footsteps approached from behind. I hoped it was Gideon, but the steps were lighter than his usual graceless thump. Instinctively, I felt my stomach clench.

"This is stupid. You should stay with the wheelchair man while the rest of us go on ahead to meet Sully," Emma volunteered unhelpfully.

Sam squeezed her eyes closed for a moment and went completely still. I think she must have been counting in her head or something. Maybe praying for strength. "I told you before. We move as a group. We're not splitting up and were not leaving anyone behind, and that's the end of it."

Unfortunately, Emma wasn't done. Reaching across, she tapped Sam on the shoulder as if she were a stranger of no consequence.

"But I don't understand why we have to listen to you. Sully didn't say anything about leaving you in charge when he left."

Her tone wasn't the least bit insolent. She honestly seemed to think it was Sully's decision to make. An irritated sigh hissed out of Sam, but her only response was to take another deep breath.

"I'm just saying we should consider other options, since Sully is waiting for us and we shouldn't keep him waiting."

It was, apparently, the final straw. Sam's eyes turned flat as all the fear and rage she had bottled up inside suddenly erupted. "I'm well aware that my husband is out there on his own! I don't need you to tell me that."

"But if you cared about him, you'd be trying to get to him as fast as possible." Emma twisted her fingers together, fully convinced of the truth in her words.

"I've tried to be patient, but you are testing my last nerve. Let me say this plainly in a way that even you can understand: while you might have bulldozed your way back into our lives, you are not part of our family, so you don't get a vote. You do as I say until we meet up with Sully again and you become his problem."

"I am part of Sully's family too," Emma corrected sulkily.

Sam's face went as red as the shirt she wore. "He's not your husband anymore! Stop acting as if you have any kind of claim over him!"

Bandit pressed into me, his whines a mixture of confusion and unhappiness. I wanted to comfort him, to offer a reassuring stroke, but I didn't dare make a move. I was worried that they were about to tear each other apart, in which case, I would need both of my hands. My eyes slid over to Gideon as I silently pleaded for him to help defuse the situation.

"Technically, she kind of is his wife," Gideon began, but it was absolutely the wrong thing to say. Both Emma and Sam glared at him, yelling simultaneously, "Shut up!"

"Oh boy," Zeb murmured, steering himself well clear.

Shaking my head at Gideon, I picked up the pace, hoping to put as much distance between Sam and Emma as possible.

30

THE CLEANER

Smith stared down at the biker, a vein popping on his forehead.

"My legs…" the biker moaned, face pale as moonlight. "Jesus, they hurt."

"I'm so sorry, sir. This is our mistake," Smith apologized, signaling for his men to move the bike off him. They lifted the bike as if it weighed no more than feathers as Smith ran his eyes over the man's legs.

The worn denim of the biker's jeans was now streaked with a dark, viscous oil. Relief washed over him as he noted the absence of blood, a small mercy in the chaos that had unfolded. In Smith's line of work, the spill of innocent blood was not only a tragedy, but a disaster for his secretive department. They preferred to settle matters discreetly, compensating victims generously under the condition of a strict non-disclosure agreement. The value of silence always outweighed the cost of a financial settlement. However, while Smith's mission was to eliminate his targets, depending on how risky his employer considered this man, it was possible this particular slate would have to be wiped clean, too.

He hoped that wouldn't be the case.

The biker attempted to shift his weight, testing his injured limbs. A sharp intake of breath escaped him as searing pain shot through his body. Still, he continued, testing the other leg only for a curse to spit out from his lips.

"Cops are gonna have a field day with you," he threatened.

Jackson leaned down to examine the biker's legs when the man waved him away. "Get away from me. Haven't you done enough?"

Jackson raised both of his hands, but glanced at Smith for his directive. Smith issued a barely perceptible shake of his head, to which Jackson backed off to await further instructions.

"We don't mean you any harm, sir. You have nothing to fear from us other than this unfortunate incident."

Smith flashed him an FBI badge, one of the many fake credentials he had in his armory. "We're from the Federal Bureau of Investigations. Unfortunately, you matched the description of the suspect we were looking for."

The biker squinted his eyes, studying Smith with a mix of skepticism and suspicion. The lines on his weathered face deepened as his frown etched itself into his features. Doubt hung heavy in the air as he wrestled with his story, trying to discern the truth. "And your man just happened to be riding a bike like mine, wearing the exact same helmet?"

His question was laced with sarcasm that he didn't bother to disguise. Smith adopted a contrite tone. The man may not know it, but his very life depended on how well and fast Smith could settle this matter.

"No. But the tracker we had placed with him lead us to you," Smith explained. It was the truth too, though a slightly distorted version of it. The biker's eyes turned dark with confusion before they cleared.

"Tracker? Your man put a tracker on my bike? But when would he have gotten the chance to..."

He trailed off, as a culprit emerged in his mind. "That jerkoff! The man you're looking for... is he a slim guy, in his mid/late thirties. Looks like city scum?"

Instead of opting for a vague reply, he delved into his pocket and retrieved a photograph. It was a picture of Sullivan, captured in a moment of relative tranquility before the chaos had broken out. In the image, Sullivan's features were frozen in a half-smile, his eyes reflecting a glimmer of mischief that hinted at the adventurous spirit within him. This was the image that was prominently displayed at the veterinary clinic during his time there.

Wordlessly, Smith extended the photograph toward the biker. The biker's eyes flicked from the image to Smith and back again, recognition dawning in their depths.

"That's him! That's the punk who stole my buddy's bike."

Smith felt a wave of relief pass through him as the biker confirmed his story. It was important not only for the man's future, but also their mission. The injured biker couldn't stop talking now, detailing each part of his encounter with Sullivan. Smith paid close attention, evaluating what he heard and asking questions where necessary. He soon had an accurate description of the illegally obtained vehicle.

Smith sent his men to contact local authorities about the stolen vehicle, and asked Jackson to take care of the biker until they could fly him to a hospital where "FBI" representatives would take over the legal proceedings. Smith knew that the man would be rewarded generously for his injuries and silence.

Having put the call out to the local boys in blue — or brown, as was more likely the case around these parts — Smith waited to be notified of any sightings of Sullivan or his family.

31

———

SULLY

What a difference two hours could make.

The bar had been transformed, having gone from empty to half-filled as a flood of mid-afternoon drinkers appeared.

With it, the noise had risen tenfold, leaving me more conscious of my solitary stay. The other side of my table was still unoccupied, though it was unlikely to remain that way for long. The empty cola can — which I had long finished — played between my fingers as I spun it first one way, then another, filled with a tension that was overflowing. I knew I should grab another drink, just so I wouldn't be encouraged to leave, but I was going to wait this out as long as I could.

Having made plans to meet up with Hipster-Pants later, the flirty girl at the bar had gone, and was now replaced by a group of men wearing ill-fitting suits and carrying fake leather briefcases. Cups of coffee clutched in their hands, they attempted to speak and joke together, yet what words I could pick out seemed forced. Their desperation clung like a cloud exposing them for what they were: salesmen, touting for business of some kind — my money was on insurance.

My eyes zeroed in on their coffees, feeling a wave of resentment toward the barman who had served them. Apparently, there was a dress code for certain beverages that I hadn't met. Any any other day and I would march right up to the punk to let him know exactly what I thought.

Instead, I stared back at the same spot in the distance that had held my focus since my arrival.

The clock above the door loomed large, its hands moving steadily, measuring the passage of time in relentless ticks. Each second seemed to echo, resonating in the corners of my mind like a drumbeat of impending doom.

They should have been here by now.

They should have gotten here only moments after my arrival.

The salesmen, the noisy crowd, and the increasingly-busy bartender all faded into the background as unwanted images crashed through my mind in vivid detail. I saw my family heading toward me in the truck when, with a screech of tires and a sickening crunch of metal, a grenade detonated, engulfing the truck in flames that swallowed my family whole. When the fire died out, I saw the road littered with the charred remains of my loved ones.

My eyes welled with tears as I imagined their smiling faces, their voices fading into the recesses of my memory. The weight of grief pressed down on my chest, making it hard to breathe.

The horrific nightmare rolled into another.

My heart leaped with joy as I saw my family arriving in the town, relief flooding through me like a warm embrace. Sam, my beautiful wife, led the way, her eyes scanning the streets until they met mine, locked in the window of the bar. A smile, full of love and happiness, illuminated her face as she lifted her hand in a wave. My chest swelled with love and gratitude; the sight of her able to dispel any fear that dared to linger.

Behind her, the familiar figures of Chase, Gideon, and my dad came into view, their faces mirroring the same happiness that radiated from Sam. But before I could fully comprehend the scene unfolding before me, chaos erupted. Bandit, sprinted toward them, barking furiously, a desperate warning that I could feel in the depths of my soul.

Chase, her eyes wide with terror, looked up at me, her mouth opening to shout a warning. Just as she was about to speak, the world imploded. Bullets tore through her body in a hail of deadly projectiles, stealing her life away in an instant. I watched in horror as she fell, her body crumpling to the ground, the light in her eyes extinguished forever.

A scream ripped itself from my throat as Sam dropped to her knees beside Chase, her hands trembling as she cradled our daughter when another bullet found its mark *and ate a path through her head*. She slumped over Chase, their blood mingling on the pavement.

Gideon and my dad, my pillars of strength, met the same fate, their lives taken from them in the blink of an eye. The world seemed to spin, the sounds of gunfire and anguish mingling into a cacophony of despair. I was frozen, my mind unable to comprehend the nightmare unfolding before me.

Only Bandit remained, his mournful howls cutting through the air, echoing the grief that gripped my soul. His cries reached a crescendo, a heartbreaking melody of loss and pain, before he too was silenced.

The can shot from my fingers, hitting the floor of the bar with a bang.

Tears fogged my vision. I fought to keep it together, knowing I had to preserve my sanity to save my family from whatever was delaying them. And it had to be a delay.

Anything else was unthinkable.

Wiping the tears away and steeled myself, my jaw clenched in resolve. *Come on, Sully. There's a normal explanation for why they weren't here yet.*

The thought of them just being lost flickered through my mind, but the devil on my shoulder chimed in, reminding me that Chase's memory was infallible and that her getting lost wasn't a likely scenario.

Well, maybe there was a problem with the truck then.

Right... The unwelcome voice in my head answered. *Because the truck was so rundown and on its last legs.*

Well, maybe the men managed to disable it remotely. In which case, they would all be dead by now.

I dug my fingers into my hands until the pain was sharp and immediate. Pain was good.

Pain reminded me that I was alive, that I still had a purpose. I needed to focus and be rational. I had to be clear-minded enough to know what to do when they did finally arrive.

Grateful that the voice had been silenced, I toyed with the idea of buying another cola when a shadow loomed over me. The barman. And he didn't look too pleased to have to deal with me again.

"Unless you're going to be buying several more and *expensive* drinks, I'm going to have to ask you to leave since I need that table."

He gestured to the group of salesmen who stood sheepishly behind him, cups of coffee in hand. I hesitated, debating between accepting the offer and knowing I couldn't afford it. I slid my hand into my pocket and fingered some change, wishing I had the coin pouch Sam had given me as a gift.

I wasn't very disciplined at using the thing the way it was intended, stuffing as many bills inside as actual coins. Consequently, there was quite a bit of cash in there. Sadly, the pouch was sitting on top of the dresser at home where I had left it.

"I'm going to need an answer from you," the barman pressed.

It was on the tip of my tongue to tell him where he could shove his answers when a weary group of familiar faces appeared down the street. My heart soared. I shot to my feet.

"My family just got here!"

The barman's face twisted with confusion. "How nice for you."

So much joy rose up inside me that I couldn't be bothered to tango with this waste of space any longer. Slapping him on the shoulder — a little harder than was necessary — I grinned.

"Yes it is."

I rushed outside. Bandit noticed me first. Picking up my scent, he barked and sprinted for me at a breath-taking pace. I caught him just as he was about to knock me to the ground.

"Am I happy to see you, boy!"

Bandit's pink tongue slobbered over my face, catching me from chin to cheek. Planting a big kiss on his snout, I looked over to the others.

"Did they find you? Is that why it took you so long to get here?" I asked, unable to stop myself. Walking toward me, Sam had a giant smile on her beautiful face when someone crossed rudely in front of her path.

Emma.

I blinked, startled, having forgotten for the moment that she was even back. Then I caught myself, as my body flooded with the shame and guilt that momentary lapse in my memory caused.

"Have you any idea what I just went through?" she demanded. "None of them would listen to me. I kept making suggestions, but they kept ignoring me. If they had taken me seriously, we would have gotten here so much sooner."

Behind her, Sam glowered with an irritation I had never witnessed before. Side-stepping neatly around Emma, she wedged herself between the two of us.

"What happened to your face? Her hand went up gently to explore my injuries.

"I bumped into a friend of the guy whose bike I stole. We got into it but I managed to get away before too much damage could be done. What about you? What took you so long?"

"We were out of gas, if you can believe that," Gideon supplied.

"*Somebody* let it run dry, so we had to walk half the way here. Slowly," Emma said resentfully, shooting Sam a dagger-filled look. A nervous twitch tugged at my face. *Had the two fought the entire way here?*

"I didn't know what was taking so long. I was getting pretty worried."

"Well, we're here now. Have you gotten rid of the bike? It's the first thing they can ID and could lead them straight to us," Sam asked, stepping into her sheriff shoes.

"I ditched it in an alley and covered it with boxes. I don't think anyone will find it. Not for a while, anyway."

While we were speaking, Chase was staring at me strangely, mentally evaluating my injuries and possibly calculating the likelihood of my death.

She must have decided that the odds were looking pretty good, as the tension eventually left her shoulders. I threw my arms around her and gave her a tight squeeze. She leaned into me as Bandit flanked my other side.

"Do we have a plan for how we're getting to your friend's cabin?" Zeb asked.

"No..." I fell silent, his question suddenly reminding me of my conversation with Mark — and the bad news that had come with it. "We can't go there, unfortunately."

"Why?" Chase asked, her face twisted with confusion. "Couldn't you get in touch with him?"

I didn't answer right away. The hollow feeling that had been in my stomach worked its way up to my chest until it felt like a great weight was pressing down onto it.

"I could, but... Florence is dead. Mark told me when I spoke to him." The others gasped, the shock in their faces reflected in my own.

"How?" Sam asked. Her quiet, one-word question made my heart lurch. Until this moment, I hadn't been able to feel the impact of Florence's death. But now that words were being spoken, the truth was undeniable.

"She was found dead in her armchair. They're saying it was a heart attack, but I know better. Florence may have died, but it wasn't by any natural causes."

"What makes you say that?" Sam asked carefully. I explained about her abhorrence for modern conveniences, how she hated microwaves most of all, and how her friend had been the one to find her. "Her killers have ensured that no one will pry into her death."

Sam's eyes were troubled. She didn't comment, her mind working through the details of my revelation as if it was one of her cases. The kids didn't know what to say and stood around awkwardly, while Emma's expression barely changed. I could have been discussing the weather for all the effect it had on her.

"Who is this Florence? Was she another wife of yours?"

She asked the question without any hint of spite.

"No. She was a dear friend of ours." The word *"ours"* slipped out before I could stop it. I felt, rather than saw, Sam tense.

"I'm sorry, son," Zeb uttered his condolences. "I know how much she meant to you." He patted me on the arm as he couldn't stand to hug me.

"The people who are after us killed her. I'm sure of it. They went after Mark, too. He'd been out jogging, but then somehow blacked out. They found him in a ditch without any memory of how he had gotten there."

A gasp left Emma's lips. "Just like me."

"Not exactly," I corrected. "Mark can remember nearly everything, but there is a gap in his memory from the time he started jogging to when he woke up. Both incidents happened on the same day. It's too much to be a coincidence."

"I agree," Sam answered. Several strands of her blonde hair had fallen across her eyes. I reached up and brushed them away as Emma's eyes bored into my back.

"But Mark had a place for us. And money!" Gideon blurted.

"We can't get help from anyone?" Chase asked, a horrified look on her face.

"Not from anyone they can trace us to," I answered reluctantly, the burden of my words heavy on my shoulders.

"We're on our own."

32

CHASE

"You can't be serious?"

Usually able to keep his emotions in check — particularly if they were a cause for alarm — Gideon was doing a pretty bad job of faking it this time. Not that I blamed him. His world had been uprooted and our one chance of survival had just been taken away with a throwaway comment from Sully.

"We can't risk calling anyone and putting them in danger. I can't have another death on my hands. Florence was alone when they got to her. Mark too. God knows who else they'll go after if we ask for their help."

Sully's expression hadn't changed though his tone softened in the way I had heard him use with Bandit, whenever he'd had to do something he didn't like — like bath time.

Sam moved forward, her expression turning darker. Before she even spoke, I felt a lurch of fear in my stomach. That knot that seemed permanently wedged there grew exponentially.

"What about the people who are already involved?" she asked, her voice all the more urgent for its quietness.

"We're already here," Zeb answered, unable to understand her point.

"Not all of us," Sully suddenly replied sounding frustrated at himself.

My mind raced, trying to piece it all together. Gideon, Bandit, and I exchanged puzzled glances, our brows furrowing in confusion. Then, like a bolt from the blue, realization struck like lightning.

"Oh Jeez, you mean Doc Robins, don't you?"

Sam nodded reluctantly, her blonde curls bobbing around her face.

"Is Doc Robins another friend of ours?" Emma asked Sully.

"She's a friend of the family," Zeb corrected gently. "You haven't met her."

Sam continued, "It's possible that they haven't made the connection, and I know we haven't told anyone about her involvement with us, but what about the adopted families of all those dogs she saved? Do we really think that none of them would have said something? That there isn't a Facebook post up where she is being thanked for all that she has done for their family?"

"You honestly think they would target her?" Sully asked.

"I would if I was them," Sam replied. "She knows far too much. And she visited us at the ranch when she came for Pixie. If they know that, they would consider her a liability."

Chills raced down my spine.

"But if we call her, they might be able to trace it," Sully mused, his face growing paler by the second. He didn't have anything to do with the situation, but I knew he would take it personally. That's just how he was - always looking out for everyone, and not just humans. It's why he was Sully.

Sam knotted her fingers together. When she spoke again, it was hesitant, as if she couldn't believe what she was going to say. "That's why we'll have to go to her instead."

Zeb had been listening to us working through our options but he interjected. "In Arizona? That's a long way and we don't have the transport or the means."

He cast his eyes downward to his legs, his frustration palpable. The challenge of reaching this town had been so arduous, the question seemed to hang unspoken in the air: *what were the chances of successfully making it all the way to Arizona with him?* His frown silently conveyed this doubt.

Sully's gaze shifted to his dad. "I guess we'll figure that out. Let's just move away from here. I don't feel safe, not with all the ways we can be spotted."

Standing on the edge of the group with her arms folded across her chest, Emma voiced her concerns.

"You all keep talking about going somewhere but have you considered how? What are we going to do, steal a car? Even I know that's wrong."

Gideon shot me a look that I knew would get us in trouble.

I knew exactly what was coming next and braced myself for Sam's inevitable reaction.

33

CHASE

We sat on a metal bench around the corner from a parking lot where Sully, Gideon, and Bandit had taken off to, the latter acting as a watchdog — in all senses of the word.

After Gideon had broached his plan to steal a vehicle from the lot, as I had expected, Sam expressed some serious objections to the criminal act. Especially as it wasn't the first time he had stolen a car while being with Sully.

Not even the second, actually.

Nope, the third time was not the charm and Sam was taking real issue with this nasty little habit Gideon seemed to have developed while living under Sully's roof. Still, after her initial objections, she eventually arrived at the same conclusion as the rest of us. It wasn't as if we had much choice in the matter. Lives were at stake and not only our own.

My stomach rumbled. I crossed my hands over it, hoping to dull the sound. Food would have to wait until we were out of this town.

As if waiting for Gideon to steal a car while Sully and Bandit kept watch, and not being able to do a single thing to assist wasn't nerve-wracking enough, we kept finding curious stares tossed our way.

While the folk here seemed friendly enough, they were obviously used to a certain crowd and I guess our ragtag family loitering around was causing quite the stir.

"Why are they taking so long?"

Emma's voice cut through my nerves, making me jump. For someone who had shown such incredulity when the idea was first introduced, she had come round faster than a fish took to water.

Her piercing blue eyes darted toward the parking lot as she paced back and forth. With each restless step she took, her shoes clicked against the tarmac.

"They're going as fast as they can. Best we be calm, and perhaps lower our voices so we draw no more attention to ourselves," came Zeb's sensible suggestion.

As if she hadn't heard him, Emma glanced at Sam, addressing no one in particular. "Didn't *she* say she's a sheriff? You'd think she'd have a bigger problem with this, but no. It's only when I do something. It's only me who gets told off."

I could see Sam's shoulders tighten. She took in a long breath, then let it out slowly, refusing to take the bait.

"Can we just concentrate on Gideon and Sully? If there's trouble, we might need to jump in. Maybe we could just focus," I pleaded.

Emma's mouth snapped closed. Thankfully, it seemed she would accept my suggestion, as her only reply was to stare across the lot where Gideon had stopped by a three-rowed saloon.

I couldn't see too much from my position, only that it was an older make which Gideon had previously admitted were the best for stealing as new cars can't be hot-wired. Newer cars also had some kind of computer system, which meant it could be easily traced.

He explained how many of the electronic devices used in cars relied on satellites to pinpoint their location in order to give directions on a GPS. That same technology could be easily reversed, causing the car to emit a trackable signal. All of this just meant that every time we were forced to steal a car, it would never be a new one.

So we could forget onboard Wi-Fi, TV screens on the backs of the head-rests or even a charging dock for the phones we didn't have anymore.

It was old school all the way.

Gideon glanced behind him a few rows, at another car that he seemed to consider. This was a beaten up number with a rusty rim job and plates that were barely hanging on. I knew looks didn't count for much, but I doubted the thing would even start, much less get us across the country. Gideon must have thought the same as he turned his attention back to the saloon.

I watched, holding my breath as Gideon stooped down as if he was unlocking the door. His body barely moved, only his hands that skillfully hid the lock picks he was using. After all the tight spots we'd been in before, he carried them on him at all times, something I'm sure we were all grateful for now.

The door sprang open.

Quick as a flash, Sully and Bandit dove inside. Sully slid behind the wheel while Gideon opened the back door for Bandit. When all three were inside, they pulled out of the lot and drove to us.

They helped maneuver Zeb into the car while I folded up the wheelchair. As soon as Zeb was settled in the backseat, Sully ran back round to the driver's seat and popped open the trunk. I struggled to lift the wheelchair inside when Gideon came over and took it out of my hands. Grateful for his help, I nodded my thanks and hurried to the car to find Emma already ensconced in the middle row. Sam had taken the passenger seat beside Sully, leaving a space by Zeb or Emma.

It was immediately apparent that the curvature of the back seat would make it impossible for me and Bandit to both sit next to Zeb.

It was sit with Bandit and Emma or with Zeb on my own.

Much as I loved Zeb, I couldn't bear to be parted from my Muttface, even in a car, so there was no real choice. Sully twisted in his seat, casting a look at all of us as Gideon slammed the trunk closed and climbed in beside Zeb.

"Buckle up," Sam instructed, ever the safety girl.

And we were off.

I had one arm around Bandit — who thankfully, acted as a physical barrier between Emma and me — while Emma braced herself against the armrest. Tension hung heavy in the air, and no one spoke. We were wracked with nerves that wouldn't abate until we were out of this town and safely on our way to Arizona.

The vehicle was in much better condition than I had given it credit for, its engine surprisingly powerful beneath the worn exterior. Despite the unexpected reliability, I couldn't shake the feeling of unease that gripped me, my senses on high alert, waiting for the telltale signs of law enforcement.

I kept my eyes fixed on the rearview mirror, half-expecting to see flashing red and blue lights, and hear the shrill sirens that might pierce the air, signaling the authorities in hot pursuit of us for the stolen car. Each passing moment felt like an eternity, my nerves on edge, anticipating the inevitable confrontation with the law.

Outside the window, the vibrant shop fronts blurred into streaks of color, a surreal tableau that contrasted sharply with the tension inside the car. The world outside moved at a frenetic pace, oblivious to the adrenaline-fueled drama unfolding within the confines of the stolen vehicle. As we approached the back of the Welcome sign, a landmark that marked the edge of town, I couldn't help but hold my breath, the tension in my chest reaching its peak.

When we passed the sign, my breath finally hissed out of my lungs like a released valve, a sound that seemed to startle Emma, who shot me a look as if to ask what was wrong with me. Outside the window, the landscape changed, the urban scenery giving way to open roads and vast expanses. The town we had left behind became smaller and smaller, shrinking into a mere speck on the horizon.

"Good job," Sam finally said to Gideon, her eyes finding his in the rearview mirror. "But don't ever do that again."

"Why?" Gideon asked. "I'm getting really good at it."

She fixed him with such a baleful stare that he slid down into his seat. Sully's lips twitched but then the grin faded from his face when she fixed her attention to him.

"This is only a short-term solution. We're in a stolen vehicle, so even if those men can't find us, highway patrol soon will."

"But you just said we can't steal another car?" Gideon looked confused, his tousled hair tumbled over his eyes in a disheveled mess.

"Once we get to the city, I have an idea of how we can arrange for something more suitable."

I couldn't wait to hear how she figured that would happen.

34

CHASE

e hurtled down I-35S, the asphalt beneath us a blur as we embarked on our epic journey to Arizona. According to Sully's calculations, a trip that stretched over twenty-four hours loomed ahead, provided we drove without interruption, with three drivers tirelessly working in shifts. I wasn't part of the designated driving trio, a fact I didn't contest. If it were up to me, it would be bicycles for the win.

The rhythmic hum of the road reverberated through the car, lulling most of us into a drowsy stupor. Bandit, lay draped across my lap, emanating a comforting warmth like a living, breathing, hot water bottle. Emma had succumbed to sleep, her head resting awkwardly against the window. I was convinced she'd wake with a crick in her neck, which seemed like poetic justice since she was such a pain in ours.

In the backseat, there was a stillness broken only by the regular cadence of Zeb's heavy breathing as he, too, succumbed to a much-needed nap. I remained wide awake, however, unable to sleep. Despite the distance we had traveled, I couldn't shake the feeling that I needed to keep a watchful eye out for danger. I had to protect my family. Even when the scenery unfolded before me, an ever-changing tapestry of landscapes, and the amber fields transformed into a sprawling cityscape, I couldn't bring myself to close my eyes.

Skyscrapers reached for the heavens, their steel and glass mirroring the setting sun and casting a warm, golden glow over Kansas City. Although I had limited knowledge of the place, I knew the city sat on the western edge of Missouri and had a rich cultural heritage, steeped in jazz music and barbecue cuisine.

That last part was really all that mattered to me — I was pretty gutted we wouldn't be here long enough to sample any of it. Just once, I'd love to visit a place when we weren't on the run.

Sully navigated the roads and slowed the car to a halt in a shadowy side street, in a spot hidden from prying eyes, between two flickering streetlights that barely pierced the approaching gloom.

My stomach churned. Sitting up in my seat, I leaned closer to him. "This is it?"

My voice was a hoarse rasp that felt foreign, as if I were the eighty-year-old version of myself. Emma blinked awake, eyes growing increasingly wide with alarm as she quickly took in our new — and dubious — surroundings. Her confusion hung in the air like a storm cloud .

"Why have we stopped?" Hugging her knees to her chest, she looked like a scared child.

Sam turned to face us. I heard Zeb and Gideon stir as they stretched tired and cramped muscles. "We're here. This is where I'm going to get us a new vehicle. From the police impound."

My eyes widened, the disbelief etched on my face, as I stared at her, slightly bug-eyed. "Sorry. I must have blanked. For a second there, I thought you said you were going *to* the police?"

Sam nodded, her eyes dark with a seriousness that sent shivers down my spine. "That's right." Her voice carried a steely resolve that seemed to defy the gravity of our situation.

"I hate to state the obvious but we're in a stolen vehicle right now," Gideon chimed in, his tone echoing my own shock. She nodded again. I kept waiting for the other shoe to drop but it didn't seem to be coming.

"That's why you're all staying here, out of sight, while I go talk to them alone. Sheriff to cop."

"Do you have any jurisdiction here?" Gideon continued, unable to make head nor tails of this plan.

"No, but I think this will work. Just give me an hour. I'll either be successful or I'll come back empty-handed." She unclipped her seatbelt as if what she had just suggested wasn't the riskiest idea on the planet.

Sully stopped her with a firm hand on her arm. "I'm coming with you."

"You can't. If I'm on official sheriff business, why would my husband be with me?" Sam's response seemed completely reasonable which made it all the harder to dispute her point.

"Then I'm not your husband. I'm your deputy, your driver. Hell, I'll be your dancing monkey so long as I can come with you," Sully pleaded, a note of desperation creeping into his voice. Sam smiled, a tender expression on her face, as she cupped his face in her hands.

"Honey, they're not after me. We haven't been caught with the stolen car, and even if there was an APB out for us, it would be for two women, two teenagers, a man, a dog, and an elderly man in a wheelchair, not for Montpelier's sheriff. I'll be fine, I promise. If there's any sign of trouble, I'll come straight back."

Sully's eyes burned with intensity, his concern etched deep into his features. "I'm not happy about this," he admitted, his voice low and strained with worry.

Sam arched a blonde brow. "Then that makes two of us."

Without waiting for Sully or the rest of us to voice any more objections, she slid out of her seat and gracefully exited the car, her silhouette stark against the fading light.

"There are no CCTV cameras around here, I made sure of that. Still, you all need to keep your eyes peeled. Any sign of weirdness, any tingling in your gut and you just get out of here and head on."

"But how will you find us?" My voice trembled, reverting to the tone of a whiny, worried kid.

Sam winked, flashing a grin. "I have Robins' address. If it all blows up, I can get myself there."

A collective unease spread through the ranks, the impending separation weighing in our hearts. Sam flashed a big, determined smile, attempting to ease our fears.

"Don't worry. I won't be long."

And with those six words, she vanished into the fast-encroaching night.

35

CHASE

S am had gone, and she seemed to have taken all the air out of the car with her.

Without her, Sully couldn't relax. His fingers drummed a nervous, irrational beat on the dashboard that set my teeth on edge. I wanted to ask him to stop, but couldn't find the words. Unable to bear the tension any longer, I made my way out of the car, craving the refuge of open space and the chance to stretch my stiff muscles.

Gideon joined me as we stood half-hidden in the shadows, our eyes glued to the twinkling lights of downtown. The cityscape glowed like a constellation of stars. "I wonder what she'll say to them," he said without shifting his gaze away from the skyline.

"Whatever it takes, I guess."

We remained side by side as night descended and the temperatures dropped. Goosebumps prickled my skin and I shivered until Gideon wrapped his arm around me. His warmth enveloped me like a protective shield and I sank into him, much like how Bandit pressed against me, enjoying both the physical and emotional support that exuded from him.

Through my concern for Sam and the immediate threat to our safety, there was a new awareness dawning inside me, a realization of something unspoken yet palpable. Something was changing between us, a shift in the dynamic we had always known. Our relationship was evolving, morphing from the familiar brother and sister dynamic into something deeper, some-thing... more.

My eyes lingered on the profile of his face, taking in his strong jawline and the familiar ridge of his nose. Feeling my stare, he turned to me, his gaze burning with their intensity, electrifying us both. The hairs on the back of my neck tingled. The air between us seemed to crackle with an unspoken tension, and the world around us blurred into insignificance until there was only the two of us.

But before the moment could fully envelop us, Bandit barked suddenly, his warning tone slicing through the charged atmosphere, and jolting us both out of whatever-this-was.

We both jumped away from each other, the spell broken, and our heads snapped around to see Bandit staring intently at a spot a few cars down. Black figures approached — three of them. Hulking figures who seemed larger than life. Was it my imagination or were they deliberately avoiding the pockets of light thrown down by the streetlights?

My body tensed, fear eating away at me. Gideon reacted swiftly, tapping a warning on the glass of Zeb's window. I sensed rather than saw Sully and Zeb's attention shifting towards the front of the car. Bandit ran ahead of me, positioning himself between me and the approaching figures. His keen senses were on high alert, sniffing the air, searching for any sign that the approaching group might be unfriendly.

"Get back into the car," Gideon instructed us quietly. Normally I would have argued, not one to take orders without question, but there was something about those ominous black shapes that had me gritting my teeth.

I climbed back into the safety of the car, gesturing for Bandit to follow. The men were now just two cars away from us, yet their features remained obscured, their faces as dark as the jackets they wore.

Sully moved his hand to the ignition. He waited until the group moved closer, then suddenly, he gunned the engine, turning on the high-beams. Light shone out, blinding the three men. Startled by the glare, they shielded their eyes with their arms.

I finally got the chance to get a proper look at them.

They were older than me and Gideon, but younger than Sully. Their jackets, which had seemed black before, were actually a deep blue and had a logo of two entwined red letters, K and C sewn onto the chest. I snapped my gaze to their hands, terrified that I'd find weapons aimed at us. Instead, they were holding half-eaten burgers, still in their wrappers.

They were nothing more than three sports fans on their way to a game.

Bandit whined an apology for spooking us like that. Gideon lowered a hand to stroke him, but kept his eyes on the guys. The one in the middle, the largest of the trio, called out to Sully, gesturing at the lights.

"Hey, you mind?"

Sully flicked them back to normal, winding down his window. "Sorry, guys," he called out of it. "This is the wife's car. Still getting used to it."

The lie was quick and convincing. The tension that had ramped up dissolved immediately.

"No problem," the guy replied as he took another bite of his burger. They continued past, chatting about their upcoming game, their excitement palpable.

I breathed a sigh of relief as Gideon made it back to the car. Even Sully's loud drumming didn't faze me now.

"I'm so hungry," Emma suddenly announced. "And their food smelled really good."

"Eat another one of your energy bars then," I answered, trying not to sound like a brat but failing miserably.

"There's none left. Where's that other sandwich?"

My gaze rested on her face, looking for any sign of awareness about how unreasonable she was being, but there was no hidden agenda or shame in her expression. "Sully ate it earlier."

"While I was sleeping? He should have waited to share it with me." Her lower lip jutted out in a pout.

"I think we have some nuts left," Zeb offered with apparently endless patience.

"Well, I'm not a dog."

Her answer had us stumped for a second. It was Bandit who finally answered.

"Do you mean squirrel? They eat nuts."

Emma shrugged her thin shoulders. "Whatever. One animal's the same as the next."

Sully stared at her through the rearview mirror as if he couldn't recognize her. When he spoke, his voice was deceptively soft.

"When Sam gets back and we're away from Kansas City, we'll make a stop for more provisions."

"But that's still *hours* away!"

"Yes."

The wind was cut from Emma's sails. She settled back, sulking silently at the injustice of it all.

Time seemed to stretch endlessly as we continued our vigil, our eyes scanning the dark horizon for any sign of Sam's return. Every approaching beam of headlights sparked a glimmer of hope, only to be extinguished when the passing cars carried on

After God knows how long, my mind was beginning to crack from both boredom and pressure, and I was giving serious consideration to playing a game on Bandit's iPad. Just as I was reaching for the device, a distant rumble pierced the stillness of the night.

My head snapped up, my senses on high alert. The approaching lights, unlike the low headlights of previous passing cars, were positioned higher, casting an eerie glow in the darkness. The ground trembled beneath the weight of whatever was approaching, and a wave of dread washed over me when I realized those lights didn't belong to any car.

They belonged to something much bigger... like a truck.

Sully reached the same conclusion, his instincts kicking in as he flicked on our high-beams, momentarily blinding the approaching driver. I held my breath, expecting the inevitable crash of metal meeting metal. Instead, the massive truck skidded to a stop, its tires screeching against the asphalt.

"Little hostile for a welcoming committee," Sam's amused voice called out from the 'truck.'

Sully leaped out of the car, a broad grin stretching across his face, as the rest of us followed suit. When I was within a few feet of the vehicle, I realized it wasn't a truck Sam had brought back at all... but an RV!

She beamed at us like she'd won the lottery, her pearly whites flashing in the dark.

"Are you kidding me right now?" Gideon was practically giddy with happiness.

Sam nodded. "Welcome to our new home. I've christened her: Buffy. She may not look like much, but she packs a mean punch."

"I don't get why everyone's so excited. If the new truck stopped working, won't this old thing do the same? As usual, Emma didn't share the same level of excitement as the rest of us.

"I think we'll be alright," Sully answered. "We're in a much better shape than we were five minutes ago."

We took turns to explore Buffy and survey her condition up close.

She wasn't brand new, but there was plenty of room inside for all of us and she didn't need an additional car to tow it. Despite a few dents, the RV appeared to be in good condition for its age.

"How?" Sully was so impressed he could not formulate a complete sentence.

"Police station's impound vehicles all the time, from drivers who fail to pay their parking fines to those running criminal activity inside them. This baby was involved with the latter, but since her owners are currently serving twenty to life, they're not coming back for it anytime soon," Sam explained.

"They don't just hand these away, though?" Sully asked, straightening up from examining the tires though what he could see of it in this light, I had no idea.

"I flashed them my sheriff's badge and asked if we could come to a deal. The vehicle would only go off to auction once the requisite time has passed. I have it on good authority that there are too many issues with it for it to sell for much. I made an offer, large enough to cover the towing and storage fees, and they accepted."

"But we don't have any money?" Call it habit, but the thought was always at the forefront of my mind.

"And we don't need any. They're billing it to my work. By the time anyone realizes we were here, we'll be long gone. And this kind of paperwork takes days to get through. My deputy will try to reach me and when he can't, it'll just delay the entire process. We're pretty much good to go."

Sully shook his head in admiration. "This is exactly what we needed. Exactly what we needed." He kissed her passionately, dipping her into a dramatic pose and making her laugh.

Having experienced nothing but terror and trouble in the last two days, we desperately needed this moment of lightness, this win for the good guys. I couldn't stop my instinct to look at Emma to see her reaction. Instead of the jealousy or anger I expected, she pulled a face as if their affection disgusted her.

I don't think I would ever understand her.

Tail wagging in excitement, Bandit bounded ahead of me into the RV, his enthusiasm infectious. Following him, I climbed up the steps and crossed the threshold into our new home — and was immediately assaulted by a mix of odors. The predominant scent was that of dusty vinyl flooring. Cheap pine-scented air freshener hung on every window. I found myself standing in the central area of the RV, dominated by a u-shaped fabric sofa curving around a table. This formed the main living space, modest yet functional. Behind the seating area, there was a compact kitchenette, complete with a tiny sink and a two-ring electric stove. A mini fridge and some wooden cupboards completed the culinary setup. It was a space that seemed designed for efficiency rather than luxury, every inch utilized to its fullest extent.

As I moved toward the back of the RV, the vinyl flooring gave way to a stained carpet that looked as though it had seen better days. There were no bloodstains on it, however, which was my bar for what I could live with, so there was that I suppose.

I passed by a shower head that was mounted over the toilet and saw how the floor of the "shower room" curved upward. The entire setup made me do a double-take.

Apparently, to shower, you were supposed to stand over the toilet. Gross.

Still, beggars couldn't be choosers. If hot water could come out of that thing, I would be singing for joy. Beyond the shower room, there were two large spaces where I assumed the washer and dryer would have been if there was one. A double bed surrounded by built-in cabinets took up the rear of the place. There wasn't any bedding on the battered-looking mattress that dipped in several places. Not even a sheet.

Heading back into the main area, I checked out each of the cupboards, but only came up with a pair of plastic tumblers and four plates. No cutlery, but I there was a pan with a half-melted handle.

I flashed Sam a broad grin. "It's perfect!"

"We need to air the thing out and clean it up a bit, but it'll do," Sam replied. She crossed to the windows and snatched up the air fresheners, shoving them into a bag she had found and tossed the lot into a trashcan outside.

Of course, our enthusiasm hadn't made its way to Emma. "How are we all going to sleep in here?"

"The women can take the bedroom. Gid and Dad can use the room here — those seats look like they convert into a double bed. And if I'm not mistaken, there's another double hidden above the driver's seat."

Sam nodded and pulled down the bed when a cloud of dust fell, making us all choke.

"Sorry," Sam apologized. "Should've known that would happen."

Back at the sink, I turned on the faucet. Water came out though there was a murky tinge to it. "That's coming out of storage tanks, Chase. I'm not sure how much is left in there. Maybe you could turn it off?"

Feeling chastised, I immediately did as she suggested.

"That water is only to be used for cleaning. It goes without saying that no one drinks from it. Bandit, that especially goes for you." Sam gave him a pointed stare. I swear Bandit's cheeks flushed. He woofed, managing to make it sound like it was ridiculous for her to even consider such a thing — though we all knew he would.

He might be the cleverest dog in the world, but he was still a dog.

No one else seemed as excited as I was by the running water, but that was the thing about me: I didn't take anything for granted. Life came with unexpected disappointments, so we had to roll with the punches or we'd all be in a heap on the floor.

Take me.

When I was a kid, during one of those periods where my mom was in-between men, so it had been just the two of us, she had wanted to do something nice for me. She hadn't always been so bad. I think people have way more shades of gray about them: we're not all black and white.

I remember being on her for this dollhouse that all the other kids were getting, even the ones in the trailer park. Owning one had been my reason for living. I know now that's pathetic and materialistic, but I was too young then to know any better.

The two of us had gone to Walmart to pick up the dollhouse for my sixth birthday. The pictures on the box looked amazing, with all the dainty furniture that even included window boxes full of plastic flowers and gadgets for the kitchen. I'd watched the commercial on television for months, so I knew everything about the house.

I knew it came with a bed and an adorable vanity table that had a real mirror in it where you could see your own reflection. The bathroom had a toilet, sink, and tub that was big enough for your doll to fit inside. The kitchen/diner housed a table and chairs and these tiny dish clothes you could hang off the sink. It was as real a house as my six-year-old mind could have dreamed up.

Mom had counted out the money she had saved up, working at a local diner, trying not to wince as she forked over the bills, sharing an excited smile with me. Two bus rides and a ten-minute walk that seemed to have lasted much longer in my tired kid mind later, we finally made it home.

She had pre-warned me that the house didn't come assembled, that we'd have to put it together ourselves, but she was sure we could do it. Opening the box, she took out the instructions and all the pieces.

Which was when we realized there was a problem.

All those cute pieces of furniture we'd been seeing on the ads and even on the box itself? None of them actually came with the house.

We'd have to pay for them all separately.

My mom became so mad that she couldn't put the house together. Her hands were shaking too much. The next day, I woke to find all the pieces of the house in the trash, having been smashed to bits.

We never spoke about it again, but I learned a hard lesson that day. It was why I had to check every nook and cranny in the RV.

I had to make sure it wasn't another empty dollhouse.

When I was convinced it wasn't, I flew at Sam and hugged her, thankful that we had a roof over our heads again.

She hugged me right back, her eyes unusually bright.

36

SULLY

T he night sky unfolded above, an expansive canvas painted in deep hues of navy blue, adorned with a multitude of stars that flickered like distant beacons. I kept our RV to a steady speed, ensuring we'd go unnoticed as the lights of Kansas City gradually dimmed in the review mirror, and the towering buildings that inhabited the skyline were now reduced to small stories.

I drove solo for the time being. Sam and Chase had gone into the bedroom after the first half hour together. Ever since Chase had toured the RV, something unspoken had passed between them. Call it gut instinct, but whatever it was, I didn't want to intrude.

Emma sat at the table, not saying a word, though I would catch her staring at me every now and then. When I looked at her, my heart would surge with joy... until apprehension and guilt took its place.

I couldn't get my feelings straight about her. The whole thing was impossible.

I pushed my feelings aside and focused on the highway, hoping that she would eventually tire of boring her gaze into the back of my head.

Gideon bustled about in the kitchenette, cleaning up dishes with damp napkins. Retrieving a can of dog food, he opened it with his penknife, using the technique Chase had demonstrated earlier. I knew I was long past a meal of my own when the smell of dog food made my mouth water.

Only two days on the road and I was already giving real consideration to dog food.

Unbelievable.

"Bandit, come get some chow," Gideon called to him. Bandit jumped off the sofa beside Zeb, padding to him. I fought to contain my envy when he dived snout first into the food.

Fishing out our remaining provisions, Gideon counted out three candy bars and one last bag of nuts. He split everything into six portions including a few nuts that he passed to Zeb, who accepted the offering with a nod of thanks. His next stop was Emma, who wasn't quite as gracious, taking the meager offering with a look of disbelief.

"When I asked earlier, you said we only had nuts left?"

"No, Zeb offered you nuts, which you declined. No one said anything about candy bars."

"But you knew what I meant," she murmured. "I just so hungry my stomach hurts." Her eyes grew large and luminous. She seemed even more of a child at that moment.

"Ours too," Zeb responded. "Hang on in there. We'll get a real meal soon."

I took the food Gideon offered, nodding my thanks as he headed to the back with the remaining portions. I reached for the radio, tuning it to a country station. The music sounded tinny and emerged from only one speaker, but it was better than having to listen to Emma's continuous suffering. The male singer crooned about lost love with a haunting refrain of what could have been. The words struck a melancholy chord in me as I found myself wondering the same.

With several windows wound down, the once oppressive artificial scent of pine, gave way to the freshness of clean air. Most of the dust had been wiped away, leaving a semblance of cleanliness and order. I could hear a chorus of crickets outside, their intermittent chirps weaved into the mournful melody of the country song, providing an additional soundtrack to the unfolding journey. I hadn't felt safe enough to try any of the shops back in the city, busy as they were even during this late hour. Following my intuition, I continued driving until the moment felt right.

We cruised by numerous rest stops along the highway, each beckoning as a potential refuge. However, as we approached them, a quick assessment revealed that they were either teeming with fellow travelers, their parking lots overflowing with vehicles, or they exuded a modernity which likely meant cameras or CCTV were in play. What we needed was some hole in the ground that wasn't part of a chain, and was likely to have only the one owner.

I almost missed the gas station when it first appeared. The neon sign that would have announced its presence was dark or more likely, broken. Only the lights inside notified me of its presence. I pulled off the highway.

Sam and Chase emerged from the bedroom as soon as the RV came to a stop. I could tell by their red-rimmed eyes that they hadn't slept much, if at all.

"We're stopping here quick."

Sam leaned down, casting her eyes over the joint. "Looks kind of neglected. Good choice."

I rummaged inside my pocket and took out what little remained. Handing it to Zeb, I said, "You're in charge of the money. I want to check over the motor home quickly before we leave again; can't afford any technical hitches."

"I have to use the restroom," Zeb mentioned quietly. The admission carried a tinge of frustration, acknowledging the need for assistance that irked him.

"I'm not entirely sure the one onboard is working," Sam replied.

"Let's try the one in the gas station and grab what we need while we're there," Gideon answered.

Between us, we got my dad outside, but it was tougher than it had been going in. This motorhome didn't have any concessions for disabled users, something we'd need to address in the future if we were going to use it for any length of time.

Gideon's gaze lingered on the restrooms situated on the exterior of the building, his eyes narrowing as he focused on a poorly written sign that hung precariously on one of the doors. The haphazard placement of the sign mirrored the overall state of neglect that seemed to permeate the surroundings. "Looks like the disabled restroom isn't working. We'll have to try the regular one."

Zeb's only response was a terse nod of his head.

The two of them headed inside.

37

CHASE

No sooner had I set foot in the gas station then a gruff voice barked over, sounding annoyed as heck.

"No dogs allowed."

I looked for a sign that would back up this outrageous claim. Sure enough, there was a faded red warning stuck to the door that I'd walked obliviously past. I'd gotten so used to our friendly stores around Montpelier, where the shopkeepers knew and loved Bandit, I'd totally forgotten to prepare for this outcome.

I looked down at his trusting face as the two of us contemplated our options. It wouldn't take me a few moments to grab the food we needed. Bandit could wait outside until I was done. Still, a wave of unease swept through me at the thought of leaving him outside. I hated being separated from him, no matter how short the time.

He seemed to sense my reluctance and chuffed at me, reassuring me that he would be just fine. His jaws parted into what I knew was a smile then he sat outside, just by the doors where I had a clear view of him. Feeling a little reassured by this, I went inside.

Heat blasted out of an ancient air con unit that sat above the door, making sweat gather at the base of my neck. While it wasn't quite the height of summer anymore, that kind of heat wasn't necessary and did nothing for the tense knot of anxiety I already felt.

Trying to ignore my discomfort, I tackled the shelves, scanning through each row, mentally calculating the energy each item would give versus the cost. I didn't need to think too hard since I had already done most of my calculations on the streets of Greenwich.

My eyes roamed over a bags of chips as I felt the corresponding pull in my stomach, but chips were one of the worst things I could spend our dwindling funds on. Yeah, they tasted amazing, but the salt would make us thirsty, while the empty carbs would be burned in no time.

Reluctantly I turned away from them. I passed refrigerated units with a rainbow of sodas on display, but all that processed sugar would only provide a passing boost of energy, followed by the inevitable crash.

What we needed was protein and lots of it.

Finding the ready to eat meat snacks, I grabbed as much as I figured we could afford, dumping them into a basket. I picked up a few more cans of dog food and a small bag of dog biscuits, a brand of which, ordinarily, Sully wouldn't have allowed. Apparently, there was more bad than good in them. Still, Bandit loved the stuff, and it was cheap, so into the basket it went.

I carried on shopping until I began to sag under the weight of the basket. I'd been mentally tallying up the total as I went along, so we shouldn't have hit our budget yet. When Zeb finally emerged from the restroom alone, he came to my side, eyes wide and impressed.

"You've been busy."

"I thought I would get enough supplies here so that we don't need to stop again; that way, there's less chance that someone will spot us."

"Good thinking."

Seeing my struggle to move with the weight of the basket, Zeb took it off my hands and set it onto his lap.

"Thanks."

"You looked like you needed help," he winked.

"Is Gideon going to join us at some point?" I asked, only a little bit peeved that he wasn't helping with the heavy lifting.

"Guess he needed extra time in the restroom," Zeb replied.

I was about to respond with something smart when a movement outside caught my eye. A couple around Sully's age were bee-lining their way toward Bandit.

Dressed in typical jeans and boots, they bore a striking resemblance to us. They looked like they were on a similar pit stop, but I *really* didn't like it when strangers went anywhere near my dog — especially if I wasn't right there with him.

Craning my neck, I scanned the area for our troops, but Sam and Sully must have been on the other side of the RV as I couldn't see them. Fingers of apprehension ran down my spine. Catching my unease, Zeb followed my gaze.

"I've got this," he said quietly. "Go."

My sneakers squeaked on the linoleum floor as I hurried outside. Hearing the couple's approach, Bandit stood to attention, strategically positioning himself by the doorway so if they tried anything, we would have the best chance of reaching him.

"Who's a good boy?" The woman cooed in a friendly voice. Bandit's tail stayed still as a rock, ears pricked forward, listening for any sign of danger. It took everything I had in me not to bolt to his side, knowing the attention that would draw. Closing the distance in a few quick steps, I placed my hand territorially on the back of Bandit's neck.

"Is this your dog?" The man asked. I studied them discreetly, taking in the matching wedding bands and friendly expressions, trying to see if there was that telltale bulge of a weapon tucked under their checked flannel shirts.

"Yes, why?" I tried to keep my voice natural. It was a normal question to ask after all.

"We had one just like him," the woman explained, her eyes misting up. "He was seven when we found out he had a heart defect. He died only weeks after he was diagnosed."

My heart gave an involuntary lurch, their shared pain resonating with me as if it were my own. However, I resisted the pull of empathy that threatened to overshadow my caution. This could be a ploy, a meticulously orchestrated distraction to manipulate my sympathies. I motioned for Bandit to remain close, just beyond their reach. He pressed against my side, senses on full alert.

"That's horrible. I'm sorry."

"Yeah, it's tough. Been six months now but still hurts like it was yesterday." The man said, smiling down at Bandit. "You mind if I pet him?"

I froze, unsure how to answer.

38

ZEB

The basket, laden with groceries, pressed firmly against Zeb's numb legs as he navigated the crowded aisles of the gas store.

Despite the lack of sensation in his limbs, he could still perceive the weight of it, pushing down on him. Hurrying to the checkout, Zeb hoisted the basket onto the counter, hoping the attendant would sense his urgency and get to the job quickly. It seemed his luck was in as the attendant efficiently scanned the items. The scanner beeped and the numbers on the display climbed higher, but Zeb turned away from the balance. His gaze fixated on the scene unfolding outside the store.

Chase was engaged in conversation with the couple, her hand resting on the back of Bandit's neck. Neither seemed in imminent danger, but the undertones in Chase's body language revealed a wealth of caution. Bandit too, displayed an unusual stillness. Zeb couldn't remember a time when his tail hadn't wagged. This was as abnormal a sight as the sun not rising, creating a knot of concern in his stomach.

His eyes darted across the aisles to the restroom, mentally urging Gideon to hurry. What could be keeping the boy so long? Though Sully and Sam were somewhere nearby, their invisibility added to Zeb's growing unease.

He felt a tightness in his chest and anxiety washed over him.

Struggling to catch snippets of the conversation, Zeb's mind raced with wild possibilities, conjuring vivid scenarios of potential threats or complications. Every passing moment seemed to stretch, each second laden with suspense as his gaze darted anxiously between Chase, Bandit, and the couple. The inability to hear what was being exchanged heightened Zeb's sense of vulnerability. Fear of the unknown took a firm hold, casting a shadow over his thoughts and leaving him even more on edge.

When the register finally showed the total, Zeb handed over the money that was gripped in his fist. The attendant accepted the payment with a hint of annoyance at Zeb's apparent distraction, but Zeb paid him no mind, his gaze focused outside.

"This isn't enough."

The attendant's voice jolted Zeb from his scrutiny. He glanced at the bagged items before quickly returning his attention to Chase and Bandit. "I don't have time to go through and fish things out."

"Do you have another form of payment?"

The cashier's question hung in the air, prompting Zeb to act swiftly. Without a second thought, he handed over his debit card, his eyes momentarily shifting towards Bandit, who had gravitated closer to Chase. It looked like the couple had asked a question she wasn't sure how to answer.

He saw Chase shake her head.

Anticipating trouble, Zeb had seen enough. Grabbing the provisions, he briskly made his way toward them. When the couple saw his arrival, they showed no outward sign of guilt or alarm. Instead, they only smiled, a palpable fog of sadness enveloping them like a shroud

"Sorry. You probably don't want strangers talking to your granddaughter, but we just wanted to pet your dog." The man explained, attempting to diffuse any concern. "We lost ours and haven't quite gotten over it yet."

"I told them about Fido's problem," Chase interjected quickly, filling him in with whatever story she had concocted for them. "How he can't stop himself from snapping at strangers on account of how he was abused before."

"We've been working on that for a while but haven't cured him of that bad habit yet," Zeb continued smoothly.

"I know we shouldn't bother every dog we see, but we can't seem to help ourselves," the man's wife finished, her tone apologetic. "I'm sorry, Fido. We'll leave you alone now. Enjoy your evening."

They smiled sincerely, expressing regret for the intrusion, and retreated into the store. Chase and Bandit visibly relaxed, their shoulders dropping with relief now that the tense encounter had passed without incident.

The cashier's irritated voice pierced the moment, calling out, "Hey, mister, you left your card."

Chase stopped in her tracks, the blood draining from her face as she looked at Zeb.

"You used your card?"

The words slipped out of her mouth like an icy whisper, sending a chill down Zeb's spine. He stared at her in shock, realizing the gravity of his oversight.

"We didn't have enough. I didn't even think about it."

Chase's eyes grew haunted, her fear transferring to Zeb. "Wait here."

She sprinted back into the store, reaching the checkout counter just in time to see the attendant holding Zeb's card. However, the attendant refused to hand it to her until Zeb confirmed she was his granddaughter.

Snatching the card from the cashier, Chase raced back to Zeb's side just as Gideon finally emerged from the restroom. Sensing their panic, his expression turned guarded. Chase didn't waste anytime explaining. Grabbing Gideon's arm, she practically dragged him out of the store, hissing, "We've got to go... now!"

Hearing her urgent command, Sully emerged from behind the RV, closely followed by Sam, both wearing startled expressions.

"Get in! There's no time to explain. We just have to go!"

Chase jumped into the RV with Bandit, gesturing for the rest of them to hurry. In a daze, Zeb allowed himself to be hoisted inside, all while the sickening knot in his stomach grew.

39

SULLY

I stalked a tense circuit within the cramped confines of the motorhome as Sam expertly navigated our escape route, her face etched with worry.

"I'm sorry, son. I don't know how I could have put us all in danger like this," my dad apologized for the third time, but his remorse offered little solace on our shaky ground. His hands were a wringing mess in his lap, his gaze fixed on the floor, his complexion as pale as a sheet.

"It was a mistake." Bandit, ever the comforter, attempted to console him.

"You all seem to make a lot of those," Emma commented, her usual lack of tact not harboring malice, only keen observation.

"It's not like we have a lot of experience with this," Gideon retorted, a defensive edge in his tone that only deepened Zeb's sense of guilt. Emma, her eyes wide like saucers, turned to me, expecting me to defend her viewpoint. But, I averted my gaze, unwilling to exacerbate my dad's distress any further.

"Never mind." Emma's response hung in the air as I continued to pace, my mind haunted by the impending arrival of those men. Would they sneak up on us in stealth helicopters like Forbes' men had, on that first ranch attack? Or would we see a fleet of those armored trucks? Picturing the artillery that had lined the shelves I caught myself assessing the frame of our motorhome, hating how much more fragile our vehicle seemed by comparison.

What chance would we stand if we were attacked?

"Let's not panic yet," Sam cut into my spiraling thoughts. "It's possible that they might not be waiting for us to use our cards, and even if they were, they would only know that we were there thirty minutes ago, not where we are now."

She was trying to keep us calm but her logic didn't hold, something even Emma noticed.

"But aren't these roads straight? Wouldn't it be obvious where we were going?"

And just like that, with her usual lack of a filter, the tension skyrocketed. Sam continued in a measured tone that belied her own concern.

"Not necessarily. We've already passed by one junction. We'll reach another in a few hours. There are still any number of ways we could have gone. We just need to keep going."

"But..." Emma started again, only for Sam to cut her off with a withering look.

"A wise person once said, there's no point worrying over things that haven't happened yet."

Emma studied her intently, trying to process what she had said.

"Who?"

"Who what?"

"Who was the wise person?"

Sam froze, momentarily caught out. "I can't remember. It was just someone."

"Then why would we listen to the words of a person we don't even know?"

"It's a saying, Emma. Haven't you heard one before?"

"None that I can remember."

And there was that uncanny ability to derail a conversation again. Sam wisely decided it would be better to drop the conversation before it went further downhill and focused on the road ahead. The air inside the motorhome felt heavy with dread. I tried not to stare at the sweat that beaded on my dad's forehead; he was taking his mistake, hard.

"Dad... It could have happened to any of us. We're tired, hungry, and scared. Don't beat yourself up about it. What's done is done. We need to stay upbeat, focus on what we can do, not what's already past."

He nodded, acknowledging the truth of my words even if he didn't exactly subscribe to the theory. Bandit padded to the bag of food we'd picked up at the gas station, nosing through the plastic bag until he surfaced with a bottle of water that he held gently between his teeth.

He set the bottle in Zeb's lap, nudging it with a dogged purpose. A glimmer of hope returned to my dad's eyes, and some of the despair he was feeling began to fade away.

"Thank you."

But as he reached for the bottle, it slipped through his fingers.

A cruel twist of fate sent it careening across the floor, just out of reach of his wheelchair. A hiss of frustration escaped in response to the relentless betrayal of his uncooperative body.

Gideon shot after the elusive bottle and handed it back to him though my dad's aggravation was palpable.

40

SULLY

The night flew past as I kept my eyes peeled for any sign of activity. Every speck in the sky that appeared to be moving, every vehicle that approached, the air would grow steadily heavier until it passed by without incident.

Eventually, we relaxed enough to share a small meal, though none of us had much appetite. We ate mechanically, forcing dry sandwiches down our throats. As I choked down the stale bread — one of the disadvantages of shopping at a quiet and out-there gas station, it seemed — a beloved memory flashed into my mind.

As the family gathered around the kitchen table, a breathtaking sunset painted the sky in hues of pink, orange, and gold, casting a warm and vibrant glow that streamed through the windows. The flickering candles on the table danced in harmony, creating an enchanting ambiance. The room was bathed in a soft, golden light that accentuated the elegant details of the embroidered tablecloth carefully chosen for this special occasion.

Sam and I, a team in orchestrating this surprise celebration, became silhouettes against the backdrop of the enchanting sunset. The air was infused with the tantalizing aromas of the dishes we presented to each family member. While the exact details of the menu had blurred with time, I distinctly remember the heart-warming sight of Bandit, chomping down with gusto on the grass-fed marrow bones I'd ordered from a local farm.

We'd been so happy then. So filled with the excitement that our announcement and upcoming wedding would bring.

It all seemed like a distant chapter from a lifetime ago.

We sat in silence until I caught Sam shooting a sidelong glance at me. Her lips had shifted to one side, a telltale sign that she wanted to talk, but was having a hard time figuring out how to start the conversation.

Having no energy for guessing games, I decided to bite the bullet.

"What's on your mind?"

A startled look came over her face. She laughed, though there wasn't any mirth in the sound. She seemed on the verge of denying any concerns but opted for honesty. She shook her head, a rueful smile now on her lips.

"You know me that well, huh?" She paused, pausing to choose her words carefully. "I was wondering if you've thought about what we're going to do when we get there?"

"I've thought of nothing else, actually. I've run every possible scenario I can think of through my mind, but I've come up with zilch. I'm counting on Elora being able to assist us. At the very least, she has access to resources that can provide us with some answers."

"You mean, how Emma could possibly be back?"

My eyes slid to her still figure where she napped on the sofa, her hands tucked under her head like a pillow.

"Yeah."

"Chase's theories were actually pretty sound last night, though I'm no closer to forming an opinion either way." Sam's gaze followed mine to dwell on Emma.

"I don't know what she is. I just know that I'm responsible for her."

"Because she's your first wife?" There was a tone in her voice. Not exactly harsh, but something lingered. I knew I was treading on thin ice.

"No. It's almost like she doesn't think like an adult. Even Bandit knows better than her. She's more like a child who needs to be taken care of."

"I've never seen any kid who behaves like her."

Sam's attempt at lightness fell flat. There were too many unknowns to laugh about. It was all too fresh and raw.

"You don't have to worry. If that's what's on your mind."

Sam flashed me a small smile, but remained silent. Didn't speak again for a while, in fact. I could tell from her body language that she wanted to drop the conversation and I was more than happy to oblige.

By my estimate, we were about four hours away from the gas station when fatigue crept in. I felt myself sinking into exhaustion when Sam's voice jolted me.

"What is that?"

She stared ahead at a black object in the distance, sitting at the road's edge. As we approached, I noticed it wasn't moving.

I sat up straighter in my seat, my tiredness dissipating immediately.

"Should we carry on?" Sam asked quietly, not wanting to alert the others unless necessary.

"Let's get a little closer until we can actually see what it is. We're still a ways away; if it's a problem, there's still time to turn around."

She kept going at the same pace, her tensed shoulders the only visible sign of her concern. The black object grew larger on our approach until we finally identified it as a sedan with its hood propped open. Spotting us, a lone driver got up from the ground where he had been sitting, signaling for our attention.

"Who is that?" came Chase's voice over my shoulder.

She must have woken in the last few moments. She was such a light sleeper that the slightest sound would wake her, something which had probably kept her alive when she had been homeless.

She rubbed at her sleep-filled eyes as movement stirred in the back, indicating the others were waking. Bandit padded up beside me, his nails clicking on the cheap vinyl floor.

"Just someone whose car's broken down."

"Tough to have that happen in the middle of nowhere," Gideon commented by Zeb's side. He had been half dozing with his head on the dining table. A tuft of his blond hair stuck up like a baby mohawk.

I looked around. Nothing but dry, black land stretched as far as I could see. No lights behind or in front of us. No vehicles would be coming down this highway for a while. It wasn't this guy's day.

"We could stop, let Gideon have a look at his car?" Zeb volunteered.

"I don't think that's a good idea," Gideon disagreed. "Let's just carry on."

"But what if he just woke up with no memory, too? What if he's like me?" Emma asked in a plaintive voice. That she even thought it could be an option tugged at my heart.

"He's not like you," Chase was certain. "His car broke down is all. He can wait until the next person comes along."

"But that could be hours, days even." Emma looked aghast. I wasn't sure why the idea of this guy being stranded affected her so strongly.

"We don't have to stay long. Gideon can just pop out to see if there's anything he can do to fix it." Having lived in a small town for the last decade or so, my dad had grown used to being a helpful neighbor. The idea of lending a helping hand was second nature to him, a reflection of the close-knit community values ingrained during his time in Montpelier.

"We need to come to a decision quickly. We're almost on him," Sam interjected. She had slowed the RV right down so we could get a look at the stranded driver.

He was around my age and height, though it was clear that even under the denim jacket and black jeans he wore, his body was athletic: there couldn't have been an inch of fat on him. He smiled at us, white teeth glinting in the headlights, relieved by our appearance. We were almost with him when the RV continued rolling past.

"What are you doing? Stop! He needs our help!" Emma said, looking out the window, one hand pressed against the glass. But, behind the wheel, Sam's face was clouded with indecision.

"I don't know. Something is off..." Sam stared back at him, uncertain how to proceed. Suddenly, she did a double-take and cursed loudly.

"He's not a stranded driver. He's a scout! Hold on to something!"

In an instant, Sam slammed on the gas, causing the wheels to shriek as the motorhome lurched. Chase stumbled beside me and would have fallen if I hadn't grabbed her arm. The vehicle jolted backward as I got a brief look at the driver's face.

My stomach plummeted when I saw that he wasn't shocked so much as he was irritated.

Seeing the hurtling vehicle coming for him, he darted to one side, but Sam clipped the edge of his car, sending it fishtailing his way. He dove out of danger with an effortless agility that I knew no regular person would have been able to execute.

I went ice cold.

"Sam's right. We need to stop him before he signals someone!"

Like he had read my mind, he reached into his jacket, revealing not a phone but a gun — a gun that he aimed dead at us. As if in fast-forward, he jogged backwards like some superhero straight from an action movie.

"Duck!" I yelled, forcing Chase's head down and pulling on Sam's arm so hard that I almost dragged her out of her seat. Her foot slipped off the gas pedal and the motorhome came to a sudden halt.

Bullets pierced the night air. The metallic tang of fear gripped my throat, and my pulse quickened with each gunshot that echoed in the dark. The very air I breathed became charged with tension as I braced for impact, but the shots veered off target as the stranger struggled to aim while on the move.

"Give me your gun!" Gideon yelled at Sam. Stuck behind the wheel, and aware that Gideon had the best marksmanship among us, Sam slid it across the floor to him.

Gideon seized the gun, taking cover behind a window as the man continued firing shots in our direction.

"He's almost out," Gideon called to us.

Three more shots blasted into the night before an eerie silence descended. Without missing a beat, fueled by a potent mix of adrenaline and determination, Gideon sprang into action. He ran for the door, flinging it open with purpose as he bolted outside.

"Gideon, wait!" I called after him.

But he was already gone.

41

CHASE

I lay sprawled on the floor, Sully's hand still pressing against my head, when his cry shattered the air, snapping me out of my panic-induced stupor. Wrenching my head from under his grasp, I turned to see the door wide open.

A lead weight dropped in the pit of my stomach. Gideon had bolted outside in pursuit of the man.

Panic surged within me, my heart pounding violently. Rising unsteadily, I staggered toward the door just as Sully shot through it. Sam, still struggling with her seatbelt, fumbled with it until the restraint finally gave way.

I think her fingers were as numb as I was. She cursed loudly.

"Stay here," she commanded, as she too ran outside.

Bandit whined somewhere behind me, but I didn't turn to look at him, too scared of what might be happening outside. What might be happening to Gideon. Even though Sam had given strict orders, I knew I couldn't obey them.

I stepped out of the RV and into the open space.

The man with the gun was attempting to run away, but Gideon was hot on his heels. He had been right. The guy must have been out of bullets, as he wasn't firing at us anymore. Gideon could have shot at him, but, despite the truck full of ammo we had stolen, none had fitted Sam's gun, which meant we had precious little bullets ourselves.

Instead of wasting them, Gideon tore after him, Sully and Sam close behind.

The man limped as he ran, obviously in pain: Sam must have caught him with the RV when she rammed into his car. It was this limp that Gideon used to his advantage. As his eyes narrowed with purpose, he closed in with a calculated swiftness. With a yell that I could hear from here, he took a flying leap at the guy and tackled him to the ground.

They both fell with such a heavy thud that I thought for sure, bones would be broken. Gideon's eyes were like black pits, fixed grimly on the man beneath him. As the man started to buck him off, Gideon pressed Sam's gun firmly against his head.

The man stopped struggling.

Gideon waited until Sully and Sam arrived, winded and out of breath. The two of them restrained him before Gideon would climb off him. In a slick move that spoke of her years on the job, Sam handcuffed his arms behind him and shoved him toward the RV.

"Move."

As Sully, Gideon, and Sam returned to my side, relief washed over me. The relentless rush of blood that had pounded in my ears began to subside, and my heart, which had been racing like a runaway train, gradually slowed to a more manageable pace.

However, this was all shattered by Bandit's high-pitched whine, a sound that seemed to cut through the air like a knife and raised the hairs on the back of my neck.

It finally registered that he had been doing that the entire time we had all run outside. I had thought he was just as worried as the rest of us, but now that the immediate danger had passed, I sensed something else in his voice.

A desperate tone that I couldn't mistake.

Something was wrong.

Like really, *really* wrong.

And this wasn't about the guy who had just fired at us.

I ran back into the RV to find Emma hunched over Zeb, her left arm raised above her head while the other pressed against his stomach. Seeing my arrival Bandit — lying beside Zeb — suddenly howled.

I skidded to a stop as Emma's panicked eyes flashed up at me.

"It's not working! Why isn't it working?" She babbled. "Why can't I stop the bleeding?!"

And with that, the whole world fell apart.

42

SULLY

Blood glistened on my hands.

Warm and sticky, pooling from *a hole in his body*. Throughout my time at the clinic, I'd seen my fair share of blood, but it had always belonged to a patient.

Never had it belonged to a loved one.

"Oh, God."

Sam drew in a shocked breath behind me. Her feet, rooted to the spot. She and Gideon had escorted the man into the RV, but I had no idea what they had done with him — and I didn't care. My attention was focused solely on my dad.

On his blood that seeped out, soaking my hands that pressed desperately against his open wound.

Emma, sat back on her heels, and relented only after Chase emphatically explained that lowering her left arm wouldn't offer any assistance. It was a minute before either of us realized that she had taken Sam's instruction from the day before quite literally.

Stick your left hand above your head and put pressure on the wound.

Those had been Sam's exact words when she had found Emma cowering in the corner of the barn and had tended to Emma's own bleeding arm. And now, Emma was applying that same logic to my dad.

What a bittersweet moment for her to have finally discovered her humanity.

My dad's forehead was clammy with sweat. Deep lines furrowed across his brow, but it was the pain reflected in his eyes that was difficult to bear.

Tendrils of terror gripped me, accentuated by the realization that I had never dealt with the intricacies of the human anatomy before. Regardless, a gunshot wound was a gunshot wound. And this needed immediate, lifesaving, first aid.

Frantically, I ran over what should be done in my head, but instead of the clear points of action I needed, my thoughts were a jumble of manic noise, racing from one unrelated thing to another. I couldn't get my act together...

And my father was dying because of it.

A familiar, taunting voice slithered into the recesses of my mind — a sinister echo I believed I'd locked away for good. The voice, a relentless phantom from the past, resurfaced with cruel precision, each word a venomous reminder of years spent branding me as a disappointment. It tried to undermine my resolve, replaying a litany of past failures, each crescendo culminating in the haunting refrain that if I'd only become the surgeon they had always wanted, I'd have some idea what to do now. At the very least, I could ease some of his pain.

Dad looked at me, the fog in his eyes clearing for a moment as he reached for my hand. But then he froze, flinching, as pain lanced his side. I caught his hand in my own.

"It's not... your fault..." He wheezed at me.

Darkness filled his mouth, and I recoiled at the sight of red staining his teeth — more blood. A ribbon of it trickled out of the corner of his mouth. I brushed my thumb over it, needing to wipe the sight of it away, to erase it from all existence, but all I managed was to smear it over his pale cheek.

"I know what... you're thinking. I don't blame you." He stopped, gulping in air. Talking was too much of a strain for him. I had to get him to stop.

"Save your energy, Dad. We're getting you help." I felt a hand squeeze my shoulder and knew it was Sam. Her voice sounded in my ear, soft yet supportive.

"I'll take over here." She covered my hand with her own, gently prying away my cold fingers. When my hand was free, she held onto Zeb for moral support while keeping her other hand pressed tightly against his wound.

Staggering into the living area, I found Chase and Gideon waiting with Bandit and Emma. Gideon still had Sam's gun pointed at the shooter. The two had secured him to the table that was fastened to the floor of the motorhome. Grimly, the thought flashed across my mind that he wouldn't be getting out any time soon — if, at all — if I had any say on the matter.

As I materialized, Gideon charged towards me, eyes wide with a primal fear that appeared to have sheared years off his life.

"He needs medical help."

"I know. But we'd be walking into the lion's den. We'd never be able to avoid being seen."

Gideon turned to me, fury flaring in his eyes. "But they're the only ones who can save him!"

"The second we step foot in a hospital, his men will have us. We can't risk that." I glanced at our hunter to see if my assumption was true. His silence gave me the confirmation I was searching for.

"Not even for your own father?" Gideon's eyes flashed with accusation.

Emma stood up suddenly, rushing to my side. "I agree with Sully. There's no point in us all dying."

Her voice, earnest and well-intentioned, sought to appeal to their common sense. She believed she was helping, but her words only managed to draw a sharp gasp from Chase and fueled Gideon's rage another notch.

"I'm only saying what you already know. Why are you all looking at me like that? Why do you act like I'm a monster?" Her blue eyes usually so clear, suddenly brimmed over with tears. "I was trying to help! I did what she said I should do!"

I could never bear Emma's tears. She never had any real reason to cry, except during those heavy moments when there was nothing more to be done for an animal, and even then, there was an understanding, an awareness, beneath those eyes. But not this Emma. Despite being the spitting image of my wife, she had none of the personality. This Emma lacked comprehension of the world around her.

Ordinarily, I would have comforted her, as I would anyone who was in distress. But time was a luxury we couldn't afford. I had to decide whether it was worth the risk of going to a hospital.

And I knew I couldn't.

As much as I had come to love my father, the risk to all our lives was too great. And I knew he wouldn't want me to jeopardize the family for his sake.

"The only thing we can do is hurry to Elora. She'll be able to help him, and no one will have to find out."

Gideon's frown deepened, conveying his mounting desperation.

"You're really going to make him wait? Can't you see how much pain he's in? How do you even know he'll survive the journey?"

"I'm well aware of the dangers, but this is the best we can do. This is hard for us all, Gid, not just you. Please remember that."

I hurried to the driver's seat.

Moments later, we sped away as I prayed to the heavens that I wasn't making a catastrophic mistake.

43

CHASE

Sam and Sully traded shifts behind the wheel, their determined eyes reflecting the gravity of our situation. Two of us were always stationed at Zeb's side, as we tried to keep him calm and distracted. Trying to keep him alive.

Gideon and I hovered over him, making him as comfortable as possible, though it seemed not only a losing battle but a ridiculous one. No matter how soft a mattress was, or however much we could elevate his head, it wasn't going to do anything about that gaping hole in his stomach.

Or the unrelenting torrent of blood that continued to seep through our makeshift bandages, no matter how frequently we added another layer to them.

Just as I'd think it could be clotting (which would be a good sign), more of that crimson would blossom through. With a heavy heart, I turned away, unable to take another moment of the agony that was etched all over his face.

Bandit stood off to the side, panting with distress. Now and then, a warning growl would sound from his throat and I'd find him facing off against the man who had shot Zeb with a fierce protectiveness that mirrored our rage and desperation.

I glared at him, hoping he could feel every inch of my hate. Sam's gun sat a few inches from my hand, far enough away from him that he wouldn't be able to snatch it up, even if he wasn't bound to the table. My fingers itched to grab it. The cold metal of the barrel seemed to mock me, daring me to try and make a move.

It took every inch of willpower not to pump a bullet straight into his head.

In the thick of the silent standoff, Sully broke through the tension with a shout that cut through the air like a knife. "Did you call anyone?"

The man, however, met Sully's question with a chilling indifference, as if he had only enquired about the time.

"I said, did you call anyone?!"

When the man didn't answer for the second time, Gideon's face contorted into a fierce snarl, his hand moving faster than I could comprehend. In a swift motion, he grabbed the gun and swung it with brutal force at the man's face that he would have been knocked down if it wasn't for his restrained hands holding him upright.

The man spat onto the floor, a glob of blood mixed with saliva, testing his jaw gingerly to see if it was broken. Despite the violence, there was no anger in his tone when he spoke.

"He's going to die if you don't get him to a hospital," he stated matter-of-factly, shooting a pointed look at Zeb.

"Shut up! The last thing we need is your advice," Gideon erupted, his hand moving toward him again with the gun. But I intervened, catching his arm before he could land another punch.

"He's more useful to us alive."

The minute the words had come out of my mouth, I knew they were true. "He's the only link we have to them. If we kill him, we'll have nothing."

Gideon's tortured eyes met mine. That familiar green of his irises now glistening over with tears. Zeb's moans of pain cut through the moment. Gideon immediately rushed back to his side, leaving the gun by me.

"If you release me, I can get him the help he needs," the shooter offered calmly, as if it was he who held all the cards.

But before Sully could even answer, Sam spoke up, her voice loaded with cold determination. "We don't negotiate with killers."

"Then I hope you have a nice plot ready for him."

Sam marched towards him like a predator, her steps heavy with intent as she closed in until she was mere inches from him. Quick as a flash, her foot lashed out with a powerful kick to his stomach that sent him doubling over in pain. Snatching up a fistful of his hair, she jerked his head back and held it there in a vice-like grip until his pain-glazed eyes met hers.

"Chase is right. We need you alive. But that doesn't mean we can't make your every surviving minute a misery." She leaned in closer, her breath hot against his face. "You say anything else about Zeb — and I mean, anything — and you will live to regret it. Do you get my drift?"

He nodded, wariness flickering over his features before he schooled his expression into one of neutrality. She released him abruptly, like she

couldn't bear to keep touching him. I had never seen Sam like that before —
sparks had literally flown from her eyes.

Still giving him the evil eye, she searched him thoroughly for weapons or
trackers, finding nothing except for his wallet. She rifled through its
contents, spreading them out on the table for us all to see — a handful of
debit and credit cards under the name John Smith, two hundred dollars in
cash, a loyalty card to Subway and a photograph of him with his arms
wrapped around a picture-perfect wife and three young children.

"John Smith?" She sounded every bit as skeptical as I felt.

"Like anyone believes that." I blurted out.

He shrugged nonchalantly, as if to say, 'suit yourself.'

I couldn't believe it. This cold-hearted killer, with his startlingly plain
face and disarming smile, had a family. Three children with hazel eyes and
glossy chestnut hair, looking every bit the perfect American family in the
photograph he showed us. My mind couldn't reconcile the image of this
man with his innocent-looking kids and the brutal murders he was responsible for.

"Are those really your family?" I asked incredulously.

"Yes."

I hadn't expected the truth. I had expected lies, fabrications, anything
other than that straight forward answer unless this was all an elaborate plan
to unnerve us. Maybe he was trying to get under my skin, disarm me so that
I'd reveal some secret he wanted.

Well, I wasn't that dumb.

"You're telling me these are your kids? That you go around killing
people but you keep a picture of your family in your wallet?"

His eyes held mine in a level gaze. There was no animosity there that I
could see. None of that desperate madness that had been in Forbes or the
fervent narcissism that had driven Xavier. In this man's eyes, all I saw was
him.

"Correct."

"Why would you risk having a picture of them on you?"

"We never get caught, so it isn't usually a concern of ours," he said,
almost casually, as if murder was just another part of his everyday life. He
shifted positions, settling himself more comfortably while Bandit bared his
wickedly sharp teeth, warning him not to try anything. Smith gave him a
leery look.

"I'm just changing positions, that's all."

Bandit's responding "woof" was a guttural growl full of ferocity and
primal instinct. No hint of my Muttface remained. In his place, this dog was
ready to attack the man who had caused us so much pain.

"You don't look like a sadistic killer." And I meant it. He seemed more like one of my high school teachers than a ruthless murderer.

"That's because I'm not," he replied evenly, not a hint of irony in his voice. "I know what you think, but you're wrong. I don't get any enjoyment out of this, but it is my job. I am a cleaner. I clean whatever needs to be cleaned. The orders come from above and I carry them out. I do it for my country."

His words were rolling into one. I had no idea what he was talking about. What orders? Who were his bosses?

"Your country?" Sully said from the driver's seat. His eyes locked with Smith's, turning bright with shock. "You work for the government?"

Smith's silence confirmed our worst fears.

"That's insane. What branch of the government would allow the murder of innocent people, of kids?!"

"The kind that works to keep the country safe."

"But that doesn't make any sense? We're not a danger to anyone. You're the ones trying to kill us," I cried.

Bandit barked yes, typing into his iPad. *"You are one of the bad men."*

Considering that Smith hadn't witnessed Bandit speaking before, his reaction wasn't what I expected. Usually people were filled with awe and delight, but Smith just looked spooked, making me wonder what kind of terrible lies his bosses had filled his head with.

"I wasn't actually trying to kill you at first. If you recall, my men and I turned up at your ranch when you started firing at us. It was self defense."

I snorted, not caring how unladylike I sounded. "Yeah, with snipers! You shot at us with snipers!"

"They were equipped with tranqs. They wouldn't have killed you. Our orders weren't to kill you all."

There was something in his voice, something he wasn't quite telling us. I ran through his words in my head, remembering his reaction to Bandit.

"All?"

His eyes slid over to Bandit...then Emma. "Our orders are only for the dog and the woman. The rest of you can still live. I can wipe your memory so you won't remember any of this. You won't even remember the dog. You'll be able to go on with your lives as if none of this ever happened. It's your choice."

I backed away from him, horrified by his suggestion. Forget my Muttface? Over my dead body!

"Why are you talking like you have any option here? You're in no position to make demands." Sully challenged.

Smith licked his lips, his eyes growing dark with intensity. "Because I know how this ends. If you get rid of me, I will only be replaced by another. I don't think you realize quite how far this goes. You cannot win."

Each word struck like a hammer, driving home the chilling truth of his words.

"Is that why you're telling us this, because you know you can wipe our minds after?"

Smith nodded. "You know I'm telling the truth. Just think about your friend, Mr. Wall Street." He addressed Sully. "We did it with him. Now he's free to live his life, none the wiser."

"After you brutalized him," Sully snapped, not giving an inch.

"That's incorrect. He was only hurt as he came at us and suffered a few blows in the process. If we had managed to take him the way we had planned, he wouldn't have been hurt at all."

"Then explain Florence because she sure as hell didn't die of natural causes."

A flicker of remorse passed over Smith's bland expression, startling me.

"That was an unfortunate consequence. Her heart couldn't handle the shock. There was nothing we could do for her. I am sorry about that. Killing her was never our intention."

"But why are you targeting Bandit? What has he done to you?"

"It's not what he has done, but what he represents. What they both represent." At the word "they" his gaze shifted to Emma.

"We don't have anything in common," she cried. "He's an animal and I've already proven to them that I'm human. Why would anyone want me dead? This doesn't make any sense."

"No it doesn't," Sully agreed.

Smith looked at Emma, his stare piercing through her with an unreadable intensity.

"I don't get paid to ask questions. But like the dog, she is a freak of nature. She's a threat and must be eliminated."

44

SULLY

Thirty minutes later, Sam switched with me so I could spend more time with Dad.

His face was unearthly pale, his skin stretched tightly against the bones like a paper-thin veil potentially moments away from being ripped apart. His eyes were mere slits, barely opening to acknowledge my presence. He tried to form a smile on his lips, but it quickly dissipated.

I was shocked by how he had deteriorated in such a short space of time.

I had wanted to tell him what we had learned from Smith, but none of that seemed to matter now. Hearing my approach, his eyes fluttered open weakly. His mouth twitched as he tried, but failed to make a smile.

"We're a few hours away from Arizona, but you can make it," I said in desperation while grabbing onto his hands as if they were my last hope. My old man looked at me, a clear understanding in his eyes.

"We both know that's not true."

"Maybe I can drop you off in a hospital. We'll drive near to one. I'll take you inside—"

He cut me off with a weak shake of his head.

"Son... that won't work. Besides, you can't risk... your lives for me. I won't allow it. I've been a burden... to you. Emma was right about that."

The way he said her name was a dagger stabbing straight through my heart. It took a moment before I had the clarity of why that was.

"I wish you'd met my Emma. The real one. You would have loved her."

Zeb's chest heaved with each breath, feeling like it was slowly cracking as sorrow bled from every pore. He bowed his head, unable to bear the intense pain that gripped him.

"It is my biggest regret... that I didn't go... to your wedding. I'm sorry... I was a fool... and will carry... that... to my grave."

The gaps between his words were growing longer as he fought to catch his breath.

"Save your strength. You don't need to talk like this." And I meant it. Those years spent resenting his treatment of me melted away into nothingness. All of our arguments seemed insignificant now. Nothing really mattered other than staying alive.

His breath came again, a thin, raspy sound that whistled between clenched teeth. His fingers squeezed mine with an iron grip, giving me a false sense of hope that he'd pull through. But then, as swiftly as the glimmer of optimism had surfaced, his fingers relinquished their grip, and I heard the deafening silence. Time itself felt suspended, as if the universe paused to bear witness to the silence.

No breathing. No more raspy whistles.

Only the hollow echo of the road rolling beneath us.

"Dad?"

I whispered his name, terror flooding my body, constricting my throat so that I could barely make a sound. Praying for his wheezing breath to come again, my eyes scanned over his face, desperately searching for any sign of life.

But there was none.

His chest was as still as stone.

"DAD!"

I screamed his name. Grabbing his shoulders, I shook him violently, forgetting everything else around me. Forgetting that it would cause him immense pain. All I knew was that I needed him to move.

I needed him alive.

Only silence greeted me, and that rumble of the tarmac beneath the wheels of the motorhome. A heavy shroud of grief draped over my shoulders, and the weight of loss pressed down on me with a physical force.

"DAD!"

My voice wailed his name as the enormity of his death hit me like a freight train. My fingers turned numb and icy cold from the horror as the world fractured apart in an instant.

An unbearable void opened up where I should have been and I felt myself slowly dissolving away into nothingness.

I couldn't think, couldn't feel.

Could not speak.

Someone thundered into the room. Gideon. Beyond my stupor I caught his stricken face taking in the scene before me. He said something to me, but I couldn't hear it over the wrathful cacophony that had taken up residence in my head. A relentless buzzing ringing in my ears until it blotted out all other noise. I couldn't be in here anymore.

I had to get out of this room.

Shuffling to the living area, I stumbled past Chase and Bandit, both looking at me in utter horror as they darted past me to the bedroom. The buzz was getting louder now, drowning out everything but the one thought.

Moonlight glinted off the cold metal object on the table and drew me in like a magnet. With robotic precision, I snatched it up and pressed the gun against Smith's temple. The noise in my head grew to a crescendo, but it couldn't mask the simple fact.

He was the reason for all of this.

He was the reason my father was lying dead not ten feet from me. The ache of grief, the weight of loss, and the flames of anger coalesced into a singular purpose — avenge my father's death. Emma sprang up fearfully, hands trembling as she stepped back towards Sam.

"Sully? What are you doing?"

I heard her question, though she might as well have been speaking Chinese for all the sense it made. She tried again.

"I don't think you should be doing that."

The floor shifted beneath my feet. I felt the RV lurch to one side and the smoothness of the road vanished, replaced by the roughness of an unpaved surface as we took an abrupt detour. My finger wrapped around the trigger. The biting cold sent shivers down my spine, cutting into the fog that had wrapped itself around my head.

Everything stopped until I heard footsteps approaching. Through my daze, I caught a glimpse of blonde curls and that familiar face I loved.

"Honey... you don't want to do that. Listen to my voice, babe. Hand me the gun."

She spoke in a reassuring voice. Her calmness had an immediate effect on me, though I still wasn't able to do as she asked. I wanted him to suffer, just like Dad had, and if he died, there would be one less person coming after us.

"Sully. Please. Don't do that. You're in shock, but this isn't what you should do; we need him alive in order to have any chance of surviving them. But if you kill him, we'll be left with nothing. We need you with us, Sully. We need you so that we can fight them. I know you're hurting, baby. I know you're sad and filled with rage, but if you kill him, you'll only make things worse. You have to trust me. Please. Hand me the gun."

Smith stared up at me without any fear, only a deep resignation, as though he had always expected death to come to him like this. How could he stay so calm knowing that his life was so close to ending? His wife and children's faces flashed before me, cutting through all the noise and making me pause. A bead of sweat formed on my brow, dripping down my face, though I felt anything but warm. Sam moved closer to me, her hand outstretched, waiting for me to do as she asked.

"Baby?" She asked softly, her voice heavy with the weight of the world.

Slowly, I moved the gun away from Smith's head, unhooked my finger from the trigger, and gave her the gun. Sam took it carefully, tucking it into the back of her jeans. Then she wrapped her arms around me, squeezing me as hard as she could. Suddenly, I broke down into sobs as tears flooded from my eyes.

No one said a word.

The kids were crying in the bedroom. Bandit howled his sorrow into the night. I felt Sam's tears mingle with my own.

Only Emma stood still and silent, seemingly unmoved by our growing anguish.

I held onto Sam like she was my lifeline.

45

SULLY

I couldn't say how long we stayed like that, how long I clung to my wife as if she were the only thing anchoring me to reality.

She sat me down — sat us all down — and went to cover Dad's body with his blanket. Bandit squeezed himself between Chase and Gideon, a paw on each of their knees, consoling them the best way he knew how.

Sam made us take sips from a bottle of water, before quietly returning to the driver's seat, and setting off again. Our shock would take a while to fade, she explained, but we weren't safe out here on the highway. We had to get to Elora — and we were close, within a few hours of reaching her.

So the RV continued as if our world hadn't just shattered into pieces. The air was heavy with grief and our usual camaraderie replaced by an uneasy silence, broken only by a stifled sob as each of us grappled with our own emotions.

While Sam had cared for us, Emma had watched her intensely like a child might study an adult. Her blue eyes opened wide, taking in every one of her actions. With Sam back in the driver's seat, Emma approached me hesitantly with the bag of food we had picked up from the gas station.

"Do you want something to eat?"

I shook my head stiffly, the simple act of it sending me into a tailspin. The very thought of food caused my stomach to lurch, and it was all I could do not to throw up. She looked at the kids, offering the bag, but they turned her away too. She focused her attention back on me.

"I can get you another drink?" She asked hopefully, like that would solve all my problems. Frankly, I wanted her to leave me the hell alone, but apparently, she wasn't getting the memo. My throat felt constricted, words caught in a tangle of emotion. I wanted to scream, to release the pent-up frustration that threatened to consume me. Instead, I forced myself to meet her eyes. I shook my head again, unable to get my mouth to formulate any words.

Her fingers were tightly intertwined, and a furrow appeared on her brow. She looked lost and unsure of what to do. Eventually, unable to elicit a response from any of us, she turned to Smith.

"Would you like a drink, then?"

Chase gasped with horror, and Gideon's eye's turned flat with hate. At Smith's grateful nod, Emma carefully — so carefully — raised the bottle of water to his lips. In a sudden outburst, Gideon lunged across the short distance and slapped the bottle out of her hands, sending it flying across the room where it bounced against the window and burst, raining water over the dirt-encrusted glass.

"What do you think you're doing?!" He screamed, an unhinged man.

Emma stared at him in shock. "I was just trying to help..."

Gideon glared at her with all the fury in the world. "He is the reason that Zeb is lying dead in that room, but you're going to *reward* him?"

Confusion clouded Emma's face as she stammered out, "No... that's not what I was doing." She was completely thrown by his anger.

"Then why, after everything they've done, would you even consider helping him?"

Emma blinked at him, startled, and turned to me, as if I would defend her. "That's what *she* did. I was just trying to be like her because you all seemed to appreciate it."

Sam glanced at us from the driver's seat. Though she kept her opinions to herself, her mouth was a thin and terse line.

"Sam was trying to comfort us..." Gideon stopped, choking on his words. I knew immediately he was picturing my father with that gaping wound in his stomach. The details of his death replayed in vivid, excruciating detail. Over and over. Haunting our very breath.

Swallowing, he tried again. "She wasn't helping the man who wants to destroy our family. She's not helping the man trying to kill us."

"I... didn't know..." Emma stuttered, her voice trailing off.

"What? You don't know the difference?" Gideon spat out the question. "I mean, how could you not? Only a monster would be this clueless. The hell is wrong with you?!"

"Nothing! There's nothing wrong with me!" Emma snapped in response, suddenly angered. Throwing the bag of food onto the floor, she stormed off to the only place she could get away from them — the bedroom.

Tossing them a hateful look, she slammed the door, causing the entire RV to shake.

46

CHASE

The RV reverberated with the sound of the slamming the door. My chest was so tight I struggled to breathe. So much was happening, but I wasn't prepared for any of it. How could you ever steel yourself for something like this?

Silence hung heavily in the room, thick with unspoken sorrow and the aftermath of a confrontation that had left us all feeling raw. Gideon stewed beside me, his anger a palpable force, a shield against the overwhelming pain that threatened to crush all of our hearts. He kept tossing looks toward the bedroom door, glaring at it as if that was the source of his grief. If his rage could manifest as a physical energy, that door would have burst into flames.

Smith spoke up suddenly, his voice cutting through the thick tension that had settled like a storm cloud. His voice sounded insultingly normal.

As if the world hadn't just ended.

"She was only trying to help."

A strangled sound came out of Gideon as he leaped toward him. Sully jumped up too, his eyes relaying a deep concern that Gideon would pummel Smith to death. Part of me secretly wished he would kill him, yet deep down, I knew it would only satisfy his temporarily unchecked fury. Eventually, he would come to his senses and the weight of what he had done would consume him, leaving no trace of the Gideon we all loved behind. He must have realized this too, as instead of completely destroying him, Gideon tore a strip from his shirt and tied it around Smith's mouth so we wouldn't have to listen to him.

I wasn't sure why none of us had considered that option before. It seemed so obvious now, after the fact. Knowing that we had a brief time out from either Smith or Emma speaking for a while, a little of the tension lifted. It wasn't much of a relief, but at least I could finally breathe again.

I gulped in large mouthfuls of air, filling my lungs until my heart stopped racing and I started to feel a little more like myself — as much as I could under the circumstances , anyway.

Sully held his head in his heads, overcome not only with grief but the heavy burden of guilt. It was ultimately his decision, his choice, not to go the hospital. I emphasized with him and understood his reasoning. I probably would have done the same thing in his place, but it didn't make the truth any easier to bear.

We sat in silence, each of us wrapped up in our misery until Gideon started pacing the length of the room. At the end of each circuit, he would glare back in the direction of the bedroom. My eyes followed his every stomping stride until the muscles in the back of my neck began to spasm.

I finally mustered up the courage to ask, "What is it? What're you thinking?"

Gideon's green eyes flicked onto me. Those golden flecks seemed to glow with feeling.

"Emma."

"I know. She's difficult to understand sometimes."

"You mean all the time. Everything she says or does is wrong. She drives me crazy. I wish she'd shut up and disappear. We were fine until she came into our lives. We were happy. She's made everything so much worse."

His words made me flinch.

I knew he was right: Emma was incredibly frustrating and annoying. But she was also new to everything. She was scared and confused and trying to make sense of a world she didn't fit into. Each time I found myself getting angry at her, I would have to consciously remind myself that she wasn't being malicious; she just didn't know any better.

I looked at Sully, but the only outward sign that he had heard Gideon was a tightening of his shoulders. His eyes stayed glued to the floor, where I was unable to read them.

"She's not doing it on purpose. As annoying as she can be, she doesn't mean to upset us."

He didn't answer me. Troubled, he stared at the closed door again as if he was hoping to be able to see inside.

"Better or worse, it is her, right?" Gideon directed the question at Sully. He finally raised his head.

"That's Emma, isn't it?" Gideon pushed.

Sully didn't immediately respond. "I don't know. I guess."

"Well, if they brought her back from the dead, can't they do the same for Zeb?"

Sully's mouth fell open. I felt the ground shift beneath my feet and had to brace myself with my hands, even though I was still sitting on the sofa.

"You can't mean that?" I gasped, shock sending me immobile. The very idea of manipulating life and death, even in the face of grief, was a shocking violation of the laws of nature.

"Why not?" He snapped, daggers flashing from his eyes. "They brought her back, so they can him too!"

"Son..." Sully began in a voice deeply laden with regret, "Even if that's what's happened here, you can see she isn't right. She isn't the Emma I loved."

"I don't care how they bring him back as long as he comes back with a pulse!" Gideon roared, eyes glistening with tears. "He can't be dead, Sully! He just can't!"

His voice broke, and the emotional intensity that had fueled him moments ago dissipated, leaving him visibly diminished. Sully reached across and pulled him into his arms, holding him tight.

"It's not natural, Gid. You know that. Even if it were possible, even if we could find the people who could do that, it wouldn't be him... and that would hurt even more. It wouldn't fill the hole within you. Trust me, I know what I'm talking about."

Gideon didn't respond, but he held onto Sully, their bodies joined together in shared sorrow.

Bandit let out a long, mournful whine that somehow managed to convey how we were all feeling.

47

CHASE

Endless night passed by, a black gaping hole of nothing that seemed to have engulfed the world, emphasizing the darkness within our hearts.

Sully had moved beside Sam now, the two of them sitting close together as she steered the RV through the night, holding his hand in her lap. Though they said nothing, I could see that Sully was leaning heavily on her support. Every now and then, she squeezed his hand just to let him know she was still with him. They had a silent understanding that transcended words. She was his rock, saving Sully from the despair that threatened to devour him.

By comparison, it was like a wall had come up between Gideon and me.

We hadn't spoken since his outburst. Each time I tried, he would offer only the barest grunt as a response — that or he would simply wave me away. I wanted so desperately to talk to him, to share how we were feeling together, but instead of moving closer, he just pulled away.

He now sat as far from me as was possible in the small space.

Unable to process his grief, he had shut down, creating an emotional distance that seemed insurmountable. Even though I knew it wasn't personal, his withdrawal still felt that way. My heart, which had already been broken once tonight, now felt as if he had taken a sledgehammer to it. What remained lay in pieces, scattered over the cold vinyl floor.

What had happened to our earlier closeness? Had I imagined it all? Or did he not feel the same way about me that I felt for him?

The doubts swirled relentlessly in my mind, creating a dense fog that clouded my thoughts and emotions, amplifying the uncertainty that lingered in the silence between us.

Sensing what was troubling me, Bandit tilted his head at me and emitted a soft whine. His big, soft tongue snaked out and gave my cheek a quick lick, his breath warm, comforting and familiar.

"Don't worry Chase. He is upset."

"I know, buddy. We all are."

I smiled, though I wasn't sure who it was meant to convince. Besides, Bandit could see straight through me — he always had.

He whined again, and scooted even closer to me, his tail thumping in emphasis, *"You are my best friend and I love you."*

Those earnest words, spoken in the simple love language of my dog, cut straight to my heart. Tears misted my eyes again. I wiped them away with an irritated hand and stared at the space we had initially kept Smith. The space beneath the table was empty now, thankfully. He had been moved to the back room and now sat securely bound beside Zeb's body. None of us wanted him to glean more information than he already possessed. The fear of him using our mistakes against us had propelled us to shift him out of earshot.

Emma had seemed unnerved at first when we'd moved him into the room, but she had decided to stay in there rather than face the rest of us.

Knowing what we knew his orders were, I suggested that maybe she wouldn't want to be left alone with him... just in case. But she had shaken her head, her blonde hair flying, stubbornly insisting that she would be fine. She was so hurt over our perceived slights that she was willing to take the risk though the raw pain and visible confusion etched across her face had struck a chord in me, causing me to question my earlier judgement. Maybe she really didn't know how tactless she was coming across. What if she really was trying?

What if this was the best she could do?

I pulled my knees up, resting my chin on them, and stared outside, waiting for a light that I was afraid would never come.

48

SULLY

At the crack of dawn, our weary journey finally brought us to the quiet enclave of Elora's neighborhood — Sunnybrook.

It was a suburb filled with near-identical ranch houses, each adorned with perfectly manicured yards. Exuding an air of tranquility, it was the kind of place where people sat on their front porches, sipping iced tea while observing the joyful chaos of children playing outside.

Sunnybrook felt like a page torn from my memories of Ellington, my hometown in Connecticut, where Emma and I had once created a haven and set up the clinic. The neighborhood resonated with familiar sights — meticulously landscaped front yards, houses receiving annual paint touch-ups, and immaculate, wide streets free of any litter. Rows of expensive cars graced the driveways, an indication that the affluent homeowners had yet to leave for work due to the earliness of the hour.

This was a community saturated with class and privilege, a place where affluence was as conspicuous as the well-tended lawns.

Where, if something bad happened, the owners would be out in force to protect what they owned. This was, in a word, the epitome of safety. Nothing would be a better deterrent to Smith's men than the curtain-twitching, security camera recording, rich folk that called Sunnybrook their home.

Knowing that it would blow their cover if they attacked us here, I felt a degree of safety parking the RV by a man-made park. Still, it took some convincing for the others to let me continue on my own, even if we knew it made the most sense.

Leaving the others, trying not to let Chase and Sam's uneasy faces haunt my mind, I set off at a brisk pace toward Elora's residence, hoping to reach her house before my seemingly inconspicuous morning jog drew unwanted attention.

At a passing glance, I would be mistaken for an early morning jogger, but if they stared longer, or came up closer and saw the boots I wore in place of running shoes, raised eyebrows could be thrown my way.

I was hoping to make it to her house before that happened.

The pink-tinged sky cast a cheerfulness over the area that was in stark contrast to my heavy heart. Normally, I would find enjoyment running in the fresh air at the dawn of another day, with the springy grass beneath my feet.

Today, it only made me want to claw my eyes out.

Driving had provided some escape from the grief. The mundane task had given me something else to focus on. With each passing minute, as the sky grew lighter, a fraction of the weight in my heart lifted, only for it to plummet again in the next moment, a crushing pain that turned my heart to stone.

Shaking my head to dispel the encroaching despair, I forced myself to continue, putting one foot in front of the other. Succumbing to my emotions was not an option; the well-being of my family depended on my ability to keep it together. The burden of saving them fell squarely on my shoulders, a responsibility I carried with grim determination.

A man wearing a cozy bathrobe took small sips from his coffee, still adjusting to the early morning. He stood in front of his house, watching over his white poodle as it relieved itself. I jogged past, quick on the offensive, shooting him a smile in the hope that he would be disarmed by my gesture.

"Morning," he called out, friendly if tired.

"Looks like another beautiful day." Trying not to choke on the lie, I gave him a quick wave and continued on my way.

The tidy streets twisted through more pastel-hued houses. I ran past so many picket fences that I lost count. My feet finally came to a stop in front of a house with a red letterbox bearing a stylish cursive font and a name I recognized.

Heart hammering in my chest, I sprinted up the stone path to the matching red door. Stabbing the bell, I craned my head, anxiously peeking through the glass panels on either side of the door.

Please be home...

The words reverberated in my head, a mantra or prayer I couldn't tell. A dog began yapping, high-pitched and frantic, growing increasingly louder. Suddenly a blur of brown streaked toward the door followed by the appearance of Elora, wearing a set of pinstripe pajamas. Her usually long and dark almost-black hair — now with a new blunt fringe — was tied into a neat ponytail, her feet encased in furry slippers. She peered over her rimless glasses at me, her eyes growing round.

Seeing her, a smile, my first genuine smile, burst out from me.

Staring from the other side of the glass, she blinked, not able to believe I wasn't a mirage. It was only when I beckoned to her that she jumped out of her daze and hurried to the door.

"Sully?" She gaped, opening the door, taking in my haggard appearance. "What are you doing here?"

She trailed off, her quick eyes noticing the flecks of blood that had gotten onto my clothes but could only be seen up close. Her alabaster skin turned impossibly whiter. The door opened wide as she moved aside.

"Come inside."

I stepped past to find a familiar dog looking timidly up at me.

At the sight of me, her small body began to shake, not out of fear but in anticipation. Her tail wagged hesitantly as if she was waiting for my reaction before committing to her own.

"Pixie?" I asked, shocked to see her here.

"Woof," she answered, surprising me with her response.

She had the face of a German Shepherd, though her small size and short legs seemed more suited to a Corgi. I was fairly certain she was a mix of both of those breeds.

Although her coat had been thin and unkempt before, it was now lustrous and healthy. However, there was a small shaved patch on her head where fur had recently started to grow back. Pixie swirled around, dancing playfully on her paws. As she turned, I caught sight of a bold vertical scar with neatly sewn stitches that appeared to be healing well. It was clear that Pixie had undergone surgery not long after Elora brought her back with her.

Behind me, Elora shut the door, drawing the chain across it as a second thought. She motioned for me to follow her into the front room, where two leather sofas were positioned across from each other by a roaring fireplace. A large coffee table made of walnut wood separated the sofas, adorned with several oversized gardening books. I sat down on one sofa while Elora took a seat across from me, studying my face with a puzzled look.

"What's going on?"

I blurted out every awful thing that had happened in the last few days, skimming through the details so I could get the gist of it over quickly, conscious that every second it took for me to explain was another away from my family. I wanted them off the streets and out of danger as soon as possible.

Elora absorbed every word with unwavering attention, her focus unbroken as I recounted the events that had unfolded. She interjected only when clarification was needed, otherwise maintaining a respectful silence that allowed me to articulate the horror of what we had faced. When I was finished, her response was immediate. She grabbed hold of my hands, sympathy shining from her eyes.

"I'm so sorry about Zeb, Sully."

I couldn't do anything but nod, not trusting myself to speak.

She intertwined her fingers together, desperately searching for comforting words to ease the pain I was feeling. In the end, all she could offer was a sympathetic smile.

"I didn't want to come here, but there was no one else I could think of. I don't want to put you in any danger—"

Elora held her hand up, stopping me mid-sentence. "Of course I'll help. You'll all stay here until we figure this thing out."

Her offer came so easily that I wondered if she truly knew what she was getting into. Maybe I hadn't stressed the danger enough.

"You understand that you'll be at risk? These people shot up our home. They attacked Mark, killed Florence and... my dad... They're not kidding around."

"I understand the dangers and I'm willing to accept them."

The burden that rested on my shoulders lifted, although a small shred of uncertainty still lingered. "I'm more grateful than you know... but why? As much as I don't want to ask, I have to. Why would you risk your life to help us?"

Elora's eyes dimmed with shame. "Because I had an enormous hand in this. I was there, helping Forbes to create this mess. I should have been stronger and stopped him, but I wasn't. As a direct consequence of that, Bandit has suffered his entire life, and even now, when he finally has a life and family of his own, he is still being pursued. Still being hunted. I owe him, Sully. I owe him and by extension, all of you, and I am finally willing to put my life where my mouth is."

My gaze lowered to Pixie, who sat beside Elora's feet, her dark eyes focused intensely on me. "Is that why you kept Pixie? I thought you were going to find her a home."

Elora turned her attention to the small dog, instinctively reaching out to pet her. Pixie leaned into her hand, her expression turning blissful as her tongue slipped out at one side.

"That had been my intention, yes. When I took her from you, I had all these ideas about how I could undo the damage Xavier had caused and find her a loving family. But when I got into her head, and saw the extent of the damage he had inflicted... I had flashbacks of Bandit. It hit me then how much pain and suffering my actions had caused, even though it was unintentional."

Her lips quivered as she stifled a sob. Taking a deep breath, she fought to gain control.

"The operation with Pixie was a success. I managed to remove the multiple tumors Xavier had placed inside her. She isn't the same dog she once was. She's still smart, smarter than most dogs, but she's not at Bandit's level. All the aggression he had engineered in her. That's all gone now. She's a lovely little thing, so appreciative of every little gesture. When she came out of the op, I knew that one of the ways I could help was to adopt her myself. By helping her through her rehabilitation, and caring for her, it was my intention that she could finally experience a happy and fulfilling life."

Pixie listened to Elora with a rapturous expression on her furry face. There was no hint of the maliciousness I had seen before. Nothing of the calculating, twisted mind that had targeted Bandit. She really was just a normal dog now, one who had been given a second chance.

"I know my part in this, Sully, and I'm more sorry for it than you will ever know. I will help however I can."

I squeezed her hand in mine, relaying my thanks.

49

CHASE

An hour after Sully had left to find Doc, we gathered around her living room, choking down cups of coffee and as much toast, eggs, and ham as we could. The coffee was bitter, and the toast was burnt, but we ate because we were starving and needed sustenance. Yet, none of us took any pleasure in our meal.

We ate, all of us, except for Gideon.

He couldn't bring himself to and despite a combination of threats and pleas, he refused to eat. It wasn't until I looked deep into his eyes and made it clear that starving himself would not bring Zeb back, that he finally caved.

However, he wasn't the only one feeling on edge.

Ever since we'd walked in and Bandit had caught a whiff of Pixie, he had been leery of the dog. Waiting for the moment she would revert to her psychotic self again. He kept his eyes on her at all times, unable to relax.

Pixie appeared to remember how she used to act around him — how she had been with all of us — and seemed determined to make amends, particularly with Bandit who'd had the most issues with her. She kept approaching him, whimpering for forgiveness. She'd lower onto the floor and roll over to reveal her stomach which, for a dog, was the most vulnerable thing they could do.

But Bandit wasn't buying any of it.

He kept close to my side, baring his teeth if she came too close though he did manage to refrain from snarling, which was something. Having seen what she was capable of, I wasn't ready to jump onto the forgiveness train either, so the two of us kept our distance.

The RV was now parked in Doc's private driveway, which was flanked by some very tall, very bushy Cypress trees that hid it from view, unless the bad guys came from above, at which point, there would be no disguising its presence.

Working in shifts, making sure that someone was guarding him at all times, Sam took food and water out to Smith. Sully gave him a bucket and a toilet roll so he could relieve himself even while handcuffed. He had just the right amount of leeway to use the bucket, but there wasn't enough to tear off the tape that was now stuck over his mouth.

The hum of the refrigerator and the occasional creak of the wooden floor were the only audible sounds in the room, accentuating the tension that enveloped us. We sat around the kitchen island, Sam warming her fingers around a mug of coffee though I hadn't seen her take any sips yet. Emma perched at the end on her own, looking very much out of place despite not doing anything outwardly weird.

Doc tried but failed in her attempt not to study her. Not a minute went by when her eyes didn't stray to Emma, who must have been the greatest scientific mystery she had ever come across. Her curiosity about her was tangible. Her fingers would point toward her as if they couldn't wait to get their hands on her, but she kept those urges to herself, showing the kind of restraint I knew most people in her line of work wouldn't possess.

Gathering our empty plates, Doc carried them to the sink just as my stomach rumbled again. Her eyebrows shot up so high they disappeared beneath her fringe.

"Sorry," I mumbled. "High metabolism."

"So I hear," Doc smiled, opening her cupboards. But all she came back with was a half-empty bag of something dark and murky.

"Don't suppose you'd like some sugar free, gluten-free, nut-free Swiss muesli?"

Looking inside the box, she pulled a face. "Actually, scratch that. I think we're well past the use by date. You've eaten me out of house and home. I'll have to swing by the grocery store."

"You don't have work today?" Sam asked, swiveling that mug between her fingers.

"It's Saturday," Doc reminded her gently.

"Oh," Sam replied, looking surprised that she would forget such a thing. In that precise moment, she didn't look like the Sam I knew her to be. In that precise moment, the familiar contours of Sam's demeanor shifted.

This version of Sam was unlike the one I knew. She seemed less sure of herself, revealing a vulnerability that was usually concealed under her self-assured façade. It was as if all the burdens and challenges had chipped away at the tough exterior she typically presented, leaving behind this scared and uncertain version of herself.

As if he knew how she was feeling, Sully chose that moment to return.

"My shift's up," Sam murmured. Giving him a small smile, she headed back outside. The thought crossed my mind that she actually looked relieved to be leaving, although I wasn't sure why. Seemingly not picking up on any of the strange vibes, Doc found a box of organic cookies and handed them to me.

"I don't have anything with much sugar or chocolate in it, sorry."

I took it with a grateful smile. "When you've had to live off whatever you can find in dumpsters, you stop becoming so fussy."

Doc's smile wavered, and I had to remind myself that my mouth didn't need to blurt things *all the things*. Some people weren't prepared to hear about the harsh realities of life, and it wasn't like we hadn't thrown her for a loop already this morning. I could probably pipe down on my jaunts down memory lane unless I wanted us all on suicide watch.

"We need to discuss our next move." Sully gently steered the conversation to more pressing matters.

Doc pushed her glasses up the bridge of her nose and came to attention, suddenly all business.

"I don't think these people will tie you to me too quickly — if at all — and judging by what you've already explained, they seem to only come after you when you are isolated from the public.

Based on the description of their weapons, they could have attacked you again by now. The fact that they haven't suggests they are following orders from someone who doesn't want to be associated with this situation."

Sully nodded, having come to the same conclusion previously.

"This Smith is our best lead in finding out who's targeting you and why. My suggestion is that you all stay here, rest, clean up. I'll go back to my lab and mix up a little something that will loosen his tongue — much like whatever he used on your friend Mark. On my way back, I'll grab some food and withdraw as much money as I can. I already have some upstairs, but I'll take out the maximum amount I'm allowed, in case we need to make a quick escape."

"You can make a truth serum just like that?" I asked, impressed, and a little intimidated by her skills.

Doc tilted her head to one side. "It shouldn't be too difficult. I have some prior... experience in this area." Her cheeks flushed, and she looked away guiltily. The confession hadn't come easily to her.

Putting the remaining dirty dishes into the sink, she dried her hands. "Let me get dressed and I'll be on my way."

"I want to come with you," Emma announced suddenly, causing several heads to turn her way.

"To my lab?"

"They keep saying I'm not normal, but I'm trying the best I can. I want to find out what I really am." Emma wrung her hands, filled with a desperate need to know as I felt the shame of a hundred people descend on me.

"As much as I'd love to, I can't take you there. Not when these men are likely to be looking for you."

Emma's sapphire eyes flashed with sudden heat.

"You're just like them. No one wants to help me!"

"That's not what I said," Doc answered calmly, as if she were talking to a child or one of her terrified canine patients. "Tell you what, why don't I bring a testing kit home? I can do some basic tests here, then run the results back at the lab tomorrow. It's the best I can do for now. Does that sound alright?"

Relief surged out of Emma. Her body relaxed and a genuine smile spread across her face. For a moment, I caught a glimpse of the woman Sully must have loved once. When Emma smiled like that, she wasn't only beautiful, she was radiant.

"I like you. You're the only one who's been nice to me."

And just like that, I felt myself becoming irritated again.

50

CHASE

A few minutes later, Doc had gone, leaving Pixie alone with us.

The little dog had been shaken when it was clear that Doc wouldn't be taking her with her. Tossing us a look as if to ask if she was really going to leave her behind with us, Pixie whined anxiously by the door and had to be comforted by Doc until she finally stopped crying.

Watching how scared and timid Pixie seemed, I felt an inkling of sympathy, though that didn't stop us being cautious, having been duped by her previously. Picking up on our feelings or maybe having her own residual ones toward us, Pixie stayed away. Lying in her doggy bed in the far corner of the room, she studied us, an unfathomable expression on her face.

Having not seen any clean water in days we took turns to shower even though Doc had two bathrooms. Should the bad guys come calling, we didn't want to be caught with our pants, quite literally, down.

When it took Doc longer to arrive home than we expected, Sam had rummaged through her kitchen, throwing together a pretty decent pasta dish using creamed soup as a sauce base while Gideon and Emma flicked mindlessly through the television.

At one point, I heard Sully and Sam discussing what to do with Zeb's body, though from what I could gather, neither of them could come to any conclusions, not any they could stomach, anyway. When they left out of earshot, nothing had been decided.

I spent my time on the internet — in Incognito mode of course — I wasn't that removed from reality that I had forgotten the basic rules of the web. I looked up the Montpelier News website which was our local newspaper, wondering if anyone had reported the battle that had taken place on our ranch, when an article flashed up with a picture of our home.

Instead of the war zone I was expecting to see, the ranch had turned into a building site. I couldn't even see the house covered as it was by a giant blue and yellow striped tent. I spotted what looked like a logo of an insect on the bottom corner of it.

I read over the accompanying description.

Termite infestation. That's the story they had gone with to hide all the destruction. A snort shot out of me resulting in a questioning chuff as Bandit read the article over my shoulder.

"Those were some high-velocity termites that ate our house huh, boy?"

"*Woof.*"

It warned that people should keep away or risk spreading the infestation and mentioned that our family was happily relaxing on an insurance paid vacation while the works took place.

I turned away from the computer, a sick feeling in my stomach. Not only did these people have endless clout and resources, but they also weren't afraid to go big with their stories. If they could cover up something as huge as our home being destroyed and our entire family having disappeared with it, I didn't want to know what else they would be capable of getting away with.

When Pixie asked for a toilet break, Sully took her outside. As the one who'd been closest to her at the time, he'd asked Gideon if he wanted to do the honors, hoping to draw him out of his funk, but he'd only shaken his head, sinking further into the sofa.

When the two returned, Pixie must have decided we wouldn't hurt her after all as she went to her bed and picked up an old rabbit toy. Very deliberately, she placed it by Bandit's feet, whined then backed away, waiting for his reaction. He gave it a cautious sniff that turned into a happy bark.

"*It's the one I gave her,*" he said.

One ear was beginning to fall off from being loved on a bit too much, while the eyes had kind of sunken in from being picked up by two rows of sharp teeth all the time, but there was no denying that this was the toy he had given her to comfort her when Doc was taking her away. It was her one reminder of us and Bandit and had been his gift to her so she wouldn't feel completely alone.

And now she was saying thank you.

Bandit barked then typed his response very carefully. "*You are welcome.*"

Pixie yapped, dancing a happy little dance then settled by his side.

Just like that, they were buddies in a way they had never been before.

THE SKY WAS ALMOST dark by the time Doc finally returned. Sully greeted her at the door, his relief palpable. She breezed through equally relieved, arms loaded with bags.

"That took a lot longer than I thought it would."

In addition to her oversized purse, she carried several Whole Foods bags filled to the brim with groceries, and a metal briefcase. Sully took the bags off from her and headed into the kitchen as the rest of us followed.

"I wanted to call and let you guys know what the delay was, but thought better of it, in case they are listening in somehow. You never know how these things work, but I've seen enough Netflix shows to know it wasn't worth the risk."

Sam started unpacking an array of colorful vegetables and protein. She fished out cans of dog food and high energy snacks for us that I was relieved to see contained all the aforementioned sugar and chocolate she normally abhorred.

Doc set the briefcase onto the counter.

It wasn't very big, slightly larger than an A4 sheet of paper with a criss-cross pattern embedded in the metal. It looked pretty innocuous considering the kind of dangerous drug I knew was contained inside.

"Was everything OK?" Sully asked in a voice filled with trepidation.

"There was an accident in town that caused a jam everywhere. Nothing to do with you guys, I promise. That wasn't the only problem I ran into though. Considering I had told Sam what day it was, I totally forgot once I was out there and with the banks closing early, I had to drive to several places in order to take out this little lot."

From her bag, she pulled out several wads of notes. Without counting, I figured there must have been several grand there at least.

"*How much do you make?*" I asked without thinking.

Doc flushed guiltily. "More than I should."

"It's in there?" Sam asked, nodding toward the briefcase.

"Yes. I managed to work up a similar solution to what's used in the military. At a push, it should do what we need it to."

"How is it administered?"

"With a simple injection. Once it gets into his body, the results should be pretty instant."

Sully and Sam swapped looks, an unspoken message going between them. When Sully spoke again, it was to Doc.

"So we do this now?"

"No time like the present." Her words were breezy though the feeling behind them wasn't. Sully had a grave look on his face, after all, once we found out who Smith's bosses were, there would be no turning back. If he wanted to back out, this would be the time to do it.

I held my breath.

"Let's go," Sully finally said.

Taking hold of the briefcase, we trooped outside.

51

SULLY

Smith's intense gaze followed my every move as I entered the RV, clutching the ominous briefcase tightly in my hands. The rest of the group maintained a cautious distance, their eyes reflecting a mixture of anticipation and apprehension.

Now that we were free from the confines of the motorhome, we had relocated Smith to the main living area. The windows had been hastily covered with newspaper, shielding him from prying eyes, but this also cast the area in an oppressive half-light that mirrored the shadows inside my soul. Seeing the briefcase, Smith's expression turned wary.

I set the case onto the small, round table as a palpable tension filled the air. With deliberate precision, I opened the case revealing two wickedly long syringes nestled inside. One syringe was filled with a vivid blue liquid, while the other ran clear like water. Smith's eyes flickered between the syringes, uncertainty etched across his face.

Looking over my shoulder, Elora reached for the blue syringe, explaining, "The other syringe will render him unconscious for a few hours in case he tries to overpower us."

I felt a rush of approval: I liked a woman who prepared for all possibilities.

"So how do we do this?"

Elora turned her focus to Smith, seemingly unaffected by his presence. "I need you to restrain him so I can have a clear shot at his arm. We just need to roll up his sleeve."

"Does it hurt?" Gideon asked. He had barely spoken since we'd arrived at Elora's so this was clearly important to him. His haunted eyes darted to the closed bedroom door, thinking of the motionless figure beyond it. It must have taken every ounce of self-control for him to be so close to Smith without being able to exact any kind of revenge.

"I don't think so," Elora responded carefully.

Disappointment oozed out of him.

"I have a question too. How do we know if it's working?" Chase asked.

"When he stops struggling and starts answering our questions. I'm no expert at this, however. I have only seen this done."

We fell silent, the weighty ramifications of her words sinking in.

Approaching Smith, I considered the best way to restrain him. He was already handcuffed to a table leg that was bolted to the floor, so I wasn't worried he about him getting away. But, it didn't leave much room for maneuvering around him.

I'd have to approach from the front.

But as soon as I got within a foot of him, he lashed out at me with his feet. I jumped back, but he still caught me on the leg hard enough that I knew it would bruise.

Circling around, I lunged at him again, but he shuffled away, twisting left and right, making it next to impossible for Elora to get a clear shot at his limbs.

I pulled back, searching for another option when Sam suddenly jumped onto the couch that formed a U around the table. Quick as anything, she bent down, hooking her arm under his chin, putting him in a chokehold. Smith started bucking wildly, but my wife, my lady, stayed firm.

"I can't hold him forever," she warned.

Gideon and I sprang into action. "The left arm. Grab his left arm!"

We tackled him together as he kicked and bucked in an attempt to escape. But there were just too many of us.

Finally finding a clear spot, Elora swiftly jabbed the needle in and pressed down on the plunger with an expertise that sent a chill racing down my back. I watched with a kind of twisted enjoyment as the contents entered his body.

At a nod from Sam, we let go of him, quickly moving clear out of his way. He still had tape covering his mouth which I ripped off from him now. He stared at me, a sick defeat in his eyes, knowing the inevitable would happen.

We waited for the drug to take effect.

I stared down at him, watching for any sign that he was ready for questioning when I noticed a change in his demeanor. His expression became pinched, the blood draining from his face, and his chest started heaving at an unnaturally fast pace. Then he fell to the floor gasping for breath, and with a look of utter pain in his eyes.

"He's faking," Gideon sneered, dismissing it as a fake performance, but I wasn't so sure.

My expertise as a trained veterinarian had primarily been dedicated to the well-being of animals, yet in that critical moment, I recognized pain and suffering as a universal language that transcended species. As I studied Smith, it became evident that this language had etched its narrative across his face in stark and undeniable strokes.

His features contorted with agony, his eyes reflecting an intensity of pain that resonated with a depth of suffering. His head snapped away from me in a violent jolt, as his body began thrashing and convulsing uncontrollably.

"Sully..." Sam murmured.

From the corner of my eye, I saw Chase backing away, a look of complete fright on her face. She had seen seizures before, when Bandit had been wracked with them, and this must have brought several terrifying memories to surface.

"Out of the way!" I reached for the keys to the handcuffs in my pocket.

"Don't be dumb," Gideon snapped. "The second you unlock those cuffs, we've had it. He's a trained killer!"

"The man is going into cardiac arrest!"

"Are you sure?" Elora hissed, unable to believe what was happening.

"I need to lay him down. Move his arms out of the way."

Without waiting for their help or permission, I slid the key into the cuffs and unlocked them. Smith's arms flopped down to his sides as I carefully positioned him onto his back. Opening one of his eyelids, I noticed his eyes rolling into his head. Interlocking my hands, I laid them over his chest and began CPR, pressing down hard and fast, while keeping track of the depressions in my head.

"How is this happening?" I heard Chase ask.

"He must be having a reaction of some sort," Elora responded, her voice tinged with guilt and confusion. I knew her well enough to know that she couldn't have meant for this to happen.

"Good," Gideon spat, a far cry from his usual self. Gone was his youthful and wry exuberance; instead, there was only bitterness and resentment. "Stop helping him. If he dies, that's one less enemy to worry about."

"You can't mean that," Chase gasped, clearly shocked by his callous statement.

"Of course I do! The question is why aren't the rest of you with me on this? He's the reason Zeb is dead! You're honestly going to save the man who killed him?"

My eyes flickered towards him but I couldn't answer, not without losing count. Thankfully, Sam's voice broke through the tense atmosphere, attempting to bring calm and reason to the situation.

"That doesn't mean we should let him die. They're the monsters here, Gid. Not us. If we don't try to help, then we're no better than them. Besides, while we have him, we still have a bargaining chip."

"All I'm hearing are the words of a coward."

He was taking Dad's death much harder than even I had expected. I knew I needed to talk to him, help him through his grief.

But first, I needed to keep Smith alive.

My arms were cramping, feeling the strain but I couldn't stop. Not until his breathing regulated and his heart started back on its own accord. I wished I had a defibrillator to shock his heart, but we were all out of luck there.

My hands would have to do.

The seconds felt like an eternity. Beads of sweat formed on my forehead. Finally, just as I was summoning up the courage to call it quits, a breath hissed out of Smith's lips. It was so slight, that I mistook it for my own. But when another came, followed by another, I knew I could stop.

He was unconscious, but he was alive.

And that would have to do for now.

52

———

CHASE

We took turns keeping watch on Smith for the next few hours, making sure he wouldn't die even and that he couldn't escape. Everybody but Gideon had paired off to keep an eye on Smith. It was a silent agreement that we would never leave him alone with Gideon until his anger subsided, and for once, Gideon didn't argue.

Smith's near meeting with the Reaper had shaken me much more than I realized it would. I knew he was the enemy, that he had caused Zeb's death, but it still didn't mean I wanted him dead. I had seen so much pain and death in the last two years that it wasn't something I ever craved, not even from my worst enemies.

While we waited for him to come around, Doc performed a few tests on Emma. She swabbed her cheek, took blood, hair, and nail samples, weighed and measured her, and created a DNA profile. All the while, Emma let Doc work on her patiently. She wasn't ever this agreeable normally, which only showed just how much she wanted to know what she was. When Doc was finished collecting her samples, she couriered everything to her lab before taking a shift outside with Smith leaving Sully and Sam to cook for us.

Sully heated up the griddle on the stove while Sam tossed in some oil and butter and seasoned some steaks. Sully crossed the kitchen for a pair of tongs, simultaneously rinsing some of the vegetables Doc had brought back as he was closer to the sink. After handing off the colander of chopped vegetables to Sam, he returned to manning the griddle.

Their movements flowed together like a well-choreographed dance. I wasn't even sure if the two of them were aware of how much of a team they were, but Emma definitely did. She watched them intently, studying their every move.

"I can help," she volunteered out of the blue, surprising us all.

Sam was the first to respond with a smile. "That would be great. Can you do the carrots?"

Emma nodded eagerly, pleased to have been included with a task. Moving to the sink where the mound of carrots were waiting, she suddenly froze, staring down at them. "What do you mean by 'do'?"

Sam pointed to the peeler on the counter, miming the motion. "Peel them with that."

Picking it up, Emma attempted to peel the carrots but her fingers were as clumsy as a child's and she kept fumbling. When she wasn't dropping the carrots into the sink, she was dropping the peeler, so progress was painfully slow, but none of us wanted to take over since it was the first time she'd wanted to make herself useful. It also gave us time to consider our options. Which wasn't much in the grand scheme of things.

With Smith out for the count, we would have to wait for him to regain consciousness before trying to get information from him again.

"I hear waterboarding works well." Gideon said it in such a blithe manner that it actually sounded like he meant it.

Red from the heat of the stove, Sully raised a disapproving brow until Gideon shrugged.

"That was a joke."

I forced a laugh, trying to infuse lightness into the heavy atmosphere when Bandit piped up, *"What is waterboarding?"*

Sully shot Gideon another pointed look. "See what you did there?"

Stroking Bandit, I answered, "Something you don't want to know. It's not a nice thing to do to someone."

"Does it hurt?"

"Yes. It's a form of torture."

Bandit's eyes grew wide. *"Like being locked in a cage?"*

He was referring to the experiments conducted at Platinum Industries. Although Bandit had never personally experienced any torture himself, he had witnessed the other dogs being terrorized on a daily basis, until they were a shell of themselves, too broken and too scared to even turn around to look at me when they were being rescued. I still caught him whimpering in his sleep at night sometimes, paws paddling the air in a desperate bid to keep the "Bad Men" away.

I said a silent prayer of thanks that Doc had missed this conversation: she would have been crushed if she had heard him.

We ate our steaks although I still couldn't taste or appreciate any of the food being served my way. I was in a weird half daze, swinging from moments of okay-ness, to being hit by a wave of grief so strong that it left me breathless. Part of me wanted to shout and yell at the world, at the others even. Zeb was gone but here we were, eating and talking around a dining table. Acting as if his body wasn't outside in the RV — decaying.

Anytime I tried to talk to Sully about what I was feeling, he looked away from me. I think he knew what I wanted, he just wasn't able to deal with it yet. Not when it was all so fresh.

When we were done eating, and the food sat uncomfortably in my stomach, I stepped out into the back yard. Stars twinkled down at me, crickets chirping a happy song. I took in the fresh air, breathing deeply in an attempt to diffuse my pain when Gideon's voice snapped at me from the darkness.

"I don't need a babysitter."

He emerged from the shadows, staring at me with a hard expression in his eyes that I had never seen before. My heart skipped a beat.

"I didn't even know you were here."

I didn't bother to hide the edge in my voice. He wasn't the only one in pain, and I was starting to get a little tired of his attitude. I wanted us to support each other through all of this instead of him cutting me out. This wasn't how we behaved. This wasn't what we were to each other.

"We all miss him you know," I began but I stopped myself, knowing I had started on the wrong foot.

"No, you don't understand. No one does." His lips pressed into a thin line. He was wound up so tightly it was a miracle he didn't leap out of his skin.

"I know you were close to him, that he was like your father, but he actually is Sully's dad so think how he must be feeling."

"He didn't seem too concerned when he refused to get him help."

I threw up my hands, exasperated.

"You know damn well that was a tough decision for him, but he had more than just Zeb's life to consider. And it wasn't like he wasn't trying — he was hoping Doc would be able to save him. We just ran out of time. Are you really going to hold that against him?"

A sound came out of him, a mixture of disgust and anger.

"Of course you would stick up for Sully! Just because the two of you have a special little relationship, no one else gets a say about anything! It's just you and him, all the time. And if it's not you and him, then it's you and Bandit! I don't even get a look in over a stupid *dog*."

I reeled back as if I'd been slapped. Was this how he really felt or was this the grief talking? I couldn't tell but I knew he'd crossed a line when Bandit stopped in his tracks, on his way to us. He stopped a few feet away, his tail dipping between his legs in misery.

My heart broke at the hurt expression on his furry face. Hurrying to him, I wrapped my arms around him.

"He didn't mean it, boy. He's just upset. Don't listen to him."

Gideon flinched, and I knew I'd cut him to the quick. I opened my mouth to apologize, but he spun on his heels and stalked away.

I sank my face into Bandit's fur wondering how my world had imploded by quite so much.

53

CHASE

When it was approaching midnight and Smith still hadn't woken up (though he was in a stable condition), Doc appeared, arms laden with blankets that she set onto one of several sofas in the room.

"I only have the one spare room which I think Sully and Sam should take. The rest of you can camp in the living room here."

"Thanks, Elora," Sam responded, looking ready to crash.

Bandit and I made our way to one of the sofas, claiming it for our own. I was pretty exhausted from everything and wanted nothing more than to curl up somewhere warm and dry, with four solid walls around me.

I should have known that Gideon wasn't ready to do the same. He stood in the middle of the room, making no move to settle himself.

"I'm not leaving Zeb out there with *him*. I'll take the night watch and sleep in the RV so I can keep an eye on them both."

As much as I thought I knew Gideon, he had been acting like a stranger all day so I didn't feel as if he could be trusted with Smith on his own. Sully must have had the same thought as he replied, "I'll stay out there with you."

"I can handle it by myself," Gideon protested, a stubborn glint to his eyes. "I'd prefer to be alone."

"I want a lot of things, doesn't mean it's going to happen." Sully's tone brokered no argument though I half expected Gideon to challenge him.

"Fine," Gideon snapped back. Not gonna lie, I was pretty surprised at how quickly he had caved. Underneath all the bravado, he must have been just as exhausted as the rest of us were. Sam offered a supportive smile, and nodded her agreement.

"I hate to bring this up... but we do need to have a discussion about the body. There are certain procedures we should follow—" Elora started but was instantly interrupted.

"Tomorrow, okay? Can I just have tonight to say goodbye?" Gideon pleaded. His voice cracked at the end of the sentence and I felt my heart ache for him.

Seeing how he was barely holding it together, Doc nodded quickly. "Of course."

"I want to sleep out there too since I can't get any around here. Due to all the snoring," Emma chimed in earning a glare from me. "I'll take the bedroom."

"You understand you'll be sharing it?" Sully asked.

"With you? OK."

"No, not with me," Sully sounded flustered and I couldn't blame him. He seemed determined not to meet Sam's eyes when he spoke. "Dad is still there."

"Oh. Can't we move him then?"

She spoke as if she were talking about a piece of furniture, not a person we desperately loved.

Gideon's face hardened. "You either stay with him or it's here with the others. Those are your choices."

"I'll stay out there," Emma replied quickly. "I'll share with the dead old man even though he doesn't need a bed anymore."

All but Emma drew in their breaths. The seconds ticked away until Doc was the first to become unfrozen.

"Right," she said, looking at us all with an unnaturally bright smile. "Everyone good?"

Sully nodded, ruffled Bandit's head, hugged me, then gave Sam a good-night kiss before escorting Gideon and Emma out the door.

"Sully... one moment," Doc said, just as he was about to step out of the house.

"Go on," he said to Gideon and Emma.

I tried not to flinch when Gideon left without even giving me a single glance.

Doc handed him her cell. "In case we need to reach you or vice versa. The phone's unlocked. I've programmed my number under "Home.""

He took it from her, sliding it into a pocket. "Thanks."

Shooting us one last look, Sully left.

My stomach clenched uneasily. He wasn't going to be far, only a few feet away. He also had Doc's phone now and could call at the first sign of trouble.

Why then did I feel like all the air had been sucked out of me?

That we were standing on the edge of a cliff face, moments from pitching forward?

Trying to keep my worries to myself, I lay down onto the sofa and waited for sleep to come.

54

—————

ELORA

With her guests left to sleep downstairs, Elora lay in her bed, hoping for restful oblivion but the day had proven too much for her.

Although she had only met him once, Zeb had been a kind man and his death was a terrible tragedy. She couldn't help but feel the cloud of sorrow that clung to her friends — even the perpetually cheerful Bandit, who was only a shadow of his former self.

She wished she could do something to alleviate their grief though the only thing that would help now, was time.

While she could do nothing about that, there was something she hoped she could assist with.

Too wired for sleep, Elora slid out of bed and made her way to her dresser. She powered on the laptop that sat among her hairbrushes and cosmetics items. She kept several computers around her home, all were synced to her work server so she could look things up at a moment's notice or communicate with her team if an idea were to strike, whatever the time.

Opening her email account, she sifted through the day's correspondance, hoping to find a specific subject heading. When her eyes alighted on the topic she was looking for, she clicked on the email with a growing sense of excitement. She read through the message quickly, opening the myriad of attached files.

Information flooded her screen, of scans, charts, and impossible calculations.

The results for Emma's tests were starting to come in and they were startling. She wasn't sure how this could even be possible...

She had half a mind to rush outside and tell Sully the truth, but discovered that while she had been poring over the documents, more time had elapsed than she had expected. She had been so consumed with the findings that it was almost two in the morning. He would be fast asleep now, as would the rest of them.

She felt a rush of impatience but had to force it back down. They had waited so long already. One more night wasn't going to change anything.

Closing her laptop, Elora climbed into bed, turned off the lights and fell asleep dreaming of DNA helixes.

55

CHASE

I woke early having only had a few hours of sleep.

It wasn't the sofa's fault — in fact, it was probably the most comfortable sofa I had ever been on — but I had tossed and turned all night, plagued with dreams of Gideon slipping away from me.

I knew we had both suffered a terrible shock. We were being hunted by killers, with no real idea of how we were going to get out of this. With so much on his mind, Gideon had no time for me. But it seemed so unfair when all I wanted was to talk to him, and all he could do was pull away from me.

The babble of early morning television drifted over. Bandit sat in the middle of the floor, watching Good Morning America. The volume was low enough so as not to wake me, but was probably a little too low to actually understand, hence the subtitles on the bottom of the screen.

My Muttface was the most considerate dog in the world.

Even more surprising than the sight of my dog watching television was the fact he wasn't alone: Pixie sat close by. If I'd had a phone, that picture would have gotten a gazillion hits on Instagram. Probably would've gotten me a spot on Hellen — one of the most popular talk shows — too.

I squinted at the television, searching for the time only to see it wasn't even six yet. The door to Sam's room was still closed, I couldn't hear any movement from her. Judging by Pixie's lack of excitement I could tell Doc was sleeping too. In all likelihood, so were Sully and Gideon, but I was feeling uneasy about our fight yesterday and how we had left things.

I wanted to make sure Gideon was okay.

I slipped on my sneakers, the only thing I had taken off to sleep — when your life was in danger, it was better to have your shoes close to you and to be fully dressed so you could make a quick getaway. Rule Number 1 of Living on the Streets.

Bandit chuffed a greeting at me. "Let's go check on Gideon."

He nodding, not wanting to bark, and followed me to the door as we let ourselves out quietly. Pixie followed us then stopped, turning back to glance up the stairs, torn. She whined, wanting to follow yet not wanting to leave Elora.

"We won't be long," I reassured her. "You can wait here."

Satisfied with my answer, she went back to the television. The brisk morning air chilled my lungs, shocking me awake. Wrapping my arms around myself, we headed for the RV, but as we drew closer, I saw that the driveway was empty.

I turned to Bandit. His eyes mirrored my own confusion.

"The RV should be right here, shouldn't it?"

He answered with a sharp bark that sent another shock to my system. My heart began to pound, filling with panic. I fought to bolt it down.

Maybe they'd had to move the vehicle somewhere. Maybe someone had come snooping in the middle of the night. Hurrying, I stood in the exact spot where the motorhome had been.

But there was no sign of it.

I couldn't move. Shocked to the core, one terrifying question buzzing through my mind: had Smith overcome them?

Bandit's head shot up into the air. He sniffed, then bounded behind one of the Cypress trees, barking like crazy. I ran to him but skidded to a stop when I saw a familiar brown boot poking out of the shrubs.

Sully's boot.

My eyes traveled up the length of the boot to find his leg still attached. Diving forward, I shoved away the branches that hid him from view, ignoring the shooting pain that lanced through my hands as the branches lashed out at them. I kept going, frantically moving them away until Sully's face finally came into view.

"Sully?"

I shook him, numb with the terror that he would not wake even as my eyes ran over his body, searching for wounds. I couldn't see any, but Sully wasn't waking up.

What was wrong with him?

Bandit pawed at something on the ground. A square of something yellow. It was a piece of paper... no, several Post-It's that had been stuck together to form a note.

I recognized Gideon's untidy scrawl immediately. Snatching it up with frozen fingers, my eyes raked over the tersely written words.

I'm sorry, but I can't let him die. If they could bring Emma back, they can do the same with Zeb. I'm going to offer them Emma and Smith. This new Emma doesn't belong in our lives.
She was destroying our family's happiness, what was left of it.
This is the best way.
You'll see.

IT WAS SIGNED BY GIDEON.

I read the entire note several more times before its message finally sank in. Bandit hopped impatiently beside me, wanting to see the note for himself. He read it quickly, his tail sinking lower and lower until it disappeared from view.

I shook Sully again, harder.

"Sully! Why aren't you waking up?"

Sticking my hand beneath his nose, I could feel the warmth of his breath, and some of my numbness receded. Gideon wouldn't have done anything to harm Sully, but it was still a relief to know that he was alive.

I went behind him and slid my arms under him, intending to half drag, half carry him back to the house. Digging my heels into the ground, I pulled until my arms felt they would pop from their sockets.

We hadn't moved an inch

I wouldn't be able to get Sully to the house by myself, not with his dead weight.

"Hurry back. Get Sam. I'll stay with Sully."

Bandit woofed sharply at me and tore off.

56

CHASE

I kneeled behind Sully, cradling his head in my lap, trying not to worry over how his face seemed colder than the ground that bit at my knees. How long had he been out here like this?

Cupping his face, I tried to warm it up when something glinted, half hidden in the grass beside me. I brushed the grass away to reveal a syringe, but the clear liquid that had been inside last night was now gone.

Recognition hit me like a freight train — Gideon had used Doc's knockout drug on Sully. The realization sent shivers down my spine as the pieces of the puzzle fell into place.

A thought niggled at the back of my mind, a memory from last night. Something that I had noticed but hadn't paid attention to at the time. If only I had given it more thought, I could have — *should have* — seen this coming.

When we were discussing sleeping arrangements last night, Gideon had given in to Sully far too easily. I had even thought it strange that he'd had no objection to Emma staying there, especially after she had spoken so poorly about Zeb.

But of course he didn't have a problem with that, not when it was his plan to exchange her for Zeb. I was floored by how easily he had fooled us all.

"Chase?! Where are you? Are you OK?!" Sam's worried voice called out.

"Over here!"

She bolted around the corner, her hair still tied in a long braid that flew behind her as she ran. Seeing Sully's condition, her panic grew more pronounced.

"God... Is he alive?"

"Yes. But Gideon's gone! He knocked out Sully with that other syringe. He's taken Emma and Smith. He means to trade them for Zeb!"

I knew I was babbling but I couldn't help it. My thoughts were a mad jumble like my emotions. My heart was in my throat and I could barely get the words out.

"For Zeb? I don't understand."

Even as she asked the question, she crouched down beside me, checking to see how Sully's eyes were, pressing a finger to his pulse.

"He thinks they can bring him back... that if they have Emma, they can use her to learn how to bring him back."

Horror flashed over her face. "But that's..."

"Impossible... I know."

"I was going to say barbaric and impossible. He can't just sacrifice her like that. Her life isn't his to give."

A gasp sounded behind her. Doc had arrived with Pixie at her heels, still in a striped robe and fluffy slippers, having only just woken up. Doc's eyes widened as she tried to take in the chaotic scene in front of her.

"What's going on?" She asked, her voice trembling with concern. "Where's the RV?" But Sam paid no attention to her questions, turning instead to address me.

"Did Gideon say anything to you about this?"

"Of course not!" I replied frantically. "He was acting weird all night. I should've guessed this was what he was going to do, but I didn't." Sam's face fell and she let out a heavy sigh. "Now it makes sense why he wanted to stay out in the RV... I didn't know Sam! I didn't!"

My voice caught in my throat as I choked on a sob. Sam's expression softened, and she placed a comforting hand on my shoulder.

"We'll get him back before anything happens to him, I promise. Help me get Sully inside first. We need to wake him."

Doc took one look at the empty syringe and immediately understood what had transpired.

"That reckless boy..." she said but never finished. Working in unison, the three of us carefully lifted Sully. Bandit and Pixie lead the way, dancing anxiously on their paws as they waited for us to carry him back into the house where we laid him onto the sofa.

"I'll be right back," Doc said, disappearing momentarily before returning with a small vial that she waved under his nose. The moment Sully breathed in the strong scent, he began coughing and slowly regained consciousness. His bewildered eyes stared at our faces.

"Why do I feel like I've been hit by a truck?"

By the time Sam had explained everything, Sully's face had grown tighter and tighter until it looked like it would crack at the slightest provocation. His anger simmered beneath the surface, threatening to erupt at any moment.

"I could kill him right now!" Sully growled. "Taking Emma like that, how could he do that to her?!" Sam looked at him, her expression not quite aligning with his outrage. Thick lines creased her forehead. She looked for all the world like a concerned mother. When she spoke, her words carried a tone of understanding that sought to temper Sully's anger.

"You're more worried about Emma than you are Gideon? He's in shock, Sully. He just lost the person he considered his father. How can you be angry at him? Gideon is still a child, even if he doesn't look or act like it. He's still a teenager, no matter how hard he pretends otherwise."

"But he's a teenager who should have known better than to do something like this. Emma isn't smart like he is. She's not worldly. She needs to be protected, and he's betraying all of us with this. Even if you don't like Emma, it doesn't make this okay."

I knew the second the words were out of his mouth, he regretted them. That look of utter hurt and betrayal on Sam's face was something I wouldn't forget in a hurry. Stunned into silence, she snapped her mouth shut and dropped her gaze to the floor.

Interrupting the charged atmosphere, Doc interjected, her tone seemingly ordinary, though the gravity of her words sent a shiver down my spine. "I need to tell you something. Last night, after you all went to bed, I couldn't sleep, so I checked my emails. I received some of Emma's results and while more testing needs to be done, I feel fairly confident in saying that I think I know what she is."

Sully and Sam were taken aback, not anticipating this news to come at this specific moment. Sully's anger seemed to dissipate, replaced by a mixture of surprise and confusion. His brow furrowed, and the intensity in his eyes softened as he processed the unexpected revelation. Beside him, Sam, who had been grappling with the aftermath of Sully's harsh words, now wore an expression of disbelief, her distress momentarily eclipsed by the weight of Doc's announcement.

"What is she?" Sully pleaded, desperate to know, yet fearful of learning the truth at the same time.

"After comparing our results to your wife's — your previous wife's — existing medical records, we found that although her DNA is the same, there are enough small mutations to prove that genetically, although she is as close as she can be to the real Emma, she isn't actually her."

"So what are you saying?" Sam asked for clarification, as Sully didn't seem able to speak.

"This Emma must be a clone. Somehow, Xavier got hold of the real

Emma's DNA, cloned her, and managed to accelerate her development into an adult woman."

My head was spinning with this revelation, so I had no idea how Sully must be feeling.

"A clone? But is that even possible?" He finally managed to ask.

"Until now, only animals have been successfully cloned. And many in the scientific community find it highly unethical to clone a human, so it isn't generally attempted."

I gasped as a sudden thought came to me. "Remember when you went to visit her grave, Sully, when we made that trip back east to your clinic? You said it had been disturbed, but we didn't believe you? That must have been when they found her DNA."

"That all makes sense now." Sam agreed. "I'm sorry we doubted you, Sully."

"But how do you explain her attachment to me?" Sully didn't seem ready to accept the diagnosis.

"She had all those pictures of the two of you that she must have studied before she even showed up on your door. And we don't know what messages they could have been feeding her while she was growing. She could simply be brainwashed."

Doc squeezed Sully's shoulder. "You knew deep down that she couldn't come back to life. At least you now know why she behaves the way she does. As much as she looks and sounds like her, she isn't your wife, Sully. She never was."

Sam's eyes brimmed over with tears while Sully just looked shell-shocked. I wasn't sure what he was making of the news.

"I wish you'd been able to tell us this last night." I wasn't trying to guilt her, but if Gideon had known then, we wouldn't be in our current predicament.

"I know. I'm so sorry. I wish I had woken all of you up to tell you, and now there's something else we have to consider. If Gideon has Smith, if he really is making some sort of deal with him... then they're going to find out about me, aren't they?"

Sully had to fight not to hang his head. "I'm sorry. We shouldn't have come here."

"No, that's not what I'm concerned about," Doc replied. "The other dogs, the ones we saved. Could they and their new families be at risk?"

The world spun around me. I didn't want to think about all those poor dogs and their helpless, terrified faces when we had rescued them.

Had we saved them only to drag them into this... again?

Doc stood up straighter, pushing the glasses up her nose. "Don't apolo-gize, Sully. This isn't your fault. You're just trying to protect your family. It's these villains coming after you. They're the ones who need to be stopped. I need a moment to think."

She fell silent. I could see her mind ticking over, working through the possible scenarios.

"Unless Gideon took off in the middle of the night, he doesn't have that much of a head start. You can take one of my cars and go after him... except we have no idea where he's gone? And we don't know where Smith's people are, either. They could be heading anywhere."

She paused before changing gears.

"Can I have my phone? I might be able to summon some assistance —" She stopped as Sully reached into his pocket, only to come up empty.

"I don't have it."

"Did Gideon take it from you?" Sam asked.

"No... not unless it was after I blacked out."

Doc reached for her iPad resting on the mahogany coffee table, her fingers dancing across the smooth screen. After a few swipes, she let out a joyous cry, her face lighting up with excitement and relief.

"He does have it! Look, there he is!"

She spun the device around so we could see the Find My Phone app she had opened up. Doc beamed at us. "We can track him with this."

"But he would know that, wouldn't he?" I interjected, frowning. "Gid isn't stupid."

Sam's brows rose a notch. "Maybe he didn't take the phone. Is it possible that it fell out of your pocket when you were struggling with him?"

Sully leaned back on the sofa, taking a moment to mull over Sam's question. "When he injected me?" Sully asked, giving it some consideration. "Yeah. Quite possibly," Sully nodded.

While they had been talking, I felt myself experiencing a heavy sense of déjà vu. It was as if we had been through this before, and not even once, but countless times. And I knew with a crystal clear clarity that we would never be free of them. Not of Forbes, Xavier or the Bad Men.

For whatever reason, they would always come for us.

"This is never going to end, is it?

The doomed tone in my voice sliced through their chatter. Sully looked as if I had struck him. He reached out to me, but I stepped back. I didn't want comfort right now.

I wanted a resolution.

"As long as Bandit's alive, and especially now that we know Emma is a scientific breakthrough, there'll always be someone after us, someone who wants to be able to create 'special' dogs or human clones."

"So we'll fight them every step of the way. Or we'll run. We're getting really good at it," Sully responded. But I shook my head.

"We'll make a mistake one day. Besides, we can't live the rest of our lives like this. I think we need to do something else."

An idea struck me like a bolt of lightning, sending electric pulses through my body and setting every hair on end. It was as if the answer had been staring me in the face the whole time. I could feel the chills of realization run down my spine. I knew I was onto something.

"I think the only way to protect us is to do the opposite of what we've been doing so far," I proclaimed, my voice trembling with both fear and excitement at the potential consequences of this bold plan. The words hung heavy in the air, each one carrying weight and importance. This was it, our only chance to turn things around and finally triumph against our enemies.

They stared at me, eyes clouded with confusion. Turning to the television where the morning show still played in the background, long forgotten now, I laid out my plan.

They listened. First with shock, then increasing horror, but I stood firm, knowing it was our only chance at survival.

But there was a caveat — a pretty big one.

My plan would either save us from the Bad Men forever.

Or it would get us all killed.

57

SULLY

An intense pressure clamped down on my head, making it feel like it was trapped in a vise.

The world hadn't stopped spinning. Every few moments, I found myself hit with a wave of dizziness that would stop me short, but at least I was conscious. Not that it would help our situation all that much.

Gideon's last words echoed through my head for what seemed like the millionth time since Chase had shown the note to me. Red-hot rage churned like a volcano, threatening to erupt.

Yet alongside that anger, fear lurked, a vast and all-consuming black hole waiting to swallow me whole. I should have been able to set my own emotions aside to talk to him. Instead, like a selfish fool, I had pushed him away and dismissed his feelings.

And now we had come to this.

It'd been a few moments since Chase had outlined her plan. We'd wasted precious minutes arguing to and fro on the sense of it, but at the end of the day, despite trying, no one else had come up with a better idea.

We had no choice now but to split up.

I took in the two cars parked in the garage. Elora's usual ride, a sleek, silver Lexus, gleamed under the dim lighting. Next to it, the SUV seemed a much less flashier — if roomier — cousin. The SUV was a recent purchase, bought to help her ferry the dogs we had rescued from Platinum Industries since the other car hadn't been as practical.

I stopped by the SUV.

"We'll take this."

"But the Lexus is faster. You'll need it to catch up to Gideon," Elora objected.

"Are you sure? I can't promise you'll get it back in the same condition."

"It's a car, Sully. I can always get another."

"When this is all over, we should have a conversation about your salary and what I have to do to be making it," Chase said to Elora. I was grateful that even in our darkest moments, she was able to make a quip — a self-preservation tool — even if her heart wasn't really in it.

I fumbled with the keys, my hands shaking as I unlocked the Lexus, ducking to climb into the driver's seat. The smell of leather and pine drifted towards me, mixed with the familiar scent of my own fear of confusion, when another wave of dizziness hit. It was only when I braced myself against the roof of the car that I was able to stop myself from falling.

"You can't drive, Sully."

Sam's voice was firm, brooking no argument. She stood beside me, her sapphire eyes flashing with determination.

"The effects of the drug should wear out within an hour or so, but she's right: you shouldn't be operating any kind of machinery, least of all a car," Elora chimed in, her brows knitting together apologetically.

"I'll be fine." My stubbornness flared up. I was a great driver and I knew there wouldn't be any trouble.

Sam turned her gaze to me, her eyes hard with feeling. "Said every person in the world who then crashed their car. You're in no condition to drive and we all know it. Either Elora or I will go with you, but since there's likely to be trouble when we eventually get to him, I think we know who the better option is."

"That's certainly not me. I've never even touched a gun. I guess this means Chase and Bandit will go with me. I promise to keep them safe," Elora answered. "You two focus on stopping Gideon before he does something he truly regrets."

She shot us a convincing smile, but the stress of all that had happened in the last twenty-four hours was finally taking its toll. My body began to shut down. I felt small and vulnerable in the face of it all.

The weight of responsibility weighed heavy on my shoulders. Memories of my mother's death resurfaced, and I felt myself withdrawing into a familiar darkness. I felt like I had when my mother had died and I had withdrawn into myself. But I was the head of the family now and it was my responsibility to fix everything. I had to put us back together again.

Shaking myself out of my stupor, I gripped Chase by the shoulders with a newfound determination.

"If you find yourself in any trouble at all you get out of there, understand? I don't want you being brave or foolish. I want you safe. If you and

Bandit are at risk, then nothing else matters. So if you see danger heading your way, just get the hell out and we'll figure out the rest later."

She nodded, Bandit barking loudly in agreement beside her. Then she threw herself into my arms, her thin frame trembling slightly as she spoke into my chest.

"Bring him back safely, okay? Don't let anything happen to him."

I wanted more than anything to promise her that, but the words caught in my throat. I wouldn't lie to her. I refused to promise what I couldn't.

She released me only for Sam to squeeze her tight. We did the same with Bandit until we were a tangled mess of hugs and doggy licks.

"We won't be long. We'll find Gideon and catch up to you. You just get in position and wait for us."

Elora nodded, one arm around Chase while the other rested on Bandit's neck. Pixie sat perched beside Bandit, her head tilted to one side and her intelligent eyes taking in our every move. She seemed to understand the gist of what was going on, if not exactly everything that we were saying.

"Don't worry. I will protect Chase," Bandit said, thumping his tail in emphasis. The certainty and love shone from his eyes, and it was all I could do not to melt down into a flood of tears.

"I know you will, buddy. You just make sure you watch out for yourself, too."

It was time to leave, but I couldn't make my feet move. It was as if they were cemented to the floor. Without a word, Sam took me by the hand and gently started to pull me away.

"Come on. The faster we go, the quicker we can be back with them."

Tearing my gaze from my kids, I let Sam lead me in the opposite direction. As I got into the car, all I could think was how fragile and young Chase looked.

Yet all of our lives now rested on her.

58

CHASE

Before we could leave, Doc had to make a quick call on her landline since she had neither her cell nor iPad anymore.

I stood next to her, my hands clenched tightly as she spoke to the person on the other end of the line. Her words were rushed and urgent, explaining that they and their dog — one of the rescues from Platinum Industries — might not be in danger.

A barrage of questions came down the line, but Doc cut them off sharply. "I'm sorry, I really don't have time to explain everything. Just call the others, let all the families know. We have a plan to stop them in LA but I can't disclose what it is. Just keep an eye out. You'll know if we've been successful."

With that warning hanging in the air, we hurriedly took off.

The highway stretched out before us, a ribbon of concrete rushing past. We left the suburban peacefulness of Doc's neighborhood and were now tearing down the streets as fast as we could without breaking speed limits.

Bandit sat in the middle of the backseat, his keen eyes scanning ahead of us while Pixie curled up beside him in a small ball. Since we had gotten into the car, she had been eerily calm — she was probably the calmest one among us.

She had changed so much in just a few short weeks. Whatever magic Doc had worked on her must really have been something as she was nothing like her previous self.

Greedily, I took as much comfort from Bandit's presence as I could. As much as I trusted Doc, she wasn't part of our family and it was never far from my mind that I was heading in the opposite direction to all the people I loved.

The scenery outside blurred together as we continued on our journey at breakneck speed.

More pretty box-like houses lined the streets, their vibrant colors eventually fading into the dullness of retail stores. But as we continued on our journey, even these buildings disappeared, leaving us surrounded on all sides by an acrid, yellow desert. The sharp scent of sand and dust filled my nostrils, making it difficult to take anything in.

If you had asked me what I had seen only a second ago, I wouldn't have been able to tell you. My thoughts were stuck on Gideon and what might be happening to him. Feeling my anxiety, Bandit laid a paw on my shoulder and whined into my ear.

Doc looked at me with concern, trying to assuage some of my fears. "It's a smart plan, Chase. A clever one. It's our best chance of surviving this insanity."

Bandit barked loudly in agreement, my ever present cheerleader. I guess she didn't know what else to say or how to make small talk, even as she turned on the radio soon after. "Let's listen to some music. It will relax us. This is Pixie's favorite station."

At the mention of her name, Pixie's ears swiveled to Doc, but she remained in her relaxed position. I tried not to envy her. A mellow song came through the high-tech speakers. Instead of listening, I stared blankly out at the sandy landscape. All I could see for miles was the blue sky meeting with that yellow sand and the odd human-like cactus. As the stress flooded my body, every nerve felt frayed and raw.

My hands were clenched tightly in my lap, fighting against the urge to scream. My heart pounded wildly in my chest, causing the world around me to spin despite sitting completely still.

It was the beginnings of a panic attack.

I bit my lip, trying to tell my heart to slow the heck down. Closing my eyes, my focus shifted to my breath, inhaling deeply and exhaling slowly in an attempt to steady myself. In then out. I counted my breath slowly, letting my mind go blank until all I heard was the sound of the road below the tires and Bandit's breath by my ear.

I don't remember falling asleep, but when I opened my eyes again, it was several hours later, and we were barreling down the I-10. The barren desert landscape had transformed into a bustling cityscape. Buildings stood tall and proud, their steel and glass structures glinting in the sunlight. Both dogs were asleep on the backseat, somehow curled together so that Bandit's chin rested on top of Pixie's head, proving what I had always known — even dogs needed comfort.

My lips felt dry and chapped. I ran my tongue over them only to feel a sharp pain as the movement cracked the skin. Doc caught my reaction and reached over to open the glove compartment. Inside were several small bottles of water and chocolate bars.

"My secret stash, in case I ever break down."

I shot her a small smile of gratitude and reached for the bottle, gulping down the cool liquid. A road sign flew past my head, but I missed the words by a split-second, though I didn't need to see it to recognize the city we were now approaching.

Palm trees towered above us as we entered the city, their fronds reaching towards the sky like giant green hands. Billboards adorned every building, advertising the latest movies and TV shows in flashy lights. Everywhere I looked, there were promises of love, beauty, and unimaginable wealth.

The energy of the city was palpable. Everything seemed larger than life and brimming with endless possibilities.

As we drove through the bustling city, towering glass buildings loomed over us in every corner. Each one seemed to house a luxurious hotel, with black stone fountains adorning their entrances and sharp-dressed valets bustling about. My eyes were drawn to the LAX airport in the distance, where giant gray jumbo jets waited patiently in lines for their turn to take off.

Bandit and I both got a kick out of seeing those. I have never been on a plane, never seen one this close either, but they were *enormous*. I was actually kind of grateful that I hadn't been on something that big. It didn't make sense how it could fly.

A retro looking diner passed by, chrome metal gleaming in the sun, which I swear I recognized as it'd been featured in several movies before. Then I saw a sign with the words Sunset Boulevard on it, just like the Broadway show. If we weren't in such dire straights, I might have enjoyed this little sight-seeing detour. As it was, I silently urged Doc to drive faster.

I wouldn't feel safe until we got to our destination and one way or another, all of this was over.

Despite how unspectacular the car looked, it came with all modern amenities, including a GPS system that also doubled as a TV. We were using the GPS to guide us. It had the little map thingy on right now with an arrow above an icon that represented our car. Jazz still played on the radio, which I suspected was one of the reasons I had fallen asleep in the first place. Like Gideon, it really wasn't my type of music.

The number was just finishing when the announcer suddenly cut in. The urgent voice of the news anchor crackled over the TV.

"We've just received reports of a possible terrorist cell working in the LA area. The extremist group is considered armed and very dangerous and should not be approached. If seen, please call this emergency report line."

A grainy black-and-white image appeared on the screen. Low resolution, as if it had been captured from far away. There were several figures in the blurry frame — and a dog.

Blinking, I leaned in for a better look, trying to make out more details.

The dog had the same dark patches of color that I knew well. While I couldn't see all the figures clearly, I recognized the old man in the wheelchair, and the young girl standing beside him at a gas station.

"Oh Jesus, that's us."

Doc's eyes snapped to the screen. As she stared at the image in utter disbelief, a phone number flashed up on the bottom of the screen, followed by the words:

REWARD $500,000 if your tip results in their capture.

"How do they know we're here?" I tried to think about how they might have learned of our plan.

"I don't know." She paused, wracking her brain for a possible answer. "Oh no... What if I leaked it?"

"I don't understand?"

"There were almost a hundred dogs that we saved and had adopted. They're all calling each other now because I told them to. I was so scared that the families were at risk, I didn't even think that it could all get out."

My heart began thudding in my chest again. That panic attack I had managed to hold off was threatening to erupt this time. Doc gritted her teeth.

"Let's think about this. I only told them that we were heading to LA but not what we're going to do. They're looking for a large group of you. They don't know you've split up, or that both Pixie and I are now on the scene. To an outsider, you'd look like my kid, and since my face wasn't in that bulletin, I don't think anyone will recognize you, Chase. LA is so densely populated, they won't be able to pull you out of a crowd."

"You think so?" I asked hopefully.

Doc nodded, but there was a slight hesitation in her gesture that gave her away. Regardless of what she was saying, we both knew the truth.

We were in big, big trouble.

CHASE

The minutes ticked by, each one feeling longer than the last as we raced towards our destination. My nerves were on edge, waiting for the inevitable shoe to drop. It wasn't that I wanted to question Doc's logic, but I couldn't be as calm as she was.

The news had branded us terrorists!

Which ratcheted my nerves all the way up to the DANGER klaxon level.

Every fiber of my being screamed with fear and adrenaline at the thought of Smith and his men closing in on us. They had always operated under a cloak of secrecy and stealth, using truth serums and memory wipes to keep their actions hidden from the public eye. But now that our faces were plastered across the news, it could only mean one thing — Smith was back in control. He must have overpowered Gideon or tricked him into complacency, and Emma's life would be in grave danger.

As utterly terrifying as the thought of them being hurt — maybe even killed — was, I couldn't break down. I still had the rest of my family to save. And now that all bets were off, I wanted revenge, too.

I needed to stop these people from ever coming after us again.

Bandit lay low in the backseat, keeping out of sight, while I tried to hide as much of my face with my hair as possible. Throughout it all, the bright Californian sun shone down like a spotlight, seemingly determined to sign-post our existence to the rest of the world.

I glanced at the car beside us, worried that the driver might turn to look and recognize me when something small flew past the car that created a whistling sound. The windows were up, so I wasn't entirely sure what I had heard, but then that same whistling sound came again… and was followed by another.

Then another.

I shot Doc a confused look when something thundered into the back of our car. I screamed, fear turning my blood to ice. Doc jumped in her seat, pressing on the gas pedal too hard in her panic.

The car jerked forward, sending the dogs flying before she could get it under control again. Bandit spun around and got up to peek out the windows when I suddenly understood what was happening.

"Those are silenced shots! They're firing at us! Everyone get down!"

Bandit hit the floor immediately, grabbing Pixie's collar as he went, dragging her with him into the footrest. The two of them huddled close, out of my line of sight, but hopefully also our mysterious attackers. Doc's knuckles were white on the steering wheel.

"Who would be firing at us? Surely not the police. That would be madness!"

Even as the words left her mouth, three police cars screeched around the corner toward us, sirens blaring. Faces appeared in the cars on either side of us, stunned with shock as they moved their cars as far away from us as they could, opening up a lane for the police.

Their passenger windows rolled down, and an officer took aim at us with his gun. It was a normal gun, though, not the silenced snipers I had heard.

Which meant the snipers were further away.

I stole a glance at the towering buildings that formed downtown LA, knowing that they could be literally anywhere. I was so mad at myself, I wanted to scream.

I knew we should have dumped the car and gotten off the highway as soon as we'd heard the news bulletin.

Instead, here we were out in the open, vulnerable and exposed. Sitting ducks. I waited for the police to say something, and insist we give up, but their only reply was to fire at us.

Bullets thundered overhead, exploding everything they touched. I ducked, covering my hands over my head. Doc couldn't do the same though. She had to keep driving, keep us moving, or we'd be dust for sure. Beads of sweat flew off her face as she hunched as low as she could while still driving.

The civilian car to one side of us screeched to a halt while the other car careened into a lamppost. Smoke billowed from the engine, filling the air. The driver looked out of his window, dazed and confused, a trickle of blood from a nasty gash on his face running down his cheek.

"They can't be real police," I said incredulously. "They wouldn't shoot first. They wouldn't risk civilian casualties."

"They think we're dangerous terrorists, so maybe they would. We've no real way of knowing. I need to get us out of here!"

Doc slammed her foot on the gas. The car shot forward so fast I snapped my head on the back of the headrest. We sped forward, weaving between the now stationary cars littering the street as terrified faces watched from the shadows of their cars.

I hung onto the door handle with all my strength, feeling the metal strain under my fingers as our car scraped against another. The deafening sound of metal on metal filled the air, sending sparks flying and causing my heart to race in fear.

"Bandit! You and Pixie hold on back there!"

I heard his whine of terror as the left side of our car struck a Toyota, snapping off the mirror which flew off behind us, landing on the ground below, where it was immediately crushed by one of the pursuing police cruisers.

I spared a glance at the men chasing us and was immediately struck by their lack of animation. All wore serious expressions, but none of them were speaking. Not even a word.

They weren't the real police: they couldn't be.

Real police would have been speaking into a radio, calling for more backup, describing the surrounding chaos. Their priorities would have been twofold: not only to capture us but to keep the public safe.

But not these guys.

These men had to be cleaners like Smith.

And they didn't care if they killed us in full view of the public. I suddenly understood the reason for the news bulletin now: it gave them the perfect excuse to shoot first. By the time the questions came, they would be long gone.

Doc floored it past several stopped cars when I saw an intersection fast approaching. Our lights were amber, but they were about to turn red.

And we were going way too fast to stop.

The blood drained from Doc's face. "Hold on, this is going to be rough."

Instead of slowing down, she slammed her foot on the gas all the way to the floor.

We shot forward so fast that everything became a blur. Just as on that first day when I had met Bandit when he had saved my life at the edge of the road, details suddenly came at me in slow motion.

Like how the family in a station wagon on one side of us had a young boy whose face was pressed up against the window as he watched us, wide-eyed. Our lights flashed to red as the other lanes began moving across. Either they hadn't seen us or they hadn't been paying attention, but when they started moving, we were already hurtling toward them.

Suddenly, a car shot ahead faster than the rest. It was another police cruiser. And they were coming straight for us.

"I can't get past them..."

I heard Doc say before our world exploded.

The other car smashed into our own, somehow ramping off us and flipping upside down, before exploding into a ball of fire. Our SUV slammed to a juddering halt. The impact jolted me forward and I would have hit my head on the dashboard if the airbag hadn't deployed.

My face slammed into it, burning from the contact.

It might have saved my life, but it didn't stop it from hurting like crazy. I think my tooth went through my lip as I tasted blood in my mouth. I tested my teeth with my tongue until I felt one of them move, loosened by the impact.

For a few moments, I couldn't do anything. There was only that burning pain on my face and the world spinning. I could hear screaming, the general confusion of a disaster, but it all swelled into one great noise.

I waited in terror, hoping for my senses to come back to me — and fast. We had to get away, as we weren't safe here. Lifting my head from the airbag, I attempted to turn my head. Pain hit, my muscles screaming at me, but that fact that I could turn it, I knew no bones were broken.

Not up top, anyway.

Turning all the way to my left, I saw Doc's own airbag had saved her life. She wasn't as out of it as I was, however, already reaching into the glove compartment for some kind of knife that she jabbed into her airbag, before turning it on her seatbelt, which was locked tight. Her hands sawed back and forth in a frantic motion as she started to cut through it.

"You okay?" she asked in a dazed tone.

"I think so."

"Bandit? Pixie? What about you guys?" she asked of the backseat.

We heard a low toned "WOOF!" followed by a higher pitched one. Their barks were shaky, but at least he and Pixie were safe.

"Can you get out of your seat?" Doc asked me.

Reaching over, pain shot up my side. I think I must have banged it pretty badly in the collision. Gingerly, I felt it with my fingers, but when I couldn't feel a wound or blood, I counted myself lucky. I found my seat belt and unclipped it. Bandit popped up in the space beside me and licked my face.

"I'm okay, buddy," I assured him. "But we need to get out of here."

There was utter chaos outside. We weren't the only cars who had crashed. Cars on either side and behind us had collided into each other. There must have been at least twelve vehicles affected. Maybe even more. The two cops inside the overturned car — whether they were real or not — were not moving. I was pretty sure both of them were dead.

I didn't have time to concern myself with that though: we still had four remaining cars after us. From the corners of my eyes, I saw the dark navy-clad figures climbing out of their cars, stone cold eyes fixed on us. They were coming toward us when they were suddenly swamped by terrified civilians, grabbing hold of them.

One woman asked, "What's happened?"

Another, "Is this a terrorist attack?"

Faced with a panicked public, the eight men — the fake police — didn't know what to do. They tried shaking them off only for more to take their place. They could not reach us through the throng of people that surrounded them.

"We need to go now!"

Opening my door, I slid out as Doc did the same. Reaching over, I opened the back door. Bandit and Pixie shot out. Together, the four of us bolted across the street.

60

CHASE

Casting a quick glance over my shoulder, I could see the determined fake officers still hot on our trail. They were struggling to navigate through the panicked and frazzled crowd in their efforts to catch up to us. But we were already several steps ahead, weaving through the chaos and gaining ground with each passing second.

We sprinted down the bustling street, our feet pounding against the pavement as we turned into a quaint business block. In the center, a charming courtyard greeted us with its lively atmosphere. The air was filled with the sweet scent of climbing roses, their vibrant blooms weaving around a white wooden gazebo that stood proudly in the middle. Several benches were scattered around the gazebo, positioned perfectly to offer a picturesque view of the surrounding area. On any other day, I would have taken a moment to admire the beauty of this place. Instead, we ran right past and kept going. Doc pointed to an opening on the left.

"This way."

We emerged from the block to be met with six lanes of traffic stretching endlessly in both directions. My heart sank as I frantically scanned for a pedestrian crossing. Didn't people walk in LA? How were you supposed to get to the other side?

The sound of approaching sirens spurred us on, knowing that at any moment the cops would be on us. Still, attempting to cross this street would definitely result in an injury, or even worse, death. For sure, we'd draw an awful lot of attention our way by trying to. Neither option was particularly wanted. With no transportation or taxis in sight, panic bubbled up inside me. Had we come this far only to lose out to *traffic*?

Was this really where our story was going to end?

Bandit limped to my side, favoring his right paw. His stride was slower than normal and a little hesitant, his normally wagging tail held low and still. I could see the worry and concern in his big green eyes as he looked up at me.

Meanwhile, Doc gingerly held her left arm, her face twisted in discomfort. She winced with every step, but refused to let go of her determined expression. Despite their injuries, they both seemed laser focused on finding a solution to our predicament. The mid-afternoon sun shone down on us, casting a warm, yellow glow over our tense group. Every honk of a car or rustle of a leaf made our hearts race as we searched desperately for a way out.

"We need transport," Doc said through gritted teeth.

I was about to suggest we continue on down the street when I caught sight of one of those Hollywood tour buses idling just a block away. A line of elderly Japanese tourists, their sun-kissed skin and vibrant outfits standing out against the muted buildings, were eagerly lining up to climb aboard the bus. Each carried a camera as if it were an extension of their arm.

"There! The tour bus! Hurry!"

We ran for it, moving as fast as we could. The dogs got there first — even with Bandit's limp — and stood, pawing the ground in agitation until Doc and I finally caught up.

A chorus of polite smiles greeted us as we hopped onto the crowded bus. They even nodding a greeting to the dogs. We searched for an empty seat and finally settled in, maneuvering ourselves away from the windows while the dogs hid themselves between our legs. A bell chimed and then we were off. I didn't let myself breathe until the bus started moving away.

"Are they coming?" Doc whispered to me.

I shot a quick glance behind us. "Not yet. I think we're okay."

The words were barely out of my mouth when a looming shadow fell over us. My shoulders tensed for the inevitable confrontation.

"Is there a problem here?" The question had come from the ticket collector. Half of his face was covered by a thick gray beard. His eyes, lined with wrinkles and twinkling with kindness, reminded me of Father Christmas somehow. Despite his elaborate uniform and the old-fashioned ticket machine strapped to his chest, he exuded an air of warmth and approachability.

"Er... yeah? Why?" I asked, adopting my most confused expression.

"You look like you've been through the wars," the conductor remarked, his kind gaze lingering over our disheveled appearance. I could feel my cheeks heating up as I shifted uncomfortably under his gaze. Before Doc could speak, I jumped in with a reply.

"We're fine. Our car broke down on the way here and we tried to fix it, but you know, we have no idea what we're doing. We just don't want to be late for the taping. We waited months for these tickets, so obviously everything that could go wrong today, has. We're just hoping we'll be able to get to the studio on time."

The conductor's brows furrowed, creating deep creases in his forehead as he stared at us with a puzzled expression. His eyes darted back and forth between us, clearly unsure whether to believe our story or not. The tension in the air was palpable as we waited for his response.

"We go past a few of them. It is LA after all."

"That's perfect," I said, hoping he would leave us alone. But he continued to stand there, staring at us, as if he were psychically trying to beam his thoughts into our heads. It took a few moments before I realized why he wasn't leaving. Turning to Doc, I nudged her gently.

"Hey Mom, we need to pay the guy."

Doc blinked, nodding in embarrassment, catching onto my lie, quickly.

"Of course. Sorry about that. Don't know where my head is these days."

She rummaged through her bag, which miraculously made it out of our crash with us, and paid for the tickets. Once the money changed hands, there was no reason for him to hang around any longer. Apparently buying our story, the conductor moved away as we sat back and allowed ourselves a moment to catch our breaths.

61

SULLY

The air was thick with tension, a blanket of unease that hung over us like a storm cloud. It wasn't all due to our concern for Gideon and Emma's safety — there was something between Sam and I that needed to be addressed.

We'd been going for an hour or so, yet Sam had barely said two words to me since we'd left the others. Her usually warm demeanor had been replaced by a cool, distant edge. I knew we needed to thrash out whatever was on her mind and it seemed like now was the time to do it, before all hell broke loose when we finally caught up to Gideon. I took a deep breath and spoke cautiously, hoping my approach would soften her defenses.

"I didn't say the right thing earlier," I started, choosing my words carefully.

"Oh? When you accused me of letting my emotions cloud my judgment about Emma?" Sam retorted with a raised eyebrow. "You know how I love being told how I feel by a man."

I sank further into my seat, immediately regretting that I'd brought anything up at all. We were on dangerous, dangerous territory here.

"That's not what I meant. I meant it in another way."

Her blonde brow arched even higher. "What other way is there?"

"Just that... It's obvious there has been tension between the two of you..."

"What I'd love to know," Sam interrupted me sharply, "is how you would feel if my ex, the love of my life who I had grieved for a solid year, returned out of the blue and you were forced to spend every waking hour with him? Would you still think I was overreacting then?"

I fell silent, knowing there wasn't much I could say in response. But before I could even attempt to offer an apology or explanation, Sam continued.

"Come on, Sully! Give me some credit. I'm not a jealous little girl who can't take the added competition. I am your *wife,* who you swore to love for the rest of your life. But now I'm starting to wonder if that's true, especially when you seem more concerned about Emma than Gideon."

"That's not true. I'm just worried about her in a different way. Gideon is more than able to handle himself."

"But he's out of his mind now, Sully! He's so lost, he's actually convinced himself that Zeb can be brought back to life. I know Emma needs help too — especially after what we've learned today — but she isn't as delicate as he is right now. Gideon is the one we need to be concerned with."

She stopped to catch her breath, hands gripping the wheel so tightly I thought it would break.

"I understand that, Sam, but Emma doesn't know about the world. She didn't even know how to peel a carrot for crying out loud! How do you think she'll cope going up against a team of Smith's men? She's completely vulnerable."

Sam squeezed her eyes shut for a moment, thinking long and hard before she spoke again.

"We're obviously not getting anywhere with this so just answer me this: if this Emma *had* been your Emma, if she wasn't a clone at all but the real thing, what would you do? Would you go back to her?"

It was such a loaded question that I didn't answer straight away. Images of the two fought for attention as a movie of our greatest hits played in my mind. I saw Emma's radiant smile on our wedding day, surrounded by family and friends. Even some of our dearest animal clients and their fur-parents had turned up to shower us with love, as rice rained down upon her, mingling with her happy tears. Florence, alive and thriving and wearing another one of those stiff cotton dresses she habitually wore, had stood next to Mark, beaming with joy.

The movie changed then, bringing me to the day I first met Sam, and she had given us a ride to my dad. I could still hear her singing with unabashed gusto, filling the truck with music and laughter. She was a breath of fresh air and a healing balm to the pain that had consumed me for an entire year. Both sets of memories flooded me with emotion, making it difficult to form words. I opened my mouth to answer when my eyes caught the familiar sight of our RV ahead of us.

My mind became a swirling collage of memories, each one fighting for attention like scenes from a movie playing in my mind. First, I saw Emma's beaming smile as she walked down the aisle on our wedding day, surrounded by our loved ones and showered with rice. The happiness radiating from her was almost blinding. Then, the movie shifted to Florence standing next to Mark, tears streaming down her face with pure joy. The love and support from our friends and family on that day was something I would never forget.

But then, just like a film reel changing scenes, I was transported to the day I first met Sam. She had given us a ride and her infectious laughter and singing had filled the truck with warmth and light. She was a breath of fresh air and a healing balm to the pain that had consumed me for an entire year. Both sets of memories flooded me with emotion, making it difficult to form words. I closed my eyes and took a deep breath, willing the confusing memories to fade away. After a moment, they began to dissipate, leaving behind only a lingering ache in my heart.

I opened my mouth to answer when my eyes caught the familiar sight of our RV ahead of us. "There they are!"

Relief surged through me, momentarily pushing aside our conversation. Sam sprang into action beside me, disregarding any potential onlookers as she frantically flashed the lights as we raced towards the RV.

As the motorhome came into view, I noticed it suddenly picking up speed. In that split second, I knew Gideon must be behind the wheel. Had it been the Cleaner driving, I was pretty certain we would have had a different outcome. I derived some small joy from this fact.

"Hold on tight," Sam warned me, but I had already braced myself against the car.

I said a quick prayer of thanks for the mostly empty road ahead of us as Sam jammed her foot on the gas and we shot forward like a rocket. The wind whipped through my hair and stung my cheeks as we barreled past the RV, Sam expertly yanking the wheel to cut him off. Her hand slammed down on the horn in a deafening blast, drowning out any other sound on the road. But in that moment, neither of us cared about being loud or causing a scene; all that mattered was stopping Gideon.

As our car now led the way, Sam started easing up on the gas. Either Gideon was going to slow his roll, or we were going to crash.

He played chicken with us, his pale face staring out at us grimly in the side mirrors. It broke my heart to see how young he suddenly looked, barely old enough to drive, let alone endure everything he had in the last twenty-four hours.

Sam's eyes flicked nervously to the speedometer, watching as the needle sank lower and lower. We were inching closer and closer to the back of the RV, but Gideon showed no signs of relenting. The tension in the car was palpable as we braced ourselves for impact, uncertain of what would happen next.

"I sure hope you know what you're doing," I said.

"You're not the only one."

I held on grimly, my knuckles turning white from the sheer force of my grip, desperately hoping that he would come to his senses and stop the RV before we all died, but Gideon seemed determined to continue driving the RV at breakneck speed. Finally, just as our bumper nudged into the front of the RV, Gideon slammed on the brakes. The RV came to a screeching halt, grazing the back of our car.

My body flung forward, but I managed to catch myself before I could be thrown out of the car. Heart racing, I leaped out of the car and ran towards the RV, adrenaline coursing through my veins. My hands shook as I tried to open the door, but it was locked tight. My foot lashed at it, unable to contain myself any longer.

"Open this door Gideon or I'll break it down!" I yelled. "So help me God, I absolutely will!"

Beside me, Sam unclipped her gun from her holster and held it at the ready.

"You have a count of three before I shoot the lock off this door, Gideon. It's up to you," Sam called out, cool as a cucumber. Despite the anger and frustration that had consumed her just moments ago, she remained calm and collected. The ensuing silence that greeted us was in stark contrast to the deafening noise we'd just experienced. Widening her stance, shoulder-width apart, prepared to make good on her promise, Sam began counting.

"One..."

There was no response.

"Two..."

Her voice grew louder, a hint of strain toward the end of the callout. Only the slightest wobble of her gun-wielding hands showed the toll this was taking. She opened her mouth to say 'three' when a familiar voice called from inside.

"I'm opening the door. Don't shoot!"

At last, the door finally swung open as Gideon's tear-streaked faced looked back at us. His panicked eyes darted between Sam's gun and Smith, who was still tied up and had been moved back by the table again, but he was clearly alive.

"You have to let me do this! It's the only way we can save him!"

I pushed past Gideon, entering the RV. The bedroom door was closed. All was unnaturally quiet within, which caused my heart to freeze in my chest.

I crossed the RV in four short strides, flinging open the bedroom door to find Emma on the bed, bound and gagged. I ripped the gag off her mouth as Emma shot up onto her knees, completely outraged.

"It's about time you got here! That boy tied me up and stopped me from speaking! He wanted to give me to the bad guys, can you believe that? He needs to be punished, Sully!"

As much as I shared Emma's anger at how she had been treated, I knew that wasn't the answer. I untied her bonds.

"I'm sorry," I said sincerely. "Just wait here. I'll handle this."

As soon as her hands were free, she squirmed away from me and rubbed her sore wrists.

"I've seen where your leadership, or whatever you call it, has gotten us," she spat out. "These kids don't respect you. Nobody listens to you, so why should I? I'm going to handle this myself," Emma pushed past me towards the door.

I stepped in her way, blocking her path.

"I understand your frustration, but punishment is the last thing he needs right now. Zeb took him in when Gideon's own family threw him out. It wasn't until he lived with Zeb that he learned what it feels like to have people who loved and cared about him. He just lost the one person in the world who he loves the most, and this is his way of trying to deal with it. It's not great, I know, but that's all he's doing. Let me talk to him. I think I can get through to him. Let me talk to him before you go charging out there."

My gentle but insistent plea had taken the wind right out of her sails. I knew it the moment her eyes softened. "Okay," she said quietly. "But if he doesn't appreciate that what he did was wrong, I get to punish him after."

I didn't respond, but instead turned and left the room, shutting the door behind me. As I walked down the hallway, I couldn't help but feel the weight of Emma's words and their implications for Gideon. Inside the living area, Sam put her gun away and bit her lip in her effort not to cry over how distraught Gideon was. She pulled him into a tight hug, offering comfort in any way she could.

I knew I couldn't wait any longer. It was time for the conversation that the rest of us had already had without him.

"Gid, I know how torn up you are over this. God knows we all loved him, but you need to realize that nothing can bring him back, and before you say anything, Elora has already confirmed that it isn't possible to bring someone back from the dead. That means no one can bring Dad back."

Gideon's gaze drifted past me to the bedroom door. "But Emma—"

"Elora received some results from her tests last night... We now know that Emma is a clone. We think she must have been the result of the experiment Xavier had bragged about to us."

I could see Gideon's eyes glaze over. I wasn't sure if he was taking any of this in.

"Do you understand, Gideon? Emma is not the real thing, no matter how close she may seem. There is nothing that can bring dead people back, and I need you to hear me right now. What you are doing here is incredibly dangerous and foolish."

Gideon's face began to crumple as the words started to sink in. The realization slowly grew until he broke down into tears. He dropped his eyes to the ground as shame washed over him. "Does she know? Have you told her?"

"I'm waiting until we get back to Elora. Emma might be a clone but she is still a human being with feelings, so this is going to come as a shock to her. We're going to need to do this the right way.,

His head nodded in a slow, tired movement as he wiped the tears from his face with the back of his hand. Gradually, it dawned on him that we were a few people short. "Where are Chase and Bandit? Are they still at the Doc's?"

Sam and I exchanged a glance, wondering how to break the news to him gently.

"The thing is," I began hesitantly, "when you took off like that, you left both Elora and all the dogs she had rehired, vulnerable, so they couldn't stay there anymore. It wasn't safe."

A pained expression crossed his face as he realized the consequences of his actions. My heart ached for him.

"But Chase came up with a plan," Sam interjected, trying to offer some semblance of hope. "We think it might be the only way to keep us from having to run ever again."

His eyes widened with apprehension as he stared at the two of us. "What plan?"

I opened Elora's iPad.

"It's probably easier if I show you." As I logged onto the news channel, my heart raced with anticipation and fear. I prayed that everything had gone according to schedule, but my hopes were crushed as the footage revealed a harrowing incident unfolding in LA. Police cars screeched through the city streets, their sirens wailing in a desperate attempt to catch the terrorists wreaking havoc. My finger trembled as it moved across the screen, trying to switch to another channel for some glimmer of good news. But my stomach dropped when the faces of the terrorists appeared on the screen. And then I saw our own faces staring back at us.

"That's us." Gideon grasped.

Sam leaned in to get a better look at the screen, her expression growing dark with concern as she processed the shocking news. "I think they're saying it was Chase who caused that accident."

My mind couldn't fully comprehend what was happening as I watched the devastation unfold before my eyes. It felt like an out-of-body experience, like I wasn't really part of it all.

People huddled on the sidewalk, blood pouring from their wounds. Smoke billowed from an overturned squad car. Emergency services rushed to help those injured, but it seemed like there were too many victims and not enough hands to save them all.

This was not part of the plan at all.

"Jesus, what the hell is going on?"

62

CHASE

One of the tourists looked our way. The fifth by my rapidly growing count.

If it wasn't for the admiring looks they sent Pixie and Bandit, I would be jumping out of the nearest exit.

They were just being polite. I could see it in the friendly smiles they gave us. Normally, I would have let Bandit charm them with a few simple tricks — nothing crazy, a simple high-five or a beg, the kind that the average dog would know — but since we couldn't afford to attract any more attention to ourselves, we'd have to do away with the niceties today.

I looked out the window, but instead of the view, all I could see was Doc's pale visage reflected in the glass. She cradled her left arm gingerly, wincing in pain every so often and supporting it with her other hand. I wasn't sure what was wrong with it, but the pain that flashed over her face was a cause of concern.

In an attempt to help, I unhooked the leather belt I wore with my jeans. I looped the end of it together and offered it to her. "It's not much, but the leather's soft. You can rest your arm in it."

A grateful smile lit up her face as she took the belt from me. "Thanks."

She struggled to pull the belt over her head, but a sharp breath of pain forced her to stop. I gently took the belt from her and arranged it so that the flat side lay against her neck. With careful movements, I helped her arm through the loop until it sat snugly against her body. It wasn't much of a sling, but it would do in a pinch.

"It might be broken," she explained, wincing in pain. "I have some painkillers in my bag. Can you help me with them?"

"Of course," I replied, searching through her neatly organized bag. Everything had its own place, making it easy to find the pills. Fishing them out, I handed them to her. She swallowed them dry, waiting for the effect to take hold when the sound of an approaching helicopter caused my blood to turn to ice.

Cupping a hand over my head as if to block out the sun (instead of obscuring my face), I searched the sky, only to locate the black and white helicopter almost immediately. It was close, maybe only a few blocks away.

"LAPD" was painted onto the side of the helicopter in bold black lettering, though from recent experience, I knew that didn't mean a thing. Further away, my gaze landed on another one, circling above a different part of town. My heart sank as I spotted more black specks in the distance.

Whether they were the real police or Smith's men, the air support was all for us. The deafening roar of the helicopters overhead drowned out any other sounds, causing my heart to race and my hands to tremble. I felt a clammy hand grab hold of mine. Doc's panic mirrored my own, and we both moved as far from the window as possible, fighting the irrational urge to flee. The only chance we had was if we were smart and didn't act on our instinct to run. We couldn't draw any more attention to ourselves.

Hunkering down, we sat, tense as all hell, hoping that a bullet wasn't going to come flying through the window at us.

Amidst the chaos, the bright and bubbly voice of our pre-recorded "tour guide" sounded over the speakers from every corner of the bus. As we passed famous landmarks, she regaled us with stories that were meant to be entertaining, though I found myself flinching from her fake cheerful air. Her facts were ridiculous too, amounting to no more than general gossip at times though I welcomed the inane chatter. At least it drowned out some of those helicopter blades which seemed to be getting closer and closer.

I was more than relieved when the ticket conductor finally called out, "Last stop, folks."

Exhausted and on edge, there were only a few of us left on the bus now, most of the tourists having left already. I looked up at the giant sign that loomed above me with just two words and that iconic logo: UNIVERSAL CITY. A shiver of apprehension ran down my spine.

This was it.

For better or worse, this was where everything would change for the rest of our possibly very short lives.

Climbing off the bus, I could feel the ticket man's eyes on us. Although every instinct told me to avoid eye contact, I forced myself to smile at him. Even managing a wave with a sunny, "Have a good day."

If he did recognize us, I wanted to make it as difficult for him to report us to the cops as possible. We entered the theme park, blending in with the crowd of colorful tourists and enthusiastic families. The scent of popcorn and cotton candy filled the air, mixed with screams from roller coasters and the distant sound of carnival music. We headed towards one of many ticket booths, relieved to see that there wasn't much of a line at this time of day since most visitors would come earlier in order to get the most bang for their buck. There were actually more people peddling toys and souvenirs than there were paying customers at this point.

I stopped by one of them, picking up two baseball caps with the Universal logo. Doc paid for them without question, instinctively knowing why I had wanted them. Once they were on, they shielded half of our faces and made us seem like every other thrill seeker.

We had paid for two tickets and were just passing through the barricade when the ticket seller, a pimply guy in his twenties with an earnest expression and a terrible man-bun, saw Bandit and Pixie by our feet.

"Dogs are only allowed in specific areas. Please familiarize yourself with those areas in the leaflet I've just given you."

Doc smiled at him. "Don't worry, we're not taking them anywhere they shouldn't be."

The seller looked down his long nose at us, lording his power. I would have loved to have put him in his place, but bit down on my lip instead. After some deliberation, the barricades rose, and we were in. Ignoring the colorful array of entertainment, I poured over the map.

"This way."

We hurried past numerous food stalls lining the street. Tantalizing aromas flew my way, causing my stomach to rumble, but to my credit, I didn't look at their wares, not even once. It was strange that even at this moment, with all the uncertainty and terror, my body could still crave food. Guess I must be what they call an emotional eater.

Excited children tore around the place, bouncing from one sight to another while their long-suffering parents followed behind, arms loaded with brightly colored balloons and soft toys.

Everywhere I looked, there were people. Above, glinting security cameras documented our every move, their presence making the hairs on the back of my neck permanently stand on end. We were like sheep walking into the lion's den, completely exposed and vulnerable. I thought for sure that at any moment an army of security guards would surround us, but somehow, we made it to our destination without drawing any attention to ourselves.

The rectangular beige building was only a few stories high, but what it lacked in height, it made up for in length, reaching several blocks long.

Three colorful letters stood over the glass entry doors, "NBC", followed by the smaller worded "Studios."

Knowing what this represented, I felt the first flush of excitement, only for it to be immediately dampened when I saw the fortress of metal detectors and X-ray machines lined up before me. The guards standing diligently at their posts added to the air of security that surrounded the area. It was like a maze of safety precautions, designed to keep out any potential threats — including us.

"You don't have a weapon, do you?" I asked the Doc.

She shook her head. "Of course not... but I'm not liking the thought of going through all that security."

Bandit chuffed, letting us know he was in agreement. He pawed the ground, gesturing at a small sign for the parking lot.

"Good idea," I congratulated him.

The four of us hurried over to the parking lot, where we were met with two lanes of traffic entering and exiting the studio. Each lane was blocked off by sturdy barricades and manned by a guard inside a booth. The lane furthest from us was currently dealing with a group of rowdy college students, while the other lane's guard had a clear view of anyone approaching too closely.

Still, this was our best chance of getting inside. I turned to Bandit. "I need you to draw that guy's attention so the rest of us can sneak past him."

Bandit nodded, crouching low to wait for further instructions. I was suddenly hit by a burst of love so strong that it could have knocked me down.

Walking through the streets of New York on my own, struggling to find food and shelter every single day, I had written off the rest of my life. As far as I was concerned, I was destined to be on my own forever. I would never know what it felt like for someone to have my back, much less, love me. I fully expected to go to sleep one night in a disgusting, roach-infested alley, only for it to be my last.

Then Bandit had appeared in my life.

A skinny mutt who had been just as desperate and alone as I was.

We hadn't known then how much our lives would change or how we would need each other. Somehow, he, and the rest of the gang had become my family and if we were to have any chance of living the rest of our lives in safety, this had to be done, no matter how terrifying I found it.

With precision timing, we waited until no cars were coming down either lane before making our move. Bandit confidently strolled up to the guard's cubicle, his scrappy fur standing on end as he bravely faced the imposing figure behind the glass. My heart raced with fear as he approached.

The rest of us stole toward the building, hugging the shadows and keeping low until Bandit's arrival drew the guard's attention. He turned his back on the barricade as the three of us crept inside. We half ran, half crouched and hid behind a parked car.

"Hey fella, what are you doing here?"

Bandit whined convincingly, holding up a paw. The guard must have been an animal lover, as he understood what the deal was immediately. "Did you hurt yourself?"

Even though the guard didn't speak our shorthand, Bandit barked yes, then threw in another heart-wrenching whine. The guard's face softened. He reached down to stroke him earning a tail thump in response.

"You are the loveliest thing, aren't you? You stay right there and I'll get you help." Turning away from Bandit, he picked up a phone that hung on the wall of the booth and pushed a button. He spoke into the handset, just loud enough for me to hear.

"I've got an injured dog here. He seems friendly and possibly someone's pet. Can you send someone to collect him and check if any of our families are missing a dog?"

I had no idea what the other person said, but by the time the guard turned back to Bandit, he had already vanished back to my side.

63

CHASE

The sound of our footsteps reverberated off the concrete walls of the dimly lit parking lot. Despite the sun's brightness outside, it seemed to have no effect on this cavernous space. We walked within the shadows, making our way to the studio building only to reach another obstacle.

The doors that led inside could only be opened with the right pass and since we hadn't come via a car, we didn't have one. So, we hung around outside, pretending to be on a call (Doc was using her wallet since we didn't even have a cell phone on us), while I made a show of entertaining the dogs.

Just a forgetful mom trying to contact her husband to let her in.

Our luck changed when a family of six finally approached. They thought nothing of letting us inside, even holding the doors open for us. If I were criminally inclined, a mother, daughter and their dogs tag-team seemed like it could really do some damage.

No doubt Sam would have something to say about that.

The grand lobby welcomed us with long, regal corridors, each lined with elegant purple doors. These doors branched off into separate wings, leading to different stages that housed their own unique productions. The air was electric with excitement and anticipation as I scanned the walls, admiring the framed photographs of famous faces who had graced these halls over the years — actors, musicians, and celebrities all captured in moments of fame and glory.

When I passed by my mom's favorite actor, a rush of bittersweet emotions washed over me. She had always been addicted to daytime talk shows and soaps, and would have gotten such a kick out of being here.

Pushing her face from my mind, I ran through the plan one last time.

I had come up with the idea this morning when, in between the madness, I had noticed Good Morning America in the background. I knew that if we could just get Bandit onto one of those news shows, the world would have to listen to us. He would show everyone how special he was and what he could do. It would be undeniable and if everyone in the world knew our story, there would be no point in anyone coming after us.

The Smiths, Xaviers, and any others like them wouldn't be a threat anymore. As long as we could get in front of the cameras, we'd be able to convince the world that we deserved to be left alone. Maybe even protected.

That was my plan, anyway, and I was sticking with it.

One of the purple doors opened beside me as a harassed-looking production assistant burst out from behind it, almost crashing into us in his haste. His face was flushed, and he held a clipboard with well-thumbed through pages in one hand, while balancing a cup full of something hot in the other.

"Sorry!" He called over his shoulder at whoever was inside the room, then, activating the radio that sat in his shirt pocket, he talked, speaking faster than I'd ever heard someone speak.

"He wanted green tea, not black!" The urgency in his voice managed to make it sound life or death. Without another word, he hurried down the corridor, apparently to rectify the crime. I chased after him, tapping him on the shoulder, when he finally slowed down enough for me to catch up.

"Excuse me. Can you tell me which stage Good Morning America is being filmed on?" I asked, breathless from the unexpected sprint.

He turned to me, irritation evident in every line of his face. "Is that a joke?"

Confused by his hostile reaction, I blinked at him and shook my head. "No... I genuinely want to know."

He let out an exasperated sigh before replying. "The show's filmed in New York. Plus, it's already the middle of the afternoon. You'd be far too late for a recording even if they were filming here." With a final huff of annoyance, he spun on his heels, jogging away, not caring that he was spilling some of that black tea onto the polished floor. I stood there, rooted to the spot, feeling sick to my stomach.

"I should have checked where the show is made before rushing us out here. I can't believe we put our lives at so much risk for this!"

How could I have done this to us? You stupid, stupid girl! My thoughts berated me, each syllable a harsh lash against my conscience.

As if he knew what I was doing to myself, Bandit stepped over a puddle of tea and pressed against me to offer his comfort, putting a stop to my inner diatribe. Pixie raised her face upward to me and whined in support as Doc's calm eyes stared at me, cutting through my panic.

"It doesn't have to be that show, Chase. Any show will do so long as it's being broadcast live. That's what we've got to look for, a live broadcast."

Her words were like a lifeline, pulling me out from the depths of panic. My heart relaxed a beat, knowing she was right.

"Come on."

Giving me a gentle nudge, Doc took off at a fast pace. Following her lead, we moved quickly through the twisting beige corridors that matched its equally beige exterior. Signs flashed overhead with bright letters spelling out SILENCE, letting us know that a show was currently being recorded inside. Every door had a simple notice beside it, listing the production currently underway.

Each of the doors bore a small glass panel that I could look through. One stage contained the cozy interior of a popular coffee shop, complete with wooden tables, wide sofas, and steaming mugs of coffee. Another held an impressive replica of an apartment with a plant-filled outdoor balcony overlooking the bustling cityscape. But the most mesmerizing stage was the one that housed a snow-covered forest, its trees glistening with frost and icicles hanging from their branches.

It was wild how lifelike everything seemed, as if I could step through the door and be transported into a whole new world.

It was only when I passed by that the illusion was shattered when viewed from another angle — the seams and supports of the set were visible, but that was the magic of Hollywood I guess. Nothing was ever how it seemed.

As we continued on, my heart raced with excitement and fear. The names of several shows that Gideon and I enjoyed flickered past, but I had to push away the thought that I might never see his face again. Sully and Sam were on a mission to find us, and since they had no way of reaching us, I had to trust that they would be successful.

Any other outcome was unthinkable.

We were still searching for a suitable show when Doc stopped in front of a wall, her eyes sparkling with hope as she read the signage. She turned to me with a grin.

"Stage Eight," she said breathlessly. "That's where we're going!"

"What do they film there?"

"Entertainment Now News!"

I felt light-headed with relief. It was the perfect solution, one that I had been hoping for. EN News was always on and it had its own dedicated channel, making it the ideal place to broadcast our message.

Following the signs, we headed towards stage eight. The illuminated sign above the door read ON AIR. I swallowed my fear as I grasped the handle and turned it, half expecting it to be locked. To my surprise, the door swung open easily, and we hurried inside.

Compared to the other stages we had seen so far, this one was much smaller. In front of us were two EN anchors, a man in his late thirties with slicked black hair and designer stubble. His co-anchor was a blonde with impossibly glossy hair and a soft, appealing voice. Behind them, a large screen displayed a freeze frame of a famous actress from her latest monster movie that was currently taking the world by storm.

The set was buzzing with energy as three bulky cameras recorded the anchors' every move, each manned by a skilled cameraman. A few additional crew members scurried around frantically, checking equipment and gathering cables, while a makeup artist stood off to the side with brushes and tubes poking out from her utility belt.

Other than this handful of people, I was surprised that no one else was here. I had expected there to be far more people involved in producing a live news segment. Psyching myself up, I looked at the others.

"Are you guys ready for this?" I asked, my voice shaky with anticipation.

Bandit nodded confidently, while Pixie jumped up and down with excitement. In the back of my mind, I heard Sully comment that small dogs were always the bounciest. The flashback down memory lane felt like a knife in the heart when my twisted mind taunted me with the cruel thought that I might never hear his voice again. Doc shot me a tentative smile, cutting into my thoughts, looking just as apprehensive as I felt.

"Lead the way."

I swallowed the dry lump in my throat. Trying not to lose my nerve, I marched straight towards the EN anchors.

64

CHASE

As the male anchor, whose name was Marko, continued to deliver his lines with practiced ease, his bright smile faltered for just a second when he caught sight of me. His eyes widened before quickly returning to their professional gaze, never missing a beat. It wasn't until Bandit, Doc, and Pixie stepped directly into a spotlight that the rest of the crew even seemed to take notice.

Marko's voice cut off abruptly as he turned towards us, his attention now fully on our unexpected presence. "I'm sorry for the interruption, but we seem to have a situation here."

The crew turned toward us and I was met with a sea of blank faces. Nobody knew what to do. It was the perfect moment to seize the opportunity. I could feel all eyes on me as I stepped forward into the light. Keeping my voice calm and strong, I spoke.

"I need you all to listen to me. This is really important."

The two hosts exchanged a confused look, neither of them seeming too alarmed by our sudden appearance. I guess a girl, a woman, and their two dogs weren't particularly threatening. Ignoring me completely, Marko spoke over my head to someone in the blackness behind me.

"Is this some kind of joke or are we letting random people walk onto the set now?" His co-host, whose name I now remembered as Alicia, started to rise from her seat, clearly flustered by the unexpected turn of events.

"Where's Lucian? Cut the feed."

Here's a thing you should know about me. Aside from my mouth loving to shoot off without me thinking, there are few things I hate most in this world than to not being taken seriously. Whether it was because I was young or a girl, poor or from a trailer park, ignoring me was a surefire to earn my ire.

"Do not cut the feed! This is not a joke!" I demanded, my voice rising above the chatter in the studio. "Haven't you heard about the dangerous terrorist cell in LA? They're talking about us! Look at me. Turn the cameras on me."

I yanked off my hat with Doc following suit. Marko looked at me like I was insane, but his cohost's eyes suddenly turned wary. She pointed a finger at me, polished nails glinting in the light, and took cover behind Marko, using his body as a shield.

"She and that dog do match the description. Can anyone pull up the alert?"

An aide came running onto the set with their phone in hand, and I got a caught a glimpse of my own mug shot on the screen when they passed by. Alicia sat back down as Marko's face drained of all color.

"You heard what she said. Turn the cameras on her."

Staring into the giant black lens of the camera, I felt horribly vulnerable and had to lean into Bandit for strength. He nuzzled my hand, helping me to gain some command of myself.

"My name is Chase Ryder and I am not a terrorist. Neither are any of the people shown in those images. They are my family. We are innocent." I ran my tongue over my parched lips before speaking again.

"We are not terrorists, but there are people who are after my family right now. They are the ones who are feeding you the wrong information in the hope that you will hunt us down, or lead them to us. They are calling us terrorists to force you into helping them because they want us dead. And do you know why?"

My words came out in a rush now, my heart pounding against my ribcage.

"Because I stumbled upon some heinous illegal experiments that were being conducted. At first, they experimented on animals, but now they have moved onto humans. My dog here," I gestured towards Bandit, who let out a sympathetic whine, "is the result of one of their experiments. But they don't want you to know about him because they are worried about the conse-quences if the truth gets out."

Bandit licked my hand. Absently, I stroked his head as I continued.

"Apparently, the people who are after us believe that this kind of knowl-edge is dangerous, or maybe they just want to keep the science for them-selves. I don't really know why, and I don't care. All I know is they are trying to kill us and we can't run anymore. They have already killed one member of my family. His name was Zebediah Sullivan. He was kind and wise and...

he was like a grandfather to me. I'm not going to let another one of my family die, so I'm here to tell you our story. I'm here to tell you about Bandit."

Marko's gaze slid from me to Bandit. He knew the situation was serious — he wasn't looking at me in a way that showed he thought I was lying — though I could still see that he was struggling to comprehend it all.

"I don't understand," he finally said, breaking the silence. "Who are these people that are coming for you?"

"I don't know exactly," I admitted. "Just that they work for the government."

Marko's eyes narrowed skeptically, but before he could contradict me, Doc cut in. Her voice was calm and unwavering as she continued our story.

"She's telling the truth. My name is Elora Robins and I am a scientist. I used to work for Sebastien Forbes, who you will remember as the billionaire who died last year when he went mad and attacked an innocent family." She paused, her face contorting with guilt and sadness. "Chase and her family are the ones he attacked. He owned Platinum IIndustries, which was a cover for the illegal experiments he was conducting on animals. I know because I worked there. I... was one of those scientists conducting those unethical experiments."

Her eyes began to fill with tears.

"I knew it was wrong, but he was blackmailing me, threatening to kill my family, and I wasn't strong enough to fight him then. But I'm here now. I'm ready to tell you everything... and it all starts with Bandit."

"Okay," Marko said carefully. "You have the world listening. Can you tell us what's so special about your dog?"

Bandit barked once, though of course, the only ones in the room who knew what he meant was us. Now that Doc had laid the groundwork, however, I felt able to continue our story.

"Bandit was a lab dog," I said. "He was created and raised in Platinum Industries until he escaped, and I found him on the street. But it wasn't until he saved my life that I realized he was different from other dogs. Bandit is super intelligent and I don't just mean for a dog. He is as clever as you or I am. In fact, he is smarter than most people I know. Bandit can read and write and he can speak. "

I knew I'd lost them suddenly when a veil came down over their eyes. I could see them looking to call security. They had me pegged as a silly girl, one overly attached to her dog.

Little did they know I had a trump card up my sleeve.

"I know how this sounds, but I can prove it to you. Watch and you'll see." Turning to Bandit, I asked, "Can you say something to them?"

He barked once. "That was the first thing I taught him. One bark for yes, two for no."

Bandit set his sleek, silver iPad on the ground and picked up the stylus pen in his mouth. The crowd around him held their breath in anticipation as he began to type, each tap of his paw deliberate and precise. The camera beside me whirred out, zooming in to capture the words being formed on the screen.

"My name is Bandit and Chase is telling the truth."

Gasps sounded from all corners of the room. Alicia was the first to regain her senses. "That's amazing, but it's not really proof of anything," she said skeptically. "You could have trained him to do that. That doesn't really tell us anything."

Was she kidding? Had she been hit on the head when she was a kid?

"He just spoke to you using an iPad. I don't think there are any other dogs that can do that."

"I hate to burst your bubble, but news correspondents are taught to always be wary of things that seem too good to be true. Your dog could just be very well trained or this could all be a clever little trick."

I felt a surge of frustration building inside me as I tried to think of a way to prove Bandit's abilities when Doc spoke up.

"What about that game, Chase? The one he likes to play?"

"Jeopardy?"

"Yes," she said. "Maybe if he answers some Jeopardy questions, they will believe you."

I crouched down, getting ready to turn on the app, when there was a commotion off to the side. The aide was looking at her phone. Something was happening though I wasn't sure if it was good or bad. My stomach did a flip flop as I waited for her to relay the news.

"What's going on?"

She looked at me, hesitant to speak until Marko nodded his permission.

"The story has gotten out. Instagram, YouTube and Facebook are exploding right now. Millions of people are watching this feed."

The floor shifted beneath my feet. My knees felt weak, and I had to lean against the nearby table for support. "Millions of people are watching? And commenting? What are they saying?"

"They're saying that if your dog is so smart, prove it. Get him to play Jeopardy right now."

"That's what I'm doing. I've got the app right here."

Marko interrupted me. "I don't think they mean the app. I think they mean the actual quiz show. There's a special charity edition shooting right now."

His words were swimming inside my mind, but I couldn't quite make sense of them. Bandit too, was looking a little goofy. His tongue lolled out from his mouth and he had this bug-eyed look about him. "Wait, Jeopardy is filming here? Right now?"

Marko nodded. "Literally down the hall from us."

Before I could even turn to Bandit, I felt him somersault in the air. He typed again into the iPad, his happy voice peeling out across the room.

"Oh boy, oh boy, oh boy!"

65

CHASE

"They're filming it down the hall?" I parroted like an idiot, my mouth agape in shock.

But as soon as it sank in, a rush of excitement flooded through me, mirroring Bandit's. He spun around, tail in the air, dancing on his paws. Even the normally stoic Doc couldn't stop grinning, clearly thrilled by this turn of events.

Despite the history that was about to be made, Marko and Alicia stayed in their seats, seemingly unwilling to participate.

"I thought your jobs were to report big stories? You won't get a bigger scoop this year. I can promise you that," I exclaimed, trying to convince them to join in.

Marko finally got to his feet, shrugging with a 'what the hell' attitude as he gestured at the camera crew.

"Do we have any cameras that can follow them?" he asked. One of the cameramen, the oldest one there, nodded, picking up a much smaller camera than the massive, bolted down giants they had been steering. Setting it onto his shoulder, he turned to the man behind him. "Follow me with the cables," he instructed.

His assistant, a young man with wiry glasses and a box bristling with wires, gave a confident nod to signal they were ready.

The camera crew forged ahead, their equipment buzzing and clicking with anticipation as Marko and Alicia trailed closely behind, their voices a steady stream of excited chatter for the viewers at home.

"Good evening, ladies and gentlemen," Marko began, his voice projecting over the bustling atmosphere. "We interrupt your regularly scheduled programming for an extraordinary event. We have been graced by the unexpected appearance of this young girl and her dog. But what's truly astonishing is that she claims to be one of the most wanted terrorists in the country, with a bounty of half a million dollars on her head."

Alicia nodded in agreement before taking over from Marko. "That's right, folks. This is live on EN News and nothing about it is rehearsed or staged. According to this brave young girl, she and her family are not terrorists at all, but rather victims being hunted by the government because of her dog, Bandit. If you just tuned in this is the most astonishing story and it's all happening live right now. This is not staged in any way. I have no idea what's going to happen, but stick with us as we're about to experience what could be the most exciting edition of Jeopardy that has ever been filmed."

The maze of twisting corridors was never-ending. Our hurried footsteps echoed off the walls as we darted down one nondescript hallway after another, all of them blending into one. People tossed startled looks at us as we passed, wondering what kind of stunt this was, yet no one intruded. Not while that red light above the camera let the world know we were live on air.

Bandit trotted alongside, a pep in his step despite how precarious our situation was. Maybe he was able to compartmentalize better than me. Don't get me wrong, the closer we got to the show, the more my own excitement grew, but with it, there was also that underlying fear that it could all go wrong. That it could backfire and leave us exposed and vulnerable.

And if it did, there was no going back.

We had put ourselves out there for the entire world to see, our faces and our story now irrevocably intertwined. My stomach churned with nerves and I worried I might actually throw up.

I focused on Bandit's expression, desperate not to let the fear take over. This was such a big moment for him. For the first time in his life, he wouldn't have to pretend anymore. He would have the chance to let the entire world know who he was — and it was all happening on his favorite show, of all things.

The iconic Jeopardy logo appeared before us, its bold and curvy letters standing out against the stark white background. It was a simple laminated sign not much larger than an A4 page, encased in a plastic holder, but to Bandit, it might as well have been a flashing neon sign the size of a skyscraper. His excitement was palpable as he let out a howl and his tail whipped into a frenzy.

No one loved a pop quiz as much as my Muttface.

As we waited for the production assistant to open the door, I could feel my heart racing with anticipation. And then, finally, we caught our first glimpse of the awesomeness that was the Jeopardy set. The room was abuzz with activity and lights, and the first thing that caught my eye was the massive wrap-around blue screen that contained the actual questions. This room was unlike any other studio I had been in before — easily twenty times bigger than the one where EN News was filmed.

And then there were the people — a giant live audience filling every available seat, their excited chatter adding to the already electric atmosphere.

As we walked in, we were met with confused faces, even some hostile ones, irritated by the lights on the camera. Studio workers waved their hands in an attempt to stop us, wondering what the heck we were doing there.

The show was currently in process, but instead of its usual host, this live charity edition was being hosted by Hellen, a comedian who was now the most popular chat show host on television. She was known for her kindness — as well as her wit — and was often giving away great sums of money or cars to deserving people. She even gave away houses one time. Seeing that she was hosting today, some of my nervousness faded. If nothing else, I knew she would be kind to us, especially as she was a big animal lover with her own menagerie of pets.

Bandit's nose touched my hand. He was confused about seeing Hellen, but we'd watched her show many times together and were both fans.

Dressed in a smart pinstriped suit with her customary white sneakers, Hellen had just asked a question to the panel of celebrities who were the contestants today. I recognized all three of them: two were famous actresses, and the other, a wrestler-turned-actor, was now one of the highest paid movie stars in the world.

All four of them had stopped what they were doing to look at us. Hellen delicately touched her ear, waiting for instructions to come down the earpiece she wore.

The EN hosts took stock of the situation. Alicia, with her perfectly coiffed hair and dazzling smile, waved at the audience. "Folks, we apologize for the interruption, but this is important. Please remain in your seats."

Meanwhile, Marko addressed both the audience and the celebrities on stage, his tone serious as he explained why we were gathered there. As he reached the end of his explanation, bright spotlights suddenly flashed in my direction and I found myself frozen like a rabbit caught in the headlights.

"What's your dog's name again?" Marko asked, though his voice sounded distant, and I could barely see his face through the haze of white light that now flooded the immediate area.

All eyes were on me now. My palms grew clammy as stage fright threatened to consume me.

"Bandit," I answered, barely louder than a whisper. Clenching my fists tightly, I tried again, this time forcing my words out louder and clearer. "His name is Bandit."

"Right," Marko continued, undeterred by my nervousness. "Chase here claims that Bandit is a product of illegal experiments, giving him human-level intelligence, and we're about to prove whether her claims are true or not, right here and now. This has serious consequences — there's currently a manhunt going on for these individuals. The police may already be on their way, so if you're going to make your point, it needs to be now."

Doc's head bobbed in agreement. "Quickly Chase."

I made my way onto the center of the stage, Bandit bounding up beside me with eager excitement. But as I turned to address Hellen, my words caught in my throat. I wasn't in my own body.

This was my first celebrity meeting. Up close she was so much daintier than I thought she'd be, even smaller than me. Though she must have been so confused by it all, she sent a warm smile our way, and that gave me the strength I needed.

"Bandit loves Jeopardy," I explained. "It's his favorite show and we never miss an episode. We even play the game on our phones after breakfast. If you ask him the questions, he will answer. Then everyone will know I'm telling the truth."

Hellen's smile faltered a little, her eyes growing dark with confusion as she struggled to process my request.

"You want me to play Jeopardy *with the dog*?"

"Yes," I nodded. "Please hurry."

66

CHASE

Hellen's gaze drifted into the distance, settling on a small windowed box that I hadn't noticed before. It was tucked away behind the audience. Figures could be seen standing against the glass. From their posture, I guessed they were the people in charge. Suddenly, Hellen shrugged, flashing one of her famous grins at the audience.

"Well, it looks like we're really doing this."

There was a smattering of laughter from the crowd, but most of them seemed more bemused than amused. Hellen turned back to me, her eyes sparkling with mischief.

"So, any particular subject matter you want to focus on, or should we carry on with random questions?"

I took a deep breath, trying to quell the nerves bubbling up inside me. "Well, we haven't covered history or geography yet. But he's really into film and television, and he loves illustrated books even though he's not quite reading at an adult level yet. He's a huge fan of classic books, especially ones featuring animals, you know, like Charlotte's Web. And we watch a lot of Netflix."

There was a large rumble of laughter from the audience. I bit my lip nervously, knowing they were mocking me. One of my hands instinctively went to Bandit's head, though to comfort him or me, I wasn't sure. I only knew I felt better when we were physically in contact with each other.

Hellen glanced up at the giant wrap-around screen behind us, with several categories already displayed on it, but they abruptly reset until the categories morphed into: children's books, young adult books, Netflix, TV shows, and Movies.

I knew from experience that these weren't the usual catchy and cryptic categories the show usually featured, but we hadn't given them much time to prepare themselves, so I was grateful they were accommodating us in this way.

The studio fell silent as a tense energy filled the air. Bandit set his iPad onto the floor of the studio and gently gripped the pen-stylus in his mouth, preparing to play. Even if people thought this was the trick, they were clearly already impressed. Phones came out as pictures were being snapped and videos recorded.

I was filled with a jittery tension that wasn't solely due to the impending arrival of the police. I felt like a nervous mother, waiting for her child to perform in front of a hostile audience for the first time.

Bandit was my best friend, and he had just the sweetest nature. He had gone through so much adversity, but never felt sorry for himself. His heart overflowed with love for everyone he encountered, making it all the more heartbreaking if that love wasn't returned.

"Okay then, Bandit. Which one of those do you want to go for?" Hellen asked, her tone playful yet expectant. I had to give it to her, the woman was a pro. It was almost as if she was dealing with her usual contestant instead of this one of the four-legged kind.

Poised with the pen-stylus in his mouth, Bandit took in the categories on the screen then very carefully, he typed out the word *"Netflix."*

A collective gasp rumbled through the audience, their eyes wide with shock and disbelief. I felt a smug satisfaction wash over me, knowing that they had all doubted his abilities. *Just you wait.* The celebrities on stage, along with Marko, the host, all wore expressions of equal amazement. Even his usually composed mouth was hanging open in astonishment.

"For those of you at home who might not have a clear view, Bandit just typed 'Netflix' on his iPad. I promise you that this is live and not staged. This is actually happening. The dog just correctly answered the question by typing it into his iPad." He paused, overwhelmed by the moment. "I honestly don't know what to say right now. This is truly incredible."

Ever the professional, Hellen stepped in to keep the show moving. "Well, I guess there's no better time to begin. Bandit, are you ready?"

Bandit responded with a loud bark, earning cheers and applause from the audience.

"One bark means yes, two means no," I supplied, unable to hide my grin. It was pretty satisfying to see all these skeptics proven wrong.

"Of course it does," Hellen chuckled. "Good luck, Bandit, though I'm sure you won't need it."

"Woof woof!" Bandit barked again, exuding confidence. The audience erupted in laughter once more, louder this time.

"Now let's see those answers," Hellen gestured excitedly towards the screen, where a bunch of answers now appeared.

Instead of picking one, however, Bandit looked at me, tilting his head with a puzzled expression across his furry face. I bent down to him.

"What's up, buddy?"

"No money, just questions?"

"That's right, we're only playing with the questions today." I got back up to address Hellen, feeling amused by the awed silence that had suddenly fallen over the crowd.

"The app we play has different game types, one that's just like the show where you bet for money, though we usually just do the quick-fire round."

Hellen's face was a picture of astonishment. She shook her head as if to get her thoughts clear. "We can do that too if you'd like? Make it faster and simpler for you?"

Clearing her throat, she waited for a question to be fed to her through her earpiece. "Right folks. Let's rock and roll. First question. This mother can only protect her two children by losing one of her five senses."

Bandit's tail started swishing across the floor in excitement. He absolutely knew the answer to this as we'd watched the movie together, completely gripped all the way through. We'd even discussed which of our own senses we'd hate to lose the most. Bandit had chosen his sense of smell, something so crucial in the process of information gathering for dogs, while I had gone — rather predictably, Gideon had said at the time — for taste.

"What is Bird Box, Hellen," Bandit's youthful and joyful voice, and so like how I imagined he would sound if he could actually speak, answered from the iPad.

Hellen's head shook with disbelief, her eyes wide and stunned. "He even spelled my name the correct way."

Someone clapped in the audience, timidly at first, until they were joined by another pair of hands. Then more until the place erupted. People started cheering too, whooping as if their favorite sports team had just scored a homerun.

Tears misted my eyes as the fear that had me gripped started melting away. I beamed at Doc, who grinned right back at me. Pixie danced in a figure of eight around her, unable to contain her excitement. Hellen waved at the audience, asking for silence, then spoke again.

"Let's try another question."

As the cheers subsided, she continued. "When a young boy disappears, his mother, a police chief, and his friends must confront terrifying forces in order to get him back. Who is the special friend he makes?"

Bandit didn't even need to look at the answers, knowing this one by heart. Typing furiously, his tail thumped wildly, and he had trouble keeping his butt still.

"Who is Eleven from Stranger Things, Hellen! It's my favorite show!"

At his response, the place went absolutely *crazy*.

If there was any doubt in anyone's mind, he had just erased them. Hellen couldn't stop exclaiming over Bandit's genius, wondering how this could be happening, while Bandit tore around the stage, soaking up all the attention and barking with uncontrollable delight.

Then, in a moment of pure joy and spontaneity, Bandit leaped off the stage and into the front row of the audience.

People eagerly reached out to pet him, some nearly injuring themselves in their frantic attempts to touch him. Camera phones flashed and families jostled each other to pose for pictures with him. I watched the whole thing with happy tears in my eyes, finally believing that things might actually work out okay...

But the instant the thought came into my mind, the studio plunged into total blackness and the camera feed went dead.

67

CHASE

Sudden stillness descended upon the room, leaving an eerie silence as the cameras were turned off.

Gone was the hum of the electrical equipment, and the cheers of the audience ceased to exist, replaced by a sense of unease and confusion as people wondered what was happening. I came to my senses first, snapping my fingers at Bandit in the precise way we had trained during our safety drills. Sam had come up with this form of communication in the event that we were ever gagged or had our hands bound. I guess her time being Xavier's captive had left a lasting impression.

The sound of his paws tapping against the ground echoed through the room as he swiftly made his way to me, guided by his superior hearing and that keen sense of smell that he was smart enough to never want to lose. As soon as I felt him nudge my hand, I held onto his collar with a death grip, keeping him close.

"They cut the power! They must be here. They don't want us talking to you!" I exclaimed, my voice cutting through the hushed whispers and murmurs of the crowd.

As some members of the audience pulled out their phones and activated the flashlight function, beams of light illuminated our small corner of darkness. I caught sight of Doc's ghostly face floating towards me. Acting on instinct, I grabbed her arm and pulled her closer as she peered into the darkness, deep in thought.

"There should be contingencies for an event like this," she mused.

Someone called out from the dark. "Stay in your seats, please. Do not panic."

We couldn't see very far, so it wasn't safe to move. All we could do was wait helplessly, rooted to the spot for whatever would come next.

More phones turned on. More flashlights were shone at us, but others were now using their phones, fingers flying over the keys as they Tweeted and Facebooked. I recognized the swooshing sounds as messages were posted in their droves.

I welcomed it all. The photographs and videos being shared were proof of our existence and what we were saying.

Hellen's voice broke through the chaos. "Somebody tell me what's happening? Why haven't the emergency generators kicked in?"

The camera crew bustled behind me, partially illuminated by phone screens as they scrambled to find a solution. Here they were, with the biggest news story this side of the century, but their feed had been cut off. They scampered about, searching for a way to get their spare battery to work.

Marko's voice soared above the panic. "Folks, it looks like we've had some kind of power failure. Please remain seated for your health and safety. Do not panic. We will get this sorted. Just remain in your seats."

The four of us huddled together, feeling helpless. Doc took hold of my arm — I thought for safety — but then she started aggressively pulling me into the dark. I opened my mouth to ask where we were going when a gloved hand suddenly covered my mouth.

Terror spiked through me as I realized that those weren't the Doc's hands on me.

I bucked wildly, trying to throw off whoever my assailant was when I felt an additional pair of hands restraining me.

They had found us!

I heard a muffled squeal and knew that Doc was suffering the same fate. Bandit started barking like crazy, Pixie joining him. I knew that they could sense what was happening even if we couldn't see it.

Hearing the commotion, Hellen's voice called over at us. "Chase? Bandit? Are you guys okay?"

When I didn't answer, she yelled out. "Does anyone have eyes on them? Are they safe?"

I dug my heels in, twisting and flailing my arms in an attempt to break free. When that didn't work, I kicked out at them, but there were so many of them that I was quickly overpowered. With a yelp, I felt myself being lifted and carried backward until we came crashing through the door.

Bright light blinded me, flooding my vision with black spots. I felt, rather than saw, Doc struggling against her own attackers as several more attempted to round up the dogs, but they were so agile and fast, they couldn't be caught.

It was absolute mayhem.

After what seemed like an eternity, my vision finally cleared. My heart sank as I saw about a dozen men in the corridor with us. The ones who weren't restraining us held onto silenced weapons. The men all wore the LA police uniform though, of course, silenced guns weren't something you typically see on cops in any state. And these men moved like ghosts, never uttering a sound or issuing our Miranda rights.

There was no mistaking it — these were Smith's men.

Bandit and Pixie bolted through the doors after us, determined to stay with us, while still giving them the run around. As soon as they were in the corridor, one of the men sprinted to the doors they had crashed through and slid a long, thin metal weapon through the handlebars, effectively blocking the doors and keeping everyone else inside.

Seeing their guns, I renewed my fight against them, desperate that they wouldn't be able to use them on Bandit. The guns weren't pointed at us, however. At any point, they could have shot us and left us for dead, but I guess there were too many people around for them to finish the job. Hence the power cut. They were creating a diversion so they could take us somewhere else.

I remember watching an episode of a talk show once, when I was younger and my mom had been out with whatever guy had been her latest squeeze.

This particular episode had been about personal safety. Opal's guest that week was an expert on personal safety who had warned — women in particular — that the number one rule if you ever were attacked in public was to never, ever let them take you to a second location.

If they managed to move you to a second location of their choice, it was likely to be isolated where they could do whatever they wanted with you.

He had warned that no matter how scared we were, however hurt we might be, if they were able to move us to a different location, it would be much, much worse for us.

Remembering that now, I kicked and struggled like a wildcat.

68

CHASE

I fought so hard that the hand around my mouth slipped a little and I was able to sink my teeth into his fingers. I bit down so hard I went through the glove and hit flesh. The guy screamed in agony. The taste of metallic and salty blood filled my mouth, which I spat out like I was possessed.

Snatching his injured hand away, he backhanded with me with the other one, knocking my head back until I felt my teeth rattle in my skull. A warm liquid began to trickle down my face from my nose, followed by a sharp stinging sensation telling me that he had probably broken it, but so long as I could still breathe, I wouldn't think about it. Every ounce of thought and energy was targeted at keeping us here.

Even if I was fighting a losing battle.

There were just too many of them and they were stronger than us. Bandit was growling so fiercely that had he not been my dog, I could only imagine the fear he would have instilled in me, but he knew not to attack these men, not when their guns could easily be turned on us.

We were stuck in a hard place.

We couldn't stop them. All we could do was delay the inevitable. Our feet beat a frantic rhythm as we neared the exit, and my heart sank at the thought of the waiting vehicles outside. Sully's devastated face flew into my mind only to be quickly replaced with Sam's. When Gideon's image appeared, my heart swelled with all of our recent bittersweet memories until it physically ached.

Tears streamed down my cheeks as I desperately wish that I could have apologized to him. To tell him how sorry I was that he didn't feel he could talk to me, that he couldn't share his pain and grief with me.

I knew that once this was all over he would blame himself for whatever was about to happen to us. The guilt would kill him.

As we reached the exit doors, they were flung open, blinding us with bright sunlight and the blazing Californian sun. As I had predicted, there were several identical vans parked across from us, their dark windows a chilling reminder of how powerless we'd be to their actions once they got us inside.

We were dragged towards them when I suddenly saw the enormous crowd that had gathered outside. They were behind the studio's barriers, which is why I hadn't noticed them right out the gate, but I couldn't miss them now. The crowd stretched on for miles, like they were lining up for a Taylor Swift concert, and they all had their eyes fixed on one point in front of the building.

I strained my neck to see what the commotion was about and realized it must be another big show taping since Jeopardy — celebrity edition or not — wouldn't normally draw this kind of attention. Yet, there was an eerie atmosphere hovering over the crowd. They seemed restless, almost agitated, instead of the typical excited energy that comes with being at a live show. It was like a storm brewing just beneath the surface.

Before I could fully process the strange behavior of the crowd, the fake cops pressed their guns against our backs, forcing us toward the vans.

But then, a loud shout pierced through the tense air: "There they are!"

Suddenly, every single person in the crowd turned to face us. Rows upon rows of faces staring intently at us. I froze in shock, unable to move or even utter a sound.

Thankfully, someone took action for us.

"Leave them alone!" A voice shouted from the midst of the crowd. Others joined in, chanting in unison: "Let them go!"

The icy fear that had me frozen inside suddenly lifted. Was it possible? Were these people here *for us*?

The members of the crowd closest to us hopped the barriers, sprinting toward us with a sense of urgency. As they reached the cops, they lunged at them, attempting to free us from their grasp!

One man at the front raised his weapon and shouted, "Stay back! This is a police matter! Back away or I'll shoot!" But instead of cowering in fear, the crowd bristled with fury.

A woman wearing a bright In N Out uniform fixed him with a steely gaze.

"Hell no! You're threatening us? What kind of police officer would threaten a member of the public like that? We're not committing any crimes, but we're also not letting you take that girl and her dog."

The crowd roared in agreement, pushing forward with even more determination. The armed men were taken aback. There was no way they could stand against the thousands of outraged people that were out here.

A burly man in a builder's helmet and hi-vis vest, still covered in dust from a recent demolition job, brandished his fist at the officers.

"What kind of police use unlicensed vehicles? Where are your squad cars? Why are you using unmarked vehicles?" Turning towards the crowd, he bellowed, "These aren't the real cops. The girl's right, they're after her and her dog!"

More rumbles of discontent surged through the crowd, the air thick with tension. The men hesitated, their bodies bunching together to form a human shield. On an unspoken signal, they took aim at the crowd. One of them fired two warning shots into the sky.

A woman's scream pierced through the chaos, causing the crowd to take a collective step back in fear. They wanted to help us, but they wouldn't risk their lives for a bunch of strangers, even if they believed they were innocent. All they could do was yell helplessly as we were forced towards those waiting vans.

Bandit and Pixie were still beside us. Still barking, their yowl's growing more and more intense. I thought I must be going mad suddenly as I began to hear more barking from further away, yet seemingly all around us too, until the sounds of barking filled the air, growing louder and more intense with each passing second.

I had no idea where the noises were coming from — whether they were only a figment of my stressed mind or actually real. My heart thudded fearfully as we reached the van. The doors slid open and I caught a glimpse of several more fake cops inside when a dog burst through the crowd toward us.

It was a Golden Retriever, known for how friendly and mind-mannered they usually were, but this one showed remarkable aggression as she charged up to the men, snarling ferociously at them.

It took me a moment to realize that all of that aggression was not aimed at us, but at our captors.

A rush of barks and yelps filled the air as another dog burst through the crowd, a Boxer with a sleek coat and muscular frame. It was followed by a tiny Poodle, its fluffy white fur bouncing with each step. More and more dogs appeared, pushing their way through the throng until ten of them stood in a protective circle around us.

The crowd had fallen into a hushed awe, watching in astonishment as the dogs stood guard over us.

And then, amidst the sea of furry faces, I saw one that I recognized — a majestic German Shepherd with piercing amber eyes.

It was the first dog I had saved in Platinum Industries! My gaze shifted over to Doc, whose beaming smile confirmed my suspicions.

"They actually came," she whispered in disbelief.

"But how? What are they doing here?" I babbled, my mind racing to make sense of this unexpected reunion.

Doc's expression softened as she explained, "There were so many dogs we had to find homes for after shutting down Platinum Industries that they were sent to families all around the country. But these dogs were homed here, in LA... and their owners must have brought them to the studio to help us!"

The crowd were pointing their phones our way. If we were lucky, this moment would be broadcasted for all to see — making it nearly impossible for anyone to harm or kidnap us.

Meanwhile, it was the men who were now frozen in fear, exchanging panicked looks as they tried to work out their next move. Each time they tried to step forward, the dogs would lunge toward them, snapping their jaws so close to their hands that the men jumped back. I saw the alarm on their faces and felt a twisted sense of satisfaction.

One of them spoke, his voice strained. "We can't kill them with the whole world watching."

I wasn't sure if he was referring to us or the dogs, but either way, I was grateful for the sentiment.

Doc pointed behind us. I turned to see that it wasn't only the crowd who had a ringside seat to the show, but the massive screen above the studio which previously had advertised trailers of their upcoming movies, now displayed a live feed of all of us in the parking lot. Our faces, the dogs, it was all being broadcasted across the nation!

And then right at the back somewhere, perched on top of a car, I saw Marko, Alicia, and their trusted EN crew filming. Their cameras aimed at us as they captured every moment. Marko flashed a thumbs up at me and I had to smile.

Against the overwhelming tide of fear, hope was beginning to take hold. Here were all these people who believed in us, who were rooting for our survival. I was overwhelmed by their support and found myself thinking that maybe we would make it out of this mess alive.

Suddenly, the piercing screech of sirens filled the air. Several police cruisers careened into the parking lot, horns blaring at the crowd to let them pass.

The police got out of their cars, weapons drawn and aimed our way, but they looked on in total confusion. Marko and his crew were hustling toward them at breakneck speed, desperate to head off an attack that might see us dead, but they struggled to get through the thick crowd.

The cops didn't know what to do, frozen in indecision. One of them could be heard asking clearing over the commotion.

"What do we do? Do we shoot the dogs, the kid, or what?"

Personally, I thought the choice was obvious, but apparently, it wasn't to them. We all stood, rooted to the spot, waiting for their next move.

69

SULLY

The RV burned rubber, hurtling down the highway.

Sam, Gideon, and Emma were huddled together next to me, staring at Elora's iPad in utter horror as the scene unfolded before them.

The bright lights of an enormous crowd surrounded Chase, Elora, and the dogs like a cage, while a group of armed police pressed in on all sides. Although there must have been at least a dozen of them, their faces blurred into one. They were all white, of average build and features, and no facial hair. In fact, there wasn't a discernible detail on any one of them.

Which I was certain was by design.

I met Smith's eyes in the rearview mirror. "Those are your men, aren't they?"

"Yes."

His reply was surprisingly honest and direct. Since I'd taken back the RV, those were the first words he had said, though his sharp eyes never left us and studied our every move. On the screen, Chase was being forced toward those waiting vans. Sam's grip on my hand tightened in response.

"Isn't anyone going to stop them!" Seeing Chase in danger had snapped Gideon out of the stupor that had clouded his eyes since our arrival.

"They still think we're terrorists." As ludicrous as it seemed that a young girl and her dog would pose a national security threat, I knew that not everyone used their common sense before pulling a trigger. The situation felt more dire than ever.

A look of disbelief came over Gideon's eyes. "I can't believe this is happening."

With things spiraling as they were, I couldn't believe I had agreed to this plan, either.

Stupid Sully. Stupid.

"She looks so small and there are so many of them," Emma's normally confident demeanor faltered for once as she murmured, genuinely scared for someone other than herself for once.

"That girl of yours is quite something."

I didn't know how I felt about Smith's admiration for Chase. He had no idea of the doubts that were plaguing my mind, impressed only with the fire inside my girl even when the odds were stacked against her.

Never give up. Never Surrender.

Her voice echoed inside my head with the slogan of one of her favorite movies, Galaxy Quest. I knew I needed to take a leaf out of her own book.

"That she is," Sam replied. Despite the motherly pride evident in her eyes, it couldn't conceal the underlying fear that gnawed at her. As a sheriff and law enforcer, she held the responsibility of upholding the law, yet she now found herself powerless to protect her two of her own kids.

We were flooring it to LA now, though it would be awhile — much longer than I'd like — until we got there. I needed to buy Chase some time. Appeal to Smith's good sense, maybe. He met my troubled gaze.

"You have no idea what she's gone through. That dog was the first person — and yes, to us he is a person — who showed her any love. He was the first family she ever had who gave a damn about her and she would do anything for him."

"I didn't know that," Emma revealed quietly. "I didn't know about her life before she met you."

"She was alone for a very long time," Sam answered. "Her mom never looked after her and her step-father was abusive. It wasn't until she ran away that she felt safer. Imagine feeling safer living on the streets on your own at only fourteen years old." The weight of Sam's words lingered, painting a poignant picture.

Overcome with emotion, Emma lowered her gaze back to the tablet, staring intently as if she were trying to reconcile that version of Chase with the girl she knew.

Even Smith displayed a rare look of shame. "I take no joy from any of this."

I thought of his own family and the love he held for his own children. As alien as it seemed, I was reminded that this man was also a father.

"Then stop this madness. You can't win. Your orders were to get rid of us quietly so no one would even know we existed. Well, now everybody knows. There's no point in you coming after us anymore."

He remained silent, his expression stoic, but I could see a slight twitch in his jawline, indicating my words were chipping away at his resolve.

"Can't you get them to stop? This can't be the result your boss wanted. If secrecy is what they're after, that's all been shot to hell. Isn't there something you can do?"

A pause lingered, tension hanging in the air, his gaze locked onto me with laser-like intensity. Time seemed to stretch, and then, after what felt like an eternity, he broke his silence. "Give me your phone," Smith asked curtly.

"My phone?"

"Yes," he confirmed. "I'll call my men off."

My brows raised so high they almost shot off my head.

"It's not my style to lie, Sullivan. My orders were to keep this a covert mission, but that ship has sailed. My bosses can't risk being exposed. They will want us to retreat. But I can't call my men without a phone."

"Would you like fries with that?" Gideon snapped, his hackles raised. "Do we look that stupid?"

I shot him a warning glance before turning to Sam. She stared at me, her troubled eyes reflecting my own indecision. While I wanted nothing more than his men to leave Chase and Bandit alone, this could be a ploy. The stakes were high, and the shadows of doubt loomed over the decision I was about to make. Trusting the sincerity of Smith's words felt like navigating a treacherous path, but I was desperate enough to call his bluff.

"You're not using any of our devices. I'm taking you to a public phone."

"Fine," Smith responded blandly, as if he'd just agreed to a black coffee instead of white.

Gideon balked at us. "Are you insane? Why would you trust him to keep his word?"

"Because we don't have a choice. If there's a chance this will keep them safe, we have to do it."

Emma's brow furrowed in worry as she spoke up. "Can we please discuss this? I want to help Chase and Bandit, but this doesn't seem very smart," Emma asked.

"This doesn't involve you so it's not up for discussion," I replied without thinking, only to see the stark flash of pain in her eyes. She was trying so hard to be a part of our family, yet I had just dismissed her without a second thought. A dark cloud of guilt washed over me.

Sam sent a watery smile my way, understanding what that must have taken. As Emma's shoulders shook with silent tears, she turned and retreated to the bedroom, with Sam staring after her.

"I'll talk to her after we've made the call."

"You will?"

"Yeah. I'm finally starting to understand how she must be feeling. This whole time, I was scared and even a little jealous of your connection... but it's not really her, is it? I was so afraid you would choose her over me that I never saw how difficult this must all be for her until now."

A sudden bolt of realization shot through me, like an electric shock.

"You thought I'd leave you for her?" I asked, my voice tinged with disbelief.

She nodded, a sheepish blush staining her cheeks. "I knew we rushed into things, that a part of you hadn't truly let go of her yet. So when she returned... I figured it was just a question of time."

I squeezed her hand tightly, trying to relay everything I felt for her through that single gesture. "That was never an option, Sam. You're the one. You're my person. I don't want anyone else. Not even Emma."

She gave me a brilliant smile that lit up her face and, for the smallest fraction of a moment, everything felt right in the world.

We continued driving until we reached a rest stop. Conscious of not drawing attention to ourselves — after all, we were still labeled as terrorists — Gideon stayed in the motorhome with Emma while Sam and I escorted Smith to a nearby payphone. She kept her gun concealed within her jacket, but aimed on him at all times.

Handing Smith some coins, I watched as he dialed a number with the Washington area code. A thought filled my head, so dark, so outrageous that I dismissed it quickly. Surely his bosses weren't so high up that they were connected to a certain White House...

"It's Smith," Smith said into the phone, his voice heavy with urgency and the most amount of emotion I'd heard from him since we'd met. "Tell Alpha team to retreat. Disengage immediately until we receive further orders."

Smith looked as if he was hanging up the phone when, with no warning, he swung the phone with brutal force, connecting solidly with the side of my head. An explosion of pain erupted above my left eye, sending shock-waves through my skull. Staggering backward, my vision became a chaotic constellation of stars, blurring the surroundings in a disorienting haze.

"Sully!" Sam's urgent shout penetrated the fog in my head as she launched herself at Smith, attempting to grapple him. Struggling to regain my composure, I attempted to help, but my vision was still obscured by the stars dancing in my eyes. The sounds of their scuffle were distorted, like distant echoes in a cavern.

Someone fell heavily to the ground — Sam.

It took me a moment to fully regain my senses and help Sam up. Relief washed through me as I saw that she was only a little banged up. By then, Smith had already vanished into the darkness.

Gideon rushed out of the RV, Elora's iPad grasped in his hands. I thought he must have seen Smith attack us and was coming to help, but his eyes were glued to the screen.

"It worked, Sully! Those men are backing away!"

Sam and I hurried over to him, crowding around his shoulder to watch as the footage on the screen showed the ten disguised men who held Chase hostage suddenly retreating in their blacked-out vans, leaving Chase, Elora, and the dogs alone.

70

SULLY

After what seemed an eternity of driving, we finally arrived at the studio, our car weaving through the chaos of crowds and flashing lights.

To my surprise, the masses had only grown larger since we left. The sky was littered with helicopters, each emblazoned with the logos of various news channels. A giant TV screen displayed live footage from NBC's stations, cycling between shots of the frenetic scene below.

And right there, at the epicenter of the commotion, was Chase and the others.

They were surrounded by camera crews and reporters, their faces projected on nearly every channel. Custom hashtags scrolled across the bottom of the screen, including #geniusdog, #geneticbreakthrough, and #jeopardydog -- all trending. There was even one called #savethedogsavetheworld which Gideon had to explain was a play on a slogan from an old TV series called Heroes. Social media was also exploding, with Facebook, Instagram, YouTube, and Twitter all streaming events.

The word was well and truly out now.

As we tried to navigate through the throngs of people, I abandoned any hope of parking our RV. The streets and parking lot were packed with vehicles and eager bystanders. I got us as close as we could to then the four of us tried to make our way through the crowd but people refused to move aside. Several even turning hostile toward us.

"We're their family! Let us through!" I finally started yelling.

No one responded, not until the others took up the call.

"That's my daughter!" Sam suddenly roared in a commanding voice. "Move aside!"

Like magic, a path miraculously opened for us amidst the sea of bodies.

"Chase! It's me!" I yelled with everything I had, but my voice couldn't carry over the crowd.

Police — the real police — were still in the area and looking bewildered. They didn't seem to know what to do either until a call came over their radios ordering them to stand down. Someone high up must have given the order, but who? For a fleeting moment, I couldn't help but wonder if Smith's powerful employers had reached out their long arms and interfered with this situation. Could they have that much control and influence?

Driving those thoughts from my mind, we continued wading through the bedlam until we finally reached the ring of dogs surrounding Chase and her captors. The menacing snarls and sharp teeth made it clear that they were not going to let us pass easily. The German Shepherd closest to me turned, snarling a warning for me to stay back, but when she got a good look at me, her tail started to wag.

She whimpered a friendly greeting. I reached out a hand so she could smell Bandit's scent on me and know that I was a friend as I suddenly placed her as one of the dogs we'd saved from the lab. I vividly remembered the videos of her torture — hadn't been able to forget them, in fact.

She looked the picture of health now. Glossy black and brown coat, a healthy weight, but it was eyes that told me the most — once filled with a desperate fear and sadness, they were now bright with happiness. It was clear that her new family was taking excellent care of her. I stepped past her at the same time that Chase suddenly noticed me. The anxious, worried expression on her face instantly melted away into a wide smile that lit up her entire being.

"Sully! You're all here!"

I staggered into the circle as she ran into my arms. Bandit barked joyously, jumping up and down as he sniffed me, reassuring himself that I was well. Pixie a-wooed, an endearing sound as her nose pointed to the sky, equally delighted by our arrival. Bandit barked something at the dogs, a command, and suddenly, they moved aside, forming a gap that the others could walk through.

I had witnessed this particular skill of Bandit's before, back at my clinic when he had commanded the dogs there to attack Forbes's men before escaping to safety, but for Sam, Gideon, and Emma who joined us in the circle with wide-eyed amazement, it was their first time seeing it in action. As soon as they were clear, the dogs repositioned themselves, closing the ring and providing us with a wall of canine protection.

And the best of it was, the entire thing was captured by the cameras.

There could be absolutely no denying that the dogs were obeying Bandit's command.

That he was every bit as special as we were saying he was.

I clung tightly to Chase and Bandit, wrapping my arms around their strong bodies as if they were the only things keeping me anchored to the ground. I knew in that moment that I would never let them go again. I felt a hesitant tap on my shoulder and turned to see Gideon standing there, his expression filled with shame and regret. He reached out to embrace Chase, who released me in order to return the hug.

"I'm sorry," he whispered to her.

"I know. It's alright. I understand."

They held each other, her face resting on his chest. Seeing them like that, I realized their relationship had changed and was no longer of the step-siblings kind. Their feelings had transformed into something deeper and more meaningful.

A hand wove itself through mine as my own love laid her head on my shoulder.

Emma stood off to one side, relieved that our family were reunited, yet also feeling like an outsider in this intimate moment. Without hesitation, Sam reached out and took her hand in hers, clasping it tightly and letting her know that she was not alone anymore.

Not now that she had us.

As I looked around at our united family, I couldn't help but feel hopeful about our future. We may not know what lay ahead, but with our bond stronger than ever before, we were ready for whatever challenges came our way.

And most importantly, we would face them together — no one left behind or forgotten.

71

———

CHASE

As I gazed into Gideon's eyes, relief washed over me like a warm ocean wave. He was alive and safe, and holding me tightly in his arms. It seemed absurd to think how long it had taken for us to realize our love for each other.

We shared everything with one another, the good and the bad. He had always been there for me, even when others weren't. How could I have been so blind to our feelings? I searched his eyes, still looking for the answers to the lingering question that bothered me.

"Why wouldn't you talk to me? I wanted to help you, but you wouldn't let me."

His eyes turned suspiciously bright. "I was a mess. I wasn't trying to push you away. I just felt so angry at the world, I took it out on you the most because... because I love you. I'm sorry I hurt you. That was the last thing I wanted."

Hearing those words come out of his lips, my heart sang, overflowing with joy.

"I love you too. Just maybe, try talking to me in the future first, you know, before you do anything stupid."

His lips curved into a smile. "I deserved that."

"Yes, and I'm not sure when you're going to be hearing the last of it so you should prepare yourself."

He stared so intensely at me that it seemed the most natural thing in the world when his head dipped closer and he lowered his lips onto mine.

A cheer erupted through the crowd as I suddenly remembered that giant

TV screen. Half filled with horror, I turned to see — yup. Our faces blown up as big as a billboard. My cheeks flamed red.

I felt a rumble of laughter in Gideon's chest and had to punch him for it.

AFTER HALF AN HOUR, I found myself back inside the EN News stage, but this time, everything had changed. The once empty room was now filled with seven chairs arranged in a semi-circle, waiting for us. Even Emma was there, sitting among us.

There had been some debate on whether letting her loose on camera was a sensible thing, but in the end, we realized that, like Bandit, exposing the truth might be the only way to keep her safe. The world would be getting the entire Emma experience, whether they were ready for it or not.

Marko and Alicia were kind and compassionate as they led the interview. We spoke honestly and openly, revealing every sordid detail of our story.

I started with how I'd been living on the cold and unforgiving streets until I met Bandit. Every now and then, Bandit would chime in with his own memories, like how excited he had been the first time he was able to communicate with me. Other highlights for him had been when he had learned how to spell a word, and how his first sentence had been: "Hello. My name is Bandit and I love you."

Those were the exact first words my Muttface had said to me.

I could almost hear the collective sigh around the world when that little detail had been revealed. Our story had touched so many hearts.

As the viewers were so invested in our story, we were taking questions from them. The co-hosts picked random questions that were Tweeted in. Some were just plain crazy, like, how did we know Bandit wasn't going to kill us in our sleep and that he wasn't dangerous. I had replied by rolling my eyes and saying the same way the average pet owner knew their dogs weren't going to do that.

The outpouring of support was overwhelming. People from all over wanted to show their solidarity with us and make sure we were never hunted again. A funding page was even started, apparently hitting half a million bucks within an hour!

Doc probably had the hardest time of all. People didn't take kindly to her connection with Forbes and her previous line of work, making her the target of some seriously harsh criticism. It wasn't until Sully explained all the good she had done since, and Bandit publicly stating that she was his friend and had always been nice to him, that some of the hate lessened.

Emma didn't say very much. She was asked a few questions, but since she didn't know very much, she wasn't an exciting interviewee. We hadn't had time to tell Emma the truth about what she was just yet, and it didn't seem right to reveal that information live on air, so we had decided to save that conversation for later.

The entire interview took several hours. The other dogs sat around eagerly listening, joined by their new owners now. I wasn't actually sure how much of it the dogs actually understood, but they seemed happy just to be in Bandit's presence. I guess he was their version of a rock star.

When the cameras flashed off, Alicia gave us all a warm smile.

"You all did amazing. Thank you. Especially you, Elora. I know this couldn't have been easy for you."

"It wasn't, but it needed to be done. If it helps to keep them all safe, then some uncomfortableness on my part is worth it."

Someone came by and unclipped the mic that was attached to my shirt. "What now?" I asked.

Marko grinned at me. "Since we've finished recording, we normally celebrate with a wrap party."

"I don't know that we're up for a party," Sam said. "I mean, we've been through the wringer today..."

"Ah, my apologies for the industry term. It's not always a party per se. Usually, we just have a lot of food."

Bandit's and my ears pricked up immediately. "What kind of food?"

"Free food," he replied, grinning.

My lips stretched into a giant smile, mirroring Bandit's expression.

"Well, that just happens to be our favorite kind!"

72

SULLY

As I gazed out at the familiar landscape of my childhood home, I couldn't help but feel a sense of nostalgia for simpler times. The border of towering oaks that I used to ride past every morning stood stoically in the distance. Beyond the fields of lush green grass, a vast pasture stretched out, dotted with grazing horses. At the far end of our property, a crystal clear creek snaked its way through, providing a cool drink for our beloved equine friends. These sights were all so familiar to me, yet now they seemed like distant memories.

After being back in Montpelier for a week, our world had been turned upside down, and not only for losing a beloved member of our family in such a traumatic manner. The home I grew up in, the home where our extended family had come together — that was all gone. The scaffolding that now covered every inch of our ranch was evidence of the significant changes taking place. Even at this early hour, workmen swarmed around like busy bees, their tools and equipment creating a constant hum of activity.

Since our story had made headlines, help had arrived from some of the unlikeliest of places. Thanks to the generosity of strangers, that funding page had swollen to such numbers that none of us ever needed to work again if we didn't want to. However, whenever I made a crack about retiring early, Sam would give me this pointed look. It wasn't a threat, not exactly, but my lady would not be impressed if I became a kept man. The money we had received had been a real blessing, coming in handy as our home had been reduced to rubble.

The sounds of hammers and saws echoed through the neighborhood, evidence of the builders working tirelessly to restore our house. In the meantime, Mobile Travelers, the largest RV company in the world, had graciously provided us with two state-of-the-art motorhomes to use as temporary shelter. And the most surprising part? They didn't charge us a cent. It seemed that our story had touched their hearts and they wanted to show their support. If we wanted to show a little appreciation their way, all we'd need to do is pose with the motorhomes for some photographs making sure that Bandit was center stage.

Yes, we had all been overshadowed by a dog.

It hadn't been all fun and building games, however. A team of stern-faced FBI agents had come to question us about our mysterious government department and elusive accomplice, Smith. Despite going over our story multiple times, they remained adamant that no such department existed and claimed ignorance about Smith's identity.

Not that I was surprised.

Maybe one day, we'd be able to flush them out, but until then, I was content with living our lives and enjoying what little moments of peace we could find.

I felt a presence beside me and smiled.

"Are you checking me out?"

Sam laughed, a throaty, delicious sound that tickled me all over. I felt her arms weave around my waist as she stepped in close to me.

"Nothing I haven't seen before."

"Yet, you're still here. You must be a glutton for punishment."

She turned to face me, her eyes sparkling with love and mischief.

"For better or worse, right? You're not getting rid of me that easily."

She smiled at me, though I could sense that there was something weighing on her mind. "Have you thought about what we are going to do about Emma?"

Some of the light went out of my eyes. This had been the one ongoing problem we still hadn't solved. She still lived with us and although she and Sam had resolved their differences, none of us quite knew what to do next.

"That's going to require a little more thought."

Sam nodded, eminently patient. Not for the first time, I was grateful for her understanding; how many other women would be the same in her position? "The other day, you asked what I would do if Emma — my Emma — came back."

Sam's shoulders tensed, the only outward sign of her tension. I brushed a stray lock of her blonde hair out from her face.

"If she came back today... I would still choose you. What we have is just as real and meaningful as what I had with the previous Emma, but that chapter is over now. My life is with you, and you alone. You are my everything."

Smiling that stunning smile of hers, my wife kissed me with the heat of a thousand suns.

73

CHASE

As the sun rose on a new day, we were greeted by an unexpected surprise visitor.

Well, actually, we've had lots of surprise visitors since we arrived home. It seemed that every single person we knew in the world — and quite a few who we didn't — wanted to swing by to talk to Bandit .

He had always been a star, but now the rest of the world had cottoned on.

My little star wasn't so into all the attention, however, and wanted to be left alone with his family as we started building the next stage of our lives together. As I sat down for our usual morning game of Jeopardy, I couldn't help feeling a flash of irritation when an SUV pulled up outside. I assumed it was yet another paparazzi or fan looking for a photo or autograph.

But to my surprise, the person standing on our doorstep was a familiar and welcome friend. She flashed me a warm smile as I opened the door.

"Hey Doc, we're just having breakfast. You want something to eat?"

"I'd love some coffee, actually," she replied. "I rushed over here so quickly that the only breakfast I had was a coffee from a gas station that was more like sludge than anything else. Does Sully have some of his famous brew? I could really use a cup."

A wide grin spread across my face as I turned to her, chuckling. "Well, sure if he didn't drink it all already. I swear he's the reason the coffee industry stays in business."

As soon as he heard her voice, Bandit came bounding over to greet her. Pixie weaved through Doc's legs and the two dogs did a happy little dance together, followed by the regulatory sniffing of each other's butts, proving that all dogs were weird, even the super smart ones.

I thought it was pretty adorable how the two were friends now, especially when it wasn't even a month ago when they were mortal enemies.

"Excuse the chaos," I said, gesturing around the makeshift space. "The house is still being rebuilt, but the coffee maker works fine."

Leading her to a small table by what would eventually be our new kitchen, I pointed out the window overlooking the backyard.

"This will be our view," I said with a smile. Currently, the room was a disorganized maze of half-finished tasks. The new oven sat unconnected to the gas mains, and there was no sink in sight. Only some of the cupboards had been installed, lacking any doors, of course. Our old counter had been replaced by a sleek marble one that Sam had always dreamed of having. Though I found it a bit cold to the touch, seeing how happy it made her made it all worth it. Who was Sully to deny her this simple luxury?

Pouring Doc a cup of steaming coffee, I felt the warmth radiating through my palms. Handing it to her carefully, we all made our way out onto the porch where the others now sat around a table. The crisp morning air greeted us as we settled into our seats, surrounded by the peaceful country-side. There was a chorus of "Helloes" and "What's Up Doc?" — the latter of which sent my dog into what I think was peels of laughter.

He rolled around on the wooden deck with his paws in the air, making a weird snorting sound through his nose. We'd recently started watching the old Warner Brothers cartoons, and apparently, this slogan tickled his funny bone.

From her spot on the bench, Emma watched with cautious curiosity. She scooted all the way to one side so Bandit wouldn't accidentally get her with those roving paws of his. She still tended to be uncomfortable around him, though she had lost that initial animosity she'd had toward him.

Bandit didn't seem to mind though. In fact, he'd tried being friends with her. I even caught her awkwardly patting him on the head once when she thought no one was watching, only to frantically scrub her hands in the sink after, as if she didn't want to catch his cuteness.

Taking a seat beside Sam, Doc addressed us all with a warm smile on her face.

"I've been in communication with various branches of the government. Unsurprisingly, they still refuse to admit that there was ever a department like the one you mentioned. I doubt we will ever discover the truth of the matter. However, I do have some very good news that I couldn't wait to tell you. Despite their initial denial, I have convinced them to fund a new department that will investigate Xavier's work. And even better, they have granted me permission to oversee it, so I can make sure that no dogs or any other animals will ever be harmed again."

"That's not good news, Elora. That's fantastic news!" Sully grinned.

Doc turned to Emma, her expression softening as she spoke in a gentle tone.

"They also authorized me to delve into your origins, but only if you give your full consent. If you want to be left alone, I can do that, but you are a scientific marvel and one of a kind. There is so much we could learn from you if you trust me enough to work with me."

Before Emma could even respond, Sam interjected, her voice laden with concern. "You don't mean to use her for experimentation, do you? Because I won't allow that to happen."

Emma looked at Sam, unable to hide her shock. "You're defending me?"

"You're new to all of this, and it's all of our responsibility to look out for you, especially when you're family."

Emma's eyes widened into round circles of surprise that glimmered with unshed tears. She clutched her hands tightly in her lap, her fingers interlocking like a puzzle. Considering her next words carefully, she spoke to Sully.

"In the last few days... I've seen how happy you and Sam are, and even though you have all been kind to me, I know I don't belong. Even if you didn't have Sam, I'm not the same person you married, but I am a constant reminder of her. I think I do care about you, as much as I know how to care about anyone, so perhaps it would be best for me to leave you in peace."

She turned toward Doc and gave a solemn nod. "Yes, I'll be happy to come back with you. I want to understand more about myself."

Sam strode over to Emma, her gaze fixed on her face. "Are you sure?"

A small smile crept across Emma's lips, the first genuine one that had graced her features since arriving home.

"I'm positive."

THE NEXT FEW hours were a flurry of activity as we sorted through Emma's departure.

She didn't have much, so it wasn't so much a case of us packing her things — everything she had fit in the one bag — but we wanted her to know that even though we hadn't always gotten along, we were her family now and would always be there for her.

After her sudden decision to leave, Emma and Sully disappeared for a walk around the property. The sight of them heading off together actually tugged at my heartstrings.

From that fateful night when I had arrived at Sully's door covered with Bandit's blood, I could never have predicted any of this. That Sully had been a shadow of the person he was now. He had been hanging on by a thread… but now, inexplicably, that thread was back only for him to finally let her go.

The sound of joyful barking pulled me from my thoughts. In the distance, I could see Bandit bounding across the grass with Pixie close behind. They weaved and dodged under the sun's warm rays, their paws kicking up fresh blades of grass as they playfully chased each other through the yard, having a whale of a time.

A warm, contented smile spread across my lips as I watched them play with such delight. Bandit was such a special dog that I often forgot he wasn't very old in dog years, not even a teenager yet. But despite his intelligence, he still loved to play with all the carefree abandon of a puppy. It was thrilling to see Pixie come out of her shell too, her cautiousness forgotten in the presence of her furry best friend. The two of them had gone through so much together.

As I stood there, basking in the joy radiating from their playful antics, it suddenly struck me how much these two had in common.

Both had been subjected to cruel experiments, but while Bandit had been rewarded for his cleverness, Pixie had endured years of torture at the hands of a cruel and sadistic man.

Wrapping my arms around myself, I let myself revel in their heartwarming bond. Their joyful energy filled the air until all too soon, it was time for Doc to leave.

She waited patiently by the car while the rest of us said our goodbyes to Emma. Gideon gave her a quick hug that she returned. The two of them had never really seen eye-to-eye, but I knew he only wanted what was best for her.

I hugged her next. "I hope you find the answers to all of your questions."

"And I hope you find a cure for your snoring," Emma replied. It took a moment before I saw the corners of her mouth twitch.

"Did you just make a joke?"

"Why would I do that? I take my sleeping very seriously." But there was something different in her eyes, a mischievous glint that hadn't been there before.

Sam stepped forward, smiling warmly at her. "Good luck. And remember, whatever happens, you always have a home here with us."

Emma didn't reply, but those eyes of hers grew brighter. She gave her a small and grateful nod, seemingly overwhelmed with emotion, as Sully came around from the trunk of the Doc's car. Opening his arms to her, she stepped into them.

He held her close for a few moments, but I could see the love that he had for her was different from what he shared with Sam. It seemed almost parental, like the love he had for Gideon and me.

"Elora will look after you. Stay in touch with us. We want to know how things are going and not only when you have news. Call or write, any time."

Nodding, she swallowed the lump that was in her throat and got into the car. Bandit came around to bump her hand under his head.

"See you later, smelly pants," she said.

He chuffed, his face breaking out into a goofy, lopsided grin. Doc climbed into the driver's seat only to realize that they were one short.

"Pixie, come on," she called out.

But her only response was a distressed whine. Bandit's smile instantly disappeared as Pixie pressed up against him. The two of them stared up at us, two identical pairs of pleading eyes as Pixie made no move to get into the car.

Bandit had left his iPad inside while he was playing (and while the builders were all around), but I didn't need an electronic device to translate their meaning.

"Um Doc... I think Pixie wants to stay," I broached the subject gently. Doc climbed out of her car, her forehead wrinkled with surprise.

"Is that true? Do you want to stay here with Bandit?"

Pixie barked once in response, then lowered herself onto her stomach as if to emphasize her decision. Doc's face became flustered, clearly caught off guard by this.

"I suppose she has made her choice known. Are you all comfortable with that?"

We barely even gave it a moment's thought. Sully nodded. "Sure. If that's what Bandit wants, too."

Now it was Bandit's turn to bark. Moving to Pixie, Doc bent down until her she was eye level with the dog. Reaching out, she gently cupped Pixie's head in her hands.

"You have been such a brave and good girl. I know you'll be well looked after here."

Pixie's tail wagged furiously and she let out an affectionate bark at Doc's words. Then her tongue darted out and she showered Doc's face in wet kisses until she laughed.

"I love you too."

Climbing back into her car, Doc rolled down the window and waved goodbye to everyone.

"I'll see you all again soon."

"Don't make it too long," Sully called out.

She gave them one last wave and then the Doc and Emma were gone.

74

SULLY

The golden rays of the setting sun bathed the land in a warm and peaceful light, casting long shadows across the grassy fields. The builders we had hired to repair the ranch the way we wanted it had left, knowing we needed this time to ourselves today.

With solemn faces and heavy hearts, the family gathered around the grave Gideon and I had dug, the rich smell of the fresh earth filling my nose. We had prepared for this day all week, but hadn't been ready to see him off until now.

With Elora and Emma gone, and now Pixie becoming part of the family again, the time felt right.

We were ready.

Dad's body had been preserved in a nearby funeral parlor while we deliberated on what to do with his remains. He had left no instructions, but I knew he would want to be buried beside my mother on our property — it was their favorite spot with the best view.

As we lowered his coffin into the ground, each of us took turns dropping a handful of soil onto his casket as a final farewell.

When it was time for Gideon to step up, he faltered. Chase made a move toward him, but I stopped her. This was something I needed to do for him — to show him that I would now be there for him the way my father had been.

Throwing my arm around Gideon, I lent him my strength.

As the sun slowly dipped below the horizon, I read over the carefully chosen inscription on the gravestone one last time:

Here lies Zebediah Sullivan.
1947 - 2019
You will be sorely missed by your sons and family.

75

CHASE

Despite the months of turmoil and danger we had faced, there was finally a sense of peace settling over us. The rebuild of the ranch had been completed, but it wasn't for our whole family's use anymore. The once humble barn now stood tall and grand, having undergone its own extensive renovation to become our very own office space.

That's right, Bandit and I had our own office now.

And before you go thinking what a ridiculous waste of a nice barn that was, just know that this was totally necessary. Every single day, offers came flooding through from film studios and television companies. Some wanted to film a docu-drama about our lives (we even had an offer from the same network who produce the Kardashian show though the last thing we wanted was to live under more scrutiny), while the studios were trying to get us to agree to not one, but an entire *franchise* of movies based on our adventures.

The world was going mad for Bandit, and they all wanted to capitalize on his fame.

The idea of having movies made of our story was kind of fun. I guess we hadn't entirely dismissed the idea, although I don't think neither Bandit nor I really wanted to be movie stars. That kind of stress wasn't for us, although we were happy to make the odd appearance on a chat show — those were kind of a blast.

They would send a private plane for us, fly us all out to LA. Just the thought of flying somewhere on a private jet blew my mind, especially since I had never been on a plane before. Did you know they have entire bedrooms on planes, with a double bed, ensuite bathroom and everything? It was like a luxury hotel in the sky.

Hellen had featured us several times on her show already. Being such a huge lover of animals, she had raised a ton of money, setting up a charity to make sure that all those other dogs who were experimented on would never lack for anything. Even more than that, she also established a foundation dedicated to finding humane alternatives so that no animal would ever have to endure testing again.

The appearances were so much fun that we would have done them all for free, instead; we were making so much money for them. I'm talking A LOT a lot. Forget worrying about whether I could afford to eat again. Now I could have those little melt-in-your-mouth meringue thingies shipped in from France *daily* if I wanted.

If Sam would let me, anyway.

She set limits on what she deemed too outrageous. Killjoy.

Sam continued to be a sheriff because she loved her job and wouldn't be a 'kept woman,' even if it was the kids who were paying for everything. Sully chose to stay home with us, still reeling from the aftermath of everything that had happened.

He didn't want to be away from his family again, not after facing such terrifying circumstances. He said he couldn't go through that kind of worry again and so we spent most of our time at home, enjoying each other's company. Sully had been contemplating starting something up on our property — he had been researching local plans and permits, trying to figure out what options were available to him. At first, I thought he might open another veterinary practice but in the end, he surprised me by revealing his true passion: opening a rescue center for animals that had been subjected to cruel lab experiments. His goal was to rehabilitate these poor creatures and find them loving homes.

This was his big mission now and one we were all on board with, especially Gid, who had quit his job with Warrey (well, technically, he'd been fired as he hadn't turned up to work for days on end).

When our first paycheck came through, I admit I might have gone a little nuts. I mean, who knew there could be so many zeroes? I spent a ridiculous amount on toys and treats for the dogs, as well as an entire room that was made out of interactive quizzes for Bandit to lose his mind in. For me and Gid, I built a cool new gaming center (Sully had finally relaxed his stance on video games after much, much persuasion from the two of us). And for Sully and Sam, I fulfilled their lifelong dream of having a swimming pool in the backyard. Even after all of these lavish purchases, I was left with a ton of money.

But there was one thing I knew I wanted to get — and it wasn't even for any of us.

Ever since I knew I would have large sums of money coming to me, I'd been giving a lot of thought to what I would spend it on. Turns out, that since I'd managed to go without for so long, I only really thought about the necessities. Subsequently, I didn't really have a long wish list for myself, but when I'd been messing around on the internet, I suddenly remembered a particular property I was interested in.

With my newly acquired wealth, I was able to locate it fairly easily. It hadn't been for sale, but after offering the current owners a big enough incentive, they finally sold it to me for an extortionate price. But I knew it would be worth every cent.

Legally, I couldn't purchase the place on my own as I was underage, so Sully had to co-sign for me. His face had been quite the picture when I had told him I wanted help buying a house.

"Are you planning on moving?" he'd asked, looking kind of sick by the idea.

"No," I was quick to reassure him. "It's not for me."

"Then who are you buying houses for?"

"It's a surprise."

Suffice to say, I had piqued his interest, which is why he had followed me into my office today. I had just dialed the number for the lucky new owners. After a few rings, the phone was answered by an elderly male voice.

"Hello?"

"Hi," I began hesitantly. "I don't know if you remember me, but you and your wife helped me a few months ago."

I sounded like an idiot. Feeling like a nervous wreck, I wished I had practiced this conversation in front of a mirror before making the call. The phone line crackled with static as I waited for a response. Finally, there was a sharp gasp on the other end.

"Chase? Is that really you?"

A wave of relief washed over me at the sound of Harold's voice. "You remember me?"

"Of course I remember you, dear. Why, we've been following your incredible adventures in the news! Wait, one second will you? I have to get my wife. She won't want to miss this call!"

Harold hurried off to fetch his wife Margaret, leaving me with my thoughts. I twisted a strand of hair between my fingers while I pictured their warm smiles and gentle demeanor.

When Xavier had kidnapped Bandit and left me in that forest, I might have struggled for days if it wasn't for Harold and his wife stopping their car to rescue me. And their kindness hadn't ended with them taking me to a phone where I could call for help.

Seeing my state, and knowing how long it had been since I had eaten, the two had paid for several rounds of food for me. When Gideon had finally arrived, they wouldn't accept a penny from us, not even when I found out how pressed for cash they were.

I had been so deeply touched by their kindness, especially when I had learned that they had tragically lost a son. Yet, despite their pain, they still believed in God and practiced giving without expecting anything in return. Their unwavering compassion had stayed with me ever since that fateful day on the road.

The weight of their decision to sell the house they had raised their children in still weighed heavily on them, especially now that their son was gone. The walls held echoes of the laughter, tears, and memories they cherished. But the medical bills had piled up, leaving them with no choice but to sell their home.

But now, it was my turn to do something for them.

"Chase?" Margaret's delighted voice came over the phone. "We're so thrilled you're calling! We were so worried when we saw what was happening in Los Angeles on the news, but then that Jeopardy show! There will never be another one like it!"

We shared a laugh as Sully listened in, a smile on his face as he already knew where this was heading.

"We had no idea that what was happening. What a terrible time you have had." It was Harold again. I could almost picture the two of them huddling over the one handset as they both tried to talk to me.

My chest tightened at the genuine concern in their voices. "I know. I'm sorry I couldn't say anything to you at the time. I didn't want to lie or keep things from you. I hope you understand."

"Of course we do, dear," Margaret exclaimed. "I have to admit, we would have loved to meet your talking dog! What a sweetheart he is!"

"We are so glad to have been able to help you, Chase. Had we known what you were going through, we would have done much more for you," Harold chimed in.

I felt a lump in the back of my throat. I had barely said hello yet here they were, wishing they could have done more for me — a complete stranger that they had picked up on the street.

"I really appreciated your help. I've never forgotten your kindness, especially when I learned about your own problems. The thing is, I've now found myself with a good amount of money, and I don't even need much because I have my family around me. So, I spent some of the money we've earned... and I bought you your old house back."

There was a sudden silence over the phone. It was so quiet you could have heard a pin drop. In fact, they were so quiet I wondered if we'd been cut off.

"Hello? Are you both still there?"

Harold's overwhelmed and confused voice spoke again. "I'm sorry, Chase. These old ears aren't what they used to be. For a moment there, I thought you said you'd bought us our old house back."

"That is what I said. I know how much you love that house because it's where you raised all your children. You mentioned how all the memories you have of your son who passed away were in that house, and I just wanted you to have that again. These past few months, I've really learned how much our memories can mean to us, especially when we lose a loved one. And I want you to have him back again, so I hope you'll accept this."

"You didn't need to do anything, Chase! Any decent person would have helped you. All we did was buy you breakfast. You don't have to buy us a house!" Margaret exclaimed, touched beyond belief yet unable to accept this tremendous gift that I was offering.

"But I want to do this for you. You said to me once that God will always provide for you and this is his way of doing that — through me. So please take this house because I don't need it. I'm giving it to you. Please say you'll take it."

Several more moments of silence greeted me. "We... we would be honored," Harold finally answered, choking up.

I felt relief wash over me as they accepted my offer.

"Fantastic! The deeds and the keys will be on their way to you in the next few days, so keep an eye out for them. They will be couriered directly to you."

I'm not sure what Margaret said next because suddenly she was sobbing down the phone while Harold tried to comfort her. I strained to hear their words amidst the chaos until they finally came back on the line.

"Thank you so much, Chase. You have no idea how much this means to us. God bless you. God bless you, your dog, and your whole family," Margaret choked out between tears.

A lump formed in my throat as I hung up the phone, tears stinging at my eyes, but I also had the biggest smile on my face. I had no idea giving could make you feel so good. I had spent so much of my life desperately wanting for everything that now that I was in a position to give, it felt *amazing*.

"Kid, you really are something," Sully said, beaming with admiration and love.

Clapping my hands together, I looked at him then Bandit, laying by my feet, his tail thumping the floor in excitement.

"That was amazing! I want to do it again. Who else can I buy a house for?!"

EPILOGUE

Gideon, Bandit, and I sat in our cozy office, surrounded by shelves of books and mementos from our adventures. The latest draft of a manuscript lay open on the desk in front of us, its crisp white pages filled with words that told our story.

Months of careful consideration and countless meetings had led us to this moment. We were faced with multiple movie offers, each one tempting but also threatening to take away our creative control. But after much discussion, we made a bold decision: we would hire our own ghostwriter to pen our story, which we would then turn into movies ourselves.

Yes folks, the three of us were going to produce our own movies!

Excitement bubbled inside us as we envisioned bringing our story to life on the big screen. Our three heads leaned close together as we poured over the manuscript, already dreaming up scenes and casting choices.

The ghostwriter we had hired was a talented writer from London, who had been working closely with us for months to capture the essence of our journey. We wanted the world to know what had happened to us — the joy, the pain, and the lessons learned.

But for Bandit, it was about more than just our story. He hoped that by sharing it with the world, people would come to care about all animals and work towards protecting them from harm.

As for me?

I guess I just wanted anybody out there who had ever felt unloved, who didn't come from a fairytale family like the ones you see in Christmas movies, I wanted them to know that there was hope: their family — the one they should have — could still be out there. They just have to keep the faith and never give up searching. I honestly believe that we can all find the love and support we each need and deserve.

A knock sounded on the door, followed by the appearance of Sully and Sam. Sully's phone was clutched tightly in his hand and he wore a serious expression. It seemed like there was something important he wanted to tell us.

"You guys got a minute? We just received an email from Emma," he said, motioning for us to gather around.

"I think you'll want to hear this," Sam finished, smiling at us.

I pushed back from the table, swinging my chair to face him. "What's it say?"

Sully perched himself on the edge of the table, taking a deep breath before starting to read aloud.

"Dear Everyone,
I'm having so much fun with Elora. She's been teaching me so many things, including how to be human again — actually, I guess again isn't the right word since I wasn't really here before, not in this body anyway.

After lots of testing (none of it painful, though a few were uncomfortable and involved some very long needles!), they have confirmed Elora's original diagnosis: I am a clone of your Emma, Sully.

I finally received the confirmation yesterday. This makes so much sense now. Things are falling into place and I finally don't feel so strange. Everything I thought I knew had come externally from videos and photographs that Xavier had fed to me. He wanted me to have a link with you, Sully, in hopes of causing confusion between you and Sam. Which I did really well, for a while there. I'm sorry to say.

Elora and her team (who are all really nice) think that I can help millions of people. They say that by using the technology that brought me to life, they will be able to clone healthy organs to replace those eaten away by diseases like cancer.

In fact, Elora thinks we should be able to help people with the same cancer that killed your Emma."

Sully's voice cracked at this part and he wasn't able to continue. Sam took the phone from him, reading the rest of the email out loud.

"I now feel as if my life has meaning, and I'm so happy that I can help all these people, including you. I really am sorry that I complicated your life but I have finally found a place in the world again. With love, Emma II."

I think we all got a bit emotional after that email. Sully looked like he might burst into the ugly cry at any second, but somehow, he managed to keep it together. Taking sympathy on him, Sam looked at the three of us and changed the subject.

"Have you guys come up with a name for your book series?"

I looked over at Bandit. He tilted his head at her, nodding like a human.

"We're thinking of calling it the Chase Ryder series. I wanted to go with the Chase and Bandit series, but he said it sounded cooler with just my name. He insisted that having one main protagonist would make for a stronger story, something all the writing books he had been devouring lately were saying, but I don't agree. I mean, this is all our story, not just mine."

Sam laughed, shaking her head.

"You guys kill me, you know that?"

Gideon stretched and let out a deep sigh, squeezing the muscles on the back of his neck.

"Is it break time yet? We've been at this all morning already."

"Twist my arm," I answered, already jumping up and heading into the house where the snacks lived. The second I stepped through the door, pandemonium greeted me.

Pixie lay in a basket by the crackling fireplace where a dozen brown and white puppies wriggled around her. She had surprised us by getting pregnant very soon after moving back in with us, and the puppies were just under four weeks old now.

We couldn't have been more thrilled, even with the unexpectedly large litter, which Sully explained rarely happened for a first-time mom. Then again, the parents were extra special. And Bandit couldn't have been a better dad. He seemed to have endless patience as they climbed all over him, these wriggling furballs of energy. Literally everything excited them.

As Sully kneeled beside me, he couldn't resist reaching out to pet the nearest pup. It was a tiny ball of fur with a big brown patch over one eye and a wagging tail that never seemed to quit.

"Have you got names for them yet?"

I pointed at the one in his hand while Bandit said. *"That's Patch"*

"Because of his eye, obviously," I filled in.

Hearing the name, Patch suddenly squirmed out of his hands and bolted for Bandit, but his little paws couldn't quite get purchase on the smooth new floor and he skidded all the way across the room until he bumped into

Bandit at a sudden stop. Shaking his head, he looked up at Bandit with intelligent eyes, then sat, waiting for further instructions.

Sully and I shared a look.

They were too young to know their names, or much more than that, but it definitely seemed that Patch already knew his name and was now waiting for Bandit to begin a game or activity.

I pointed at a different puppy, one with a white shape on his rump.

"That one's Star." Bandit said.

The minute the iPad said *his* name, Star's head shot up, then he too bounded over to sit beside his brother.

Sully's mouth fell open. "No way. They're much too young to behave like this."

Feeling a wave of excitement building inside, I watched as Bandit finished calling his kids.

"Panda, Ace, Champ..."

As he called their names, each puppy jumped to attention, coming to sit in a neat row in front of Bandit until all twelve were in a neat line in front of him.

I turned my head sharply to look at Bandit. His eyes seemed to sparkle with amusement as he glanced back at me.

"Did you know about this?" I asked, feeling a mix of shock and excitement. "Did you know they were super smart, too?"

He snorted out of his nose, laughing at our shock. Sully and I exchanged a quick glance, the same startled expression in our eyes.

"But..." was all Sully could say.

I at least managed two whole words before the full ramifications of an entire household of super smart dogs could hit me.

"Oh boy."

THE END

A NOTE FROM THE AUTHOR

If you've got this far then hopefully you've liked this book, maybe even loved it (yay!) in which case can you please take a few minutes to review this book and the series?

I'm an indie author which means I write on my little computer from my little rental home (London is expensive, y'all). The websites, paperbacks, advertising... everything is done by me so if you love my books and would like to see me become successful as an indie author, and you know, maybe

finally buy myself and my cats a little home that I own, please help by
<u>leaving your reviews.</u>

The more people that know about my books, the better they will do and the more time I will have to write you more books!

And if you would like me to continue this series, do let me know in your reviews and FaceBook ad comments. This is how I judge what projects to focus on next.

Thank you so much for reading!

— Jo

WE'RE NOT DONE YET!

Jo has another series that you might like!
Continue reading for a sneak peek of her new romantic suspense series.

There is love, laughter, suspense, danger, a hot yet tender man, a complicated woman in need of help, and a super adorable dog in every book!

Perfect for fans of Nora Roberts, heartwarming romantic suspense, and dog lovers.

(Available as ebook and paperback.
Audiobooks and large print coming soon!)

UNTIL THE STARS DON'T SHINE - PRELUDE

He had just come off a trying assignment and was looking forward to some R&R when the call had come, smack in the middle of what constituted packing.

A few shorts, his trusty camo shirts, briefs, and cargo pants as beat up and put through the ringer as he was, were being shoved into a canvas backpack when his phone had buzzed.

The melodic rap by D'angelo that had been blasting from the old school sound deck that provided his one luxury in life stopped playing, replaced by that annoying ringtone that seemed to reverberate around the tin walls of the Airstream Travel Trailer he called home.

Though it was only thirty feet long, the trailer had everything he needed for full-time living: a bedroom with a double bed that connected to a small but serviceable living room that also doubled as his kitchen and office, with a shower room and laundry at the other end of the trailer. And it came with one of the most glorious views of the Malibu ocean that he would never be able to afford in his lifetime if he wasn't living in a mobile home.

Truly, it offered the best of both worlds. And the icing on the cake? When he inevitably felt that siren call to move, he could simply shift his home and his life by attaching it to his truck and hauling it off to the next place.

The ringing continued its insistent call, interrupting his thoughts. Lips turning down with disapproval, he looked for the phone but couldn't locate it anywhere near him.

"Bud," he called out. "Fetch my phone."

The German Shepherd who had been snoozing by the bed sprang up and raced into the lounge, letting the rings guide him. When he padded back, the phone was gripped carefully between those two strong jaws of his. Intelligence shone from his brown eyes as he looked up at his owner for approval.

"Thanks, Boy."

He took the phone from him and ran a hand over his dog's smooth head in the way that he liked. Bud chuffed happily, lifting first one paw, then the other before returning to his position by the foot of the bed, circling round in the way that dogs do before lying back down.

The man stared down at his phone, at the name of the lowlife who dared to interrupt this most holy of times — that of vacation.

He'd worked long and hard, and this downtime was due him. People knew better than to bother him when he could almost taste the grit in his teeth and feel the desert air whistling through his hair.

It was going to be him, his bike, his trusty dog and the unforgiving outback of the desert.

Which was just how he liked it.

His eyes slid over a shelf of framed photographs and knick-knacks collected from a lifetime of experiences. Landed on the only picture he had kept from high school, back when he hadn't been half as tough or rugged as he was now.

The two teens in the picture were skinny things, all arms and legs with glasses and unfortunate zits that were the cause of many a beating from the jocks that'd had their run of the school.

After a pretty miserable childhood being bullied and living under the roof with a drunk for a father, and a drug addict for a mom, when Kane Turner suddenly grew two feet — seemingly each way — he'd fled to the marines as soon as was feasibly possible.

Disciplined, driven, and relieved to be getting out of his crummy home situation, he advanced up the ranks quickly due to formidable physical skills and an almost sixth sense for danger.

Didn't matter if he was in the sketchier parts of downtown or conducting a dawn patrol in Afghanistan, Kane always knew moments before contact with a hostile was initiated. It was this uncanny ability that had kept him alive throughout each of his tours when so many of his brothers had fallen by the wayside.

Despite being so good at his job, he never enjoyed it.

It was in his blood to protect and serve, but he didn't like fighting people, didn't like hurting them, however misguided they were. Still, he would have stayed a marine if it wasn't for the devastating loss that occurred in Operation Condor.

It was supposed to have been a routine expedition.

A simple patrol in a small town in the middle of nowhere where only a handful of people lived. They were to show their faces, let the locals see that the US controlled the region when an IED went off as they neared.

The car ahead had flipped over, though luckily, Kane had felt that tingle in the back of his neck, that flutter in his stomach that had warned him something was amiss.

Slowing down his vehicle as he scouted the area, he had been far enough back that the bomb only did surface damage. The wounds he sustained would leave a few wicked scars, though they were nothing compared to the devastation his marine brothers faced.

Suffering through weeks of agony, their injuries finally proved too great as a number of them died one after the other. Those who clung to survival did so by a thread: tormented by PTSD, they only made it through the day by medicating themselves with whatever was available.

And those were the lucky ones.

Unable to work or return to normal civilian life, a few became homeless, sleeping on the streets before vanishing off the face of the earth completely.

Kane hadn't wanted that for himself.

He hadn't survived his childhood to let that be the end of his story. He knew he had to quit before his number came up.

After he returned to civilian life, Kane flitted around from city to city, working various manual jobs from construction to bartender to a stint as an Uber driver, until his high school buddy Wilson had called, offering to employ him.

The class nerd, Wilson had gone on to make a major success of himself and now ran one of the most sought-after VIP security services. Having heard that Kane was struggling, he wanted to help the one person who hadn't made his life a misery at school.

The money was decent, and it was fun to mix with the Hollywood elite who were as eccentric, as out of control as a person would expect. From well-organized "sleepovers" featuring some of the country's best-known faces to basement S&M dungeons, Kane had seen it all.

Despite some of the crazy things he'd witnessed and how he could likely fund the rest of his life if he would only pen a book detailing the madness he'd been privy to, Kane was a consummate professional and would never betray his employer's trust.

This kind of integrity was a quality often missing in LA, and so he found his services in constant demand, particularly when the employer happened to be a bored and lonely housewife.

Many fell for his brooding good looks, while others simply loved the challenge.

Kane frequently found himself in uncomfortable situations where he would catch his client walking around in nothing more than a thong and a smile.

He never took advantage of the moment.

The women who threw themselves at him? He never found them attractive. He didn't like their too-tight facial features so often caused by surgery, or the voluminous breasts that never moved. The fake tans made him think of overcooked frankfurters on a grill. In fact, he hated fakeness in general, which was why, although he was seen as a catch, he still hadn't found The One.

Not that he believed in that kind of thing.

Having seen what a loveless marriage could do to two people, he had sworn off the idea. This was just as well, as none of his previous relationships had been at all successful with an average lifespan of only a few months — if that.

He knew he was far from perfect, but he'd considered himself above average in many respects and most of the women he came across tended to agree... until they came home with him for the first time.

Apparently, his tiny tin home didn't hold quite the same appeal for them as it did him.

After the first night, many didn't bother returning while the ones who hung in there he would inevitably find fault with.

What was it about the women in this town that made them all so focused on fame and money?

He'd lost count of how many celebrity parties he'd worked at where women initiated conversations with potential "love" interests by asking them what job they had or how much square footage their house contained.

It all left a bad taste in his mouth.

Having finished a trying job with a diva pop star who'd acted very badly when Kane had rejected her drunken advances, he had packed a bag and was ready to take off on his Harley for a week in the mountains. Now, the one person in the world he couldn't ignore was calling.

"Wilson," Kane answered his phone. "I'm literally walking out the door so this had better be good..."

"I know, but this just came through," Wilson responded with uncustomary excitement.

Mack "Stonewall" Rockefeller, the well-known movie mogul who owned Pinnacle studios, was receiving death threats. This wasn't unusual in and of itself — the rich and famous were always being targeted by money grabbers and weirdos. However Wilson was particularly concerned as the threats were coming from the same source...

And they seemed to be escalating.

The Rockefellers had a daughter who they had managed to keep out of the limelight for most of her life. Not much was publicly known about her other than she was about to turn twenty-five and an enormous yet "private" party was being thrown to celebrate the occasion.

Wilson explained how bad an idea that would be: Stonewall would essentially be opening his home to thousands of strangers. If anyone wanted to do something to them, there wouldn't be a more perfect opportunity.

Stonewall and his movie star wife Mandy were resisting, however, and were in the process of finalizing the firm they would go with for the job. In particular, they were looking for a bodyguard for their daughter. The literal King and Queen of Hollywood, Wilson had fought for their business for years. If he was able to win this contract, it would set up the company for life.

"So what's the problem?" Having had all this explained to him, Kane wasn't sure the point of his call.

"I'm stuck on this detail in DC right now and none of my usual men are cutting it. I need someone different, someone who might shake things up."

Kane ran through what he'd been told about the family in his head. "They sound high maintenance and I just got done with a job like that."

"Just meet them. Talk to them like you would any other client. If they don't go for you, fair enough. But I'm telling you, every firm I know is fighting to land this gig. It would mean a tremendous amount if we could win the account."

Kane glanced over at Bud. His ears were pricked high as he listened keenly, picking up on his reluctance.

"I already told Bud we were going. You know I hate disappointing him."

As if he understood, Bud sighed, staring at him with sad, accusatory eyes designed to pull at his heart. He tossed a rubber bone at him that Bud snatched out of the air with his jaws.

"Tell him there's a giant marrow bone in it for him if he'll wait just a little longer." Wilson sounded hopeful, knowing his pleas were working.

"Tell him yourself," Kane grumbled, shaking his head. He looked longingly out of a window at the faint outline of the mountains that seemed to be moving further away into the distance.

"Thanks man. Appreciate it. Get the job and you can have a long break after. As long as you want."

"Don't forget the marrow bones," Kane reminded him, determined that Bud would not lose out.

"I'll have a box shipped over," Wilson laughed. "You'll need to get there this afternoon. Go flash them some of the Kane charm. Clara will collate a file and send it over to you ASAP."

Clara was Wilson's assistant. She'd worked with him for close to five years now. She wasn't the quickest, but Wilson swore she was loyal and could be trusted with anything.

Kane hung up the call and sent Bud an apologetic look.

"So... it looks like we're going to have to put a pin on that vacation I promised you..."

Bud responded by groaning and covering his eyes with a paw.

"Don't be such a drama queen. At least you've got bones coming."

At that, Bud perked right up. His tail thumped against the laminate floor tiles.

"Let's grab a walk before we head over there. I've got a feeling this job is going to be rough."

Barking with the kind of excitement that would make a person think he had never been out on a walk before *in his life*, Bud raced to the door, jumped up to the handle and tugged on it with his mouth. The door swung open. Light and sea air flooded into the trailer that had his mouth opening to capture it all, but he stopped short of going outside.

He was too well trained for that.

Kane nodded, giving a hand signal. "You can go."

At that, Bud bounded outside, yapping and barking like he was a puppy again and not the grown-up three-year-old that he was.

Rolling his eyes at his dog's antics, Kane joined him outside.

You've reached the end of your free preview.

To continue reading, get the book HERE!

ALSO BY JO HO

ROMANCE

Silver Screen Secrets Series

A heart-warming suspenseful romance series for dog lovers!

If you like Nora Roberts and our four-legged friends, then you will love this series!

Until The Stars Don't Shine, Book 1

Until The Sea Runs Dry, Book 2

Until The Last Leaf Falls, Book 3 (June 2020)

Until All Color Fades Away, Book 4 (Fall 2020)

YOUNG ADULT

The Chase Ryder Series

Read this heart-warming thriller trilogy to learn the story of a mysterious dog who has escaped from a sinister lab, a lonely homeless girl surviving on wits alone, and a grieving veterinarian still haunted by a past that he can't let go of.

Can they keep their new family together while fleeing from the army of a ruthless billionaire? Will they even survive?

Gold Medal Winner of a Readers Favourite International Book Award

Wanted, Book 1

Haunted, Book 2

Hunted, Book 3

Twisted Series

Between her bizarre roommate, standoffish new friends, and overbearing father who's followed her to campus, Marley's first year at Blackville University is off to a rocky start. But when a strange night out leaves her with magical powers, college starts to look a lot more exciting...

What Doesn't Kill You, Book 1

Beware The Signs (Book 2)

See No Evil (Book 3)

The Blood That Binds (Book 4)

When Trouble Comes (Book 5)

Bad Habits (Book 6)

Left Behind (Book 7)

Hell Hath No Fury (Book 8)

In Her Skin (Book 9)

First Date Jitters (Book 10)

Grave Matters (Book 11)

Plus more to come!

Standalone Books

Who is the boy next door? A thrilling mystery that will keep you guessing until the very last page!

The Boy Next Door

See them all including her special discounted boxset deals at:

www.johoscribe.com

ABOUT THE AUTHOR

A proud geek and video gamer, and champion of complex female protagonists, Jo brings her page-turning screenwriting style to books to weave well-crafted, suspenseful stories with twists you don't see coming. She writes YA books under Jo Ho and heartwarming suspenseful romance under Joanne Ho - most of them featuring dogs!

A self-taught screenwriter, Jo's writing life began when she created the groundbreaking, critically acclaimed CBBC action fantasy television series, "Spirit Warriors," which introduced leading actress, Jessica Henwick ("Game of Thrones," "Star Wars: The Force Awakes") to the screen. Granted the biggest budget ever given to a CBBC show at the time, it was nominated for "Best Children's Programme" at the 2011 Broadcast Awards, with Jo herself, going on to win the Women in Film & Television's "New Talent" Award in 2010. Jo even made history for being the first East Asian person - man or woman - to have created a British television drama series.

Since then, Jo has worked with some of the most acclaimed producers in the world with several television shows and movies currently in development, she also writes for games. When she isn't working on her own stories, Jo helps others with their work - she is one of the BFI's (British Film Institute) recommended script consultants.

Jo suffers from MCS (Multiple Chemical Sensitivities), a debilitating condition she has developed over the last few years which has left her mostly housebound. Unfortunately, it is still not officially recognized in the UK despite the World Health Organisation listing it as a physical disability. There is currently no help for sufferers of MCS in the UK. Unable to travel or attend meetings and writersrooms, she has lost many screenwriting opportunities but has refused to allow the condition to rule her life. Despite the wrench life has thrown at her, Jo started to write and publish books.

Her debut novel WANTED, Book 1 of the Chase Ryder series has been a bestseller in 15 YA categories. It also won top prize in the YA Sci-Fi category for the 2018 Readers' Favorite Book Awards. It is her dream to bring all of her book series to screen and she believes she can make it happen with her readers' help!

Jo lives in London and hopes to travel across America one day in a super kitted out, MCS-friendly, Zombie-apocalypse-ready RV with her lovely fella Matt, and three equally lovely kitties.

Don't forget to SIGN UP to her mailing list for updates, book release details, gifts and exclusive offers at www.johoscribe.com

Check out her romance books here: https://www.amazon.com/Joanne-Ho/e/B081QVSCH5

facebook.com/Johowriter

twitter.com/johoscribe

instagram.com/missjoho

SIGN UP TO JO'S NEWSLETTER!

Be the first to hear Jo's news, book releases, and giveaways.
Apply for her ARC teams (she has one for ebooks AND one for audiobooks)
to get free, advanced copies of her books to read/listen to and review.

Plus, you'll get a free book as a thank you for signing up! What's not to like?

Sign up and join all the cool kids at
www.johoscribe.com